LIFE WITH BEAT

LIFE WITH BEAT

The Book Girl

Sim Elgin

Library of Congress Control Number: 2023911892

ISBN:	Hardcover	979-8-3694-0189-7
	Softcover	979-8-3694-0190-3
	eBook	979-8-3694-0191-0

Print information available on the last page.

Rev. date: 06/27/2023

To order additional copies of this book, contact:
Xlibris
844-714-8691
www.Xlibris.com
Orders@Xlibris.com
849278

CONTENTS

Chapter 1:   Atmospheric Testing.. 1
Chapter 2:   One Girl's Obsession 9
Chapter 3:   Age Nineteen 19
Chapter 4:   College, 2Nd Year 30
Chapter 5:   Her reservation 35
Chapter 6:   Consolidated Depot 47
Chapter 7:   Departure 57
Chapter 8:   Disastrophe 69
Chapter 9:   Black thunder 77
Chapter 10: Train life 89
Chapter 11: Lost again.. 96
Chapter 12: Xanthallado 106
Chapter 13: Commodore 114
Chapter 14: Hogan forth 128
Chapter 15: Monday... 133
Chapter 16: Tuesday.. 143
Chapter 17: Cocojo 152
Chapter 18: Wednesday 165
Chapter 19: Thursday 181
Chapter 20: Friday aM 203
Chapter 21: Friday PM 226
Chapter 22: Saturday am 10k 239
Chapter 23: Garden Center 257
Chapter 24: Main beach cruise... 270
Chapter 25: Erotic passage 284
Chapter 26: Tony the crude 295
Chapter 27: Pizza again.. 308
Chapter 28: Dancing binge 321
Chapter 29: Mall trip.. 329
Chapter 30: Interview... 341
Chapter 31: Jungle ride... 350
Chapter 32: Wild ride home 361
Chapter 33: The party 376
Chapter 34: Cardiff shores... 385

Chapter 35:   Light house... 400
Chapter 36:   New implant 411
Chapter 37:   Shattuck visit..419
Chapter 38:   Longlead-UP evening 426
Chapter 39:   Pool side sun... 439
Chapter 40:   Wild ride home 454
Chapter 41:   Airport 461
Chapter 42:   Boarding pass 468
Chapter 43:   No spayah bayd 482
Chapter 44:   Cable car... 493
Chapter 45:   Nightmare.. 500
Chapter 46:   Gunter interlude 509
Chapter 47:   Packsaddle...516
Chapter 48:   Catching on 526
Chapter 49:   Spinnaker 534
Chapter 50:   Aquarius 544
Chapter 51:   Interlude 555
Chapter 52:   Last run 567

The winds swept back in. Cocojo's rocky south shore glided by at a lashing speed. The catamaran flew by Le Tournepier, that stood atop a tall sea-side cliff. The uncombably out-of-control pile's Beatense said to sail in close to this sheer rock, but Shean told that the surf would smash them into it like tomatoes. Lorraine, nervously, asked all that tumbled hair how she picked Emeraldeye for her visit. Working the jib, eyeing her spindly legs, the beach blonded, beanbag bellied, bamboo built and bitch blacked body believer looked up. Formed cheeks, wide placed processing eyes.

"Hah? Oh, it was this advice letter, in *Chez Health.* Me being me, vidi veni."

However the microphone Me, no baddy, timid and paint store right now, format also forces the teensy, but sea breezes and consult with their very insecure to spill were just $600 away! So staff to find the best their deepest and most one jet and shuttle van colors to put up. Plus agonizing insecurities later I was a backpack don't forget wallpaper to the entire room. It hostel initiate! It was as you shop!

The newer can be of help to some right on the ocean, and types go up easily, so people, it gives a new lazed back! This sunbug in a few hours you can angle. But facing your Elee ran me down to the creatively revamp your pain, where this creep fabulous Cocojo lawless apartment! Fabrics can is spying on you, this beach! All week we made also be used to a nice wouldn't be advised. A chocolate mad at us! effect, and you can do quiet

life is all you The hostel let us both great things with them need, this will slowly go nude! Party Saturday to liven your digs up! bring healing. I thank night, danced hips hot, Come home from work to you for writing, all lost all control, got your fancy pad! Wadya victims can relate and fooked, again! Prim me! waiting for? Send us a (Cont'd pp 159, col 2) (Cont'd pp 201, col 1) picture! *Chez Health*

1

ATMOSPHERIC TESTING

Despite their shore summers the olden wealth juniors were fearfully, passively pallid. They were jeered at as sissy, but their later bomb-test era cousins were raved over taut and tan god perfects. The isotopes granted too their forceful cheeks, direct eyes and tuffeted peeky-ears hair. Us impressed less-money lessers all envied their toasty arrogance, but we never tried for that free prestige ourselves. And unlike...

The finer-breds we failed in mind and make, we had buzz cut hair and we went baggy jeans and T-shirts un-prestiged. But with 1965's Varsity 10-speed advent, the nascent atomical athleticals saw lethal prospects. In a twenty year nation-wide romp on sand, grass, street or court, these self exalting warrior slims, just in their cuffed-up butt-cut cut-off shorts, were proudly feared for their sun clashy long waist uppers and sun clashy long legs lowers, as they strafed saddlery shined. Until the winter fade.

But the sea or ski jetters stayed demoralizingly ever luxuriant. Low folk resented their striking ostentation, but then 1970 these betters went shock ennobling with two, three or four year hair, inter-shifting spilly thick. Decadent, overtly extravagant, even more demoralizing, but aso free. For the low folk this excess meant societal ruin.

This Cannot Be. But overlooked, many of their own sons went plentiful to look insolent, only to look innocent. But for me, no appeal: Clumsy, nerdy, underweight and anemically buck-toothed pale. I died seeing Roblon, a pepsi cola saturated (not exaggerated) terror, who gave swim meet fame to our local Woodvue pool. His games play with his admiring but befuddled friends stressed in his leaned lines, while Erick's chlorine crispy blaze also gave a race team edge. And down-the-street sun pro Jeff flashed a breathtakingly metallic nose to toes shatter. Pre-teens also shattered.

We saw this deity in Barton Park. Mark griped, "Lucky brat's ski boat hosing." Barty Park, that upper realm where both his stellar sizzle and stellar shape were for that enclave necessities. In white knee-cut deck jeans on his banana-seat Stingray bike, slouching with belly sunken, he viciously glared. So did an in-shorts ball-player just ten, already by June ice cream bar fatal. For those older the sun vicious Scott of the trim tennis shorts. At the time girls weren't responsive to the bomb genetics, but Scott, his little brother Nack and whole youth armies were sun sadistic.

Or a neighbors and parents revered sun star, a flagrant distractor on a look-at-me walk, and swim class Bob, each superbly fifteen and pan fudge slathered. Or prodigy Essen's sinister sun session slayings: Sullenly sensational ten-to-two torchings.

But others simply loved that sky lantern. The lazily lanky Lang, a burned copper no-shirter, his muscles flexed only upon need, like tossing rocks in his uncle's torrid quarry. On grey days, morbid. The limber Paeter's fervor conferred his bran velvet blur, or neck-beads Dryden washing the car, also fudge blurred, with sudsy chest.

Also sand specters, park lagoon fawns, teen scantlings, boater hawks, avid new sunners, miracle sun farm lads, a tail-gate seated corn seller and a hot day rural bike boy, all pristine brilliant and dense deep radiant. But with their capri-kini lay-outs and lordly sailing-shorts strolls the monieds deep radiated too, and they were martial arts, dirt bike, steep ski, ice hockey and surf or skateboard radicals.

Many elaborated their rebelly anthems with pretentious mid-back cascades, and the ten speed resplendents flaunted scruffy haystacks or abundant dried shucks.

Also during the 1970s, the worshipful mothers on their own enabled provocative, spirally unsnipped garlands for their gifted, creamy pure or sun kissed celestials.

Back in 1965, that Barton bomber was a fellow Woody. Yes, we belonged, but I wasn't otherwise distracted, the girls there were plainfully doughy bland, and wore their ugly orthopedic swimsuits complacently. They didn't follow the lead of their vivid sun crazed brothers, so the doughs were later eclipsed by the nuked next generation.

These spontaneously lightweight selects, in their 1970 spring tropic travels, even the academics, on maddened impulse, dared to wear the criminal new string bikinis. And back on campus they faced the *Hey, Peanut Butter!* razzing of their friends.

Dorm-plaza hot baking (a few bravely blatant) they presided with a peach, pelvic and patella agitation. As the old prude rules were upended, in their spurning the 1950s of dim memory, their first effulge stay-overs got them the response, Well why not.

Those tie bikinis edged ever more risky, until in public settings, some in nothing. July of 1983, a boy-tough pretzel with white breasts pressed out, lay blithely bared on her sand cot within a beach mob, in startling teasy view. Willfully relaxed, chaste she decided to be not. Staring as I walked my bike by her she elbowed up...

To give my butt-cut shorts, tan beating and my sailboat's spiffy rudder upon my shoulder an appraisal. Her proclivity went back to when her library love fell to the alluring 70s itch, and her hitting beach or pool in her birthday twelve top-patches and banana peel. If fun parents, pills too. When I saw her as a collegiate, life for her and all skinny adventurists was a wanton hoot. But actually their expected and *accepted* effulging, triggered by their willowy statures and floaty frock or leggy jeans enticing, they owed to those early beach-walk striding string intrepids.

The family-beach pushy Sylphire led the charge: Beddy ready, aristocrat lineage, sky blue mini-kini and eyes, kaffe rays deluged, squirmy belly. And this hitch-hiker. Stately stern, wispy twisty, twin triangles, tight hip-hugger jeans, kaffe rays deluged, squirmy belly. These and all top quality outlaws made badder better, so the sensible achievers, sensitive artists, staid scholars, silly daughters and steady workers all felt free to deluge and effulge indulge. Their sun addiction hit with utmost disturbance turbulence back during the active radioactive era, that except for the rare exception test-ban faded away. But back in the thrilling days of high fission yesteryear...

The impudent faced pool devotee Matt, an un-cut hair, head tossing archetypal physique sun ravager. In 1969 I saw him ride Hill Street by all the proper shoppers. Then, walking his $1200 racer bike back through the crowd, belligerently brown and threateningly out of place, in spite of his mid-teen proportions, that seething sheened cut-offs clad marauder commandingly intimidated those fearful, fretful fools.

I noted; this stab at old era decorum took real audacity, so I thoughtfully did my own vitality education. But a sun scarce week of work, dirt mud. In 1971 at sunset Scott and Roblon patrolled their Varsities along, as they shimmered with alarming violence from their drought infusions. Horrified, I took off after.

I caught up shaking and eyed those ultraviolet lashed heroes, and the sure long thrust of their strenuated thighs. Like with downtown Matt, the sun danced upon the smooth succulence of their arched backs. They looked at me in surprised contempt, for my queer chase and pitiful deviance. I fled in pathetic confusion.

Years later got a look at this happy moptop of twelve fishing. He was just in high cuffed cut-offs set to his hips and neatly creased into his wee buttem. Pole in hand, precisely pretty and door key yarn hung, he gleamed so room lighting incandescent brown he just swarmed. I looked. Bar thugs would look too, from the safety of their faked disinterest, of course. Saw him again fishing with friends, unforgiveable.

Then 1983, this light, tight lass in her smart winter coat, leaning into the corner of the elevator, perusing her *Finance Journal*: Cookie complexion with her eyebrows inquisitively set. Ethereal. That is, not quite of this world, nor that of the Beyond.

That serene, blue eyed conceit. First time I really looked. So with this new interest, that summer, done sailing with boat stowed by ten, I laid out in the adjoining park, right in with the all-out aggressors. Also present, the tender, earnestly...

Overdone maidens, in their micro tie-pieces. Less courage than that sand cot craver, who abused the law's tacit lenience. Also abetted, me foraying my toxic sun intensity with expo walks, and campus, city and country bike rides. With me so inexplicably deluged, reactions included fright, friendly protest, revulsion, disbelieving merriment, fellow fanatic respect, impressed awe, gay suspicion, wistful envy, flimsy excuses to look, or sincere honor. But sailing, stray boaters only.

So, the two boys burst into Scott's house, laughing at that faggot run-in. Scott's parents chuckled but they were alarmed by their account, because of the potential danger posed by *me* as the resident perv. The question was, how did Scott, and the eyes widening Roblon, make it this far without other run-ins? They were merciless in showing off, tempting other losers, so they decided to vacate Scott for awhile, to get him out of my deviated sight. Like, blame me.

They told him they needed him to check out their investment farm up north in Clarendon, tended by Sid Muggert and family. They expected a fight, but Scott was ready for this trip, not guessing he was being exiled. Nor did the precocious Nack (in real life, Matt's little brother), who begged to go too. Scott was convinced.

Also he was a suburban boy; this was a chance to get honest soil underfoot and *even drive a tractor.* Thus at the local Maher Ridge station he boarded the thousand foot Queen of Steel (the only way to make the trip, no jets in the north) with alacrity.

In trademark butt-cut tennis shorts and chest-cut tank-top he got the crabby old conductor to look twice, from the safety of his position, of course. The Queen was a mighty streamliner from days long gone, and Scott, a good kid really, settled into his Roomette smiling with expectation. But as fast as the train roared northward he felt confined, until just in his shorts from car to car he got himself *noticed.*

As Scott stepped from the Queen in Arrolynn the farmer Muggert was drawn to him, with the excuse of asking if he knew of this Scott feller. He about fell over when the boy (a boy, with all that long hair?) said he *was* Scott. He had never before seen anyone so divinely put together, and like everybody, I too, to my humiliation, he was struck by his breathtaking magnetics. What would the family think?

For Scott, it was surprising how crudely misshapen everyone here was, and how backward this land was. He took out his cellular phone to call home, only to see *Searching For Signal.* Instead he had to use a phone booth, that was provided with a built-in stool, and a light and vent fan that came on as he pulled the door shut.

Waiting for the connection he saw an echelon young lady with scratty volumned hair walk erectly by with a few magazines. She too was a sun fiend. But worse.

Damn, if I just wasn't on this stupid... "Oh, hi, Dad? I'm here!"

As they drove from the station Scott saw that all of the cars were old styled, just like in the vintage car shows back home. Great towering buildings of grey stone loomed over the busy streets, and their stores at sidewalk level had tall, narrow signs alight with multiple colored bulbs, that spelled out the businesses vertically. A strong smell of vehicle exhaust filled the air, adding to an odd hint of foreboding Scott felt.

The downtowns he knew were friendly social places with parl benches, modern statuary, fountains and flowers. Not here. The commuters fleeing to catch their fifty foot streetcars (*What the hell are those?*) were all tiredly haggard and worried.

But the boy did notice that he had been stared at in wonder, and this was better than back home, where stand-out that he was, he was but one of many, in spite of his lurid beaten-in tan. Everyone marveled at his long hair and firm blue eyes.

Their interest gratified him, but it didn't make up for his eventually finding out that there were no hamburgers or pizzas, nor a single one of those paragons of kitchen expediting, the microwave. TV, *black and white?*

Scott was funny, won the Muggerts over. The daughters took to him. He helped with the chores and errands in the morning, then when the family took their naps he lit out. As soon as he was out of sight he ditched his T-shirt and ran on. He didn't think he would be seen in the rural isolation, but he was, which got back to his hosts.

Mr. Muggert said he reckoned it would be plumb foolish for him to help with the cultivating or second cutting all hot in his shirt. So in just his butt-cut tennis shorts he stacked the hay bales, muscles singing. Next day he rode with to the suddenly silent feed mill. In shorts he also sat down to meals, where he snapped with such energy his lath-like form seemed to hum. The mother, girls too, felt quite dizzy, as they took in his influencing looks, crackling aura and hair longer than any woman's in these parts.

Family visitors stupidly mumbled. Scott pushed his luck and outside alone, took off his shorts. He ran the sweltery trail bare to the creek to get decent sun, and one day he came upon that magazine girl. *Yes! That brush pile of hers! And that tan!*

She was bare too as she lay upon the flagstones. He already knew of her. She and her father were running a survey just a mile away, and the family talked of her animatedly the other evening. The girl was so hair explosive and sun rotisseried she was famous, and all libraries had books of her explicit photos.

She was said to be working the Foxdell Road survey stitchless. This is why the family let Scott go similarly dressed, if out of sight. And now like himself the girl was lavishly sunned. He was on intimate terms with the all-night gymnastic acrobats back home, but this complex creature, was infinitely beyond them.

He stood breathless. The nymph smiled, sprang over to him, her pert baseballs jiggling. Her nerves always unsettled, she shook in panting anticipation.

"Hey, how's it going?" *Oh n-not b-bad.* Nervous laugh. "Glad to meet you. I'm Beatense." *H-Hi, I'm Scott.* "Hey, Scott. Wanna lay in the sun with me?"

Cross-legged, facing each other, sunk curved bellies sultry sweat wet.

Later her father, in search of the girl after his tavern lunch, came upon the two. Quickly backed off and lit his pipe. Then, "Beeter! Where the pisspot hell are you? Yer not fixing for me to do all this work myself, ain't you? Come outta hiding!"

They part at last, laughing. Girl splashes away the fluids. Runs off.

The boy then heard all kinds of yelling, and he crept behind a bush to watch. He saw who would seem to be the girl's father cursing and shaking his fist in stamping fury, but to Scott's surprise she just laughed and shouted right back. She pointed out her own list of his faults. Their dispute abruptly ended and the two companionably walked side by side back to their work site. Scott was in a quandary, what to do, but then ran after the combatants. He didn't know how to find them, but he heard more arguing and homed in on it. The girl saw him.

"Scott! Pop, meet my friend here! He's the one! The best ab exercise!"

The boy felt jittery about this remark: Their act, plus his clothing lack. The surly old surveyor greeted Scott by spitting aside in disgust. Actually impressed. *Wow!*

The car-slowing primeval zephyrs helped run the county road's offsets, while the father swore nonstop. Scott laughed nonstop. At day's end he was invited overnight for the beach the next day. One AM, Stan returned from Smitty's, grousing.

"Big mistake, that desert surveying camp, plus tan camp. Girl runty thirteen, ran blackety nakie, tornado hair, little jugs." *Scott, you can't stay!* "Ah, that's why sofa empty! At camp they take her to clinic, fixed her. Didn't pass test, at fourteen camp again. Back home, at beach kid nakie as usual, agent spots her, sets up photos with her and Xanthallado boy Slat." *Scott, no, I... Uh-Aghhh!* "Good, he's staying. Book published, with pay-out baby buys Spook, races very bareback." *Agh! Agh! Agh!*

So, Roblon pulls up on his bike by this sun pro older guy just in hip-wrap cut-offs. Mixing time, place, fact and fiction, this was me, that chaser of years ago. This goes back to my first college year 1967. April Saturday, everybody outside, in long pants and sleeves I hiked the nearby countryside. Came to nice spot, just my underpants, four hours sun. Sunday early, tawny me! In mirror, still reedy, but more developed. Didn't see this come in, even as the cafeteria put out full spreads.

Made cut-offs, nine AM left the dorm, crossed street into farm fields. Took T-shirt off, native scout me! Laid in sun six hours, cut-offs rumpled for half-mast butted line. Redwood me! From many more outings, all slop oil rubbed, got heavy sun impact. Needed to publicize this, so one afternoon laid dorm-side. But with no overkill greed yet, and my oiled-up tactics looking too frenetic, back to distant seclusion.

Striding along in my cut-offs, with the cuffs snugged up high and belt loops just held, setting off my long weavy waist, I roamed ridge and road far afield to get alone. Then returning my walnutty impact to campus, I discretely entered the dorm's far end stairwell. Walking our floor, loud protest. In T-shirt and the same butt-cut shorts, I nerved my obnoxious face and long limbs into class, library, cafeteria and stores.

Next three years same, with summers 1967 and 68 just-jeans surveying. In senior year: Peeky ears hair, winter sunlamp, which later amplified real sun. May, imposed an overkill greed campus walk-through, to and hours later from far-afield drenching.

But school end 1970, UV BS only. Home again, backyard basting. Then my first apartment, July 1973. Week off, no backyard. Forced into Matt-like public shows. In cuffed butt-cut cut-offs, strut-narrowed and matching old penny Lang, I shot my racer bike with the to-work traffic, towel and olive oil pint back on the rack. Arriving beach empty, I slopped on the oil. By noon elbow to elbow, old penny me old pennier.

Nine all-daze cruelty tortures, seems Sylph wanted a wink. Riding home exuded my vibrato deluge, abusing hundreds. Photo proof, the deluge, 165 pounds including hung biceps, shaped shoulders, jutted collarbones and hips, presentation chest and placketed sunk belly. In stores, other indoors, more arms and legs nerve. But 1976, morbid crisis, got fat. Worse, these kids: An oozing-dark steed rider, a bar-bending tennis show-off and Laguna surfers, all beer bottle braised and sit-ups rippled. But in skiing 1978, shamed by an arabica faced racer boy, got plackets and impact back.

So, my sailboat pier-side and old-penny bikini me slouchy belly sunk, sat in talk with these kayak women. More events, then prairie epic, Bondi NSW and Acapulco. Also eight summers riding to saddle shirtless, and once, butt-cuts only, galloped half mile no saddle. Same butt-cuts, sailed over to my singles club picnic: Loud protest.

Misguided invites too: "Oh, get that shirt off!" But 1994 fail, quit bike, broil, boat, downhill, horses, and the later six mile runs. Got all flabbed and no arabica boys to shame me. But as roller-bladed, biked, weight lifted and all-day lush sunned back to deliberate overkill guilt, in the 2008 Pacific Beach summer, with my gleaming impact (photo proof), yet again the slendy-bendy **D** sacreds looked.

The intelligence **D**iligents exert their proficient authority as a reluctant duty, and seek sun to enforce their assured sensual poise. The tinty-tanty **D**eniers (magic Jan, Bulacci, others) are showy-glowy shy, but friends or family might get them to try sun effort. The grim, high-heat thriving **D**eplorers summer simmer out of regretted need, then coerce sickened stares with their exotic bearing.

The equally grim **D**eployers wreak their voltage with cold aimed impunity. Bodily assault is unlawful, but by legislative lapse these elegants do inflict and conflict. The **D**edicateds (Meghan, Alder, Elita) in their determination are ardently self focused six hour layers. The **D**elighters are lively kindred spirits of sportsy/outdoorsy impossible brown. Many all-night joyous, like the Diligents and Dedicateds, on beach or by pool, they revel in that benevolent sun, all fervently trusting, I too, *This I must be.*

The **D**s all share in uncommon the glorious **B**s. **B**one, where the muscles are tensioned and aligned to exactify their lyrical frames. **B**lood, or hungered character, inherent pride, tested fortitude and pedigree. And **B**right, luminous health.

2

ONE GIRL'S OBSESSION

Beatense Colwell, at twenty, yes runty but stalk steeled and self focused profoundly tan, riffled through her *Chez Health*. "So, not only beach indiscreet, like fearful modest me, but she's altogether in that lodge? Ah, here it is."

Cont'd from pp 69..... so if you're made right out of science fiction Early the next morning you look right. Another at its wackiest worst! Elee and I ran to Coco fact, quite true, but a And with its balconies dare bared! So are you university study showed hovering at five story weary dreary? Tired of that every toddler will intervals like gravity your rut? Need a quick by preference go to the defying golden haloes, <u>realign? Go jet! *Bitsy*</u> nimble pint-sized girls and with its sea green Yo Bit, involved much? present, but the larger exterior of mis-placed Nice photo! Exemplary! plain women in the room bathtub tiles, how can But ease off that sun! caused fussing. Perhaps our poor attempt begin Cuz our mag advertises a killer blow. But face to describe this weird SPF! You might lose us it, we all take to wide spectacle? Be sure you some sponsors! But bed eyes and nimble bods! put this uggo building action? No prob! *C/H* Cont'd pp 287, Col 2 in your itinerary! *C/H*

"Is that a dream! Nimble me better look into that hostel! And that Cocojo!"

That other article brought back memories. At age ten little Beatense read this story, *Jam Session At Abby's,* about a girl who hoped to have her choir group over to practice, but she was ashamed of her wretched smelly old apartment. She thought, maybe a little paint would help. She asked her father, and he said yes, so when her friends came over they exclaimed over the inviting new look.

9

Beatense closed the book and looked around at her own prison bedroom with its stained, dull ocher paint and age blackened bureau. With trepidation the girl went to her father to ask if she could paint her room. He was cold, distant and mean. After much disapproving comment he asked how she expected to pay for this paint. This was awkward for her, of course she had no money. But he actually pulled out a ten and without a word went back to his box scores.

A disaster. The idea of painting her room did seem easy, but the reality for this picked-on, sad little girl was a blotchy, splotchy mess. Her father heard her defeated sobbing and peeked in on her. For the first time since Trudy died he felt sorry for his lonely, and paint splattered, daughter. He wiped his own tears.

"Now, here there, darter, lets me shows yer how yer do it. Yer gots a good start, but the trick is long, smooth strokes. Here now, watch how I do this."

The two worked together and the girl's bedroom was transformed into an awful Peony Pink. She loved it, but more important, she and her father laughed and got to be fast friends. The dresser next, hideous Plessy Ferguson red.

Father and daughter went to Rentschler's and they decided on a cozy little bed, a bedside table and a just right desk for doing homework.

"Now there ya are, darter, I knew it! I wents and got yer all spoilded! Fancy this and schmancy that! Next youse will wants ter paints the living roomie!"

"Well, Pop, as long as you brought it up..."

"You jest hesh! We ain't paintin no living room, sech foolishness! But if we *was* to paint it, *ahem*, what color do ya rackermand, all these *notions* of yers!"

She fell onto the nearby sofa laughing. The flattered father pointed it out to the clerk and said, "Aye, we'll be taking that too, her blubbering it all up!"

The living room was done in Lettuce Snow. Clothes next, Beatense picked out a dozen nice new dresses, quite the rarity in this parsimonius world.

This was a land of endless, gritty slums. Of kids playing in trash can lined alleys. Of walk-up flats and flowers set in empty pickle jars. Of fish sticks, liver, pot pies and sardines. The father, sitting at the table in his sleeveless T-shirt, would get two full scoops of tuna glop, while the son in high school got one scoop, plus a little more. The mother and young sister would each get one. It was never enough. You gotta give McDonald's credit, until then us poor people didn't know food had actual taste.

The high school senior above had to wear his father's flapping old flannel suit to the prom, but as mortifying as this was, he knew that the other guys heard the same coarse shouting, "What's wrong with it? It's a perfectly good suit!"

When the truck came to deliver the couch it got everyone's attention. What the deliverymen dreaded was the five flight hike. The old sofa was typical; the cushions were worn through top and bottom and the cotton stuffing was coming out. Car seats were the same way, but those cushions couldn't be turned over. The smart motorists put in seat covers when their cars were new, thinking this would save the upholstery, but with the action of their getting in and out the fabric wore through anyway. There was talk that down in Xanthallado clothes, furniture and rugs lasted for decades.

Travelers returning from there swore that they saw ten year old cars there that looked like they had never been driven. They had quiet, tuned exhaust.

The drawback with little Beatense's new dresses was that their bright floral prints enhanced her high color, making her different. All too dependably, summertime her color was accentuated, a skin contamination she detested and tried to avoid. I too.

One asset the girl did have was her little tuckets of bone over her eyes, that gave her a probing perception that people quite deferred to. Not I. And her quick dexterity as she got older made Beatense one of the first picks for gym or street play.

Ten below winter, age twelve, she ducked into the big train station near home to warm up, and strolling around on one of the waiting benches she found a women's magazine from that storied southern province, Xanthallado. Thrilled with it, she went on to frequent the depot and she grabbed any other magazines that were rarely left behind. Their pages showed tan as a need, worthy of one's investing entire days.

Beatense saw the possibilities. So still twelve that summer she tagged along for the farm surveys, and in her play alone in the back field heat, with no one to see she went nothing. Cradled in silent sun surrender she excitedly got herself iron rusted.

Her father was glad to see her smiling for no actual reason, but he objected to all the magazines she collected. For all his shouting she had a big stack in her fuchsia room. He lectured her as she paged through them at the kitchen table.

Those small, iron rusted arms in play, she absently repeated, "Oh, shut up!"

"Them maggies are keruptin ya, darter! I tain't never seen no sech trash! Them raggedy clothes tain't fittin to wipe up an axeedent runnin to the bathroom! That's if them libberteen corndogs gots no clothes on at tall! Which they never ain't!"

"Oh, shut up! Just because they're teaching me what's what in life."

She didn't care to mention what that What's What was, or her interest in it.

"I'm telling yer, darter, them mags is fillin yer nog with all silly idees, the way you run them fields without nothing on! And the roofie too, I might add!"

Her head jerked up. How did he know about her rooftop escapades?

"You know about that? But I'm always hidden! Anyway, I am pretty legal at the beach. You don't know it, Pop, but I sent for this bikini I saw in *Cheap Sluts*, yellow, with the pieces string tied, that I wear under my extra long T-shirt to get there."

That shirt didn't hide that her growing bones were pulling her freshened muscles into a light, hardened efficiency. Still, she managed to have nourished little teacups, quite separated. Her father really had no objection to her careless tendancy, and the news of her disruptive tie-bikini was no revelation; he knew all about it.

But he acted out great anger. "I seen that beekanee! Don't think you hads me fooled! And I'm thinking to make you wear it out in the farmer fields too! You wear it over by that river beach? So yer little pertoot is in plain disgusting sight?"

Yes, thong styled, it was. Beatense's smooth doeskin patina had a remarkably captivating life deep and dark within. Just in her long T-shirt she started helping with the bank surveys in town, but for the rural work with old Julius helping her father, the girl ran free despite her father's threat. She was less free when they platted out any new subdivision tracts within the city limits. But if they were helpfully enclosed by tall weedy growth and excavation piles, the girl got away with her top and bottom or even just her bottom as they staked out the lots and ran the curb and gutter alignment.

One evening, "Yer catching on quick, darter, not real quick but quick enough, so I'm thinking to send you out to this surveying camp. That way you can get yourself licensed and you can stamp your drawings the same as me or Julius."

It was hot, she was in her bikini. "Me, licensed? But Pop, I'm only thirteen."

"It's a two week term. You just have to get certified out at that camp and sign up for the city licensing exam. We can charge more then. And I can pay you full rate."

"Yeah, right. Full pay, Pop. Sure." Beatense smiled.

With that she fell back into the dusty old armchair. In the dim living room lighting she appeared as a sapling of knotty pine heat, a wrenching look. Being indifferent to food the girl's hips stuck out and her belly lay sunken, but her apples bulged into the tiny triangles of her top. Her impolite, uncouth hair was all atoss. She stunk of sun.

She sprang over to the hall closet mirror. A backside look at herself gave her a jarring shock as her bottom's vertical string lay unseen within her butt divide, and this coverage lacking, with that woefully edited bottom strip, did persist frontally.

Her firm breasts were petite, but the bridging cross-tie of the flimsy triangles lent them a very pronounced visibility. Her father smiled, heart pounded. *That's me!*

Dawn the next day the girl broke her bikini in for streets use by venturing out in it when they were still grey empty. She ran thirty blocks. Later, the sky hot, Beatense took to her building roof. Several ladies hung their laundry as she hid back of her peach crate barrier in her tie-pieces and melted butter. By noon left alone she untied into a ninety degree flotation. Five, as re-tied she bolted down the building stairs.

She re-ran the now busier streets. Just some yelling so ever after she ran to the beach tie-pieces only. Her camp application required swimwear photos. Father took them, accepted. Midsummer the two left for the surveying camp at the Superior and Commercial Oil fields, out in the great Geode Desert, the main reason for the photos. In fact reflection panels were by the pool.

Surveying lab mornings, class evenings, afternoons free. The camp was six miles from the Allegan River Gurney branch.

Also on the river was the lonely Nywot Transfer station. No agent, no nothing. It was just a waiting room with vending machines at Desert edge for the trains or those foolhardy vehicles making the Clarendon-Xanthallado hell trip. Boats also stopped.

Beatense and father got off of the southbound Queen Of Steel here to await the camp bus. Girl swam, then, father snoozing under the overhang, in olive oil only she waylaid a luggage cart. This began her desert sun epic. Long night in waiting room.

Beatense got more sun, then the Xanthallado train pulled in with those campers, just as the bus also arrived. Girl put on her tie-top and butt-cut shorts, gave father a hug and ran over to the noisy other kids, forty in all. She saw that they all had clever looks, starved detail, rampant tans and shaggy hair. Petro intern Lesta stepped out.

Skeletal, elitist, all-over sun immersion. "Hey, losers, no laws, no AC, so strip!"

They did, Beatense also. The sole Arrolynn sign-up, yet like the other kids, with hair wild piled she was cute, strap strong and fiercely tan. She sat with young Soler, who said she had a medical clothing exemption for school, stores, even the train.

This stick little, sunk belly nature-creature, everyone, called Beatense Puppet.

Next day pool-side the thin sunned intern guys coached the barbells. That night the intern gals hosted disco heat at the club, and even the lamb-like academics snaked their snaky selves in nude need. Puppet wickedly writhed. Dance end she trustingly went to Lesta's follow-up party. Video taking, milken gay Frond worked Soler. Then.

"Hi, Puppet, don't be afraid. Hold him. Real deep in, he will make you happy."

Better instincts forsaken, shaking child held. Lesta talked her through that scary deep in, that with her springy build electrified her. Loved it, so next day Lesta set up her implant. Like her tent-mates the tan fevered activist went too active, waylaid her survey studies. And Geddy, the chemist's lonely daughter, one of many on-site kids, warned that it was all very wrong. "Hey, GidGad, let *my* belly do the aching! Idiot!"

Afternoons, Puppet and Soler swam, clanked iron, panel reflectored, ran, battled tennis and joined in savage gallops from the small stable. After class, still bared the two played pool at the club with Geddy and parents, then danced up recreation.

Trip home, Puppet hit Nywot. In just her Lesta-given thick-knit crochet patch and Camp Gurney tummy-tee, she conspicuously sprang from the train. Tearful hugs.

"Naked, Pop! In class or helping with lunch, or in the lab logging the diopters, or riding Feisty! Plus dancing and just fucking! But poor Geddy scolded me for that."

Saves me the trouble. Once home, fueled by her fluids, moody looks and black attack, Puppet burned to continue bare, but her father told her, rural only. She wept. Like the Deployers, I too, she benevolently yearned to assert and hurt. People stare, as if this is soothing. Like the Deployers, I too, Puppet cared to comfort them.

"Just be dang glad I'm lattin you keep scaring the beach in that beekanee!"

Except, insatiably she later ran crochet only. Arriving, item off. One day in patch and her bathed glistening, she went from beach to library. Police escort home.

"Pop, I was just returning a book! And this is lots more than at the beach!"

"What's that, more than at the beach!? You tain't all nakie there, are you?"

"Like kinda, yes. I got restless, I began running there no top, and getting to the beach, I just went bare. I run, swim, get drinks… The lifeguards just look at me!"

As usual he tried to look angry, even as the blinding miscreant stood before him within her scrap, which with demure concern she did wear for the book visitation.

The police were troublesome at the beach too, so Beatense had to find out how culpable her all-over pine knotty naughtiness made her. One evening, in the roomy white cotton office shirt she found at Zanderhechts, sleeves rolled to her elbows and four buttons appallingly open, she returned to the library and, disregarding the hostile staffers, she found and studied the municipal codes. No mention of exposure, so by default her naughty naughtiness wasn't so naughty. *So, they can't arrest me!*

Even now, but for her long shirt the girl, in nothing. On impulse, removed. Heart pounding, she held out her long, slim leg and eyed its live vibrance. Shirt off as she left, everyone stared. Back on her street she played tag in nothing, and rooftop next day in just butter, worked her recent weight set. This was still summer thirteen. At workday end, in zero she hopped from her father's truck over to their building. Beach visits, evening street play and runs caused more commotion. *I'm as bad as Soler!*

Not enough. "Pop, let's move out to the Gurney! I have to retake the class, and they need a surveyor to stake out the new wells and pipelines. And for me Soler is gone, but there's Geddy and Lesta, and I can go bare and run Feisty over the desert, and fuck! Even fifth graders begged, me next! Plus I fitted in there, unlike here!"

Yes, the idealized depictions of damsels in portrait art, books or garden figurines, always showed them as exquisitely waif-like. But in this derelict world any beings of this look were limited to young Miss Colwell of the complex eyes, compelling cheek points, small low chin, angled up nose, dark rank hide and forest princess hair, that straw-like fell about in hopeless dry tangles. Again that winter, her etched butternut face and tumulted hair set her apart. Then summer fourteen, another try at camp.

Nywot again, bus came, girl got on her patch. Forearm held protectively before her, she confronted her father. He cursed and threw his hat down, but he had never seen such a jolting sight. Golden rusty black, Puppet was intricately emaciated with hard survival stamina. Her sun-imbued, bone chiseled face had a look of all kinds of evil secrets, and her rays-blonded auburn hair strayed tously fly-away, as if she was never civilized, and would kill anyone who dared to tame her.

Her dark eyes bored into her over-awed father with majestic menace. Her small breasts were lifted with nips stuck out, her little butt was carved into two tight bulges, and the restless annealed huntress sinuously flexed. Father winked, went with to the bus, affably met the good-influence Lesta. Reunion surprise, the lecturing Geddy.

After round of hugs the other campers fell silent as Puppet hopped on the rattly bus. Played pool again with Geddy and indebted parents, for her friendship and this year demanding she bake out. Set her up with milky gay, talked her through rapture. Wise father took trembly, bonier novice to clinic. Her slight self, poking hips, delicate arms and legs, throbbing tan and delight in play all gave her a popular, dreamy life.

Driver from supply barge told of big elderly boat camp. Lesta led the stable and wheelie-snarling dirt-bike kids in raid. Club victory video, blackety wet Geddy reined over as blackety wet Puppet tackled an old grey from the unruly Feisty. Blackety wet boys kicked him. Last view, the girls with other riders flipped off to run back to camp. Watching, whooping, whippy waists whipping, the twin nudes writhed up delerium.

Heading home, Puppet hit two ghastly days Nywot. Then on train, blackety dry.

In the later summer photo session, Puppet and the twig-like sleepy Slat, a tanner the team brought in from Xanthallado ($18,000 fee) did lard oil barbells and city runs. At the beach they swam and got lard oil sun, but in their public wrestling the shy Slat went stiffened aim only. Night secret camera, hours deep in, and the poor tired child got to keep the lard oil quart and ultra-tight three-inch zipper jeans, that she wore for the uproarious, calamitous about-town no-shirters. Last chapter, *Fairy Flies Free*.

Using part of her $48,000 up-front, the fairy bought the flying steed, Spook. With her good humored engaging looks, coat hanger shoulders, gaunted collarbones and hips, out-shifted peaches, sunken belly, hung biceps, her feral hair and surreal grey photo tones, frail Slat's too, altogether with its edgy portrayals, *Fourteen* sold mega. Their night dimly lighted, stores, even libraries and schools, could safely offer it, and Puppet's camp videos in Xanthallado's NetField raised demand there, gaylords full.

But as finally certified, the Book Girl still helped with the lowly surveying.

"Pop, I pulled the pin before I set the point! We gotta redo that line!"

"I saw that coming! Nakie or not you jest watch whatcher doing stedda yerself!"

Not easy, I often eyed myself myself. So with everyone in Beatense's sad world homely and ungainly, they didn't interest her. Unlike back at camp, no one, in Maple Ridge too, had her projecting Presence, look of insight, uncanny muscle and sun self focus. That summer, as if stricken with her tan propensity she deflected the curious attention with snooty irritation. She had that persona of educated, sheltered care, of meticulous priorities transcending animal need and passionate brown, so bare at the beach, with her forbidding power, she affected stately stern distaste.

Her father was quick to trip her up, but she still stood out. Back in the old 1950s very few of us stood out, but the supremacy boys we saw did. We marveled at those superiors, but for truly strenuous specimens, it's bad form to be or see. In the rural surveying, with seers rare, the in-patch sprite was free to be. Impatiently fast, the girl ran the range pole ahead for the foresights while old Julius held the backsight pole. And for the topographic contours (she did the maps) they got two level rods going.

If a sight line was obscured by brush the hot streak of hot muscle flailed at it with the machete like a fury. And sweat wetted she clacked the transit legs together and ran it on her shoulder to the next turning point, then set the transit back up, with the plumb bob centered in seconds on the stake driven in with the last set-up. She then took the backsight on the range pole held by Julius.

Pipe smoking Mr. Colwell turned the angle to the next corner, then put the pin on line as held by Beatense, who then ran dragging the measuring chain to set the new point. On cooler days she replaced her absent sweat with liquid lard.

Meanwhile there was Spook. She found him a stable, but with his restless blood he required lots more time than she counted on. All good. She took off days as a registered surveyor to ride, getting to the stable on her clunky bike.

Once astride she tossed aside tie-top and crochet patch, and she galloped ridge and road in bareback abandon. Her few witnesses watched in worship.

School start, awaited bell in tie top and butt-cuts. Refused, of course. Her deep vee white shirt, again denied. Back home, put on a filmy mail order dress, and long legs stepping, was finally allowed into ninth grade. At first she worried her teachers, but despite reputation she took her classes seriously even as she lit up the room.

In her fifteenth summer, offered a tent counselor job, the girl begged to return to camp, "so I can fuck again, Pop!" He almost let her but did not, so she went on with her beach, farm and roof cloth-lacking. As the Sarnia Street celebrity, her neighbors watched fondly as she played in the games of tag, baseball or Run Sheep Run in her crochet, lightly flitting and yelling nonstop with exorbitant tan flashing.

One day at noon in this fifteenth summer, she came upon Scott. At last, another union since Slat, who bothered her with his silly caution. Public working would have paid her a full five dollars per book, even beyond her contract of one hundred eighty thousand, which sadly was closing in fast. Once she hit this, her two dollars a copy would fall to a measly one dollar, even with the night play.

Beatense, in deciding to fly a chancy beach run, told her father she wouldn't be helping the next day. *Oh? Help, you call it?* Towel aflutter, in-zero Beatense sprang the stairs to the street and started out fine, but running past her own block she felt a little iffy, so she ran full tilt to the safety of the beach, six blocks. Then later the trick was getting back. The girl felt all sunned out, unusual for her but it was humid.

In a lethargic fog she walked. Even in this foreign stretch her startling state was popularly accepted, because she was already patch-famous through here. And the book did set her up for special rights. And so she planned to go total ever after, but told her father that some indoor venues, unlike with Soler, might be ill advised.

"Absolutely, darter! I always thoughts yer was smart, and this proves it!"

"I think we can calmly discuss my concerns without your ignorant obstruction!"

"That's right, I forgot what subject we was on! Yer being modest, right?"

"That, and inspiring is what I am, like with poetry, fine art or symphony."

The inspirer's working rural bare was easy for her, but for any tracts in town, she paused. Crochet topless, a good dodge. Otherwise, beach bare. Later as a hopeful new sophomore Beatense approached the high school, butt-cut shorts only.

Stared upon, awaited the bell, her irrespresiible shine burned painfully dark. Of course, refused. Returned, white shirt, four buttons open. Let in, then took shirt off. To the principal. She tried to cite the city's lack of laws but he said, "Aha, Miss Book, except we have posted rules." Shirt back on, same buttons open, stayed.

Girl later learned in health class that genital activity led to corrupted ruin.

"Just like Geddy at first, old Miss Cole said fucking for fun is bad, Pop!"

"I tain't so sure you shoonta done that, darter, imprapper as it twas!"

"So I said that having sex got me a hundred thousand, so how is that bad?"

"Don't get cocky. Another eighty grand yer take will be cut in half!"

Living in a scrabby flat, nice things always out of reach, Miss Cole resented how this slut's evil ways made her wealthy. Everybody else could feel this way. Arrolynn was a weary pit of grinding labor, but to its citizenry's credit they quietly endured their bleak lives and kept up standards that one star notoriously waged war on. Casually she got away with every outrage. Miss Cole bitterly resented this.

Beatense, by chance seeing her enter her decaying old building, was torn with guilt. She lingered after class, visited with her, but to no avail. She persisted, at last her wide placed eyes and regarding forehead had effect. "You silly little toothpick."

Summer sixteen Beatense ordered a tight fitting, airy sunsuit done in gold satin, that featured an inexcusable, slinky navel plunge. Despite her faded book fame, she still had great power. The new principal stared into that russety black gap and at her russety black arms and legs. He rasped, "Today only." This was her junior year, leading to another summer of riding, sunning and surveying.

In that summer the girl cut a T-shirt off like her old Gurney slash crop. First day senior year, in that and butt-cut shorts, all russety black. "Today only."

At year end the girl got an undeserved break, from the combination dirigible mooring mast and antenna atop the Inctin tower. At graduation the DWBD manager saw her solo *A Sad Sad Goodbye,* as her voice's rough crackles intruded on its light silvery tones. After the ceremony he waylaid the girl, already brown within her gown, and offered her a job singing ads. Her irritated look. "Well, I suppose."

Beatense and father entered the palatial lobby of that landmark edifice, and were escorted to the studios on the 69th floor. As they discussed the details the Presence gazed in wonder at the view. There were two options, either wait at the musician's union and take potluck as they answer the phone and one by one call over the tiredly hopeful other singers, or DWBD could sign her as direct inhouse talent. This meant lower rates, but then she wouldn't have to loiter at the hiring hall for placing.

With the new summer in progress, Beatense readily contracted for that.

Her sessions took place in any of the smoky, dim, low rent, grubby second floor studios uptown. At first as the girl did her gigs the union singers resented her scab ploy, but her singing about soap, coal or cereal got their attention. Beatense brought along Flora Cole, they always dined at Whitman's first. Her father took an interest in her and went with, cussing as usual. They got to know many of the legendaries who kept the city's tube-set radios and phonographs warm at night. One time a no-show.

"Hey, teacher, can you sing?" Got $75 and contract. "What a traitor!"

3

AGE NINETEEN

Beatense's hair was a waterfall; its massed profile shag density hid all but her nose, cheek points, mouth and low chin. It rather distracted from her charred, long drawn thighs, with that light pack of fine muscle, and her decorative small arms.

This summer had been different. She was often left home to draw the maps and run the slope stake calculations, and just wearing a slop of melted butter she set up shop out on the fire escape. She was right in sight of the other buildings across the way, but she got used to this and no longer felt exposed. She had to carefully pin up her hair for these sessions, because otherwise its full shaking weight fell down her back, blocking the sun. During this past summer she often went entire days nonstop fabric-free, running to the beach too, and now she was on her way to college.

"What's wrong with my dress, Pop? It's raw unbleached cotton!"

"Oh yeah, for the $600 you paid it's got the seeds showing like a feed bag!"

"That's the whole idea! What you really object to is it's cut kind of short."

"Short! Look at that, not one inch of them legs is hided! It's disgraceful!"

"That's the way it's supposed to be. And it is a little longer if I'm standing."

"Well, yer better do a lot of standing when we gits down to the college for yer registrationing! Darter, they are likely to kicks you right off campus, but don't look at me none for no ride home, wearing that disgusting rag! Yer nippies almost shows!"

"It's got a wide, deep vee cut. It's a way of showing I'm proudly healthy."

"Healthy? That sucked in belly of yorn looks like I don't hardly never feeds you none! And yer running nake all over tarnation don't help! Now hesh!"

"Now don't you go and blab, Pop. I don't want anyone down on campus to know I'm the ad singer, so I'm going to be way more modest. Fall's coming anyway."

"They'll know it's you! Plus they're lining you up to sing records too!"

"There's no record deal, that was just studio talk. Or it better be. Now look here, you're managing my welfare escrow account for people who can't pay the rent or buy food. I put in fifty thousand for that. I don't want anyone kicked out or left hungry. Of course I do look hungry myself, being the picky eater I am."

"Picky is right! And tell your evicted friends to quit their damn drinking!"

"That's why I want you managing it. You can tell a drinker better than some fool social worker, being such a wasted, bumbling and useless slosh yourself."

"Oh now listen to this! You got your own slosh with the sun, darter!"

"Well that slosh has got me worth 185 thousand, minus that fifty."

"You takes that fifty back! Them boozers, it's their own damn fault!"

"Boy, I wish I brought Spook with. But the school does have a riding club."

"You ride decent, you hear? You say riding nakie yer at one with yer horse! You think if you gallop fast enough no one can sees yer are nake, and okay, I gives you that, but you go plodding along right along the road, too!"

"Well I have to rest Spook down to cool him off. And myself, of course."

Mr. Colwell grunted with bemused satisfaction, but said, "Well, no more of that! Winter is coming and that might pound some sensicals into yer idiot fool head! Flora says it's time you civilize yerself down! I agreed but said it's hopeless!"

"She says everything I do is wonderful. So here we are, Pop, driving down to campus in this old dump of a truck, famous me riding like a piece of freight."

He gave her an absent gaze. "I cudda and shudda stuck you on a bus!"

"Why didn't you? But just hurry and get there. And try to find some back parking lot so no one sees me in this rattle-trap. A girl has to have some pride, you know."

"Oh, pride now! I thought you was the shy type! I just learned something!"

The girl laughed and gave her father a shove. He scowled, eyes twinkling.

Registration and orientation would be the next day; this was move-in day. As she entered the lobby she had her usual effect, especially in her frock, that showed just how under-fed a girl could be. She was no longer the famed Book Girl, that was five years ago, but she still cast a spell. She set her elbows on the counter and told the staring fumbling attendant her name. After signing the forms and getting her key and linens she asked if there was roof access. The bewildered reply was no.

As she and her father carried her things up Beatense worried about how to take advantage of the waning late summer sun. She didn't care to break these people in to her habit by lying out in the dorm plaza, yet, but roof seclusion was denied her.

But getting herself established in her little room (her roommate Trinket had yet to arrive) a look out the window reminded her that her dorm was right across the street from a woods, that invited investigative exploring, as unencumbered.

"Ay, darter, yer wants we get some eats at that truckie stop we went by?"

She was about to say no, the sun called to her, but thought better of it.

"Yeah! It's just eleven so I should be back here by noon, to get… *Settled*."

"Yeah, darter, I know what kind of settling you have in mind! You get good and kicked out of here and I'll get you backs home where yer damn belongs!"

At last twelve-thirty they stood by the old panel truck, that looked like it had been built with flat sheet metal and then inflated. On the side was painted,

STANLEY COLWELL
Land Surveyor

The two hugged, and Beatense failed in hiding her tears.

"Pop, I might take you up on that, coming back home, but… I have to stay!"

"No one wants you there scandalizing the whole neighborhood anymore than you did already! Now things can settle down and be normal for a change!"

"Oh shut up! I might bring Spook here, so expect me home next weekend."

"You cares more about that broken down foundered horse than me!"

Beatense watched the truck wheeze and gasp its way down the street, while the passersby stared at her legs and that hair all down her back. She ran back in to her room (still no Trinket, probably giving her pig a final hug) and got off her dress.

On went her new jeans over her patch (she outgrew the Lesta one), both ordered from a *Chez Health* ad, and her self-cut T-shirt. She stepped into the hall and faced several girls with cold aplomb, her skin and hair popping out their eyes. Unlike her hemmed Gurney shirt, which kept its shape, her present tee's scissors cut was curled up. Her turgid apples pushed the shirt out obviously.

She said hello and stepped into the stairwell and took them down two at a time. She burst out into the busy lobby filled with parents and students lugging clothes and boxes, and she sprang out the door and across Pinewood Street.

As soon as the trees half obscured her she stripped to her crochet patch and ran off through the woods, that conveniently had a network of paths. She came out into open fields and put a sandy ravine to hot use. It was sloped into the sun's angle so it aimed the rays, but this wasn't enough to make up for the lateness of the season and her tan knew it. She put in three hours and then explored the countryside, and found an old quarry. This was at the mile distant dead end of Pinewood, that in this rural stretch was a gravel road. Despite the threat of any cars coming oby she followed this back toward her dorm, at the extreme southwest corner of the campus, and town.

Ducking in the woods she put back on her hidden jeans and barely there T-shirt and ran over and entered the dorm. As she walked the hall to her room, in turning aside to let several staring girls go by, her tan did seem too loud. For Beatense this was an ill-timed first impression she made, and as if they had all been just discussing her the girls suddenly went quiet. The girl got to her room and saw that Trinket had moved in, and she was most likely in that group that had just cold shouldered her.

Most likely they were on their way to the cafeteria for their first meal in college, a fun adventure that Beatense was excluded from. And now even with her reserved pride she knew deep fear. Four years lay ahead of her of being a social outcast, and just these few minutes were painful enough. She could not and absolutely would not go by herself to that cafeteria; she would have to sit at a lone table while everyone stared at her. That tuna sourdough and cherry pie would tide her over nicely, so just now she didn't need to eat, but there was tomorrow and the next day and the next.

The floor lay dead silent. Trinket had an old wind-up alarm clock, and its noise seemed to bounce off the walls. Everyone had gone up to eat. For the first meal the cafeteria would want to put on a big feed, including thick slices of roast beef heaped with mashed potatoes and arm-matching gravy. Beatense imagined a rattly old cart wheeled through the tables, from which big hunks of chocolate cake were given out, with ice cream. The girl sighed, then tensed as the door opened. Yipes!

Trinket was a dull blob, and for the first time in her life Beatense wished she had the same common looks: That indifferently pudgy array of mis-matched body parts, along with scraggly hair and corny thick glasses. As a farm girl, Trinket had enough sun exposure to get the usual muddy beige smudge.

"H-Hi. You're Trinket? I'm... I'm glad to finally meet you."

"Hi, but tomorrow I'm going to the housing office to get reassigned."

"No! If I'm making you uncomfortable I should be the one to move."

Trinket seemed disarmed by this concession. "Well, I guess we can see how it goes. How did you get so... So rotty banana? You're not a gypsy, are you?"

"No, you can leave your things lying about. But I might throw that noisy clock of yours out the window, though. Er, wh-what did you guys have... To eat?"

"Eat? We just went for a walk around campus. They're not serving yet."

"Yet, meaning this evening, or yet, meaning not until tomorrow."

"Breakfast. The doors open at 6:30 AM. Then registration. oLet's jump right up there, Beatrice, to beat the... Boy, you sure are skinny. Like a toothpick!"

She laughed. "That's two of you who called me that. But Trinket, I did mean it about moving if you want me to. I don't want to put you in a difficult spot."

"We're both physics majors. I think... I think us two better stick together."

Beatense had to turn away, looking in her closet as an excuse. She took out her cotton office shirt. Watching as she put it on, Trinket shook. That hair, and the faded and swirl-stitched jeans that fit very tightly, stretching the girl's legs into stems, and were set so low to the eleven inch hips they had a three inch zipper. The back seam cleaved her rear anatomy into two tight curves, giving that take-charge look.

The tall girl's face was awash with tan, giving her bone sculpted cheeks a strong, projecting force. Her carelessly wind blown, sun lightened fronds enframed her face and long neck, and of special threat was the profile projection of her tipped nose and long jaw from out of this back lengthed, shaking mass. This, and she was hard.

"B-Beatrice, you're just so... Just so... You're beautiful!"

"Finally I get some credit. But it's Beatense, Trinkle. Anway, this is what I'm wearing tomorrow, by the way. I do have actual dresses, but one last fling."

"Well, you m-might button your shirt up a little more! You almost show!"

A few other girls entered the room, and they too noted Beatense's child-like size and sun steeped skin. They felt her as an energy, especially with her shirt almost all opened. She replied to their question by saying she had gone out on a hike; as a licensed surveyor it was almost inbred for her to get the lay of the land.

She said she had a pesky little horse, described in the ad as a push-button, but was not. They smiled; they knew all about it. She left out that Spook was actually a stamping and snorting thoroughbred that she just-sweat galloped.

The next day in her gold satin sunsuit, with slim legs steppy long. No one had preparation for the human creature so drawn out and personality facial-detailed. And she wore her look-twice volcanic tan and long hair as if they were points of pride.

The girls got their classes lined up in registration, then they went into the Main assembly hall for the usual welcoming speeches and warnings to study hard, and to avoid an activity which "cannot be named" but would result in punitive expulsion.

Beatense was the only one who knew what the dean was getting at, and hoped that no one would find out her ravenous history. But she wasn't about add to it; as expected the guys here on campus would never show up in any photo book.

They all had that dull look of agrarian confusion, especially as they beheld that springing, coffee-colored filly with the light, tensiled lines and scattered hair.

Beatense wanted to get back to her sand patch that afternoon, desperately, but she played at being sociable to allay any lingering doubts the girls had. She iced the deal by lending out her magazines, which in this strange land were the equivalent of contraband. The girls stared in amazement at the photos.

One feature they noticed; all the women in the magazines seemed to have the same cosmopolitan no-food look that Beatense did. Or the other way around.

As she entered her classes for the first time there was a suppressed shock that turned to delight, as if it was a plus to have her. Word had gotten round about this special new girl on campus, and everyone beheld her with deferential curiosity.

With her proudly exclusive hauteur she modeled her casual styled dresses from Xanthallado, that enchantingly flowed to her every inspired move. In comparison the dresses the other girls wore were dorky, shapeless and crummy. With this talented girl's example they saw the importance of the right clothes.

As time went by Beatense helped the girls on her floor in ordering new dresses. Like string bikinis being proper for the lanky only, she tactfully guided them to more functional styles that went with their unenlightened, proletariat proportions.

She had a natural interest in sleeping bare, and hopping up from her bed with a lusty stretch. Then her morning exercises. Just in patch mid week she was given a look by the varsity track coach, and a quickly gathering crowd. Went out for the fall schedule; the sun was easing up anyway. All training after four. Coach was right about her thighs, in her effortless lightweight sprints her feet didn't touch.

First Saturday, no meet yet scheduled. Beatense left Trinket to her dreams, and just in crochet patch and practicing for track she ran west along Pinewood, with towel and lard oil. She was on her way to the quarry, out at the end of the road's gravel stretch. She stepped warily into the digging and lay back between two rock piles at a good angle. Despite the season's waning days the concentrated sun hit in with the restoring effect of the rays themselves, and a stifling ninety degree bonus.

She figured she would be nicely secluded here, but in the late morning a party of students came hiking out along Pinewood with their walking sticks and busy ideas of sturdy exertion. Eyes closed, Beatense heard their voices as these intruders entered her sanctum, then they fell silent as they espied her. Unfortunately she should have picked a more hidden spot but did not, and as the suspense continued she knew that her visitors were edging in closer. Crochet set aside, she was a horrifying sight.

She lay oil-slopped dark brown naked within her saddle of white stones, and her jutting hips and collarbones proclaimed just how fearful of food she was. The four by eight inch oval of her long waist, together with her sunk belly, as accompanied by her stretched limbs and fertile baseball breasts, was paralyzing.

At four hours she turned onto her front, and her later visitors saw her better side. Despite its rude exposure no one felt offended by her wee, twin lobed butt. But now her waist looked even slimmer, as compared to the eleven inch width of her hips and the upward widening of her shoulders. Her lines had a steeled, fluid flow.

The trick was re-entering the dorm in just her piece. No prob, the west end door and stairwell were rarely used. She hid back of a tree until the coast was clear, then ran for the door, in and up. Sadly she met a few girls in the hall. Trinket was mad at being excluded. Beatense tried to explain that her cauldron had hit ninety degrees, plus her silent rays obeisance would have seemed a tad anti-social. This was a risk Trinket accepted, and she watched as Beatense lay out the next day at the quarry.

Considerately she kept her patch on, and Trinket observed how its thongs were hooked ever so lightly to her strange friend's stick-out hips. Her belly lay sunk.

Beatense wasn't responsive; as usual she zonked out barely conscious. Trinket took care of her theory of equations and then turned to her econ. Beatense slept.

She finally woke up, wet with sweat and espresso obscene in the hot glare.
"What? Are you still here? Trinket, you fool, this heat is dangerous!"
"It's not as hot as our loft with the bales coming up every twenty seconds."
"They made you do that? You should have some muscles then."
"I do, but they don't show like yours do. Come on, let's head back."
"Another hour. And then I'm going through that lobby like this."
"No! Use that west end door again. Okay, one hour, old buddy."

The gravel road was a mass of heat waves but 99% nude Beatense reveled in it. She and Trinket entered the neglected door and took the equally neglected stairs up. She recklessly walked the hall again in just her patch, live with tan and hair, and she ducked into the bathroom where the fluorescent lights added a smoking heat to her day's coloration. The results were gratifying, a shock to all, but sadly her last bake.

Even if she had the freedom, the next Saturday was a misty cold bust. The meet was at home. Allowed to run in her buttcut shorts and camp tummy tee she did four tape tears. Her spare lines and gapped five-inchers were unbeatable. If no conflcts she also worked the football sidelines, writing the coach's remarks on a clipboard.

She also joined the campus riding club, and despite the chill, as nude later in the season she galloped Truman bareback in the lonely fields. Even if it was cloudy, as oily blacked, the medaled heroine rode at most in her crochet patch, and she hacked with other club riders along ridge and road, all over the township.

Beatense settled into a sunless life, so she didn't mind the long bus rides to the away meets or the football sidelines. For speed she had Trinket shorten her hair, and she gave out the long glowing locks. Her wins made her popular, but she built a real circle when Trinket found in their mailbox the envelope from DWBD, rubber stamped with the legend, **CONTRACT RENEWAL**. So, that enigmatic girl was the ad singer!

As far-flung as the local stations of her friends were, they all ran her ads, so they often heard her jingles. Once track season ended her dorm-mates proudly attended her volleyball games, although as golden faded she didn't exceed or excel.

Meanwhile, the girl was a student. Her class friends noted that despite her reign she took careful notes and was always raising her hand. But there was a reason. She could feel that tension as any cold hearted teachers looked around for any hapless victims to pounce on, so she asked stupid questions or stirred up noisy discussions to spare them from any public embarrassment. Many times I cudda used her.

She always smiled, as if sharpening a pencil was a delight, or as if handing over her cafeteria meal ticket to get it punched fulfilled her with deep happiness. It was an act, but not entirely a cynical one. She had that zest of being kid little, but her active engaging with everyone was driven by her first fears of ostracism.

Back home she could be very aloof, even as a kid, but here she could start over, which is what college does to a lot of students. Her roommate was her biggest fan, because in the fall she had come to campus as an awkward nonentity, but Beatense worked with her, and Trinket blossomed into social demand.

Trinket accompanied her once when she went home one weekend, first to annoy her Pop, second to catch up with Spook, and third, to sing up commercials. Trinket watched her in the studio. She was very impressed, but was also surprised by the deprivation of Beatense's home life. A gritty neighborhood and, despite the bright paint, a basically dingy apartment. Her father fussed and yelled. It took awhile for Trinket to catch on that he liked her. Beatense read a letter saying they wanted another book. Cool! And with that prospect of more to come she sat down and wrote out checks totaling another $50,000 for the various local charities.

When the semester ended the school officials saw that there was an uptick in the grades for the classes she attended, where the students worked to avoid looking like fools to her, as if her opinion meant more than their own futures.

In registering at semester break Beatense had the foresight to get off a couple afternoons a week, even though at the time it was dead winter. As spring came she returned to the quarry, where even with snow still present the rock walls held the elusive warmth, while the stone piles focused the sun as she lay tucked within them. The girl, with hair regrown to upper back, started on her renowned tan.

Whenever at the barn, with little concern about indecency she put Truman in the side ties and brushed him and picked his hooves. She led him out and hopped on his back, which actually was wistfully envied by any rider less svelte.

"Hey, Sarah, heading out? I'll run Tru out in the arena until you're ready."

The girl was slouched so that her ripples were almost painfully curved in.

"Er, uh, yeah, okay. B-But is... Is that all you're... W-Wearing, again?"

It was. Once or twice a week Beatense joined the little groups as they scatted off along the dusty roads, with her faithful patch tied around her neck in case of trips into town. As a born horseman she always rode bareback, even as her ride suspiciously bucked at any blowing leaves or candy wrappers.

The girls wanted her to lie bare in the dorm plaza instead of going off to that rock quarry, and since she was riding nude this seemed like a reasonable idea. But she wanted to test her limits first. And so one hot weekday afternoon as the girl returned along Pinewood from the quarry, she was dark brown in butter only.

She met some hikers and gave a cheery wave. As she drew near her dorm the campus area was busy. Classes had let out, but the west end door was isolated as usual. No. The outlaw slung on her patch and shockingly entered the lobby almost naked, and after checking her mailbox strolled to the stairs. She walked the hall, and everyone crowded to watch her shower off her dairy grease with foamy suds.

The head resident informed the girl that where Pinewood was paved she was on campus and had to be decent. The stable was also school, and for that matter her horse as school property was considered campus too. "Oh, really."

It was a mistake for the Dean of Women to call the scandalous girl in after this lecture. She was aflame with blazing energy, and this was what confronted the fretful official as the truant entered her office. Instead of a dress, she wore her menacing, paint-tight, swirl stitched jeans. With their lethal three inch zipper they had a low, hips riding fit, and her white cotton shirt was tucked sloppily in, and rudely opened four buttons down. The resulting, shiny deep half showed her separated peach breasts, right to their fingertip nips. Her elbow rolled sleeves bared the dried finish of her thin, aesthetically flowed forearms, while within her clothing her muscles were exactingly stretched, shaped and aligned to fit to her lyrical frame.

Her thick cascade of wantonly tousled auburn, blond tipped hair formed a profile privacy curtain for the animal, and the lower lid drooping of her coldly skeptical eyes showed that she resented this arbitrary interruption in her important affairs.

Top cut girls have favorite ways to proclaim their assets, that include being Baked, Bulked (muscled), emBoldened and Bedded. Presently Beatense was active in just three of these. She sat in a slattern slouch, aggressively exuding her sexually sensual, splitting power. The brownist was a weightless athlete in the medals, and her bacon smoke sun-smell filled the room as if with an aura.

Dr. Appleton had of course known of her, few did not, but this was her first close sight of this bone-tight scofflaw. Awed by her prowess and Presence, the frumpy lady had no protective assets as the supernatural child irritatedly faced her.

"Young lady, what do you have to say for yourself?" said the old matron, as she tried to stifle her breath's terrified huffing. *She's… She's beautiful!*

"I'm not sure why I'm here. I admit I do walk nude along the unpaved part of Pinewood, and have entered right into the dorm that way, being quite concerned about my ventilation needs. More tamely, I also have been seen topless."

"That. You must try to accept that our classes are meant for the sole purpose of seeking and acquiring knowledge, not for gratifying one's exhibitionist whims."

"But I am decent in class. So is this about my gravel pit excursions?"

"We can't control what you do off of campus. But you ride horseback nude and that stable is a school facility. You ride nude along remote rural roads, which is bad enough, but even along main traveled roads. You entered the city limits in plain sight. People are complaining. And in your running on your own, it seems you're doing this now before it's half dark. That is disgusting. You play tennis, I admit skillfully, in just that tawdry scrap of yours. For girls swimming you're naked in the pool."

"We all are. Thanks for the opening remarks, but why am I here exactly?"

"What? You dare ask that question? Do you not have any morals at all?"

"I'm not sure what that word means, from your angle. But for me it means as a kid I had intercourse a hundred times at surveying camp. But I am open to compromise with you. In class I will restrict myself to my dresses only if I can, without any of your arbitrary interference, work on my tan nude in the dorm plaza. Agreed?"

"You don't seem to understand what trouble you are in. I have here a letter of dismissal that is addressed to the Registrar if you refuse to cooperate."

"It seems it's addressed to the Registrar whether I cooperate or not. Or do you mean you will send it if I don't fall into line with your notions of decorum."

"Your attitude is unaccept... I was told you're a nice girl. Why do you have this hostility? I'm only telling you how you can keep yourself in school here."

Slumping, "Okay, I'm sorry. But hey, I do wear actual dresses to class."

"True, but what about the stable and Pinewood Street, out to the quarry?"

"You said I could be naked off-campus! But I could wear my crochet piece."

"I heard about that crochet piece. How did you ever acquire such filth?"

"Mail order. Sixty dollars. But these jeans are just like the photo shoot ones."

"Yes, those tight jeans. All that convoluted stitching. But photo shoot?"

"My book. The jeans here are all baggy, but these I got mail order to replace my old book ones. Which I can still get into. The idea is to look all set to unzip, for even sweet faced, homework-doing precious young girls. It's just that we just do what we do, including very naughty but very fun activity, with whoever."

"Whomever. But let me tell you, all those spontaneous girls of yours are on the road to ruin. Yes, they might be enjoying their fun now, but they will all end up broken spirited and degraded. I would take that as a warning, young lady."

"I already said, I had sex all out at surveying camp. And I'm better for it."

"I'm appalled. Another point, your costume and stray hair show disrespect for the Dean Of Women. This is a disciplinary hearing. Groom appropriately."

"Oh, pish pish. Wanna hit the Union for coffee, Happy Appy? I can buy."

In love with this girl, she almost exploded. "I'm afraid that... P-Perhaps."

As usual Beatense drew huge interest, so the Dean felt her stock edge up.

"Your request, my dear, for nudity in the dorm plaza. We cannot refuse you per se with nude models in use in our art classes. Also this being college, one is expected to confront values contrary to his own. Still, we must deny you."

"Hey, Stinks," said Beatense later to her roommate, "nudity denied!"

"Can you be more specific, you old sweathog? You mean on campus?"

"She said in the dorm plaza. So I guess I would be legit anywhere else."

"Sure, you're nude off in some field, but how about tennis with me naked?"

Her heart pounded. "There again she didn't specify that as off limits."

Later that afternoon with friend, Beatense entered the tennis court in her long-cut T-shirt. Set aside. Just in her blackety wet skin, she had a magically mesmerizing interplay of boned muscle. Drew crowd. Shirt back on, dinner in cafeteria.

Then no-shirt blackety wet at the Dean's door. Pulled in.

At ten ran back through the campus, blackety wet entered dorm lobby.

That summer the administrators argued this situation. The new school rule-book faced a printing deadline, so should they target this trophy-case athlete? Her nudity was popular, and GPAs were up, too big of a coincidence, it had to be that rebel girl. Dean Appleton proposed that any new rules codify interpretive options if reasonable concealing steps are taken, as deemed by the perpretrators. *Yes! Oh my, yes!*

4

COLLEGE, 2ND YEAR

And so Beatense received a letter urging her return. She opened it after a long day of high heat atop the roof, and in the subdued lighting of the kitchen she looked viburnum reddish black. She read that she would be accorded certain freedoms with her habits, but to use concealing precautions.

"What do they mean, as determined by the perpretrator?" she raged.

"What's the prab, darter," said her father, lighting his pipe.

"It says here I have to use concealing precaution! But then it also says that it's up to me to decide this! Well HP Bulgebottom, I'm just going to go naked then!"

"Let me read that letter. I thought it would be kicking yer out of school!"

"Not yet. I guess I can look on the bright side. If I was a slow runner they would just kick me out instead of trying to humor me! And actually if you read this carefully, it says I can do the campus nude. Like me all over town, here."

"You been pushing that too far, darter! Plus yer singing all them silly-assed loonie tunes on the squawk box raddio like a caterwauling hyena!"

"Oh, I forgot! I have to go in to see them! I have more ads coming up!"

"There ain't no stations safe from you no more! I can't git no peace!"

That evening while Beatense worked her bedroom barbell set, every so often a neighbor skulked by on the fire escape and glanced in at her, shaking. Finishing up she sprawled out on her bed, right by the window. Later, bared but for her mail order Tri-Flites she went for a run, right through the theater row crowds.

The next day surveying she checked the scope crosshairs to verify that the pins they set were on line, then ran for the stakes and sledge. As her trusting father held the stakes she drove them into the holes of the removed pins. Then she ran back to verify that it was both on line and at exact distance. This was also the procedure in setting the corners of a rural plat, or for aligning the curb and gutter for a subdivision. All this was done with Mr. Colwell's ongoing cussed fault-finding, that had the shining nude happily arguing back. Even humdrum old Julius chimed in, laughing.

As the students returned to school everyone was relieved to see Beatense back on campus, now as a sophomore. The fear was that she would be lured away to Clarendon Poly for their track program, but by some miracle she had returned to the lowly ag school. Ready to defy those *concealing tact* limits, once settled she saw off her Pop, and did a campus run just in her thong patch. Then in oil only she ran from the dorm to the quarry, and put in four Nywot-like hours.

But prior to registration and the dull welcoming speeches next morning she was collared for a talk with the Dean of Academic Affairs. Inexcusably she was just in her Appleton-denounced thigh gap jeans and short-hacked T-shirt, but she had no prior warning of this meeting. But just like people admire a good fisherman in their midst, or a golfer, he accepted her condition. Without having to demonstrate as with golf she was obviously very good at what she did. Her bacon and maple sugar smell filled the office, and her four by eight waist oval seemed to be straining with tensions.

And with the confidence of being fun and cute she purposely showed a delight in life that included the Dean in her smiling benevolence. Taken by this fetching kid he made perfunctory comments and let her urgently hurry to her orientation session.

Yes, Beatense no longer felt the need to confront people with her attributes, but instead shared them. Trinket, who should have been mortified at her account of the torn shirt, was in awe. After the talks they got their books together, but then Trinket was miffed when Beatense escaped back to the quarry, alone, for the afternoon.

Trinket and friends got the idea of spying on her, and they hiked in the deep heat out to the quarry and sat atop the low enclosing cliff and watched. In contrast to that roiling glare, the oily wet shine of the slim girl shimmered coppery black.

After two hours the tanner got up and speed-flung egg-like rocks at the cliff wall, luckily facing the other way. At sixty feet she hit the same spot repeatedly and hard, bringing to mind the possibility of the spring baseball try-outs. She then lay back with wet pink split open. The girls shook at the sight. When she got up to leave the girls scurried down and "by chance" met her at the quarry's entrance.

Beatense was glad to see them, unaware they spent all afternoon watching her. As they returned to campus she stayed naked, and sat on the building steps right by the busy sidewalk. A campus policeman ticketed her. She took the citation, smiling guiltily. She mailed in her token fine of $25, which of course was refunded.

After all, she did add to the trophy case. The girl made her way to her first class Monday morning in a leggy frock of light cotton. As she entered the room everybody sighed, not knowing she would be joining them. Despite her anti-social attitude she smiled at her fans. The professor stared at the long muscles of her racer's legs.

Speaking of, she ran both track and cross country, and this ended her Saturday afternoon sun worship even if the meets were home field and the skies clear.

There are students who are parentally forced to go to college; so they try to flunk out. None of this took place with this girl who was familiar with everyone on campus. Never were pool cues ignored with more intensity. The test scores and grade points inched up again, and the students who actually did fail felt as if their lives had no use as they packed up to leave. If possible, they got to these track meets, for sure.

"Hey, Ed! Ed! You flunked out, hah? I might just be joining you in that, ha ha!"

In the Academic Affairs Office they were clever enough to see that there was a correlation. This was why that letter was sent, and why her freedoms were allowed. Anyway with fall's chill Beatense ended any controversey by dressing normally. But she did ride Truman shirtless in her three inch zipper jeans even with frost in the air. Guys who had little interest in horses suddenly saw the merits of the equine world.

After track Trinket asked Beatense to go home with her for the weekend, but she said she had already been asked by Rosa, and she was planning to go.

"But you're not friends with Rosa! How could she even ask you?"

"She was so nervous she could hardly get the words out. So I agreed."

"Beatense, you have to stop being such a do-gooder. Rosa's family is very poor and you'll be lucky if you get one actual meal. Of course, with the way you eat you'll be stuffed. But I'm warning you, they have an old dirt farm."

Beatense was shocked at the dirt farm's poverty, but Rosa's parents were even more shocked that this incredible famed girl came to visit. Word spread fast and the Sudecks didn't have to worry about the eats; stolid farm folk came in from all over to share in a huge potluck. By popular demand Beatense sang to long applause atop a picnic table. Rosa never was so happy. An old woman wept; she never knew such beauty existed. The smiling girl told her she ate three slices of her pie.

"Hey, if you think I'm cute now, wait until that double crust pie hits my genetics!"

There were parental concerns, but that night Beatense slept with Rosa.

As winter came Beatense didn't fade; during summer the Physical Culture Club invested in sun lamps and she put these to active use. At 600 watts they had more power than the sun, and with their primitive design their spectrum had more burning rays, and so Beatense got darker but cancer risky results. The girls on her floor had to face the long winter with her massive hot shine, and this year in butt-cuts and tie-top she turned sedate volleyball into war. As a sophomore, finally lettered.

They flooded the soccer field and Beatense skated with her friends. She actually was awkward at this, and even shivering in her crochet patch she watched the others float around sick with envy. She managed a sturdy, sure glide while the lesser girls almost did ballet. But Rosa loyally stayed by her. She was famously in love.

For the spring semester registration once again Beatense managed to book two afternoons off. But it would be months before she could work this. She kept on with the deadly sun lamps, so that during swimming class, under the violet hue of the new mercury vapors, her muscles were highlighted as she glowed stick skinny black.

The sun lamps had smoked in a burned-in heat that kept Beatense in constant pain, the feeling her skin was too small. The girl found it helped if she rubbed herself all over with lanolin cream, and with shaking hands either Rosa or Trinket massaged her back. The assembly of bones yelped and squirmed in delight.

Once Beatense went from the sun lamps to see an enthralled Dr. Appleton.

"So what is the problem, my child?" said the Dean, who sat transfixed.

"It's Rosa, on my floor. I went home with her for the weekend last fall, and I was warned that they just had this decrepit farm, but I was still heartbroken to see their poverty. They still use an Aerotor windmill and they just have a few mangy cows, but the problem is their tractor. It's a decades old Clafferton Nifty Farmer, with iron lug wheels and just eightteen horse at the drawbar. It doesn't have a three-point hitch or PTO; instead it just has this side-mount belt drive flywheel. I mean, you don't care about all that detail, but it's just that they won't be able to scrape up her tuition for the next fall, and so I would like to set her up with an all-expense scholarship."

"Ahem, back to the tractor," said the Dean. "How will you pay for this?"

"Oh, I have thousands, but it's her tuition, not the tractor I'm worried about."

"You won't have to do this. I can set up a fund for these kinds of cases."

"Oh, perfect! Now what about my case? Can I walk the campus nude?"

"That is despicable, you irritant. If you were a fictional character the editor would return the manuscript. No one could possibly be that insensitively crude."

"A crude nude. So, somehow I have to get them a new Thorvald 560."

Six endless weeks later Beatense was able to get to the quarry for her first real sun of the new year. The cliff-like enclosure, plus her lamp tan, helped resist the fifty degrees. But just in shine she did feel an invigorating chill walking the road back to campus. She went in the end door. In her room she studied her mirror. She saw how her bony, sun caressed face defined her noble hungered character.

Word got around about her throwing skill, she made fastball only relief pitcher, no fancy curves, sliders, change-ups. It helped that all games were under the lights.

The 560 was delivered, with the explanation it was a factory test model.

"Trink, in the daily rag today it tells of this new agriculture scholarship. I'm going over to the diamond, so if you see Rosa before me, do mention it if you are sober."

"Yeah! Okay! No prob! I hope they chase you with five homers."

If Beatense was done with classes by noon she was set for sun, but to be handy for the late afternoon infield practice kept her on campus. Her dorm was atop a low slope that gave optimum sun angle. She lay here in her crochet. The authorities let this slide; the dorms were staying full up. But to get in a quick gallop she ran the fields to the stable and back. She joined the other riders, hacking bareback.

Once they stopped at a root beer stand just in town. The naked girl had to stay mounted, but one fellow brought her a cone. She traced a cold milky streak from her separated peaches down to her sunk, sweat black belly, slouch curved.

The trap with sun worship is that it takes firm control. After a day of extreme sun Beatense was always humming with healthy contentment, so she happily made ever more disgusting shows of herself. She played tennis and sand volleyball and swung the hanging rings just in her crochet, and like back at home after dark she ran at high risk right through town. Beatense waved as the headlights caught her.

Good thing she didn't know it; she could have popularly run at any time.

The book people came. This latest would be in color. First, the girl strolling the campus in her crochet. Her father trailered in Spook for the stampede photos, where she chased wild horses. Then the quarry. Watched by the crowd, Beatense slucked lard on her blackety self. Mr. Colwell quietly left for lunch, then the imported Scott got her sunken rib-ledged belly working. Video got it all. Kids later $60,000 each.

Midnight they made secret dean visit. With her approval, on Art Day among the other works, model modeled herself live naked. That evening gala athletics banquet, girl got an award. Feeling of doom, last week of class. Then finals and school over.

When the dorms vacate at year end, we quietly exit with no farewells. Even with the empty campus I hiked off for a hidden last bake. Beatense did not. Feeling sad she walked the campus at high risk, few saw her, then hit the dorm-side slope.

5

HER RESERVATION

The two were heading back to Arrolynn with Beatense's things in back. With a towel laid over her seat the knees-up girl rode naked, legs in arms.

"Aye, darter, were you the last fool idiot on campus, were ya?"

"Almost. I saw a few lonely souls, probably staying on for summer school."

"I thought you said yer finals would be done up two days ago! So why didn't yer comes home yesterday instead of carousing around there all by yerself?"

"I wanted to walk the campus naked, which I did. Thanks for hauling old Spook down, by the way. It was sure fun showing him my Truman trails."

"Yeah, you made the evening news! You was nake right in town!"

"Sadly on black and white TV. And I feel really sad right now, I'll miss everybody so much. Yeah, I walked the campus naked but no friends to scream at me. I actually turned out to be popular here, I knew half the student body names."

"Speaking of body, your art exhibit in the yearbook was plain disgusting!"

"All those photographs and not one posted in the FieldNet to hype my sales."

"That latest book, it's plain disgusting yer gettin paid all that money for despoiling that nice kid Scott! It don't seem right, sixty thousand just for a few pictures!"

"And the videos. They said I was skilled enough for that advance. And hey, that was hard work! It's different being on camera, with everyone watching every move."

"Poor girl. So, you're back to being the Book Girl! Now if you could just do something about all that tangled hair! Then I could stand being seen with you!"

"If I had normal hair I would be two hundred thousand less rich."

"Speaking of, darter, they got pre-orders for forty thousand books! It ain't right!"

"It is right, Pop. It's very right. Girls should be rewarded for being natural."

Mr. Colwell leaned forward and saw her moist pink split. That piece of anatomy would make her a million. Maybe there was justice in that. And she was a nice kid.

"Oh, and yer might stop by Maverick. They got more addies for you to mess up!" The girl turned the rear view mirror to admire herself. "Hey! Leave that be!"

"Give me a break. I got a crick in my neck from looking down at myself."

Once back home, Beatense quietly decided to attend to life more modestly, with the proud satisfaction that she could subdue her baser instincts and be civilized. She made what she assumed would be her last just skin run. But next morning looking in her mirror, she compromised. So, in her short cut T-shirt and butt-cuts worn with her lone patch, she joined her father who was cooking eggs in their primitive kitchen.

"About time yer wakeses up! Look at that, clothes you gots on, hah?"

"You guess right, oh great seer. But my jean overalls, not. Why?"

"I already got a look-see on today's plat, and it tain't nothing but pricker bushes, thistles and brambles! Yer bestest wear them overalls today!"

"Well, shit! Can't you do better than that for my homecoming? Why not a nice traverse of remote, bulldozed acres of sandy subsoil full of roasting rays?"

"Yer wants some eggsies whiles yer settin there complainin?"

"No, I don't like the way those poor embryos never get a chance for at least one breath of air before they're sacrificed for the greater good."

"Or greater bad! Wait, you better wait on coming with! Yer gats to wreck up a couple addies today! The studio boys called to say they got some lined up for you!"

"The way they work, that could take all day! I better stick with you."

"Shit. Darter, I wants work done today, not yer settin there sunnifying!"

"I hope. Oh, I better bring my boys department overalls while they still fit, just in case it's as bad as you say. Make me some toast there, servant. Quick, now."

"I already made ya some, but yuh sets there yapping so I ate her down!"

Beatense and father took the stairs. There was some kind of secret telegraph in the building, so everybody knew if she was on the move. Several doors opened, the reason being to see this remarkably made girl after her latest absence.

They were disappointed to see her in shorts and cut-off T-shirt short as it was, because often this stairwell, roof top too, found her naked. She even did the laundry down cellar dressed in that way. And people along the streets awaited her running naked in the evening. Beatense hopped out and down the front steps onto the already heat waving sidewalk, and she opened the creaking right-side door of the truck.

"Pop, I can buy us a new truck, honest. Look, see? I have to lay my towel on this filthy seat to keep my legs clean. Good thing I didn't put on my oil yet."

"Yer ain't putting on no oilie today! This ain't school no more, you know!"

They drove along the gritty streets, that swam in the heat. They picked up Julius and kept on. As Beatense insulted him she had an out of kilter feeling as they drove along, past the shuffling, soiled humanity wrecks on the sidewalks.

"Just where in hell are we going, Pop? I take this way to the stable!"

"We are going to the stable! I got yer bike in back, under the tarp, and once yer done with overworking yer pore old horse, you can ride to the beach!"

Beatense eyed her rolled up towel with its bottle of olive oil secreted inside with heart pounding. She had assumed that she would be lying on some sand bank over lunch, but now she had a whole day of real sun before her.

"Well, shit! Give a girl some warning, will you?" she said by way of thanks.

Once the girl said hi to everyone and got Spook brushed down and spoiled with Oatalene, she led him out of the barn as he dutifully, patiently followed. Stripped and ready, she hopped on and galloped off bareback. Riding hard takes effort, especially for the horse, and so with her sweated belly flexing Beatense slowed down to a light canter alongside the gravel road. Quite out of character she then recklessly bolted her horse through the empty meadows and fields.

People nudged each other as she set her bike in the stand at the beach, for she had arrived in just her patch after riding fifteen miles on her clumsy bike.

She was slendy bendy enough to oil her back all over, and she untied and lay on her front. But it wasn't any fun, the beach was pitiful; the river had recently flooded, staining the sand with old mud. Barges full of ore slag and coal floated by, and near the park there were grubby warehouses, liquor stores, shitty pawn shops, and dismal taverns popular with the trembling local refuse.

Clarendon was strangely backward, it refused to adopt the technical progress of the ocean-caressed Xanthallado far to the south. Luckily they did develop the basic industries on their own, so that telephones, electric lights, refrigerators, automobiles, diesel locomotives and propellor airliners were in use. But they didn't accept digital computers or even photocopiers, and television was grainy black and white, and like the radios and the few computers they worked with vacuum tubes. Air conditioning was found only on passenger trains, and in movie theaters.

With their unrelenting ugly old fashioned lives, everyone on the beach stared in confusion at the oiled saturation of hot dark the famed star publically presented. As she did her back her dainty breasts lay pressed out, and the saddle-like sling of her lumbars lay low between the tight bumps of her little butt and the spinal curve of the widening rise to her shoulders, with waist at eight inches, hips at eleven.

With no escape from the heat, by one the great city of Arrolynn had fallen into a stupor. More mothers brought their squalling children to this Stoker Flats beach, and they played in the warm, smelly water and dug in the sand.

This was beneath Beatense's dignity, but the only alternative was her building's hot tar roof. At two the girl got in line to buy a drink, then walked the sands.

Back at her towel she slopped her poured-on oil all over her front. Her firm apples wriggled like rubber to her rough massage. A policeman stared as she lay back, split showing, and awkwardly placed her thinned arms. Her separated breasts angled out left and right, and her sunk, hard belly of tensioned silk could bounce a dime. Her hips and collarbones sharply jutted. Nice curve of bicep.

"Well, I didn't have any killer urges, Pop," said Beatense later, as she broke the orange she had peeled into sections. "I laid nude before all at Stokes as usual but I just couldn't get myself to flaunt myself by dancing in front of those shabby women."

"Lucky them! But yer wants to go nude there again tomorrow, do yuh?"

Her heart pounded. "Of course, but why… Why are you suggesting this?"

"Because I wants you arrasted so's you'll quits this damn foolishness!"

"I hate to say this, Pop, but I was in total nude with police enablement!"

"They should gits yer fer disturbing the peace, is what they should do!"

"Oh, yeah, like that foundry down the street with its sixty ton trip-hammers?"

"Well, leastwise with that the womens don't have to blindfold their kiddies!"

"Those kiddies came right up to me. Anyway, I stopped by the train station on the way home, and one of the magazines I found was actually quite recent."

"Them junk mags is trash and yer gonna toss them all out! Now what about yer miserable ad singing? Is that studio there despite you? You better call them!"

Beatense sighed and she turned to grab the phone and set it on the table.

"Hey, Monty, it's me. I'm back for the summer. Any jobs lined up?"

"Why, welcome back, Puppet. Yes, we have a couple regular ads, but this other one is a multi-talent number, where you lead in to me reading from the script with a muted clarinet background, then you close it out. It pays 250."

"I'm on flat rate, or is this a side job. Anyway, expect me at 8 AM."

Beatense made two pieces of toast and added cheese for a sandwich.

"Once I'm done with that, Pop, I'll try Stokes beach again. If I'm arrested at least I can bail myself out, with that 250 talent fee. Okay, I ate. Time for a bath."

"You just stay settin there! I ain't eaten yet! Try showing some manners!"

That evening as she lay upon her white sheet in the dim lighting of her still pink room, Mrs. Skillet looked in from the fire escape. She saw the curved furrow of the bare girl's spine as it traced up from her baby's butt to her delicate scapula blades.

In that particular lighting she hummed metallic golden black. The ugly lady stood rigid in fear. Beatense was aware of being watched, and making little fists she loudly stretched. She set aside her magazine (with its enticing Bitsy letter) and hopped up and watched by Mrs. Pickey too she began hefting her weights. Her shined muscles were tight like carved soap. With barbell on her shoulders she studied her mirror as she pivoted it back and forth, painfully twisting her long eighteen inch waist.

Later the girl tied on her mail order sport shoes and sprang down the old smelly stairs of her building and burst out the door for a run. She loped the deserted streets just in her sun heat and floaty hair. She was obsessed with that exciting Bitsy letter, telling of her crashing that party as a nude. Beatense knew all about that.

She followed her alley routes that would avoid all but a few stragglers, then raided theater row. She pelted out four miles with heavy tresses airborne. Once home, the girl wrenched her barbells again. She rubbed in lanolin lotion, to ease the starchy dryness of her day-long beach burn, plus it soothed the tightening effect the hot sun gave her too small skin. She re-read that article. She had to get there.

The next morning Beatense, in her tight, three inch zipper jeans and wrinkly shirt opened four buttons down, ran to the corner with her pint of melted butter rolled up in her beach towel, and hopped on a streetcar, named Inspire. This was a huge jolt for the already tired passengers resigned to the hot day ahead. The famous girl had to stand, and she smilingly refused a seat that was deferentially offered to her.

Eyeing her bare arm as she held to the grab bar, she read the corny aspirin and scrub brush ads over the rattling windows as the rumbling streetcar hummed along.

Later she stood at the microphone that looked like an outboard motor housing, as Monty played the intro on the piano. Then smiling at him she sang in that in-demand strained voice of hers, that seemed to echo from countless years in the past.

> *If your old albums*
> *Are giving you problems*
> *If you're having problems*
> *With your old albums*
> *Try Winthorpe photo mounts today-ay-ay!*

At that Monty chimed in. "Yes, how many times have you reached for that old photo album, only to have half the pictures fall out? Way too often?

"Well the folks at Winthorpe solved that with a new adhesive for their photo mount corners that will never dry out. Available in black and ivory white, and now offered in an attractive new smoke gray option. Stop in at your photo dealer today!"

> *If your old albums*
> *Are giving you problems*
> *Try Winthorpe photo mounts today-ay-ay!*

"That's got to be the dumbest ad I ever sang," Beatense said, as Monty felt the power of her thick, spirited layers of light auburn hair that enframed her exertive face and lengthy neck. Her abundant hair gave her noble head an uncanny Pesence that made people hesitant to address this thinned, dark brown girl, nice as she was. "Are they seriously paying me $250 for that? And what about the clarinet?"

"Called in hung over. So the piano. Let's have a cig and coffee. Oh, I heard from Mercaphony again. They want to sign you with a $5000 advance."

"Not after I hit the beach naked again today, all the static. Hey, I better get going before my melted butter solidifies. Let Mercaphony know I might do it."

Monty wobbled as he eyed the authoritative, seventy inch up-thrust of her leaned lines, as exemplified by her eleven inch hips. Her shirt was opened to where he just saw her breasts, and his strange reactions to them persisted long after she left.

If only Beatense knew she would have undressed. She took the return car, now named Desire to the stop for the beach. A few mothers led their sadly unappealing children out the back door of the car, that opened five feet wide to speed up the exit process, because the streetcar tracks didn't curve in to the curb, causing the traffic to stop. Beatense stepped off after them, and as she crossed the patchy grass onto the beach sand she caught a whiff from the nearby foundry.

They were pouring molten iron again that day, and the dull smell invaded the air. Also, having read of Bitsy's misadventures Beatense had higher standards than this grubby mud dirt beach. Shirt half off and then all off, she dashed to catch the clanging Inspire streetcar. As stared at she hopped on and went back to the exit door.

Several boys playing ball in the street tiredly watched the car ride by. Beatense couldn't help but irritatedly compare them to the pretty sophisticates back at Geode.

She entered her building and took the creaking stairs up to the tar beach, or the rooftop. A few ladies were hanging out their laundry, and Beatense greeted them merrily, which was unexpected. They responded with delight, and the girl lay out her towel. She took off her jeans and slucked on her butter, taking care to oil her split.

The camp nurse told her that slight girls of strong build who get so tan hit the eye with powerful reactions: Fear, anger, despair, laughter or honored respect. For this attention she had to be unbending. This she was. She lay back grunting.

The shocked ladies stared, and with arms carefully placed the girl settled in. It was ninety-seven at eleven as she began her therapy. At two she propped up on her elbows to give herself a caring study, then turned over to hit her back.

She eyed the windows of the taller building across the street, and she saw some residents observing. Some watched until she quit three hours later.

"Well! So's you was uppity on the roofie today, hey, darter?"

"Hi. Yeah." It was five as she sat down with a banana. "The foundry was pouring iron, which stunk. I'm getting sunned out. So I can help out tomorrow."

"Oh no you ain't! Old Julie needs a little extra money, so you stays home!"

"If I do I'm going to the depot first to book me a trip to Xanthallado. I need a tropics beach with surf, sand dunes and coconut palms, and free legal nudity."

"You gots a brain like a coco-nut! That costests money, yer knows!"

"I sang up $400 today, and Mercaphony is giving five thousand to sign up."

"You can use that to pay me back for all yer useless college-itating!"

"It wasn't useless at all, not with their 600 watt sunlamps. And stable."

"Hesh! You eating tonight? You better! You're gattin too damn skinny!"

"Maybe a peach. How did the survey go today? Wish I came with?"

"Hah! We was going so fast old Julie slowed us down for the billable hours!"

That evening Beatense lay bare on her bed with dainty legs held in her arms, and as she awaited sufficient darkness to head out for a run, she thought about that Bitsy yet again. A trip to the still hostile library earlier gave her some basic information.

The trouble was, to afford it she would have to sign up with the record company, but would ask to do all recording at Monty's studio.

It seems she forgot her worth was pushing two hundred thousand.

The girl got up and worked her weights and finally went out. Upon returning she restlessly slept because of that day's high sun energy. Morning, just in a rude, towel rubbed shine of lard oil she entered the kitchen.

"Oh, awake are we now, darter? Hurry up now, and git something on! We gots a dab a work today! Yer mights look that word up in the dictionary!"

"Oh, ha ha. And I thought you said I didn't have to work. But I do want to, Pop. We had a haze layer yesterday that intensified the sun gloriously, but with the extra burn it gave me I couldn't sleep. So working today will cool me down."

"Well why don't we just brings yer along a feather beddie, then? A nice nappie whiles the rest of the world is at work just might do ya some good!"

"Father, you keep trying, don't you. No, I'll give you eight good productive hours today, running the whole time to speed things up, even if it cuts your billable hours."

"How much money ya got saved up from all that cursed singing of yers?"

"Not that much, me having to pay Spook's board and farrier bills. Why?"

"What you want is a holstein, so's yer can git yer sunny butter free!"

Beatense held her arm protectively. "Melted butter is a very powerful tanning accelerator, especially if it's hot. Also lard. This closes this discussion. Try to decline any further speech in lieu of affirmative grunts, whistles or hand claps."

"Agghhh, git on with ya! Whistles! And move! Do I see brackfist? No!"

Sighing, the girl rolled her eyes up. But as she turned away to the old icebox her ever vigilant father saw her smile. His absent look betrayed his amazement that this problematic girl was his daughter. In this lighting her skin shined black, as ever.

"Are ya gittin brackfist er not?!" came the yell, as she got out the eggs.

"I can scramble these quicker by smacking them on your empty head."

"Yes wastes plenty a eggses on yer own head! What mag was that in?"

"*With It Woman*. The eggs mixed in the shampoo give the hair manageable body and shining highlights. But mine is too far gone for the manageable part."

"Oh is that so? I never saw sech a disgusting mess! If yer ever wondered why the wimmins pulls their kiddies close when you go by, well now ya know!"

Beatense's lower eyelids had a world weary drooping that was soul probing.

"Quite the opposite. They all point me out to them. *There she is!"*

"They's saying that to the coppers, so's they can arrast you!"

Beatense fell against the counter laughing. He just never gave up.

"Don't slobber all over the counter there! And are you eatin this marn?"

"Maybe some cut up cantaloupe. Why!?"

"Well then we'll stop at the café instead! Better chance of survival."

She ignored that. "Yeah, I can get some coffee, maybe even some pie."

"Use a fork this time! You don't eat no pie like no sammich! And put them eggses away before your clothes rot in the closet and you *have* to go nakee!"

"I do anyway. Now look, I found a home for you father, with a friendly staff. Three meals a day and a new activity room. Two day-pass outings a month."

"Okay, I'm the one who's crazy! Leave the eggses out then! Now let's git!"

"First, I want to go to Xanthallado for a couple weeks, Pop. The train down and back will add a few days. I saw an article about this one Emeraldeye town. There's this hostel right on an actual ocean beach that charges just a hundred a night for the bunkroom, Hoganforth Lodges. It looks bona fide. I can get sun on real sand, and while I'm at it I can also buy a laptop for our surveying. They can close a ten sided traverse in two seconds. Like, any objections?"

"If yer leaving right now, none! Especially if yer brings me back a case a Birdie's rum! And what's this just $100! That's what we pay for a whole month's rent!"

"Prices are higher in Xanthallado. They have an actual economy there, you see. And to meet the expenses I can do some more of that shittin singing."

"Hesh now! You just damn hell son of bitch watch yer language! And don't we hears you enough on the raddio as it is? Now, Xanthylahlah, hah? Well, if you bring me back a case of their fine rum, like I said, I say go ahead!"

The girl never thought she could get his okay this easily. But ethically, with her needs always at high alert she had to warn her father of a certain detail.

"Ahem, I will indulge in sex. The magazines all say how great it is, and I found it true, even as a kid. But the camp nurse said to not overdo it, which I went and did. Okay, I said too much and the trip's off now, but I do want a month off this summer if I stay here. I want to get all-over sun over at Muni

Pool. Yes, nothing on but lard or butter!. The chlorine will give my tan a crispy rich dryness, along with being hot dark."

"No! All the folks here knows ya! If you wants to burn yourself into joining the licorice lobby, they say Ain't she cute! But way over at the public pool all nakie or in that butty bare tie-twine of yours, yer gonna gits yerself locked up! Now let's go!"

With Beatense in crochet the two went through the tan energizing Lettuce Snow décor out into the hall. There was a smell of last night's fish, plus that stink of fried eggs. The secret building telegraph brought out two old neighbor ladies.

"M-Marning to y-you," said Mrs. Schesky, nervously, staring at the shocker girl in her gorgeous hide, amber black in this lighting. "Heh heh, my n-newspaper."

"And m-my milk," said the ogling Mrs. Rindal, bending slowly over to pick up the dew wetted quart bottles. Beatense almost warmed them. "While it's still cold."

"Hey, hi!" said the girl brightly. "Wow, fun seeing you two so early today!"

Mr. Colwell fell back against the wall. His conceited daughter was always fairly polite when they were town or country, but as was her right she was quite reserved in their own building and neighborhood. So what was going on?

The unfortunate old ladies were dumbstruck. Beatense's high tension waist always lightly flexed as she stood, and she rubbed at her arm as her rank bacon sun smell rolled out in waves. The two almost went into eye-popped seizures.

"Oh, say, guys, do any of you know when the iceman cometh?"

"L-Later t-t-today, I believe," said Mrs. Rindal, with trembling effort.

"Thanks! I never can keep track. Pop so tight, we still have an old icebox!"

"I could take it in," said Mrs. Schesky, and Beatense gave a one-armed hug.

They took their leave and started down the wooden stairs. They were lit by dim twenty-five watt bulbs so that the residents wouldn't steal them. Mr. Colwell saw that Beatense continued to smile, as if that meeting was the greatest luck.

'So I'm cheap, hah? And what are you smiling at?"

"Oh, I just never realized how nice those two are."

He stopped. "Wait a minute, darter! Are you... Are you, er, feeling okay?"

"Well, yeah! It's just that, speaking of ice, I have to break some of that with our neighbors here. Tanning nude up on the roof and all, I need their goodwill."

"You been pushing it since you was a kid! But leastwise yer don't gots no one track mind! You can go a minute easy without thinking of your damn skin!"

They stepped out into the hardscrabble old street, with shabby stores built in more optimistic times, but now were decaying with still-trying-to-make-it neglect. Deprived laborers shuffled by, on their way to awful jobs, and they started at the sight of patch wearing Beatense. Compared to them she had a ruling stature and poise. But the famed girl surprised them with a wide smile, giving them hopeful flickers of shoulder straightening self respect. Father and daughter got into the steamy truck and rolled down the windows. Already hot, this was a merciless city.

"Fans of yers?"

"That one guy had Robusto in his pipe. I did them. *Make it mild and make it smooth! Hmmm! Smoke Robusto in the morning!* They want me again."

Mr. Colwell was impressed. That stray whiff and she knew the tobacco?

He started the anemic engine, that made it abundantly clear that it resented this imposition. They pulled out and started down the oppressive street that already was misty with a smoggy heat haze. Awful tanning conditions, Puppet noted.

"Palm trees, Pop. I want to see palm trees. And tumbling surf."

"Hesh! I tain't a going to put up with no nagging about Xantylahlah when I already sez youse can go! Just so's yer stays in line, thinking of what you said!"

"Oh, you can think? But I am not staying in line! I want screaming recreation."

He couldn't help but smile proudly. His daughter had her own ideas.

"Darter, I never tolds ya how stupid yer are, letting you find that out yer own self! That ain't happened yet, so I'll just lets you keep on being all wacko until yer finally catches on! Then you'll come to me crying, Why didn't you tell me?"

She gave that flat look. "This was too easy, your going along with this. You got some backhanded little scheme up your sleeve, don't you."

"Yeah! Right at boarding time I'll say we gots too much work, you can't go!"

"Whew! Boy, you had me worried there, being so agreeable. But can I go ahead with my reservations, Pop? If I do sign I can pay for it."

"You can buy the whole train! Your interest alone is a hundred a day! From your just hinkying around! So I can't stops ya none! Now there tain't will be no mores talk about it! You won't listen none to my valuable advice anyways!"

"I'm still not convinced you mean it; your promises have a nasty habit of being forgotten overnight, but I am calling that Hoganforth Lodges."

At the job-site the bare girl applied her lard oil. In the heat along the tractor trails through the corn she felt herself bake darker within her oily glaze of sweat.

She ran the range pole from backsight to foresight with highest alacrity.

No footwear, but the dried stubble, sharp stones and thorn prickers had no effect on her flying, callused little feet. It was good to get back to this work.

In patch, in the kitchen that evening she took the wall phone, giving her father a menacing glare. He shrugged and stepped out onto the fire escape with his pipe.

Tall Beatense sat cross-legged on a wobbly chair and took a drink of chocolate milk. With hands shaking she dialed. After twenty seconds a ring and a click.

"Hello, Hoganforth Lodges, this is Zapo. How can I help you?"

She took a deep breath. There were mysterious buzzes of static, and even faint garbled conversations. It was almost dizzying for the girl to think that she was now talking with someone in tropical Xanthallado, thousands of miles away!

"Hello. I'm... I'm, er, inquiring into reservations."

"We can handle that, but what are you looking at?"

"What am I looking at? Right now, the wall!"

Laughter. "No, I mean when will you be coming?"

"What's all that noise? All that music and talking!"

"Oh, unusually we're having a party. So, what... What are your plans?"

"Well, I expect to get there in three weeks and I want to stay two weeks."

"Well, sorry, but we can just give you one night. We're really full lately."

"One night! But you don't understand, I have to stay two weeks!"

"I think we can make it two... Just a sec. Hey, Viturna! Did that one dude ever confirm that one night for the 19th? Did you hear back from him?"

Zapo apparently got the answer. "Yeah, we can make it the 18th and 19th."

"Well, that's twice as good, I guess. But wait, what about that one Cocojo nude beach? It is nude, isn't it? I have to know that before we go any further."

"Yes, Cocojo is open, but you don't have to go way down there for that."

"Why not?" Her heart leaped. "This Bitsy in *Chez Health* said she did."

"Yes, lively Itsy. But she was here awhile ago. What happened was they voted in nudity for all local beaches. It was getting that way anyway. We have young women staying here naked the whole time. No luggage. You don't need Cocojo."

"Boy it sounds just gorgeous there. I mean I'm always naked here, but it's like they're giving me a special allowance because I'm so famous."

"You're famous? How are you famous?"

"I'm the Book Girl." She said it like she said she was a meter maid.

"Monkey HP Shit! No way! Well, welcome to old Emeraldeye! I'm impressed! Great, super videos! Look, I'll give you Viturna. She's trying to run this druggy dive. Ah, she just lurched over. Half wasted! Okay, here's old Vitty."

Emeraldeye Beach! It's a vacation just talking to these people!

Viturna sounded like she was older. "Hello, who am I speaking with?"

"Whom. Hello, the Book Girl. I'm Beatense Colwell, calling from Arrolynn, up Clarendon way. I was telling Zapo I was hoping for two weeks."

"You're the Book Girl? How are you getting here, private jet?"

"Hey, good idea! No, by train, the Northern Geographic Steel Queen. I rode her before, to Nywot Transfer. Unfortunately I can't fly down even if I had a jet."

"I better sit down. Move, Zape. Zapo, you shithead, get the puck up! Okay, so I take it you don't have a credit card to confirm your reservation?"

"No, the last one I saw was in a magazine. You mean I can't come then?"

"Well, it's just that... Zapo, what? Yeah, give him the key! Hah? He did?"

Beatense's spirits sank. She had bad feelings about this.

"Sorry. A misplaced key. Okay, I assume you're a sun nut, right?"

"Plus a muscle nut. Just now I match our cherrywood spice rack, but that's just these anachronistic 40 watt bulbs, is why. But can't I get two weeks?"

"That tan? I don't think I want you here. But look, we normally allow at most one week. This is a hostel for actual travelers, we can't give rich bitches like you a cheap vacation. And in any case we can't even give you one week. But no credit card? No prob there. We'll let you stay free. It's our honor. And so you're set. We can book you. Two nights. If anything else opens up we'll let you have it."

"Thanks, but I'm sorry, Viturna, I can't make that trip for just two days!"

"Well, here's… Zapo, what? Tell him to tap the quarter barrel! Okay, where was… Oh, anyway, uh, we always refer those who do want to stay longer to this Hideaway Motel. We use it for any extra staffers. I can just tell old Cheevy you work here and he'll even give you our discount. How's that, Bookie?"

Bookie! "Oh, you don't know what this means to me! This is wonderful!"

"I can call him and give him a heads up. Now, we will book those two nights for you here, and set you up with another twelve nights down the street."

"Darter! Ain't you done in there yet? All this yapping! Hurry it up!"

Almost weeping from happiness, Beatense completed the booking details.

"You can't go, darter! I just changed my mind! All this plum foolishness!"

The girl laughed. "I'm going for a run to get more naked practice!"

The girl ran, then still sweat naked played pool with her father at Toodle's Bar.

6

CONSOLIDATED DEPOT

Beatense was just in her slimming jeans and a well cut off yellow T-shirt as she boarded the bus the next morning for the trip to Mercaphony. She wasn't in her stylish dressy suit, but she could still sign a contract, if one was offered.

The prude lady in the drab office said, "Y-Yes, Mr. M-Morley will see y-you in a minute, miss. He is pleased to have you try out with us. Do have a seat."

"Th-Thank you, but I might not be good enough for actual records."

Offices in Arrolynn were painted just a few colors. Pastel green, salmon orange, ocher vanilla or pale blue. Sometimes they painted the green, orange or blue about four feet up as wainscoting, and continued on up with vanilla beige. The lighting was done with white glass globes that were very courtroom-like. The play of the dull wall color and dim lighting made young Beatense look especially dark, and so Mr. Morley visibly gulped when he stepped out of his office.

"M-Miss Colwell? How n-nice to see you. I have your book. Do come in."

He was pudgy faced in that respectable, community solid, stuffy and quite above reproach way. In comparison haystack Beatense was a wildcat.

"I understand you're interested in a recording contract with us, young lady."

Beatense saw the plaques and awards, and the various photos of the artists that performed for Mercaphony. She saw Keevy Hazleton. *Wow!*

"Yes, but I'm afraid I've just been doing commercials. I can give a sample."

"No need. We'll do your audition in the studio shortly. If you prefer your actual work will continue at Maverick. But for now, are you familiar with *Westward Wind?*"

"Why of course! But that's an old one of yours. Will I re-record it?"

"No, no. You will just sing it for your audition. But first, let me ask..."

The questions over, the girl was taken into the studio. She shook hands with the producer, the recording engineer, the mixing technician, the horn players and pianist. Some she happily already knew. She glanced at the sheet music. The score was the same as for the old song; she just needed the lyrics.

"Okay, Herb, bring in your intro, ready on the horns. One, two… One, two!"

Beatense sang the piece a few times, but her voice sounded too cynically jaded to succumb to a desolate heart. She then sang Papa Say Do No Do six times.

"Ah, yes-yes, marvelous. But we need a more peppy tone, Miss Colwell."

"Well, this is the way I sing. Don't you have any morbid songs I can do?"

"Benton, give her Hey, Don't Wake Me Up! Herb? From the top."

Beatense began to worry about the sun out there. This was ridiculous. Why all this horsing around? She hated how people could be so content to be pale.

Under mounting high stress, she sang Hey, Don't sounding like she didn't care either way. Her weary sad voice put a new twist into this lighthearted tune, giving it a cheap slum hotel and broken hopes pathos that was haunting. Maverick was booked for any possible recordings, but this was a take. She signed the papers and left at noon with a surprising $20,000. First the bank, then a far too delayed hot bake.

In the week leading up to her train departure Beatense indulged in several butter splashed roasts, plus for both subdivision and rural surveys she ran in just her patch. And even roof or beach she wore this, because she wanted to fade in string lines.

She figured that more modest look would appeal to the high moralistic instincts of any friends she expected to spend multiple spine lashing effulgent nights with.

She was dedicated to get as tan as possible before she left on the train, because except for Nywot she would be enduring three horrid days trapped in a steel tunnel. She was satisfied that even in full, sand reflected sun she looked golden rusty black, and she had leaned herself far skinnier. Still, she fretted.

"Damn it, Pop, I'm going to fade to nothing on that train! Plus being shit decent! That recording session the other day was torture enough, but three days?!"

"I thought it was just an audition, ya did!"

"No, they're pressing Don't Wake Me Up now, with Westward on the B side. And so I ended up with that twenty. I can get a bonus if they use my photo, which they already took, on the cardboard jacket. For the sleeve they use grocery bag paper with a circular cut-out, so that the record label itself tells what it is."

"I knows how they sells records, darter! Go look in the cabinet there!"

"Well I'm just explaining! Anyway, they say that with my photo on the cover they can get upfront music store placement because I'm already famous. They just came right out and say I'm beautiful, but just as an incidental plus for merchandising. The trouble is they say I'm too tan, so they want me to fade up. I strictly refused. But Mr. Morley did say I have this tropical look they can use for this new *Red Sails* album, by Mindy Dott. So that probably means a shoot when I get back from Emeraldeye."

Beatense reflected. A photo like that, the song would be secondary. But with permission the record company ultimately used a picture from her latest book. Sales were so big Mercaphony was compelled to pay her and her publisher royalties.

"So what's up tomorrow? Not that Toppelson survey! Most of it's in the woods! I can't get any sun there! I mean, yes, I can be the stealthy jungle girl and all that, but I'm trying to fade in tan lines, but how can I do that if I'm stuck in a woods fading all over? Pop, let's do that Swanton plat instead. Acres of sand!"

"We tain't got no blueprints for Swanton yet. But I can let you off at Topp so you can cut some of that brush. We want open sightlines, darter."

"Yeah, perfect! I need the workout! I've been doing swings and sways with my barbells on my shoulders until I'm wet, and I'm doing extra long runs. I have to get myself ready for whoever I'm up against, all those women beach professionals. Plus fucking. But why am I worried about the train ride? I'll be in an actual Roomette!"

"What are you wearing on the old Queenie? Can I break in to ask?"

"Normal clothes. I don't want everyone saying, that's the Book Girl!"

When father and daughter (she in jeans and vee-opened white shirt) left for the station in a yellow taxi, she was carrying 25,000 dollars. An unseasonal gloomy gray chill pervaded the day, that deepened the exhaust pungency of the cab interior. The majestic depot lay in the heart of Arrolynn's downtown, where stately granite buildings with colonnade pillars towered over the crowded streets and sidewalks.

The taxi alternatingly raced and then bumper to bumper crawled by monumental banks, graciously dignified old department stores and prestige landmark hotels. It also went by coffee shops, theaters, tobacconists, haberdasheries and news stands. Also opresent, lunch stands, menswear and millinery stores, shoe stores, dime stores and novelty shops. The elevated trains, trucks and buses together generated rumbling, sub-audible vibrations that filled the air and actually shook the pavement. The myriad tailpipes spewed into the smoggy air a sharp, aromatic-enriched smell of vehicles on the move, that permeated indoors and out alike. The smell of downtown.

The sidewalks were crowded, with the occasional couples holding hands. For many it was quitting time, and the doors of the restaurants continuously swung as the released employees stepped in for the evening dinner in the uptown metropolis, that would be immersed in the bustling drama of the proud city's nonstop activity.

The lowly bow-tied clerks held to their posts. They felt honored to man their sales counters, to attend to the presidents and financiers who were their customers. "Yes, Mr. Aldorf, Rexton cigars and Plus X film. Yes, a touch of cold in the air today. Bag these up?" The important officials tolerated this familiarity; all day everyone cowered uneasily in their presence. "Oh, no, Mr. Griffith, I would wait for our sale next week."

These minions lived in dreadful walk-up flats, and cooked on hotplates and sat on straight wooden chairs and with a glass of milk read the papers assiduously for the evening's diversion. They worked years at the same counters, at the same low pay.

"Mr. Murchison, I recommend the blue stationery. All occasion, you know."

Beatense, in white shirt of library notoriety and low set stitchy jeans, studied the bustling sidewalk throngs with a benevolent pity. The girl wasn't real sure about her visit to the tropics, but she did look forward to her trip on the train.

"But the main thing, Pop, I'm famous down there too. So, they want me at the Hoganforth. I'm going to see a whole new world, and grow as a person."

"Well, you didn't mention no hijinks. Yer might already learned something."

"I will take the situations as they come. But nothing wrong with readiness!"

The cab stopped and the driver pulled on the hand brake.

"Here we are, darter! Shake a leg! What's it come to, sarge?"

The answer, sixty cents, came as Beatense with flowing moves got out.

"Sixty cents! We were stopped at red lights half the time! Here's fifty!"

As the driver got out the luggage Beatense slipped him a tenner.

"Thank *you*, Miss Beat! Bought your book. But is this little case all you have?"

"Well, you should know! You were the one who put it in the trunk!"

"Quit that chitchat, girl!" This was an attempt at his usual gruffness, he seemed to have an edge of fright, that of trying to stay in control. "Now git moving!"

In her own turmoil Beatense was oblivious to her father's plight.

The cab pulled on ahead to the busy stand, leaving the two standing in awe before the Consolidated Depots Terminal. Built in the Imperial Classic style, it was such a vast structure it took two whole city blocks. But as imposing as it presided outside, it overawed with even greater grandeur within. But Beatense was used to all this, and nodded familiarly to the doormen as the two entered the cavernous interior. The PA speakers were booming out in a babble of echoes as they announced a departure.

"Come on, Pop! These announcements are making me nervous!"

"Darter, you run on ahead! I'll grab me a pack of cigs!"

"Get me some too! I'll be over at the Northern Geographic windows!"

Mr. Colwell paused to gaze up at the soaring, deep blue marble pillars, that were crowned with capitals of lustrous gold leaf. These pillars supported broad groined vaults of veined green granite, that were embellished with broad heroic murals that depicted Railroad Might. Far below these lofty aeries, row upon row of wax polished wooden benches were arranged upon a gleaming lake of black marble, which was speckled with gold mica. However, with surging crowds present, the station handled over 50,000 riders per day, this showy touch at the mortal level was rarely seen.

The pigeons flying free within had the best view.

There came what might have been a track call. With the muffled echoes it was difficult to tell. A railroad, the name of the sailing, a final destination, and a tedious listing of the intermediate stops. Drawing stares, Beatense crossed the wide floor, slipping through the thronging herds, toward the ticket windows.

Drawing more and more stares, she spotted a magazine on one of the benches. She always picked these up as left by the Xanthallado women, but took it reluctantly. After all, she was actually leaving for the place where they came from.

Rolling her sleeves to her elbows, the girl approached the wide, oaken paneled wall of barred ticket windows, where the vested and visored agents held court like spiteful judges. She found the windows labeled **NORTHERN GEOGRAPHIC** in cast brass letters and got in line. She looked up at the giant scheduling board above the cages, that posted the Arrivals and Departures of the dozens of trains stopping here every day. The chalkboys up on a catwalk hurried to update the entries as they read the ticker tapes. The three-runs-a-week Queen Of Steel was marked as *On Time*. The Esquire was delayed by a faulty switch, but this was the only late train. A train was called late if it came in one minute after the posted time.

The trim young lady over in the next line had to be from Xanthallado. She wore tight, faded jeans and a yellow jacket with blue shoulder panels, whose bulky size called attention to her diminutive form. Her steady blue eyes took in the busy scene with a quietly poised intellect and patience, but indeed, her rosy flushed cheek points and her taut curved, regarding forehead told of a critical fortitude that would brook no disagreement. She was sunny complexioned, and her blond hair was softly tousled with a loose held ponytail. With her cool observant cool gaze she was a person who knew she was infinitely valuable by merely existing. Recognizing her as a fellow ethereal, Beatense admired her. The two caught eyes and nodded.

"Aye darter, I thoughts you would be plumb gone by now!"
Beatense turned to her father. "Not in the line I'm in, as usual!"
The agent called out. "Next! Are you ticketed? Step up!"
At that the line moved up a notch.
"Next! Come on, next!" the agent called in the line to the right.
The yellow jacket casually leaned against the counter in careless disregard. The agent tried to fluster her, but she solemnly gazed into his eyes.
"Next! You there! Step up! Next!"
Beatense felt a wave of panic as she stepped to her window.
"Are you ticketed? Hand it over!"
"Pop, give me my ticket! Quick!"

"Darter, you got the tickie!" He also felt the wrath. "It's in your purse!"

She was on the charts, but dug in her tiny purse with fingers of putty.

"Come on, hurry! Others are waiting!"

"Here it is, sir!" the girl yelped, and she slid the ticket under the brass grill. The granite of the counter ledge had a peculiar ink stain that apparently defied all effort to remove it. The girl noted her tight forearms. "It might be a tad smudgy."

Yellow Jacket strolled away with ticket in hand, unimpressed by her agent's hostile impatience. She had the detached elan of a princess-like bearing.

She's beating me at my own game, thought Beatense. *And I'm famous!*

"You have taken a Roomette?" The agent consulted a chart. "Unfortunately it's presently occupied! You can't have access until the party detrains at Evert!"

"Well, what... What do I do, then? Stand in the aisle?"

"Proceed over to the Conductor's Office and confirm your Roomette assignment! You will board Sabbatical Quest at Sign H, Track 9, for your temporary coach seat!"

"Temporary, I hope." Once again the girl gazed upon her heated arms.

The rubber stamp twirled in striking and hit the ticket with loud thumps.

"Thank you, sir," said Beatense as she took back her ticket. "But where..."

"Out on the platform! They have these signs! You're H!"

"No, I mean, where's the Conduc..."

He indefinitely waved, apparently signaling left. "Next!"

"And where do I check my suitcase, sir?"

"Freight Office! Next!"

"Darter, you're going to needs yer grippie on board, ain't ya?"

The speakers sounded. "Attention please! We have a track assignment for the departing Antares! At the call for boarding proceed to... Track 28!"

"Missed it by one. Oh, yeah, you're right! Now to find that conductor!"

"Ay, darter, I'll find us a spot over at yon lunch counter! Travelers Rest!"

Mr. Colwell wandered off, and Beatense suspected that he just wanted to take in the sights. But strolling around in this madhouse would take effort.

Beatense was recognized as the radio girl, the Book Girl and singer. If she was rusty black like back at desert camp she would have been stupefying, but being just pine knotty brown she got smiling appreciation for her worthy achievement.

But her wide vee, opened yet another button, did seem mercenary, so even the many employees, some who saved the magazines for her, felt wobbly.

The Freight Office the girl went by was a counter, a long, mobbed counter. The passengers packed in before it all looked anxious. Precious few suitcases were crossing the gouged wooden surface, and the luggage clerks seemed to take pride in their slack indifference. A worried traveler demanded to talk to the station Manager, and the bemused attendant confronting him blandly dialed his telephone and held it over to him. Flustered, the passenger backed off in defeat. The other passengers looked upon him in contempt, wasting all that time.

Back of the counter the freight elevator had only a dozen bags on board, but with departures imminent nothing was being added. But at last the rubber stamps began, and showhorse Beatense moved on. Another train was called, and if anyone in the waiting crowd proceeded accordingly, he was a master of deception. Beatense kept going to the Conductor's Office to get her Sleeping Car assignment. The fellow here was actually quite friendly, so Beatense guessed he was from Xanthallado.

She took care of her reservation and started for the restaurant, but then saw the luggage shop. Backpacks! Xanthallado backpacks! Beatense picked one out, and transferring her things to it she ditched her ratty old suitcase. By now she had been looked at a thousand times. Of usual interest, her unkempt auburn hair was scattery sun bleached. Also of interest, her separated cream jugs showed right to their nips.

At a distance, Beatense saw her father enter the Parlor Room Coffee Shop. She was concerned about how diminished he seemed here. How could she even think to leave him like this? Adding to her misgivings was all the cash she was taking with her. But she would be bringing back a laptop, which would make them the fastest metes and bounds experts in ten counties.

Beatense entered the crowded restaurant. Big black ceiling fans hesitantly turned, and the chrome edged pedestal stools at the counter also turned as the patrons either sat down or got up. There was a clunky clatter of crockery as the hurried wait staff dumped the dishware into tubs under the counter. Soiled rags were used to wipe off the counters after use. Mr. Colwell was sitting at the red linoleum counter with two cups of coffee. Gazed upon, Beatense slid in beside him, by a fruit drink Jet Cooler that sprayed a blue liquid out against its clear plastic dome interior. She matched her coffee until she added the cream. The counterman gave her a sour look.

"Pop!" the girl cried, lighting the offered cigarette. "I can't go and leave you like this, just so I can get sun! I do appreciate it but just give me a vacation here!"

"Yer wants to git sun serious, don't ya? I won't get no peace until yer so royally slapped up with sun yer half crazy! Now what's that yer got there?"

"My new backpack! I ditched the suitcase, almost falling apart."

"I don't sees how that backiepack is all you need! Aintcha takin no clothes?"

"I'm going to be nude legally nonstop, but I do have my patch. Hey, you know, I wonder if they have those laminated maps of Emeraldeye Beach. Be right back."

The newsstand had them. Beatense bought one and the first thing she saw was the **Cocojo Open Beach and Dunes Shore**. *Wow! WOW!*

They had ample time, but Beatense felt antsy, and so the two made their way to the phalanx of heavy, glass-paned doors. Each had a marble slab above, that was inscribed with the almost comically redundant message, TO TRAINS.

Father and devoted daughter stepped out onto the granite promenade, that was situated as a ledge balcony above the glistening rails that swept through the station.

Many streamline passenger trains were present. The trains departing south had their locomotives hidden within the tunnels that ran in under the balcony, and in turn under the station building itself. Those trains heading northward had their engines hundreds of feet ahead, equally out of sight. Between the tunnels, steps of whorled agate led down to the gritty boarding platforms, that extended out between the track pairs like long piers. This track area was sheltered over with a single broad roof of gigantic dimensions, under which the close stale air was wreathed with stuffy clouds of diesel exhaust, coal smoke and steam. This hazy amalgam wafted slowly up to the smudge fouled lights above, causing then to cast an unnatural vivid glare upon the proud streamliners presiding below. Despite her...

Many magazine hunts Beatense always felt awed by this sight, that of the long waiting trains and their hurrying or patiently standing passengers. She watched the Metropolis head out, as its revving diesels and tractive generators pounded with an Engines of Earth fury. Beatense leaned out over the balustrade as the long, black roofed cars were drawn one by one into the yawning, arched tunnel beneath her feet. Then a lightly swaying glass roofed dome car approached. The girl felt like a spy as she gazed upon the complacent passengers within.

The track area was mobbed, between the moving or stationary trains there were surging crowds. The doors of the various baggage cars were open, and the iron wheeled carts set by them were stacked with luggage. The hostlers were oblivious to the roar of the crowds and engines as they urgently flung the parcels, suitcases and mail bags on or off board. Other hostlers were perched atop their ladders, icing the Dining Cars through the rooftop hatches.

Anxious father and lordly tossed hair daughter came to the stone steps that led down to the tracks 9 & 10 platform. According to the big clock suspended overhead, whose milky glass faces had those anitquity I, V and X numerals, the time was just pushing 3:30. The Queen was due at 3:45. It was probably in sight up the track as it worked its way through the yard with its bright headlight leading the way.

As she started down the steps with her father Beatense spotted another girl from Xanthallado, whose union suit underwear shirt had such a widely scooped neck, that her collarbones were as exposed as with Beatense's own open vee. She seemed to feel sure of her place here, but at odds with this, her soft blue eyes were engagingly touched with pathos, as if she had recently wept, and her red lips were shaped with brave uncertainty. This look of vulnerable emotion was made even more poignant by her long, loosely rippled blond hair, and her golden skin. She walked with tensioned poise until she reached the steps. Then with a guilty smile she hopped up onto the polished stone banister and slid down it to the platform, just like the typical, forever child-like college girl that she was.

Beatense had often done this herself, but now she impatiently sprang down the steps. Time ticking away the girl and her father worked their way through the crowd, past the cast iron letter-signs as the travelers recognized her overkill hair and tan.

As the two reached Sign D there was a stir of the waiting passengers, and a loud calling of horns. A distant bright white headlight had appeared up Track 9, that grew larger and larger. With her diesels lazily, but massively, puttering, with clanging bells and steel wheels clunk-*thunk*-thunking, the Queen regally trundled into the station.

She was hauled by four locomotives, a front A unit with cab and three B units behind, that disappeared into the tunnel. After ten cars went by the train lurched to a stop with a steaming shriek of the air brakes. The vestibule entry doors had their top halves already open, with carmen standing ready. They swung the bottom doors open and raised the entryway hatch plates, exposing the steps. They hopped down to the platform and set the yellow step-up stools in place. The coaches began disgorging a flood of passengers, who milled toward the station in a noisy blur.

Few riders cared about the train, but Beatense her father certainly did, admiring every detail of the heavy eighty-five foot cars. The two saw the six ton wheel trucks with their coiled springs that looked impossibly burdened. There were the cast iron handshake couplings, and the thick black steam hoses that connected the coaches. The yellowish orange paint scheme was accented with two red stripes that ran above the sweep of long, rectangular windows.

Beneath these a broad band of brick red bore the proud signboard:

Northern Geographic.

As already observed the corrugated, curved roofs of the coaches were black, as was the paneling beneath the coach bodies. These concealed the hissing air tanks, junction boxes, compressors and generators crowded in beneath the coach decks.

Beatense peered up into the dimly lighted entry vestibule interiors as she walked by them. She saw two conductors confer with each other as the mighty Queen was readied for this new departure. The new passengers were being met by these and the other trainmen as they stepped aboard. The blue painted Commutator Champion just over on Track 10 portrayed a similar scene of depot activity.

"Attention, please! The Cardiff bound Northern Geographic Queen of Steel is now boarding on Track 9! Time is limited! All aboard, please!"

They came to Sign H. The Sabbatical Quest stood ready.

"Okay, darter, you got yerself two weeks! I got old Julius filling in, so don't come back early!" She felt dizzy. How that long yellow train burned her blood! "But is yer gettin brownt worth all the money yer tossing to the wind?"

"Father, I protest! I'm already brownt! But I do plan to get brownter."

The PA speakers had been booming all along, but now their message had sharp relevance. "Last call for boarding the Queen of Steel! The last call!" They hugged and the girl hopped up into the vestibule. She tearily turned and waved.

The father pretended to cough to hide his own tears.

Unaware of this tragic poignancy, the diesel horns impatiently sounded. *Blawwwwwaaaaat!*

7

DEPARTURE

The vestibule Beatense sprang up into was painted within with that glossy dull orange enamel that seemed to be used exclusively for passenger train vestibule interiors, and bulldozers. She saw that both the upper and lower halves of the entry door on the opposite side were shut, and the hinged iron deckplate there was closed down over its steps. Once the train was underway the trapdoor that was opened up beside her steps would be closed too, so that one could stand at either door over the covered steps to watch out its window. The vestibules were where one coach was joined with the next up or back, and these car-to-car transitions were enclosed with heavy rubber accordion pleats.

Beatense returned the startled trainman's (her open shirt) nod, then admired the brake wheel and curved grab bars by the closed trapdoor opposite. She also spotted other details, including the diamond pattern of the decking. But suddenly she wanted none of this. She squeezed down by the other boarding passengers and leaped off the step-stool. She whirled her head in panic looking for her father, then spotting him she chased after him by her car through the thinning crowd.

"Pop! Wait! I'm not going!"

He turned back with a tear stained face, and they grabbed.

"Darter, what the hell you doing? You git on that train!"

"I can't, Pop! I'm staying here! Me running naked isn't that important!"

"Now yer makin a liar of yerself! Now hurry and git back on board!"

"Boarrrrrrd! All aboard!"

Mr. Colwell warned her to be wise up, the two hugged, and the girl raced back to the entry of her car. The trainman had stepped off, only to see a repeat of that tight belly as the girl ran over. "Is… Is everything quite all right, m-miss?"

"With a father like that how can it not be."

The two stepped back up into the dimly lighted vestibule, and the trainman closed down the deckplate and swung the lower door shut.

"So that's how they do that! But, sir? I'm not actually ticketed for this car."

"Any seat that's empty, miss. There are a few. Three to be exact."

She entered the corridor, that immediately turned left, then right, jogging around the rest room lounges. The hallway was so narrow that even Beatense brushed the tubular bars guarding the windows. These windows were too low for one to actually look out, being set at the same height as the windows by the seats.

The Queen of Steel lightly lurched to a start. It began to crawl ahead with a shrill metallic creaking and shuddering groaning, as the heavy running gear was stirred to action. The girl, truly alive as only trains could make her, stooped to look out.

Ever, ever so slowly it looked as if the still stopped Commutator on Track 10 was dragging by, window by window. A late passenger came flying, holding his hat, and Beatense turned into the long passenger compartment.

The décor was typical. The curved ceiling was painted in beige enameled steel, with metal luggage racks along both sides. The windows were framed in dark wood with rounded corners, and the panels between were plied with plaid fabric. The seats were done in harvest straw kimbric, and the grooved rubber tread of the aisle was flower pot orange in color. The linoleum under the seats was light beige flecked with grey. Coming from behind, the seat backs were too high for Beatense to see if any were available. As the letter Sign G outside crawled by, she submitted herself to the ordeal of looking from side to side in search of a place to sit, while attracting her usual jolted stares of skin and hair recognition.

"Miss, would you like assistance?" It was the trainman who boarded her.

"Isn't there a seat? I'm missing everything outside!"

"A window seat is open at up 6A. A lady in blue is sitting by the aisle."

The girl thanked him and hurried forward. She came to the heavy, agrarian looking woman in blue, who was frosty in her expression despite her homespun dowdiness. She had lost the weight war and possibly the one for IQ, if any.

"Er, I was told this seat is open, lady." No look of recognition. Good.

"It looks open to me." Shirt pulling out untucked the girl shoved her backpack up into the overhead rack, then hurried for the vestibule of Explorator Quest ahead. Its deckplate was still up. Beatense hopped down the steps and hung out of the coach clinging to the grab bar. By now Sign D was moving slowly by. She saw her father and she wildly waved.

"Pop! Thanks! See you in a month! I… I, er, okay, I'll spill, I love you!"

"I love you, darter, but for how long I don't know, you'll git yerself kilt!"

"Yeah, and no refund on the ticket! Bye! Give old Julius my regards!"

The stay-behinds and station loiterers longingly stared at the moving Queen Of Steel. As she peered out Beatense could feel the wheel truck trundling under her, as its spring coils minutely flexed to the track's irregularities.

The stone balcony facade drew closer as the train rolled faster, but two porters pushing baggage wagons kept a step ahead. The black mouth of the tunnel drew closer, then Explorator entered the bowels of Consolidated Depots. Beatense watched from her door as this low, dark world of heavy concrete pillars and arches screeled by. She saw the multiple pumps for refueling the diesels, and with the freight and baggage consignments marshaled here, a rack of clipboards fluttering with bills of lading glided by.

A group of redcaps and porters stood by a row of iron wheeled carts stacked with mailbags, idly watching this legendary train.

As the grey daylight from the far end of the passage began to wash out the dim lighting of this grimy underworld, Beatense returned to her seat in Sabbatical.

She was just starting to feel that moving, shaking sensation in the floor.

"Excuse me, please. I'm back, lady."

She coldly eyed that frontal coloration. "Sit down. I ain't stopping you none."

Beatense rolled her eyes up, stepped in and sat down. She pushed her recline button and leaned back her seat, and she pulled the leg-rest up with loud clicks. She watched out her window, looked at her front exposure, then to the lady.

"Name's Beatense, Beatense Colwell. Beatrice and Hortense combined."

"Cornhill, Ida. Quite a pair of jeans you have there. Thigh gap tight."

Well, the old girl has taste, anyway. "Thank you. They cost enough."

"I can see your breast side-on full. You might button hat shirt up."

The faster moving Queen was thunking, clunking and lurching from track to track through a bewildering maze of switch turn-outs. These had all been pre-set for this very departure, and as the accelerating train moved through they were already being reset for the next trains. Looking over the swarm of tracks Beatense saw the Inctin Building through the misty rain, whose dirigible mooring mast was so tall it was lost in the low hanging clouds. There were other tall buildings, but farther down the track the buildings quickly dropped in height and importance, and they took on a grubbier tone as well. They all had ugly fire escapes, and Beatense lived in one.

Down at storefront level the crowded sidewalks were overhung with frantic signs, including giant spectacles, mortars and pestles, violins and false teeth. And running alongside the signs were suspended lines of electric utility wire, hung from poles that had at least six crossbars each. Unseen from the train, in the main window display of the Fells Department Store, sat the famed life-sized mechanical clown, that soundlessly threw itself around on its stool, swooping its rigid head while blinking its lighted glass eyes. That and the shoe department's X-ray machine were popular attractions. The store was decorated within to take its patrons into another world of refined elegance.

The accelerating train was passing by a series of crossing gates. Their red lights flashed and their loud bells rapidly clanged as the bulge-contoured autos drearily stood in wait in the dribbling drizzle. The train ran by the gasworks, a forsaken flat of huge round tanks that telescoped up and down within their iron frames depending on the production of the coal gas and its use.

The long train rounded the tank works and coke gas ovens in a sweeping curve, and the municipal incinerators appeared. Here as the cars and trucks pulled up the workmen pulled open the massive iron covers that lay by the road, and the eternal orange flames came leaping out as the visitors threw in their trash. The incinerators marked the entry into Milltown, a cheerless region of foundries, coal piles and blast retorts, that lit up the skies at night with their hellish glow.

The workers lived here in squalid hovels that were set right in among the factory mills, the work houses and gas flares, and the gritty shunting tracks that bore coke, scrap iron and hematite to the waiting fires. Dozens of smokestacks could be seen, and as their heavy, black clouds rolled upward, mournful whistles called day's end.

And the start of the next shift. The commonly seen amputees and cripples in the city were excluded from workday pay. Beatense watched with eyes wide as the now faster train barreled right down the middle of a cluttered street. Crude children and a woman wrestling with a cart stopped to gape at the express thundering by. Beatense briefly felt the need for political reform. Unlike that lady, she was cared for.

She turned back to her seat-mate. "I won't be sitting here for the whole trip to Cardiff. I have a Roomette, but I can't get to it until we get to this Evert."

"You have a Roomette? How did you luck out on that?"

"As soon as I said who I was the agent said he had one for me. I said, Don't give me any special consideration, but he insisted. I'm going there on vacation."

"Wait now. You're making a visit *to* Cardiff? You tarn't from there?"

"Actually, I'm from town here, but thanks for thinking I'm a Xanthallado girl."

"I better see your driver's license. I would swear you were a Xanthie."

"Yes, I plan to be very, very Xanthie by getting some sun on this trip."

"You want *more* sun? How t-tan do you get?"

"What you see is what you get. But out in Geode I did get real ultra dark."

"Geode? The... Desert? What were you doing out there?"

"Oh, back when I was thirteen I went to this surveying camp. I was..."

"You're Puppet! Our library has your books! I thought you were familiar!"

She smiled with delight. "Ida Cornhill, of course! Wow!"

The appearance of a cranky looking conductor ended her happy moment.

"Miss? Sorry to disturb you, but it was reported that you foolishly protruded your person from the vestibule entry as this train was departing. Leaving those lower side and trap doors open was in neglect of Rule 887 of the Operating Code, as revised. The trainman responsible has been warned, but we ask that you try avoid any such hazards. And another point. That's as indecent as you're going to get on this trip, young lady. We will not tolerate that bee-kini of yours."

Her mouth dropped open. "Why, I remember you!" She stood. "I thought you were such a meanie, after me for my skimpy habits. But you didn't know I slept naked under my blanket. Boy, it sure is great seeing you again, sir! Old friends!"

"Well, heh heh, we just ask that you be careful, miss. Welcome aboard."

Beatense gave a quick hug and plopped back down. "Plus you, Ida! Shit, any more coincidences like that and the editor returns this manuscript!"

"Not with you as the main character. What a wonderful gift you are."

"I know. My books are sell-outs. The second one revived sales of my first title, *Fourteen*. But surveying camp out at Gurney was almost a homecoming, Ida. My father was on this surveying team laying the territory border between Periebanou and Flageria. My poor late mother was with him. I got into her tummy at the time."

"Well, that explains how you get so dang blasted tan. Parts of Geode are full of uranium, which affects conception. And so many young women take to the desert for the genetics. A lot of our interns too. They went for those skinny tan petro boys."

"Yeah, those petro boys. Katrinka and Soler both just eleven did no one else."

"Katrinka rules the camp. She's very slight, but a muscled body builder wildcat. Just to stick it to us oldies she lays out dark brown naked by the pool, so we stare. From her face and eyes you might think she's too proper in mind to be so physical. Like your friend Geddy. She's a tan little bean pole, sweet in looks, but very active. She's an intern, like Lesta was, who's now a geologist. Naked even in her office."

"That's nerve. And Geddy, good to hear she's managing okay, without me."

"One boy sent in a fake photo, he was actually fat and pale. Geddy had to…"

Just then the conductor who had set up Beatense's room booking back in the station stopped by with his ticket punch. His deferential uniformed presence was evocative of horizons ahead via those twin streaks of steel.

"Hello, ladies. How are you two doing? I need your tickets, please."

"Yes, just a second," said Beatense, pulling her ticket from her little string hung purse. "Just hope giving you this doesn't expose myself to any undue danger."

"Ah, yes," said the official, noting the girl's *exposed* situation as he punched both tickets. He tucked them into the window shade spring clips. "That was Mr. Colton Westergard, miss. The head conductor."

"I knew him from six years ago. But sir, can I get to my Roomette at that Evert?"

"Oh, yes. You're assigned to Cabin C in Tellurian Quest, ten cars forward."

"Tellurian Quest," the girl repeated. "Quite a stretch for a name, but it beats Sabbatical Quest. So anyway, can you tell me how fast we're going?"

He cocked his head. "Eighty-five. We'll make Evert in two hours."

"Eighty-five, hah? Wow, Cocojo, here I come!"

The official laughed and moved on, and Beatense settled back.

It seemed curious to her that both conductors were wearing the same uniform, or the special, short-cut coat with medallion buttons, the watch-chained vest, the side striped pants, and the widening upward drum shaped hat with its slim black visor, but although their suits lent both officials a formal air, with the one the uniform instilled a fearful dread, while with the other it inspired friendly reassurance.

One hour and one stop later a white coated porter came down the aisle, moving with the swaying of the coach as he lightly touched the seat backs for balance.

"First call for dinner!" he called. "First call fuh dinnahhh!"

Beatense signaled him. "Excuse me, sir. Which way is the Dining Car?"

"Two, miss. Six cars forward, or ten back. First call for dinner!"

"Two choices, Ida." The porter moved on. "Which one should we try?"

"No, go ahead, miss. I got my own food. And I guess this is good bye."

"Oh, my Roomette! I'll be moving into that. Okay, nice seeing you again!"

The girl started for the forward Dining Car. Other travelers also got up, but the consensus seemed to be to wait until later. The speeding car was lurching; the girl found it tricky to keep her footing despite all her riotous bareback riding.

Up at the head of the car the girl paused to look at the neo deco Queen of Steel medallion, that was set in the birch veneer bulkhead wall to the left. Beatense pushed the passage door's activating handplate, and with a tired gasp the portholed door slid jerkily open to the vestibule's roar. There was no insulation here, the thunder of the distant locomotives was loud, and the tumult of the iron wheels hammering the iron rails below was even louder. Beatense hesitated at the pounding threshold, leery of the grinding, sliding plates of the vestibule decks. With the wheel trucks and couplings at war just underfoot, the narrow door of the car ahead was jogging from oside to side. And in that faint light the girl saw the rubber shroud pleats work like a giant bellows, swirling the stagnant odors of hot oil and blue exhaust.

Beatense made a heroic step across the shaking deck toward the opposite door and caught the grab bar. She checked for oncoming traffic through the door's round, rubber gasketed porthole, and turning the D-handled latch she led the small party into the Explorator Quest's lounge corridor. The abrupt silence, once the door was shut, was as startling as the noise itself had been. Beatense quick buttoned her shirt.

As the party worked its way up Explorator's aisle, a rough stretch of rail sent them staggering. A young couple laughed as if this was all great fun, and they joined in. From their looks Beatense guessed they were from Xanthallado, and so in the next vestibule she managed to collide herself with the teen-look husband. That got her invited to join the two, dazzling tan Tiffany and unmoose-like Moose.

The next car, Special Quest, had only five rows of seats. It was one of the dome observation cars, featuring a stepway that led to the upper deck. The party took the other steps to the left, that led down to the side tunnel that jogged beneath the dome just above the ground. Tiffany and Moose let out excited wows as the rectangles of light from the windows raced along the track outside. Beatense wondered how they could have missed that effect during the trip up. With three days on the train they had plenty of time to catch these details.

The group emerged from the detour and forged on, and reached the Dining Car, Enlightening Quest, at last. They got in the line in the narrow corridor that ran beside the galley, where they were kept out of the service area proper.

"I wonder what they'll be serving," said Tiffany expectantly.

"The usual Hitsy Titsy A La King Babette," said Moose. "Anyway, miss, did I get your name right? Beatrice? I'm sorry I crashed into you like that."

"Oh, it was my fault, er, Moose. But I'm not Beatrice. It's Beatense."

"Be Tense?" said Moose, laughing. "Ha, I never... You're the Book Girl!"

"Stray genetics. Centuries and centuries of chromosomes trading all these traits back and forth, resulting in the statuesque huntress you see now."

"Yeah, er, nice shirt. Ouch! Tiff! I just recognized her, I didn't propose!"

Tiffany laughed delightedly, but it seemed she didn't quite know how to.

But being cutely beautiful, she happily voiced the ha-ha laughing chuckles. With her bone gifted cheeks and pinned-up, almost living black hair, which was lipped out over her elegantly angled forehead, her alert dark eyes were quite disarming.

Despite her bright energy and deep sun complexion, her eyebrows conveyed a pathos that was at odds with her brightly tender looks. She had on trim black plaza slacks and a form-fit vee-neck sweater of knitted mesh, whose snug short sleeves showed what really capable little arms she had.

Moose wore a polo shirt with a team emblem and multi-pocketed sport pants. He was slight, as if put together for lithe athletics, but he also seemed awkward in that adolescent, stumbling, ever confused way that makes people smile.

But Beatense quickly forgot these two. An impressive Xanthallado looking fellow with a humor conspiracy grin entered the car. He paused at the end of the line, and then he boldly came forward, past the resentful stares.

"Hi, I'm Craig," he said. "There are only three of you. Mind if I join you?"

Tiffany the extrovert smiled widely, and Moose nodded. Craig smiled, shyly, at Beatense, not recognizing her, and she smiled back. The porter led them in.

There were enough four-place tables to seat forty-eight patrons. Each table was spread with a starched linen cloth, adorned with candlestick and bud vase, holding a rose. Crisp linen napkins folded into crowns stood at each setting, that included sterling dinner, soup and coffee spoons, dinner, salad and dessert forks; and dinner knife and butter knife. The silver gleamed, casting little haloes upon the linen. Red velvet curtains with gold brocade added the luxury touch.

The kids were shown to their table, and as Craig sat next to Beatense a waiter poured ice water into their leaded cut crystal goblets. The haughty Chief Steward left off the menus, done in distressed Merico leather, oxblood colored.

"Damn, nothing edible," said Moose, eyeing his antiqued vellum listing.

"I know. I haven't had a Whooper in weeks," said Craig.

"At least the prices are half cheap," said Moose. "Even in the hoity toity Fancio Schmancio Grille back at our hotel. But you just want junk food, at any price."

"Yes!" said Tiffany. "I would die for a pizza! Just a heaped monster!"

They all groaned in longing, including Beatense, who had pizza galore back at camp. If not for that she would only know of it from her magazines.

Stealing looks at his neighbor's remarkable forearms Craig studied his menu. He saw Creamed Tidal Bleche Oysters, and Rib Roast Beouf Flambe. Between looks at Beatense he also saw Spring Milk Chicken and Pork Tenderloin Cutlets.

"Again, I'm Craig," he said, easily, casually, but Beatense's terrible tan and looks were taking their toll. "H-H-Hamiltyn, w-with a Y."

"I'm Moose Venter, and this is my first wife, Tiff… Ouch! Tiffany!"

"And I'm Beatense Colwell. Not Be Tense, as a reminder."

"Or Beatrice," added Moose. "Also known as the Book Girl." Craig started.

The Steward returned. "Could we possibly order now?" he demanded, turning to menacingly watch his waiters working the other tables.

"I'll have the Black Line Grilled Mountain Trout!" said Tiffany brightly.

She had a charming, child-like voice, and like a child she was proudly sitting up very straight. Beatense admired her as a worthy adversary. The light of the candle lent her dark eyes a moistly earnest glow, while enhancing her threat of a tan.

"I'd like a Haute Dogeau," said Moose, "with Sousse de Muztard and Ketchoup, and Fries au de Pohtahtoh. Any chance of that?"

"Most assuredly not!"

"Okay, the Red Snapper Mar… Marchale, however you say it."

"A hot baked potato with butter and lots of sour cream, please," said Beatense, as the nearby passengers turned to look. "And what soup do you have today, sir?"

The Steward suddenly knew who this girl was. That singer. As she gazed up at him, her all-knowing lifted irises made him feel like the fourth stooge.

"W-W-Well, yes, of course. Th-That would be Bisque of Lobster, my lady."

The lady leaned her head in her hand and laughed. "Ick. So how about a cut up tomato and mayonnaise? Oh, and chocolate milk. I'm hungry."

"That isn't much if you're hungry," said Craig. "There's a whole menu here."

He didn't know her stomach was the size of a softball. In fact a good question was, with belly so obviously tightly sheathed, how would even that fit?

"You're right. Sir, I'll have buttered toast with that also. And cherry jam."

Moose and Tiffany stared open-mouthed. Now they knew why this girl was so famous. Those centuries of chromosomes conspired toward perfection.

"I'll have the Shepherd's Pie," said Craig, "and chocolate milk." He winked.

The Steward wobbled off and Beatense sat tight belly slouched. She knew that back of the tied-aside curtains were train-and-bus typical rounded window corners.

Ah, yes. "Well, gosh, Tiffany, what would be your favorite magazines?"

"Favorite magazines, Beatense?" --/-- "Like, you know, *Career Achiever* or *Chez Health*. All those." --/-- Tiffany screwed her lips lopsidedly, as if she was afraid to answer. --/-- "I, er, don't... I don't read any of those, Beatense."

"What, how can you not? Of course, it's different with you, living right there in Xanthallado. But me, those magazines are the only way to keep in touch."

"Yeah, no offense but, I mean, it is kind of retro up here. I hate to say it, but that Inctin Building looked kind of corny, with those weird balconies."

"Yeah, I agree. I read something like that in one of my magazines."

"But gosh, if you're from Arrolynn that sure is a great tan you have!"

"Thanks. It's just this deep primordial instinct I have, to deeply bake. I guess I'm out of place in my jeans on the train like this, but in my camp days I was worse."

Craig wished that damn food would come. He could hardly breathe.

"And I have muscles. Barbells, I worked myself up to eighty pounds."

"Oh hell, eighty," said Moose. "That's nothing. I do a hundred. Ounces."

Craig couldn't respond with another joke to cut down the stress. Haggardly he eyed the outspoken girl's delectable forearms at rest on the table, that spoke of artist paint brushes, piano lessons, library books, hot cocoa, collie dogs, tree climbing, ball bats, potters wheels and rifles. They had a darkly fresh glow.

"I also run. Track, and with my Pop surveying. A lot of running in both."

"S-Surveying?" said Craig, staring. "Th-That's your line of work?"

"Well, it shouldn't be that big of a mystery. They got a few pictures of me at the transit. And then I sing radio ads and I have a few records on the charts."

"The problem is," said Craig, forcing himself to talk calmly, "is that..."

A porter came down the aisle. "Evert! Evert is the next stop!"

"Oh, Evert! I can get into my Roomette now," said Beatense. Her plate was set before her by a properly servile porter wearing white gloves. "Oh, wow, that potato is lovely! And look at how thick that toast is! Perfectly golden!"

"What? You were waiting, too?" said Moose. "They overbooked on us."

"Yeah, they said I had to wait before I could get in it, once they prep it."

Their porter, who from the luck of the draw got this table, served the other plates with slow, fastidious care. He took another glance at Beatense and was astonished that the star smiled. She seemed like a nice kid. And years ago Craig had flittered through her first book at the library, and now here she was.

The train began slowing down for Evert as they started to dine. The town was isolated and dreary, with sad old stores that probably saw few customers. When the train started up again, the next stop would be Shoglatt, in four hours.

"So, I've been a naked sun nut since twelve, and I hope this trip gets it out of my system. What do they call it, Tiffany, maxing out?"

"It doesn't work," said Tiffany. "You just get all the more hooked!"

"Going north for our honeymoon was the only way to ever see her," Moose said. "She would lay out every day for a month, given the chance."

"Oh, I would not!" Tiffany then made her laughing sound. "Ha ha ha!"

"It looks like you... You soak in sun pretty quickly," said Craig. He was directing his comment to her as a backdoor way of also complimenting the other amazon. No way could he say anything to her without choking up in terror. "You... Y-You might even get... *Huff! Huff!* G-Get pr-pretty dark?"

She caught his breathing difficulty. "Me? Ha ha ha! Maybe once I did."

"That's her city fade now," said Moose. "I mean for her Tiff is faded."

The girl smiled proudly. It seemed her proclivity was often the butt of joking remarks. She was probably also teased about her skimpy swimwear, and to Craig's relief Beatense didn't add to the commentary on the subject. Then...

"Just like me at thirteen and fourteen at that desert surveying camp, I was super crazed. So when we raided that camp this is what I had." She lifted her shirt.

Craig made fists under the table. He saw her sunk flexing black ripples.

"Those old people were so helpless, it was hilarious galloping after them."

They all had Meuniere Cacao Latte Torte for dessert. Moose pointedly looked at the dark chocolate and then to Tiffany, shaking his head. She laughed, or tried to. Beatense felt full but she crammed the fudge cake into her mouth.

"Well, now what," said Moose as they finished. "We can all stumble back to that Sky-Liner Car at the end of the train. Or we could go back to that Dome Car."

"At night?" said Craig. "What can you see at night?"

Abruptly, riding in a darkened Dome Car appealed to Craig strongly, after he had just axed the idea. His new (he hoped) friend might have sat with him.

"Let's find the Club Car," said Tiffany. "I'm old enough now."

"Oh, topping," said Moose. "We can get good and jolly well trashed."

"Attitude readjustment," said Craig, grinning at his clever originality.

"Wait," said Beatense,: my Roomette is just a couple cars up, I think, in Tellurian. Can you wait here a sec while I run back to Sabbatical to get my things?"

"We have to move ourselves," said Moose. "Let's meet in the Club Car once we get downloaded, heh heh. Get it? Downloaded?"

"Er, uh, yeah. But let's do that, good. And what's my cut of the tab?"

"I'll pick that up, Miss Colwell," said Craig, reddening. She unbuttoned her white shirt to make a deep vee. "And... And... Why not have a porter bring your things?"

Craig stopped the Steward and Beatense explained her situation.

"Very well, miss, we can accommodate you." --/-- "Oh, good, thanks! So go on ahead, guys, I can find you! And Craig, thanks for treating me. I'm stuffed!"

"It... It didn't come to much." He grinned cheesily. "But any... Any time."

But despite the gratitude Craig wasn't asked to join her. He felt like life had no meaning if they weren't better friends. Meanwhile, as she headed forward Beatense happily recounted the events. She suddenly had three attractive new friends, with a possibility with that Craig. And it was fun walking the swaying corridors to her car.

Her Roomette in Tellurian Quest came far too quickly.

She slid her heavy, windowed door open, adding one wee rumble to that of the train, and she paused to look at the 24 volt lights shining upon her seats.

Her two bunk Roomette was a tiny cabin in a line-up of other similar rooms along both sides of the narrow aisle. Beatense sat in the forward facing single seat of the twin pair provided. The seats could be pulled out toward each other, so that together they made a cozy little berth. A bunk was tucked in above, that simply folded down sideways. Since the girl was alone, it would be unused.

She pulled her door and its floor-length curtain shut, and awaiting the porter she watched out her gloom darkened window. The forlorn lights of the countryside swept by in a relentless, ever changing pattern, while the locomotive horns sang out into the lonely night. There! A light tap at the windowed door.

"M-Miss, I have... I have your things for you."

She slid the heavy door open. The porter stood bracing himself. The train, of course, and also the close presence of this star. Sacred eyes. Wide placed eyes.

"Oh, thank you, sir. I could have gotten these myself, but me being in the Dining Car I was conveniently so close to here."

"Yes, miss, the Steward mentioned your saying that."

"Oh, he did, did he. But could you fold out my bed now? The lower one?"

"I can do that," he said, "but you'll have to step out into the corridor."

She did that. The aisle was lined with windowed doors like her own, twenty total, and paneled with beige enameled steel. The lights overhead dimly glowed, and the narrow hallway rocked with the train's movements. Several Roomette doors were softly alighted, and Beatense heard snips of muted conversation.

The porter snapped the locks and slid the seats toward each other, so that the seatbacks lay flat with a spring click. Then he lowered the upper bunk and laid the made-up bedding stored here out on the girl's lower berth. He hung her backpack in the narrow closet squeezed in between her seat and the aisle wall.

"Now this is your vent control lever, miss, and this is your night light and reading lamp switch," the attendant said, pointing. "And this is the release for lowering your sink. Towels are on the lower shelf in your closet, and the car's restroom lounge is forward, up the corridor. Basic toiletries are provided, plus there is coffee."

Beatense looked upon her little bed as it flew through the night. The lights softly shined down upon the blanket with its insignia and the turned down sheet.

"You know, I always dreamed of this. My last trips were just in a seat."

"Ahem, so I heard. I... I bought... I-I bought your record. *Daddy Say*."

"Oh, great! I appreciate it! With or without picture?"

"With. With. But... B-But it doesn't compare to you in... In person."

8

DISASTROPHE

They grabbed and hugged and the fan left. The girl eyed her inviting bed. She almost felt like staying put here, but she would be missed, even looked for. Shirt in hand she walked to the ladies lounge at the end of the hall. It had the typical layout: A small room with the lavatory cubicle in the corner, and a counter with two sinks was tucked in beside it. A thin padded settee, fake leather armchairs and a wobbling ashtray stand completed the actually spacious arrangement.

The toilet was an inverted stainless steel pail, with a forbidding seat of hard black rubber. The girl stepped on the flush pedal and a little hatch opened to the jet roar of the train's speed. She exited the compartment and at the sink she opened a fragrant bar of Cashmere Bouquet and washed her hands. Re-wrapping the bar for next use Beatense put back on her shirt, vee opened, and left in search of her friends.

She walked the swaying corridor of her sleeping car. Not all curtains had been closed, and the girl espied these other passengers. She felt like she was on a fool's errand. How could she find her friends in twenty cars? She pinballed through the thundering and diesel smelling vestibule into the next sleeper, and re-entered the Dining Car. Here she saw a sixteen year old Xanthallado girl in a rumply sweatshirt, who was having dinner with her parents and young sister.

Despite the looseness of her shirt she was obviously narrow in lines, with a long and thin toughness. Along with her dark hair she had black eyes, that with her dark eyebrows had a pleasant but determined set. Her refined features and moist skin of sun mellowed ivory gave her proud face a classic, pure simplicity. Her piano playing hands were shaped with the utmost caring exactitude.

The young sister wasn't a girl after all; the remarkably tan faced child was her brother, pretty and long haired. He had that masculine edge to his looks, he definitely was a boy, but he had wide dark, dreamy eyes, and such a startling abundance of loosely curly black hair, shags of it, he could easily be mistaken for a girl.

Beatense, gazing upon him as she went by, saw a gold chain necklace that gleamed from his firm, tan neck. A necklace! And long hair! A camp boy!

The pretty boy saw her interest and gave a little jolt. Smiling at his typical reaction, which everyone else had, Beatense went on to her Sabbatical and she went by the snoozing old Ida. Other passengers were also in transit, and politely made way for each other in the cramped walkways. Everyone made way for the famous Beatense, who fakely smiled with a shy, fetching delight. This would be a long trip. She went on through fifteen coaches and finally found her friends in the Recreation Car.

"W-Well, welcome b-back!" said Craig, standing as Beatense walked up.

"Hi, Craig! Hey, you two, did I miss anything?"

"No, we're just starting Sheeps Head," said Moose. "And don't say you don't play it, because Tiffany just loves it so much."

"Oh, yeah, ha ha ha! Hey, let's play gin rummy!"

Beatense looked around. The others in the car were reading, writing, or quietly conversing, or studying her. A glassed-in cubicle held a private party, and children were busy with toys in a play area. At the darkened far end a silent comedy featuring the usual 2x4 on the shoulder knocking everyone down was being shown, and at car center a steward stood back of his counter, ready to dispense drinks, mixed or not.

"Wow! Is this ever neat! Sheep, you say? Deal me in! Penny a point!"

Sheephead is an obscure farmer game that Beatense knew well, but Craig had trouble with it. Plus he was so flustered by the vee-shirt girl that he trumped at the wrong times, and he gave up pat, club filled hands to pick Schnitzel.

But Tiffany's far more unfortunate blunders, along with her guilty looks and fake laughter, took the heat off. Craig was just to Beatense's right, and shirt now open he could see the ripple-writhing of her sunk pine knotty belly.

It bothered him that she looked like she knew better than to make this display; it seemed she had a mentality that should have transcended any animal sensuality.

On the other hand with her high quality she did have her rights.

After a few loud arguing rounds the family Beatense saw before in the Dining Car came in. The steward carried a stack of 78 records over to the cabinet phonograph, and he nudged the dazzling long haired boy into playing them. He had never seen a record player before; it quite captivated him. He set the needle in the lead-in groove, and after a long, suspenseful, static filled interval as it worked in, the familiar old tune started up, "*...Step aside, partner, it's my day...*" Beatense sprang up and she sang along to the chorus parts. "*... Of a real live sea-to-sea excursion...*"

It was a big mistake, for the last doubting hold-outs knew her now. Moose began to air play the trombone, and Craig began tapping on the table in time, shaking. *Boy, can she sing! HP Shit!* Tiffany nodded her head, also in time, and when the smiling boy put on *A B C D E F G H I Got A Gal,* the newlyweds began to dance.

Beatense sang to this song too, and at the final crescendo after the fake end she pulled Craig up for the next song, *Bugle Boy.* The steward gave a concerned look as they crazily jittered to the music. But this was the radio girl. Hugged old Pete.

As the train rocked along others swung to more songs that the showy boy put to needle, including *String Of Beads,* and then a jumpy song called *Patriot's Point.*

Beatense was wild; her breasts showed, and Craig quietly decided she redefined the word flexible. When the Recreation Car closed at ten, no one cared to leave, but the steward chased everybody out. The friends went through the darkened cars to Tiffany's and Moose's Roomette in Solitude Quest. Goodnights were called, and Craig counted the cars as he accompanied the humming Beatense to her door.

If only the train was longer. A lot longer. Could he dare ask to see her again?

They entered Tellurian Quest and the moment of truth came.

"W-Well, Beatense, I... I hope you d-didn't mind all th-that dancing."

"Silly, I roped you into it! Oh, and thanks again for picking up on the dinner. But I'm... I'm wondering, will we, er, see each other again, Craig?"

He almost laughed out loud. All that fearful dread of The Question!

"Sure, I-I would like very much for us to s-see each other again."

They looked into each other's eyes. The shaking and rumblings of the flying train momentarily disappeared. Again Craig was sweating it out, what to do. Suddenly he grabbed and kissed her. The girl's hands were all over his back.

They separated, panting. "C-Craig, we gotta be careful. I mean, you know..."

He went rigid, was this an invitation? He was from the old school, where girls of class like Beatense were above this. Maybe not, he saw those ravenous videos, and book. It came as yet another shock as she took off her opened shirt and unzipped. She shoved the jeans down from her small hips and sat with legs held out. Shaking, Craig got off her $800 running shoes and $1200 jeans. The Arrolynn shirt was five.

"Thanks, but don't get any ideas. I'm just undressing for the night, Craig."

"Are you sure about that? If there was ever a come-on, this is it!"

"Not at all. I'm a naked sun natural all the time, since I was just twelve."

Wide placed eyes, smoky with desire. Shine stretched skin, real dark brown.

Sadly with just a foot of space between door and bed, the mechanics of intimacy were awkward, almost by design. Also Beatense had been broken in on the thin tan intern boys, who were picked for their desert resilience. Girl kissed Craig goodbye.

Left alone, she dialed the thermostat up a few degrees. She turned off her light, pulled up her sheet and watched out her window. This was the Sad Lands, isolated ugly towns swept by every few miles. At Ballard a telegrapher stepped away with his orders hoop. He had just handed a message up to the lead engine. Its horns called out as it shot through this old forgotten outpost. Then the clanging of a crossing bell, that was drawn out and twisted by the rocketing speed. Watched by a few lone souls, the train swept through Waknuk, Meadowlands and Sugar Loaf. Bandana and Baskin were sucked away in turn, followed by Gothic, Mountain Slag and Bridgeport.

Then Beatense felt a catch of the brakes, or did she. A little lurch.

The train began slowing down. The porter came through, quietly calling out the next station, Shoglatt. This backward city of 400,000 did almost nothing to light up the night sky. As the train shot through the dismal outskirts Beatense saw the countless squatter shacks that unreeled through the candle and kerosene lighted gloom.

This city was famous for its endless slums, all filthy, noisy and dangerous. Aside from the multitude scrap lumber shacks there were houses in Shoglatt, most of them rented, and the Queen raced by endless gloomy residential dumps built decades ago when times were even worse. Internet 1920s and 30s street scenes tell the story.

Shoglatt's dirty factories made mousetraps and fly paper rolled into smelly tubes. They manufactured thumb tacks and snelled fishing hooks. The factories made apple corers knobs for police radios made and used elsewhere. But the main industry was wooden fruit crates (the fanciful, multi-colored paper labels that looked upon the bare Beatense atop her roof were printed here too). With pay so low it was far cheaper to ship whole logs to the Shoglatt sawmills from the distant forests for the crates.

But the workers were so careless and conditions dangerous they were injured or even killed in the mills daily, to the great amusement of the others. Collections were never taken up. In fact the dying victims had their wallets cleaned out.

The Queen swept by saloons, taverns and stout alehouses. Hotels, dance halls and bottle goods stores came in throngs. The same dollar bill would travel up and down the same street all day, most of the time buying gut liquor. Every place was open, even grocery stores, barber shops and shoe stores.

Any cars with enough self respect to start were out rattling along the brick paved streets, and the broken sidewalks along them were mobbed. Ghoulish children were up and out at this hour, and they ran in and out of the forbidding alleys, or they stood smoking with bottles of beer, and there were shoving matches and even fights.

The train sounded and the brakes grabbed, and the Queen glided to a halt. The platform of the depot ran right along the street, and Beatense shuddered at the decrepit old cars parked here. Slovenly cheap women and gaunt overworked men paused to look at the Queen with coughing wonder, or they purposefully shuffled along carrying decayed rope-tied cardboard suitcases, as if they intended to board.

Horrors! Beatense didn't want this trash on her train! She had to see if anyone was actually boarding. And she wanted to look around. Maybe a healthy run! She put on her jeans, athletic shoes and famous white shirt, for once with no deep vee, and stepped out into the corridor and met the conductor.

"If you're thinking of stretching your legs, miss, stay close, for we'll be departing Shoglatt shortly."

"Oh, I'm just after some Thunderbird wine, sir. Muscatel. You're Bernie, right?"

"Yes, you can please call me that, Miss Col... Er, Beatense. But listen for the horns, okay? This is not a restocking stop."

"You got it. But no one from here has boarded Tellurian, right?"

"This clientele has their own car with a bypassing side corridor. Hurry now, and I better go myself. I see a bit of unpleasantness outside I better attend to."

"This whole town is unpleasantness. It's worse than Arrolynn!"

Bernie hurried off laughing. *Geez, she has an energy I could actually feel.*

The Tellurian's vestibule trapdoor was tipped up, conveniently exposing the steps. The girl hopped down onto the cobblestone paving, but almost turned back. The stale air reeked of foundry smoke and fetid humanity, and the ancient grape-like street lamps, that so dimly lighted the station house area, revealed shabby cruddy derelicts huddling in the stagnant shadows, with their collars turned up and bottles in hand.

Beatense carefully detoured around a coarse, vulgar, low family that was cursing poor Nicky's leaving the city, involuntarily, with handcuffs and a deputy escort.

The ragged mother bawled with a face of shapeless putty, and the dirt brothers of the convict looked as if each was vowing deadly revenge. Probably prison would be a better place for Nick. And the train for sure.

Beatense looked up the windowed length of the mighty Queen Of Steel, feeling proud of how out of place and modern it was in this shitty swamp. Further up the girl saw several rabble destitutes as they boarded their quarantined car.

But others, with little else to do at this hour many came to the station just to idly view this attraction. If not vomiting, dirty children chased around, cursing and yelling. Beatense stepped guardedly by other upstanding (most of them, anyway) citizens on the brick paved platform, across from the team of locomotives. Their puttering and thrumming idle trembled the pavement as she drew near.

The girl walked up past the front of the train and turned to admire the massive engines. Their ABBB consist had the same color band sweep as the baggage cars behind and passenger coaches as continuing down line. But despite the spectacular horsepower of the four engine line-up, twelve thousand, the big split windshield of the lead locomotive had a sadly droopy look as it curved over the headlighted hood, with lighted number boxes on each side.

The faint abrupt call of *"Boarrrrrrrd! All aboard!"* quickly ended Beatense's study. A red lantern was swung in an arc, and the 140 dB horns blared. The girl jumped. Brass bells began clanging, and with a volcano of smoke and a shaking of pavement the sixteen cylinder diesels powered up. As the wheel trucks began to clunk forward with another burst from the engines, the girl whirled her head in panic.

She ran for her car, hoping the door was still open.

"This is crazy!" she yelled as she ran by the moving cars, dodging the human excretia blocking her path. "This is insane! Just who wrote this book!"

The screeching, steel-on-steel lament of the accelerating train was growing ever more urgent as passenger and Tellurian Quest quickly met. The upper half door was invitingly still open, but the lower door was snugly and smugly shut. The girl ran on, hoping to find an open door further down as the speed increased. After all, she hung from an open door in Arrolynn, did she not? She even got in trouble for that! Mutely she watched as Sabbatical Quest came and went, all those lighted windows with the passenger silhouettes on their shades, and her terror was complete.

The rest of the Queen swept by in a roar, window after window, car after car. As the crushing final insult the girl saw the oscillating red tail light of the Skyliner lounge car sail on its merry way. She stumbled in a shell-shocked trance as the increasingly distant horns called back to her from out of the infinite night.

Beatense could not believe what she was seeing. She couldn't dare believe.

She danced, shook and sprang about in mad paroxysms of outraged, cursing fury, but the Queen Of Steel kept rolling on, as if her selected verbiage had little, if any, braking effect on its progress. She stamped and shouted aloud as the train's figure eight swiveling, red stern light grew ever fainter.

The girl frankly discussed the situation further, shaking her fist at the black sky, then she clutched her head and reeled drunkenly.

The bystanders cackled, hooted and jeered, as if this traveler's predicament was part of the evening's entertainment. They trumpeted their hands and shouted out whatever gems of cheerful encouragement that came thoughtfully to mind, but the girl was too wildly distracted to even notice. And yet, and yet, she did spot the depot house, that she had run past in her manic plight, and she ran back to it with the faint despairing hope that therein lay the escape from this frantic hell.

"I had to get off! Oh I had to get off!"

She burst into the antiquated waiting room and sprang over to the barred ticket window, where the bespectacled old station agent, stooped in his frayed black vest, was patiently setting up an itinerary for a lone (thankfully) customer.

But it quickly occurred to the trembling girl that this didn't bode extremely well. It seemed as if there was some blubber lipped confusion.

"Well, she don't stop in Leak Run, but she will in Gascola five miles up."

"Hmm. Well, you see, it's urgent that I get off at Leak Run."

"We better check the Official Guide again. Let me see..."

"Of course, if there's a hotel in Gascola, that might work out."

"They have one, but I must inform you, its dining room closes at eight."

Beatense grabbed at her hair. She was reminded of its overgrown tangles.

"Indeed. Oh, and I might add that our lodge is planning to go by Northern for our annual convention. If you have some brochures I'll bring it up at our next meeting."

"Why not have our booking agent at the main office make a proposal?"

Beatense hyperventilated.

"Splendid. I'm glad I thought to bring it up. Do you have his number?"

Gasleak left at last and Beatense pounced.

"Sir! I was on the Queen just now and it took off without me!"

He gave this thought. Stupidly, it seemed to Beatense, glancing around.

"Now hold it. You say you were on the train, but it left without you."

"Yes! I mean, here I am! How much proof do you need?"

"Ah, yes. Be with you in a minute."

"A minute! But my train just left! I have to get back on it!"

The agent looked up from sorting through his paperwork. "Young lady, if the train actually pulled out, you can't get back on it, can you?"

She stepped away, looking again for someone else. *This fool is alone here?*

"I suppose your bags are still on board?"

"Yes, of course it is! Even my purse! Which I usually never carry."

"And your ticket, I suppose. Where were you heading, by the way?"

"I guess it doesn't matter now where I was going. Cardiff, Xanthallado."

"I'll wire Dispatch to see what we can do. Your name, miss?"

"Beatense Colwell. The radio girl! And please use the phone! It's faster!"

The agent limped over to his telegraph key, that was on a counter within a bay window alcove overlooking the platform area. Humming, he sat down in his creaky wooden chair, and as he filled his pipe Beatense all but tore the bars of the window loose. He shoved aside a noisy clutter of way bills and train orders and reset his specs, then consulted his big Operations Book.

With maddening patience he paged through it, very slowly, licking his finger every twenty seconds. Then with infinite care he ran his finger down the columns on what must have finally looked to Beatense as page 350. He turned to her.

"It spells it out right here, miss. Section 18, Paragraph 45, Article xxxi. I wire the Dispatch to drop a signal on her."

"Drop a signal! What do you mean? You knock a tower over on it?"

"Stop her, miss."

"Oh! That would be wonderful! But... But where?"

"Altura."

"Altura! Where's that?"

"Oh, she's a fur piece down the pike."

"A fur... A far piece down the pike! How far is a far piece?"

"Oh, nigh onto a hundred miles. She'll be there in eighty-two minutes."

Beatense gasped. "A hundred miles! Can't you stop her sooner than that?"

"Well, miss, Altura is the only station with a long enough side track. Old Queenie will be waiting there for you until you come in on the bus at seven AM."

"A bus! Seven AM! But can't I get there tonight? Can't you call me a taxi?" She stopped. The automobiles here would never make it. Nor the drivers.

"No ride tonight. Sleep in the waiting room, if you want. Okay, hold on. Wait a minute! You ain't the singer, are you?"

"How... How do you know that?"

"You just said you were. And it's all up and down the wire. You are plumb cute at that. But we can work this out for you, being who you are."

"Oh no! I don't want any special treatment! Thanks for the offer, but no."

"Well, how about if this happens again I help the fellow the same as you?"

"No, because what about anyone before? It wouldn't be fair to them!"

"Until now everyone had the sense to stay on the train, miss."

"Oh ha ha ha. Okay, go for it! Every second counts!"

The de-de-dees flew out into the enclosing night as the agent tapped his round black key. It seemed that the responses coming back had a certain intensity, but the agent kept doggedly on. The girl had no idea what all those dots and dashes meant, and wondered about them racing along all those miles of wire. Wasn't it possible that those distances could cause those minute impulses to garble up together, so that the message would arrive all different? What if it came out to say, "Go faster." Or, "Unhook last ten cars." Or, "Tell radio girl to await return train to Arrolynn."

Plumb cute. In this crisis at least I have that going for me.

"All right, miss, I got your return Confirm. But I had to kind of explain this to the Dispatcher. He said he don't care who you are. But he agreed."

"Tell him a world of thanks. But what will he do, assuming he does do it?"

"Wire Altura to stop the Queen to await famous passenger, is all."

She couldn't do it, hold up the Queen until dawn because of her own stupidity. Trusting stupidity, yes, but stupidity. "Well, thank you, sir, but I can't have that entire train and all those passengers just sit there until morning waiting for me. You better just let her go. But I want a *clean and safe* hotel room! No HP Lovecraft!"

She surprised herself saying this, but she had reached the wearied point where she was resigned to her fate. She even felt a little ashamed of her crazy antics. And for his part the telegrapher, a devout Railroader, was touched that this beautiful girl would sacrifice her own interests to keep the iron rolling.

9

BLACK THUNDER

Beatense rolled her sleeves to her elbows, brightening the place noticeably.

"We got a freight coming through south in fifteen minutes. I'll wire Dispatch for an unscheduled meet order. You just relax now."

"A meat order? Do you think I'm hungry or something?"

"A *meet* order. One train is ordered at meet another at some point."

"Oh, that meet! And so you mean I ride the freight down to the Queen?"

"If you care to. The caboose. You'll be back on board in a couple hours."

She wept. "Oh, thank you! Thank you, thank you!"

"Tush, now." He gazed at her one full minute. "Okay, back to the bug."

"Sometimes it helps to be famous, I guess. With stared at plumb cuteness."

The girl had a friendlier appreciation of this cozy place now. She gazed upon the Bluerock batteries, track levers, lanterns, the signal tower relays, telegraph sounders and paper filled clipboards. She saw a candlestick phone with dial in its base, and a Superior and Commercial Oil calendar. *Hey, no shit!* Presiding over all was the old pendulum monitor clock. The agent worked his key and presently a response rattled back, stridently, and the agent returned to the window.

"Well, miss, this is what we worked out. Dispatch wired Mickelburg to slow the Queen to sixty. Then she and your freight will make Altura together."

"Well, why don't they just stop the Queen at Mick… Mickelberg?"

"I just told you, no siding track. Now, until that freight gets in have a seat."

"No thanks on that, sir. I'm too wired to sit down. But I really appreciate all your help, and especially your admiring me. I'm sorry I got so unhinged."

"Someone will catch hell for that. I vouched it twarn't your fault none."

"Thanks. But sir, where would I ride in that freight? A boxcar, maybe?"

"Nah. We'll set you up in a caboose, I said. Nice and cozy."

"Hey, that'll be fun! Okay, I'll try and relax now. Ten minutes, seriously?"

The telegraph began to rattle with other urgent messages, and Beatense toured the bleakly spare four-bench waiting room. The grim yellow walls were covered with blackened old wainscoting to a height of three feet, where a small ledge was littered with empty matchbooks, gum wads, pencil stubs and other stray items. At both ends of the scratched up old benches brass spittoons stood in befouled readiness.

The dour lights hanging above gave their tarnished brass a dull shine. Just like at her home depot Beatense saw an old magazine lying upon a bench, and in paging through it she saw that it was printed on pulp paper in black and red ink.

It was full of tasteless ads for brillantine hair oil and fifteen cent lipstick, and comb and brush sets and curling irons that are heated on the stove. An article was entitled, *I Was Warned He Was A Cad*, and for ten cents one could order either a secret spy ring or a handshake buzzer. Ventriloquist gizmos (that don't work) were also offered, and peanut cans with jumping snakes. Beatense was tempted by X-ray glasses.

The distant call of an approaching train's horn sent the agent hurrying over to the pullchain hanging in his office, and he gave it a tug.

"Gave him the board," he said, as stepped outside with his orders pole.

Moments later a freight thundered by, heading north. Or so Beatense hoped.

The agent returned, shivering, it was a cool night, and he took to his creaky desk chair to report the train in and out. More telegraphy.

"Won't be long now," the agent said, when the chatter ceased.

"Yes, I think I'll wait outside now, sir."

"Well, warmer in here," the agent said, nodding toward the cast iron wood stove standing in the corner. "But she'll be here quick. Just left Sloat Avenue."

"Of course, Sloat Avenue. I could have guessed that."

The telegraph began to spark again and the agent hurried over to it to take the message. Beatense went out onto the platform. She had forgotten she was in the middle of a large city, and as she peered down track she wondered if she would be able to see her train's headlight. No, too many other lights, even in this old time warp city. She looked up at the signal semaphores atop their tower, one whose light was glowing so unmistakably red, silently guarded the track to the south. All signals were interlocked, so it would be nearly impossible to route opposing trains onto the same track. Somehow the dispatcher kept every detail straight, so that minute by minute knew where all his trains were and their speeds at the time. Probably stopping the Queen forced the rescheduling of ten trains. Beatense grimaced guiltily.

The agent joined her. "Ah, there she be. Won't be long now."

Beatense saw the distant but bright light and her heart leaped. She could hardly wait to hop aboard that caboose and get... She looked up the track again. A steam locomotive was on its way! Its mournful whistle sounded four times.

Wauh-Wauh-Wauh-Wauh!

"Whistling for the board," said the agent. Beatense looked up at the signal tower. "Otherwise he would be highballing at ninety."

"Oh! He wants you to change it to green! I get it!"

"He thinks I'm getting forgetful in my old... Wh-What was I just saying?"

The girl laughed. With bells clanging the red blinking crossing gates swung down as the behemoth chuffed in. With rolling clouds of hot steam it hissed to a mighty, towering and earth shaking stop, and Beatense felt faint. This was no junk greasy teapot, but a crack express streamliner, the royalty of the rails.

Strikingly enameled in gleaming midnight blue, it was gorgeous. But maybe the engine was too frighteningly futuristic with its long stark shape and yellow pin-striped lines flowing back from the sun ball circling the headlighted snout. The massive steel tank of the stretched, sleek boiler presided above four seven-foot drive wheels.

As giant discs these did not have those old see-thru spokes. The cowcatcher, or pilot, cleared the track by just one inch. Beatense gazed up in delicious fright at this sinister dinosaur, as the steam from its twenty inch cylinders wafted around her legs, and as the boiler heat from its rumbling fires warmed her face.

The engineer waved from his 2x4 foot side window, that seemed lost in the titanic bulk. His forward window set in by the boiler cowl looked barely big enough to stick out a rifle, but somehow the engineer was expected to use this to watch the track ahead, past sixty-six feet of raging, iron encased fury.

As she and the agent walked to the end of the engine, Beatense vowed that she would either ride in the cab of this hulk, or die under its wheels. The narrow door back of the side window opened inward, and the engineer clambered down the ladder to join the two. The fireman stood in the door, ten feet up. The roar and rumble of the boiler permeated all thought. The nameplate read *Neptune*.

"Evening, Abe. What's up, old man? Getting forgetful in your old age?"

"Was just discussing that. Anyway, howdy, Ike. Got old Neppie tonight?"

"Saving a deadhead. Why didn't you give us the board?"

"That's what I want to know!" shouted the conductor, who came running from the caboose. "That's twice we were stopped tonight!"

"The Queen left without this here young lady, who sings all them radio ads and does the naked pictures, so I got a meet for you down at Altura."

He resented her lanky height, brown face and hair, unknown in this cesspool city.

"Oh, hell! Here, give me it to sign and let's go! And you miss, expecting special favors doesn't interest me in the slightest. But we're committed now so I have no choice! Ellery, do you have the new train orders? Hand them over!"

The brown face was even less enthusiastic now to ride at train's end.

"Er, I don't want to ride in some dumb old caboose," she volunteered.

"Oh? Why couldn't you decide that before we were stopped?" the white haired conductor snapped, as he scribbled on the slip. "Do you come or not?"

"I'm sorry, sir, but think who you're talking to. Yes, I'm the famous singer, and nude, but more important, I am, er was, a Roomette passenger, First Class. I stepped off the Queen Of Steel here and unexplainably it left without me."

"Well, we'll take care of that! Pull the boose up, Elwood!"

"Hold it, I'm not going to ride back in that caboose and have you nagging me the whole time, when this whole thing wasn't even my fault!"

"All right, I'll spare you that! I'll ride the cab! Pull her up, Elwood!"

The engineer didn't care for the conductor's companionship either.

"Miss, we can't hardly ask you to ride forward, anyway. It's hot, dark, bone rattling and noisy. Besides, only road employees can ride the tractives. Rules."

"You ain't working for the road, are you?" said the agent, promptingly.

"Not me. My father." The girl hoped that track survey long ago counted.

"Well, then you see, Ike? She can ride up by you!"

"By spit and by gum, she can! Of course, it is terribly dangerous, miss."

She visibly brightened at that, and the conductor whapped his forehead.

"Oh, all right, if that's how it is! Now can you give us high iron, Ellery?"

At that the conductor stalked away with heels chinking the stone ballast.

"Let's fly, miss," said Ike, as he also signed the order and handed it over. "But watch your step. See ya, Elly. I owe ya, getting him out of our roost."

"Well, he would be quizzing you from that Rule Book the whole time. Now stretch old Neppie's legs, Esky's a coming, and Paulie wants you on Track 2."

"Well, damn it to hell!" said Ike, winking. "Track 2? Son of a bitch!"

The trainmen laughed. Beatense, perplexed, missed the humor. "I didn't know freight trains had conductors!" she said. "And who's this Esky?"

"The Esquire, running late, mad as hell. You stay well ahead of him!"

Beatense gave the agent a hug. She took hold of the iron ladder and climbed hesitantly up the ten feet into the darkened interior of Neptune's trembling cab. The fireman nodded to her, and with a grin he stepped down on an iron pedal rising from the steel plate deck, and the firedoor clanked open, half to the left, half to the right.

The girl stared at the livid bed of burning coals that was exposed, where orange flames fought each other with a buffeting roar. The dim light showed that the cab's interior was painted with bright industrial green, while the complex network of steam pipes were black. The round valve handles were bright red, and like the DeluxTru gauges these numbered over two dozen. The firebox door halves clanked back shut, cutting off the heavy red heat, and the engineer tapped Beatense on the shoulder.

He hollered. "Take the jumpseat behind the fireman, miss! And hang on!"

She hollered. "Yes, sir!" Sign language would work better.

The girl folded down the padded seat, that was hinged to the left side door. The fireman took the seat in front of her, and the engineer sat over on the far side of the wide, curved roof cab. Between the seats the firebox's enormous, slanted backhead jutted out over three feet. This held many of the gauges.

The engineer pulled the whistle cord: *Wauhhh! Wauhhhhhh!* He pushed what Beatense guessed to be the brake lever, for a loud, vapory wet *whoooosh* escaped. He pulled the whistle again and pulled the throttle cut-off lever down.

Amidst the shellfire racket of giant, bedrock fracturing stresses, along with sharp explosions and shrieking storms of steam, Neptune trundled in reverse.

"What… What are we going *backwards* for?!"

"Taking up the slack!" the fireman yelled. "For a flying start!"

"Oh! You had me scared there! But what's that infernal roaring noise?"

"Them's the air jets! They kick the coal around on the grate!"

"But don't you shovel the coal?"

"Not on old Neppie! Take four men!" The fireman pointed to a grip release lever as the train continued to ride in reverse, closing together the cars. "This here handle controls the worm screw back in the tender! Feeds in the coal automatically."

The locomotive eased to a stop as more steam hissed in billowing escape.

"We got green! High ball!" the fireman shouted, pulling his stoking lever.

"*High Bawlll!*" the engineer called back. "Sit tight, miss!"

She was already doing that, as she verbally pointed out to the engineer.

He hit the whistle again: *Wauhhh! Wauhhhhh!* He set the direction lever and throttle, and the mighty engine lurched ahead. Steam laden black smoke erupted up from the low profile stack, actually zero profile, in multiple volcanoes as the first few yards of rail groaned by. Suddenly earth shaking lunges almost tossed Beatense off her seat, as the drivers suddenly broke traction and screechingly spun.

Sparks flew, as the seven foot discs caught. Each boxcar down line was nudged into forward motion, and the locomotive jolted wildly as it shunted onto the next track. With rapid blasts from its zero profile stack Neptune began to accelerate.

Beatense was wide eyed. The speed rocketed up and continued to climb as the buildings and houses of the city flowed by. By the time the shanty town outskirts hit, the piston blasts had merged into a single pulsating roar. The piston-driven half ton connecting rods driving the drivers were flying back and forth in a blur, if one was to observe them, and the screaming jets of steam were violently loud.

Somewhere in that thunderous din Beatense heard an insistent pounding. The grate shaker. She could feel it throb at her $800 shoes through the bucking of the deck. Her seat was also in motion. She had to hang on to stay seated.

Wauhhh! Wauhhh! Wau-Wauhhhhh!

"Green!" the fireman called, as his head swayed from side to side.

"Green!" answered the engineer, as he stared intently forward.

Her eyes wide, straining, the girl hardly knew what to think as she braced herself against the flying locomotive's wheel on steel shaking. To be a part of such enfuried power, of that ninety mile per hour impetus, drove her mad.

She wanted to shout, and actually she was. As the hurtling engine lurched over the uneven tracks the wild rocking and pitching did concern her about how well the wheel flanges would hold the train to the rails, but she forgot these doubts when the fireman stood and waved her to his seat.

"Keep her at 260, miss!" he shouted. "I gotta check the drive box! The clutch is slipping! Good thing you're along! Hurry now! We're losing head!"

"That... That isn't 260 psi, is it? That high?!"

Wauhhh! Wauhhh! Wau-Wauhhhhh!

She never got an answer. Beatense traded places with legs of rubber, in spite of their hard muscle. She saw that the DeLuxTru gauge had already fallen to 250. She pulled the lever, and the quivering needle magically crept back up. Her heart leaped. This was better than hot day nudity! The fireman opened a hatch in the deck, and he worked at the gear mechanism with a wrench. He returned and pulled another lever.

"Feed water, miss! Watch that sight glass! Green!"

"Green!" responded the engineer, as Beatense, like him, stared ahead.

Peering ahead through her 6x12 inch, cowl hugging window, that was three feet distant from her wide placed eyes, searching past the massive length of boiler and its bursting jet of smoke, the pile of hair saw why green was such a popular color lately.

Far down the track, so far it was just a speck, she saw a faint green light. The crewmen were calling the colors to each other, to mutually verify that the up-line iron was clear. The green light shot by, turning red, and the next one appeared.

"Green!" she called out, glancing at her jumping gauges.

"Green! Thank you, miss!"

The fireman finished his repair and shut the hatch. He stood by Beatense.

"You're doing a good job, so I'll have me some coffee now!"

She whooped in reply. The fireman took the jump seat. Looking out, the girl saw another light, a bright white star far ahead in this blackest of nights.

"What... What's that?!"

The fireman poured coffee out from his Thermos ©. "Oncoming express, miss! Engine 17, lead end, Gunderson! You know her as the Citadel!"

"Oh, why, of course! The City Slicker!"

The fireman put the vacuum flask back in his black round topped lunchbox. His casual action did little to reassure Beatense that the intruder was on its own track. In fact she was sure it was not. After all, did they not switch to the second track? The light grew rapidly, and still they relentlessly flew toward that cursed glare. Paralyzed, as if in a dream, the girl watched their locomotive ram into that great white eye.

As if in a dream she watched their boiler's seams rupture bolt by bolt in a hyper volcanic eruption. Then blessed reprieve, the Citadel's silvery coaches torrented by just a foot and a half away, at a galactic and terrifyingly loud opposing speed.

"We're down to 250!"

"Oh! Sorry!" Eight seconds later the Citadel's last car blasted by. "Green!"

"Green!" *Wauhhh! Wauhhh! Wau-Wauhhhhh!*

They burst into a small town. Houses flew by, a school, stores, a feed mill, more houses, and after thirty shots on the whistle the place was gone. By now Beatense noticed that their track ahead looked awfully narrow. Now it curved to the right. For her, sitting on the left, it disappeared altogether. Not a sign of it! The terror of the head-onner with the Citadel was nothing to Neptune's plunge toward the illuminated speeding curtain of trees, just a stone's throw ahead.

The curve swung left. Now the engine seemed criminally bent on flying off the track. And no steering wheel! Even worse, the swirls of smoke often obscured her view far ahead completely. But she kept her levers pulled and called out her signals, rather able to face explosion, wreck or hurtling derailment with infinitely more serenity than the fireman's reminders. If only she could get at that whistle!

Wauhhh! Wauhhh! Wau-Wauhhhhh! "Green! Another town, sir!"

"Green!"

"Mickelberg, miss! Jake's got a note for us! Excuse me!"

"Wait! How much further is this wretched Altura?"

"Forty miles! She's dropping! Watch your gauge!"

At ninety miles per hour Mickelburg lasted ninety seconds. Just about two miles. The fireman leaned out the entry door and caught the telegrapher's pole borne order, as the ties beneath him peeled by.

The dark night returned. Beatense, even now self focused, saw more lights.

Wauhhh! Wauhhh! Wau-Wauhhhhh!

"Is that another town? Green! What one's that?"

"Green!"

"Check your water, miss! Give her a… Good! That's Endicott Junction!"

"Never heard of it, but I'm sure I'll be impressed!"

Beatense felt more confident, she watched as the fireman gave the orders to the engineer. He glanced at it with a nod and looked right back ahead. It was probably just a Confirm for their meet order at Altura. The girl returned to her vigil just in time to hit her levers and see another signal.

"Green!" *Wauhhh! Wauhhh! Wau-Wauhhhhh!*

A wild succession of more curves careened by, then the Neptune speeded up as she bulleted ahead along a beautifully smooth straightaway.

"Gr… Red! I see red!"

"No miss! That's the Queen! We're drawing up on her! Green!"

"Green! So we must be coming up on Altura, hah?"

"No, she's thirty miles on yet!" *Wauhhh! Wauhhh! Wau-Wauhhhhh!*

Beatense watched as the figure-eight oscillating red light of the Queen drew ever closer. Their closing speed was thirty per, but it seemed that old Neps was taking a maddeningly long time to catch up with her train. She finally saw the rounded end of the Sky Liner come into their headlight's beam, and the engineer throttled down their speed. They drew along side the Queen, but from her high vantage point Beatense saw only the roofs of the coaches as they crept by.

"Green!" --/-- "Green!"

"Hey, Tommy!" She knew her friend's name by now. "Take over!"

"Sure thing, miss!"

"And thanks a lot!" She stood away from her seat. "That was fantastic!"

She stumbled across the shaking deck to the cab's entry door on the right. She saw through its window just how close the trains were to each other, just a foot and a half. That didn't seem like hardly enough, not at these speeds.

"Green!" --/-- "Green!"

As they continued to inch by the Queen crafty Beatense had an idea. The other train was within an arm's length. With it being that close, couldn't she just jump over to it? She went back to her friend, who was staring ahead as if transfixed.

"Hey, Tommy! If the Queen has an open door I could save you guys stopping if I hop aboard her from here and that would be that! Would that be okay?"

"What, miss? Oh, uh huh. Fine. We'll get there! Sit tight!"

With that Beatense returned to the door, as the dim train ran beside them. She glanced over to Ike and Tommy and opened the door and started down the ladder. The sudden exposure to the wind tore at her, concentrated as it was by the howling tunnel she was in. She was bombarded with sandy cinders swirling with smoke and steam, and as the gravel flew by in a blur just beneath her feet, the loud hammering of the giant drive wheels and connecting rods stopped her heart.

But she had to go on, for at present the two trains were traveling together at the same speed. The girl shut Neptune's door and opened the conveniently handy door opposite as she held to her ladder. Good thing they had outside handles.

Wauhhh! Wauhhh! Wau-Wauhhhhh!

The diesel horns also sounded. *Bwaaa! Bwaaa! Bwaa-Bwaaaaa!*

Beatense stepped into the Queen. She closed the steel door, and suddenly there was a huge silence. She dusted off her hands and started for her coach. She hurried through several darkened cars, including the sectionals, where the facing coach seats were converted into curtained bunks. As she entered the corridor of Enlightenment Quest she found her conductor.

"There you are! Thanks for taking off and leaving me!"

Bernie's face froze. "M-Miss Colwell! Wh-Whatever are you d-d-doing here?"

"I think that's for you to explain."

He jolly well wasn't ready for any chat. "Miss Colwell, upon my word, this simply will not do! I don't know how you got here, but you must get back on that train!"

"What? Bernie, this is saving you guys a lot of trouble!"

"Oh no, it isn't. If Mr. Westergard finds you here there will be an inquest. You and everyone else will be clotured for it! You must get back on that train!"

"Clotured. Isn't the word cloistered?"

"Yes, it… No… It's… Miss Colwell, there isn't a moment to lose!"

"But…" She looked out and saw a boxcar. "But…"

"We'll go back and get you on the caboose again! Come on!"

"No, I was up in the head end, Bernie! The engine! And I can tell you, that conductor is much infinitely worse than Mr. Westergard."

"Baerwolf. Okay, we'll have to go over the top, then."

She guessed what that meant. "N-No. I-I can't. I could get killed, Bernie!"

"It's quite safe. The boxcars are ten feet wide, with catwalks, and you jitter along sideways for balance. Freight service, we do it all the time. But we have to hurry, we're coming up on Altura, and we absolutely don't want Mr. Westergard to find you."

Bernie retrieved two lanterns and gave Beatense one. He opened the entry door. The girl leaned out and grabbed onto the boxcar opposite's ladder as it came within reach. She gave a last look at her train's cozy warm interior, then with her lantern's rubber coated bail held in her mouth she swung across and began her climb up to the roof, in a fiercely loud, shaking darkness. Bernie followed.

Wauhhh! Wauhhh! Wau-Wauhhhbwaaa! Bwaaa! Bwaa-Bwaaaaa!

The girl, in addition to regretting this trip, was worried about making that bend to get on top, but she found a life saving rooftop rung. She pulled herself up onto the broad roof. Bernie was right. She crawled over to the catwalk along the ridge of the roof, that was lipped out to meet that of the next car. The fugitives stood gingerly up into the driving blast of cinders, wind and hot ash. The thunder of their heaving and swaying boxcar should have terrified the girl under all that whipping hair, but she saw the experienced Bernie's sublime indifference. He moved easily to the rocking.

"Come on, miss! We have about ten cars to run! Hurry!"

"We don't have to worry about like any bridges, do we?" the girl shouted, just as the trains sounded together. *Bwaauhh! Bwaauhh! Bwaau-Bwaauhhhh!*

Bernie's lantern aimed down as normally carried. At the time it was lighting the corrugated boxcar ends, as it drew the girl's eye down to the couplings, and the blur of racing ties below. But as menacing as this was, the faint sparkle of Altura's lights sprang her forward. She hopped across to the treadway of the next car ahead, and she danced sideways ahead of Bernie along its narrow spine. Occasional billows of heavy smoke engulfed the two, and Beatense struggled with her footing on the shaky rocking car even as the wind tried to drive her back.

They reached the next car. The more nimble girl sprang the gap and ran on and sprang to the third car. A crosswalk of signal lights approached, and the two fell flat. Neptune began slowing down as the Queen pulled ahead. Bernie took Beatense along five more cars, whose clatter had quieted markedly.

Wauhhh! Wauhhh! Wau-Bwaaa! Bwaaa! Bwaa-Bwaaaaa!

"I have to get back now, miss! The tender is just ahead! The water tank deck is first, then the coal! Jump down into the hopper onto the coal and watch out for the worm screw! The cab roof has a hatch you might have to open! Good luck!"

"You owe me for this! I just lost half my tan! And my singing voice!"

He laughed and ran back. Beatense came to the tender back of the engine and negotiated the top of the tank. It actually rode steadily. She reached the coal bunker and shined the light in. Just a three foot drop. She jumped down. She clawed and scrambled her way forward in the rocking depth. The loose coal gave a very chancy footing, and since it was sloped higher toward the front, she climbed it on all fours.

She got to the forward ledge and hands on cab roof she got to her knees. She looked down through the opened (good) roof hatch into the cab. She saw the boiler backhead, with its iron fire door. This had a fiery gleam around its edge, but was a welcome sight. The girl found a handy ladder and climbed down to the deck.

Wauhhh! Wauhhh! Wau-Wauhhhhh!

"There you are!" said Ike, turning. "You weren't in the tender, were you?"

"Uhh, no. No!" She was obviously lying. "I, er, heh heh, just looked at it!"

"Well, you just stay out of there. That worm screw will cut your leg off."

Setting down her lantern she faked embarrassment. "Oh, I, uh, I'm sorry."

Ike pointed to the whistle. "One long, miss. Wake old Queenie up."

Ahhh! She grabbed the cord and dropped the steam to 200 as Neptune rumbled into Altura. *Waaaauuuuhhhhhhhhhhhh!* With bell clanging they drew up alongside the Queen, that had just stopped for them on the siding track.

"There you are, miss. One of those car roofs is yours."

"Wow! Thanks, guys! That was wonderful! No one will ever believe this!"

The crewmen smiled proudly, and fondly. Never saw anyone so energetically full of life. Beatense gave the two joyful hugs and climbed down the curiously unmoving ladder to trackside. As she got used to the solid footing a trainman came running toward her, carrying a lantern. She recognized him as her head conductor.

"Colwell? You're on our shit list."

She wasn't sure which shit list. It could be a mildly bad one or the very bad one Bernie had out of kindness persuasively mentioned. "Er, heh heh, why's that?"

"You know why! From now on try to stay seated for those local stops!"

"That's what I say!" said conductor Baerwolf, who had run to join the discussion. "Westergard, can you not keep your people on board?"

"He had nothing to do with it!" said the girl loyally. "I foolishly got off at Shoglatt without his instigation. The trouble was that the train left right on time, and based on *other* railroads I have traveled I thought wrongly she would pull out ten minutes late!"

"Yes, our operations are sound! Now excuse me, I have a 31 to sign!"

Mr. Baerwolf went up into the opened door of Orchestral Quest and crossed over its vestibule out the far door. Colton Westergard watched him with a sigh.

"Ever the diplomat," he said wearily. "But look here, miss, explain this."

"Didn't you get the wire from Dispatch? This wasn't my fault! And I gave you a huge break by chasing after you instead of making you wait until seven!"

Another figure joined them. The forward conductor.

"Bernie! What's going on! You said I could get off!"

"I'm truly sorry, Miss Colwell, it was all my fault entirely. We received a telegram from the local police informing us that an escorted prisoner would be late in boarding there, but in fact the convict was present as we arrived. I led the criminal aboard, and in my assisting the police I neglected to wave you back aboard."

"Yeah, I got that impression."

"Now let's get this straight," said Mr. Westergard. "We don't coddle convicts, he should have been stowed in baggage! How did he end up in coach?"

Bernie nervously pulled at his collar. "Black lung, heated quarters required. But despite his infirmity he put up a struggle, and there was a bit of a scuffle."

"Per Rule 878 he should have been ejected, North. But with or without that our Miss Colwell was left behind. For which I apologize, miss."

"I'm exposed to dangerous subhuman criminals? I sue, you cad!"

"But looking into this further, didn't you see she wasn't on board, North?"

"How could he?" said Beatense. "He was wrestling with that Nicky!"

Bernie started, and Mr. Westergard pondered that. "Hmm. Well, I'll draft a report on these events tonight and submit it to Operations for review."

"But no inquest?" said Beatense, as she shivered from the cold.

Bernie's eyes widened in alarm as Mr. Westergard's narrowed.

"Now where... Did you pick... Up that?"

"Why, heh heh, the engineer, Ike. He said I might be held for questioning."

"He might be right at that, miss. Let's rip." He laughed. "Cad, indeed."

Mr. Baerwolf returned and Beatense faced him. "I decided to forgive you."

He really did wish he had her company in the caboose. Her alighted brown face was inutterably boned beautiful. She was slim, tall and strong. She hugged him.

The impromptu between-train conference ended, and the interlopers hopped up into Orchestral. Beatense gave a wave to Neptune and her friends who had been looking on. The conductor waved his lantern and signaled the Queen to proceed.

The engineer was impatient; she began moving immediately.

As Beatense started for her cabin she intoned to herself, "Green! Green!"

10

TRAIN LIFE

Early next morning Beatense opened her curtain and saw that the Queen was driving through misty rain. This, along with that cloudy gray light, made her feel safe, cozy and warm, and she wasn't missing out on any sun! They were racing through a deep, forbiddingly uninhabited forest. The stalky girl sat bare on her bed, happy to be an ignorant and lazy passenger once again.

She wondered what her hair looked like after her boxcar escapade. The night before she had stopped in the restroom and laughed out loud at her sooty face. She then washed herself in her miniature sink but her hair needed an actual shower.

She opened her backpack and got out her pocket mirror, which she used to eye her back while laying in the sun. She decided that her stormy hair was beyond hope and put the mirror back, after studying her life improving face. Then she rested back on her elbows and admired her adventure loving tan and hard belly. This she had cruelly worked most recently with Scott, but it was still eighteen inches around.

She dug out her "Tropics Pulse" bag, that held her Gold Digger string bikini, that she had recently ordered and would at last see a real beach. She pulled the suit out and gazed upon its iridescent gold metallic fabric. The bottom was the size of four postage stamps, narrower than her infamous crochet and thong.

If required by law the girl would wear this out on the beach instead of going bare. But her new bangle bracelets and a shine of oil were all she hoped to disagreeably wear otherwise. It took away some of the fun with her father so amenable to all this, but he knew her habits by now.

The girl got up and folded down her little sink. She felt comfort performing this mundane little task on the train, that of washing her hands and face. Her doing this under these conditions (the sink was as big as half a melon, and she had to brace herself against the train's shaking) was the stuff of which Civilization was made.

The plucky girl finished and put on her tight jeans and smoky greyed vee opened white shirt. She sat on her bed and absorbed the train's movements as a kind of restorative tonic while she read the info brochure. "At our various stops step off and take a stroll." *Oh, sure!* She stepped out into the passage and found her porter.

"Good… Good m-morning, miss. I understand you h-had quite a night."

"Hi. Yes, but it wasn't my fault. Hey, look, is my hair non-presentable, sir?"

It embarrassed him extremely to gaze *into* that face. It had a strong projecting character, giving it paralyzing force. Her hair was a cat scratch mess.

"It… It w-will do. Now, you just have time to make the last breakfast call. While you're gone I'll change your sheets and ready your seats for the day."

"Leave the sheets, Walt. Back home I go weeks not changing them."

He held his heart as the girl went on after another hug. She went through the rocking train as the passengers who encountered her looked upon her with honored respect. Word had gotten around. Or not. The girl went on to the Dining Car, where the wait staff was cleaning up. She was led to one of the many empty tables by his lordship. The occupied tables were filled with people nudging each other.

"Here you go, miss. Anything at all, anything." He offered a menu.

"Yes, as long as I don't sue anyone. Thanks, I'll just have toast and coffee, sir."

"Well we have two leftover fritters that I can give you quite cheaply."

"Yeah, sure! Except, what… What are fritters?'

"Fried pastry dough rolled with raisins and bits of apple and cherry. Ahem, after your adventure last night you do need the nourishment."

"I beg your pardon, I don't have the foggiest idea what you're talking about."

At the sound of her voice a head turned. Craig.

"Beatense! Hi! Is it okay if I join you?"

"Sure! Come on over, Craigie Weggie!"

He almost knocked over his chair in his urgency. He sat back down at the girl's precisely laid out table as an honored waiter poured her coffee.

"Sir? Shall I move your things over?" --/-- "No, I'm all done. Thanks."

Beatense leaned forward. "He wants a tip, you ass," she whispered.

"Oh, er, I'm set, sir, thank you," Craig said, blushing, thrilled Beatense called him that. He left a dollar and returned. "Greedy bastards."

"Yeah, no shit. All those damn son of a bitching hints."

"But anyway, you look great this morning, Beatense. That white shirt is, er, really like cute on you," he added, noting that it was again opened down to quite a vee.

"It's my *Isn't she nicely modest* outfit. But the impression I have is that down in Xanthallado a quality girl's total focus on self is commended. Like, out at surveying camp these intern women were just ultra hot but still considered best of breed."

"Y-Yes, you mentioned that surveying camp last night."

Beatense gave a recount of her unexpected locomotive excursion, and she smiled up at the porter as her fritters were served. Again superb thick toast, and the coffee had a snap to it; it was actually good. The girl stuffed the fritters into her mouth as Craig watched, with a smiling laugh. Left behind like that! She daubed more butter onto her toast and almost swooned eating it.

"I have to compliment your singing again, Beatense. You were a sensation!"

"Oh, that. Thanks. But my cover is blown, what little I had. Ever had. Like my first book is back in publication, a hundred thousand more, my videos and photos are all over the NetField, and my music here is sold as CDs and USBs in Xanthallado. I stopped counting after I hit a quarter million. But most important, I'm kind of brown."

By coincidence, it was the record boy with the necklace. He was in white cotton buttcuts and a short sleeved white shirt all open, showing his stupifying stab of a tan. Kind of brown. Each of his fresh muscles was purposefully shaped, and his long hair seemed even thicker today. Beatense revered him as a fellow sun fanatic.

The Steward's crusty face broke into what one might call a smile.

"Well, Master Hayden, and what can we do for you?"

"Muh paants waant a pat a caffee," the kid regally replied, with nose tipped. "Ah pahhtuh is tayning up al the bads in ahh cah, so Ah hafta gat it."

"Very good." The Steward snapped his fingers and gestured to one of the staring waiters. "Coffee here for the lad! Ambassador service!"

The Steward offered Hayden the silver flask, and he took it with elaborate muscle flexions. His rippled belly drew in tighter, richly shifting in color.

"Sand a pahhtuh to braang it baaack."

Beatense watched the boy's long rust drenched legs catch the shine of the lights as he marched up the aisle with hair aflutter. The other patrons stared too.

"H P Shit, unbelievable!" said Beatense. "He beats the desert rats! And me!"

The Steward appeared. "You already ate the fritters, young lady?"

"Yes, I broke my hardly-eating habit. But boy, sir, like my trips years ago I never ate in such luxury. A prestige establishment like this, I wish I could stay all day."

He finally got some credit. "Heh heh, well, we do try."

The Steward floated off, and Craig laughed admiringly.

"Boy, you sure got old Ahab as a lifetime friend. He must be a fan too."

"Everyone is. So, shall we meet for lunch? Or meantime, maybe we can fuck."

"B-B-But w-w-we hardly know each other!" Shaking, Craig briefly looked out and saw a bleak, sodden town fly quickly by. He realized that there might be something very wrong with this girl. "L-Let's, er, n-nap together after... Lunch."

"Craig, don't be tiresome. Waiting to get to know each other is stupid."

Panting, Craig paid, but the girl's giving the Steward $100 for the staff to divvy up decided him that indeed putting off this hauntingly beautiful creature was stupid.

"Well, where, Beatense, yours or mine?" he offered, once they emerged from the pinball machine vestibule of the first Sleeping Car.

"What? We're waiting until after lunch, I thought. Or maybe supper? Then we can spend the night for repeats. Do you have a wider bed? We need the room."

They reached Tellurian, and the two parted with a quick hug. Beatense entered her cozy little cabin and sat on her forward facing seat. She closed her eyes and waited until she was sure obstinate Craig had gotten back to his Compartment.

When she stirred the Queen was pulling into Solon, which marked the entry into the Deinlowica province. A few bundled up forms huddled through the drizzle across the trackside pavement. The train went on through the dank forest, and to dispel its gloom Beatense changed to her self cropped T-shirt and stepped out.

Drawing multiple approving stares she reached Triumphant Quest and went down through its gut, with feet just over the rails. She took the steps up to the observation deck to hopefully find herself a seat. The arching windows left just a two foot strip of center roof with vents down the middle. Moving forward she went by Hayden and family. His girl-like long hair crowned him with an aura of snooty superiority. He shook back his heavy tresses, exposing pierced gold earrings stars. Beatense got her own star struck looks as she moved on to the front and found Moose and Tiffany.

"Hey, Beat!" said Moose. "Sit down! Your shirt shrink? How's it going?"

"Hi, guys! Yeah, just warming the place up, like that kid back there. What time is it? Later I'm going to my Roomette for a flying eighty mile per hour nap. A nap by myself, Craig being such a dullard. I said I wanted sex and he just froze."

"I would too," said Moose. "Really! Tiff kept hinting and suggesting and there I was, no way could I ever, ever make it worth her while. Not with what she had."

"Has," said Tiffany, blossoming at his indirect compliment.

"Well, maybe he is intimidated. But did you see that one record player kid? Like, I should tell you about surveying camp. He would right fit in. Like I did."

"I saw him, yeah!" said Tiffany. "Ha ha ha! That tan at his age!"

"Stand in the aisle, Tiff, so she can take your seat," said Moose. "I... Ow!"

But Beatense stood and looked out the wide front window at the speeding line of black roofed cars stretched out forward like a giant, segmented spear in flight. She was thrilled at how the coaches jolted and lurched, and as they cruised along in such chaotic coordination, the trees close by the track shook. The sky western sky was a band of blue, and above that were dramatic brush strokes of vivid grey. And now the sun's peeking out added starkly contrasting effects that even Beatense noticed.

Impressed, the girl sat down, and the other passengers quit their staring.

"As I said I'm heading for Emeraldeye Beach, guys. Ever been there?"

"Was I ever!" said Tiffany brightly. "For my first spring break. We went to this Bum For Sun dive and these guys kept buying us drinks! We ended up with them in our room, and we partied until dawn! Then back to the beach!"

"Ahem, what do you mean, partying?" said Moose.

"That's a polite way of saying we were all passed out."

"Oh, good. I was starting to question your character."

Tiffany laughed. This time it was real. They were mad for each other.

"But what about the beach?" said Beatense. "And did you see Cocojo?"

"Nah, it's way south," said Tiffany. "But I did want to try it for the nudity."

"I heard Emerald is nude now. This guy I talked to where I'm staying said they finally legalize it because so many girls just went nude legal or not."

Beatense went on to tell of her desert camp sun meltdowns.

"I was thirteen and repeat fourteen. It was beautiful, those bareback gallops."

Tiffany looked at Moose, *Oh please can we do that?* Beatense then related her adventure the last night, omitting the boxcars, and the two were gaping wide eyed.

She felt validated. Her world did have some tricks up its sleeve.

"Wow! You helped run the engine?" Tiffany raved. "Ha ha ha!"

"Say, Beat, we might be getting into a Compartment after all," Moose said, once the discussion ended. "This one is sitting empty, and we might get it."

"But I thought you had a Roomette!"

"They messed up our reservation!" said Tiffany. "So *instead* they set us up in a Roomette, but like you we had to wait until we could even get in it! Now it depends on if the party reserving it boarded or not! Our porter is checking it out."

"Hey, if you do get it, guys, can I tell this lady in coach about your room?"

"Sure, fine," said Moose. "Hey, are you leaving? What about lunch?"

Beatense stood. "Thanks, but I better go tell Ida so she can get dibs. And I might skip lunch. And anyway I forgot my cigs. Okay, nice seeing ya! Bye!"

The fellow in the seat behind offered his pack. "Wow, thanks, sir!" the girl said as she shook a cigarette out. "Mall Pall! Mild, and they are outstanding!"

There is something about walking back through a train. In every car but his own one feels as if he's somehow intruding. But of course everyone welcomed the singer, in her curled up slash T-shirt that hung free a scant two inches from her poking nips. Beatense wasn't ticketed for Sabbatical, but it was her original car, so she felt a fond loyalty toward everyone here as she entered. Right. She found Ida.

"Oh! Hi! I thought we parted company, Puppet! Our little singer!"

"I try. I just came to tell you, Ida, that you might be getting a Roomette, only if these friends of mine can get this Compartment that looks empty so far."

She leaned anxiously forward. "Honest, girl? I'm too old to travel like this."

"It isn't definite, yet. But did you see that kid with the tan parade by?"

"Nowhere near as tan as you. How you ran naked in the desert."

"I plan lots more running naked. Right on public beaches!"

Ida laughed, delighted. Puppet's excited antics tickled her so much.

Bernie entered the car and stopped by the ladies, one of abundant hair.

"Good morning, Beatense, Mrs. Cornhill. Did you need something, miss?"

"Well, Ida here needs the Venter Roomette, if they get that Compartment."

"I'll quietly arrange that. I'll get back to you, Mrs. Cornhill."

"Oh, thank you!" Ida replied urgently. The conductor smiled and moved on. "I sure appreciate that, child," Ida went on. "Browner than any oil intern, you are. Their lives are a joy. They're beautiful, free and desert whipped into top athletic shape."

"Well, make sure you disregard the athlete right beside you! But wanna go back to the Sky Liner? I found out last night the Queen has one."

"Do me some good, the walk," the lady said, heaving herself up. "And yes I'll be making the Dining Car run from now on, too. I finished off my own food."

"I bet you did," said Beatense, smiling knowingly.

"Well listen to our skinny little dandelion! You sound like all those slat built tech brats, lecturing you on carbs, LDL and trans fats. Nicely, of course."

"You almost make me want to catch the bus again at Nywot Transfer."

"Oh, if only you did. You were such a little sparkplug."

The two started down Sabbatical's tossing aisle for the distant Sky Liner. Entering the restroom corridor, Ida stopped. "Wait for me a minute, dear."

Beatense peeked in past the partly open curtain and saw that the armchairs and settee within were occupied. "Sure, leave me out here to rot."

"There is a mirror over the sink, if you need something to do."

Left alone, the girl spied the water cooler, standing flat against the bulkhead wall beside the vestibule door, in wait for no one's thirst. She didn't see why the railroads bothered with them. Cups were provided in a long silver tube, but they were small, conical things made of thin paper that took forever to fill from the dribbly spout.

Ida emerged from the lounge, Beatense gulped her water, and cup discarded the two went on to stumble through ten D-latched, orange painted doors into the roaring, bucking vestibules, then went through an equal number of pneumatic doors out of the vestibules. As they entered the Etruscan Bar Club Beatense saw Craig with another woman. She was slim and bone tight, a sharp careerist right out of *With It Woman: Important and collected.* She was outfitted in a trim blazer and mid-thigh cut skirt.

Her sheer black hose lent a formal flair, and also turned her long legs into leaned instruments of decisive go-getter action. As she walked her shining dark hair would waft impatiently out with each heels-poised stride.

Beatense grimly walked by the half occupied armchairs and settees, separated with lamp tables. As she and Ida exited out the rear door she glanced back and saw Craig look at her. Except for a twitch he barely reacted. The two ladies reached the Sky Liner at the end of the train. The girl last saw this externally the night before.

The Sky Liner had a rounded stern, with a bomber cockpit's assembly of shaped windows that arched over the wrap-around settee at car's end. The ladies sat here, and Beatense watched the trees rapidly shrink away from them, as the tracks flowed out from under the train. Ida asked the steward for two bottles of Banana D beer.

Beatense started in on an account of her escapade the night before, no boxcars, and just like in the dome car the nearby folk gave an ear.

Among them, a dapper sharpie with curved sideburns and collar lengthed hair, to show he could still grow it. He wore a flashy sport coat, zigzag patterned trousers without belt, and step heeled, two-tone ankle cut boots with buckles and snub-boxed toes. When Beatense finished her story he laid a grubby five on the bar and glided smoothly over, and though he had an eye crinkly smile, Beatense didn't like him.

He had that creased look of far too many cigarets in too many poker games, and too many drinks from too many days spent in too many bars. But for his congenial conversation (raspy from smoking) he solicitously did include Ida. Johnny B Lucke (actual name Luckenwitz) was full of funny stories, but they all took place in different cities, implying he was a drifter, and somehow they all had police involved.

"...and Gladys, now there's a classy broad with real smarts, but a bitch streak? *Hooooweee!* I'd lay odds it was her that nabbed the cops on us! But hot damn, my old parole officer Pinkie was in on the raid and let me off! So, little lady, more beer?"

The girl declined and excused herself for the restroom. She ran into Craig. "What do you want? Go back to that new friend of yours!"

"Beatense, she has an account with us. So, can I join you and that lady?"

"No! I have met a very fine gentleman just now, and he's waiting for me."

He blocked her path. "Beatense, I'm coming with." They entered the Sky Liner. Johnny stood in threat. "Hey, welsher, that's my snatch you got there."

Craig quietly made a fist and carefully studied it. Johnny held his hands up in mocking surrender. He went back to the bar, shaking his head. *Women!*

"Ida, this is Craig. Craig, this is Ida. We met in the Dining Car last night."

Ida liked this fellow's looks a lot better. "Nice to meet you..." She looked at her watch in shock. "Oh, no! I better find out about the Roomette! Er, bye, kids."

11

LOST AGAIN

Beatense spent an adequate hour with Craig, then well restored ran hot naked back to her Roomette. Sadlly, no one saw her. Later upon awaking she stared out anxiously at the misty, sunny dawn. No grey sky to calm her today; there was huge sun she would miss out on. Sighing, she tugged on her jeans, that after last night's efforts seemed to fit looser, and again put on her yellow T-shirt of dangerous cut.

She stepped out into the shaky corridor. She was to shortly meet Craig in the Dining Car, but she had another (better) idea. The forward end of the train was just ahead, and Beatense decided to investigate this first. She passed on through four Sleeping Cars and entered the fifth car, the side-bypassed Shoglatt coach. Then the baggage car. The girl dodged through and around boxes, skids and piled luggage to the forward door, and she peered through its porthole at the locomotive just ahead.

Beatense was enthralled by the pulsating roar of its engine, pounding loud. She pushed the hand plate and the door helpfully hissed open. There were no enclosing rubber pleats here, this connection was open to the air. Like atop that boxcar the girl looked down in fear at the massive iron couplings and speeding track as the furious dynamos raged even louder. The noise was like a hundred baseball bats beating on hallway lockers. The girl took hold of the D-latch of the metal door before her.

It turned! She stepped across the gap into the rear locomotive, that had a V-16 diesel engine gunning at full throttle just ahead. The intruder had to both stoop and grab for balance as she worked toward it, because of the radiator plenums, hydraulic pipelines, conduits and ducts overhead. She stared wide eyed at the engine's giant tractive generators, as the armatures hummed at over a hundred decibels, and she gazed at the rapidly spinning shafts, fan belts, sprockets and gears that drove the auxiliary pumps, generators and compressors.

Actually forgetting herself Beatense was thrilled by the locomotive's mighty rage, as with the head three it shot the train ahead, the deck plates shaking under her feet. The sidewall portholes let in little daylight, and the wire caged bulbs glowed dim, but the resulting semi-darkness only heightened the otherwise vain girl's reverent awe.

She paused by a lighted gauge panel and watched as the red needles quivered with the steaming lifeblood of this rocketing behemoth. She stepped on and found the engine itself, a hulking mass of green painted cast iron whose exposed valve rockers and push rods moved in a clattering blur.

Alongside the engine a raised steel deck with steps and yellow pipe railings gave access for maintenance or adjustment. The eight cylinders of the twin piston banks made for an incredible 12 foot length. Every detail was clean to museum standards.

After gazing in worship Beatense turned and started back. She reached the rear passage door, but its knob turned uselessly in her hand. She tried again.

"Oh, great!"

She peered through the window, both fearing and hoping to see someone come through the baggage car. The plan of meeting Craig for breakfast was temporarily dashed, and the girl anxiously hovered in wait by the door's round rubber gasketed window. After five minutes of that she looked for a place to sit down.

A low bench set over a pump housing was just over by the door, but an electrical relay enclosure was just over it. But she had to sit down, squished or not. One more minute of stooping with the locomotive's rocking and bucking would stoop her for life. And the loud rage of the engine, so thrilling before, was getting to her.

Beatense couldn't even watch out the side portholes. For a continuing flow with the windows of the coaches they were placed at too low of a height.

The girl sat bent over on her bench and settled into a good, long wait.

Craig found Ida in her newly assigned Roomette.

"Excuse me, Mrs. Cornhill, hi. Have you seen Beatense this morning?"

She could barely hide her disappointment. She did accept the night frolics of the sun crazed drilling interns, and even more so of the self worshipful Puppet. She had felt it in her bones that she and her congenial friend would spend the night, but here was Craig, looking for her. *Damn it!*

"Why, no, young man. Have you checked her Roomette?"

"I did, after waiting for her in the Dining Car. We were supposed to meet."

"Maybe she stepped into the restroom."

"No, I looked past the curtain and she wasn't in there, that I could see."

'Well then, you don't suppose she… No, not twice."

"Ida, I'm really worried about her. It's maybe too soon to say that I love her, but I do. Did she wander by here at all? Maybe while you were still asleep?"

"I did sleep late, after that horrible first night. But maybe she went back to that Sky Lounge. She might have gone back there and lost track of the time."

"Of course, how stupid of me! I'll head back and probably find her. Plus I can check the dome cars. I wish I checked the two I already came through."

"I'll check them. Tell her I'm cross at her for worrying us."

Ida went forward, and after checking out the first observation deck she ran into Bernie. She almost told him about her beloved absentee, but what if she then found her in the next dome car? Or maybe Craig had found her by now and was scolding her. If only those two did sleep together. Why were they so silly about it?

Finding the rear conductor, Craig didn't hesitate. "Cedric, hi, good morning. Did you happen to see Beatense recently? That is to say, Miss Colwell?"

"You mean the singer girl we left back in Shoglatt? Goodness, not again!"

"I take it you didn't see her, then, hah?"

"No, sorry, Mr. Hamiltyn. Let's give Westergard a call."

Thinking of that struggling little child under him, Craig was led back through the next two coaches to the cubbyhole used by the rear trainmen for their office.

The conductor squeezed in at the built-in desk and pulled the candlestick phone out on its scissors bracket. He dialed a single digit and there was a sharp click as the other phone was picked up. "Captain, trouble, missing passenger, that singer again. A Mr. Hamiltyn hasn't seen her. Yes, sir. Thank you."

"What did he say?"

"Gilmore Valley is coming up, we'll stop there and wire back all the stations. But Westergard says we should have heard by now if she was left back."

"But how would we find out? By radio?"

"No, but the telegraphers at any of the towers we passed last night should have poled a message up to the cab as we went by, or signaled us."

"Well, she must be on board then, sir. I was just checking the Sky Liner."

"I was just there and didn't see her. Her, you... Notice. But give it a try."

Craig hurried off, more confused and worried than ever. No one can truly hide or disappear on a train, their being confined. Maybe she had gotten to know someone, perhaps a charmed older couple who just wanted someone to talk to, and she was in their Compartment or Drawing Room now talking away. Look at how she befriended Ida Cornhill, who was hopelessly out of her league. She unfailingly smiled as people recognized her. She acted like they were the stars.

Passengers were just stirring awake in the seats-only coach cars as Craig hurried through. He went through the Etruscan, empty, and burst into the Sky Liner. He saw Johnny Lucke, who already had a drink. Well, at least he wasn't the reason she was missing, if treacherously he had suspected that.

Wait, maybe Beatense was with Moose and Tiffany! Those funny two, she would certainly stop in for a visit if they saw her. Especially with all that beach talk. Craig hurried the long, rocking way forward again to Anticipation Quest.

And Ida encountered Bernie again, and this time she spoke up.

"Bernie! Have you seen Miss Colwell? She isn't anywhere to be found!"

"I know the situation, Mrs. Cornhill. We'll find her. Don't worry."

"But where can she be? You can't find her if she's not on the train!"

"We will be stopping in Gilmore Valley in thirty minutes, and we'll telegraph all stations down line. If that doesn't do it, we start knocking on doors."

"Well, can't you start on that now?" Somehow the image of the uniformed train personnel deferentially tapping on the Sleeping Car doors was reassuring. "We have to know as soon as possible if she's not on the train."

"I'll call Westergard on that. In the meantime, Mrs. Cornhill, it's better to return to your Roomette and relax. Then we can find you when we find her."

"Why can't she stay in one place?"

Craig now knew black fear. Moose and Tiffany, despite their playful jabs at each other, seemed to be very, very loving at the moment, if the baby's happy squeals that came from within meant anything. They obviously did with Beatense.

He stumbled away, concerned about little Tiffany, who seemed too innocent for ecstacy. Did her wedded status really make that moral? Well, he didn't care to be a crank, especially since his time with a certain recent teen was almost pedophilia.

Beatense, chin on her hand, recalled that the engine had those raised walkways. She could sit upright there. She went back forward and saw that the platform on her side had the Stuart Garner fuel injection system crowded between it and the engine.

It looked like the engine's other side had more room. She was just stepping over the hammermill's spinning propeller shaft, when there came a sudden sharp blast of compressed air. Beatense jumped back startled, then a moving lever changed the transmission gear with a loud clunking. The cadence of the engine began to slow as the gears clunked again. The horns sounded, none too quietly, and the stooping girl peered out the right side entry door's porthole. The train was entering a town, but it seemed odd that they were stopping here. She had studied her timetable earlier and they had nothing scheduled until noon. *Unless it is noon!*

The Queen Of Steel glided majestically to a halt, and Beatense's nearby engine eased into a driving window-rattling idle. The girl welcomed the relative silence. She saw from the sign on the station house that the town was Gilmore Valley. It was full of gracious old buildings, like a movie set basking in dream-like yesteryear.

The platform had a few loafers and hangers-on, but in the seconds it took for the trainmen to cross over to the station, the townspeople began gathering to greet the train's arrival. This was probably a big event in their lives, and an army of kids came swarming from the various houses, with their wide veranda porches.

It seemed as if there was an effervescent sunny day outside, full of those elusive fragrances and balmy vapors, great for tanning, but the sun deprived Beatense only had burned oil to smell, and ozone from the generator armatures.

More townfolk came strolling over to admire the train and have a relaxed bit of discussion, and Beatense hatched a desperate plan. She would open the entry door on the other side of the engine and hop down to the tracks, and then run around the front of the train and innocently mingle into the crowd.

It was a big risk, what if the Queen upped and left as she watched? Anyway, she wasn't nude, good thing. She almost was. But her T-shirt would certainly clash with these good yeomen. They all looked like they had just stepped from their tractors.

As Beatense skulked by her window contemplating this, the station master came by accompanied by the conductors. Within their uniforms, except for the local bankers and lawyers, probably they were the most formally attired gentlemen within fifty miles. Grey faced and severe, the town's utmost citizens were on the scene, too. *We can't have this happening here!* Then Beatense saw her chance.

A pack of noisy boys ran by on their way to the head of the locomotives, probably to gaze in awe up at the cab. Moments later the horns burst to life, echoing, and the boys, capering back in sight, excitedly danced. But what Beatense hopefully noticed were the older girls who seemed to stand in watch of the kids.

Their older sisters. If she could just get in with them! Of course, they were in full old fashioned dresses, but they might hide her! As the engine kept up its lazy idle she leaped over the stilled drive shaft across to the left access door. She peered out its porthole and saw townsfolk over here, too, but this couldn't be helped.

She opened the door and waved. The small crowd buzzed over this unexpected turn of events. She climbed down the short iron ladder and hopped off to the gravel. She ran up past the engine that had been her prison and the three others up line.

As she made her channel dash Beatense saw that Gilmore Valley was an idyllic village, isolated and quiet. There were barns right in the town proper, and she could hear the cackling of chickens and the lowing of cattle.

The truant saw a homey little gas station, Motolene, where an attendant paused from fixing the punctured tire of a boy's Phantom Flier. It was the kind of town where the boys climbed trees and carried cane fishing poles on their shoulders, and knew of any strange "veehickle" that might happen into town within minutes.

The Queen was one of those *veehickles* at the time.

Beatense stayed in close by the nose of the lead engine as she cut around it, so the crewmen wouldn't see her, but another anthem from the horns almost made her leap to the windshield. Ah, there were those high school girls! As the station master and conductors continued their conference, turning as the telegrapher ran over with some message, Beatense made another dash into the midst of the startled boys and their watchful sisters. She quite didn't blend in after all. She was tall, thin and dark brown of face, arms and belly, and inexpressibly fine.

Rather too excitedly everybody exclaimed over her arrival. "Shhhhh!" she urged, waving frantically. "I need your help! Can you all gather around me and go with me down to my car past those conductors so they don't see me?"

The girls cried their agreement, absolutely mad.

"You must be the famous singer they're looking for!" one of them added.

"What? What do you mean?" It seems they didn't know about her books.

"They stopped the Queen Of Steel here to telegraph the stations to search for a lost passenger! Clem says they're looking for you all up the line!"

"Technically that would be down the line, but, they... They are?"

"Yes! The Queen Of Steel normally rolls by here going ninety! We just get the freight locals! Boy, you really *are* brown, like they say! Lilah, look at all that hair!"

"People think lots of hair means fertile health. If only. Okay, let's go."

The boys were smiling with delight, and they began a loud head-turning chatter.

Beatense decided she better turn herself in after all. But then as a matter of fact she didn't have to. Colton Westergard turned and saw her, and she was cooked.

With a cheesy grin she walked up to the conductors as if she had been out for a stroll while the train was stopped for scheduling reasons.

"Miss Colwell? This time you did make our shit list. And just where in blessed tarnation were you, if I may be so kind as to expect an answer."

"I... I was in the rear engine, sir. But it wasn't my fault! You should keep those doors locked! Or at least make them so you can open them from inside to get out!"

"You pull the knob toward you. But you're right, Rule 829. This whole crew will be furloughed after this trip. Myself included. But you're not hurt, Miss Puppet?"

"My ears are ringing, you cad, and my nerves are shattered. Also I'm fading!"

"Well, by now you are expendable. Let's highball. Thank you, Clem."

"This young lady does get around. She'll be a topic in this town, I reckon."

As everyone turned and nodded, a voice. "Beatense! It's you! It's you!"

"Craig! Er, excuse me. Craig!"

The two grabbed, and Beatense was glad to see him. He really did make a fun interlude. But meanwhile, too bad she wasn't injured, to give drama to their reunion. But the girls, on seeing that their heroine had a romantic friend, were gulping in their worship. Beatense waved to them in parting and hair flouncing climbed back aboard the rumbling, waiting Queen with the others.

Moments later the horns called, and the little town returned to its sleepy routine of blacksmith forges, fishing worm hunts and milk cans.

And Beatense, Craig and Ida made the last call for breakfast, as the girl told Mr. Westergard her account for his second report of the trip. Everyone laughed. The two went on to Beatense's Roomette and they just sat, quietly smiling.

That afternoon the train rolled through a land of old, rounded green mountains. Beatense sat restlessly with Craig in one seat in the rear Dome car, and Tiffany and Moose sat across. Scattered in the rolling hills and shadowed valleys were lost little towns. With the long uphill grades the train rounded the winding curves slowly, so that all of these snug hamlets seemed to crawl by.

Beatense, in spite of this steady progress and having shocked the whole train by changing to her legs-showing four inch shorts, felt increasingly desperate. She loved train travel but she wanted to hurry things up. She had made this journey before, as decent and indecent, and she knew how endless this part of the trip was.

Craig showed an interest in the old tractors and barns he saw, but no one could miss his staring upon one tan girl's twitching child-like figure. Moose also did some of his own fake indifference, but his wife didn't feel jealous; she had credentials of her own, and unlike many women who frequent health clubs, she responded brilliantly.

"These towns and villages look so quiet, don't they, Beatense?" said Craig.

"Yeah, I'm used to the city myself. Sirens, traffic and jackhammers."

The girl wished she could instead spend the afternoon holed up in her cozy little Roomette. She could hyperventilate without being asked if she was all right. Or why not another way to relieve stress, like with Scott, or Slat. Or raiding that camp.

By the time they were seated in the Dining Car Beatense, back in her jeans and vee-opened white office shirt with half rolled sleeves, was ready to scream. She did blame the confines of the train and not getting sun instead of her friends. And with Craig, it wasn't as if he was in one place and she in another, so that they had their separate lives until they saw each other. No, on the train there was no escape.

"You're so quiet, Beatense. But how are your mashed potatoes, are they okay? Having them mix in that chopped bacon sounds inspired."

"Yeah, I kind of eat weird if I do eat. But it's nice to pile on the butter without my Pop complaining about how much I'm using. Even though he doesn't pay me."

"Well, it would be like he was paying you to work on that beautiful tan! So how about after we finish here, Beatense, if we sneak a drink in the Sky Liner?"

"Are we invited?" said Moose, and Tiffany kicked him. *You idiot.*

"Yeah, I think I'll have a Northern Comfort New Fashioned, Craig."

"As I said, I'll be coming down to Cardiff for that trade show Friday. By then you'll be at that Hideaway. Maybe… Maybe we can get together."

"Yes, there is a certain way of getting together that I prefer. Thank you again for our fuck last night, by the way. And you can call my tan beautiful all you want."

Craig reddened, she was a little outspoken. "But say, Beatense, I was thinking of your going down to that one Cocojo beach. Your map showed it's kind of remote, so it could attract all kinds of weird types. I wouldn't go there alone."

"Well I was planning on asking about it, that is if I ever do get to that hostel. But why not extend your ticket and join me down there? You could escort me."

Now it was Craig's turn to need space. "Oh, heh heh, I would but I have to head into work to report on my trip and catch up on paperwork. But we do have that trade show this weekend coming up. Then we could work something out."

"Oh, yeah, perfect. But Craig, what is your job? You never said."

"Oh, I sell ledger logs and actuarial journals. Arrolyn is hot turf for us, because lately of course in Xanthallado everything is done on computers now."

"You just sell… I mean, oh, you sell ledger books?"

"Yes, I'm selling for Kueffel Actuarial Ledgers, Inc. But I'm looking, which is one reason for me to hit that trade show. I'll leave our booth every so often and see if I can pick up some job leads. If you were with me they would hire me, bam!"

They mutually decided on one event only, then sleep separately. The girl was reaching the tanner's limit of endurance. Early the next morning she sat restlessly in her Roomette as the train rolled inexorably southward. She was just in her crochet patch of happy memory, and a rubbed in film of lard oil. Feet resting on the opposite seat she had a good view of her slimmed, pine knotty thighs and pine knotty belly.

She gazed with worshipping wonder into her pocket mirror.

The terrain here lay wide and flat, but ranges of vague hills lurked in the infinite distance. As Beatense grew ever more suspicious that the day was turning out to be drought hot, she felt desperate. Considering the many days of clouds and rain back home, she just assumed that this was a gross waste of precious sun.

Beatense turned her burning eyes from the racing scenery and saw Tiffany just outside. Good, but what could she possibly want at this hour? She smiled and used her foot to slide her door open. "Hey, Tiffy bitch! Hi! Sit down!"

"Wow, nice outfit!" She closed the curtain. "Are you just ever ever brown!"

"Yeah, well, it's just from radioactive uranium. I thought I had statuesque hunter genetics but I'm nothing but a nuclear mutant, fuck getting as the results are."

"I might be a bomb brat myself. Because otherwise there's no family blood for how tan I get. Of course I do spend all day laying in the sun!"

"Yeah, it really takes over who you are and what you are. But structurally you're beautiful and so am I, sun or no sun. Unlike people up my way, who are all at best pitifully plain. So the radiation must affect that too. But meanwhile, Tiffany, I'm not sure about that Craig. He sits there wearing these stupid suits. Too respectably adulty and responsibly mature in attitude. And not thin. Like, you know, Moose."

"Yeah, Moose said he will always be a college student no matter what."

"I'm spoiled, out at camp I had sex with all these intern guys, who were all picked because they were thin and could take the heat. The young women interns too."

"What a dream," said Tiffany, and she opened the door's curtain and stood.

"Leaving so soon? I wouldn't hear of it."

"Moose wants to make the first call for breakfast. Wanna join us?"

"I feel too antsy to eat but I might stop by for some of that thick toast."

Like lesbians the two hugged and kissed, then Tiffany left. A little later Beatense saw Craig and waved him in. He stared pop-eyed at her lanky, explosive slouch.

Both thighs were quivering with tension. He gaped at her apple breasts, and her long, sunk curve of gaunt belly. Her bleached auburn hair was all a tumble, its natural state. Her skeptical face was boned exertive. Her baked burn stung the eye with its shifting shine. Each of her light muscles was exquisitely disciplined and shaped for graceful strength, and their spare size left her with stark, hinged shoulders.

All these as combined were lethal. With her, her morality was no morality.

"If... If I didn't live up to your standards last night, Beatense, it was my fault."

"How stupid. As a a nature girl I loved it. Except, this trip is depriving me of sun and so I compensated by working you hard. Don't think I got exercise? Take a look!"

"I'm looking, I'm looking! I understand you completely. In comparison here I am just a desk rat. But not for long. I going to get me a job in Cardiff and find me a studio on the beach, and instead of retiring to the beach I will live there now."

Her eyes widened in delight. "Oh, wow, Craig! You're not quite as idiot dull as I thought! The trouble is, you can do that but I can't. After just a couple weeks sadly I have to go back home. I might as well not be rich!"

"You're rich, baby, in hundreds of ways. I... I love you."

"Well, there's a declaration that I accept. But my tan comes with, you know. You can't filter that out in lieu of my other qualities. I gotta be brown. Get undressed!"

They had an event, except for Rosa the first time for the girl not just physical.

Beatense put on her jeans and white shirt, left deep vee open. The two left for breakfast and went through the staring train to the Dining Car. Adoration in torrents poured upon the girl from the staffers and other diners. The Singer.

"Welcome to Xanthallado Territory," greeted the Steward, eyeing her front.

"What? This is it, Xanthallado? What did I do, sleep twenty-four hours?"

"No, my dear, but it's the territory, not province. In a couple hours we cross the Allegan River over by the Nywot Transfer. That's a station by the edge…"

"I know all about the Transfer, sir. I baked nearly black there, waiting for the oil company bus to go to surveying camp. Comparatively I'm sickly now."

Craig shook his head. This girl's sun energy could power three cities.

There are magazines on the newsstand that normal guys disregard as they look through the car or gun issues. But if they're morbidly obsessed they will look at the fashion or health magazines, elaborately shaking their heads to assure those nearby that they're just trying to see how "bad" they are. The same is true of the beaches, a guy has to show indifference. But the Book Girl, indifference was impossible.

12

XANTHALLADO

Craig decided Beatense was the embodiment of evil vanity, but society poured upon her wealth and honor. But despite that, there she sat with a toast sandwich of bacon and runny egg, positively in transports. She smiled at everybody as if now her day was complete, and she looked upon Craig himself with eyes absent in joy.

She never once eyed her half exposed apple-like breasts, nor did she cast loving looks upon her gleaming bared forearms, that alone could changes lives.

But lurking back of their idle conversation was their sport together. The girl didn't seem to have the slightest constraints before, during or after. In fact, during she had raved with enthusiasm, coaxing her friend with nearly fainting ecstasy.

Just as with her helpful friends back at camp, Craig felt each of her tight muscles and every square inch of her dark brown skin working in skilled coordination, to bring the struggling girl convulsions of overpowering brain dead pleasure.

"So anyway, we could stay over at the Transfer, Craig, so I can catch back up on sun. We could sneak back into these nearby dunes to play. That will tire us out for the long night in the waiting room, on those wretched benches."

"No, I don't have your sun enthusiasm, that wouldn't be tempting to me at all."

"If only this train had a gondola car, I could lay out there and still travel!"

Craig laughed. "You're not one-dimensional, are you?"

She took the pack from her shirt pocket and lit a cigarette. "No, I do have other interests. When the nurse examined me for my implant back at survey camp, she said my swollen buds give real high sensitivity. So that makes me two dimensional!"

Implants were far too predatory for Craig's taste. They awarded young women, kids too, the floodgates to indulge repeatedly, which they did proudly, shamelessly.

"She said I'm long, lean and lanky, increasing that effect, so I should run and lift barbells to dissipate my urges. I was already running, and doing the weights. I bought a set for home and had the store deliver them up to our building roof."

"W-Well, you added great results to your already great shape."

"Oh, there was no change. I was always muscled. My fission genetics."

Craig sweated. Adding to her shattering tan impact, that hair, and face. It wasn't fair that she should have all those qualities and attributes, while others did not.

But in her case that didn't mean it was wrong. She was very deserving.

"Hey, Craig, let's us dissipate my energy by going back to the SkyLiner."

As they left the Diner the Queen was slowing up. They looked out the vestibule half door. Their train was gliding through a presentable enough little town, but there wasn't much by way of Xanthallado glamour. Its buildings, stores and houses had a basic rural life functionality, except… Beatense, as Craig watched, looked again.

She saw palm trees! She saw thick bushes that sagged with tropical blossoms. She saw big, rugged pick-up trucks cruising along, and mini-vans, and quad traction sport vehicles. The girl saw sleek performance cars that until now she knew of only from her magazines. The train trundled by ranch style houses, followed by a store purveying bagels and muffins. Then one that sold coffee rolled into view. Beatense saw a computer store, a cellular phone store and a health food store. A convenience store with self serve gas pumps went by, and the girl saw her first Penny's. She saw a massage spa and branch bank. She saw a skateboard and blade skate store.

Two kids in shorts and T-shirts flew by on that type of skate. Beatense felt angered by them, their wasting this sun. Then the train station, a structural steel building, dull putty grey with wainscot brick facing. Beatense expected the train to stop here, but as she opened her shirt another button it ran back up to speed.

In the coach cars everybody turned their wide open eyes upon her near bared breasts. She seemed to make them feel as if she was smiling at each person alone, even as her slender, regal bearing gave her tall dominance. Craig didn't know how practiced she was at this, how her entire city lay at her feet.

Back in the Sky Liner the conductors were seated at a small table as they quietly compared their notes on the operation details. Bernie read the names of the current passengers and the rear conductor, Cedric, checked them off. They gave Beatense startled nods as she entered with Craig, but in evaluating her outfit, her friend Colton Westergard rolled up his eyes.

"Miss Colwell, we have standards on what is properly worn for rail travel."

She tossed her hair. "That's why I wore this shirt, sir. No bikini for this trip, like after camp. So why didn't we stop back at that Douglas? We just slowed down!"

"We had a meet order, miss," said Mr. Westergard sternly, eyeing her tan.

"A meet order! There wasn't another train there that I saw!"

This degree of knowledge clearly wasn't expected. "It was a freight, miss," said Bernie, "over on the other side from your Roomette."

"Oh. But we weren't there at the time. Funny we didn't see it. But how can we possibly be still on schedule after that inexcusable break in progress?"

"You're a fine one to ask that!" Mr. Westergard shot back, and the relieved other conductors laughed. He turned to the steward. "Stand them."

"Thank you, but we actually just had breakfast," said Craig.

"Tell Holden your drink order then. You know, Miss Colwell, we picked up a wire from Rail Operations at Douglas. No more tickets for you, ever."

"Oh, come on! Yeah, like I really believe that!" Everyone laughed.

Johnny Lucke, who overheard, came over and patted Craig on the back. "You can have her," he said, and Craig laughed with mock misgiving.

But then he put his arm around the troublemaking firefly. She accepted it.

The two sat back by the wrap-around back windows, and the steward took their order. They lingered here, as the train rolled through desert and semi desert.

At noon the train slowed to a stop, at the Transfer. Beatense half jumped.

"Nywot! Boy, this sure came up fast! Oh and look at him, that criminal!"

Craig saw a thin hot tan youth in cotton shorts, with scruffy hair like Beatense's.

"Well there's my competition today," the staring girl said, as the boy came over, apparently to board. "Must be a camper. Only explanation. What a sickening blow."

Craig agreed. Like Beatense, he felt threatened by the kid.

"I don't know why I'm going to that Emeraldeye, Craig, really. Distracting that I might be, there's going to be boys and girls like him by the hundreds. Younger than me, same age as me, and older. Those magazine photos shudda scared me off!"

"You're the last person who should worry about any competition."

"I know. And it would be good to take a hit if I'm not that great. Wait a minute, selling ledgers. Is that really your job? What do you really do, anyway?"

"I'm a Lextango systems consultant. I've been trying to land some accounts in Arrolynn for a good year now. I hate to say it, but everyone there is so mule headed they decline our proposals even if they see we can really help them."

"It's the not-invented-here attitude. We still use vacuum tubes." She turned to Cedric. "Hey, what's taking so long here? I could be out laying in the sun!"

"We're waiting on the oil bus, miss, plus other traffic. Could be two hours. Go ahead. Others are getting off. Engine will give you all a warning toot."

Minutes later Beatense and Tiffany lay steaming black naked in the desert sun up at platform end, hidden by a freight wagon. Craig and Moose, sitting on a bench under the overhang, saw the hot tan youth hop off the train and run to join the girls. Then Hayden in bikini, hair tossing, went over with astounding connected hand springs.

"Must be real cultural shock for the Arrolynn humdrums to see that," said Moose.

"It's culture shock for me," said Craig, laying his sport coat beside him.

In answer to Beatense, the now bare teen youth said he wasn't from the Gurney camp; he had gotten off on leave from the cargo barge he was working that summer on. Age eighteen, the boat deck glare had burned him coppery-flickering dark.

"I just loop the ropes over the bollards at the locks, and pull them back off."

Moose and Craig climbed through the vestibule and went over to the river beach where train escapees were swimming. Moose stripped and ran in. Damn tan, Craig noted sourly, loosening his tie. A packet boat emptied riders for the train, then a bus came. At last three-thirty the train was satisfied, and at the horn everybody ran over. Culture shock nude, the four sunners returned to their quarters as the train started.

The panting, restored Beatense saw groves, hay fields and pastures fly by. She saw stretched off to the distant hills scattered stables, ranches and oil wells.

She noticed that the tracks here were dead flat smooth. Instead of that bucking that before made any walking fairly difficult, here there was a hushed steady velocity, punctuated with a faint *dhunt... dhunt... dhunt...* that could calibrate a watch.

Beatense watched as her cabin's front bulkhead wall swept the many sights into hurried view past her speeding window. The sense of powered speed was dizzying, this was nothing like a car going equally fast. *Dhunt... dhunt... dhunt...*

She slid open her door when she saw Bernie. "Yo, there! Smooth tracks!"

His jaw worked. "Er, er, uh, hello. W-Welcome to libertine Xanthallado. And yes, they are smooth. Doing one-ten. Making up for your getting sun at the Transfer."

The girl's later excursion was an evening stroll, no grabbing things to hold on. In gold satin sunsuit, her renewed tan dark shined. After their wrestling oil spree she hit three hours. Her bare limbs passage through the train got the usual admiration.

She stepped up into the first Dome Car and found Craig and the pop-eyed Ida.

"Hi, guys! Well, this is it, Ida, Xanthallado! What a paradise place, hah?"

"And y-you got some sun, I see" said Ida. "N-Nice outfit there."

"Got it when I was sixteen, still fits!" She sat by Ida. "Oh man, what a bake-in! I rubbed off that butter oil with my towel but I still look wet! If I didn't get so dang shit brown, I would die. Like that Russ. He works on the river barges, endless sun!"

Craig sat there worried. Unlike his friend, Tiffany and Moose he didn't do well in the sun. And unlike the gangly Moose he just had an average build. And that Russ boat boy: Light muscles, near molasses match, ton of blond hair. He wondered if the boy and Beatense did anything. But look at her: Insatiably bony starved, tan wild.

As the Queen slowed down in prosperous little Bradley, Beatense saw four smiling young boys waiting on their fancy BMX bikes. She knew what these were, thanks to an article about single mothers and the sports they could get their sons involved in.

The boys were wearing team number jerseys and buttcut shorts. Their tan faces and rumply thick hair shined in the hot sun. One lad held up a wee finger in greeting, and his friends covered their mouths and laughed, eyes sparkling.

"Nice little ginger snaps, aren't they?" said Ida. "Color-wise."

"Like our author," said Beatense. "And me! Let's see, Maher Ridge next, right?"

"Where I get off," said Craig. *How can she be so unaffectedly talkative, that tan?* "So, okay, Beatense, Friday I come down for the trade show. I'll find your motel."

The talk went on and the girl gave the kids thought. Their feathery lashed eyes were narrowed from the sun, so that together with their delicate eyebrows each boy seemed to convey a warily discerning intelligence. As the train moved on Beatense then saw a stern faced girl of twelve who wore a sleeveless T-shirt that covered her shoulders, and short-cut shorts. Her dark hair was pulled back into a long no-trouble tail, and she had a remarkable tan. This was pure color without shine or golden glow, as if from a drought heat. And this was why she had that scowl, all the attention.

She eyed the intruding Queen with some misgiving, with her fine eyebrows knit together in serious concern. She had defined muscles, quite unexpected with anyone so young, and like her thighs even her neck had taut lineage. A team swimmer?

"She looks like she's a budding body builder!" chirped Beatense, with a smile at her alliteration. "But I know from surveying camp, that look can come very naturally."

"All too true. But I better get ready to get off," said Craig, and Beatense went with him to his cabin. They sat facing each other as the semi-tropics speeded up.

"Okay, what about this Maher Ridge, Craig? Why does it sound familiar?"

"It's just an obscure town that just made the road atlas. But glad to be back after so long. Except for you, I hate to break away for that trade show. Now look, I know how crazed you are for sun. I know I would always take a backseat to that. So in other words I knew I'm probably not right for you, Beatense. I got zero sun at Nywot."

"You're not going to get rid of me that easy, Craig. I just need four hours a day."

Bernie's call for Maher came. The girl followed Craig out onto the track platform, which was quaintly paved with brick and it was separate from the parked cars with a white picket fence. The girl saw how the townsfolk gave her second jolted looks, but otherwise they stayed stable. She was famous down here, but no one suspected she was The One. Just another self loving tan stick. Craig saw his parents get out of the car while Beatense said, "Boy, Craig, I'm so glad I got that sun. I feel so much…"

She started. Perched upon the narrow saddle of his Carbotek racing bike, and menacingly slouched like a leaned, drawn back bow, was a thin teen-aged boy who was burned so deeply tan all over, he was literally awashed with liquid sun.

He just wore a trim pair of white deck shorts that he and his long legs fought with from his baking, and the seared skin of his taut belly curved neatly in under the low, loose hold of the elastic waistband. All shined with sweat, he was breathing himself down as he coldly beheld the strutted arm he held crooked out before him. The boy's chest and belly, his shoulders aimed his insanely dark tan upon his viewers.

"…Better. Oh, that is… Sick. I'm furious! He's getting sun all day!"

Craig felt threatened. "Oh, that's just that Nack kid. He never lets up."

"Nack? That's Nack? That's Scott's brother! Wow, no shit!"

"You know Scott Grimaldi? How would you know *him?"*

"Are you kidding? Scott is in my second book with me!"

He didn't know this, he had been away. Library, saw her book, walked on by.

By now the proud youth was aware of her attention. His cheek points and slack opened mouth betrayed his troubled wonder at the girl's interest as his heaving chest continued to work. His long blond hair enframed his hard face. The novel visibility of his muscles staggered Beatense, but what truly devastated her was his courageous ostentation. Just like herself, even presently in her comparatively tame sunsuit.

Craig's parents had to detour around that picket fence. They returned his wave.

"Hey Mom! Hey Dad! Say, Beatense? I better warn you, this isn't a long stop."

"Sorry, I was staring. Trust me, that's weeks of painful lay-out that kid has."

Beatense was just going hop over to Nack but Craig's dumpy parents walked up and the horns sounded. Comfy greetings were exchanged: Nice to meet *you!*

"Look, you better get back on board, Puppet. You know what can happen."

"Oh my, yes! Young lady, you don't want to get stuck in this dull town, ha ha!"

Beatense laughed obligingly, outdoing Tiffany. Craig kissed her and she sprang aboard the train, grabbing hold and waving. They waved back, but then as Bike Boy turned his critical gaze upon the sweated brown of his quivering disciplined belly, the girl felt like one of her own victims. It was a cruel outrage that this pouty kid was not only soaking in that brutal heat, but he was mercilessly flaunting his tan as a bonus.

This had always been her game, I too, to make total strangers hate their lives.

The train started, and a young mother came walking by with her little daughter. She didn't have that naturally authoritative look but could give orders. She was petite but athletically fibered, and she was tawny warmed in a natural way. Her waif's legs were fully bared by her drawstring tied sweat shorts, while her sleek waist was bared by her not-quite-store-acceptable cropped T-shirt. Plus she was barefooted.

She was cute, not that of being silly or ineffectual or foolish, but due to her alert eyes that always showed a warm but ironic humor. Like oil tech Lesta.

Beatense, with a last appraisal, hopped up the steps into the vestibule proper as Cedric, the rear conductor, stepped in to shut things up.

"Cedric, I don't know if I can take much more of this Xanthallado. First that one disgusting Nack kid so dang tan, and even the mothers are beautiful here."

"Most mothers are, my dear."

She laughed. "I didn't mean it that way. But why are we going so slow?"

"Track repair ahead. I'll leave the door open for you."

"So I can see the ties and rails stacked hither and yon? Gee, thanks!"

She stood in the doorway as the Queen groaned along. The wheel trucks beneath her feet made a low rumble from their rolling iron on steel contact. The train trundled into an orange grove. A track crew in a seething stretch of sand and rock stopped working. The thinned young heroes, with jeans held to their light hips, were shirtless, and so insidiously brown in that blurring glare, with their poetic muscles they looked unnatural, fake. Barge Russ would fit right in. And the oil interns back at camp.

The girl wobbled even as the guys noticed her and reacted. With height to hip width ratio of six to one and pine knotty, she too could fit right in. But little comfort.

The wheel truck rumble and the trembling idle of the locomotives was just heard, then they revved back up to speed. Beatense watched the boys glide away.

She returned to her Roomette and later saw the first signs of the city. She felt increasingly uneasy about what lay ahead. It all depended on that phone call so long ago. And was the place really on the beach, or was it stuck in some stupid alley five miles away? Beatense got out her fold-out map again as the Queen galloped along into Cardiff. Yes, Hoganforth was right on the beach, barring a printer's error.

They were well into the city when they went by the airport, and here jet airliners came dropping for a landing toward and right over the train. One came in so low it seemed impossibly, dangerously suspended, rocking its wings up and down.

The Queen pounded along between the backyards of split levels or ranch homes, then along the backsides of plush apartments, with tantalizing pools that lay unused. Suddenly, expressways. They were glutted with traffic, some of it zipping right along, while other vehicles barely moved. The highways had big green overhead signs that sent the traffic either on or off the exit ramps like beads on a necklace.

The ramps were elevated, and they flew up or over or between the roads. Going eighty, the Queen sliced on. Off in the still distant city center Beatense saw Cardiff's office towers, that loomed dozens of stories tall, and with their metallic glass facades they were so spectrally dream-like they could have been, or maybe were, apparitions from outer space. The Queen entered a rail corridor, and kicked into high gear.

It flowed smoothly by endless lines of stationary freight cars and passenger trains at a fearsome, driving speed. Some trains were just eighteen inches away.

"Cardiff! Cardiff, Xanthallado! End of the line!" It was Cedric. He paused by Beatense's door as the ninety mph express rocked and shook. "Look, miss, we'll be slowing down into a wye track and backing into the station," he said. "Sit tight!"

13

COMMODORE

With the windows in the opposite Roomette Beatense felt like she was a rock splitting a river torrent as the cars on both sides of the train shot by. Then the brakes caught, and the train slowed down as the track curved to the right through a slum of aging shabby factories. This neighborhood was neglected and dirt ugly, with pawn shops, liquor stores and saggy bars prevailing. The train's entry here tied up traffic, then it stopped and stood maddeningly in wait. The vent fans were suddenly loud.

What are we stopped for? Another meet order? Beatense silently raged.

She felt like jumping out of the stalled train. The train finally lurched and began gliding backward, toward the station hopefully. As the curve straightened a twin-deck commuter train raced past the Queen toward the nearing station.

With her iron trucks clunk-clunking the train backed in under the great boarding shed of Commodore Station. The tracks were roofed over here with blue enameled structural sheet steel, supported by heavy I-beams with PA speakers mounted. The pace was slow but steady as the train worked in along the platform.

Beatense turned on her overhead light (now needed) and got her things into her backpack, then heart pounding changed to just jeans. Her backpack straps legalized her breasts or so she hoped. She stepped into the corridor. The lights here, always dim anyway, seemed dimmer now, and the other passengers in line gave a feeling of claustrophobia. But she responded to their good-byes with a smile, although truly it was quite an uncertain smile. "Sorry, we have no record of your call. Next!"

The track platforms here were raised, the trap decks were left down for a direct walk out. Her backpack hidden by her hair, the girl stepped out into the migration.

She quickly found out that people here had a deep, serious admiration for a lean, light and tight beach girl. Even dowdy middle-agers gazed into her shocking corded belly with full approval. People stepped over to get a better look, photos were taken of her with no hesitation, and the girl overheard many favorable remarks.

"Look at how tan she is, Mom. She's like just so... Dark!"

"Where does she get that nerve? Just so brown! That is sick!"

I walked the San Diego airport in butt-cuts and T-shirt, reactions non-verbalized.

Beatense had that arrival satisfaction of striding by the Queen's coaches one by one as she and countless others headed for the distant depot. As she looked in the windows she saw that passengers were still waiting to get off. A wafting of steam came out from under the cars, that old sign of destination reached, jouney's end.

The trainmen in their uniforms were answering urgent questions, while porters were helping some of the passengers with their luggage. They paused to gape.

Beatense caught up to Ida to walk beside her. Ida's husband, Herbert, met them. The girl always thought he was a little stuffy for the baked naked intern girls.

In the noise Ida was just heard. "Herbert dear, hello! You remember Puppet!"

"Why hello, young lady, nice to see you again. That tan, no mistaking you. I can recall your logging in the mud data that time when Glendice was sick. No errors."

"No, it was diopter scans. And she wasn't sick, she was bedding Andy on the sly, and finishing up I had to run interference for her by knocking on Benton's door."

Herbert hesitantly laughed and the ladies hugged and the couple went on.

Beatense half ran, anxious to get to those coast bus shuttles Bernie had told her about. Jogging on, ignoring the comments, Beatense saw a girl standing alone.

A slim child of fourteen was arrestingly beautiful, and as expected, sun-loved.

Beatense caught up to Moose and Tiffany, who were hefting their luggage along. The young wife was striking in her plaza slacks and belly baring camisole top. The three stopped, and Tiffany took some of the heat off Beatense, as did this bony, tall, duress-tan young lady who came striding along in her sarong wrap skirt and tie-top.

"Hey, Tiff! Look at the competition we got! Aren't you looking, Moose?"

"I can't notice things like that anymore. Tiff goes half ape... Tiff! Ouch!"

"There's millions like that," said Tiffany, turning from chastising her devoted (no wonder) husband. "Wait until you hit the beach. They even beat me there.

Me and Moose went by this Murderers Row on Troubadour Island. Every one black as you."

They exchanged laughs and parting hugs. Beatense looked back to the girl.

She was in a tucked-in T-shirt and tight blue jeans, and she stood with her thin arms crossed under her delectable breasts. She was born to surf and sun, all toffee warmed and shined, and her rippling long hair had a deep honey color. Despite her blossoming youth and deceptive slack stance, her graceful form was sensually alert. Her wide, green eyes seemed to convey a responsibility in important matters, so with friends she was always the one in charge, the one to hold onto the tickets.

She had bone defined cheeks and a dainty chin, and her measuring eyes had tuckets of bone placed above, like Beatense, shaping her all-knowing eyebrows with skeptical doubt. But what truly set her apart was the perceptive clarity of the lenses of her eyes, as seen at an angle. They gave her intelligent character.

Beatense approached her. "Hey, what are you just standing here for?"

"I'm wait... Wow, what... A tan! Anyway, waiting for my Dad, on the TriPax."

This train was due at any time, for a wandering herd came toward them.

"Oh, does this TriPax go out to Emeraldeye Beach by any chance?"

"No, that's the South Coast bus." She pointed, extending her toasted small arm with wrist neatly cocked, as if to have it admired. "Out front. Follow those straps!"

"I just might! Thanks! But boy, it's sure... Oh, that must be your train!"

The gleaming twin-decker came thundering in under the station roof, on the track opposite her own Queen. As it loudly stopped Beatense said good bye and started toward the glowing yellow letters posted on the distant station wall, that spelled out...

COMMODORE

The silver twin-decker's doors opened. As Beatense kept going the few Sunday commuters, but mostly leisure riders, flowed with and by her. Heart still pounding Beatense conspicuously walked along, in full command, as the natural flexions of her long, Geode freshened waist drew stares. But in this land of beach combatants she would face tough adversaries. Her appalling nerve was a critical need. A security guard stepped toward her, but from previous encounters knew he would get a fight.

The tracks ended at a wide windowed wall. Trains in wait were snugged up to heavy iron stanchions here, the end of the line. Beatense gave the Queen, in fact its SkyLiner, a last look, then breasts half hidden stepped through the station doors.

This modern station was hugely different from the Arrolynn edifice. It had a low acoustic ceiling with fluorescent light panels, and rows of molded plastic seats. No wood benches. Over to the left a long, open counter stood, where the ticket agents conferred with the travelers. Back of the counter TV monitors displayed the many arrivals and departures. A PA announcement: *The Stanton Surfer now boarding.*

Over on the opposite side Beatense saw a Deli Court, an enclosed area packed with dozens of busy tables for the walk-up restaurant counters. She paused to look, then another girl caught her attention, a young woman whose preoccupied face had a cultured frailty, a delicate poignancy that her dusky complexion and bone refinement exquisitely complimented. Beatense admired her even as she had been breaking necks herself almost all her life. But did wonder why she wasn't tan.

She was thrilled to see the other proud women here, they reminded her of her intern friends. Many had haughty expressions as they displayed their smashng shit tans. They pulled their luggage pieces behind them, on little built-in wheels, seemingly with the bland attitude that these were invented just for them.

Another boarding call, the Sleazy Slider. Beatense laughed, and went on by the Travel Now gift shop. Both her books were on display in the window, $75. She went on to exit the front doors of the station. With the confusing sights and sounds of this new city confronting her, she followed the curving walk-way of the drop-off loop.

The heat was welcome, after all that A/C. The taximen smiled and swept their arms invitingly, but the girl shrugged in apology. There was also a line-up of shuttle vans and limousines, but the girl went on to the bus she was after,

SOUTH COAST BEACHES

Unlike the old bread loaf buses Beatense knew, this one was a big cracker box, with broad windows. The luggage bins were open. The backpacker stepped up.

An aristocratic skinny lass hopped from the bus. In fact she was stretched into runner's form. She wore a white cotton office shirt, whose sleeves were unevenly rolled to her elbows, baring her sun kissed arms. Her shirt was open three buttons down, showing a baked neck and baked chest. Her leggy, faded jeans had such an exacting tightness they seemed to poise her hips, in a way that said, "I'm in charge here." Or, "Shall we?" Her fine shaped forehead was angled just slightly back, as if from being hurried, but her round blue eyes told of a pleasant patience.

She had a curved nose, a mark of distinctive lineage, and her cheek points, low chin and long jaw conferred her all-wise face with a boned focus. But Beautiful.

Her officer's hat was tipped back upon her loose blond hair, tousled by sun and surf. She was a sunner, who had to be real deep tan to be happy, or even alive. She handled the waiting passengers and turned to Beatense.

"Hey, great tan! The Book Girl! I'm Kathy! Ya want South Coast?"

"Book Girl, hah! They got my books at $75, but all I get for my newest is five! What a racket! But if you go to Emeraldeye Beach, yes. But are *you* the driver?"

"Oh, so far. Where ya heading to in Emmy Eye?"

"Hoganforth Lodges, if you know of it. This beach hostel place."

As the two talked other passengers bought their tickets and boarded.

"Yes, but I'm warning you, it's rowdy there. If you prefer a quiet place..."

"No! I've been quietly moral long enough. Hey, what about that Cocojo?"

"If I blast the sun weekends there, I can face the work week calmly, but not always worth the hike. Or you can park in Sorel's parking lot and quick run into the dunes, but you gotta be fast if you're uncivilized. Odd thing is you can be nude right along the Coastal Highway in Emmy, if you're on the ocean-side, but in Sorel you go back fifty years. A way bigger danger for you with that crazily conspicuous tan. Wow!

"Now at old Hoggy they will ask you, a sex or non-sex room. Say sex. And no dress code there. You can just wear nothing. Okay, a ticket is eight bucks."

"Here's a tenner. No change. No, make it a twenty. And I'm Beatense."

Kathy gave the ticket, showing her golden herringbone wrist chain, that glowed against her sun warmed baking while detailing the delicacy of her forearm.

"Wow, thanks! Sit up front, across from Bobby. We'll be leaving quick."

A starved young lady walked by in a mesh sunsuit with appliquéd breast circles and a four inch appliquéd hips band. She was sharply tanned, with a dried finish that looked as if she had scrubbed herself with lava soap and a loofah. At ninety pounds, she pulled her phone from her string hung purse and thumbed it.

"Ted, hey, just got off work. Want me to pick up anything? Yeah, okay."

She wore that outfit on the job? Well, this is how it should be if one wishes to forego normal clothes on any given day, especially if the one is life changing.

"What kind of work?" Beatense laughed.

As she turned a petite girl who was approaching wore a tiny black velvet dress, baring spindly but strong, heels flexed legs. Medical science had likely studied her sixteen inch waist. Her amassed hair was glistening black, her skin was of warmed ivory, and her black eyes had an exotic, wide almond shape. She pulled her luggage along with such casual aplomb, she turned it into a key fashion accessory.

She purchased her ticket with a light crisp voice and carefully stepped up into the bus. Beatense wasn't in Arrolynn anymore.

She followed the emaciated child up into the cavernous coach, and sat just kitty corner back from the driver's seat. A teen-age boy was sitting across from her, by resting back against his window as he lazily propped his bare feet on the armrest.

His shining blond hair swarmed long, heavy and full, with ends curled randomly. He wore faded blue jean cut-offs, and a tan of impossible saturation. His bright skin carried deep, deep within a shattering dose of the sun's energy.

"Hi!" this actually beautiful boy said, smiling. "I'm Kathy's brother, Bobby."

She slid off her backpack. "You mean Kathy, my driver, Kathy?"

The boy stared. "Y-Your driver? Yeah, her. Who are you? Where ya going?"

"Beatense. The Book Girl. Going to Emeraldeye. Th-That's quite the tan."

"I know. You too. I saw your book! You must beach out worse than me!"

Although casually topless Beatense felt herself strangling. Bobby was so tan he seemed to vibrate. He was far browner than barge Russ, Nack and the track crew boys. The stretch of his light muscles gave the thin boy a crispy hot shine. He had a chest, and as a barbell enthusiast Beatense knew the exercise that did this. He had worked his slim belly too: Rippled. He was other-worldly. And then, cute faced.

"That's… That's an incredible tan. You… You can melt butter at ten feet."

Bobby smiled proudly. "Hey, I better remember that line! But you, your tan is famous! Hey, if you're coming down to Tucumzozo let's lay out together!"

"Nope. Emeraldeye Beach. But I heard that's nude there, hah?"

"Our beach is too. It's just us locals. *Totally* open. We can even love pile!"

"I can guess that would be a big draw. Good beach for me to check out!"

"Oh man, you would rip the place open! Only Authenticity has your tan. Half the time she doesn't even know what clothes are. She just goes naked! And fucks!"

Beatense couldn't argue that healthy life. There came an under-floor clunking of the luggage doors as Kathy swung them shut. The last of the riders filed on, they all stared as they saw the two. Kathy jumped up into the bus and, rolling her eyes at Beatense, slid lightly back of her big steering wheel. Now she looked quite small.

She levered the door shut and leaned over and started the engine. Ventilators filled the coach with conversation muffling air. She took the microphone down from over her windshield, big as a billboard. The side windows were big also.

"Hey, guys!" she said, holding the PA mike in one hand as she lustily ground the transmission into gear with the other. She eased the bus out from the curb as she twisted around to check for traffic. "You're on the South Beach bus. The first stop is Cardiff Shores, in 45 minutes. We're scheduled for 35 but this is high rush."

The bus turned into the street. Beatense gazed up at the tall office towers, which stood back of the busy plazas that fronted them. She saw magnificent department stores and fabulous hotels. Under their portico awnings lordly doormen in swanky uniforms whistled up the cabs with imperial flourishes, or they attended to the sleek limousines that oozed in. Even Beatense would blanch at the nightly rates.

"Bubble Breath drives one of those," said Bobby.

Beatense was glad to finally get moving. "Wow, Kathy, no kidding?"

"I don't drive it, I aim it. Ha ha ha."

"Bobby, what do you know about Cocojo?"

"It's a great beach, all sand dunes, but it's hard to get to. No way in north, you have to come in from Sorel and their lifeguards are all pissy. I burned black in those dunes. My skin ached for a week. But aren't you from around here at all?"

"No, all the book photos were taken up in Clarendon, way up north. But I know all about aching skin. It's like it shrinks and your bones stick out and chafe against it."

Kathy nodded in firm agreement. She had gone several blocks and was turning onto a ramp off their street, to make the elevated expressway ahead. Moments later they jostled into the racing torrent. Beatense was impressed by Kathy's skill as she pressed the coach ever onward. She had four frantic lanes to watch, but she simply sat slouched with one little hand on the wheel. This was unheard of, that this girl, or any girl, could handle this vehicle with such lazy indifference.

For the bus drivers in Arrolynn there was none of this jaunty hat angle or blue jean stuff. And what jeans Kathy had! Like Beatense's pair their butt seam shamelessly creased deep into the cleavage, cleanly shaping the anatomy here while giving the spare young women wearing them a springy active look.

The bus glided along past factories, restaurants, shopping plazas and residential neighborhoods, and reservoir lakes. Beatense was fascinated by the alluring names on the big green signs overhead. One sign got her attention:

Beaches

Exit Right   1 Mi

"Kathy! Did you see that sign? Do you turn there?"

"Yeah, I do. When we hit the beach us guys won't be so unique anymore!"

A minute later the coach was curving the banked exit ramp down toward a new highway. It had just three lanes per direction, but the traffic moved just as fast. The bus slid in to become a part of this sluice-way, heading west into the sun. They passed shopping malls, office courts and towers, medical centers, more restaurants, and car dealerships. There was just no comparison to Arrolynn.

"Just look at the strong economy you guys have here, Kathy," Beatense said, still looking out. "Unlike where I'm from. It all looks so prosperous!"

"Credit cards. That's where all this economic activity comes from. But hey, if it means everybody has a negative net worth, party on."

"She's just mad because she thinks her limo payments are too high."

"Well, they fucking are high. And with stocks heading down, shitful tips."

The highway began curving south, and Kathy exited again, swinging onto a wide avenue of slower traffic, Embarcadero Drive, that ran parallel to the original highway. Along the left esplanade luxury hotels came one after the other, behind a line of palm trees spaced every fifty feet. And off to the right, across shimmering acres of open sand, and reaching to the infinite horizon and beyond, lay the bright sea. Beatense watched a majestic succession of sunlit waves roll leisurely into bursting oblivion.

But her interest lasted one second. For out her window, in full view of traffic, she saw a triumphantly browned, aristocratic-faced twig in just a tie-strip proudly striding with breasts flexed out, right among the other pedestrians on the busy sidewalk.

"What the... That girl was topless! I thought it was just me with that nerve!"

Kathy had seen her first as they drove along, through her windshield. Other brave and braver individuals were ranged out far ahead. She saw them everyday.

"If she doesn't a friend for the night, she will," she laughed. Beatense still looked back. "This sidewalk along here is considered beach, so she's within the law."

Beatense was manic. Palm trees, hot sand, exclusive hotels, and that girl. If she wasn't such collegiate old money quality, even her assumed plans she could handle. No family standards for her. Two more twigs came by, talking with lively gestures.

"There's a nude on my side!" said Bobby. "Walking right past the Rameer Palms Hotel! I didn't know they could do it on that side of Embarcadero!"

"Where have you been, Bobby?" said Kathy. "Okay, we're stopping at the beach here, Beatense. Be prepared." She took down the mike. "First stop, Cardiff Shores! And just a warning, bikini girls and nudes will be boarding. If offended don't look!"

Kathy turned into the parking lot that had appeared. The bus rolled by row after heat waving row of parked cars to the last line, right along the by sand. Kathy turned and idled along, toward the big, old time looking beach house ahead.

Here nude and topless girls walked by with an unaffected lack of conscientious concern. A starkly tan young boy in a bikini rode by on a BMX bike. His leaned back was hooked into a slouchy bellied curve that cruelly flashed with sun.

Beatense was stunned, even after her surveying camp sojourns. Brown animals were cavorting, running, and playing without the slightest sense of inhibition. They were distant from the street traffic, but the big hotels just yonder had a nice view.

And in any case there were plenty of sun lovers right along Embarcadero to calm the held-up drivers there. Beatense saw tan waifs on towels in bake, totally nude or nearly nude. Others carried surfboards, or they raced the sidewalk or parking lot on those peculiar inline skates. Naked sticks weighing just ninety pounds kicked lustily along on skateboards or scooters. They shimmery shined in extreme dark contrast to the hazy acres of powdery white sand. This was no rooftop or stone quarry.

These pre-teenage, teenage and college age boys and girls all had smiling, sun and salt scrubbed faces, and they were gracefully light and tight. All were celebrating being wild, brown and beautiful on this hot day. The smiling all boys had thick, long, sun lightened hair like Bobby and Russ, and they had their elaborate muscles.

Their young lovely sisters also seemed to know little of boring demure chastity, as if it did quite escape them that long ago there had been rules of decorum.

"That girl's getting on that guy!" said Bobby, half rising. "Woo!"

Beatense wildly scanned the beach, and she saw a sweet faced girl in her teens sitting frog-legged on a boy, working as she smiled down at him.

"Yeah! She's riding! She's trying to hide it but… Yeah, he's way in her!"

Beatense found little comfort in her own sordid history of that, public or not.

They stopped at the old beach house. Kids ran over and sprang aboard the bus, and they filled the ventilation air with a strong sun smell. They laughed and noisily pushed each other. Several sun worshippers came over to the bus as they modestly tied on their bottoms and/or tops. These hot-baked bony women were muscled like wildcats. If tall they looked small; if small they looked tall. Tans tight stretched.

As they boarded they laughingly shivered from the cold air, skin flashing.

Kathy started on and puttered along further along the beach, and Beatense, the wonderful mighty Beatense, the famous singer and all that, the Book Girl and Puppet too, even as shirtless helplessly stared out her imprisoning window. *This shit bus.*

At the southern end of the parking lot the beach was emptier, and ahead on the white sand a thin young woman drew inexorably near. With heels propped she was lying on her surfboard, making nude use of her remote location. Her thin arms were flung out, her hips were bone out-jutted, and her sharply dark tan was in a close battle of oiled bake versus sweated burn. It was her surfboard that crushed Beatense, far more than her raw nerve. A skill she lacked.

Beatense was wild. Beach gear toting people walked by on the sidewalk a few yards from the nude! But they pretended not to see. Maybe they were used to it.

She raised to her elbows to observe them, as this outlaw's impassively mirrored sunglasses didn't convey any interest in their presence. Her peach breasts stuck out from her as defiantly as their eager nips did from them. In spite of or because of her ravening small build, a blurred aura of the deepest hot brown seethed out from her in waves. She saw the bus, then in recognizing it she sat up and raised her hand. The white plastic key tube that hung between her seamlessly tan breasts came to view.

She sprang up and turned to pick up her board, showing her waist narrowed backside and wee hardened butt.

Bobby made a face. "She had her skegs dug into the sand again!" he said in disgust, watching as the sports girl carried it over. Kathy hopped out and opened the forward luggage compartment, and she shoved it in with a loud scrape.

"Easy, Sis!" Bobby cried at the sandy screech, but they didn't hear. He turned to Beatense. "You gotta try surfing. But go easy on the equipment."

The two boarded the bus, and the surfer carefully lay her large towel on the seat beside Bobby. She visibly crackled with a beautiful hot bake. She flaunted a small waist and flat belly, which looked as if it could take the hit of a spiraled football.

A hard tuned carnivore. But modestly, as a nude, she had boarded with hand placed. Kathy shook her head with smiling disgust.

Beatense morbidly realized that suddenly she was just nobody here.

"Hey, Canty! How did it go last night?" said Bobby, the skegs forgotten.

"A good six hour ride." She fell beside him with knee up and tensed belly empty sunk. "I was totally sore all over this morning, but the surfing gave me new aches to consider. Then the sun baked all my…" She had turned to Beatense. "Hey, you got some sun in yourself. I'm dethroned. Did you get on up by the bathhouse?"

"No, I got on at Commodore, uptown. Er, I have to commend your nerve, getting on the bus bare like that. I should have rode the train that way!"

"It's called survival, stuck in an office, all those piss meetings. So I took time off. Sunning out in devotion to my skin, bar dancing naked and fucking, I'm at peace."

"Boy, I know the feeling! I lay for hours in devotion to my skin, and yes, I fuck. I first got active as a kid. I was just meant for it, like being all-over tan in the sun."

The bus was moving again, slowly because of the building line of cars.

"Exactly. Our natural state is nothing, but early on clothes are put on us, so then we get this fake need to cover up. Going bare, we're just returning to the primordial state we were meant for." Beatense thought of Soler with her judge order. "When you live half your life in just your skin, and fuck in celebration, that shows your priorities."

"Well us girls have to give ourselves credit for being bony, brown and beautiful."

"Yes, and we can't be defensive about it, either. None of this modesty shit. Me going into work you should see how skimpy I dare myself. They never said anything."

Canty's svelte form raged rye crust shattering upon the white cloth of her towel. Admiringly, Beatense thought that any clothes she wore would do little to lessen her impact. She could alter lives wearing a feed bag with a neck hole. Of some interest was the stark protruding of her hipbones, a feature that along with her sunk blacked belly Beatense also boasted, and she glanced down for reassurance.

"Say, er, heh, th-they call you Canty? I mean, that can't be your real name."

Her answer that her name was Canterbury Biscotto impressed Beatense. Beatense Biscotto. Perfect for her record label. She had to call them!

"So what's your name? Don't tell me it's Tiffany or Courtlyn, or Ashleigh."

"No, I'm unusually named Beatense, which always raises a few laughs."

"Not from me. Your name, it's the thought that counts."

"She's the Book Girl," said Bobby, and Beatense rolled her eyes up.

"Oh, those books are great classics! Perverts image me at the beach, but me, I just end up in the FieldNet, with the library computers blocking free girls like me."

Kathy chiggered the bus along an road that didn't hook back to the expressway, but instead it eventually swung into the Coastal Highway that Beatense had seen on her map. The bus passengers were welcomed by a corny, but lovingly kept up, old wooden billboard that announced the first beach town along the Coastal Highway, Stony Arbor. Where Kathy's real work began. Her problem was the range of foothills running down the coast and pinching the towns, resulting in just this one main road.

This was scheduled driving at its worst, because of the fun resort atmosphere in these busy beach towns. Mr. Father ahead there, barely moving as he searches for some motel with a name like Seashell. And the oblivious tourists all seemed to think that the busy Highway was just a handy extension of the beach, and they strolled out into the stalled traffic like trusting lambs. Teeth gritted, Kathy braked repeatedly, but Beatense used this slow speed to study this new world.

She was vaguely disappointed that this Stony Arbor wasn't the little tropical jewel that any brochures would make it out to be, but there was a balmy seacoast flavor here. She saw gift shops, surf shops, art galleries and fashion boutiques. She saw beach bungalows and fancy condominiums, and comfy bed and breakfast inns.

There were hotels and motels and snack stands, and rigging works for sailboats, and coffee shops and ice cream parlors and sidewalk bistros. There were bars with names like "Jammers" or "Blue Pipe." Dull ordinary stores were present too.

And back-dropping all this was the sea, that kept tantalizingly popping into sight. Kathy halted in front of a pottery store, where several starved teen-age girls waited. They were stretchy thin, and they wore polo shirts and shorts. Very tan, they noisily tumbled onto the bus and, with screams at the three in front, they went to the rear.

But a raging tan girl who yelled good bye didn't get on. She was stark naked, as noticed by the frumpy tourists walking by, and she was enriched with a sweat filmed burn. She drank from her bottle of spring water with a jaunty hand on her tipped hip.

Beatense yawned, not wanting to clue Bobby in on this sight. As the bus pushed on the girl, with springing feet, ran alongside, amazingly fast. Her friends opened the window and cheered her on. Kathy could finally stop for her a block later, where the bare girl hopped on board. She filled the bus with an effulgence of sparkling heat.

"Thanks for stopping, but as you can see, I don't have any money on me," she explained, panting as she held the grab bar. "Hey, Allie, buy me in!"

But Bobby jumped up and paid instead. The girl elaborately leaned on the seat immediately in front of the wide eyed Beatense. Running shoes only!

"Thanks! I'm Smoky! I was going to run home, but I remembered that I left my bike at Forsythia's! You're almost half tan! Where do you hang out?"

"Tucumzozo Main. I'm Bobby."

"Hey, Bobs, I'll check it out down there! I can bring my board!"

The happy lad flopped back down. Smoky rejoined her friends, who teased her mercilessly. The bus rolled into Madeline and rolled past a big marina, whose piers stretched out to sea. But overall this town with fewer stores seemed more residential than Stony Arbor. No public beach was in sight. But waving palms beckoned.

As they neared Emeraldeye Beach the road angled just a block off the sea, then the bus rolled by a wooded bluff along to the right. It cast the bus in an enexpected shadow as it also cut off the view of the ocean. As the bus got past the hill a picnic area and skateboard park appeared, and beyond this stretched a world class beach, that was nestled against the bluff's broad south flank. Its sands covered acres. The bus stopped at a dignified old hotel built in the days of rest cures, and a few actually clothed people got off. Kathy hopped out and to handle a couple of worried looking tourists, who had decided that this wasn't the seaside respite they expected.

"Okay, Hoggy Hodges!" said Kathy, as with unwitting grace she sprang back into her seat. "Except I have to park out on the Highway; I can't get in and get back out."

"Either way," said Beatense, who was getting more and more agitated.

To the west the green sea gleamed, and to the east the tall foothills lay golden in that late afternoon sun. Beatense thought of the surfer girls native to this world as being golden, too, but in truth they looked like escapees from the shoe polish factory. Even the younger girls walking the busy sidewalk seemed to be commited to a life of tan, and but for the near undectable thin strings of their thong pieces showing upon their toasty skins they looked as indecent as the kids running free back at Cardiff.

Yes, to the dismay of a shell shocked Beatense they wore their thongs right on the sidewalk. Many were topless or nude. And not just the girls were so hot blasted tan. One shining slim hero at Beatense's age was neatsfoot buffed black. He was the most astonishing sight for her so far in this particular hundred feet of street.

Plus he had muscle. His faded jean cut-offs were cuffed up to bare every inch of his long, starchy dark thighs, and riding loosely low to his light hips, they publically let half his butt show. Beatense felt stupefied, besides Neatsfoot she saw more young athlete women in ever greater numbers, who flashed with a fierce heat.

They were brilliantly perfected with the three **Ls: L**ong, **L**ean and **L**anky. All of them had confident, strong white teeth and confident, strong brown faces.

The bus went on and stopped for the light at Smoot Street.

"Okay, this is it, Beatense. There's old Hoggy. When the light hits green I'll pull ahead and stop. We have to hurry, we'll be blocking the street."

Her heart leaped. She spotted the Hoganforth. It was a couple buildings in from the Highway, at the end of the half block of Smoot that ended at a cement ledge. Beachers were walking, running and biking along what, per her map, had to be the Beachway Walk, as edged along by that ledge wall. Edged from what? The *beach!!* People were in motion, near and far, beyond the wall too.

Kathy nudged ahead and stopped. Beatense slung on her backpack, hiding her nips again, and giving Canterbury and Bobby a jittery smile, followed Kathy out. Bobby made a quick decision, called goodbye to skin-only Smoky and he got off also.

"Bobby, what are you doing?" said Kathy. "I said we have to hurry!"

"There's still good sun. I'm running home from here."

"No, go back in and make friends with Smoky. I want her in the family."

"Me too," said Beatense. Bobby laughed, but she did Geddy, Soler and Rosa.

His tan was intensified in the deep sun. With his slim waist and barbell chest he was a tall up-thrusted burst of boy. His cut-offs were cuffed up to hold snugly to his stretched thighs, while the belt loop band sagged down in rumpled looseness, baring a brave curve of split. Like Neatsfoot's, and mine. Canty got off the bus too.

Bobby high-fived her and Beatense, then loped off in reaching strides as the hot sun lashed at his brown back and long legs. Beatense gazed after the sunbeam in springing flight. Like Craig the other dudes going by were too adulty to interest her; she had an instinct for slight thin. But the guys were definitely interested in her, and they noticed just-skin Canty with a jolt, followed with appreciative laughter.

"Look, I gotta go," said Kathy. "Canty, get back in." She offered a business card. "If you get down to Tucumzozo, look us up! Or call if you need a limo."

Beatense, regretting her tight but prude jeans, took the card. They shook hands and the girl started for her hostel as the bus rolled on. Her long journey had come to an end, and for the first time in three days she could finally stay put, if they had her booking, that is. She had grave doubts. But the ocean beach, straight ahead!

What excitement! The air was alive, and her Nywot worked tan fit her right in!

The beach was indeed just over that low ledge. Beatense walked by the hostel toward, it and she jostled through the walkers, runners, bikers and skaters thronging the Beachway. She felt like weeping, the sight before her was too glorious to bear. Just like back at Cardiff, the mighty surf rolled in and burst into airy foam, but the sea here lay just two hundred feet away. Ranging to the north and south were lifeguard towers, and from the closest one the PA blared out.

"Hey, you swimmers by the flag! That's a rip tide area! Stay close in!"

A military helicopter flew by. *Dut-dut-dut-dut-dut-dut...* It was then followed by an airplane pulling a huge fluttering banner advertising Balboa lager beer. A policeman rode an ATV across the sand, that was scattered with tanners on towels and runners on adrenalin. Others were grouped in conversation or playing catch. Yes, glorious.

"I want to move here," said Beatense, as the tropical energies infused her.

14

HOGAN FORTH

I want to move here," Beatense repeated. "This… All my life… Finally."

She recalled Craig's talk about finding a little studio crammed in with dozens of others, and this was the place for that. She looked south, down a long line of motels, condominiums, houses, cantinas and various shops that were ranged along the busy Beachway. And apartment buildings. Dozens of palm trees fluttered in the warm sea breezes, and along the walk there was a steady parade of walkers, runners, skaters and skateboarders. Beatense saw four frail girls in tans only walk unaffectedly by.

So right there in public she got off her jeans, and she dug out her crochet and tied it on. *Ah, justice!* She held her backpack under her arm. Right away she got looks.

Out on the hardpan sand a teenage girl slowly rode her bike. She was a local, knowing that one could ride the wetpack. She held a little foot out and gazed in open worship upon her slim leg. Beatense knew the feeling. She sat and swung her legs over the ledge and standing against it she let the late afternoon sun scorch into her.

In spite of the urgency of checking in she got in a good belly bake hour. People walking by slowed to ogle or just stopped. The sea-gazing girl ignored them.

The gouged and scratched wooden door that matched the green painted cement block building in terms of degraded condition, had a curious push button combination locking device. Backpack under her arm, in patch, Beatense was ready to push the bell, but just then a fellow happened to come out. His mouth worked in horror.

"Uh… Uh… Y-You want in?" He turned. "Hey, Z-Zapo! A new guest!"

"Yeah, yeah! Stuff it, Webster! Send him to the office!"

Beatense stepped nervously in. There were several guys and girls sitting at the two picnic tables in this main area, and they all turned to look at her, but in a friendly way. In fact she was an unexpected upgrade to this dumpy dive. A fellow gestured with his thumb over toward the half-door set in the wall that was covered with fading posters. The girl crossed over to it under the jungle hut roof of dried reed matting.

A fellow was at the computer in this closet sized space.

"Hi, er, excuse me, I think I have a reservation here. I hope."

He shook. He was just getting used to tan million dollar girls. No, not quite. HP shit! All that hair, and one of the tannest starvelings he ever saw! The Book Girl!

"W-Well, let's see if... If we do. I know who you are, but your name?"

"Beatense Col..."

"Yup, the Book Girl! I set up your reservation! I'm Zapo! You're all set! We got you in a twelve bunker, if that's okay. Hey, Vitty, Beatense is here! She made it!"

"I'm in the laundry," came a distant, harried voice. "Welcome, Bookie!"

Zapo stepped out and led Beatense to the stairs by the entry door, where a tiny kitchen branched off. They climbed to a walkway, that gave a scenic view of the lobby room roof, and the sand and ocean beyond. Towels were hung to dry on the railing, fluttering in the hot wind. They entered the bunkroom, and three nude girls, who met the three **B** and **L** check list for finer living, and who ranged in tan from dark to just criminal, and also were slight in that meal disciplined way that gives the looks strong force, smiled at Beatense. They were rubbing their heated skins with coconut cream lotion (per the label) after their beachy day, as four guys watched from their bunks.

"Er, hi. So, this... Er, Zapo, is this a sex room?" said Beatense. "Because I'm extremely interested in attracting and indulging in conjugal relations."

"Us too!" one of the athletically bony girls answered. "Preferably all night!"

A shaking Zapo showed Beatense her bunk, a lower one. The messy beds were heaped with tangled up clothes and towels, with shampoo and toothpaste and other toiletries tossed into the clutter. There was a half opened dirty window, the sun gave the dust a bright glow. A breeze filtered in and shook the faded café curtains.

Beatense tossed her backpack onto her bunk, as the guys watched warily. That electric tan, and tensioned belly and waist meant bitch. And dark tan girls often had that stern look, as if they couldn't justify the time and suffering effort put in.

But this one was cute. Impish. And all that hair... The Book Girl! Smiling!

This interplay took two-tenths of a second. "Hey, dudes," Beatense said, seeing their interest. "Sorry I blurted that out about sex, but it and tan are ever on my mind."

"Well, your mind has two nights, miss," said Zapo as he left, still shaking.

The sticks introduced themselves as Afton, Bedbug and Scabby, and Beatense shook hands. She bumped fists with the guys, as learned at camp. A fourth girl, a plain nonentity she had overlooked, had obvious suspicion.

"Hey, Molly, plus you sweathogs, I'm Beatense. Let's go swimming!"

"How... How did you know my name?"

"Easy, I saw your name in the diagram for this room. Joining us?"

"I don't think so. I can't compete, so I don't fit in out on the beach."

Beatense was just in her patch. "Come on, or I'll drag you. So let's go!"

The guys looked at Molly in entreaty, as if her refusal would derail the jaunt. She was never that interesting before, and uneasily got up from her bed. The guys quick changed and the three girls tied on their strips. They ran down the steps and chased out the door. They vaulted the low ledge wall and ran across the sand and splashed in for a surf tossed romp of grabbing, screaming and running crazily to and fro.

Beatense jumped up onto Molly's back and they all began chicken fighting. Others joined in the noisy riot. Tired out at last they stumbled ashore. Heading back to the ledge Beatense held Molly's hand in friendship, the two widely smiling.

"Okay, let's hike the Beachway, everyone! I'm new here, give me a tour!"

Their noisy party included Molly, four topless girls, and at least for the present the four bunkroom guys. As a camp and campus savage Beatense nee Puppet walked along breast bared, even as people bumped into each other staring at this annealed bodybuilder with all that hair. They headed south, slowed by the others present.

After fifty yards Beatense said, "Wait here! I gotta get some money!"

She ran back and rounded the corner to the Hogan front door. Oops, she didn't know the combination. She knocked and a young woman in her late 20s opened the door. "Oh! You're Beatense! I'm Viturna, my last name, actually. Nice to have you, even with that shitty tan. Where are the others?" The shitty girl stepped in.

"Waiting for me! Nice to meet you, Viturna I'm just here to get money, to buy some blade skates. I'm told nudity is allowed here? I appreciate the lenient policy!"

"I gave up on enforcing decency. Hey, Zapo! Check on that pizza!"

"I did! The Breeze is hosting a poolside pizza party so it will be awhile."

It was explained to Beatense that pizza would be served, at $3 each.

As a near nude she hopped up the stairs and dug out $1000. She quickly rubbed on lard oil, to give a new zest back to her surf fresh tan. She flashed back down and ran to rejoin her friends who were in wait sitting on the ledge. Looking out toward the surf she saw volleyball games in progress, with others nude sports in active display. *Stupidly they picked me for the Book Girl! Look at that!* The girls and guys at play were less interested in their winning points than publicizing their splendid health.

Calvin whistled at Beatense's beautiful polishing of oil. But in a way Molly was a better pick, and despite her being pudgy and pale she was having fun conversations.

"Yeah! Those waves kept knocking me down! Then she's on my back!"

The party shuffled on. Beatense's heart pounded, she was born to commanding display, and here she was in a mob of hundreds. But many college age women and teen girls young or older were carelessly nude. One small slimmed mother of horrific tan majesty, navigating her stroller and toddler, did modestly wear a tape strip.

Good idea, Beatense thought. There was a carnival-like atmosphere. Beatense was excited to see many open-air bars and cantinas along the sidewalk, and most shops were also open fronted. It was fun to see casual nudes as customers in these places, and they seemed to have zero self conscious concern for their state, while old people stared their morality distress. And the still hot sun baked in, giving a dizzying effect to everyone. Despite her Transfer session Beatense especially felt this.

She untied naked. Walking this crowd she felt a joy of liberation. With the blood quality of her tan, lines and face Beatense attracted pained interest. Shaking guys stumbled backwards taking CVids, all headed for the NetField, also called Old Netty. As closely watched, she hopped atop the ledge and walked along it. Upon coming to someone in the way she did a gymnastics class handstand-flip off.

And along the Beachway superior girls and boys of the teen and pre-teen years walked, rode their bikes or ran. From their free, beachy lives of hot sun they were all so proudly browned they glowed, and matched the oil camp kids. Playful nights.

But most of the people on the walk were just hated tourists, with no life changers among them. Even the studio apartment dwellers sitting out were very average. And of course the elderlies. But still there was a festive air that only the sea can bring. Beatense looked into the busy stores, cabanas and bar patios, that were open to full view. The guys in their group and Molly, worn out by the dynamic energy that Afton, Scabby, Beatense and Bedbug radiated, entered a patio deck for a bottle or two.

Except, on a padded bench a skeletal, yelling tan nude was getting a massage.

Beatense had trouble too. A shock brown, thong-bare blade skater racing along twirled to a halt. Scoping out the Book Girl the regally skinny teen rolled backwards. He had a clear washed complexion, and he was agleam with towel rubbed butter oil.

"He beats you, hah, Beatense?" said Bedbug, laughing at her expression.

"I think... I think I know him! But who ever, I need skates exactly like his."

The boy skated off as people stared. Scabby watched. *I better get it tonight.*

"He was wearing no more than a handprint," Beatense said, still puzzled.

Her friends laughed as they continued jostling through the crowd. A patrolman rode by on his ATV; he gave Beatense a nod. Widely smiling, she was enthralled by this wonderful new world. Here sunny freedom ruled by day and night. Dozens of bikes kept going by, and skateboards and blade skates. Girls ran by in thongs, or no thongs. Like the guys many of these steely, athletic women carried surfboards.

Younger kids too, many sculpted with inspiring muscle. In answer to Beatense Afton explained that surfing could be very strenuous, but they also worked weights.

Like the camp kids, Beatense thought, living for sun and fuck. And why not?

The party went by a line of vacation condos, with motels tucked in. Palm shaded sidewalks branched off the Beachway, leading the one block distance to the Coastal road. These were lined with jammed-in houses and studio efficiencies. Loud music was in the air here, and the palm fluttering warm winds also fluttered their curtains.

They came to a beach gear filled surf hut and went in. With much good advice and after almost falling down as she tried them on, Beatense bought a $400 pair of blade skates. She also selected a $75 pint of professional sun speeding oil.

The girl also studied the skateboards. She belatedly asserted her discount rights but just got a neck hung key-tube and a roll of modesty tape. They headed back and got Choco Delite cones at a squeezed-in snack stand. Struggling to carry her blade skates, Beatense worked on her Big Stupe. The four girls conspicuously entered the lodge only to see that a stack of pizza boxes was just being delivered.

In minutes the main room was full of hostel guests. Beatense paid the tab, with a tip equal to one of her cheaper ads, so it was a free treat for everybody. The Stupe already filled her, but she ate three wedges just to get to know this friendly crowd, even as she kept her back arched in flexing out her proud peachy breasts.

Beatense, Afton, Scabby, Bedbug and Molly refilled their poly cups with pop and went out to the patio deck to watch the Beachway. Beatense, still unaffectedly nude, talked and laughed with her friends. Later a keg appeared on that same deck.

With music playing, and bathed by the floodlights, Beatense put her camp dance skills to work, whipping her whippy waist with her arms raised and breasts lifted. Far beyond the walkway's continuing parade and darkened sand the white surf rolled in.

Beatense later danced with the latest guest, an older guy with thin muscled lines, whose butt-cuts and high effort tan were out of sync with a normal bloke's attitudes, especially at his indefinite adult age. That pushy show off, me 2007, but no dancing, slept alone. Elgin, not. Beatense led him to bed, and he shot sparks into her craving nerves. She then fought Gibbs, Daniel and Erven, and finally wrestled with Molly.

15

MONDAY

Beatense excitedly awoke at her usual 5:30, thinking of calling her father. She got up, leaving Molly to her slumbers. That Bitsy was right, this was the place for a reset. And it was so joyously antithetical to moral standards. She delighted in being really evil, but that playful fun didn't seem real bad. She didn't know that a third book was planned, and the selected amateur photos from the bus ride on would give her a future $90,000 advance. They anticipated that these Netty postings would raise her first title sales, delaying other publications. They decided on $8 a copy, retroactive.

Unaware of her far greater wealth Beatense went into the moldy, filthy bathroom and quick washed. The air was cold but she went downstairs freshly bared and ran over to the office half-door. She expected to find Zapo, but it was another staffer.

"Hi, Hawk," she said to the abruptly wide eyed attendant. "Got a phone?"

"Y-Yeah, b-but, er, heh heh, you're… You're up this early?"

She rested her light forearms on the door ledge. "Yes, but why do you ask?"

"It's just that y-you had a real work-outs last… Last… All night."

"Well, dancing and fucking, if you call *them* work-outs." She took the phone and dialed, and there came a faint ring. "Hey, Pop, I'm here! Hot sex already!"

"Well good, darter, you gots that outta yer system now so git on home!"

"It's not out of my system yet. I'm just starting. But congratulate me."

"I tain't corngratutating no girl who ain't here doing some honest work!"

The arguing continued then the girl hit End Call smiling, wiping a tear. "Thanks, Hawk. He lets me do anything I want. But hey, is it cloudy out there?"

"Oh, th-that's just the morning fog. It'll… It'll b-burn off."

"Foggy! Good, it will hide me for a nice naked run. Thanks again, Hawk."

He tried to sit down but half missed the chair and fell on the floor. But Beatense was already pounding up the stairs. Afton was up, they quick hugged.

"Hey, kid. Up already? All that dancing and then you yelled half the night."

"Did I? But yeah, I'm going for a run. Where are my shoes in this mess?"

"Don't be gone long. We have to get skating before the tourists come out. But I better ask, were you protected last night? That Elgin guy got you pretty intense."

"Yeah, I wonder how old he is. But I had an implant since turning thirteen, so I'm good. But it's funny how that little thing in my arm obliterates all doubts in doing it!"

"Who has doubts? Why not make a beautiful life even more beautiful?"

She felt weepy, beautiful she was, she would bake tan all day, then more fuck.

"But hey, I gotta find my shoes. They cost $800 but won me medals. I gotta run while it's still foggy so I can fly nude, even though my cussed hide will beacon me!"

"You can run nude anyway, Beatense. Even over along the Highway. No cute and beaten brown bony bodyists like us should be denied reasonable freedom."

"Berry brew, especially sex. But I still want the fog to hide me. But did you get a chance with that Elgin, Afton? It's okay for girls to just bake, but with guys it's iffy. I mean those are all day lay-outs you see with him. Just super brown."

"No shit. I mean, shit yeah. He might be an odd duck but we did one hour!"

Minutes later, with a smirky smile of being bravely bad, Beatense flew off north instead of the slightly more familiar south. She wasn't hidden like she hoped; in fact her dark tan did cut the fog so she was seen coming. But the fee expecting cameras were stymied; the skinny shaft of muscle was just a fast moving blackety blur.

The walkway in this direction turned into a long lawn and palm edged plaza that was bordered with motels and restaurants to the right, and the gloomy beach to the left. Flitting along, bare Beatense saw several surfers miserably wait with their boards.

The plaza narrowed down to run along the front of the Breeze Hotel's swimming pool, and continuing through here the girl sprang on at a 50 yard dash extension and came to the fenced in skateboard park, then a wide picnic area. The beach walkway finally ended at the great wooded bluff Beatense saw from the bus, Holiday Hill.

Her map showed it as home to little cabins connected by winding one-laners.

As she returned southward the fog lifted enough for her to see the Cliff Diving Rock, two hundred yards out to sea. Its lofty peak caught the first of the sun's rays burning in. The girl saw the lifeguards trudge out to their towers. As she got toward the lodge, all wet glaze shined, the butt-cuts bared, sick overkill Elgin, (not me, didn't run there) coming up from the south looked the same. Embarrassed greetings.

The sun was shaking off its mood; a hot day on its way. Both sunbather hearts pounded as Beatense fiddled with the combination and burst into the building. A few fellows at one of the picnic tables gave her, then obnoxious Elgin, a startled look.

"Hey, guys. What are you... Oh, toast? Where did you get it?"

Hawk came over to her with a rolled up piece of paper.

"You're all over old Netty," he said, showing the spread. "Take a look."

"Well, I better get used to this. Where did you get this?"

"I just printed it out now. But yeah, the toaster is in the kitchen there."

"No toast yet," said Afton, coming down the stairs with her skates. "Blading first. You too, Beasty. Hop up and get your skates. Elgin, I saw you had skates."

"Okay, but check out these pictures, Afton. I can't complain, they show me way dark. I hope they get you today, Elgin. Your tan, I could either laugh or cry!"

The deluged yellow butt-cuts Elgin went up and returned with his skates, and the very average other guys made that grim he-must-be-gay smile. What irked them was he was more youthful at his age than they were. In 2007 I was reaching sixty, but I baked in sun every day, and wore my butt-cuts to proclaim my suspect obsession.

"Hey Elgin," said Beatense. "You are skating with us deathly pale bitches?"

He looked. This girl was unreal. "Yeah. Running I saw good pavement south."

Others came into the room, some leaving with backpacks strapped on. Beatense said goodbye to them, having partied and danced with them the last night.

Generous kid. She ran up to get her skates, and rousted out Scabs and Beddy. Elgin and the bare girls took their skates outside to the ledge by the beachway.

As the surf worked far back of them they buckled them on. Beatense saw that in this misty golden light she, and the yellow shorts Elgin, looked ruste deep dark. She stood, wildly lurching, and grabbed onto a signpost as sore exercised belly reacted.

"What is it with these things? I've been on skates all my life!"

"You have Class 7 bearings," said Bedbug. "Be really careful at first."

"Gee, thanks for the tip. These things are mur... Agh! Murder!"

At this early hour the beachway was already busy, but these people were sports minded locals, not tourists getting in the way. Out upon the beach tractors groomed the sand, and a trash truck came along and workers emptied the barrels.

They took off southward, and Beatense's thin arms waved erratically as she fought for balance. The sun coming between the buildings gave her bare tan a soap filmed richness, so the athletic locals were tolerant of her poor form. The other four skated with a practiced but still edgy skill. Rusted also, I skated shirtless at times.

Beatense's sloppy style and the bearings distracted her from the fun of this ride, but by the time they reached the shop where she bought her skates she was cruising with confident power. Her belly visibly strained with the effort, and her thigh muscles writhed like snakes. The other four too. Their vibrato deluges abused hundreds.

Included were the early rising elderly misfits, who smiled in sad defeat at these obscene sexuals all along the walk. Naked Beatense delighted in upsetting them. It was better than that camp riot, because that just lasted two hours. Here, all day.

The Beachway ran past cantinas, now sadly closed, tucked in cottages, lodgings and swim shops. A coffee shop did have disconsolate customers sitting out on dirty plastic chairs. The beach was still being groomed, and several people were walking their dogs along the surf. On the path itself the Hogan five raced by the college aged locals, who were running, walking, skating or biking. Some carried surfboards.

Miles south the walkway ended at the Windemere residential street, consisting of crammed in private homes and more studio apartments. Beatense spotted For Rent signs as the five skated along here, but at the time there was the difficulty of broken pavement. They turned back anyway with some urgency; the sun was calling.

Also per Afton's warning the tourists began to emerge from the hotels, motels or rental condos, and their presence cluttered things up for the locals.

The visitors didn't understand the path and its "rules" so they just got in the way. They put on hopeful faces as they bumbled along in their vacation shirts, while their wandering was too unpredictable for blade skating, because of its chancy nature. But the butt-cut one and nude four blazed by them as they rewound the sights in reverse.

They took off their skates and went back into the lodge. By now the picnic tables had a dozen toast eaters, and Scab was volunteered to make some for the other four as they sat in wait. Zapo wasn't on yet but he lived on site, and during the party last night Beatense had told him she was looking for a studio. And so now he came over with a Greg's List print-out. The rents started at a shocking $1200 for the off-beach studios and got up to 2500 for on-beach. *Good luck, Craig.* In 2008 I paid eight.

"Yes, thanks," she said, looking at the listings. "This will really... Help."

Her tuned health troubled those watching her. Zapo's photo set was respectfully handed around, also was troubling. Ched, who was one of Beatense's bedmates, joined the group, rubbing his eyes. The two looked at each other with nods. Beatense sensed he regretted it. But she had been far too aggressive, a fucking machine, and she looked just sixteen. The only proof she wasn't a kid was the Lodge's minimum age of eighteen. On the other hand it turned out that athlete Elgin was pushing forty.

That didn't concern Beatense. "We're getting sun later, Elgin. Wanna join us?"

"Okay, but I'm warning you, I don't socialize. I'm in full concentration."

"Looking at me, how do you think I handle it? I totally zonk out."

"Where is that toast?" said a perturbed Bedbug. "Scabby, hurry!"

"Yeah, others need the toasters too!" Viturna added.

"I'm more worried about missing out on sun," said Bedbug.

Beatense and Elgin nodded to each other. This would work.

Scabby came out with the toast. "Here's a whole stack, everyone!"

Beatense felt funny sitting with everyone in tan only. Just for the memories, they said, photos were taken of the group, and with her slouching back curved and belly sunk right at the end of the table, taking her was dream easy. She looked right at the cameras, despite knowing that she would be all over the NetField again.

Bedbug was called that because she was quite active, last night too. As they got ready for the beach she gave Beatense a couple brass ring bracelets to clash accent her tan. The girl put them on and they clinked together. Metallically ringing, back down in the common room she slucked herself to a dripping wet shine with her $75 oil, and with care she also slupped it into her split. Everyone gasped at this breach.

"Beatense, we don't do that," said Viturna, beginning to count the hours.

"It's just that I feel sore there, juicing it all night. I'm wasted all over, and my abs ache, all that deep effort. My waist is way sore too, all my twisting as I got in orbit."

The way she just said it. Molly came down the stairs. "Twisting! You were wild! But I got burned yesterday. Not real bad, but enough where I have to be careful."

"If you put on some sunblock you can still join us laying out," said Afton.

"Say, I better not. I, er, don't have any sunblock."

"No prob," said Viturna. "There's left-behind tubes on the bathroom shelf."

"Check the dates," said Scabby. "Some of that stuff is older than I am."

Beatense ran up and found a crumpled partly full tube, ending that as an excuse for Molly to avoid the beach. But the way Beatense took those steps flattered her.

Beatense was working her blackety baseball breasts with the wet oil. "Molly, just give us a couple hours. No, three hours. That will make noon. Okay, I'm ready."

Everyone was starting to loathe her. Her eighteen inch waist didn't help. It was her lapse that she was irritatingly too perfect and too ravenously self worshipping. In fact she went over to the dirty full length mirror between two posters and stared.

"You ARE going to the beach?" said Viturna, now counting the minutes.

The girl laughed. "Well, duh!" The five girls, and Elgin, felt the heat hit them as they went outside and went through the gap in the cement ledge onto the sand.

"I hope the author can get you out of this pickle, Beatense," said Afton.

"What author? What pickle?" --/-- "Your oiling up all naked like that. You better tone it down. And you don't have to fuck everyone to make friends."

"Well if I oiled up upstairs they would still see it downstairs. And I didn't fuck that much, just Elgin and those three other guys. But yes, I will Ease... Up."

"No," said Elgin. "Did I ride in that Harvest Day parade just in my shorts? No, stupidly I eased up. Except, always at the stable after a hot day's ride I was royalty."

Slight, nude and wicked brown, Beatense's heart pounded. "Me exactly!"

"Here's a good spot," said Afton, rolling up her eyes. "Right in the crowd."

"What crowd?" said Beatense, looking away from the tumbling white roar.

"Oh, it will fill in. We will be surrounded by hundreds, by noon."

"They will all wonder why you have me along," said Molly. "Me so white."

"We need you for contrast!" said Beatense. "Like Elgin's yellow shorts! But why don't we go to Cocojo?" the girl continued, lying upon her front and watching the surf fifty feet away, then eyeing her arms. "Actually that's why I came here."

"Too far, and you got that Sorel in the way," said Afton. "The deal is, you got two social levels, the takers and makers. We're the takers. We lay in the sun all day, we dance half the night, then fuck. Hip parents like their young daughters following our example. There are actually twelve and up disco bars. But the makers, they hate us and our pleasure, so they go to Sorel to escape us and their shitty factories, garages and oil fields. You go there with that volcanic tan, Bookie, you'll need life insurance. They can handle their lives if they're not reminded of our easy, fun, beautiful lives."

"You're talking about my hometown! Drab and grim but they love my antics."

"Don't worry about any dislike of you at the Lodge, Beatense" Scabby said. "With the turn-over they have, except for us everyone will be gone tomorrow."

"I get the same static," said Elgin. "All kinds of reactions. If you're a golfer or a hunter no one knows it unless you bring it up, and those are socially legit. But being a tanner there's no hiding it, obviously, and for a guy to lay out all day is a little iffy."

"Not with your results," said Beatense. Up on her elbows she looked around and saw the grand panorama of buildings they walked by yesterday and skated by today. Palm trees waved in the hot, stiff winds. The walkway was busy with skaters, bikers, runners and walkers. The air was bright and crisp, and screaming kids were heard over the surf's muffled roar. The sensual girl decided to hit her front first and turned over with legs out vulgarly wide, and settled into a good bake with eyes closed.

Her friends noted her sunken belly, and protruding eleven inch wide hips.

Beatense had angled her towel so the sun would sweep both sides evenly as the three hours went by. She felt a rich healing burn from the tropical intensity, so even with her public nudity she felt safely relaxed. She squirmed with excitement as the loving, basting rays roasted her, in her deepest tanning experience since... Nywot.

By eleven the beach was mobbed, and the girls were surrounded. At noon Molly left, and everyone but Elgin ran to the water. They played in the surf, and later when the others went back to their day's work, Beatense walked the shore bared to let the hot wind dry her persisting oil shine. Even the pale pudges watched approvingly.

Beatense encountered several guys and she exchanged laughing remarks with them, as they hugely pretended to see nothing amiss. She returned to her towel and set it for the afternoon sweep. Renewing her hot oil shine she lay on her front to tan her back. This side too would bake fast, hot and dark. Her friends noted that her backside exposure seemed to stretch her waist, giving it even tighter tensions.

People walking by diverted their paths closer. Photos and UVids were taken.

"Well here's a kid who's in the naturist set," said Bedbug. "Check it out."

It took all of Beatense's control to show minimal reaction, but in fact she felt as if she was slammed againt the wall. This was the problem with Xanthallado, she was now on the receiving end, unlike back home where she alone ruled.

He was a slender youth of late teens, just in saggy jean cut-offs whose four inch top to bottom hip wrap bared an extremely deep, unnatural tan. The lad was golden shined real dark brown by the hot sun, and perfectly muscled. His jean cut-offs had their cuffs pulled up tightly snug to his long runner thighs, and like mine the belt loops rumply sagged to publically bare half his butt. County roads, rode my bike like that.

His intelligent cheek points placed his dreamy blue eyes wide apart, while making his low chin look ever so delicate. Completing the enchantment, he had long, silken blond hair that fell in scruffy, unkempt thick shags. He eyed the sun and laid out his towel, just over from Beatense and party. He lay on his back; she was pop-eyed.

Her turmoil only increased as the slim waisted angelic gave a furtively guilty look from right to left, and he hitched his hips up and slipped off his shorts.

The very thin boy lay upon his front legally naked, but still it was disturbing.

"How... How c-can he d-do that?" Beatense rasped, in rigid shock.

"Oh, like everybody else here, you mean?" said Afton. "But he is a jolt."

"Hey, you sun-phobic kid there, come on over by us!" Scabby called.

He raised his head smiling with delight. He got up using his towel to conceal his proud eight inches, and his long baked legs stepped him over and he re-established himself. Beatense gazed upon the starchy salt-shine of his back, and stretched legs. His also-stretchy waist was quite as narrowed as her own.

"I'm Keter, thanks for asking me over. Boy, are you ever tan! I get that way in the Geode Desert. My family, we camp there, and I just slam real dark."

"Yeah," said Beatense. "As another plot-changing coincidence, I was also out there in that desert. Surveying camp. But you might know this teen kid we saw on roller blades yesterday, desert dark also. Thin muscled. Disapproving blue eyes."

"Taylor. He and his older brother Dyno, the tourists all fear those two."

"I get feared too," said Elgin. "Like this prairie campground? I'm disgusting."

That Taylor looks like Slat! "Keter, I want to see that older brother!"

"Oh I think he's off catalog modeling. Swimwear. Now who are you all?"

They told their names. Keter said, "Being on this part of the beach, you must be Hogies. Me, I'm local. My family and I live on Moneta two blocks in."

"You must make those two blocks a lot," said Afton dryly. "No job at all?"

"I do ice cream at Once Upon A Chocolate, up the Coastal Highway by Barnett. Evenings. Hey, don't buy any ice cream along the Beachway, it's pure junk."

"Too late," said Scabby. "We might stop by this evening, for comparing."

"I might do a little comparing myself," said Beatense cryptically, noting the boy's obvious nude habit. "But what's your age? You don't seem that old."

"I will be a sophomore in high school but I'm also taking morning classes at the community college. I'm doing the ice cream as my summer job. Weekends it's all tourists. Last week I was late from the beach so I showed up in just my cut-offs. Mr. Worth wasn't there so I just worked that way. Estee and Lorelle, being tanners too, changed to their bikini tops. The fluorescents made us look unreal. Later Mr. Worth found out. He wasn't mad, he said we had a massive take that night, but the codes require shirts. He said he would try and get a variance."

"Boy, I would quit if I was lectured like that," said Beatense, half panting.

"Cut-offs," said Bedbug. "You should try a boy bikini, Keter."

"I sail in my boy bikini," said Elgin. "But once I didn't, even hiking out. But my biggest triumph was sailing across the lake and landing at this park beach where my singles club was having a picnic. The women raved at how brown I was."

"Wait a minute," said Afton. "Lake? Singles club? There's some déjà vu here."

Viturna came over the sand towards them, wearing relatively modest tie pieces. She was thin in that classic, light framed way that either told of driven athletics or the wasting of a continuing frugal diet. She was tan, or perhaps her tint came from blood heritage, or both together. Her active face told of sad trials long ago, but there was also that wise expectation of defeating life's future hazards.

"Hi! Mind if I join you? Oh, am I interrupting anything?"

"Keter and I were just going to initiate," joked Beatense, rubbing the boy.

"Oh, Scab, we found a $10 bill on your bed. It's in the office."

"Thanks. Appreciate the honesty. Bea… Beatense, will ya lay off!?"

The named girl was still rubbing the flowing curves of Keter's back.

"Can he stay with me tonight, Viturna? We will need just one bed."

"I would let you two take a private room if we had any left. Sorry."

Viturna lay out on her towel, deciding that her earlier Beatense misgivings were unfounded. But her wanting to bed an obvious teen-ager was odd.

The party fell silent in rays commitment. Two hours later Keter stood and pulled his cut-offs back on. He snugged their cuffs high to his thighs, then let the belt loops sag, badly. He said good-bye to everyone and radiantly headed across the sand.

"I regret having that sex with Ched," said Beatense. "Now that I saw Keter."

She decided to do the Beach Walk bare and alone. She buffed in a deep coat of her expensive oil, giving her tan a fresh deep intensity, and as she told of her plan her friends wished her luck. The girl walked south, past the swimmers and sunners. But after a hundred feet she cut across the populated sands toward the walkway.

Heart pounding the girl jostled into the crowd, glistening wet nude and alien dark. Any electric agony she caused was subdued, but from the corner of her eye she did see guys nudge each other. Anyway, they were used to the confident naturists who were proudly notorious for wearing brown only, even in inappropriate situations. So Beatense inflicted herself undisturbed, her nips leading the way.

Just how brave was she? Heading south she stepped up to a raised beach club deck and asked for bottled Red Duck at the bar. She was given it despite obviously having a lack of funds. She went back to the fence, and leaning on it watched the hordes go by. Even happy pre-teen girls were nudies.

"Good to see kids free like that," she said to the shaking fellow who stepped over to her. "They're not stupid. They can make those decisions. I sure did."

"Looks... Looks like you m-made that d-decision a lot."

"Starting age twelve. That and an even bigger step, if you can guess it. But why don't you go and pay for this beer for me? I'll wait."

He returned and Beatense was sitting on a stool leaning against its back so that she got full frontal sun. "Oh, hey, thanks! You brought another one. The last time I was nude in a bar setting, I was with my father at Toodles. It was a joy. He always let me do whatever I wanted, even sex. He knows how important it is to me."

"Do... Do I see possibilities here?"

"Well of course, idiot. Come over to the hostel tonight. Ask for Bookie."

"Wait, there's gotta be a catch. I'm Roke. And you're..."

"Bookie, I said." She tossed the`bottle into a trash barrel 20 feet away.

"Hey, that was recycleable!" --/-- "Color too close a match. Okay, bye."

The girl went on, again noting the sights. Along with the surf shops, walk-in bars were spaced along, and open air cantinas. Tiny private homes were in abundance, many of which had small patios enclosed with low brick walls.

The fabulous larger houses had glowing tinted windows and balconies with stylish chrome railings, and their stucco facades of pastel hues gave a striking effect. There were also condominium rentals and five star motels that went for $5000 a week.

The sidewalks leading over to the Coastal Highway from the Beach Walk were arched over with tropical foliage. As seen before these inviting little by-ways were jammed with more homes, and studio buildings. As Beatense walked along, in her preoccupied state she forgot she was sweat naked. This is as it should be, where an ethereal can go free with so little self awareness it's second nature.

Beatense went another mile south and turned back, still noting each detail, and finally returned to the Hogan thrilled with her exploration. Many of the beach girls she saw were brilliantly tan and thin, with pride, spirit, character and pedigree. But these were bred-in credentials; it was how they handled them that mattered.

What this visitor didn't know was that these women faced a fierce environment, where they had to be exemplary as students in training for the careers they had to have, often squeezing in part-time jobs with their schooling, while keeping up their all important bed and beach images. Then, once hired, the pressure was worse.

Beatense entered the Hog with her usual strife, and found that Elgin and Molly had left. In tie-pieces she, Afton, Scabs and Bugs walked the Highway to a tropic tunnel that led to a beach-side hamburger joint. Next they saw Keter at Once Upon. Back at the Hoggy Roke was waiting, and the white-shirted (only) Beatense and friends went with him to the surfer hang-out Sails West. She danced bare, and later took Roke on. Hawk kindly waited to kick him out. She then got in bed with the new guest Mort.

16

TUESDAY

Early next morning Beatense awoke in her *own bed* with a leap of heart. This was especially true in summer when she felt truly alive. And now in this magical land she could indulge in the public display she craved, and sex, with no limitations. Like now. She slipped from her bed and went into the bathroom.

Because of the early hour everyone still slept, so the girl had the gungy sink and sewer tub to herself. Stepping from the tub she studied the smudgy cracked mirror, marveling at how quintessentially black her shower-wetted tan shined. Probably this was how the girls here could get away with going nude; like her own their attentively worked tans had artistic aesthetics, giving a soothing appeal even for those olds.

As Beatense perused her ratty and disheveled hair she did wonder if there was some consequence. Her life couldn't be this perfect without penalties of some kind, a "Now we got you" payback. But no, it's the homely prims who fail, while the tanning, barbelling, dancing and fucking girls live a dream. For example, last night Beatense saw Roke off, then back in the room Dal entertained her after his initial surprise.

There is the consolation for the drab, that in time the useless twits will age and circle the drain and get ejected from the popular whirl like so much junk, while they, with patience, will come out looking pretty good after all. Because, with old age thin turns to shrivel and tan turns to sag. I just have to wait, Doris Schpluk says to herself hopefully, horrified by all the smiling, skinny brown nudes all around this hostel dive.

After a careful study of herself in the mirror, followed by slopping on her costly professional oil, Beatense tied on her shoes and sprang down the stairs, only to find sitting apart from the few others at the picnic tables at this gloomy hour, a nondescript girl, plainer than Molly. The mentioned Doris Schpluk.

Beatense stood just opposite her with one foot parked up on the end of the bench, opening her moist split.

"Hey, welcome to the Temple of Doom! Did you just get here?"

The girl was surprised by this eager attention from this quivering animal, but this casual display of hers was an unwelcome and offensive imposition.

"No, I have a private room and I got in late last night. But do you mind?"

"Oh, sorry!" She put her foot down, switching the focus to her flexing belly. "But hey, a private room! Let me stay with you, hah? We can divvy up the rate!"

Viturna came out of the office. "Well, what do you think, Doris?"

A light framed youth that Beatense would have entangled instead if she knew he was a guest came hopping down the stairs, just in butt-cut cut-offs and dramatic tan.

Doris stared, never any rest, but this cute faced, shy boy gave her an out.

"If… If I'm g-going to have a… A r-roommate, I w-want him!"

Being the friendly good boy that he was, he laughed, red face flattered.

"Anyway, welcome, Doris! I'm Beatense, the stymied hostel slut! And now with it being so early I'm going to do a naked run despite fewer witnesses!"

"No, Beatense, no naked," said Viturna. "This dive has an iffy enough reputation. You go right up there and get something on."

More hostelers came into the room and Zapo set out two loaves of bread on the counter in the kitchen. Beatense put four slices in the toaster and drew out some coffee. She went over to say hi to Hawk, at the desk in the closet sized office.

"Hey, shitball, any more photos of me? Hey, what's that you're watching?"

"Oh, Misty and Fawn. Eleven and fourteen. They post two new videos every morning. It's a dollar per view so they make over $10,000 a day."

"Unlike any videos of me. Speaking of, anything of me, heh heh?"

"Let's just see." He typed in Today's Beach Girls and scanned through the little thumbnails and clicked. "Ah, here. The Beachway and Sails West nude!"

"Wow! Is that slick! And boy, am I black! But it's just all the glare, really. Now how did they get that one? That's when I was on the patio deck of that one bar with Roke! They gave me a free beer, me quite without money."

Beatense ran upstairs and got her Gold Digger strip on, her oil wetting it, and coming back down she sat down to toast and coffee served by a worshipful Doris.

Beatense looked up and as she saw Viturna she had a thought.

"Oh, when do I have to check out by, Vitty?"

"Your bed will be taken by eleven, but you can hang out here all day."

"For the rest of my life, I wish. And where is that Hideaway?"

"Down the Highway a few blocks. I can call to make sure of your booking."

"Nah. Who would want to go there if they can come here. Be serious."

Viturna laughed. She had already realized that since this crazy girl was on the premises, everyone was on his best behavior. There were always the occasional personality conflicts or the fools who drink too much. But no one cared to get all pissy with this kid around. She even had fun jokes for Molly and now Doris.

"Yeah, Beat, it's a saggy old fleabag but it's cheap. And, *accommodating.*"

"Yeah, so I heard. Okay, thanks, Little Vittle. More coffee, Doris? Now!"

Beatense went out on the patio deck and worked the barbells there all this time. Then she and Afton went for a run, along the wave-wetted hard pack sand, a route with fewer witnesses than the walkway, but the tumult of the surf was exhilarating.

Both needlessly strip-decent girls were barefooted, bonied and baked.

"Just look at that sight, Afton, all those beachy buildings. And all those tall palm trees, just waiting to get their beach back when civilization ends."

"You call this civilization?"

"If an athletic beach girl can get an implant and put it to heavy use, it's civilized!"

The two ran down to where the walkway ended at Windemere, then cut in to run along the cement wall, on its sand side. Those on the Walk on its other side were fortunate enough to get a fleeting look at Beatense. What was noticed in particular about her, besides her tan and joyous smile, were her skin-tight abdominals.

Framing the six pillowettes of her taut transversals were the linea semiluminaris stretched at each side, that gleamed with tuned strength, correctly indicating that she worked muscle and bed like an obsessed maniac. But the trick was to display a light thinness while still looking well fed, to avoid that veined stringy look. But Beatense's healthy build had smoothed tensions that gave her staying power even as a kid.

The girl was smiling because of the now friendly familiar sights before her as she ran, and because of everyone's neck snapping admiration. The elderly people out for their after-breakfast strolls could only sadly stare. Decades ago their beachwear was neck-to-knee confining, and the stifled ladies could not show or especially act on any sensuality whatsoever. But here these happily satisfied sexuals were flitting along in their minimal strips, that had the same weight as aspirin bottle cotton.

The four girls got ready for another day of sun. Pointedly, they ignored their strips; they would all go free again all that day. The policeman on his ATV cycle was in a quandary as the four girls flitted across the sand at 9 AM, laughing and yelling. Nudity was allowed, but some girls pushed it too far. Fucked right on the beach even.

Like Beatense, Afton, Scabby and Bedbug had come to Emerald for a tanning odyssey, and getting settled they had an oiling orgy, then lay back with eyes closed.

Beatense was grateful her friends took tanning so seriously, otherwise they would talk and fidget. The four lay as if dead, and with bellies so sunken maybe they were dead. As more people came the noise levels increased, but the girls silently baked.

Beatense didn't have to quit just after four hours, but despite her present ecstacy she felt increasingly edgy about getting into that motel. She told her friends where to find her, but they said their week was up and they were leaving the next morning.

This led to hugging goodbyes, and bare Beatense with towel in hand ran across the hot sand over to the hostel, with its patio deck wall. In skin only she ran in and hopped up the stairs. She grabbed her backpack off Scabby's bed (being technically checked out, someone else's things were already on her own bunk) and with Lesta's crochet strip chastely in place she ran down to pay up.

"Zapo, you're on! Well, this is goodbye. Off to the Hideaway. Just awful."

"Well, it is quieter down that way, but you can visit here anytime."

"It wouldn't be the same. Oh, I better get my top on for the Highway."

"Stay on this side and you're legal. It's the other side that's off limits."

This lobby area had a constant stream of guys and gals, all staring at the girl's nearly nude, obscene tan. She didn't recognize all of them, with the transient nature here. Beatense herself would be leaving, and she went out and found Viturna doing clean-up duty out on the patio deck.

"Boy, hate to see you go, kid. These were happy days." --/-- "I go way beyond happy myself. Sorry about my going naked so much, and keeping people awake."

"Well, if you don't like being splashed all over Old Netty, that's my revenge."

"Yeah, especially since I don't get any money out of it. Like Fawn and Misty!"

The two hugged. Beatense came back into the common room and sadly gave a wave and stepped outside, with backpack shoulder hung. She ran the half block over to the Highway, because if she walked she might have turned back.

Her skill in baking in stinging hot tans near black in depth was from her genetic abnormality, from the radiation. And it wasn't based on a trained ability for which she would earn some kind of recognition, like mastering the violin or running.

Still, word of her had mysteriously spread, and so although this was a humdrum weekday, suddenly it seemed to be a good idea to go for a walk.

Heads pivoted, panting people stared with teeth clenched, and on the Highway cars blatantly paused to await her, then drove by the girl slowly. No one honked, if anyone was going to hold up traffic, this was definitely the time to do it.

Some popped out of stores, or others jogged ahead of her and then dug in their pockets in acting like they had forgotten something, then turned back for a look. Still others emerged from the flower shaded walkways that led out to the beach.

Beatense didn't know that this was any more activity than usual. Instead as a newcomer she felt proud that she had a basic familiarity now with this world.

She walked past the shops and stores she saw the last evening with her friends, including the One Stop Grocery and Emerald Wave Bar. She saw Wacky Wearables and Skate Street Boards. Another surf shop she recalled seeing was called Radical Wave, and then came the Oro Grande Restaurant and the Hideaway Motel.

This was a sad old one-story building whose ell shape enclosed its crack filled parking lot, as also bordered by the Highway and Bastian Street. Of course the old manager had no preparation for her as she burst in back of her nips. She leaned her thin arms on the counter and shook back her piled hair by way of openers.

"Hello, sir, I'm Beatense Colwell, and as I understand it, Viturna at Hogan set me up with a staff reservation here for the next ten days."

"Why-Why-Why, y-y-y-y-yes, m-m-miss. I m-m-mean, y-yes!"

"Don't tell me you're smitten too, sir. All the way here I had people bumping into each other or walking into lamp posts. Like, am I the only beach girl in town?"

"Well you are the Book Girl, and y-your costume is a p-persuasive factor."

She laughed. "Oh yeah, right. Now let's make my check-in quick, sir, because I want to get down to that Cocojo. Oh, could you tell me? That beach is nude, right?"

"It… It has… It does… Yes. But I d-do warn you, it's v-very open."

"Oh, I know about that. I'm all over the Field, being very open. Some good live action. And of course surveying camp in the Geode Desert. And then my books."

The girl was the most beautiful creature he had ever seen, and in this coast town there were hundreds. Her extreme tan flashed and snapped, and with its near black depth and baked golden gleam, it lighted up the walls. But a closer look at her face revealed that the kid could be dearly friendly in that good old chum way.

"Yes, m-miss, th-this is your… Y-Y-Your k-key. Can y-you f-f-fill this out?"

"Sure! And you're Mr. Cheevy? I'm Beatense! Nice to know ya!"

Bicep rounded she extended her strong hand and gave him a smile that almost seemed to have an uncertain shy edge to it, as if she truly hoped for his approval.

He didn't know his heart could still pound like this. It was comforting that he just wasn't eligible anymore. For him a huge victory would be if she acknowledged his existence beyond that of a functionary, but already she went way further than that.

As she filled out her registration she kept looking up at him, quizzically, and she made little faces as she worked, tongue showing.

"There! I'll throw my backpack on the bed and head down to Cokey Jokey!"

He was still shaking. "M-Miss, will you need water? No services there."

Beatense agreed and Mr. Cheevy handed her a 24 ounce spring water.

When she stepped out he sniffed the bacon and brown sugar sun smell she left lingering. The girl opened her door. The room was the same loud pink her bedroom once was, but the dressing table mirror had those side lights. And for the first time in her life she had a queen sized bed. Wow!

This motel was not on the beach, and indeed it lay across the Highway from the jungle of apartments, lodgings and houses lying between. This put Beatense in an awkward spot because she would have to maintain at least basic decency until she crossed the busy road. Also the Sorel State Beach wasn't open to free expression from what she heard. And so she added her paired-triangle top to her crochet.

She took her rolled-up bed sheet and water and oil bottles and stepped out. She crossed the parking lot and stood waiting for the green at the corner, causing turmoil with the drivers going by. She saw a squad car come and wondered if she was legal enough. But the cop gave her a finger-pistol greeting and drove on. The walk light came on, the traffic came to a halt, and the last thing the drivers cared to witness as Beatense hopped across the street was that wee twin-coconut butt.

The girl was heading for a beach where she would be escaping this unwelcome scrutiny, plus that of the retired elderly, who were so scandalized by the brave bares and their lax morality. Sadly these old visitors were important guests for the charming old seaside cottages and motels, so their owners resented the girls too.

Unaware of this controversy, Beatense decided she was now safely within the beach's sphere of activity, even as the traffic whizzed by back of her, and she untied naked. That's better! She ran down Bastian with a flash of spindly legs, by a line of brightly painted tourist rentals. She hopped across the street that ended Bastian at a tee intersection, the familiar Windemere. A low stone wall stood here, with a gap for entry. Beside it was a faded old metal sign labeling it as Bastian Street Beach.

A reedy teen child in trim shorts and T-shirt came up the cement steps from the beach below. She was grimly responsible and skeptical in looks, with thin, tawny tan limbs. She eyed the statutory legal one with wary disapproval. A sensible kid.

Beatense heard a noise and turned to face a thick grinning fellow who had come up behind her. As he stared the girl held her light arm protectively. Unlike everyone else in town, he was a sun-phobic landlubber: Pudgy, with a bland nondescript face and active red bumps. His flat topped crew cut was about as sporty as a mousetrap, and his adult maturity was stupidly out of place in this sunny world. Wearing service trousers and a billowy white shirt half tucked in, he probably was as dull nerdy as he looked, but his eyes had a somewhat clever glitter. Beatense gazed in horror.

"I... Heh heh! I, er, uh, heard about... About y-you! Heh heh!"

"Well, no one will ever hear of you so I guess we null out."

"You know what that *means*? I work with null meters all the time!"

"I suggest you check those meters for calibration. Now, kindly egress."

"W-Wait, my police band radio said just you did the Highway nude!"

"Sorry, I was just topless. So, anyway you're..."

"I'm B-Buck. B-Buckland Hendrickson. What's y-your n-name?"

"Cockamanie Calliope. But where did you come from so suddenly?"

"I p-parked just over there. I... I deliver pizzas, and I like to check out all the different streets so I can... I can f-find the places faster at night."

"Hmm, I would think as a local you would know the town by now."

"I'm... I'm still learning. We do Hoganforth a lot, where you're staying!"

All this time he tried to control his shaking, to show he wasn't affected.

"Were. But how did you know that? This is getting weird. Fuck! Off!"

He got into his cavernous, old grey Burroughs, built in Arrolynn, and sagged in defeat, black and dreadful. He thought she would be delighted by that bit of intelligence. Now he could shake. Naked! Buck clutched at his steering wheel, with eyes bulging and breath strangled. He pictured her belly, placketed bow string tight, and with her every move its muscles instinctively flexed. He never saw such a slim waist. He couldn't hope for any involvement with her now, that disastrous encounter ensured that. He had her books, his only consolation.

With Buck gone the bitch looked northward. In a majestic suspended panorama she saw the entire sweep of coast, all the way up to that Holiday Hill. And she saw Main Beach, that she had seen as a runner and bus passenger. Looking south, she saw the long pier down at Sorel, which was on her map. She sprang down the cracked and broken cement steps. A lifeguard saw her, jaw dropped.

It was his civic duty to maintain friendly relations with the beach visitors. He, ahem, stepped over. "H-Hello th-there, m-miss. I, er, you're the B-Book Girl!"

He tried to control his shaking. Now he knew the reason for all the hysteria.

"Yes, perfect and gaped at as I am. And you m-might try talking without all these d-double consonants. So how far is this Cocojo, anyway? Which is where I'm going."

"No n-need to g-go there. The b-beaches here are nude, Miss Book."

"Try and let me decide what my options are. I'm used to getting my way."

"Hey, back off! Don't unload all over me! I was just saying!"

"Oh, sorry. It's just that this Buck guy was making a shit of himself."

"Oh, him. In seach of the most scenic babe ever. Good luck there, pal."

"Yes. I sure didn't qualify. Now look at them two, and I get the static."

Beatense saw two young teen sisters, just in 1x3 inch white tape strips, devotedly baking their sacred, thin selves upon their backs. They were lush oiled tan, and their nips stuck offensively out, all set for any old cranks who might visit here.

"They go to school like that, some judge thing." She thought of Soler. "But going down to Cocojo, you first go by the Bolingbroke and summer home beaches, and the Oxhead dunes beach. All nude. But Sorel, really strict. Even bikinis get static."

"I'll just bulldoze through that sicko time warp. Oh, speaking of the time…" He looked at his watch. "One… Even. B-But you sure are total shit tan."

"Yes, it and fucking are making me hundreds of thousands of dollars."

"Somehow that doesn't seem right."

"Of course it isn't! But you can see that I'm winning in life. Okay, bye!"

Bookie regretted losing so much sun since leaving the beach earlier, but as she turned to go she turned back to the rescuer. "Hey, you got a phone at all?"

"Back at the chair. But I thought you had to get to Cocojo."

"Shut up." She went with her friend to the tall lifeguard chair and dialed the Hog Lodge. "Hey, Zapo, it's the sex crazed Book Girl! I left my skates there!"

"We got em. Why don't I, er, bring them by tonight? I can leave… Early."

"And stay late! Room 8. Maybe we can catch a drink somewhere, first."

Now she was set. She thanked her friend and ran. If she made Cocojo fast she could bake four hours, if slope angled into the sun on a sand dune. She came to the Bolingbroke enclave beach. Several people were here, ranged out far ahead.

Girls her age and youngsters too were naked in the sun, romping and swimming. The rich life. Deep within the wooded enclave the girl caught glimpses of homes that were brilliantly dramatic in style. She glanced down at her breasts. *I got assets too.*

Farther down she came to a small group of low sandy mounds, home to a small grove of the classic, umbrella topped palms. These trees had strayed out from the heavy growth behind them, and sitting beside them was a yellow catamaran sailboat with a tall black mast. As the girl kept running, awkwardly holding her things, the trees and foliage were replaced with low dunes laced with sand grass.

Back of these were some fine old summer homes, that had grand screened porches facing to the sea, and dormer windows for the bedrooms in their attics. They also might have wooden floors painted with shiny enamel, and breakfast nooks that would be perfect for tea and toast. They would also have old stone fireplaces with flower or artist brush filled jars on their mantles. The furniture would be mismatched, old and creaky, but beloved by visiting grandchildren, who could actually prop their bare feet on the coffee tables with no yelling.

Some of those grandchildren, and others, played the beach now. Beatense was heartwarmed that they too were deep brown and bare. In a little sandy nook a boy and girl were together. Beatense ran on, toward the distant Sorel beach. Between it and the end of the summer homes the dunes swept on, identified as the Oxhead on her map. The girl ran by a broad pathway, which led up and over a low saddle between two dunes, into the salt grass dotted hills. Wheeling gulls completed the scene.

Beatense was beginning think everybody was right, Cocojo was too far. But with the loud, wind driven surf tumbling in she ran on. She stopped at the Sorel border to sling on her patch, and kept flying. Tree shaded picnic grounds beckoned across the sands, and appropriately there was an old wooden bathhouse and snack stand set back of the wide beach. The park visitors along the shore were arranged on rumpled blankets or in beach chairs. They did look like low laborers, Beatense observed.

In running through like a wasp, startling everyone, she went past nifty little utility trucks parked in a row. A suddenly alert rescuer jumped out of one in pursuit of her, but the illegal girl easily kept ahead. Running the broad low angled slope coming up from water's edge, she ran under the massive pier's entry ramp and on to Cocojo.

17

COCOJO

Beatense saw that the lifeguard had stopped, so she paused and took off her patch, and gazed out over Cocojo's gleaming blurred sands, that lay as powdery soft as a cloud. The park had dozens of visitors, but with the infinite spaces their random placement gave a greater sense of solitude than if the sand lay empty, because they looked lost in all that space. The dunes shimmered as if haloed, and back of them, atop steep banks of sand, stood the tall trees of a verdant jungle.

The hunter girl's heart pounded as she stepped into this magic realm, aiming for the dunes at a long angle. A sunbather lay just ahead, nude. Glowing very dark, she lay roasting under oil on her big white towel. Oops, no, wearing a thong. No top though. Beatense went by four girls on big bed sheets. They were militantly tan and bone built and tight, but they chastely wore both pieces of their micro tie bikinis. They smiled and, in recoconizing that they were sensually elite, Beatense agreeably smiled back. But she was somewhat disappointed. Bitsy had made it sound like this beach was all full of exciting action, but it was very quiet here. Too few to victimize with her famed shattering tan., and some people were instead riveted by her rank hair.

Beatense reached the sand dunes and explored their wavy edge, feet squeaking the clean sand. She was in search of an inlet, that would lead back to a sanctum of deep seclusion. Not that privacy was precisely desired or necessary, but in fighting it out with the sun she needed to be undisturbed in her battle.

She found a likely looking draw and followed it in. It turned back on itself like a buttonhook, perfect for intensifying the rays. She lay out her big sheet in her hidden cove, against the rise of the sand, so she would be aimed directly into the sun as the afternoon hours baked by. Shaking, like those sisters she slopped on her oil and lay back with her limbs flung out. Already she felt the sun burn in.

In this secret hollow the rays embraced her on all sides, so the directional placing of her sheet wasn't so terribly necessary. The girl raised up to her elbows and gave her twin peaches and rich, wet black tan an appraisal, like she first did age *twelve!*

Her rib ledged belly lay sunken, with ripples tensed as always. Her pelvic bones stuck out an inch and a half, stretching her skin, and as she rubbed there she felt a protesting tingle. With heart pounding the vain girl lay back again, with long legs and needful split opened wide, and the muffled surf lulled her into a naked cruise.

Besides Geode this was more lethal sun than she had ever known. It was the latitude. Up north she could gain thirty degrees by lying against a slope, but this was cheating and her skin knew it. But here the angle added such great power, even her outrageous Book Girl tan couldn't keep up with the fierce energy burn of the rays.

The intense heat back in here got Beatense very excited, the same as getting it deep, driving her into narcotic ecstasy. But with her water running out she had to go. So over two hours later she got together her things and followed her narrow pathway back out to the open sand. She was surprised to see that many more people had arrived. She spotted a worthy competitor, an obvious athlete, with carelessly astray, loose black hair. As Beatense got closer she saw that her probing dark eyes had a smoking intensity, while her directed cheekbones focused her personality.

Along with her being baked to a shiny hot livid darkness, she was bare. Not as a tanner, but as a natural creature. Beatense was one herself; if her bedding counted. Uninvited, she laid out her sheet quite oclose by the other girl's and sat on it, leaning back on her hands, with the hot sun aimed into her well opened legs, and with her royalty paying oily shine agleam.

"HP Shit," the other said. "Look at that waist! Boy, can you fuck with that!"

"What my waist does, I'm pretty much unaware of it, when I'm in action."

"Me too. But like, if you came that way, how did you get through Sorel nude like that? They prohibit even bikinis, and of course topless, needless to say."

"No kidding! I wore my crochet bottom and boy did this lifeguard chase me."

"You're a walking anatomy chart, all that muscle, is why. Too agitating."

"My tan too. Mention that. Anyway, I'm Beatense, lately of Hoggy Lodge."

"That notorious dive. I'm Sienna, hey. But what do you mean, lately?"

"They kicked me out. I could only squeeze in two days there."

"They shudda let you stay, kid. Bump someone else. Where ya at now?"

"The Hideaway. I will be staying amost two weeks there."

"You shudda stayed at old Hoggy. You don't want an dump fleabag."

"It's cheap. But they let me be downright naked at the Hog, just hanging out or dancing, plus I was reminded of my noisy disturbances right in the bunkroom. Still, I do have some shreds of morality, but if kids can do it here, as I applaud, why not me?"

"Kid, if you want me to keep my hands off, shut up! Hey, you're not…"

"Yeah, the Book and FieldNet wonder. Just the videos make me famous."

"Yeah, I saw them. But your books, too expensive. Went to the library."

"Tell me about it. But my take only comes to a dollar per copy for the first book. For the second book they paid me sixty up front, plus five dollars a book, but the way advances work, no pay until they use that sixty up. I might have hit that. I would do a third book here, but I just did the second book, and I don't have my horse."

"Those riding pictures are unbelievable. You were bareback at full gallop!"

"So was the camera truck. But it's the other riding I did that's the interest. Scott was amazing, plus Slat. But hey, these young girls I saw up at Bastian, laying in the sun in just these strips. The lifeguard said they go to school that way. Court order. I knew a girl at surveying camp who did that too, Soler. Kind of inconsiderate."

"Oh fuck that. You get so tired of hearing you gotta cut people slack. Like, is anyone going to give you credit if you go around in some burlap bag?"

"Hmm, never tried that." Beatense sat with the sun aiming at her back, to try and catch it up with her front. "Those old people up in town would sure like it."

"You don't get old unless you wanna get old. Wanna go body surfing?"

"Oh, good idea. But I was planning to learn real surfing, Sienna."

"Any surfing instructor will tell you to body surf first. So come on!"

The girls ran over into the surf. Disregarding the cold water, they dove in and floundered as the heavy swells lifted and lowered them. A white wave-top curl raced toward them, and the stellar Sienna stood in wait. Beatense watched doubtfully as a mounting breaker bucketed toward the two, a bellowing elephant. It hit.

Sienna let out a whoop, just as Beatense was grabbed underwater and smacked into the sandy floor. She was shaken and tumbled like an old rag doll in a tornado. She struck at the sand with every part of her flailing body, but at last she was dumped off in the shallows. As the flooding backwash sizzled past her she crawled her stick thin self toward the dry sand, gasping.

Sienna flopped down beside her. "You look like hell. What happened?"

Coughing, Beatense compared her own sleek, muscle laced, wet, dark tan body to Sienna's. They were almost twins. Even their pre-wetted hair.

"That body surfing isn't fun at all, plus I got all these sand burns!"

"How can ya fuck up body surfing? Well, it is your first time. But next time spear yourself right into the heart of the wave, hey, just before it hits."

As a confident sun annealed athlete Beatense ran back in and swam out as a couple of minor waves lightly lifted her in sliding by. She stood as a rumbling hulk careened toward her. She waited until it was just ready to break over her publically bared, slimmed iron tough form, and she dove into its throat.

Sienna lied, this was far worse. But she had enough air this time, and she rolled herself up in a ball and bounced along the bottom. *This is life!* She clambered to her feet, as skinny boys and girls, bare and brown, ran over from the dunes and lay out blankets. They were alight with that active dissecting intellect that transcended them above the usual plane of plain human existence. Highest pedigree.

The lovely boys had long thick hair. The lovely girls had long thick hair, and in spite of their slight builds, the kids had live muscle. One lad with a child's face and voice excitedly cried while he and the others sprang for the surf. Beatense then saw the deceitful Sienna awaiting a rumbling breaker. At the precise moment she turned and dove with it, and she cavorted in like a seal. *So that's it!*

The girl ran in and caught the next wave. She flew! The air was energized with screams as the other kids played, either in the surf or as they bounded like deer in circles upon the sand. As Beatense turned to run back in, she saw a teen boy run hand in hand with a sun-child lass over toward the dunes. They looked warily back, then slipped in. Beatense knew what was next.

She made more runs with Sienna, then they lay on their sheets. A bared mother came over from the dunes with her ravishing son, who owned quite girl-like hair, all fluttery long and at odds with his developed muscle. Both were tightly thin and tawny pale. They oiled each other and lay upon their sheet some distance away.

"Sienna, yeah, two of those other kids snuck back into the dunes for recreation."

"Hah? Oh, that's a switch. Usually they just do it wherever."

"Well I wish they would do it wherever here, instead of all hidden."

"Just wait." Sienna took her oil and rubbed it on in a rough massage. She lay sprawled back on her sheet, in a slinky, lanky stretch. She was thinly built, but like Beatense her muscled toughness lent as much rigidity as her hard fine bones. And although she was shrieking hot dark in the glare, Sienna was actually pretty.

The lovely kids ran in from the surf or ran from their running. Oil squirted in all directions as they played, the girls shaking with excitement. Then they went to work.

"That's so beautiful, Sienna. I know what it's like to have sexual intercourse as a kid, me thirteen. And me just black tan and crazed for it, once I started doing it, not knowing it was what good girls didn't do, and me implant safe, I fucked really a lot."

"Yup, good girls don't do it, you say? I didn't think it was bad at all. My Mum didn't like me active at just twelve, so I got me an implant secretly at school. And she rags I'm just a beach bum, but I'm brown and hard as a muki nut, and fuck really a lot."

"Isn't it great? Because that's why I'm here! So you don't work or go to school?"

"What the piss is this? Yes, step right up! It's career counseling time!"

"I was just asking the question! So, you live with your mother?"

"The hell! Us girls got this shack back in this coconut grove south of Turtle Rock. Torrey paints and pays the rent. We help out but she doesn't care either way. She's pretty slack about it. She gets high prices. Hey, they could be here by now. Funny they didn't look for sociable me." Sienna stood. "Let's go scout them up."

Beatense wanted to stay but she also wanted a closer look at the family duo. As the two walked by, the boy angel was lying companionably on his mother, innocently with no possibility of being in her. Beatense smiled as Sienna kept going.

"Come on! Yeah, so Torrey paints us naked sluts laying out, quite tropical, and also paints herself in, using photographs. Hey, do you think I'm a gypper?"

"Hah?" Beatense then decided that her new friend was gypsy. Her hair tumbled down in that typical ratty, dry abundance, like her own. "I... I think so, yes."

"The hell! Gypsies hate sun, not knowing the skin needs its life and vitality."

Both girls had life and vitality. Their melanin proteins were crushed together in a shifting golden blur. This was also true of the many slender boys and girls from the pre-teens to twenties here on the beach, and even the young girls had biceps.

Yes, Cocojo was like Bitsy said. Beatense gaped at the finer specimens as the girls walked. Several proudly nude teens were flying a plastic plate back and forth.

"How do they make that thing turn around like that in mid-air?"

"Huh? Oh, that, a Whizbee. The wind does it. Nice *swimsuits*, hah?"

"I can't argue. I've been a nudie since sixth grade. I'm in my element here."

Sienna looked upon her with new respect. She passionately lived sun too.

Beatense had seen the Cocojo sand hills as she entered the park, and then went back in them, but as the two walked by the long parade of the rolling dunes now, she looked upon them with greater interest. Tucked into the inlets were sun worshippers, alone or in small groups. Out on the sand there were low key beach games, as if no one wanted to be too distracted from that sun seeking agenda. All these celestial beings, including even the tender youngsters, had a firm lay-out belief in naturist sun.

As they kept walking south, Beatense accepted the presence of the plain pudgy pales, even if they didn't belong here. The dunes marched on, but the distant wall of rock seemed to mark their end. Noisy gulls were whirling overhead.

Sienna was talking. "I was just a kid when the thongs first came in, so I had to steal one. You have to be a born bitchorexic to dare them. Yes, sweet shy waif girls crave them. Despite those soft, persuasive eyes they don't hold back just because they're young. They know it can be frowned on, but they go almost naked."

Showing common sense, thought Beatense, who saw a nearby sand baked little sophomore walk absently by, just in thong, with delicate breasts bared. She had the widened eyes of puzzled distress. The child watched the action of her wee feet, and thrilled with her divinity, she was blissfully ignorant of the early trailblazerswho made proud self worship and sensual freedoms a morally upright part of modern life. For her and girls like her sex and sun were unreservedly honored and abetted needs.

Sienna pointed back up the long stretch of beach. "Hey, he's coming! It's Jesse! On Windfire! You have to see this, Beatense!"

Beatense saw a distant horse come charging down from Sorel at a gallop. As cheers called out moments later a tan young boy flew by bareback on his racehorse. With long hair airborne behind and small arms in control, he shot over the aftercrash fleam of the freight train breakers in a wild, triumphant blur of bursting spray.

The kid's whipstaff profile was warhawk flexed as if for reining back a runaway, while in his beautiful freedom there was nothing between the sensational dark baking he sported and the sea breezes. He shot on to the tumbled rock wall closing off the south end of Cocojo, and skidding his mount to a stop he pulled him around. Horse and rider bolted back into the shimmering dunes, and the evil brave was next seen driving his fury in leaping lunges up the tall sand bank into the wood.

Beatense's dark eyes were alight. "Wow, that's incredible! Who was he?"

"Jesse! Gyp, speaking of. But unlike them he's a tanning addict, as you might have noticed. He makes the rip down from Main all the time. Sorel tries to stop him."

"They did me too. Well that makes two of us in town who fly bareback."

"Hey, I ride too! Bare! That is if I can get Jesse to borrow me ol Win."

They continued their trek, and down by Cocojo's south end, where the rider had ended his attack, they came upon three girls on a big bedsheet by the dunes. One burgundy brown girl was personally beautiful, with long hair of soft honey gold. Her character looks would make people very deferential and covetous of ways to get her approval. Waitresses like these rake big tips. On the job she was the type to wear tailored tweed slacks, a mid butted turtle neck sweater, and step arched zip boots.

That has to be the artist, Beatense thought. Torrey. A work of art herself.

"Hey, hi! Sit down!" one of the other girls called out. "Grab a beer!"

"But Senny," said the third girl, who also had a caring love of heavenly brown, "You're... Joining us? I thought you hated us fucking sorority cunts!"

"Fucking sorority *bitch* cunts. But you shudda been looking for me!"

Torrey laughed. She had the clear, direct blue eyes of the highest strata in human perfection. The detail of her face told of admirably methodical habits and thrift.

"So listen up, guys, this is Beatense. I'm not kidding, that is her name."

The three girls, impressed already by this visitor's painful tan, and shocking hard muscle, happily laughed at that. Be Tense. And so Beatense was accepted.

"And, her dancing has been all over old Netty. You can see why."

She rolled her eyes up as she endured their adulation. The other two girls were Staranne and Summer. Beatense smiled at the introduction but needed to catch her back-side up. She lay her sheet out and sat on it cross-legged, facing the girls while the sun deep heated her. Everyone noted the taut inward curve of her belly.

The girls weren't in any sorority; this was just Summer's flippant remark. Her job was a pre-dawn paper route, ridden on her bike, while the painfully brown Staranne picked produce naked with the gypsies. But if she wasn't called in she helped Torrey with her art. The three girls quietly subsidized the proud Sienna.

"That's a history making tan," said Torrey. "And how did you get that waist?"

"Barbells. I'm in my eighth year now. My poor father, he can hear my clinks and clanks any time of the night. The secret is, your linea transverse muscles are fibered horizontially, so sit-ups don't work. Instead you heft your barbells on your shoulders and do twist-swings. That brings your abs in nicely."

Again, Beatense's black belly was tightly curved in, showing gaunted ripples. As she told of herself, including her Book and ad singing, a petite, trimly athletic girl sat with them. She wore a swim team one-piece maillot that fit like spray paint, but its sleek fit didn't prevent her small breasts from bumping proudly out. She had tailed back, coppery blond hair and an exactingly cultured tan.

Beatense deplored her glasses, an office girl nuisance that warned others of her prudent caution. But this Tenacity's pair didn't detract from her being steeled thin and strong. Her unique name was appropriate for her scholarly glasses look. Their small lenses sat well down on her nose, giving her a cute busybody look.

After introductions Beatense recapped briefly, then continued her story.

"...And it was all because of that article, and so here I am on the majestic and magic Cocojo Beach. But you would think this would be solid hotels here."

"It's some kind of nature preserve all the way over to the Highway," said Torrey. "Which means, as soon as they get the financing the hotels will take over."

"I don't suppose that will stop those young kids up yonder from their sex."

"Probably not," sighed Torrey. "It's like there's this collective intelligence of what we conceive as right and wrong, and maybe we're pushing the needle into dangerous territory. As the years and decades go by, there's a constant flux in the behavior and attitude rules that society finds workable. But it just seems that as we drop all these inconvenient traditional guidelines, we're not replacing them."

Beatense nodded. A preciously slim and hot basted lass, whose ice blue eyes clashed with her tan, came out from the dunes and kneeled on her towel by the girls. Despite her self important naïve looks, making her touchingly tender, she was bare.

"Hi, Krinkles," said Torrey. "Finally you join us. Back in the bowl again?"

"Hi, guys! Yeah, for six hours, Torrey! I just got extra, extra baked today!'

"Congradges," said Sienna, wearily. "Don't let my sick envy stop you."

"You, envy me? Anyway, at Clem's last night I met this really nice guy, but I felt real bad, he admitted he never had sex yet. So when we were in bed I was teaching him how to do it I had to put him in me, and then really work to ride him deep!"

Somehow that last tidbit was alarming. Beatense ironically thought, *And she's a decent kid!* But what an enrapturing play this trusting child would be.

"He fed you a line, Krink," said Sienna, "but it worked out. See him again?"

"Tonight! But you're new. Boy, I thought I got the tannest! Just, *wow.*"

Other commendations followed and Torrey said, "Starry, sadly we gotta go. We got that show up by Holiday Hill later and we need to load up the car."

"Wait, Sienna says you guys live in a coconut shack," said Beatense.

"It's cheap but horrid. We're totally isolated, bugs, and the heat is awful."

"How meretricious. But does your painting really pay the bills?"

"It depends. I just do slop-it-on primitive, so it sells cheap but I sell lots. I don't have the technique for subtle coloration. Kringle, need a ride? Got your stuff?"

"Just my towel and my piece." She held up a one by four inch tie strip. "But thanks, I want to stay here. Maybe I'll absorb some of Beatense's tan!"

Torrey and the other three said goodbye and ran offl. Beatense, excited to have Krinkles to herself, continued her back, lying on the slope of the dune. The sun was still raging hot, and over the next hour both girls felt new tan soak deep in.

The two got up and walked through Cocojo to Sorel. The sign posting the hours said that the lifeguards were off duty, but the kids tied on their strips. Beatense was impressed by Krinky's unaffected simplicity of soul. They went under the pier access ramp, going between the support timbers, and went on to conspicuously walk the Oxhead and summer home beaches. Of course everyone stared.

"Hey, Krinkles, how far ya going? Wanna see my motel room?"

"I would like that, Beatense, but no lez stuff. I have that new friend."

"Okay, I understand. I of course just do guys."

They came to the Bastian beach. The two sisters were still lying tape-strip inert, now on an old embankment-tilted sidewalk slab. Beatense and friend hopped up the steps and the short stub of Bastian, going by the intriguing little tourist rental jumble done in bright painted stucco. At the light the two sprang across the busy Highway to the customary chorus of honking horns and screeching rubber.

Beatense first led Krinkles into the office, where Mr. Cheevy was signing in new guests. The baked, near nude girls were an exorbitantly uncalled for intrusion.

Beatense interrupted. "Hi, Mr. Cheevy. If I have a guest tonight, is that extra?"

"N-N-No, young lady. Y-Y-Your friend here will be w-welcome."

"No, not Krinky. She's not staying. I mean a guy. I met him up at Hoggy."

The staring manager shook, as did the offended middle aged humdrum couple. The fine, starved dark brown faces before them had a captivating radiance that stole into their hearts, so they recalled the days when life held more promise.

In mutual attraction they clabbered together on the big bed. Then the spent duo stood before the lighted mirror. Their nerves tingled with health, but their shiny hides were at war, struggling to sort out the day's influx of rays, brown versus burn.

One reaction was their saturated gleams of darker tan, while the other was hot burn. No problem, this would glow in beautifully overnight. The two friends oiled each other just out the door, then in their respective 99.7% nudity they strolled along the Coastal Highway. The beachies were met with strongest acclaim. Kids pointed, cars stopped, and cameras caught their fierce tans. The book people later saw millions.

Further up Krinkles crossed the Highway to the walk leading to her sex institute studio, as a slender, near nude shaft of sweated bake. Beatense almost went with to check out her digs, but she spotted a dark tan youth with long yellow hair carelessly slouched upon the sun heated brick ledge of the Red Dot Shop.

Keter aged, he was just wearing blue jean cut-offs that wrapped to his hips like toilet paper. Feasting upon the sun's glare, he was inflicting himself on the last remnants of the work-a-day traffic. He was slight but tough in build, and he openly admired his deeply brown legs and sweat-seared concaved belly. The girl stared, hoping her slow approach wasn't obvious in its intent. Breath strangled she gaped at the boy, whose cat-like blue eyes studied her with cold disinterest.

She wanted to stop, to look; she was helplessly caught in his web of power, but as her ears roared she forced herself to keep going. Shaking, she crossed over to the Strings N Things, and escaped inside. For effect, the store was dimmed.

An older lady (her name tag read Tess) anxiously asked if she needed help.

"Yes, I need a new thong. My crochet here is too mod… Oh, look!"

She stepped to the tri-paneled mirror she saw and, turning, admired herself.

Watching, the lady was reduced to helpless submission to this bag of bones. But Beatense had played this game before: Inflict uncalled for cruelties, then warm her victims back up with disarming charm. She didn't know which of these was the real her, but in her continuing sensual intensity she didn't care. But she did take friendly interest when Tess wrapped the yellow tape around her and read 18 inches.

"No change in size. But look at those Le Nakees, just like my friend's." She held up a string-tied one-half by three inch fabric piece, like what Krinkie and many other girls wore, to be offensive while remaining unindictable. "Yes, just right for when a skeletal surfer like me wishes to display the ultimate in daring."

"You walked in here doing that, miss. I do admire your lovely nerve, but at times decorum does take priority over the baser instincts. Let me show you."

Beatense dutifully followed the lady, looking out across at the Red Dot boy.

"Check out this cropped top, miss, with an open hang." She held it out. "It's casually beachy in style, and its pink and yellow swirls have a bright appeal."

"I saw T-shirts like that in one of those beach shacks. For way less."

"For the tourists. Wash it a few times and you have a pile of lint."

"Well, it does hang openly, I see. It would make me look nicely hungered."

"Y-Yes, perfect for your slim waist and taut, adolescent lines."

The girl put on the swirl shirt. She stepped back to the mirror and saw how its open hang and colors brilliantly called attention to the leaned tensions of her flexing slim waist. Trembly Tess, admiring the upturned nose of her cultured girl profile, was reminded why she loved these high quality, under fed, arrogantly spoiled brats.

"Okay, but I'm not wearing it now," she said as she took it off, returning to her topless state. "Shit. It looks like some of my butter grease rubbed off on it."

Tess did observe that she was thickly wetted with shiny rich nutritive oils.

The lady showed her a light dress, a Grape Stomper, made of soft synthetic mesh weighing but four ounces. It bared all her legs, and its torn frontal cut gave wicked exposure. The girl took it, and a fine gold belly chain twenty inches long, and a gold chainlet that Tess clipped to her knobby ankle. Plus Beatense jumped at the risky "Aunt Clara," a horse collar of lacy linen with a plunging oval cut. As worn, this hung back of the neck and over the shoulders as it hid the breasts frontally only.

The shoulders baring webbing was like crepe paper, just three inches wide. The items in her bag she left with were charged, $787.

For those awaiting her outside, they acted as if they no interest at all in that door that would not open. At last it did. The girl emerged in her $100 Nakee, that gave a good compromise between showing one's tan and civic responsibility.

Unappetizingly, the BurgerSpa restaurant was located across the road from the Red Shield blood donation van at the Ivy street corner. There were picnic tables out front, in use by several tourists. The store featured a greenhouse-like annex of grey tinted windows. Beatense had no money, but she pulled open the glass door anyway and approached the counter as she read and re-read the lighted menu sign.

The clerks and other patrons read and re-read her.

"Hi. I'm not carrying any money but will settle up later, like at that Strings store. I want a Spa Royale, please. That's a hamburger, right?"

"The... The last t-time I ch-checked. Want it w-with cheese or b-bacon?"

"Why does everyone talk like that? But y-yeah, cheese and b-b-b-bacon."

"Anything to dr... Drink? F-Fries w-with that?"

"That Agricola. Medium. And yeah, fries. Had them at camp. Large. But how much food is this going to be? My tumtum hurts if I at all eat too much."

He looked at her latticed belly, as if assiduously adjudging the situation. "Y-Y-You can-can-can handle it." *What a waist! Like she's twelve!"*

No money, but Beatense sat down with her latest hamburger, which had been flame grilled. Like with the Humungus fries she crammed it in.

As she left the place she saw another distraction across the Highway. The light changed and she crossed over to a store parking lot. Here a thin boy of sixteen was selling corn piled up in a pick-up truck. Just in faded jean cut-offs, whose cuffs held high to his thighs, and whose belt loops were very low in sag, he was deluged with a fierce agrarian tan. His fine arms gracefully played as he filled a bag for a wide eyed lady, and as he lifted the heavy bag his fresh biceps bulged and his ripples tensed.

Beatense, shaking, casually strolled over to him, watching as the athlete set the bag in the car's trunk. As the kid dug in his pocket for change he withdrew a curious silver foil packet about two inches square. The lady, with a not unfriendly look at the newcomer said, "Kedzie awaits, Shanty!" and she got in her car and drove off.

The youth sat perched in a sun heated, sunk belly curved slouch on the tailgate. Noticing his new visitor, he flicked the packet up and caught it with a quick clap.

"You're... The Book Girl! In actual real life your tan is unbelievable!"

"Finally I get some credit." Beatense admired the smiling boy as he caught the packet again. *Clap!* "But corn? Who wants stupid old corn?"

"Lots of people do." *Clap!* "Fifty cents an ear, five dollars a dozen."

"What did she mean, Kedzie... What is that thing, anyway? Can I see it?"

"Useless prop. Here." It read, BRD of ED ISSUE PROPH EX LG H3317

The girl said, "Extra large, hah?" and gave it back. She always refused their use. "But anyway, fifty cents is kind of pricey, ain't it? So give me a sample, and I'll eat it raw right now. So how d-did you get... So t-tan? By selling this corn?"

"Forget me! You're the one with the tan! Your photos were not shopped!"

This boy had long blond hair with girl-like wisping curls. He laced his fingers together and extended his thin arms, causing leaned snakes of tricep muscle to appear. His long, enriched tan legs had a fresh appeal, and he had a shaped chest and shoulders. He was sport leaned to poetic perfection, and he was cutely eager.

Russ, Keter, Ledge Boy, and now this. "So, do you... Do you raise this corn?"

"No, I just water it, pick it and sell it for this farmer Josten. Lots of sun."

Indeed, thought Beatense, eyeing this liquidically brown, golden dark boy.

He took an ear and expertly tore the husks away off with a quick snap. His biceps bulged, again, with that capable boyhood look. "Here. E-X-L-G!"

"Fun-eeee," she laughed, then gnawed at the corn. The kernels burst moist and sweet. "Not bad. So again, what's the deal with this Kedzie?"

"Car goes by, young girl sees me. "Daddy, *stop!*" He says, $50, son. "Nice try." I unzip, she holds me. *"Daddy! Please!"* Kedzie. He pays 200, but do her free now."

Unaware of two cameras Beatense said, "I should charge." She crossed the street back toward the picnic park, now hosting an outdoor art fair. The near nude entered the snow fenced enclosure and looked around at the hopeful variety of offerings. She was carefully ignored by this metro crowd, with many of their own daughters naked.

"Hey, look at this one, Mom!" a thin teen-age bright face said, as he pointed at a cracked and faded painting of a sad eyed clown. "Angie just wants it so bad!"

"Later," the mother said. --/-- "No, come on, just look at it!"

She sighed and looked at it and tiredly shook her head. "Yes, very nice."

The adorable kids laughed at their pestering joke, then recognized the Book Girl, but they were too well bred to eye even her peaches. But there were many smiling actual nudes. Beatense saw Neatsfoot, ultra brown shirtless in tight hips-held jeans. Dizzied, she came upon two brawler types in sport shades and sleeveless tank-tops, arguing the price of a surf scene tapestry, rendered on prestigious black velvet.

"No way, man. They got the same thing at Cash-Lo for half that."

The seller looked like a gypsy with his scraggly mustache and sun-creased face, and the bandana that was tied like a cap over his greying fly-away hair.

"Machine painted crap! This took me hours! I'm bleeding at fifty! Dead!"

"Forty, man, or nada." The hold-out saw Beatense and lifted his glasses. *Whoa!* "So, heh heh, how do you like this piece of gar-bazh?"

"Hey! Get out of here! Serious inquiries only! What us artists put up with!"

"I swam in surf just like that today. A bunch of us! My muscles still ache!"

"Okay, man, fifty, *sixty*, if *she* hands it over. Hey, Davy baby, divvy up."

The epicures took the prize from the surf girl, and the gypsy tiredly sagged. Still politely ignored or admired, Beatense saw Torrey and ran over to join her.

"Beatense, hi! Nice Nakee there! Very artistic, and legal, too!"

Torrey herself wore butt-cut cuffed white shorts and a shock mini triangle tie-top, both at war with her day's livened vivid heat. Her works were of ancient misty forests with gloomy distant castles. These works were brilliant! Their atmospherics glowed.

"Torrey, what were you talking about earlier? These are gorgeous!"

"Oh, those. I'm selling them for an art house. I get a cut. Them are mine."

Crude, yes. Beatense perhaps recognized the friends she met today.

"I like these better, the solid colors. They're very energetic, Torrey."

The artist rolled up her eyes, and turned to sell two more energetic works.

"Thank you, sir! I hope you still like these once you get them home!"

"Even more. But can I leave these here and pick them up later, miss?"

"No," said Beatense, "be seen with them and show everybody you're a patron of the arts. But gotta go, Torrey. I'm hitting that bloodmobile, just over."

"You donate too?" Then to the patron, "The Wharf Sunday evening, sir!"

Torrey let Beatense take her pick. And so as she left the fair she carried, along with her skimpily filled Strings bag, Sienna as amateurishly painted.

She stepped up into the van with its lush twelve volt lights, jolting the staffers and the one other donor. At only 100 pounds Beatense as usual lied about her weight.

The needle stung in, and as she worked the grubby rubber ball her blackety hot child's thighs, small breasts and sunk belly clashed in contrast to her pale, upturned arm. After lemonade and donuts and the mandated fifteen minute wait, extended to thirty by the *concerned* nurse, she left with bandaged elbow and the warning to avoid exertion. "Is blade skating okay?" she asked. "It really is effortless."

"We were never asked that before. If you feel faint, stop right away."

"Okay, but no way I'm stopping a good *ahem* fling, if I'm that fortunate!"

Beatense stopped by the Hog and retrieved her skates. She found out that her three friends had gone up to Once Upon, and she had just come from that way and didn't care to return even with Keter as an attraction. She buckled on her skates and took off, and she rolled up to the drive-up window of Burger Spa and paid her tab with the ten she borrowed from the office, with the picture as hostage. Then she skated home, gliding right with the catatonic traffic to avoid the sidewalk tourist clutter.

The girl had invited Zapo to go out for a drink when he came over, but when he showed up, with picture, not the skates as arranged, they stayed in because she had just donated. They discussed the *terms* for Zapo's paying her debt the next day.

Kneeling on his legs, the girl worshipfully adored his useful length. Taking hold, she kissed it, and testing her patience she mouthed him, a delaying trick she learned as a kid at camp to excite herself joyously. A camera peeked in through the gap in the curtains. At last she moved over him and eased him deep in. She worked.

"Zapo, we're just starting! I just need this so..." *Aghhhhh! Aghhhhhhhhh!*

18

WEDNESDAY

Early the next morning Beatense sniffed in her bacony and brown sugar smell of sun as she appraised her ever tense, coppery dark belly. Because of her writhing efforts to reach excitement with Zapo, it reacted even as she breathed.

He watched. "Hey, babe, the author had a good idea. I can set you up with pay per view for your videos on the Net. Just give me your checking account and routing numbers and you could easily make a thousand a day, like Misty and Fawn."

"I thought you said they make ten. But I don't have those numbers."

"Easy, open an account here. Let me know. But gotta go, Miss Average."

She grabbed him with her whooping they joined. She went to the door with him and saw a grey sky. Disappointed, she hoped to return south and bake in a blaze of glory. She later got her skates on and, in belly chain only, rolled the parking lot and shot across the still quiet Highway. The air was chilly; the bare girl became shined from the damp mist. She coasted the Bastian slant down and leaned hard into the Windemere turn. She streaked this street out onto the Beachway Walk.

This was already busy with locals and earlybird tourists. Beatense hit full speed, avoiding the cracks and bumps by pure instinct. In contempt, she noted that the old tourists all looked mortally wounded the among the dozens of bed fulfilled, hot beach sexuals running in tie-thongs, or nothing. One miss hip-snapped an old guy down.

Puppet flew by the closed up sales huts and cantina bars, that were now familiar sights. Some motels had sad shivering refugees out on their balconies, watching the dreary surf. A Beachway coffee bistro had a slow trade going; everyone turned to watch the nude flash by. She saw a news team ahead, and a fellow with a headset and mike waved to intercept her. She slowed to a stop, smiling widely from her very bad but very rewarded life. A dozen news analysts stopped too.

"Er, hello, miss. I'm Brock Mencar of ONUJ TV and I'm wondering if you would agree to an interview. This will be shown in our *Beach Happenings* at 5:30."

Brightly assenting, she replied to the remarks as the camera played on her bony face, her small breasts and flex tensing belly, black aglow in the grey light. The happily surrounded immoral child laughingly admitted, "In answer, yes, I fucked all night!"

Yes but no, not all night, but Zapo might see this. "One of the few times I wasn't caught on video! They even got me out at that Geode surveying camp!"

"Then, y-you must b-be the Book Girl!" --/-- "You voyeur! Okay, bye!"

The girl left and skated on by Hoggy's patio deck, that had a sodden empty look. She swept on through the wide plaza, that anchored Barnet Street. The ghostly sun was just emerging, and the threat was that this would attract more tourists.

Beatense wisely turned back. But not soon enough. She shot through the rapidly growing congestion, at times cutting between husband and wife, and she careened around those shitty clumps of tourists that took up the whole path.

She didn't know the author had the same problem. He had to skate at 7 AM.

She finally got down to Windemere, that as a residential street had no draw. The girl, now sweat splashed, raced up Bastian to the Highway. She crossed at the light and shot to her room. Pulling off her skates she got together her beach items, and burst out the door. Beatense sprang across the Highway and ran down Bastian and its beach steps. No rescuer yet, but the two sisters were at it.

She ran southward. Alone in this silent realm, feet scarcely touching, she flitted along the light surf, as her stretchy thighs ripped her by the verdant retreat of snazzy homes, just visible through the gaps in the lush jungle foliage. The yellow catamaran was speckled with dew that sparkled in the still mist-obscured sun. Beatense hit the summer home beach at speed, and an older woman, a grand dame matriarch, came out from a sand trail leading up to a fine old house with a wide porch.

Naked Beatense gave a wave and with snaking flexes of her tightened waist she ran past the Oxhead dunes next, chasing the sea gulls. As she drew near Sorel she loped down to eye the sands ahead. Empty! She could chance it! With her Nakee bundled up in her towel sadly she had no choice. But as she got closer the park was filling quickly, just like the skateway. The girl ran by the staring folk with no concern, but danger lay ahead with the lifeguard party down by the pier. They were raking up the slimy piles of kelp and hefting them into their truck.

The girl aimed away from them by angling over toward the campground. But she saw a park policeman ahead, luckily before he saw her, so she had to veer back toward the relative safety of the seaweed crew. Seeing her, they stopped in mid lift. They stared incredulously, panting. Beatense ran up to them and stumbled to a stop, panting also. She was gorgeously sweat muscled and of course black in this light.

One of the lifeguards, she noticed, merited attention. He was tall and athletically built, with an air of quietly wise command that his friendly look didn't quite overcome. That wise command caused him to grab her wrist.

"Let me go, you suckbag! You don't know who I am!"

"She's that Book Girl!" said one astute rescuer. "All over the FieldNet!"

"Miss, we don't allow nudity here!" said her captor, still holding.

"I have my belly chain on!" She momentarily considered kicking her knee into his stomach, but she chose diplomacy instead. "I said let me go! I demand to know what grounds you have to detain me, a young girl who happens by statute to be legal!"

The nearby park visitors ran over. They were shocked by this wild savage. Her thick hair was fly-away shaggy, and repeat her tan shined near black. Noticing them, with a clink of bracelets the slight nymph held her free arm protectively.

"Who are these losers? And let me go, you creep! That cop is coming over!"

The shaking lifeguard let go her arm as the policeman clumsily ran closer.

"Oh, *now* you let me go! Sure, with the cop coming! I'm real sexually active, all last night, so write me up for that too! Ah, the out of breath officer slows down."

"You... I will get you off," said the enforcer. "This one time."

"Okay, thanks. For nothing! And like... Ahem, what's your name?"

"I'm... I'm-I'm J-Jerry, m-miss. I'll clear you with Officer Molen. Now go!"

The rescuers got as much of her as they could in those few seconds before she turned and ran. Despite her aggressive tan, with her upturned nose she was high pedigree. Her long waist was frighteningly slight, and although her fibered muscles were lightly shaped to move her with an airy grace, their only real use was aesthetic beautification. The lifeguards began stabbing again at the kelp absently, but seeing it as a red, humming blur. As Jerry told the officer he gave her provisional permission, for just this once, they saw her enter Cocojo and stop to greet a startled surf casting fisherman. The policeman warned that this wasn't correct procedure and he headed back, as the truant was seen laying out her sheet, just over the line, by another sun worshipper they noticed before, who in that shimmering haze also looked black.

A lifeguard watched through the Rescue-Use-Only binoculars.

"Here, Jerry, take a look. She's oiling up. You won't believe this shit."

He waved the binoculars off, but he couldn't dismiss her powers that easily.

The fellow with the binoculars shrugged and looked again. "What I hate is those skinny beach girls all work out, dance and just fuck, and that's bad enough, but then they go and get so shithole tan. How the hell are we supposed to handle that?"

Beatense's neighbor wasn't Sienna as she had first thought, but she was a good second choice for companionship that day. What they both had in common as a true basis for a deep friendship was that both girls were iron rust tan.

"Hi. You awake?" Beatense said, and the other girl, also bare, started.

"That tan! Give some warning!" she said. "Did you just get here now?"

"Yeah. I was attracted here by *your* tan. No shit white for me. But look, with the sun still low to the east let's go lay on the far side of that one dune there."

The other girl self-introduced as Bondy agreed, and they found just the right slope. Beatense grilled her back until high noon. She flipped over and lay propped on her elbows, noting how her gold chain glinted upon her belly. Her poking hips sunk it to hungered depths, but her firm little breasts were full. Her night tightened her belly.

She looked at Bondy, who had a violent rays saturation that crackled against her white sheet. She stirred and reclined back on her elbows like Beatense, in blatant admiration of her child body, a vain caring study that included her half-melon breasts and boned handle hips. Like all true tanners, she affected hateful scorn.

She was boy-like in the youthful simplicity of her body, and blasted tan.

Beatense stared. "Did you get that much darker just now? she gasped.

"It's just the glare. Bigger crowd now. Wanna show them how to swim?"

First the bi-sexuals squirmed in play. They came out. Beatense saw that Cocojo had a far bigger population. The high heat was bringing in visitors by the hundreds. The sprites broke into a run and bounded into the driving waves. Bondy was an eel. The surf kept driving the two apart but she flashed right back. At one point the joyous girls stood mid-thigh deep in boiling white froth, each a proud shaft of sun burnished muscle skeletally leaned. Beatense grabbed Bondy and they hugged.

A boy who attended the Soler school of no clothes swam out on his board and danced in like a demon. After five or six runs Bondy asked for his board and did wild dancing of her own. As she watched, swimming, Beatense saw Sienna.

She swam over and dove under and took hold of her ankle, and as she surfaced Sienna half smiled in greeting. They swam together in the scrubbing roar as Bondy continued her black streak surfing. She exemplified what it is to have a young body that can respond to the most strenuous sport action.

Beatense thought that surfing looked reasonably easy, so she borrowed a board from a fellow (he could hardly refuse her) and paddled out. She let a likely breaker pummel by her as she watched Bondy handle it. *Ah, you just turn and race ahead of the wave and hop to your feet!* Beatense sat on her board, that felt nubby and rubby from its waxy preparation, and within a minute another wave approached.

She quick lay upon her tummy and swiveled around and paddled like mad. She glanced back and decided that this was the moment. She held the board and jumped into a squat, and held on with one nervous hand as the wave caught her. The board was tippy, but its skegs and the speed of the wave lent stability. Beatense carefully stood and whooped out loud as she rode right into the shallows.

No way was she going to give the board back. She flopped to her stomach and headed out again and joined the other surfers, all glad to see this hodad. She keenly watched for the next top. "Here it comes!" came a yell. Just before it hit she spun her craft around and fought for speed. Onto her feet, another thrilling ride. Instinctively making the right moves flexed her waist with poetic style. Her long years of barbell work and galloping bareback were paying off; she took to this sport as a natural.

"Hey, you're already standing!" said Bondy, as they floated together.

"Yeah but, what am I going to do? That dude wants his board back!"

"You sit tight! I'll go fuck him! I want some anyway! Which one is he?"

"Can't you tell? He's the one waving. Oh oh! Another wave! Thanks!"

When Beatense ran over to give back the board later a towel-clawing Bondy was on her knees and elbows, in urgent concentration. She gave a quick teary smile.

Sienna knew Bondy. She joined the two girls when they went back to their dune and lay out again, now on its seaside. Beatense had to do her front now.

"Are the other girls here today, Sienna? And how did Torrey do last night?"

"Six hundred. She's painting today, and Star is framing. Tenny and Summer are back in the bowl. Say, Bondy, ain't you sailing today?"

"That's later. But hey, Beat, wanna come? My friends have this cabin Shefield, Med Studs, and we're heading out for an all nighter. Come on along!"

"Sounds fun but I have to do my front now. I really do."

That forged deep bonds of respect in the other girls. She had priorities.

"Oh, come on, Beater, it's just that with those warm tropical breezes out on those gentle, rocking waves, beautiful things can happen."

Beatense saw a plain and pale blob in her late twenties nearby, who seemed to take a defeated envy in this invitation. It occurred to her that she was woefully out of place here at Cocojo. A lesson had to be taught to this non-sensual intruder.

Resting back on her elbows, for Chubbo's benefit she openly admired her sizzly hot tan. With a haughty snort she shook back her hopelessly tangled hair.

"Oh, they wouldn't want nerd me along, Bondy!" she belatedly replied, affectedly laughing. "By midnight I would be all fucked out and wanna sleep! Ha ha ha!"

Yes, Chubbo wilted in that exchange. Good. But Beatense then saw that Bondy was actually quite plain herself. She was an ordinary shop girl.

The unruly type who smokes only because her worried mum nags her not to. No one would look at her straight, mud yellow hair twice, either. It was all scrappy, as if she wanted it to look uncouthly offensive. But the girl had marvelous, strap tough muscles. And her vibrant tan was the darkest Beatense saw since her own, and that Jesse kid's. Yes, and Neatsfoot too. At that art fair people bumped into each other.

"Well, unless drove here too I guess you can't go with anyway."

"Bondy, it's just that my one boyfriend is coming Saturday, and he won't be real understanding if I went off on a tropical binge cruise without him!"

"Yeah, little inexperienced you," groused Sienna. "I saw your last night vid."

"What video? But speaking of, this morning my friend Zapo said he could set me up with pay per view in the Net. I'm supposed to set up a bank account in town, so if anyone watches me he has to credit card in, so I could add to my book and record royalties. The trouble is, me leaving town in a few days the videos would just end."

Chubbo wilted at this bit of info so Beatense added, "I'm worth a quarter mill."

"Not enough. I would scratch every cent you can, Beatense," said Bondy. "Your videos will keep playing forever. Meanwhile, boat-wise, you two join us Saturday!"

"Hey, that would be a great activity for us! Just in case he wants to idiot golf!"

The friends laughed, and Chubbo sagged in cruel defeat. But Beatense sensed that she actually took morbid pleasure in missing out yet again, which was made far worse by her frustrated resentment toward her. She began appraising herself with curled lip disdain. The other girls, including the non-ethereal close by, admired her coltish balance of delicate versus durable.

Truly, if she weighed one pound more or less, it wouldn't work.

"So Bondy, sailing?" said Sienna. "But what about your waitressing?"

"I'm expendable. I do cocktails at this shit Sunset del Camino dive, Beatense, at least until I get fired for not coming in tonight. Which I will not. But I'll get another job within a couple days, believing as I do in *paying my own way.*"

"Maybe, just maybe, I'm fucking up my life," said Sienna.

Beatense laughed. She wanted Chubbo to suffer worse. She eyed the sun and shifted herself to align herself with it, with the additional benefit of giving her a vulgar view as she opened out her legs. But after horrible torment Chubbo was distracted; Tenacity came out from the shimmering dunes and joined the three bitch sluts. She was just in oil, and her muscled form was other-worldly dark cherry browned.

Beatense stared; yesterday she was just paper baggy. With her striking tan she had a charming body overall: Slim, musically graceful and strong, all crucial traits. A girl's build is her identity as much as intellect or personality, just as bony looks shape character, or character shapes bony looks. Somehow it all works together.

"Hi, everyone. Krinkles joined Summer back in the bowl. I'm escaping from that heat." Her rounded voice would tell of a high quality and ready humor even over the phone. "Did you get any tips last night, Bondy?"

"A mere pittance. But I'm not the type. I'm not cute or bubbly or some innocent wide eyed, laughing little sophomore, so the most I ever get is a tenner."

Beatense was surprised to have her earlier thoughts voiced like this.

"That's true for any job," said Sienna wearily, "which is exactly why I don't have one. I don't have to be fakely bubbly, I live on my own merits."

Tenacity and Bondy smiled at each other knowingly. And Beatense looked over toward stupid Chubbo, who was close enough to overhear the lively blather of these magnificent women quite closely. *Good, listen up and learn about life.*

"Oh, it was so funny," said Tenacity. "Before Summer came a couple gays were moving in on me back in the bowl. I was nude, so did they look!"

"But you're so obviously a girl!" said Sienna, eyeing her warheads.

"I was laying on my front. They must have thought I was a young boy. I sat up and they almost dug a hole in trying to get away."

"Yesterday I met this Buck," said Beatense. "I bet he's gay."

"Buck?" said Bondy. "Good old Pizza Buck? If only that creep was!"

"Why does he even try with us?" said Sienna. "He's just torturing himself."

"He's junk," said Bondy, and Beatense felt her hostility was vindicated.

Summer and Krinkles came out of the dunes and joined the party. Bondy began spraying Beatense with her aerosol bottle. The fogged-on mist made her shiver, and her muscles reacted within her oiled, stretched skin. She tossed and shook.

"Aghhhh! Bondy!" she yelled, for Chubbo's benefit. "Ease up with that!"

"It's seltzer, from the bar. The droplets of water give the sun more power."

"Oh, douse it on!" She gave Chubbo a look. "I am trying to get half brown!"

Pointedly she looked over at Chubbo again with a heavy groan of luxury.

She was being bitchy, but since she perceived the world with her eyes only, it was uniquely her creation. If things went badly for her in this virtual world, her trials would be hers alone. So could not also her pleasures be hers alone?

Now it was Krink's turn for the spray, and she yelped in spasms. Bondy set the bottle down and got up to presumably head for the marina.

"Now, Beats, get this. Saturday when we land offshore here we'll row the dinghy in for you. That white gelcoat will really clash with that tan."

She gave a careful study of her arm. "What's jell coat?"

"The deck. It's painted with gelcoat. White gelcoat over fiberglass."

Beatense pondered. That gelcoat sounded fun. *How about you, Chubs?*

"Oh, like the yachts in the magazines! So when should we be here, then?"

"What? Beato, we have a sailboat! You can't set any exact time! We plan to up anchor nine or so, but that can turn into ten real fast. But then if there's an adverse wind we might not make it until afternoon. So just get down here and lay out until we show up! Got that? Whether or not you do, see ya then!"

Naked, she ran for the dunes, leaving her things behind.

"Here, Beatense," said Krinkles, "Get on your front, I'll oil you all up!"

Beatense submitted to the kid's hot massage with eyes half shut. She squirmed and grunted, solely for her fat neighbor's benefit. She studied her thin arms, trying to decide if they were as dark as they looked, or if she was being misled by the glare. Krinkie had her turn over and did her front, expertly working her limbs into all kinds of awkward positions. She tantalizingly worked her hands all over her breasts and belly, ever closer, then stuck fingers deep. Beatense began writhing, tossing and yelping. The child kept tickling, then finished her off with the spray, and a panting Beatense turned back over. Summer traced her finger down her long furrowed spine. She flexed like a snake in reaction.

"Summer, you idiot, you're giving me the shivers! Now let me do my back!"

She continued her back for another hour, then got her things together.

"Im heading up to Main," she said. "I gotta find this guy as tan as me."

The girls were puzzled as she first walked south. But a short distance away she turned back and, proudly springing as she flitted by, she cheerfully waved.

Her tangled hair tossed upon her long baked back, her slim waist flexing again.

Chubbo choked helplessly in agony. The newest babe on the beach then ran on into Sorel and stopped to tie on her Nakee, out of deep concern she would be halted, being only half legal. Yes, a lifeguard came toward her.

"Miss, we... You... You're the same... The same girl this morning!"

She knew him as one of the kelp rakers. She held her arm protectively.

"Yes. Odd, isn't it? Now let me through. I have my legal Nakee on!"

"Look, I don't like the rules myself. But this is a family place."

"Well it's about time these families learn some Brown's Anatomy!"

She ran on, aiming inland toward the campground tents set back from the sand. This area formed its own busy little city, with fewer rules. She saw a girl in a floral tie bikini brushing her shiny long hair while looking in a mirror hung from a branch.

Torrey could paint her easily; she was a chocolate figurine. Now why didn't the stupid lifeguards get *her?* Nearby another chocolate rendering, a mid-teen boy was tapping fly balls out to his even tanner friends. It was all these wonders could do to keep from looking down at themselves as they lightly chased over the baking sand.

And how their pretty faces lit up as the call came from within the camp: "Hurry it up, kids! We got burgers on!" Beatense watched the long-haired boys run, laughing and pushing and shoving. The figurine girl ran and joined them.

Beatense ran on through the park watching for the tall Jerry. She saw him up by the pier as he lectured a half dozen worshipful Forester Girls. He swept his arm out toward the now placid sea in making a solemn point. One of the girls pointed out Beatense, and the lifeguard gave her a dirty look, probably for her upstaging him.

Beatense broke into a hard run just to show the low people here the joys of tan youth and health. As a track star she flew through the rest of Sorel, then on past the Oxhead and summer homes. And still at high speed she ran by the modern digs.

Throughout her travels all paused to watch her fly by. She came to Bastian and untied naked, and saw the two girls, and yesterday's same phone lending lifeguard.

She walked up to him. "Hey, I want to buy a surfboard."

"Don't get a longboard. How good are you? And are you experienced?"

"Only when I'm in a purple haze. But yes, I can surf. What's your name?"

"I go by Curt, miss. People call me Curt. What's yours?"

"Beatense. Hi, Curt." She winked. "Er, busy at all tonight?"

His blood absolutely pounded. It was her waist that did it for him. But how could he arrange this? That's the trouble with living together. It sounded good but a guy is just as tied down as with marriage. When he worked up at the health club, all those tight, slight women vibrating with tan, but home he went.

"I... I actually am, er, Beatense. B-But I can help with the surfboard."

"No, I just realized, I can't get one. What would I do with it back home?"

"I thought you wanted to move here."

Her jaw dropped. "How did you know that?"

"Easy. Everyone wants to move here. Okay, then, see you tomorrow?"

"I'm not leaving yet. Which beach is best for meeting guys, Coco or Main?"

"Cocojo? That's Flake City with all those bipolar nudies and gayboys."

"Hey, if I'm not criticizing the cretins on your mediocre beach, you lay off mine! Anyway, everyone seems okay there. Except, Tenacity did see some gays."

"Tenacity. Glasses, right? Down on her nose? Like a scolding teacher?"

"You are good. But it's a maxo beach. I borrowed this guy's surfboard and my friend Bondy, like, helpfully kept him *occupied*. But anyway, bye, Curt."

The way she already used his name, *Bye, Curt.* "Yeah, b-bye. Later."

Beatense headed on north as everyone's eyes feasted upon her. She felt a wee bit iffy even though she was legal. The rules might have changed.

As she got to the end of Windemere the girl could have walked over to take the Beachway Walk, but she stayed at water's edge. Fewer people. Or so she thought. She had told TV land that she would be on Main that day, and in sad disappointment many individuals spent all day looking for her. And now here she was after all.

Her admirers ran over to watch her walk by, and equally morbid family fathers turned into shaking red eyed wrecks, despite their closely watching wives.

In the distance Beatense saw a small figure dive off the Cliff Diving Rock. Well, that gave her a reasonable destination. Her fans seemingly aimlessly moved on with her, and out to sea the planes and helicopters flew by at intervals, closer and slower than usual, it seemed to Beatense. Five minutes later the diver made another drop. Even at this long distance she saw that he was just a kid, who was falling through a good thirty feet, equal to the roof of a three story building.

The girl went on by the Hoggy Lodges. It stood in a the long line of beach bars, cantinas, surf huts, restaurants, vacation condos and motels, that came to an end at the Breeze Hotel. This towered up over its stretch of beach, so that its overhanging penthouse ballroom looked to move against the clouds. The palm hut cabanas upon the sand were cordoned off with red velvet ropes, and the hotel featured a glassed-in swimming pool terrace atop a flight of concrete steps. This entire complex on the beach and off was very busy with paid guests, some with Beatense's caliber or better.

North of Hoganforth the Beach Walk had widened out into the plaza Beatense had skated along, and this had a slight uphill grade as it approached the hotel. And so from here northward the promenade was ten feet up off the sands.

The phantom death-dropped again. It *was* just a kid! Beatense walked up and joined the gathering on the shore, that eyed her approvingly, but then turned back to watch his side canted spirals, that seemed to unwind in slow motion. The height he negotiated had to be forty feet, more than she first guessed, and the angle of the sun gave a flashing effect to his vile hot hide. The audience cheered at his butterfly dive, and then he climbed the rock again. This in itself was a feat. The boy performed a dying quail tumble, then pulled his surfboard off a ledge. Like a fury he danced into shore on a roller, gorgeously wild.

The fans crowded around the small, black tan kid as he heroically arrived on his board, and Beatense was startled to see that he was the bareback dashing Jesse of yesterday. When their eyes caught (causing him to look twice) she saw he was the most beautiful creature she ever saw, even counting her mirror. His eyebrows trailed off into self important little points, that made him a baby face in spite of his legendary prowess. And his daring shafto lock garlands fell down his back in thick abundance. Yesterday they were afloat behind him. His muscles were sublimely expressive; he could convey a symphony of motion just by opening a pickle jar.

Even though he had a relatively young age, he had command of the crowd. His attraction went far beyond the diving; with his dense tan, muscles and looks the boy had an irresistible star-like quality. He was a happy boy, and even though he proudly held court, he had a disarming shyness that was very unexpected.

Beatense pushed through to him. Two splendids in confrontation.

"Nice diving, but I'm more impressed with your Cocojo ride yesterday."

"What about my tan? We're almost twins."

Everybody laughed, even as others came hurrying over. Here was the innocent excuse they needed to look at this girl; that convenient boy.

"Okay, let's lay in the sun tomorrow at Cocojo."

"I don't know, I might make another run. And who are you, anyway?"

"Beatense of book fame. I was at Hogie's, but now I'm at the Hideaway."

"I'm Jesse, and I know Mr. Cheevy from way back! Er, uh, bye!"

The girl had walked on and Jesse staggered as everyone gently laughed.

Beatense looked ahead toward Main Beach. Properly, all the beach north of the individual street beaches was Main, including the Beachway so popular with the see and be seen set, and the similarly useful plaza, but the hotel was a kind of landmark that acted as a divider for the beach-going crowds.

North of the Breeze a grey concrete retaining wall ran along back of Main. Along its top was a railing for the walkers here, and the restaurants, motels and shops that Beatense saw from Kathy's bus. In the wall itself, at sand level, dark windows rented out surf and sail boards, and umbrellas and chaise lounges, and other windows sold snacks and drinks. One grim little dungeon with limp plastic pennants was where the blood-stirring catamarans crouching in wait out along the shore were rented.

How lethally poised these sleek craft looked with their knife-like, rakishly battened mainsails! Their trampoline decks and banana shaped pontoons were exciting for sailors and non-sailors alike. All this was presided over by the many lifeguard towers, manned by work-out heroes sporting whistles and sunglasses.

But for all their sun on the job they just didn't have the tans that the women had. Lying on their towels or playing upon the sand, these wild sea lasses were pipe-stem limbed and thrillingly brown, and all these lissome devotees of risky bare were nude. Stately Stacey's and Budget-wise Bridget's exuberant self celebration flowed through them with an erotic energy that they put to every-night dancing and bedtime use.

Beatense also saw petite, soft voiced tenders, who were so sweetly delicate and twig-like sheltered, they would patiently await the walk light with no car in sight. But like Krinkles they weren't shy about what they did or did not wear. And bed habits?

The shoreline eased gradually away from the retaining wall, so the beach fanned out wider as it continued north toward Holiday Hill. The retaining wall angled slowly down to continue the raised concrete walk beyond the retaining wall. Unlike at dawn the walk was mobbed. Beatense came to a tin sign that warned,

NO SWIMMING! SURFERS ONLY!

This unwelcoming rule to those who didn't surf conferred an exulted status upon those who did, giving even its youngest cohorts a disdaining pride. Many were actually young kids, but they were all hard faced from their expert skill, and as if forged by a daunting regimen of salt and sun they were cruelly hot tan. Their taut tuned muscles quivered with strength. Beatense admired the rippled bellies and trained chests that even the pre-teens had, as they in turn reacted to her.

Boys and girls spent hours floating on their boards far out to sea, like menacing birds of prey, and Beatense could proudly think, *Me too, me too.*

Dodging past the racing tongues of the spent waves, she kept northward, where the shore ahead curved out to meet the mini-peninsula Holiday Hill bluff. This was protected from the waves by rugged boulders scattered before it. The surf hit these and shot mightily up, then roared on to storm the narrow strip of beach at the bluff's foot. Distant figures appeared and dashed for the beach proper.

As the next wave came one fellow was too slow. The trees on the hillside above him gave a nice back-drop as he was swept by them into shore.

As she kept exploring Beatense was dazzled by these broad acres of sand. She felt as if she was taking part in a great pageant just by walking through here. Then,

NO SURFERS! SWIMMING ONLY!

Holiday Hill was a mass of normal leafy trees, but its lower flank along the beach was fronted by mounds of sand. Beatense was now walking the notorious College Alley, bounded by the hulking Holiday bluff to the north and the tourist areas to the south. The guys, who were a little tipsy from too much beer, were fully aware of the babe paradise they were in, and with wise, sloppy smiles they were giving all the nut baked rowdy girls their caring attention. One such girl turned and crossed through the Alley toward the access ramp that led up to the Walkway. The iron pipe railing was lined with suddenly interested admirers as tan champ Beatense climbed up.

Still watched, she found herself at the Cemented Passion Skateboard Park. An acre in size, along with its admissions shack it held a maze of waving and curving pathways, half pipe culverts and bowls. Tan boys were hanging around inside with their fancy boards, and others were snapping off some truly gravity defying tricks.

They dove down into the open bowls and shot up skyward on the far side, then flashed out sensational twist-flips and rotations. Beatense, watching as she was in turn watched, was quick to credit only the muscled tan marauders with these extravagant hot fueled tricks, but some of the performers were cheap punk drop-outs.

Even in this heat they wore baggy black T-shirts along with floppy old ugly pants torn off below the knees, which made their anemic legs look like white sticks. They had no interest in sun, nor in portraying an attractive image. From their crude, snorting laughter as they noticed Beatense, they obviously set out in life to be repulsive ugly misfits. They didn't have the fine, quick minded looks the tan athletes had, boys and girls, but instead they were shapeless and diseased looking.

Reassuringly, the show-off boys had the same vain arrogance the surf kids did, and though people might doubt the value of their fond self worship to this society, at least their lives were directed toward constructive purpose. And the young surf and skateboard girls could be praised for the same reason. They were hard trained body builders, but they had such fetching cute faces their muscles were quite disturbing.

Beatense walked along the skate park and turned onto the walk-way, as a trio of toasted girls in thong bottoms blasted by everyone on in-line skates. They pressed their southward flight along the broad, sweeping arc that was this promenade. This was also home to ordinary tourists, mothers pushing strollers and the elderlies.

Beatense came to a drink stand on wheels and got in line even though she didn't have any money on her. The girl working the counter had active green eyes, and a raspy voice that sounded like her vocal cords were lightly tied together.

Skinny, T-shirted and tan, she never stopped laughing and smiling as she deftly made the drinks. She had loosely full, shining reddish blond hair. Some customers called her Tuffy. Carefully watched by all, Beatense stepped up.

"Hi. I'm afraid I don't have any money, but I'm really thirsty."

Tuffy laughed. "No pockets, hah? Well, do you promise that if I give you a drink, that you'll pay me back tomorrow? Or do you just want water."

"Water. I can't promise to pay you back, it depends on the beach I'm at."

The fellow behind Beatense stepped up. "I... I can h-help you out."

"Thanks! I honestly will watch for you, to avoid paying you back."

Loud laughter. Tuffy thanked Davis and gave Beatense a Mega lemonade. She drank half of it in a gulping chug, and Tuffy refilled it. Beatense thanked Davis again and took her drink over to the edge of the promenade.

She folded her sheet into a square and she sat on it propped back on her hands with feet dangling. The later afternoon sun was still intense, heating into her chained sunk belly as she worked her drink and watched the beach. Everybody walking by paused to watch her. She stayed until six, getting good rays. When she got up to go she gave Tuffy a wave and headed back south. She got as far as a massage table.

Screaming, writhing, she was butter rubbed naked. Drew a crowd

At Bastian Curt was gone; the sisters too. She dashed up the steps to the street and hopped across Windemere. She ran up Bastian past the small shops and pastel painted tourist lodgings along here. Her heart pounded, she was still naked. At the corner a car racing to go through on red screeched to a stop. Beatense, all butter shined, flitted for her motel and stopped rather noticeably by the office.

"Hi, Cheevy!" The manager looked up in commendable shock once again.

"G-Goodness, girl, I-I-look... L-Look at all the... The s-sun you've gotten!"

"Exactly! But sorry to just barge in on you indecently!" On legs so slender she teetered on them, she sprang to the counter, reeking of sun, and spotted a computer over to the side. "Hey, you got a computer here! Can I look at it?"

He was violently shaking. "W-W-Why, c-certainly."

She was quite out of place in this drab office, a bony, skinny girl dark beach tan and wet with oil. Her lack of clothing lent a disquieting effect, and her fertile breasts quivered with firmed readiness. Her tangled auburn blond hair was tumbled thick all over her hardened little shoulders. Her surfer tuned body sang.

Rank with greasy sweat, the muscled savage stepped around and she sat at the keyboard smiling widely. Her gold-chained black belly was gauntly curved from her slack posture. The girl's bangle bracelets clinked and jingled on her wrists.

The monitor showed a blank guest register form. The border was green, the form yellow, and the gridlines were bold black. Beatense was enchanted.

"Wow! Is that ever cool, Mr. Cheevy! Tell me what to do!"

He trembled. "Why, y-you can enter your own self, y-young lady. Here, take your registration card you f-filled out when you f-first came here yesterday."

Head turned she began typing with the classic erect posture. A haggard looking tourist stepped in the office with his even more haggard looking wife.

"Hello," he sighed. He blinked at the wild clerical temp. "D-Do... Do you have anything? W-We got bumped down at Sugar Beach."

"I never quite agreed with their policies, sir," said Mr. Cheevy. "But look, my assistant will be happy to help you. Bring up the vacancy menu, miss."

The girl stared at the screen uncomprehendingly. Mr. Cheevy reached, shaking, and clicked. A new field appeared, that showed a diagram of the motel. Beatense gasped. Amazing! The two open rooms were shaded in green.

"Yes, sir," said the clerk, happily all business. "We have two vacancies, so let's see, the charge is... Wait!" With thin arms at play she clicked to the Rates screen. "This is midweek, so for the two of you it will be... Mr. Cheevy, are there any special events going on for a higher rate? Besides me being in town naked?" She winked.

"The Art Fair, but we don't count that, my dear."

"I went to that art fair! Okay, smoking or nonsmoking?"

"Either, miss." The husband had to mask his interest in this smiling assistant.

"Okay, sir, it will be ninety-five dollars, plus tax. I need your credit card."

Beatense went on to fill out the registration right on screen, and she warned that the room (now shaded pink) had a previous reservation for Friday night.

"...but we can find you a place for the weekend, if you would like."

"Why, that would be wonderful! Yes, thank you! Thank you very much!"

The couple joyfully left and Mr. Cheevy cleared his throat.

"Young lady, we do not normally offer that service, I'll have you know. I'll be on the phone all day tomorrow!"

"Ha ha! But boy, is this slick! My Pop and I could really use a gadget like this for our surveying! Here, now I'll do my own self! Let's see…"

The leopard finished her entries, and the manager wobbled as she stepped back out. He put her card back in the tin box. This he would always keep.

He called out. "Stop! I forgot, I have a letter here for you, Miss Nauti-Gal. But unfortunately we enforce policies here, no shirt, no service. It's policy and law."

"Some law! I'll run and get my new shirt."

Before he could halt her she was out the door. Seconds later she was back with her swirl shirt. She pulled it on over her head. Mr. Cheevy watched as she gamely tugged it down over her breasts. The shirt's fruity colors gave the girl a lush browned glow, and its open hang gave her waist an unearthly leaned editing.

"Okay, that's my part of the deal. Hand it over."

She took the envelope and fakely smiled. Craig. She didn't need him, her heart fell as she tore it open. Well, she could handle his company for two days. The only difficulty was she was hoping to ensnare that Neatsfoot art critic, who had far more appeal to her even with just that glance from the bus. He wasn't all adulty in build.

"Okay, he says he's coming Friday afternoon, but he can't see me until the next morning, because they have to set up for his trade show. Well, what shitfulness! I can't just sit around here Saturday in this old fleabag waiting! Oh, I better call home, Mr. Cheevy. Do you charge for that if I use my room phone?"

"Sadly I can't waive the fee, the owner checks all phone use closely. So why not use the office phone here?" He said this casually. "Come by th-this evening."

She smiled and went to her room and got her shirt back off and stood before her mirror. She had burned ever dark brown, giving her muscles a new, sleek tightness. Grabbing some money she headed out and hopped across the Highway to Wacky Wearables. She held her arm beside a yellowish-green *Psycho Sunner* T-shirt and took it, and she selected a ribbed, tank styled sleeveless undershirt done in circus peanut orange. Everyone in the store pretended great disinterest.

From there she went to One Stop and bought two peaches (firm) and a quart of chocolate milk. Back home she quickly ate and got on her skates. She rolled across the parking lot, aware of how the poly wheels smoothed out the bumps. The skating was an erotic dream. The girl easily glided with traffic up the Highway, and at Strings she paid her tab. She cut around the skate park and flew back along the beach, and stopped to pay the massage guy ten tens. Returning, she went into the office to call home. After a few stiff criticisms her father told her to call Mercaphony, they needed her okay to press *Papa Say Do No Do.* "Why don't they just go ahead on that?"

Smiling with mischief, Beatense turned on the No Vacancy light.

Mr. Cheevy had my *age* problem, but the girl's coaxing got him nicely in.

19

THURSDAY

Thursday morning Beatense awoke at 5 AM and sprang impatiently out of bed.

She was wide awake even though she gave her friend four hours. She tied on her running shoes and sprang again, out her door. She was bared and readied for a run. She took the same route as last evening; she loped the now empty Coastal Highway up to the skateboard park, then she pelted down along the walkway back to Bastian. She got back to her room and quick got on her blade skates, and took the Highway again. The dawn haze gave way to a clear sky.

Her heart pounded. By now there was more traffic on the Highway, and the cars almost collided as the drivers watched her. The early sun gave her tan an unusual depth, as it also added a glow to her shining muscles. And of course her apparel selections were minimal, a few bracelets and a belly chain. As she got over to the Beachway she sprinted up to a reckless speed, glazing herself with sweat.

Others were along here at this wakening hour, all locals who were trying to get in their dog walking, skating or running before the yapping tourists came churning out and wandered along four abreast. As a local Beatense got a few whoops and cheers.

The girl returned to her room and sat cross-legged on her bed, in wait of a magic, mystical odyssey of tan surrender, where she would heat her pan fudge darkness by baking it impossibly wicked black. She admired her face in her hand mirror and the tears came. Besides Krinkles she never saw anyone so wondrous.

But what beach today? She wanted to try Main, but she wanted the risky thrill of running naked through Sorel on her way to CoJo. For that she had to get going now, before all the park lifeguards were out, ready to pounce. She pushed back her blond streaked, tumbling hair and pondered this. True, she could make it through now, but the afternoon would be rife with hazards. She didn't want to drag her Nakee along again because of a crowd of dipbags with weird ideas.

Beatense rolled up her sheet, not the motel one, her own, with her surf shack oil and sadly, her Nakee. She ran out across the parking lot, surprising a few guests loading their trunks, and she leaped across the Highway.

Down by Windemere, she saw a familiar face. "Oh, hiya... Buck." *Damn.* Amazing luck. He was on his way to down to Curt to repay his $5 loan.

"Wh-Why, hello! I... I don't hardly r-recognize you, miss, that t-t-tan."

Her bony face registered irritation. "Oh, I don't know, I might be darker."

He dry swallowed. This talk wasn't going well, but they never did. But now the miracle, the girl lowered her eyes and smiled shyly. She had an idea.

She could use his phone to get that Mercaphony call out of the way. "Gee whiz, Buck, you got a phone on you? Can I use it? It would be so helpful."

He handed it over in seconds and she tapped in the number, that she knew all too well. She pressed *Send* and the phone at the other end uselessly rang. *Damn, too early!* No voice box in Arrolynn. And now she had made a slave of Buck. She gave the phone back with a smiling shrug of gratitude.

He almost grabbed her. Despite her tan, she was so delectably sweet he could hardly resist, he wanted to feel her tough little muscles work against his own as she struggled. But at the same time he worshipped her, he could never force himself on her that way. She was the only beautiful woman who was ever more than civil with him. In fact her face opened up radiantly.

He looked behind him. "Who... Who are you smiling at?"

"You accept me naked. Some people get so pissy about it. Well, bye!"

She hopped down the steps to the beach, and she was happier to find Curt. He was doing the inevitable raking. The girl whimsically watched.

"Hi, dirtball! Why so early today? You even beat the two sisters."

He pointed to his idled surfboard. "Hi, scum bitch. I was hoping to surf."

"Oh, yeah, not good waves, hah? Well, did you change your mind?"

He was jolted by her stunning nudity. "Ch-Change my m-mind about what?"

"Surfing with me, as in, let's us have an All-Nighter. Here I am, sensitive and clever, culturally restrained and computer adept, and demurely agreeing to take that tawdry journey into Fleabag City. I'm unfailingly promiscuous, so let's fuck!"

He leaned on his rake panting. "Th-This m-might not be the best way to..."

"Am I too pushy? Well, it's not my fault. As a kid thirteen when I got my implant the nurse said I had real touchy receptors, so she warned that this with my lack of maturity this could make me like sex way too much. And I did!"

"Hey, Buck!" *Yeesh!* "You're delivering a pizza down here?"

Beatense saw the gentle clown trudge toward them in his billowy white shirt, his leather wing-tip shoes and clip-on bowtie. She held her arm protectively.

"Hi, Curt. I... I just saw a m-mermaid, is all. And I owe you that five."

"Oh, yeah. Anyway, she seems to be pestering me to befriend her."

"Oh, like, twist it all around! With the derelicts and gays down at Cocojo and the jails full of convicts on phenobarbitol, I would pick a loser like you?"

"Anyway, Buck, this is Beatense, and Beatense..."

"Yeah, I know Buck. Curt, how about in secret? I won't spill." --/-- "No!"

"Well, I can take a hint. But I'm wasting sun. See you two!"

She ran off, then turned and waved in weightless, springing side-steps.

They watched the feathery, brown young mermaid flit southward as a nude with trailing sheet and hair aflutter. That butt of hers... Those legs... That tan...

"Nice kid, but she's a flake, Buck. Not quite the young maiden in her restraint."

Slut Beatense reached the summer homes and cranked up in hard acceleration, speeding like scared buckshot, as she happily noted the live action of her legs.

Then as she ran the Oxhead she also noticed how her brass bangles were so shaky and clinky loose on her thin unencumbered arm. The few people on the beach either smiled, laughed or stared in offended disapproval.

Beatense thought about Buck. She never could be big, like him. Look what he missed out on in being large! In her case, her trim stretched waist, together with her light hips-set and twin coconut butt-set, had flexing tensions that were shared by the rest of her firm tuned body. No adult male could ever know the supple efficiency that she and other petite teen-likes lived with. Excepting guys like Neatsfoot, and Elgin, they never woke in the morning with that leap of excitement in being vitally attractive. Indeed, she thought skinny girls could be so perfect, and could be so inviting for bed, she found it hard to stay humble while being one.

Beaense slowed to a prudent walk as she entered Sorel. Anyway, she actually was slightly winded. The day was already hot, lots of people were out. Sadly it was too late to get through here nude. But she could just wrap up in her sheet!

She huddled within it and walked on, more modest than she had been since last winter. She did catch the tall Jerry's eye, who at the time was driving a tractor that raked the sand, and he gave her another coldly annoyed look.

"Wow, he let me by," Beatense muttered, giving the rescuer a stately look.

Cocojo had a widely scattered clientele. Beatense found an area with just one human nearby, Chubbo. She stopped, just far enough away to make any overtures difficult, and removed her sheet. It had the desired effect, Chubs recoiled in shock.

Heart pounding, and regally ignoring the other, Beatense sat on her sheet and plied on her greasy rich lard in a soothing ritual. She became sloppy wet, and she gave herself pouting study, as in disapproval of how dark tan and thinly sex sensual she was. She recklessly flung out her limbs and let out heavy groans.

The only trouble was, this was really just for Chubbo's benefit, because the sun's low height meant it had no power. She needed a slope angle at this early hour. So she abruptly sprang up and ran with her things into the dunes.

She lay in hot baking of her back for three hellish hours. She woke and groggily turned to get a look. Her lower back, her tight butt lobes and shapely legs gleamed with an outrageous tan. With head spinning, now sun drunk, she sat up and debated her next step. It was gorgeous back here, but the sun was high enough now for the flat sand and any possible partners upon it. She had two addictions. Both took hours

She ran out and returned to Chubbo's vicinity, and propped on her elbows she brazenly eyed herself. She lay back with legs opened, and she fell asleep.

"Hey, Beat, wake up! You're melting!"

The girl awoke, in a fog. This was from the intoxicating effect of the sun, or its sweating out her electrolytes. Sienna sat cross-legged on the sheet beside her. She had sandy white patches all over her crisp dark hide.

"Oh, hello, Sienna." She sat up. "Do I look any tanner? I'm using lard."

"Lard, hah? I wish I had a slick of that on myself awhile back. These frat zeroids, I did a hot, orgasmic dance for them. They wept. Can I lay here?"

"Well, this beach is public. I can't say no even to Buck. What a dink he is."

"Tut tut. But I mean on your sheet! Can I lay here?!"

"Well, it is big enough, but get that sand off first. What time is it?"

"One. I came by before; you weren't here. Where were you?"

"Back in the dunes. Hey, Senny, if Bondy is out on that boat will they stop here? Because I got a letter from Craig saying he is coming, so I just want to connect with her, is all." She gave a look over to Chubbo. "It's all set up *at my motel* for us to *stay together* Saturday night! First dancing, then fuck! Unless we take that cruise!"

"You better ask Bondy. But you're back, though, hah? No Main today?"

"Yeah, as if I matter. But I'm going there now to find a place for us for when Craig comes. He wouldn't like Cocojo here. He might not even like Main. But you know, if it's one, I got in three hours for my back and an hour for my front!"

"You do need it. You got some genetic thing that scares me."

"Wait, we sail on Saturday! I *can* stay here! I can hit Main tomorrow!"

"Okay, but you see that tall, odd looking hill with the cliff up yonder?"

The girl looked. She noticed that geological oddity her first day here. Back within the forest standing back of the dunes, there stood a craggy rock hill, with a height all out of proportion to its breadth, like a small volcano.

"That's Lookout Mountain. You can see for hundred miles on top, and there's a hidden little ledge will give you the most dazzling, rock reflected bake."

"Sienna, I do have at least a week to go. Try me some other time."

"Your hair is turning blond pretty fast. Come on, speed up the process."

The kid was tempted, but she needed to borrow a phone. Obviously Sienna didn't have one. Chubbo probably did, but she didn't dare ask after her antics.

"It's silly to go up there, Sienna. Sun is sun."

"Yes, but picture yourself moving through those trees like a forest predator."

"Trees! But what about that ledge up on the mountain?"

"Well, you obviously have to go through the woods to get up there."

"Sienna! How long will that take? I can't break my rays momentum!"

"Okay, I'll give you another massage. How did you like that yesterday?"

"Krink could do that for a living. Why don't you? Yesterday afternoon I paid this guy like two hundred to massage me naked right on Main Beach. Drew a crowd."

"Anyone recognize you?"

"Oh I suppose. But what about water up there, on your ledge."

"Jesse rides a gallon of water down on Windfire every few days, for us laying out up there, himself included. Plus there's a pond in the woods."

"Tempting. I might lay beside that pond sometime."

"It's in the shade. So, you coming? I have to know sometime today."

"No! Now let me keep on with my front! Can't thin girls get tan around here?"

Sienna ran for the dunes, and with an irritated look at Chubbo Beatense tossed back her sun tousled and blonded hair, then ran for the surf to cool off. She emerged with skin fast drying. More lard, then it was time to explore this pristine sea world, to commune her bared brown skin with it. And find a phone.

Heart pounding, nips athrust, the naked foundling strolled along the gently rolling surf. As a nature child, the powerful tri-hull runabout she came upon, pulled up onto the shore, her shore, offended her deeply. She held forth her arm protectively, as if fending the boat off, then with a tossing snort she looked away to banish the sight of this mechanical fuel burning monstrosity despoiling her beloved tropical shore.

Forsaken and alone in that dazzling sunlight, yet aware of the fluidic poise and allure presented by her light form, she bunched her massive hair up in her hand and gazed back northward. The sea starkly silhouetted her slender form, as the boaters, sitting nearby, stared helplessly. She turned from them with scorn. In her being so tanned and sleek muscled, she had made a commitment to self perfection that she strenuously, obviously fulfilled, making her royalty. With a distressed look of concern she aimed her gaze back to the boat boys. They recoiled in shock.

With thinned legs hot shining the seeker knelt upon the sand, and she sifted a handful of powdery sand through her fingers. She leaned lankily back on her hands, and her rib ledged belly sunk sagged as her hips jutted. The fellows shook as the seared intensity of her tan exploded into their rabidly bulged eyes.

They were mesmerized by her long, small waist, and that open split. They had heard about the liberties down at this beach, but this girl buried all expectation. Her bony face exerted an aristocratic pride; she was built with hung biceps, and her surf scrubbed buffing gave her buttery baked tan a live sizzle. She wanted.

Her shape had a symphonic flowing, and her pelvics protruded so gauntly they stretched her skin. Between them, her rippled belly could bounce a penny. Her slim waist and aggressively thinned thighs warned of her inner fires, and the child-sized girl's tan and sparkling gold belly chain were cruelly teasing.

Beatense wondered what she was up to; she would welcome a fuck but for now she wanted to use their phone. She had to call the studio and okay that wretched song. She glanced at her victims, and saw that they were okay. Their driving stares, with no assumed indifference, had a charm. And their baggy shorts were favorable. No one could take himself seriously wearing them. Neatsfoot adored himself.

They were on a ratty old blanket, that was probably torn from an unmade bed in their haste. A cracked and faded plastic cooler sat ready, and a seventy dollar boom box with detachable speakers was rasping away in dying battery agony.

Four pairs of eyes continued to stare. Finally one fellow took the plunge.

"Tha... That's quite a t-tan you h-have there, m-miss."

She gave an annoyed look. One reason was that Chubbo was walking by.

"As an athlete I have deeply committed myself to being brown in the sun."

Unbelievably she... She answered! She... W-Wait a minute!

"Hey, aren't you that interview girl? We saw you on TV last night!"

"The Book Girl. But look, any of you guys have a phone, well charged?"

They compared their bars and a phone survived the shaking as it was handed over. She entered the number and this time got through, after the 2000 mile wait.

"Hey, Dixie, it's me, Beatense. Is Mr. Morley in? He is? Okay, thanks!"

"Hello, Miss Colwell, I have good news, we added 30,000 to your account."

"But that's not the only reason you wanted me to call, just that."

"Er, no. We need a B-side to *Papa*. Can you sing us it now?"

The girl explained that all she had was a cellular phone, and even with a regular phone the dynamics would be suppressed. She was told that with this particular song, *Desmond*, they required subdued fidelity. Many people wanted the scratchy, static filled old gramophone sound back. The four guys stared.

"I can't sing that! I don't know the words! Let me do *Chances!*"

"Unfortunately that's our label. Do you know *Greys In The Night*, my lady?"

"...*My mama done told me*... Well, it's an okay song so get the tape going."

By now a small crowd had gathered, including a slim youth of indefinite age, who had been walking by. He was a stunner: Golden toasted by the loving sun and poetically light muscled. Some boys bake tan to look deadly, others from a love of nature. Some bake to become perfectionist athletes, while others, like Beatense, hope to diminish people. But this boy simply loved being brown, and thin, with all his dear heart. His jean cut-offs had their cuffs snugged up tight to his long thighs, and they sagged low in a rumpled wrap that half bared his butt. His cheek points conspired to widely place his dreamy blue eyes, making his low chin delicately dainty. Completing the enchantment, he had shaggy long blond hair.

"Keter! Hey, hi! Stick around! I'm gonna cut a record!"

Beatense stood before her first actual audience and sang into the phone, and only three cuts were necessary. She smiled for the flattered applause and explained that the instrumentals would be dubbed in later, and her fans nodded knowingly. The girl shook hands with everyone and they left. But the smiling boy stayed.

"I… I just wanted to compliment your singing, Beatense. If that's okay."

"Keter, whatever you want. But let me scam these four guys here."

He laughed and lay out his sheet. He slimed on his oil and lay back.

With him unconwcious the four guys felt like they had proprietary interest again.

She turned to them. "Thanks for the phone. Hey, mind if I lay here for that sun I mentioned? And then can you hitch me a ride down to the Breeze?"

They readily agreed and Beatense ran and got her stuff, with a look of hate at Chubbo. Then sitting on her sheet by her friends she lard oiled her front. The guys pretended interest in everything else as she kneaded the oil into her skin, so that the tight fusion of sizzly tan to sinuous muscle gave it a luminous shine. Her long thighs and waist were working to the motions of her hands, and her limb muscles had taut tensions, as if she worked barbells.

Her baseballs were pertly alert, almost bursting despite their size, and her small, hinged shoulders had a dearth of bulk. Her oiled skin glistened with luxurious, fresh energy, almost blurry. She lay back on her elbows, with heels dug in.

"You… You d-don't have to lay right there just because we lent you our phone," said one of the fellows. "So you're the Book Girl? No wonder they used you."

Distant cameras aimed as she said, "Half the women here way outgun me."

Her hipbones stuck out an inch and a half, her collarbones were ropes, and her pinks poked like fingertips. Her belly plackets flexed as she breathed.

"So, what's with the boat? Pretty snazzy, if you ask me."

They introduced themselves. Their seeming leader was Calder; the others were John, Ted and Dale. As befuddled as they were at having her stellar company, their nervous smiles were charmingly at odds with their guyish looks.

"So we took that one out today because of the light surf," Calder offered. "These runabouts with their triple hulls aren't good for shit in rough waves."

"Yeah, back where I'm from the boats don't have that fancy triple look. So where do you keep it? That marina up in Madeline, that I saw from the bus?"

"No, the Gates River north of Cardiff. This isn't a sea-going boat."

"Okay, with that settled I'm going to float into a nice full frontal bake now."

Chubbo stumbled by, and Beatense was angered that she likely would sit herself nearby again. *Okay, bitch!* She got to knees and elbows with weeping, wailing and gnashing of teeth. Then she lay back, legs opened and thin arms carefully placed.

"That run-boat does impress me," she said dreamily, eyes closed, "like you doing me. Wow! But better to impress with one's own self than with external peripherals."

"Well you sure have us there," said Dale, "but not by much, of course."

"Ha ha. Anyway, I'm so shit tan people think, *This Can Not Be*, but they buy my books." She looked over. After watching her event Keter was back to tanning, but spoiling the view, there sat Chubs. *What is it with her?* "But look, I gotta bake now."

"How about a beer before you get started?"

"Oh, good idea! I didn't take water along and you guys sweated me out!"

She sat in an inviting, cross legged slouch, and she took the can and like at camp cracked it open. Foam spilled out. She sucked at the beer noisily, tipping it too far. The foam dribbled down between her breasts and then slid over her quivering rippled belly. But perhaps some beer did make it into her sun beaten, whip-like abdomen.

Her vitality was felt as a physical force, as strong as her squirmy sex reactions.

The girl set down her can and burst out with a loud sigh. That won them over, if they could still be doubtful. It was odd how they welcomed her friendly conversation, but if she was plain they would actually resent it. But that got back to her top quality, her sacred character and pedigree. Plus she gave of herself, all four of them.

"Oh, in case you don't know it, you guys did me hot! And thanks for the beer!"

"Yeah, it was still half cold, despite the cooler, not because of it."

"Don't change the subject. What's the job situation around here?"

"You could ask Jesse," Dale said. "He knows all about that kind of thing."

"But he's just a kid, isn't he? How would he know about jobs?"

"He just does. Do you know him?"

"I'm planning to ride his horse pretty soon. So how do you know him?"

"Holiday Hill is his second home. We live up there, by the way."

"Yeah, I saw on my one map that it has all these stray cabins on it. How stupid. But I thought you came down from that river north of Cardiff."

"That's where my parents live," said Calder. "We stole their boat today."

"Well, good. We don't want any loose ends to confuse anyone watching my Net videos being made today. See that camera? Okay, let me get back to browning."

Beatense baked for just an hour and then announced it was time for the ride.

"It'll only take you a minute to get me up there, so I don't feel guilty."

"Nah, we better head back anyway," said Calder. "We're getting waves."

He flipped into the front well of the boat and with a swish of ice cubes Dale gave him the cooler. Beatense waded alongside the hull and admired the boat's high tech interior. White vinyl seats and ten gauges back of the alloy steering wheel.

"Wow, this boat is gorgeous, you guys! This will be an honor!"

"Our... Ours too," said John, as he handed in the cassette stereo.

Calder stepped back between the low profile, acrylic windshields and sat at the wheel. Beatense looked back at the envious Chubbo with contempt.

"Er, I don't want to put you guys out. I can just walk up to the hotel."

"No, come on, the Breeze is on the way. Help Ted push us off."

The two pushed so hard their feet dug into the sand. Then as the Evader floated free John held out his hand and pulled the eager naked girl up into the forward well.

"I hope I don't get seasick, again," she said warningly, "heh heh."

"Just puke over the side," said Dale. "That's what we *usually* do."

Beatense called good-bye to Keter, and he waved with his usual smile.

It seemed he had the easy ability to burn darker brown in just fifty-two minutes.

Ted the back-to-back seats down to make a sunning settee. But the girl didn't lie on it; she sat on it with back against the padded gunwale. The white vinyl made her look oiled black, which was some consolation, except that Keter, leaning back on his hands cross-legged, was fondly admiring himself. The four guys reflected on this.

They spent their teen years just hanging out, video games, TV, the mall.

Calder saw that the boat had floated out far enough, and he started the V8, that was within the enclosure Beatense rested her feet on. She gave a last look at Keter.

It angered her to see that he had fallen into conversation with Chubs.

Calder shoved the lever forward and the 220 horses leaped to power, heading to the north. Beatense changed sides so she could watch the distant shore go by. She was enough of a local that she knew all the sights. Cocojo was succeeded by Sorel, the Oxhead and the grand old summer homes. Next in line, the fancy house enclave and then Bastian Beach. Beatense saw its broken old cement steps, and the sisters, as the people along the shore absently watched them go by.

The Evader was a good hundred yards out, so as its vee wake tumbled into the sand, it poorly imitated the surf. The many palm trees and multi-colored buildings all made a glorious scene. Calder roared by a gracefully picturesque sailing yacht at a lovely tilt, and Beatense gazed back at its tall sails, now more interested in Bondy's invitation. The boat swung around the Cliff Diving Rock, no Jesse, and headed in for the rapidly approaching Breeze Hotel shore. Calder cut the throttle back just in time and they lightly nudged into the crowded Breeze beach.

Calder shouted over the high revving idle of the engine.

"Nice knowing ya, kid! I'll buy your books! Hop out! The surf is building!"

Dale handed over her things. "Here you are! Shove us off, okay?"

"At last, an actual use for my famous muscles! Okay, nice fucking! Bye!"

With hot tan flashing and bendy build flexing, the nude tossed her bottle of lard and rolled-up sheet to the sand and sprang back. She leaned into the bow, pushing the chug-chugging craft free. Calder clunked the engine back into gear. The fellows waved and regretfully left her behind as they turned back out to sea. Their fun friend had an audience, so she gazed forlornly after them. She felt eyes morbidly burn into her as the boat ran out to the Cliff Diving Rock and then veered north. There was no lack of witnesses for her dramatic arrival, dressed as she was. The cabanas obliged her with longing stares, while the balcony birds suffered dropped jaws. The steward over in the Barbarrosa Hut literally went rigid, even though many of his young lady customers confronted him bare every day, wet with oil and bony baked.

It was a combination of sensual impacts: Her stark nakedness, her healthy, dark tan and light lines, her hopping out of that high-tech boat, and the play of her young muscles as she pushed it back out. Her hair was surfer bleached reddish blond, and her long, slim waist and legs were also a factor in the interest.

Thin young women who play in sports aren't always aware of their royalty status. They're athletes, trained to their games. If they do catch on, many become common and play up to their attractive endowments. But serious competitors disregard their tans, looks and lines, and are embarrassed by active admiration.

But there are the younger sports girls who start having little inklings that they are entitled to worship, a thrilling revelation. They realize that they can change lives.

Beatense's state of mind went far beyond inklings. She picked up her things, and with a dismissing glance around at these people, started north.

A hotel lifeguard confronted her. "M-Miss, are you a g-guest here?"

An eager crowd quickly gathered, using this encounter as an excuse.

"No, but I do appreciate the landing. I'm not a guest, so I'm moving on."

"She isn't the Book Girl, is she?" said an older fellow, hoping for laughs.

She smiled for a photo. "The video girl, unfortunately. Okay, I am leaving."

The lifeguard was startled, he saw those clips. "Well, j-just k-keep going."

Shyly she tied on her Nakee and headed up toward Main, wondering if he was more concerned with her full nudity than her non-guest status. The tie-thong bikinis were just as daring in their day, but now they were the go-to uniform of choice for the young and younger daughters of even the most stodgy tourists. And with the public beaches accepting active nudity Beatense was commendably quite legal.

She entered Main's southern edge, and as she looked down at herself she felt proud of the cold fear and hell envy she caused for the unkempt tourist wives. They didn't dare turn to see if their husbands were looking at her, but of course they were. Sweating paralysis blind-sided these family men. As they had come into town they hoped to see those famed beach girls, but the Murderers Row reality hit hard.

Although it was midweek, Thursday was another busy day. Beatense went on to College Alley, looking for a likely spot, as the legions of student and career singles recognized her and nudged each other. She saw a fervent sun maniac, whose hot dark hide clashed with her blond hair and probing steady blue eyes.

She was glistening and shimmering as she relaxed back on her hands amid the crowd, and as her brick brown tan roiled in the raging heat. Her heels were propped, so the one last chance she had for restraint in her mini-thong was willfully neglected. She also wore a gold tummy chain, that made a talking point of her intrusive abusive tan and taut trunk. Her out-shifted breasts seemed to yearn for fevered action.

For once Beatense was impressed by someone else. She lay her sheet just by her. Incredibly there was an open spot in this prime location. Untying bare she lay upon her front in the midst of the large, noisy crowd, a mob scene.

With the freedom of the times that made nights of rapture expected of even the earnest child lambs, Blue Eyes exemplified those crazed tanners who, on any given beach, are joyously freed from school or job. As athletically hard and leaned as she was, and as blatantly as she admired herself as she baked, she had a wide smile for everybody walking by. Indeed, she was exploiting being a hot lightweight girl with a morality-mocking tan to the fullest. Sex, obviously!

But for all her enthusiasm, her white bleached eyebrows gave a purposeful set to her strong willed face, and that might have been warning off the fellows seeing her. However long she had been out here that day, this rifle shot was still alone.

Presumably working out the kinks from her long day of lying still, she lay back on her elbows and with a wicked flashing of tan and a twisting of her slinky waist, she swung her long leg over to extend it to the other side of her sheet. Then she wrung herself the other way. This working of her sleek middle showed how whippy-slim her stretchy waist was, quite matching Beatense's own, and her steeled lines presented such a carved flow of muscle, she had to be a surfer.

Her shagged yellow hair and horizon searching blue eyes exemplified this. This girl was an elaborately tuned and tensiled practitioner of combative sex.

The lass finally straightened herself, and her hips re-emerged, sticking right out. She flipped over and lay upon her front, and smiling with delighted guilt she re-opened her legs. Beatense shook. She was actually getting hit with her own weaponry.

The mortal blow was now her enemy untied naked. Why not? And her breasts, that pressed out from her, carried their own threat.

A half hour later a fellow on a nearby towel picked up his cigarets and found the pack empty. Within a twinkling the alert twisty girl hopped over, sitting cross-legged. Her open split proclaimed that she would become very excited upon intrusion.

"Here, I got one for you!" she said, holding out her pack.

"Oh, thanks," the startled fellow said, as he shakingly took a cigaret.

"I should have one too," Blue Eyes offered brightly. "I'm Karen. A terrific day for sun today, hah? Finally I'm getting results! I hope I don't get arrested!"

"Y-Yeah. Y-You look like you've b-been laying out all w-week."

Karen shyly, and slyly, lowered her gaze. "Well, all month. But did you get into Emeraldeye just today? You probably need a guide. I can show you around!"

"Oh, yeah, I would appreciate that, but…"

"Well, you probably just want to kick back the first night. Myself, I just like a nice quiet evening, watching a little TV. Not many guys go for that, like you do."

"Well, I never said…"

"I got this sundeck summer rental right on Main here, on top of that pink building just up from the Breeze. Nice and real private, you know?" She pointed, and her new pop-eyed friend obligingly looked. "Stop by, Suite 402! I'm just hanging loose."

"Y-Yeah, I g-get that impression. So is she over there. Boy, she's a dark one."

Karen looked at the sudden-threat Beatense in irritation. "It's senseless to invest all that time and effort into just your skin like that. I mean, get a life, loser!"

"Well you just said you were laying out a whole month."

"For the beach vibes, yes. That's different. And anyway down at Sorel I start lifeguard qualifications next week. An actual job, not just laying there like her."

"She could almost be the Book Girl, tan as she is. You saw her books…"

"Oh, yes yes yes. I'm a lifeguard, certified for heavy surf rescue, but she gets all the credit for a few stupid pictures. So anyway, nice knowing you. And you are…"

"Rudd. And nice knowing you, er, Karen."

"We can know each other way better. I'll buzz you right in if you come by!"

"Y-Yeah, I might just d-do that."

"I can sustain for hours! Not that I'm hinting, Rudd, ha ha, but I love working out! Only prob is, speaking of work, they said I can't wear a bikini down at Sorel, but I can wear my tan-thru maillot! At least with that I'll lose the few lines I still have!"

Beatense felt a chill wind blow. If that twit started work down at Sorel she would never have a chance with that lifeguard, especially since he hated her.

"Well, th-thanks for the cigaret, Karen. Uh, see you later."

Smiling cheerily, but also showing grim displeasure, Karen lay again on her sheet. Pretending to lie in blissful repose, in an unguarded moment she looked as if perhaps the bumbling ineptitude of these stupid men irked her. *Doesn't anyone want to fuck?*

Beatense knew what the problem was, her frizzled, intent eyebrows. Like herself she was too purposeful as a sun tanner. She turned to face the other way, and was surprised to see a couple fellows cheesily grinning at her from their towels.

"Hi!" one of them said, smiling at this hottie. "Are y-you from around here?"

"Sort of." She raised to her elbows. "I got into town a week ago."

Their blood roared. "Us, t-too," the first fellow panted. "Well, actually Sunday for us. Wh-What have you done b-besides getting that g-great t-tan?"

"This? This is mostly burn. That Karen over there is genuinely dark."

"Th-That's some burn. So you've j-just b-been laying out?" *Cock bite!*

"Well, it's pretty obvious, isn't it? But I just came up from Cocojo, where there's fewer people. Here it's so crowded you can't hear yourself think."

"Y-Yeah. But wh-where are you staying? We're at Red West Sails. A week of double occupancy and the airfare and all gratuities are included."

"Gosh, what kind of deal is that?"

"A package. It also included a free welcome party but we didn't go."

Thankfully they didn't recognize her. "Why *not?* A free party?"

"All they do is load you up on all these expensive tours to take."

Seeing this was an unexpectedly talkative girl, the other fellow spoke up.

"With our twin occupancy, we worried about what to do if one of us had a *friend* stay over, but that hasn't been a problem as of yet. We can hardly talk to any of the women here, but who can blame them. They have it all."

"The only woman who talked to us at all had timeshares for sale."

"Oh, timeshares," said Beatense knowingly. She took hold of her Nakee. She was concerned about a lifeguard who seemed to be moving her way.

"And the tip sucking waitresses. I'm Gene, by the way, and this is Will."

"Hi, guys, I'm, er, Trinket."

"Hi, Trinket," said Gene. "Cute name. So, er, are you here alone?"

"Yes. No one would want to join me in the schedule I'm enslaved to."

"What schedule is that?" said Will, his spirits rising. *Alone! Alone and nice!*

"Laying out. My friend is coming Saturday, and maybe then he can get me to do something else, like golfing. This is my fifth day of laying out, but I earned it."

Gene and Will felt keenly disappointed that this friendly girl wasn't so alone after all, however that did take the pressure off. But they could brag back home that they met this beautiful beach girl, and they had a great talk with her.

"Five days," Gene gasped. "F-Funny we haven't s-seen you, then."

"I told you I've been mostly down at Cocojo. Maybe that was a mistake."

"Very true. So how do all you women get so tan, anyway? So far we got squat, ourselves, and we're the only ones even half trying."

"It goes back eons. Us women scouted out the deer for the men to hunt, and for stealthy sneaking we evolved into blending into the trees like forest felines. Then we started to hunt ourselves, and you men have been useless ever since."

Gene said, "Wild game. Is that what you girls are still scouting for?"

She laughed. "Without much luck, and I'm even single occupancy."

They laughed, relieved by her candid admission. Will said, "So, like where have you been eating at? Or I should say, not eating. Any decent places?"

"I hunt and skin my food, but I want to try that Hard Fought Café."

"Hey, maybe we should meet there tonight," Gene suggested, casually.

"I'm not sure about tonight. I might just hunt up some food at the One Stop, and skating after that. I got new in-lines. Pretty slick. What do they have?"

"Hah? Oh, the restaurant. Steak, pizza, ribs, chicken... The usual."

"Steak? Pizza? Quite a spread. I had grilled steak out at surveying camp. Six and then seven years ago. We don't have it grilled up in Arrolynn where I'm from."

The girl let that sink in as she looked around, observing the beach blanket bingo. She saw that Karen had a visitor, who gave her a frantic stare as he sat upon her sheet. Light in proportions and drenched to an agonizing hot dark brown, like Elgin, this butt-cuts bared all-day tanner sat in a cross-legged slouch as he and she eyed each other. His belly was curved as it hooked into the low held elastic of his yellow shorts. The gold ring bracelet on his thin arm and gold neck chain both betrayed his self involved pride. He had wind ruffled, long cut dark hair, and his tuned biceps and shaped shoulders set off his shaped chest, and he was long, lean and lanky.

But Beatense saw his stupid wire-rimmed mod (me, 1970s) glasses.

"Th-That sun sure is hot today?" he said nervously.

She looked up. "Yes, but hot or not, now I'm trying to bake myself, alone."

He quavered. "It's just that, if y-you r-remember, I was j-just over from you here Sunday afternoon." He was more nervous now. "I w-wanted to s-say hi."

Karen, now in her own tightly curved, cross-legged slouch, gave this mod hippy glasses wearer a cold inspection. "I don't remember, but hi, I guess."

"Plus I w-wanted to c-compliment your t-tan. It's really, er, n-noticeable."

He obviously wanted his own effort noticed. She shrugged indifferently.

"B-But anyway, I w-wanted to go out s-sailing today, I'm w-working nights, all this week, b-but the w-wind is too light. But would you maybe l-like to sail s-sometime?"

"So, can we meet at Hard Fought?" Beatense heard Gene say, *damn him*.

"Er, uh, maybe tomorrow," the girl answered, to put him off.

"I'm not interested in sailing. I think it would be boring. Like you. Sorry."

He stared into her hunger sunken, bake beaten belly, as if in disbelief such a thing was possible. "W-Well, l-like I say, the wind... You know..."

She took her arm away. "It's too light, is what you said. Shit happens."

"Where are you staying, Trinket?" Will now. *Of all times to get talkative.*

"Oh, at the Hideaway, up on the Highway there."

"Oh, cool. We know where that is!"

"We ate at that Oro Grande Restaurant," Gene put in. "Kind of ratty."

"S-So, I guess I, uh, will j-just ride my bike now, since sailing is, er, out."

She squirmed, flexing her waist. "You repeat yourself."

"It was n-nice talking to you. Er, c-can I ask your n-name?"

"Karen. But look, this fucking shit needs to stop. Go ride your trike."

"Are you here on vacation, Trinket?" Will again.

"Yeah, didn't I say I was?"

Sailor Boy stood with mouth open. "O-Okay, s-see you later."

Karen lay upon her front in ugly dismissal. The sizzling Sailor Boy, with a look of horror at Beatense, who was a black, lean streak of muscle, left in defeat.

"Boy, she sure shot him down," said Gene, lowering his voice.

"He was a fag," said Will. "You saw the fucking tan he had. Fags do that."

"But he was going after a girl. Fags *don't* do that."

"A woman like that, even a gay will be smitten. Or should be."

If only Craig had that look, or at least wished he had it, thought Beatense.

She regretted her situation. If it wasn't for these two clunks that loser might have stopped by her instead, and she would have been far friendlier. But why didn't Karen respond to him? Because his tan took control and beat her at her own game?

It was the rare guy who carried a tan like that, one that showed useless hours of self centered effort. This put him at odds with the other guys, who didn't at all try.

But now Beatense understood why Sienna hated Main so much. Down at Cocojo one could quietly indulge in sun without dudes and babes all dialoguing each other.

"What time is it?" Beatense said. "I need an hour more doing my back."

"It's two-thirty," Gene replied, looking at his clunky black sport watch.

She shined her back with oil, then lay back on her elbows. Gene and Will stared. Her sunk belly was placketed with formed muscle. Her hipbones were ready to burst her skin, and her small breasts also looked ready to pop. Her rib ledged belly burned the eye with its dark rust bake. Her opened legs indicated that she would become very excited upon intrusion into her waiting ganglia. After those first years of parental and societal doubts, girls having sex was now accepted as healthy, happy and beautiful.

But not just anyone qualified. High pedigree only. They could be very active.

"Okay, guys, I'm going into a hyper bake now. All conversation ceases."

"Th-That's okay. Gene, d-dig us out a couple b-beers and w-we'll be set."

The girl took this reply at face value, not reading into it the sad implications. So they stared in blood boiling turmoil as she lay upon her front, pressing out her fertile breasts. Bracelets clinking, she groaned in delirium, happy, healthy and beautiful.

Her long back looked coffee dark in color, with a lustrous goldeny tint. The sleek tight muscles flanking both sides of her lazily curved spine lined her back vertabrally with a cacao sheathed furrow, and complimenting that graceful flow were her delicate shoulder blades and vulgar twin butt shapings. Her intricate legs also had a smooth flow, in continuation of the lovely form that was her light body.

Her belly chain and bracelets completed her ensemble.

Actually her friends were miffed by this predicament; it looked as if they set up by her just to scope her out. Karen, seeing their problem, and ready to ace out her competition plus likely get a good bedding, gave the fellows a wink.

Beatense wasn't aware of it. She gave her back a grueling half-conscious ninety minutes. The sun's heat lulled her into a lazy, hazy dream.

She awoke with a tossing shake. She flipped over and lying on her elbows she gave her front-side a perusal. After all day her tan was still mad for these lethal rays. She was tan saturated so extra deeply she shined espresso dark. She saw that her friends had left, but their blanket promised their return. Should she stay? She didn't need one now but it might be a later fuck. She saw that Karen was also gone.

Beatense guessed it was only four but she decided to head home to get on her skates. Her skin actually ached from so much sun. She rolled her sheet up and started toward the shore. This was like a dream, having baked bare before all these people, and now she walked among them. She was starkly tan amidst a crowd of hundreds. But her honored video status (cameras in action now) ensured that she could get through without anyone daring to confront her with clever remarks.

Then she saw saw him. Neatsfoot. Like the boy at the campground he was hitting flyballs out to his friends. The girl moved closer and stared in horror.

He was a tall, elegantly slendered college youth in ragged blue jean cut-offs, very radically dark. The armies of radical tan deep within his skin were jostling with each other, so that they leaped forth in a baked radiance of golden blurred black. He was thin, but like Sailor Boy's his slimmed shoulders were rugged shaped, and his proud chest was barbell bulked. The chancy careless hold of his cut-offs to his narrow hips was enabled by the snug grip of their folded-up cuffs to his runner boy thighs, so that they were rumpled down so low fully half his white butt was in stunning open sight.

Like me Oval Beach 1969, only I was half mast butted, no white showed.

Beatense shook. With pretty biceps nicely rounded he swung his bat, flexing his waist and turning his shoulders with lovely effort. Beatense watched as his latest hit sailed through the air, right into the hands of magnificent Karen. Will and Gene both had to pull up short in running for the flyball to avoid colliding with her. They laughed, she laughed, and the bare brownie drilled the ball back in a line shot.

Neatsfoot tapped the incoming ball with the bat to stop it. He tossed it up and hit another lazy lob, and one of the other catchers in the rye colored sand caught it. The two traitors made funny remarks to Karen, and with belly ripples tensing she laughed like they were old friends. Beatense felt brutally betrayed.

She had to get even, and Neatsfoot would work perfectly. Well, maybe not. With breath rasping, heart pounding, she stepped closer. She saw to her agony that this hero was adorably boy cute, with eyes that looked as if he was sleepy, afraid or lost, and he had an absolute thatch of curly black hair. She had to take action.

With Sailor Boy, Will and Gene history, this was another chance, a gift from the gods, if any. She did have a queen sized bed.

She dropped her things. She knew that the youth, in running to catch the ball coming back to him, would eventually see her. He finally did dance by her, and Beatense gazed down in chaste reserve. She peeked back up, just enough to see Neatsfoot obligingly lower both bat and jaw. She quickly looked back down.

Now what? In such close proximity there was only one thing she could do, show indifference. Springing lightly for effect, the famed bare dancer ran for the surf.

She dashed in and dove deep into the sea's unwelcome coldness. Surfacing, she surfaced and swam like a porpoise as she repeatedly pulled herself under.

She turned toward shore. *There he is! He came come out after me!*

With the foamy water to their slim hips they warily eyed each other, genetic freak versus genetic freak. Despite the lower sun dozens of cameras caught this classic scene, as two back-lighted profiles with hair alight.

"Er, hello," said the perfect boy. "I l-like your t-t-tan. How y-ya d-doing?"

She elaborately yawned, with heart pounding worse. "Oh, f-fine. My tan, too."

"I never saw you before. Wh-What's your name? If I can ask."

"Trinket, but I don't think guys should just swim out after a girl like that, with whatever intentions. So, anyway, ahem, wh-what's your n-name?"

"K-Kitanning. Kit Gilman. Er, w-want to p-play ball with us?"

"Well, I don't know, but thanks for asking. Bye."

She turned and flashed away, wondering what stupid shit made her refuse that fabulous athlete's invitation. Playing ball, innocent fun! And with that flash of energy that sizzled between them, even a fuck was possible. The girl watched helplessly as Kit returned to shore. *Is my being a slut working against me?*

She reached shore too, only to realize that her things still lay close by Kitanning. Chillingly, coldly, she went over and picked them up, and as then she cut through the gaping players toward Holiday Hill, through tacit agreement Will and Gene didn't look at her. Instead, Karen, who ran and caught another one, with upraised hand.

Spinning around, she whipped it back, stumbling as she lost her balance. The light muscle-pack of her long gap thighs gave her the most delicate little knees; she was a sports girl: Light, strong and free. Beatense was out-gunned.

She tied on her Nake and went on to the north end of Main, where the trees of the bluff loomed above. Beatense entered the sand mounds here and saw girls tanning nude privately instead of in public. She turned and followed the curving shore out to the Hill's narrow strip of beach. This shore was guarded by big boulders and rock formations about twenty yards out. The girl turned at a sudden loud uproar, a scuffling of hooves and the screams of a raging stallion.

"Windfire! Knock it off, you fucker! Settle down!"

Young Jesse. He came out from behind the rock pile further up the beach as his fiery, golden maned bay nervously trembled and side-stepped beneath him.

The horse pawed at the sand and reared, and the tan wild boy held on. He was almost frightening to behold, a living art form in wet antiquity bronze. As the celestial cliff diver pulled the reins back to his chest, curving his spine with his effort, his sweat plaited belly, liked Beatense's, looked to be the very epicenter of the sun itself.

The kid was so dark, so pupil shredding burned black, he was almost a match for the disarrayed auburn extravagance of his plentiful hair. And but for his gold bracelets, this sun baked warrior boy was oil-bathed bare. Beatense staggered in shock; first Russ, the track boys, Keter, then Sailor Boy, Kitanning and once again this kid.

This latest inflictor pulled his bucking ride around in a hard circle, and favored his spectator with a wink. His look turned to smiling surprise, and with a yell he touched heels to steed and rocketed off. He dashed through the shallows to the Main Beach shore, where in turn he galloped southward, savage and bareback freed.

Driving up sheets of spray he scattered the strollers, and cheers rang out as he continued his flight. Watching his flight, Beatense felt some of the vicious stress she happily caused in others. *So this is what the receiving end is like. Oh oh.*

She saw Kitanning approach, with bat perched upon his fine black tan shoulder. She thought of waiting for him, because a "chance" kismet run-in would be so perfect for a second try, but he would see through it. She started up the path.

The hillside was very steep, so the sandy path threaded upward right to left in succeeding ramps. The soft, shaded sand felt cool to the girl's feet as she climbed. The trees angled the sun's rays in misty streams, and she breathed in soothing pine fragrances. Birds distantly called, and the ascending trail went up through the trees and bushes thick with tropical blossoms. Beatense got to the top and looked out to sea. This view through the leafy boughs was magical.

Beatense would have lingered, but Neatsfoot was coming. She started back in along the wooded sand trail, toward a proudly baked girl carrying a surfboard. Her draped towel made Beatense suspect that her tied slingshot thong was all she wore. She turned and saw that indeed she was topless. *Well, duh.*

Beatense went on and came to an old, unpainted wooden cabin, one of dozens scattered throughout this woods. She went by an ancient, rusting sixteen foot trailer, built back in the days when trailers featured that nautical flair, with yacht-like details.

Its round cornered entry door had a porthole, and the other windows had rounded corners. Other similar trailers, and cozy cabins, abounded. The sandy path came to a narrow roadway of broken cement, that ambled from cabin to cabin.

Beatense crossed the confusing intersections, where shady byways snaked away through cabins and trees, and where old iron-posted streetlights stood guard. Along one stretch colorful party lanterns were strung from tree to tree, in keeping with the name of this place. Holiday Hill was as idyllically charming and rustic as its miserly landlords unwittingly made it, right down to the chintzy café curtains in the rattly old paned windows. There were also piles of cordwood set about for the cold seasons.

One could easily imagine the inviting, halcyon appeal of the music and laughter drifting on the warm evening breezes here, as the dim orange, red, green and yellow party lanterns cast their friendly glow.

Beatense felt reassured by the benign squalor here, plus its scarcity of cars. So she wasn't the only one without a big fortune in town. But as she went on she had no sense of direction, an irksome lapse for her as a surveyor. But with the sun obscured and all those maze-like intersections she had no idea which went where.

She saw a guy coming toward her, a slight, perpetually bewildered college youth lugging a grocery bag. He wore 30L jeans and white T-shirt, and he had a pure, sun fresh complexion. The college boy looked with a start at this near bare girl, and he nervously pushed back his hair. Beatense saw he had nicely crafted hands, but his real weapon was his tousled hair. The two passed by each other, and as Beatense paused to look back at him she saw that this boy also turned.

It wasn't as if she had just turned to sight-see; she directly caught his eye. She had to laugh; this was like Neatsfoot all over again. This broke the ice.

"H-Hi," the boy said, also with a laugh, an uneasy one. "N-Need help?"

She inspected her arm. "Now why would you ask that?"

"Er, this road goes to a dead-end."

She dutifully registered surprise, but quickly recovered her composure.

"Okay, I'm exploring. What's the vacancy situation up here? Any idea?"

"Well, I think everything is rented here if you want your own place. But I know a couple girls who could use a roommate, uh…"

"Never mind. Okay, you win, I'm Beatense. You saw me in Netty as the nude dancer, plus they got me fucking. The bastards. Hey, it's like half scenic up here."

"Oh, yeah, I saw you! In that motel! B-But anyway, I'm K-Kenny, and uh, yeah, the only place is with those girls. You could try the Hit List but they charge a fee."

"They got me with Zapo? But money is of no consequence to me." *She has that fuck tan, and she's rich, too!* "But mainly because I don't have any."

He laughed. "Join the club. Are you ever... Are you ever just so... So tan."

"There's no cause to be especially impressed by me just because I happen to be in ownership of camouflage. Kenny, how dare you overlook my other qualities!"

"Sorry, but that's all I'm seeing right now. You are awful tan, though."

"That's better. But wait, if I do look into those roommates, can I retain you for a character reference? I'm abstaining, reliable and honest. Where can I find you?"

"You went by that one cabin with the oil tank? There. North loop, B12."

The girl turned. She shrugged. "Well, I'll find it. And where is their cabin?"

"Too hard to explain and I don't know their address. But I think if you..."

"Well, I think if I ask someone else I might have better luck. Bye, Kenny."

His heavy bag was as nothing. Beatense kept on and eventually found the long service drive that rose up from the Highway. Ringdon Terrace was paved with twin strips of cement like the oldest driveways in Arrolynn. The girl started down the road, leaving the silent Hill behind. She came out on the busy Highway oat its intersection with Trenton, a dry gulch following road that cut back to the foothills.

It was home to a few shabby businesses and a sad group of ratty mobile homes. As Beatense started south along the sidewalk, maybe feeling a little too nude, a young woman approached, apparently on her way home from work.

She wore satin harem pantaloons that fit closely above her born delicate ankles, and a white rib-knit top with sleeves pushed up to the elbows, showing how capably elegant her thinned tan arms were. She moved with a tall, proud carriage, and her humorless expression told of her weariness in having people try to catch her eye all day long. She was classically slimmed with refined features, whose emaciated erotic portents to her regret revealed that she did mate in spite of any reluctance. She also had a rippling, full triumph of long, dusky blond hair, and her tawny sun color promised an overpowering tan at any time she tried. Her regal, wide placed eyes were intently blue, and their complexity showed that she had a self deifying superiority stance, that made her disinterested, disengaged and dissatisfied. Many others like her.

Beatense knew her stare would be unwelcome, but she had to look. Some girls are so other-worldly, their lives can be as difficult as those with physical deficiencies. Like everyone else Beatense had to read her eyes and establish a connection.

That completed (and reciprocated, but of course she was famed), she came upon the picnic area that held Tuesday's art fair, and with cars honking at her as a near nude, she walked by the Highway's inviting clutter of stores, restaurants and hotels.

Way down at the One Stop grocery Buck came out, stock still staring.

"Why, B-Beatense! Hel... Hello!"

She felt regret that she was friendly earlier. "Oh, hi, Buck."

He stared at her dark browned skin. "W-Were y-you on the b-beach today?"

"Of course I was. You saw me this morning, on my way to Cocojo."

"T-Twelve hours ago, yes. I w-wondered if I would ever s-see you again."

She looked puzzled. "What, did you think I got kicked out of town?"

Something had gone wrong. "No, I d-didn't th-think that, b-but..."

"And Buck, there's lots of people you will never see again. Me also."

He shook in terror at this well meaning gaffe. "Yeah, but... Uh huh."

"And... Were you really counting the hours like that?" Buck chose to simply grin foolishly. "Well, okay, see you around, Bucko, but don't count the hours."

He muttered a reply and stumbled away in defeat. A gang of young aquatic surf stars then walked up. The boys and one brightly cute girl, all obviously bodybuilders who could kill, carried surfboards, and they all had a hard day of dangerous sun.

The boys had vibrant, fascial chests, and for all the kids their sullen, lurking bellies closely matched clipboards in hardness and color. In faded jean cut-offs torn to just four inches, these proud surfers were grotesquely baked, with skin like hot burnished fine leather. They showed severe disdain for any tourists that dared to behold them, me included. But their finely traced eyebrows and the curved crescents of their black eyelashes actually made the boys femininely attractive, and like the heart-warmingly adorable girl, very much at odds with their steely baked and tuned preeminence.

They were brilliant. Gobs and gobs of unkempt stray hair, like Beatense's.

One youth affected stricken distress, as if he was explaining how he had lost his homework. Another strikingly perfect lad of fifteen was viciously brown. With his intelligent features and provocative, ends-curled, lengthy blond hair, defiantly he was both girl and boy. Gabriel, the others called him. They saw Beatense, yes virtually naked, but other women they saw all the time were similarly undressed.

The surf boys, and the sweet faced, muscle laden maiden, with hard tuned belly ripples, watched Beatense go into the store, where as stared at she bought six glaze donuts on credit. At Butler's she also charged a quart of cocoa butter oil with free neck-hung key tube like her other one. She finally got back to her room.

She applied the oil, she buckled on her blades, and after saying hi to Mr. Cheevy she glided up the Highway with the traffic. She rolled right into Butler's and paid her tab, then settled up at One Stop. She continued northward along the busy Highway, again right with the astounded traffic. It was very hot.

She turned into the first street south of Trenton, Harding. She cruised by modest but well-kept bungalows and boulevard palm trees, toward a thinned, bursting brown mid-teen boy. He had a wide smile, probably from inflicting his feared tan upon his neighbors. Like legions of the local sand boys, his cut-offs were cuffed snugly up, for the same saggy, rumply ride Kit and Keter enacted. His thigh muscles snaked under the russet shine of his lengthy legs as he paraded along, and the shaking Beatense bored into his belting belly and chestnut chest. Going on, passing him, she looked back at his baked back, and almost fell. Blades can be tricky.

Getting her own reactions from the humble neighbor folk, the girl skated south to the next street, Marie, and took that back to the Highway and crossed to the crowded Beachway. Progress was slow; all the tourists in the way. She finally got home and after dining on her six yeasty donuts she went in to see the staring Mr. Cheevy.

"Hey, guy. Excuse my modest costume. Any messages?"

"Z-Zapo fr-from Hoganforth is… Is on tonight. He w-won't be making it here."

"Well, us two can fuck. A repeat! Wasn't that beautiful? I thought so."

"My dear, it was beautiful, but at my age we sadly better wait a week."

"You can just rub me! But this woman I keep seeing on the beach, I wonder why she tries. These guys who took me out in their boat today didn't even notice her."

"Well, I've had many plain unfortunates staying here, discouraged and alone."

"Hah? What do you mean, discouraged? I mean, she has to face facts!"

"Forget her. She's here for a vacation but it's just depressing her. No biggie."

"No biggie! Mr. Cheevy, you jerk! I'm not forgetting her! That poor thing!"

20

FRIDAY AM

Early Friday morning Beatense took a quick warm shower, still half crazed with the publisher's mail packet Mr. Cheevy had given her. It held multiple photos of her getting off the bus, and then for the next three days. Her favorite was her kneeling beside a back-lying Hogan friend as she held his length in dread. Yes, a third book was preparing, when the project was complete her advance would be 120 thousand. Pre-printing demand was so high the retail would be $100 a copy, her cut would be fifteen for the initial sixty thousand. Also she would get catch-up royalties for her first titles, netting her eight each. Accounting was tabulating the final total, then the funds would be sent to Meredith Safety Bank. More critical for Beatense, Darcy Publishing had secured for her full nudity for all of Emeraldeye's public areas, providing that the new edition featured tourist attraction promotional scenes, along with a royalty cut.

This freedom didn't apply to the other beach women; as naked they had to stick with Main Beach and the west side of Highway, but topless in tie-bottoms they could walk the other side. Like Beatense did with Krinkles, who would be awarded twelve thousand for her photos. The open door got quality views of their bed play. In fact a book was debated for Krinkles, along with Bondy, Sienna, Torrey and Tenacity.

It was half-light dawn as Beatense stepped outside. She could see that she was screeching dark brown, with a healthy, golden tinted and oil-wetted shine, giving her the highest status a surf girl could hope for. She saw the couple she had checked in; they exchanged warm friendly greetings. Then she bounded off as the nascent heat added sweat to her oil. It was just after six; plenty of time to also run Sorel naked.

Flaunting her wet tan, the athlete impatiently danced on the corner, tossing her belly chain, key tube and yellow streaked hair as the cars slalomed by. A gap finally came, and she sprang across the street and ran Bastian past the pastel hued tourist rentals, and she hooked right onto dull Windemere for a quick pre-Cocojo run.

She was running her route in reverse, and she found herself facing a much more thrilling view. The northern sweep of coast gave a feeling of promise as the new day began. Leaving dull Windemere behind, she ran toward, or with the other athletes on the Beachway as she leaped ahead on her thin legs. The sleepy tourists drinking their coffee on their lodging balconies stared in turmoil; they had presumably just got into town the night before and didn't yet know of her, unless they saw her videos.

Beatense reached the Hoganforth, and she saw that no one was out on the patio deck yet. She picked up her speed, and showed herself off as she ran by the snooty Breeze. She passed by the skateboard park and ran the picnic area to the Highway. This was emptier now; the cars before must have been shift (shit) bound. Ha ha!

Beatense ran the centerline. She got back to her room and tossed in her shoes. No water; she could mooch off others. She ran down to the beach and found Curt, as the first airplane-towed banner turned inland.

"Hi, Curt. Hey, if that's your surfboard can I take it with me?"

"It's just a rescue board. Your hair is lighter. Are... Are you bleaching it?"

"The sun is. I better get going! Sorel you know. When do we fuck?"

The girl took off, and the shaking, blindsided Curt saw that little butt work with her effort. She ran along lightly, her feet scarcely touching the sand. The few people on the summer home beach stared, down here nudity was still iffy, unless a cute local granddaughter felt the urge to bake bare. Then of course it was okay. The matriarch lady walking her dog gave her a fixed smile. Despite the private doubts they might have, progressives have to show how progressive thay are.

It was hot. Sorel already had scattered visitors. Most of these were scions of lower classes, or those folk who work at ugly, low paying jobs to enable an economy prosperous enough that starved sun bitches can tan all day and fuck all night. These abused lessers stared at Beatense as sprinted by, true aristocracy among them. But despite her speed trouble was brewing; as she ran toward the pier one fool seemed offended by her, whatever, and he got up and hobbled over toward the lodge, slowly, but yelling. Beatense ran faster. Could she make it to Cocojo?

She saw Chubbo. *At this hour?* Beatense flew over to her and skipped to a stop before the startled girl, without taking one extra breath. She was heavy sweated, so her muscles shined in carved relief. Her tan looked black.

"Look, you have to hide me! Let me lay under your blanket! Quick!"

Smiling widely, Chubbo pulled her blanket aside and covered the scared refugee with it as she flopped to the sand. She lay her newspaper over part of the slim form, and rested ever so casually upon the other. She saw a lifeguard searching.

"What's going on?" came a muffled voice.

"They're looking for you. Try and suck in your big butt. What did you do?"

"What did I do? I was naked, you dolt! Now what's happening?"

"One guy has binoc… Oh oh, shut up! Don't move."

A second lifeguard walked by, obviously puzzled. He caught Chubbo's eye.

"Hi, er, did you see this really… This really, like tan girl run by… Naked?"

"Why, er, no! What did she *do?*"

"She was naked! We're going to kick her ass."

"How awful. But sit down here! Standing there, she can see you easily, and if she ducked into the camp or a Tote A Toy she won't leave until you're gone."

"Nah, we're checking the potties. You laid your blanket in a funny place."

"Kids and their useless digging. They must have buried a friend in the sand, and he probably's still in there. But he's comfy. Well, good luck."

The lifeguard wandered off and Chubbo gave Beatense a nudge.

"That was hilarious! But I didn't appreciate the part where you asked him to sit down. I wouldn't be able to breathe! So is he gone?"

"Yes, but Beatense, what made you think I would help you out?"

"Good question. I've been nothing but a shit to you, and if you can accept it I'm apologizing. This isn't because you hid me, I thought of it before. Honest."

A fellow walking by stared toward the disembodied voice.

"Hey, hold it down. What makes you think you were shitty?"

"Well, I squirmed and squealed when Sienna oiled me, and then I ran by you all springy, and I made this big show of being with those guys yesterday."

"That's okay. After you left this Keter sat by me. He was a real nice kid."

"He moved over by you? He wasted himself on just you?"

She laughed. "Yes. I was in shock. He said you're the Book Girl."

"I'm the hiding Book Girl now. Anyway, too bad that Keter is so young."

"Yes, just eighteen. Some older teens get all adulty, but he's still skinny."

"Yes. But in forty years he will be fifty-eight, so think of that. His present videos will live on even as he starts using a cane. Hey, how do you know my name?"

Chubbo laughed. "I overheard it. You sure have beautiful friends."

"Sure, leave me out. Can I leave now, Little Miss Laugh At Anything?"

"Not yet. But anyway, it was nice talking to him. It rescued my trip."

"Yes, I was worried about my shittiness to you. What's happening now?"

"This one lifeguard is scanning the area with binoculars, and another guy is out checking the pier. But look, Beatense, you don't know what a sensation you are. You think you do, but you don't know the half of how people react."

"Can you shut up? Someone's going to see your big mouth flapping!"

"It must be a dream to have a body like yours, Beatense."

"It's turning into a nightmare. Is anyone around? In particular, lifeguards?"

"Er, uh, no. I mean, there's two lifeguards over by the pier, but they're with this policeman. I think you should worry more about him."

"Officer Molen. He's fat. Maybe I better run for it, over to Cocojo."

"They'll follow you right over there! You broke the law *here*, remember?"

"But this is a state beach! Look, how about creating a distraction, Chubbo."

"Chubbo? Who's Chubbo? Where do you get that?"

Despite her color, coverage and predicament Beatense burned red.

"Well, that is to embarrassedly say, I guess I, like, got your name wrong. I'm really... I'm really sorry, Chubbo. Even if you did steal Keter from me, bitch."

She laughed again. "Oh oh, here we go again. Sit tight."

Searching, the lifeguards and the policeman walked up to Chubbo.

"Sorry, miss, but we're wondering if you actually did see that nude girl. She was seen running into this area. No one saw her run into Cocojo."

"I was reading. See? This is a newspaper. Reading it I saw nobody."

"Wait a minute, just what is under that blanket?"

"Sand. All heaped up. I picked this place specially, for the comfort."

"No, they groomed the beach. She's under there. All right, come on out!"

The fugitive sighed and threw off the blanket and stood. All sandy, but they didn't expect this adorable treasure. They could have picked hundreds of other girls for the books, but her face was what sold tens of thousands of copies.

"Well, well, well, we're going to write you up, young lady, plus your friend here will get one too, for aiding and abetting a *fugitive* from justice!"

"Some justice! And don't write her a ticket! Write me up, I am naked, but I'll kill you gladly if you give Chub... If you give her one."

"What's your name, miss? Chub what?"

A small crowd of jurisprudence minded beach-goers quickly gathered.

"Adalyn." She stood. He called her miss! "Adalyn Chubbo Sudberg."

Beatense saw her irritable, tall lifeguard friend come toward them.

"I'm letting you off with a warning," the Officer Molen continued. "But I need your naked friend's name for the records."

"I'm a transvestite, Fred Jones." The promising lifeguard arrived. Beatense felt exposed in her costume. "Hello dere, Jerribaldi. Again."

"What the hell is going on here? We talked to you about this before!"

"Wait a minute now," said the policeman. "How many offenses were there?"

"Several, of me being a little too naked. But cut old Chubby Wubby some slack. I threatened murder if she didn't hide me. Which she did poorly!"

Everyone laughed. If this was her jury she would get off.

"You threaten that a lot, it seems. Okay, Jerry, no write-up. When this foul criminal wraps up in her towel, make sure she gets down to Cocojo."

"Okay, come on. There's a nice beach over yonder for your kind."

"Now just a minute," said Adalyn. "I don't like the sound of that!"

"That's okay, Adalyn. I can stay here because I don't have a towel."

The officer finished his writing and gave Beatense a pink slip. She ate it.

"Well, Adalyn, old girl, thanks for trying to hide me. I hope to see you later."

Old girl. Already! "Hold it, I'm going with. I owe you for not killing me."

Everybody laughed and the crowd broke up. Beatense ran in and splashed off, and the rescuer Jerry escorted the girls over to the Cocojo border.

"You little shit." He laughed. "No one will believe this story, ha ha ha!"

"Well, that episode was a waste of good sun. Bye now. Come on, Addie."

"Not so fast. You... You w-want to do a steak tonight?"

"Yes, I love eateries so much I bake in the sun long hours just to get myself invited to them. But that's my secondary motive, I also bake tan for equilibrium. If you guys want to act all snocky about that, that's your shithead prerogative."

"With that t-tan, how can I not have a prerogative? So is that yes?"

"Not tonight, trust me on that. I'm hoping to snare another better lifeguard."

Jerry offered his hand. She took it with a firm grip and a swell of veined bicep. She could murder at that. She looked right into his eyes.

"I appreciate that you asked me out, Jerry. I just hope I don't over-dress."

At that she ran into the surf. Jerry and Adalyn watched the little sprite play like a seal. She frolicked in the rolling waves and in swimming underwater she popped up a hundred feet away. Her key tube went front to back, back to front.

"Cute kid. But a tan like that... Wow. I mean, terabyte wow."

"Forget the tan," said Adalyn. "She's a nice kid. Who would think?"

The two entered Cocojo and went by a whole city of wind screens, tents and canopies. Sun culturists, with kids. The girls went on to a remote spot down at the beach ending rock wall. Beatense lay with Adalyn on her disgraced blanket, and she squirmed as her friend slimed her back with her key tube oil. She knew the impact of her dark tan and the tight flow of her muscles was a huge overload for her admirer.

"Th-There, B-Beatense. Now you j-just lay there wh-while I read."

"Thanks, Addie. I just want to get a little brown today, in this nice sun."

"A little brown. Most women would kill for that *little brown*, Bookie, sickened me included. That's the darkest tan I ever saw. Tell me what it's like to be so tan."

"Well, just the feel of being tan is fun and energizing. You feel happily complete and full of expectancy. And it isn't just me. All us beach girls. Like yesterday there was just this ungodly brown girl up at Main, blond hair, and like me her tan made her happy, it weaponized her, it made her a part of nature, so being brown was what she must be. And for me everyone knows who I am, with those fool books, and videos. I don't get anything for them unless I set up a Netty site."

"No, it's too late, Beatense. They're already out there. And it's too bad, you should get paid, the way your slim waist and belly jerky jiggled your hips."

"Oh, you're talking about the dancing. They got me fucking, too, at the hostel."

"What a dream life. And not just you. All you beach girls."

"Look, Adalyn, lots of cute women have to fake it and act all foolishly ineffectual, because it's expected of them if they're small and have extroverted looks. Imagine diminishing yourself like that. Being beautiful can actually drag you down."

"Yeah, but any customers we have sure light up when Lissy says hi."

"Who's that?"

"I work with her, we're both tellers. And boy do they go to her instead of me if we're both open. But I can say this, she is adorable. Golden skin. Delights in everybody and everything. Shares funny stories with me like we're old chums."

"Yeah well that's where I fall… Hey, you didn't use up all that oil, did you?"

"Kind of, I did. There were only a couple ounces. I can go buy you more."

"No, the closest place would be way back up at Sorel, and you would just go and get the wrong kind. I can just scam someone for when I do my front."

Adalyn told about herself, and her friend's ala Tiffany laughter flattered her, as if being an assistant teller was the stuff of hilarious misadventures.

The next two hours drifted by. Beatense grogged out in sleep. Later…

"Beatense, do you want anything to drink? I can run back to that stand."

"It's too far, I said. Look, there's lots more people. Ask them."

Adalyn laughed. "But Beatense, you know, there's this spirit to this beach where it almost seems like it's a living soul. I mean, if Cocojo here was some isolated beach with no one ever on it, it would be just sand."

"You know, you're not all that stupid. But yeah, it's far but get me pop or beer!"

Adalyn wondered what her reception would be as she entered the park; she was never on the lam before. Unnoticed as usual she got in line. She returned with the bottled beer and oil and saw a newly arrived neighbor just yards away.

Sprawled back on his towel in yellow butt-cut shorts, the nearby penitent was so drenched with tan, he was a torturing horror. He was lightly thin, with slim shoulders and limbs, and the panting Adalyn saw that he had a bulked chest, a leaned-in belly and bone poked hips. Photo proof, I was an extremely deep deep brown.

Beatense pointed toward the little yellow sailboat pulled up onto the beach.

"Sailor Boy," she said, taking her bottle. "A boding coincidence. Thanks, Ad."

Kneeling, Beatense drank noisily, as Adalyn admired the curved tensions of her stretched thighs. This and her eagerly out-skewed breasts dizzied her.

Beatense stepped over to the intruder. He started as she kneeled beside him. Teasingly snaking her slim, gold chained waist, with small bicep flexed and a sliding clink of her gold bangles, she drank of her bottle. Some beer spilled and it foamed between her pulsating breasts, wetting her tummy. She was rusty dark brown, a strap tough whip of muscle. Her bleachy hair fell in curling weed patch tousles.

"So, you spotted me and ever so casually laid out five yards away. Did I get your attention while you were out at sea, or after you landed, you fuck creep."

Shocked by her presence, he helplessly stared into her wet black belly.

"I… Are you… Are you… Ever… But I… I can be here if I want!"

"Well, at least we're equally matched. I do appreciate that. Too many fuckbags think all they have to is be guys and I'm all over them. Let's go sailing."

"H-Hah?" He had switched to goggling her hinged, knot tight shoulders.

The nymph sat cross-legged, ankle to ankle, her wet split opened. She was so slouched her belly sunk almost horizontal. She rested back on her hands, shifting her small apples further out, as her corded abdominals spastically squirmed beneath her slimy, foam streaked shine. Her poignant eyes had an exotically commanding, lower lid drooping. The druid forest princess walking among the coarse peasants playing their concertinas and balalaikas couldn't have been a more startling visitor.

This girl was so beautiful she could tame wolves. The distant cameras aimed.

She pointed over toward his little boat and shook back her hair. "I said let's go sailing." Holding her bottle, she stood and pulled the confused sailor up. The girl had to admit, he had boyish lines. His shoulders and hippy-fit shorts focused his tan.

The naked girl waved over to Adalyn. "Be right back, Baddy! Sailing!"

"Just make sure it's sailing sailing and not sailing sailing!" --/-- "Both!"

The boat was just twelve feet long, with a white propylene, scow type hull and yellow propylene deck molded with a broadly countered, shallow well.

It was more of an *on* boat than an *in* boat. Wading, they pushed the fragile craft out into the light surf, and the wind swung the striped sail back and forth.

They bellied themselves up and on, or in, as the boat tossed. The sailor shoved the keel into the raised housing's slot and levered the rudder down. In contrast to his shorts and the poly deck he was hot deep brown. Beatense, settling lankily in with a swig of beer from her long necked bottle, goggled his intensely baked belly, drawn so trimly in. Despite the over-big lenses of his dated single-swinger glasses, like me his sizzling proximity in the confined boat was electric. Beatense definitely had plans. The two sat side by side, actually they lounged, back against the low right counter.

Beatense raised her knee, to show her pink split. The sailor shook.

"Get those shorts off. We're naturists here. How do we make this go?"

With a hesitant smile he slipped off his shorts. No white, as expected.

"It... Well, we..." He did stiffen, the girl noticed, relieved. "J-Just w-watch."

He pulled on a rope that tightened in the boom, and he turned the rudder and they glided off. Cocojo's shore retreated surprisingly fast. Smoothly. Quietly. Magically.

And now all business, the sailor glanced at the sail, judging the wind.

The slight girl beside him was forgotten, until she brazenly took hold. He hauled the rope tighter and set a southerly course. This delighted Beatense, she was in full sun. Her chain sparkled upon her dark tan. Not that she ahem noticed.

"Okay, let's know each other. These readily openable legs belong to Beatense."

He smiled. He actually had expressive cheek points.

"I'm Sim. N-Nice to meet your legs. They... They d-do open nicely."

She laughed. "Thanks! Anyway, how come you're so tan? Are you gay?"

"No! I'm just good at it, and it's fun how people react to my showing off."

"You're gay. So anyway, I saw you on Main Beach yesterday talking to that bare bomb." He showed anxiety. Despite all the power of his tan, he was an insecure wreck. "You lit Main right up, I recall. But did you see me?"

"Y-Yeah, did I ever, b-but you were… You were with th-those guys."

"They were with me, was the situation. Boy, I wish you were in my book."

Double-take. The boat bucked the waves as it cut along at a nice tilt. The seaborne airs picked up and Sim sat up on the deck ledge and leaned back out for balance. His belly was tensed under his baking as he worked rod and rag.

The wind picked up and Beatense also leaned out, whooping as their boat slapped along, dashing the two with spray. Five minutes later the wind fell and they sat back in, with pretty legs resting again on the opposite counter. They were two miles out.

Atop a distant cliff, a heat hazed sweep of rooftops lay along the rugged range of foothills. Bony Beatense, feeling like an adventuring explorer, pointed to them.

"Sim, you're fun. But where are we? South of Cocojo, is all I can guess."

"That's Le Tournepier. But… You s-seemed to like that little zip we had."

"Yeah. Seeing it from shore, sailing does look dull. But was that slick!"

"A perfect wind. Er, that's my apartment building, up on the hill there."

She looked toward the wide panorama of the town. Along with the requisite palm trees that made this land such a paradise, she saw a tall concrete building sectioned into grim cell-like balconies. In its prison drabness it loomed over the city between it and the cliff. Still, it was a wonderful scene she beheld.

"Is that it?" The girl threw the empty bottle into the sea. It floated away with its exposed neck bobbing in that characteristic way. "That big cement jobbie?"

"Nice throw, but you should have filled it over the side first. But yeah. It's got a swimming pool out back. Plus by eleven I can lay out on my balcony naked, right in town. Once the pool naked. But hey, want to take over? We have to trade places."

They made the move. With knee back up the girl took sheet and stick. This was new to her, but she did work the wind. The exertions swelled her hard biceps.

Her thighs were also shapely tensioned. She sailed out to sea and let the sail loose. They drifted in a quiescent bake. The girl was blacked naked; she desired an event of shaking explosions, but the sailor was oblivious to her. No, he panted as he stared, but he didn't act. Beatense took hold of him again. He throbbed.

She panted too. "S-Sim, you know from my b-books I do… Fuck. Shall we?"

Frog-legged, she sat onto him so he went deep in. The trouble was the boom, swinging side to side. Arms propped she worked her friend with head lowered, as boats in the area moved closer. The girl kept at it even as a flying bridge deep-sea craft got within ten feet. Sim started, was about to yell them off but she said, "Relax, they're just taking photos for my next book!" Her working in a five inch travel still left a tickling two in. She acted to the cameras, screaming. Finally they got going again.

They swung back north. An hour after they set out Beatense made Cocojo. Sim pulled up the centerboard and they hopped off and waded the boat in. Loyal Adalyn, patient in wait, came hesitantly over. Sim impressed Beatense by politely asking her out. Despite his nudity the surprised Adalyn agreed, they glided off with waves.

The boat looked vulnerably alone out on the mighty sea's expanse. They did a quick tour north up to the summer homes and returned. Sim got his things, abruptly said goodbye and headed back out. Beatense thought he should have joined them.

"How was your voyage, Beatense?" said Adalyn, gazing upon those two breasts. Eager, freshly firmed, they were made for a lover's caress. "Wasn't it fabulous?"

"Indeed, Chub, it was surreal out there. But why he didn't stay with us?"

Concerning this, Sim had actually come to Cocojo to work an all day bake, plus scope out the tanxotic women on the occasional walk. With his stark tan and youthy lines he did get greetings from the college and career girls he encountered, but they quickly saw he was too tan obsessed, somehow overlooking their own manic hours.

He did have wins: That Madeline marina pier interlude with those excited kayak girls, plus when he sailed in to his singles club picnic, much to the disgust of the other guys, as the women raved. And the campground attendants, that cashier, others.

So, today in landing his boat and seeing black Beatense, too aware of his spotty record, he was helplessly drawn over to her. But she went *right* at him!

The girls returned to their spot and Beatense sprawled back on her sheet so fast she beat her shadow. With that crooked placement of her arms her breasts aimed outward. Adalyn stared at the thrust of her nips. Her clean cut navel lay just four inches off her towel as she squirmed, and her bony hips stretched her brown skin.

Her bleaching hair lay out in a willfully entangled extravagance.

She rose to her elbows. "Adalyn? I wish to tan super deeply. Slop me up."

She saw her glistening skin gain in darkness from the oil splash. Her gaunt hips seemed to jut out ever more sharply, and Adalyn's clumsy hands made her gasp and squeal. Beatense lay back, deliciously groaning. Her friend divided her rapt attention between the illustrious creature beside her, and her book. A parade of staring fellows stumbled by in agony. Adalyn could tell it was tempting for them to stop for a look, some even "dropped" an item as an excuse, but even here there was a social stigma that kept them from outright staring at that prune dark stick with oozing split.

And so as two hours roasted by they kept ambling by, with the helpless, trembling stares, the shaking shock, the burning, fevered anguish.

"Beatense, you awake? You might be burning. You better turn... But hey, look, that sailboat just dropped anchor, and they're lowering the sails!"

She groggily raised to her elbows only to get a look at herself. She saw that she was rusted fudge black, great achievement, but typical of every ardent sun worshipper she felt curiously detached, as if she was unwillingly admiring a rival.

She yawned, watching as the sails of the spiffy yacht came fluttering down.

She looked more closely. The girl tying up the jib looked... It was Bondy!

She sprang up. "Adalyn, we're in luck. I'll be right back!"

Naked, Beatense ran for the surf. She dove over a breaking wave and swam the fifty yards out to the heavy craft, which was rolling in the swells.

"Bondy!" She swam to the bow. "It's me, Beatense! Ahoy, there!"

"Beater Pie! Swim back around to the ladder! Hey guys, we got cump!"

She swam back and started up the chrome ladder but she slipped one one of the steps and whacked her shin. She was helped into the cockpit by one fellow, and as she rubbed at her leg two other fellows froze. They saw the legs, the tan. Plus, just weighing a hundred hardened pounds, she was so casually and naturally naked.

Bondy, modest in a thong, gave her a shove, and a second woman, in her early thirties, in stunningly tight jeans and an open necked, rib knit top with elbow lengthed sleeves, smiled as if to say, "I'm dethroned." She was older, but she had hard, reed like lines and a toasted pecan shine. Her cheek points, although not connected to her mentality in any way, told of a strong will and character. Ethereal.

"Hi, I'm just nobody but they call me Bob," the fellow who helped her in said. He offered his hand. "Rolling thunder, that's a killer tan. But you're Beater Pie?"

"Hi, Bob." Her smiling handshake had a good grip. "Beatense, actually."

One of the other fellows, getting his wits back, said, "Hi, Booker Beatense. I'm Chet, and this is Hank, and this is Sylvia." Staring, he gestured helpfully.

Sylvia had a forceful voltage, as her cheekbones warned. Her interpretive blue eyes almost looked as if they should have had star shaped pupils, but they twinkled with ready humor. She was one to get a bemused kick out of the reactions guys had toward her, still, and to playfully laugh them out of their trauma. Even her blond hair was aggressive, an easy-care boy cut shaped to her head, and curved out just out at her shoulders. She gave a very welcoming smile.

Two boys emerged from the cabin. Both had tuned chests and ripples, and both were burned to the high royalty of upper middle class or higher brown. This and their classic muscles marked them as pampered elitists. They were both world improving beautiful, with shaggy full, tarnished golden hair that made them mistakable as girls. The older, teen-aged youth was showing off his heated tropical hide in a capri bikini, and the fiercely tan younger boy was in hips-held, trim white clamdiggers.

"And these are Sylvia's boys, Jhardon and Shammey," Bob concluded.

"Hey, guys. Chamois? And which is Jar Don?"

"Yo!" said the cute older lad. "The actual Book Girl, hah?"

Proud of his vibrant energy in a happy unthreatening way, Jhardon was a darling athlete boy. He untied his bikini. "Hi, Be Tense! Nice tan!"

But the superior, bored Lord Shammey only looked at Beatense curiously. However he did join his brother in matching his clothing selection. No lines.

"And last but not least, I'm Hank. So, can you stow away with us, miss?"

Happily conscious of her effect on these startled people, she watched as the tall mast lazily swayed back and forth. A week ago none of this was possible.

"Sure! But my friend is back on shore, and I wonder if she can join us."

"Right on! Let's do the whole ball of wax! The more the merrier!"

"But can she swim out here?" said Chet. "Or should we row in to get her?"

"I can," said Beatense, eyeing the bobbing plastic dinghy tied astern. "But I better confide this in you first. My friend Adalyn is… I mean, she's… Well, she's heavyish, and… Not perky. Look, if she can't come, I can't either."

The angrily baked Shammey rolled his eyes up. His facial expression even at his age was unnerving. Few people equaled his peerage and he knew it.

"Get her on the double," said Hank. "You got two shakes of a lamb's tail."

"Yeah, Beat," said Bondy, "what do you take us for, high school shits? But talk about shit, are you tanner? My world is a broken wreck of defeat."

"Me too," said Bob, fearing for his own world. "So go get her already!"

Beatense wanted to weep. These guys were okay. Only Bob was shirtless, he sported loose cotton pants tied with a drawstring. Chet and Hank had on polo shirts and baggy shorts, hardly the choice of self-involved types like Karen's erstwhile visitor the day before, and since then her own satisfying sailing host.

"Okay, thanks guys! Be right back!" She dove off the stern, and muscled herself up into the bobbing boat. She set the tiny oars in place and rowed in for shore. She was thrilled that her light self was so capable for this active life of hers. And she was wealthy because of it. Approaching the shore, she waited for a wave to crash in, and as it ran back out she rowed in. "Addy, get over here! On the double! Chop chop!"

Adalyn stood uncertainly, then ran over. "What's going on, Beatense?"

"Get in! We're going sailing, man! Twice in the same day!"

"We… We are? But what about the stuff?"

"Shit, that's right." She jumped out. "Here, help me haul the boat up!"

They almost stumbled over, it was so light. They pulled it up onto the sand as the next breaker reared up and tumbled in. Adalyn stood in hesitation.

Beatense held the dinghy's gunwale as the surf flowed toward it.

She saw back of Adalyn that several guys had come by to watch. This was the glamorous life her bare miracle tan gave her. But just now she disregarded this.

"What? What's the matter, Addy?"

"They don't want me. They want young beach babes like you."

"Chubbo, come on! You're being included for once!"

"Beatense, I can't. I like it just fine here, so go on ahead, and good bye."

"Do I have to break your arm? I already explained to them that you're just out of prison, on phenobarbitol psycho drugs! Come on, we're all waiting on you!"

She shaded her eyes and gazed out at the anchored yacht as it swung and rose and fell. Two fellows gestured in waving invitation. A brilliant girl actually waved too.

Her eyes stung. "Beatense..."

"What! Skedaddle, woman! Try not to take all day, like, okay?"

Adalyn stumbled with laughter as she ran over and grabbed their things. As she realized that Beatense could have abandoned her, she was blinded with tears as she hurried back to her friend. Dancing upon her long thigh gaps, snaking her waist and shaking back her now dried avalanche, Beatense yelled a farewell to the audience.

They laughed, pleased by the eighteen inch waisted girl's noticing them.

"You are so beautiful," said Adalyn, holding to the boat. "Radiant, actually."

"Fine. Come on, as soon as this wave hits we'll ride out with the back flow."

The two stood poised: One leaned, hard and rust browned, and wired up for this adventure, and the other pudgy, soft and oatmeal beige, and not so sure. But both were intent. The awaited wave tumbled in, and it broke up and glided toward them. Beatense tensed, although her muscles were always tense, one reason for her life.

"Now!" she cried. "And don't fuck this up, Adds!"

They shoved the dinghy forward as the driving flow buried their knees. Beatense helped Adalyn in, then as the water turned back she flipped in herself. She sat and then with spindly legs set she flashed out the oars.

They were swept out to sea as Adalyn clung to the gunwales in the tossing shell. Glancing over her shoulder, while admiring it, Beatense dug in with the oars. Adalyn, ignoring the noisy tumult all around, stared at her worshipfully.

"You're so heroically athletic, Beatense! I wish you could see yourself!"

She laughed. "Oh, I can see just fine!" In fact she couldn't move her eyes fast enough as she studied herself. Her rowing gave her small armsbeautiful action, and Adalyn stared at the working, tightly knit cords of her depleted belly.

They closed in on the big yacht and Adalyn looked at it worriedly. MED STUDS. But a smiling fellow stood at the stern, and he extended the boathook. Adalyn took hold of it, and Beatense grabbed at the ladder to steady the boat.

"Hi! Come on aboard!" the hooker, Chet, said. "Three PM, just in time!"

Jhardon appeared. "Yeah, welcome aboard! Watch that first step!"

The bank teller cast a fond look of gratitude at her benefactor as she held to the ladder, but the nude was stowing the oars. The yacht was bobbing up and down in a very nautical way. Adalyn watched for her moment, then climbed. She was thrilled, never dreaming this (additional) adventure could actually happen to her.

"Hey, I seen you before!" Beatense heard Bondy exuberantly holler, as she flung the painter up to Chet. "Whaddya drink, old gal? We got gin and bionic, vodka and renegade, and a shitload of wine ghoulers! Even beers for tears!"

Beatense snatched Adalyn's things and handed them up to Chet, who stared as the girl climbed the ladder and swung her long legs in over the stern. Adalyn was taking a bottle of beer. Beatense watched as Hank and Sylvia raised the mainsail up on the cabin roof. They used a crank, just like in the movies.

"Get the bloody jib, too!" Bondy called out. "And sit tight, you there!"

"Wow, is that cool!" You There cried, as she too watched the sail billow up.

Jhardon smiled delightedly, proud to share this event, even as Shammey sprang onto the narrow ledge or counter that ran by the cabin. He agilely skipped forward to the bow. His tensiled muscles at work, he began readying the jib.

"I hate that," said Adalyn, "when they waste tans like that on fool kids." Jhardon smiled as Adalyn studied him, half laughing in bewildered disbelief. Like that of his brother's, his tan was astonishing. "Can I rent that tan from you?"

"Gosh, er, Miss Adalyn, most offers I get are to buy it!"

He was lounging on the side bench, giving himself an appraising look.

"That is pure sick," Adalyn muttered. She looked up at the masthead. "Oh, what are those peculiar little stick things up on the pole there?"

Beatense didn't care about stupid little stick things. The sails now raised and the halyards made fast, and Sylvia lightly hopped back down into the well. Bob headed forward to help Shammey with the anchor. Hank was atop the cabin, sitting with legs hanging down. Chet was staring at Beatense, dry gulping. He saw the Sim video.

"Stick what?" he said, looking away, looking up. "Oh, those stick things! Well, they're for seagulls to sit on. An old tradition. And your name is? I'm Chet."

"I'm Adalyn. I'm on vacation rebounding, and talk about rebounding!"

Everyone laughed, and Beatense felt justified in dragging Adalyn along.

"Rebounding!" said Bondy. "I just got fired! I should rebound myself!"

Hank turned to Adalyn. "I'm Hank, chief cook and bottle washer, all bright eyed and bushy-tailed, at your service. Hey, how's them bananas?"

Beatense rolled her eyes up. The rumbling sails drew taut as the sheets were pulled home and Bondy spun the wooden wheel. The boat heeled over as the sails filled, and everyone cheered. Hank clambered into the well.

"Ready on the anchor!" he called. "Rise and shine! Up and at em!"

Young Shammey pulled the line in hand over hand as the coils presumably fell in precise loops at his feet. He stood during this procedure, he rode to the now gliding boat's random lurchings as steadily as on a sidewalk.

Both boys were apparently born to boats and boating, and their privileged young muscles knew their workings intimately. With wet tan flashing Shammey wrested the dripping iron hook from out of the deep, and Bob stowed it.

Boat now in flight, the grim boy returned, shined with spray. He looked browner, worth another million. Beatense watched as he entered the cabin, wishing he would stay on deck for her study. But he came right back up with a quart bottle of oil.

Bob climbed back down into the well, and he took the bottle and shook it. "Old kitchen oil. It might be rancid, you two, but go ahead and use it up."

Its condition wasn't a worry. Within seconds the boys were atop the cabin, both sleek oiled and giving their all to the munificent god of sun. These were the type of boys who intrude on summer events like art fairs just in shorts, to show off. For me it was ever disconcerting in the 1970s to see baked young barbell brats, with long hair.

"Well we got rid of them," said Hank. "Good riddance, heh heh."

"Isn't enough enough?" said Adalyn. "Can't they take a day off?"

Beatense felt red fury; Adalyn didn't understand sun worship. She sat on the lee bench in the sun next to Hank, who took the helm. Both Adalyn and Bob were to her left. On the opposite bench Bondy sat back against the stern, so that Chet and the taut Sylvia were squeezed by her feet against the cabin bulkhead.

"Are those your kids, Sylvia?" said Beatense. "They really are treasures."

She smiled, with an ironic, chummy sideways twist. "So where did you get the ludicrous idea they're treasures? Try one day with them."

"Both of them are top drawer. They reek of money, if I can say it."

"Thanks, we do reek of wealth. I work at the Coventry Department Store, at the Black Canyon Mall. I have a ten year old car that's leaking oil."

"Yours waited ten years?" said Adalyn, hoping for an answer from this creature. "My heap's radiator is leaking after just eight!"

"I didn't say it started at ten years," Sylvia laughed. "It's continuing at ten years. My poor boys are embarrassed to be seen riding with me."

From the rough edged but cultured duskiness of her voice, Beatense knew that Sylvia was of fine academic breeding, but some mishap occurred that put her on another track. But she was of no less value to self or society.

"Say, Bob, can we trade places?" Sylvia said. "I want to get sun now."

They made the switch, grabbing onto things as the boat bucketed along, with its bow spanking the waves like a frisky colt. Beatense held her hand out to the dashing spray, and when she turned back in both Sylvia and Bondy had moved to her bench. Sylvia was right next to her, and Beatense could feel her powerful sensuality as she unaffectedly became bare. Her formidable tan lashed out.

Adalyn was seated opposite these three cheetahs, whose presence of bone and blood crushed her. They were browned, steeled and thinned, and only wacky Bondy made a concession toward decency, wearing her tasteful tie-bottom.

"Adalyn, how about taking over here?" said Hank. He eyed the sail's flutter, a tactic Beatense knew. He fell off a little. "Strike while the iron is hot."

"How's that again?" said Adalyn.

"Do you want to take the helm, kid? Nothing ventured, nothing gained."

"What? Are you absolutely out of your mind? I don't know how to sail!"

"I'm giving you a free lesson. Don't knock it until you tried it."

"I'm going to kill you for this, Hank," said Adalyn. She wobbled up. "You and the other boats, when I ram them." She traded places. "Okay, what do I do?"

"You should have picked me!" said Beatense. "She's too stupid to do that!"

"Just aim for that salty piece of land lighthouse," said Hank, laughing. Adalyn was giving Beatense the finger. "Remember, in sailing, steady as she goes."

"It isn't fair!" Beatense went on, turning to hide her tears for Adalyn's sake. She spotted a town drifting by, two miles distant. "That's Le Tournepier!"

"Yeah," said Bob grimly. "You can see it ten miles out because of that big ugly building. The whole coast is beautiful and then they go and build that."

Beatense had seen the building earlier but kept her own counsel.

"So, you're the Book Girl," said Hank. "I came, I saw, but I didn't buy."

"You fucker. Yeah, I'm the Book Girl, but I also want to be the Video Girl."

"You already are. Earlier we just saw your latest, out in that sailboat."

Her mouth dropped open. "What the... It got posted that fast? Is nothing sacred around here? I suppose you me fucking Sailor Sim. Well, I want to be paid for that! My one friend Hawk said I could set up pay per view and get a dollar per time!"

"Nah, I don't recommend it. You have too many videos out already. No one is going to pay to see additional footage, if you have previous videos free."

"But Hawk said these young kids Misty and Fawn make $10,000 a day!"

"They might or might not, but they have a production company that controls who sees what very carefully. But they're still hacked by pirates."

"Well that's perfectly stinkful! Here I just want to make money! What good does it do me to be the tannest, most beautiful girl in ten counties if I cant exploit it?"

"Well you are getting money for your books, right? That comes to a little."

"Very little. Sales are dropping off. I'm never going to bust 800 thousand!"

Now other mouths dropped, and eyes popped. Adalyn almost gibed.

"I shudda had them make a book of me," said Sylvia. "And my boys."

"It's a racket, Sylly," said Beatense. "I shudda hired me an agent, the bastards. I get five dollars a book, but at Commodore Station they sell for seventy-five!"

"They have way high prices. You can online them from Amazin for sixty."

"That's still a ridiculous percentage, for all that work!"

Hank shook his head. Poor girl. "You're doing great, Adalyn, but watch that luff. The boat is most stable with a bean reach tight sail. Keep up the good work."

The boat felt as if it was being towed along by a submerged cable. It raced along in dead silence, or at least the sound of the wind and bow-slapped spray wasn't fully commensurate with the speed. The boat made random movements, gracefully slow and dignified, as it gently rolled and yawed. It was intoxicating.

Beatense swayed to the shifting motions. "I could fall asleep," she said.

"Let's hit the sun on that foredeck, Beat!" said Bondy. "Sleep on that lovely white gelcoat! Like I told you about!"

"Yes, that gelcoat. Adalyn, this is okay with you, isn't it?"

"If we tip over, you'll be the first to know. But yes yes yes, go ahead, Beatense! And look at me, steering an actual yacht! Wait until I tell the others at work!"

"As one low paid employee to another," said Sylvia, "they will hate you."

She was cartilage hardened, quite out of spite, and her tan was burned in from difficult sun sessions. Smiling back at the gulping stares, she lay out on her front on the lee bench with feet angled against the cabin bulkhead. Beatense, watching this unfold, gave Adalyn an apologetic shrug as the animals climbed up on the windward counter, taking hold of the mast shroud cable. But reassured by her cheerful laugh, she teetered along the bouncing ledge in pursuit of the sure-footed Bondy.

Crouching low as her legs wobbled her along, Beatense held to the tilted cabin's coaming with her left hand, but the cable that was strung along the low pylons at the narrow deck edge was just knee high, useless for a respectable handhold.

The seas were cleaving by alongside, at a terrific speed.

Bondy hopped out onto wide foredeck, that had a threatening wind tipped cant, and Beatense crept out after her. Bondy lay out on the starboard, or the preferable and safer high side of the deck, leaving the lower port side to Beatense. She lay prone here, clinging to the edge of the open hatch fearfully and bracing her feet.

Indeed, her tan had to be hotly dark against the white paint, but as she anxiously watched the huge oncoming waves she was jiggled back and forth in slippery alarm. The riding bow bucked through the waves, and the spray flew.

Bondy tied her thong to a nearby cleat.

"I'm getting that fucking oil bottle, Beastie!" she yelled. She stood and reached back along the cabin roof to where the boys slept, oblivious to the boat's bucking. "Ah, got it!" She slid back down the angled cabin front, and just to show what an old seadog she was, she oiled herself to eliminate all friction.

"Now, this is living, ain't it, kid? Want some of this?"

"N-No, I'm f-fine, Bondy!" The cold spray caught her. "Oh-h-h-h!"

"I'm getting some beer! Want one? I'll polish you up when I get back!"

Bondy sprang up and ran back along the ledge.

"Hey, Hank!" Beatense heard her yell. "Toss me some of that cat piss!"

Med Studs lurched and Beatense grabbed to a cleat. She gazed out across the vivid, sparkling green seas, that held such menace. Dozens of other boats like their own were at all distances. The day was glorious. More spray hit. Wild Bondy dove back down onto the deck. She gave Beatense both cans to hold, and she sat astride her, and excited by her own skinny thighs, she oiled her friend's long, widening back with the rancid ooze. She finished and sprawled out in relaxation. Both girls were toothpicks, slippery shined and grotesquely tanned.

Beatense craned around to look at her twin butt bumps. She was relieved to be out here in this nautical solitude, having given the cameras the slip. Observing the toughened swelling of her opposing triceps and biceps she snapped her can. Despite her chances of getting tossed over the side, her heart pounded. *This indeed is life.* She swigged her beer. The flying spray beaded up on her oily dark rust shine.

"Bondy, do you think Adalyn can handle ours and Sylvia's lack of tact?"

At that the two heard Adalyn whoop with laughter.

"She might pull through, but where the angel food did I see her before?"

"She was just over from us up at Cocojo, Wednesday it was. She angered me because she kept giving us this sad sack look, and so just to get her I got all squirmy when Krinkles massaged me. And I ran by her all springy, too, just to get her."

"That explains that maneuver. So how did she get to know bitchety you?"

"I was running through Sorel naked this morning, and the lifeguards chased me. She hid me under her blanket. She was actually friendly even though I was shitful to her before. But she did dig her elbow into me." --/-- "Naked in Sorel!"

"Plus yesterday I took off with these guys in their boat, as she watched."

"What happened, anything?" --/-- "Yeah, before that they gang fucked me. Odd no one mentioned that, but they did say they saw my fucking Sim out in his boat. My first sex video was Milky teaching me out at surveying camp." --/-- "Pure classic."

Ruined Beatense lay in affected relaxation, despite the sailboat's unpredictable heaving pitches. Also, in her nudity she was more exposed out here at sea than she expected, with other boats drawing close in. But perhaps with the romance of sailing yachts heeling along, their interest was in that and not her.

The girls slept. When they awoke the foothills were reduced to tangled hills of dried vegetation. The boat still bore southward, silently, steadily and alone.

"Bondy, where the hell are we?"

"Way down off East Bluff Sunk. You can't build there, the ground keeps shifting. Some fault zone. Billions of dollars worth of frontage going to shit."

Several boats were pulled up onto the shaky shore, and tents were pitched on the forsaken shore. Perfect sand, but this desolation gave Beatense the creeps. A hand on her bony shoulder caused her wet oiled black coconuts to tighten. She got to her elbows, wriggling in protest. Chet, who had traitorously just sent the girls to the Net, was beside her. He drew his finger down her long, muscle furrowed spine

"Sorry, kid, I couldn't resist. I came to warn you we're coming about soon."

"Hey, I know what that is!" the girl said, flexing her waist, unwittingly adding to the considerable effect her coffee bean baking had. "It's turning around!"

"Exactly!" Chet lifted her oily chain and let it drop. "So be ready. And that's a beautifully deep tan. And your waist is like a hunk of rope. Hawser."

"Okay, Chet, thanks for the warning," said Bondy. "Next time grab me."

Shaking, Chet made his way back as Med continued to jill along.

Beatense's heart pounded from his crude attention. But not crude enough.

A call from the distant stern, "Ready about!" Jhardon raised his pretty tousled head. "Ready about!" he relayed. Bondy hopped to her knees. She grabbed the jib sheet and jerked it free from its jam-cleat, and she unwound it from the bollard. The sail rumbled. "Haul away!" rang Jhardon's bright voice.

Adalyn at the wheel, Med Studs was ponderously turned into the wind, and with a loud rappling thunder mainsail and jib swung over to starboard. Bondy warped the sheet around the port bollard, then grabbed a crank from its bracket and wound the bollard to pull the sheet tight. The same action took place in the stern.

"Boy, is that slick!" Beatense yelled, as the sails filled again and the showy boat settled into its new northerly heading. "And we're still in the sun!"

When Sim's boat had come about the first time Beatense resigned herself to the sail shading the boat, and her, but she was surprised to see that the sail still hung in toward shore, and she and Sim stayed in full morning sun. The same occurred here. In their coming about sailboats simply pivot under their stationary masts.

"Say, Bondy, why are you out sailing today? I thought you said you wanted to sail tomorrow instead. You specifically said that. Ask Adalyn."

"I got myself fired, so here I am. But tomorrow is still on. Watch for us."

"And who are these guys, anyway? That Chet is kind of... Grabby."

"Well, you were naked and black as molasses, so no shock there. Anyway, the guys bought this boat from these doctors and kept the name."

"Oh. But I don't like to think about doctors. What... What are you doing?"

Bondy was working the loose rope. "Just getting the off sheet nicely coiled."

"Yeah, see, you're neatening it up for appearance's sake."

"Not appearance, you fuck! You want all lines in predictable readiness!"

"Oh, hey, where was Sienna today? I never saw her at Cocojo."

"With Jesse. They rode the horses up the Palisades, north of town."

"Those luckies. It was bad enough seeing that Jesse ride, but Sienna too?"

"Yeah, she rides Windfire and Jesse rides his brother's horse, Specteriffic. Ned doesn't like anyone else using Spec. Very sad case. Let's go back now."

Beatense teetered back with Bondy. She rubbed off her oil with an offered towel. A cheery mayhem reigned as Med Studs bucketed merrily along.

Jhardon sat slouched with bony shoulders pressing into the stern corner. Bondy precariously rode the port gunwale, sinuously flexing. Shammey sat perched beside her. His belly ripples also flexed to his natural balancing movements.

Chet led Beatense below-decks to show her the cabin arrangements. The tiny galley had a cleverly miniaturized stove and sink, and Chet demonstrated folding the benches of the table into a bed that could sleep two. Two other confining berths ran coffin-like back under the benches in the well. Chet then took the volubly impressed girl ahead of the mast into the fore cabin under the front deck, where berths on each side were curved narrower to fit the point of the bow. Their quilts were turned neatly down, and wooden lockers were tucked in over the beds.

The open foredeck hatch and the curtained portholes gave a subdued light. The tossing seas were heard sloshing against the speeding hull, and bent over in the low headroom, the girl had to grab to keep her balance.

"Wow, is this ever… Oh!" She was flung onto a bunk. She righted herself and lay propped on her elbows on the bed. "Is it ever cozy down here!"

Trembling, Chet sat on the opposite bunk. The girl had delectable muscles. Not those of the grimly capable athlete, although they were similarly tensioned, but those of a kid who would be fun to take along on a hike. Always scampering ahead, climbing trees or rock piles, breaking sticks, pointing and yelling.

"B-Beatense, you better get up. Y-You have th-that oil all over you."

"No! You saw me rub it off! I might still look little shiny, though."

Indeed. Her skin had a violent, toasted shine, muscle stretched. In that dim light the sun-smelling desert girl glowed rich black, and her gold chain lightly kissed her. Her baseball breasts caused Chet great trouble. He took her thin arm and nosed her bangles. Her resilient muscles, that were live anyway from the unexpected moves of the boat, tensed, and her nippets readied. She became awash with sweat.

Her breath shook. Her dark eyes became large with wonder. Long thighs working, key tube wobbling, she backed herself into the corner. Cornered as she was, she seemed too fawn-like small and young.

Chet was maddened to take this browned sandpiper. She worriedly locked eyes with him. He patted her sunken belly. Panting, she shook, with hipbones yearningly protruding. Her taut muscles twitched within her tan's vivid heat, her split opened.

A face showed in the hatch above. Jhardon. "Whoa! Sham, check it out!"

As the kids put them on the Net the two paired, the girl screaming. The two went back up. The girl was offered the wooden-spoked wheel, which wasn't the same as Sim's potato chip at all. Her plunging yaws and rolls had Adalyn in tears.

But as they swept by Cocojo Beatense stood poised and expertly spun the wheel, leaning into her majestic turn. The sails rumbled over and Shammey dropped the hook. As the boat wallowed Adalyn burst with gratitude.

"Oh, thank you! Thank you, thank you! This was the best day of my life!"

"I myself have to agree," said Beatense kindly, winking at Chet.

Beatense rowed back to shore. Hank went with. He admired the working of her arms, shoulders and belly. Everyone did. The girls got out, quickly drawing onlookers, and Beatense pushed Hank back out. The two returned his waves.

"Well, Beatense, my beautiful, brown banshee, I have to hit the road."

"What? Us two have to hit the bars tonight, Addy! What's a banshee?"

"I'm already checked out. I have nowhere to stay. It's a marauding spirit."

"Oh. That's me. But you can stay at my place, Chubs! Girls gone wild!"

"No, sorry, kid. I'm ready to return to my life now, after this glorious day."

"Two glorious days, bitch. But go in the morning! We can just watch TV."

"No, honestly, I have to go. I seriously have hours tomorrow, the drive-up."

The banshee went with her friend into the Sorel parking lot. People stared as this unlikely pair stopped by Adalyn's car. Beatense waved as she drove off. She felt a little miffed by her friend's abrupt exit. She started on her way northward and people stared in fear as she sprang lightly along, suspecting the very worst.

Her painfully slimmed, long waist flexed like a snake as she ran, flaunting those indefinable signals that she was very sexual. She showed these homely shlunks the contempt they expected and deserved. Their quiet day at the beach ended as primal instincts long dormant were set afire by her bared skin.

The lifeguards let her through because technically by now they were off the clock. She ran the Oxhead beach to the summer home shore, where an enthusiastic girl of fourteen was playing a spirited game of sand soccer with her four brothers.

Her large eyes had a bright sparkle, but her being so aesthetically muscled and boned frail, her dark eyes also had a heart melting luminescence. She was a child, living only for beauty and love. Surely her adoring brothers would watch out for her, here on this shore and the big heartless world at large, sheltering her from its rough edges. Except, the roles were reversed; in fact she was the protector.

As the lovely browned bikini boys bounded across the sands they wildly waved, calling, "Maum! Maum! Ovah heah! Ovah heah!"

"Rawss, queeck! Petah, let heem keeck eet! Theyah! Guud one!"

Now that was a shock. Four sons! That sprite had to be in her thirties????

Beatense got their attention. The mother and the boys stopped play.

"Maum, look at how tyann *she* is!" the astonished Ross whispered.

"Wah, Ah dew buhleeve yah the Buuk Gehl!" Maum said. "Nyked oz evah!"

"How did you guess?" said Beatense, drawing laughs from the fine boys.

Also bared, lay a nearby blond teen-aged girl. Her white sheet, by virtue of its contrast, gave her tan a healthy fullness that her oily shine richly enhanced.

These gracious old homes had been in the same aristocratic families for generations. The dedicated heroics of Stephanie, which might be her name, were probably indulgently tolerated by these residents. After all, she was that cutely spoiled Amherst girl being the Amherst girl. But if outside renters came and their daughters took to the sun with the same fury, it wouldn't be proper. But young Stephanie, what a sunbug!

Beatense deeply envied this life, with summers spent on the shore.

This girl suddenly sprang up and ran for the cold surf. Here again her life of hot long summers on this shore gave her an advantage, being toughened to the sea she dove in without a flinch. The soccer sons whooped and followed.

A slim, tan young woman came half running toward Beatense, dragged along by her dog. She too was a summer girl, she wasn't flaunting herself like the typical vacation beach slut. Living here she could pick her times. Her thick blond hair was pinned up in that hurried way with sport girls. She was sunny brown flooded of face, with strong, forceful cheeks, that were set off by her authoritative sunglasses, and her regal forehead showed that she was decisively confident in place and purpose.

Beatense sighed. She was top pedigree, but not in noble lineage. She ran on to Bastian. No Curt, but the sisters were there. She continued north up to Main. This was already glutted with weekenders. They hurriedly checked in, emptied their cars, and hit the beach within minutes. The new arrivals gave Beatense startled stares.

This was when she realized she was getting a blowback effect. For each of the victims she rattled, this just hyped her up almost unbearably. Then she saw trouble ahead to make things far worse, Neatsfoot, resting back on his elbows.

The vain lad was openly admiring the finely sculpted, deeply oiled darkness that was his devastation tan. He lay panting from the heat, and the impact of his own tan. His jean cut-offs were shoved low, suspending the belt loop band loosely from hip to hip. But of chief interest was his exposed edge of pure white.

Otherwise this slender youth was burned dark brown, that the light blue fading of his cut-offs seemed to deepen to black.

Wobbling, the naked girl approached him. "S-Say, er, K-Kit?"

The boy sat up, and his slim frame slinkily adjusted to his new position.

"Hah? Oh! Oh, it's… It's you!" He sprang up. His cut-offs enticingly just held precariously low about his lanky hips. He stared. Bitching naked! "H-Hi…"

"Hi, er, Kitanning, I guess y-you got mad at me for when like yesterday I stupidly panicked and swam away from you, so let me apologize for that."

"*You* apologize! Let me apologize, B-Beatense."

"You remembered my name?"

"You… You reminded me of mine?"

They laughed, both very nervously. The dance began.

"Look, Beatense, I… Well, that was the proudest moment of my life."

"It-It was? My swimming away?"

"Yeah, a guy isn't a guy if he isn't shot down once in his life."

"But I didn't mean to shoot you down! I just got flustered!"

"I also." He took a shaking breath. "But I-look, c-can we ever, er…"

"This evening? I'm-I'm st-staying at the Hideaway. Room 8."

"I can't, I work nights over at the Breeze, tending bar, and I won't b-be done until one-thirty. Too late to p-pay a call, isn't it?"

"I'm not sure what the protocols are here, but I don't go by any rules. Stop by."

Shaking, fuck arranged, the two looked into each other's eyes. Kit's ruffled dark hair was the picture of schoolboy innocence as it touched upon his fine forehead.

"I c-can st-stop by, and why not lay out with me here tomorrow?"

"I would love to, but I'm on for sailing tomorrow with my, er, with like my girlfriend Bondy. Do you know her? How… How about S-Sunday?"

"Even better. I guard the Breeze pool that morning, and after that I'm off until the next morning. But I better go, I have to set up my glassware. Bye, B-Beatense."

Just color, his tan, but it leaped at her, burning her eyes. "B-Bye."

She watched his long, lovely, bare back as he left. He had that weavy hip-tip effect. And how those curled lockets of piled black hair tickled onto his long neck!

Cell by cell he was so perfected, Beatense wondered why one of them couldn't have thrown in some flaws, just to make him a little human. Kitanning, that radiantly slender shaft of sun, turned and waved, and the anticipating girl waved back.

She had that big bed all set. The sun's power was waning, it had to be pushing seven. Atop the promenade, the closed-up drink stand was being towed away. The eager Tuffy, the epitome of all tan and kid-like college girls who thrive in T-shirts and shorts, sprang down the ramp to the sand.

Free at last! She ran through the crowd for the Holiday Hill beach with tan legs flashing. Beatense followed her path in reverse, toward and then up the ramp to the Beachway. Naked, she ran this south toward Windemere.

She ran by the Hogan's patio deck, where the usual beer birds sat watching the passersby. Of course they saw her and loudly hooted. She finally connected into Windemere, where the beachies rarely ventured, too residential, and she raced up Bastian. Two minutes she was getting on her skates.

She added her thong crochet for a characteristic modest touch.

She rolled into the office. "Hey, Cheeves, empty bed tonight. Shall we?"

"No, my child, it isn't good for you to lie with old garlics like me."

"Just as well. I might have a friend coming at one anyway. Tan as me!"

"Ah, that would be young Kit." Oops, he gave away his watching her in the Net.

"How did you know that?" --/-- "I, heh heh, was just scanning Today's Beach."

She smiled and rolled out. Mr. Cheevy, watching her cross the Highway, started as she fell. A crack in the pavement had caught the wheels of her skate at a rather bad time; the light had just turned green. Smartly she used that very crack to brace her skate as she got up, so it wouldn't zip out from under her. But it was an awkward maneauver, and Beatense made some futile grabs at thin air as she tried to get back up while salvaging her dignity. She gave a toothy shrug to the waiting cars and shot over to the far corner, where she grabbed the lamp post, awash with sweat.

21

FRIDAY PM

Beatense raced down the Bastian Hill, and she leaned hard into her turn onto Windemere. She glided along and connected onto the Beachway, where the beach crowd was giving way to strolling locals and tourists looking for likely places to dine.

Of course the girl was a bit of a jolt to everyone, but for once she was half legal. She flew northward all the way to Ivy Street, and went by the hopefully parked blood van. She took Ivy across the Highway and on to Preston.

Here lay a small neighborhood park, featuring a timber fort, a crawl tunnel, a chain plank bouncing bridge, and climbing obstacles built of tires. Of higher interest was the tennis court, where cliff diver and bare rider Jesse was at play. Drawn by the sunny flashes of his black skin, the wide-eyed Beatense skated over to watch.

Along with his bracelets and belly chain the kid wore a gauze tie-bikini and sport shoes. He also had a lingering patina of banana oil, that his explosive tan shined through in a rich glow. Selected locks of his hair tossed at mid-back. It was so grabby thick, like Beatense he was top heavy with dense live masses.

He was playing against a middle aged Mr. Modern with styled greying hair and designer frames as unfortunate as Sim's. His eager opponent was wildly whirling all over the court, purposely overrunning the ball so he could make dramatic whip flying intercepts. He was ever watchful, gauging his power to his friend's readiness. If he saw he was off balance he returned the ball with an easy lob.

Or if his friend had his footing he shot it back like a jet rocket, exerting his every fiber in controlled, flexing moves. The hero was exalting in the sinuous, upthrusted flowing that was his glorious build. His muscles bespoke of the supernatural.

He was burned rusty black gold, Beatense noted, like herself.

She leaned right against the fence to watch this wondrous spectacle before her, this splash of live sun. Prancing lightly around with spring steeled grace, drawing his ripples inward as he breathed, expanding his barbell chest, the bedeviling boy was statuesque and resplendent, a snorting proud thoroughbred colt. Impatiently at every chance, the shock savage shook back his fiercely ostentatious, long fulled anthem of looping feather tressed hair, that had those embellishing, free spirited spirals tickling past midback. *I could be looking in a mirror*, Beatense thought.

And springing nimbly to the attack he was flashing with professional skill that rich residuum of that summer sun, that scorching hot and enriched enfeastment of brown invading his skin. Appliqued to his muscle and bone points just so, it was alive with hurrying under-flickers of lurid bronze. Again Beatense could congratulate herself.

But despite her own show she felt run over by a bulldozer. And that long hair of his, intended only to remind lower people of his pedigree. He had every superiority, and now this kid presented a heart stopping tennis tutorial.

Staring in shock, a bloated sweat slob of about thirty oozed up to the fence. He was a craven voyeur (me, 1977). Filled with loathing, Beatense moved to the nearby bench, observing that the fatboy didn't notice her.

Jesse called for his friend to hit the difficult corners, and like a phantom terror he met the ball, chinging his racket with his drives. Another trick he had, when the ball was rolling astray on the ground was his flicking it up with a snap of his racket, while he also flicked his eyes down to note the ripples enlivening his ever-tensed belly.

Ripples at that age. Well, most kids here did have them, as did Puppet.

His cocksure, heaving tan chest was more difficult, with the angle too tight for the grounded ball pretense. Apparently his breeding kept him from studying himself too openly. Although his muscly build did have a classic, chieftain's first born detail, and although it was a magical alliance with his beguiling intelligence, whereby his physical self was in a natural alliance with his spiritive essence (ethereal), he was just a typical local kid who took his sensational brilliance a step further.

The game ended. "Come on, Frank, you can't want to quit now!"

"Sorry, Jesse, not being thirteen..." In sotto voce, "*Check that one out.*" The two swiveled and looked. Beatense ignored this, she was expected to.

Frank sighed. "Anyway, not being thirteen I'm in a state of declining decay, and I have a big day tomorrow. We have to man the booth at that piss assed trade show."

After a rudely long look Jesse turned back. "Well, what about the 10K?"

"No way can I work that in. You'll understand someday."

"Not me!" The thirty year old lard boy continued to stare. And then he and Beatense both turned; the brown Harding boy spring stepped out onto the court. He knew he was getting attention, perhaps one's instinct to stare at a beautiful tan has a lot to do with a sunner's delight in self. "I'm going to raise and train horses," Jesse went on, after an assessing look, "when I'm not on the skiing circuit."

"Speaking of, there's still snow up at Hammersley. You might check it out."

The Harding stick-boy was dancing around, hitting his ball into the backstop.

"They always do in mid summer!" Jesse said, giving a last look at his rival.

"Not like this. They had twenty feet of snow this winter."

"Well that would bury the chairlifts. Are you sure about that?"

Frank laughed, shaking his head. "Our little lawyer. Anyway, thanks for the game, kid, and remember what I told you."

"Not to try playing tennis when I'm old and decrepit?"

"True enough, but that isn't what I said! I was talking about the snow!"

"Yeah, all slush, ice and muddy bare spots. And thank you yourself, sir."

The youth extended his hand over the net and the two shook. The boy came over and sagged down next to Beatense on the bench. He stared.

"S-So you decided to p-put a b-bottom on? To hide your being so pale?"

"Ha ha. Say, er Jesse, does this Preston go all the way to my motel?"

"The Hideaway, right? Yeah, but it's kind of home-ish and housey, this end. Plus it crosses Barnet, and that's a real busy retail area. Lots of traffic."

Frank gave her an ahem casual look as he went by. The boy waved to him and untied his bikini, and he picked up his jean cut-offs and slipped them on over his big shoes. He pulled them over his knees, then pressing his shoulders against the bench, he bridged himself up and pulled the shorts fully on. His gold ring bracelets slid down with a clinking ring again as he bent down to retie his shoes. Torn between him and the Harding lad, Beatense stared at his tan blackened back.

The unwitting target of her study straightened up and looked at her.

"If I were you I would get back on Beachway or the Highway."

"Nah, I'll try Preston." Beatense felt the clash of his fierce skin against her own. "That neighborhood needs some excitement, besides his."

He looked. "Yeah. But I can ride with. I live down that way anyway."

The beautiful Harding Boy was hitting the ball with more power now, smiling his joyous pride. The homo shook as he gripped the chainlink.

"He likes tennis. But yeah, I could use you. You can run interference."

The striking pair started south on Preston, as Jesse on his stunt bike rode at an easy speed beside the skating Beatense. They got looks from the solid worthy folk, and the girl felt her heart pound. She was deeply aware of her intruding into this residential setting, and adding to her abusing the neighbors, Jesse's incredible nerve and verve as he displayed muscle and tan. He looked upon himself in admiration as his tan assaulted these people, just as the tennis boy did everytime he went by.

And Beatense, who earlier had enough doubts about her free nudity to wear her patch, still felt the trauma she was causing. As the sex wild girl she represented the forces of immoral evil, and much to the worried fear of the few chastity believers left, the wrong side was winning. Except, that honey browned dog-walker abstained.

They crossed Barnet; it didn't have a light. This was no problem for Jesse on his bike, but Beatense needed a clear shot from both directions so she could skate across without stopping and falling. Barnet was a retail area, with multiple tattoo, massage, coffee and health co-op stores., and restaurants. There were enough attractions for heavy foot and vehicle traffic, and Jesse stopped at the corner with leg set to prop himself. The girl observed the tight concave curve of his rippled belly.

The pedestrians stared at the two, and Beatense noted the unfriendly, but mostly friendly, surprise she and her friend caused everybody. After all, she was topless. Jesse yelled "Now!" and they tore across and kept going. The houses continued, but there were occasional businesses tucked in, including a nail spa, a hair styling salon, a sub sandwich gallery, and a lost looking paint store Then a post office, good to know about, and in the next block the library. Houses and apartments made up the rest.

The two finally got to Bastian and the motel. *Will Kit come? I need therapy.*

"Jesse, I liked that neighborhoody street. I might run it tomorrow morning."

"You won't be able to. The big 10K. Hey, would you want to run it? Six miles, up through Madeline. This year it's open to naked runners."

Her heart pounded. "Shy me? But is it a race? A running race? I ran track."

"Y-Yeah." He stared. "We're like twins! But yes, *hundreds* of runners."

Beatense opened her door and held it so the boy could enter first. The following camera wasn't expecting this. Door still open she got off her crochet and blades and fell back into her cheap, pea soup green vinyl armchair with a knee up.

He sat staring on the edge of the bed. "Are... Are you sure you want me here?"

"Yes, but don't get any ideas. The rule is, no one younger than me."

"Young, shmung. Down at Cocojo women prop me all the time. But it goes the other way too. There's rangers after young girls, and they jump for it."

"Probably ugly creeps who can't make it with women their own age, hah? If you need an example, that filthy blob watching that gorgeous boy on the tennis court."

Beatense then reflected on her own older partner exploits back at camp.

"I hope you don't get the idea for me to leave. I mean, I could ahem stay."

The girl was half tempted to give of herself. Jesse's energy was smoking in its projecting proximity, as the baked essence of his vibrant being sparked across the space between the two. There was a sheer, crackling power in that hot-xotic skin of his, that had a high sun smell. And within that deep, breathing chest his life excited heart and fire-charged blood were racing with active health.

He almost hummed. The kid was so replete with tan he was divine, and the light chain hung loose about his middle lay golden against his sunk, blacketed belly. His splendid array of youthfully pretty muscles constituted a lesson in anatomy, and his tumultuous black hair belabored his advanced superiority.

He was a woodland secrets elfin boy, wild and quivery and beautiful.

He broke the mood. "Hey, wanna order a pizza?"

"I can't eat all that. Myself, I might add. So, I hear you have this brother."

"Two brothers. Which one are you talking about?"

"Well, Sienna, or Bondy, said you have this one brother who's insufferable. Not in behavior, but impact. And Sienna mentioned this Ned, whose horse she can't ride. Until now I thought they were the same kid. Which one's which?"

"Ned's fourteen and he's a problem. Always very sad at how life is treating him; he's just never happy. Shean's sixteen and gets as tan as me, and this summer he might beat me He, on the other hand, has I have to admit a fun enthusiasm."

"I think he's the one I'm inquiring about. But I'm sorry about Ned."

"We're hoping it's just a phase but it probably isn't, by now. You have to walk on eggshells with him. If you say the wrong thing he just doesn't forgive. If only he and Shean could average their personalities. Shean could use some toning down. He works at this garden center just in his cut-offs, to pull in the traffic. He works out front so people going by can see the brown beach boy with all the long blond hair. It's like advertising, they stop to check him out and end up buying a bag of fish meal."

"Yeah, like that corn boy, or Keter. They say they attract sales the same way."

"Shean look-alike Keter. And I ride with Shant and Cimarron up the Palisades."

"That Shanty rides? I might defer my rule. But the Palisades, what are them?"

"Up back of Madeline. They're cliffs. They just glow in the sunset."

"Oh, I saw them from the bus, coming into town. Wow. A lifetime ago."

The faun lay upon his side with his pretty head propped on his hand and his hair spilling through his fingers, and he was unspeakably lovely. With his wide placed and smoky lashed and openly soft, trust sparkling dark eyes, and with his baby boy nose tipped mouth and expressive dimple-kissed cheeks, and his remarkably fresh bright complexion, and with his neglected orphan's head of shining hair that fell so rebelly unsnipped and random frondlets tously, enframing face and neck, and with the heart stirring depth of inspired character his looks had, he was so decoratively luminous, he looked like a mythical girl who looks like a mystical boy.

But it was the girl in the armchair the camera wanted, but it was out of sight.

"Oh, how about that Holiday Hill? Does it have any vacancies at all?"

He sat up again. His tight, concaved ripples shined with deep intensity.

"Well, there are two women who urgently need a roommate."

"Yeah, that's what that Kenny said. But are they okay? Honest? Reliable?"

"Lorraine and Virginia? They're too stupid to be anything but! A shit, total lack of imagination. But I can find out if they still got that empty third bed."

"Yeah, could you? How often do you get up there?"

"All the time. Hey, should we order that pizza?"

"Pizza? That's the best food. Yeah, call and order *me* one. Small."

Jesse rolled across the bed to the phone. "Okay, what kind do *you* want?"

"I don't know, how about salmon, eggplant and spinach?"

"Tempting." He dialed. "Hey, Sarah, me. Get a heaped Manhole Cover to the Hideaway, room 8!" After other words, he hung up. "Okay, we have to wait."

"You won't be here when the pizza comes, I hate to tell you."

"Oh, yes I will. I got dibs on a couple pieces, by all rights."

"Oh, I suppose. I mean, it's nice to talk to someone tan as me for a change. Like that Sim I sailed with today, he did have this all-day lay-out obsessed intensity, but even at that he was just four stars. But we rate five."

"Good analysis. But you sailed with Sim? Sailor Sim? A yellow boat?"

"Yeah. Why? A little weird, maybe, but one must respect that dedication."

"His age, I hope I still have his dedication. I wonder where that pizza is!"

"Yeah, forty seconds now. But anyway, us professional tanners, girls and certain guys too, we want to be taken seriously in other aspects of life. But our being just so sick tan is a distraction, upstaging our other contributions and achievements. It's like your mother is the teacher and you get straight As, everyone says, Uh huh, sure."

"Dumb example, and it doesn't apply to me. My mother... Died years ago."

"Me, too. When I was a kid, like visiting a friend, I would hear these noises in the kitchen. The refrigerator opening and closing, the oven skreeking open, the rattle of silverware, the egg beater, the faucet running, singing, all that. Then I get home and our kitchen is just silent. I tried to put a brave face on it, to fool my Pop."

"Well for me if I wanted to skip school I didn't have a Mom to fake being sick to. And if Dad believed me he was the one who wrote my excuses."

"Another subject. Okay, Shanty showing himself off like that with his customers, it's okay because it's their choice to approach him or not. He isn't forcing himself.

"But in other situations he's pushing it. Me, I'm always pushing it. I got this killer instinct for vulgar display, so I force myself on everyone with full cruelty."

"Yeah, I saw the reactions in your videos. And I know all about it myself."

"Yes, we don't have all our bundles of hair to be nondescript. That and those artistic muscles of yours, and mine, make our tans terror revolting. How can people respond? What qualities do they have for reassurance that they also matter in the great scheme of things? But instead if you deprived yourself of showing off by going fully dressed, would they give you any credit for your thoughtful modesty? Totally not. So when you or I hit with both barrels it's a way of punishing them for that lapse."

"I... I think I follow that."

The camera out by the street did not. Talk talk talk. Dead dog waste of time.

"Now that Neatsfoot. He goes way beyond that honest pride in oneself, and he glories in his tan openly. But with Shanty or Keter, anyone seeing them feel uplifted, the beauty of youth and all that. What healthy outdoor sun lovers, they say, smiling. Or that Harding kid just now practicing his tennis. I saw him walking along his street the other day and his brown skin was actually flashing sunbeams onto the houses as he walked by. He was thrilled to make that death shock display of himself. But you and me, we go too far. We should be indicted as reckless killers."

"My brother Shean too. Worse than any of us. But who's this Neatsfoot?"

"His first name is Kitanning. He works at the Breeze."

"Yeah, shit, I know him. He even sets me back. I run into him and within a half hour I'm laying in the sun to get even. At least I have that fall-back."

"Exactly, we can fight back. But you get these pudgy homely nonentities, they have no assets, nothing. They just sit there being quietly sickened."

"Speaking of, want a chaser to that sailboat ride?" --/-- "No!"

Beatense told Jesse to stick around in case the pizza came and went into the bathroom. She stood in the tub, and looking over her shoulder at the mirror she admired her long, hot burned back against the white tiles. Her waist looked even slimmer from this strained angle. Her shoulder blades stuck out.

She turned and appraised her severely blackened front-side. She vowed to be ever more cruel in her inflictions. Why not? What punishment was there? At last she put on her four inch shorts and swirl shirt and came back out.

"Jesse, how long will it take for that pizza to get here?"

"It has been too long." Way too long, he added privately. But he was relieved to see the girl was decent. "I was just going to look out to see if it's coming."

Beatense fell into the ugly chair, and compared the pea soup green of its arm to her own arm, yet another reminder of her famed tan. Every second a reminder.

A car pulled in, at the still opened door. The girl saw Buck get out with a grubby padded container box. Should she entice him? Was she that desperate? Yes, as a fresh, attractive young girl she always wanted it. In this world these joyous attributes quite innocently led to more joy, all deserved. She ducked back into the bathroom.

Jesse greeted Buck at the door. "Oh no! They sent stupid fool you? You didn't carry the box under your arm again this time, did you?"

"Look, Shattuck, if you give me any more of your crapola I'll wrap your head with this. Now come on, shortstop, who's paying for this? With tax and soda it comes to twenty even. Let's see some money, honey."

"I'm not the one paying for it. What happened was, my gal pal saw your ugly face and ran for it. Sorry." --/-- "Then you pay for it, runt-o-rama."

"We'll eat it first and then catch you later if we don't puke. But I'm warning you, Buckable, if this pizza is as shitty as the last one you let get cold, I'll get you fired by saying you jumped me in the back alley for immoral purposes."

"You mean tripped over you in the ba... B-B-Back..."

His head made a little jerk. He saw Beatense come from the bathroom, and step over to the two. She shyly cast her eyes down. Good thing she put on her shirt, she looked and was sweetly tender of heart. Buck saw how snaky slim her long, chained waist was. She sang very dark, brown, with, a, nice, shine.

"H-Hi, B-Buck. I d-don't suppose you remember me at all."

"Uh-Uh-Uh-Uh-Of course I d-do! That was just y-yesterday I saw you!"

She blushed as much as possible for her complexion, and stole a glance, gulping visibly. "Yes, in front of the g-grocery store, I think." The child swung back and forth self consciously, like she was caught taking the last cookie. "I-I just c-came up f-from the b-beach. M-Main Beach. Me and my silly habit, I laid in the sun all day."

Buck felt his corpuscles rage within. Jesse stood openmouthed.

"Oh, y-y-y-yeah! Uh huh!"

Her look turned sad. "All I do is get sun. So... Wh-What do I owe you?"

His mouth was working like a pneumatic stapling machine.

"I... It's-It's on m-me, miss. P-Plus t-two c-cans of Whiz F-Fizz!"

"I thought it was Agricola," said Jesse, gritting his teeth.

She gazed earnestly into the visitor's eyes. Jesse rolled his own eyes up. "Don't be dumb, Buck. Twenty, right? When you spend it, th-think of me."

"It-It's not m-mine to spend, b-but I'll th-think of you!"

She looked lost in the clouds, her densely browned face alight with celestial bliss. It was an astonishing transformation; her sacred eyes impressed Jesse deeply.

"Oh, you're just saying that. Okay, twenty. Should I make it twenty-five?"

"N-No, t-twenty is fine!"

"I underestimated you, Buck. You're very kind."

He shook as she pressed the fives into his clammy fat hand, holding her boned wrist just so, jingling her bracelets. They cast little dancing glints on her enriched skin. Her wee golden hairs added to the effect. Crippling, even if he saw the day's Net.

"Th-Thanks! And b-bye! I have to go! B-B-Bye!" He turned and tripped over the threshold. The girl clapped her hands in delight as Buck grinned back apologetically. He came back in and retrieved the pizza carrier. "Heh heh, I forgot this!" He turned and smacked into the door jamb. "Sorry! B-Bye!"

He finally stumbled out and a laughing Beatense waved an elegant arm and shut the door, as loud whooping could be heard out in the parking lot.

"Beatense..." --/-- "Hah? Okay, that should be enough time. Stay here."

The kid stepped out into the balmy twilight. Buck's key stopped in mid air before the steering wheel as the key's owner beheld her gossamer approach.

"Hey, I thought I spotted a Burroughs out here! Good pick! Just let me look in at that familiar old interior, Buck, with its Sonic-Caster radio and Jet-Flite compass built right into the dash. Do you have the Quad-Flo Infinite Variable tranny?"

Buck nodded and nervously pressed himself back as she rested her skinny arms on the door and leaned in. Things seemed to be moving too fast here. Maybe not.

Beatense was genuinely attracted anyway by that *Transvue* dashboard, with its deco styled gauges, knobs, and chrome strips. So her interest should have allayed suspicions that she was just working a ploy, despite the missing rearview mirror.

She reached for the celluloid shift knob and jiggled it with her dainty arm.

She touched his arm. "I... I guess you'll be working kind of late, hah, Buck?"

"M-Me? N-No. I mean yes! I'm w-working until twelve!"

"Oh! That's when I was planning to go for a run along the surf! I just love running the shore in the dark, but it's kind of risky, being so alone like that. But maybe a nice walk along the surf would be okay, with a friend. Then a nice private spot, and..."

Thinking of that she luminously gazed into his eyes, her breath trembling.

"Oh, er, y-yeah. Y-You have to b-be careful! Well, b-bye! S-See you!"

"S-Soon, Buck, I h-hope. Bye bye."

She withdrew with uncertain misgiving. He didn't respond right. Buck started his straight eight and backed out with an after-thought wave. He swung around and the girl watched as the dumpy old automobile turned the Bastian corner.

Jesse eyed her narrowly as she stepped back in, doubtfully smiling.

"Do you mind telling me what's going on?"

"What's the big deal? I was mean to him before and made it up to him."

He wasn't satisfied. "You're not playing games with him, are you? Million dollar beach girls like you have never gone for him. No girl, period."

"That I believe, but I just appreciate his admiring me without sizing me up. He's genuine, Jesse, the way he even tangles up his words."

Tears showed in his eyes. He loved Buck. He was overjoyed for him.

"Well, I'll just have a piece or two of this pizza," he said hoarsely.

Beatense was actually hungry, and she inhaled the pizza. The Fizz was a perfect vintage. When they finished she closed the grease stained box.

"Toss this in the trash on your way to your next uninvited intrusion, Jesse."

"Intrusion! And you're not kicking me out, are you?"

"Of course! I have to get ready for... For when... Buck comes back."

"Oh! You made plans?"

"Sort of. I mean, yes. And look into that roommate thing, will you?"

"Sure! If I can find them. It is Friday night. You can hear the bar music."

Jesse finally left. Beatense had two hours. She watched a comical show on TV, something about switched luggage. He opens it only to find women's clothes, a gun and a hit list. She got in the tub and languorously soaked her baked body. Panting, she oiled her wet skin and rubbed it in with a towel. She gazed into the mirror.

She worked on her jeans, which fit so tightly to even her legs. She realized that except for her wrinkly white office shirt she didn't really have anything to wear with them. And she didn't want to wear her undanceable running shoes, either, in case Buck wanted to go out. She got on her Aunt Clara and skates and she shot up the Highway toward Butler's, where she had seen colorful, soft vinyl shoes for cheap.

It being Friday night, the sidewalk further up was full of idly bumbling tourists that Beatense almost mowed down because of their random moves. She rolled right into the busy store. She got desperate looks; the fluorescent lights gave her a strangling darkness. Her quivery peaches in the profile view gave the cameras a profile view.

And she was small but strong, very shiny and famously tortured tan.

Beatense pawed through the big close-out box of translucent, pliably soft shoes until she two that matched. She straightened up guiltily; it seemed that rummaging through discount clearance junk was bad form.

A truly beautiful, brown young woman who had baked in hours of sun all day, and whose flushed burn was searing the ascendant tan that was her born right, watched her curiously with her moodily reserved eyes. She had assertively proud eyebrows, and her projected cheekbones and high noble forehead told of academic prowess.

But in her discovery in her earlier years that she was one of the magnificent, she had taken on commendable sensual aggression. She was of intimidating top quality, and her hardened muscles amplified the image. How did she reconcile her divergent talents, that of urgent wild versus intellect? She took a box of Ecstasy Thrillers, was how. Beatense recognized Honey Brown, no dog this time, who rolled her eyes.

The high minded athlete set the item on the counter with troubled eyes that were uninvitingly diverted. Looking away, the also disturbing Beatense saw a pipe rack of shirts, and in recalling her errand she rolled over and selected out a ruffled white one with large collar and large neck opening. It was dashingly styled with long, full sleeves and barrel cuffs, and it had a longer cut in front, as if for a cavalier or swordsman.

She also picked out a skateboard and skated to the counter.

Despite her blasting impact she blushed as she set down the cheap shoes.

The clerk gulped, it was a hard night. Karen came in. Beatense saw her look of disdain, because she had her own weapons. She wore a string bikini top, made shockingly of show-all gauze, and shorts made of flimsy diaper cloth, measuring four vertical inches. Thinned, live with magnificent muscle, she was stinging brown. With bulge of bicep she picked up a twelve pack of spring water. Taking it to the counter she waited back of the just familiar Beatense, looking disinterested, disengaged and dissatisfied. The cameras got the two, adding to the beach baseball set.

"Yo, Kare," said the clerk as he recognized her. "Running tomorrow?"

He tried, anyway. No answer. Beatense realized she had her own power, she could rescue this guy. At her turn she smiled into his wide open eyes, then with the flexion of her own bicep she selected an item stacked on the counter.

"I need this, too, top dude" she said, peepy eyed. "Soothing cocoa butter!"

He was grateful, until she removed her Aunt Clara. Deciding on Once Upon she skated south. The sidewalk was still glutted with revelers and confused tourists.

There was a restless ferment in the air. A lanky, teen twig ran by in tee-shirt and shorts, her face showing her athletic intent. She was one of those sports skilled girls who are brilliantly active machines, but shruggingly disregard this. If they're tan, they made no effort and know this only from the compliments.

Beatense realized that she had been missing a great venue for showing off. All these crowds along the sidewalk gave a live energy to the night air, that carried right into Once Upon as she went in. Keter greeted her happily and the tourists stock-still stared at the two as the girl took her raspberry fresco double. They had heard about these tan beach kids here, but... But... Shirtless? Topless?

The scofflaw got back to her room and put her new ruffle shirt on. The soft sheet cotton felt glorious, and like old times she left it unbuttoned enough to bare her front with disastrous lack of tact. She put her gel shoes on, ready to dance.

She brushed her hair. The stray, salt dried tangles from the sun's bleaching had taken away its last obedience, and her hair was a shaggy mess. The mirror revealed the loose fit of her troubadour shirt and just how small she was in it. It's fresh white cotton set off her darkness eagerly, and her jeans gave a whip taut slimness.

If it weren't for these effects she would await Buck bare.

She heard a knock at the door. Just eleven! She threw it open. Craig. *What the...* She staggered back, then recovered herself. She smiled.

"Craig, my gosh, what are you doing here? Hi! Er, come in!"

"Hi, honey." He stepped in. Her shirt was opened to a deep vee.

"W-Wow... You're... You almost I-look like y-you're going out!"

"No, this is a new shirt I'm trying on. So sit down! What's going on?"

"S-Sit down? N-N-No hug?"

She bopped her forehead. The two embraced as he felt the dynamic strength of her hard, truly dark brown body. She watched out the open door, worriedly looking out for Buck's miserable car. They parted and stood back.

He shook. He thought she was tan on the train but what he saw now tore at his pupils and left their edges in shreds. And her hair, all surfer girl blond!

Beatense, watching him stare, gave a smile.

"Oh, glad to see you, Craig!" She eyed the clock. "Sorry, no sofa. Take that revolting chair." *But don't really take it.* "Typical motel room, heh heh."

He playfully shuddered as he sat down, and the girl sat on the arm with her legs draped over his. Her jeans-steeled thighs sang long and tight. Craig tentatively took her hand. He was slugged by her tan. He had no idea a tan like this was possible. Now he knew why her books sold and her videos had such play.

"Am I... Am I interrupting anything at all, B-Beatense? You seem uneasy."

"Do I? I'm just kind of flustered at seeing you again is all, especially at this inopportune hour. So how did you know where to find me, heh heh."

He sensed a difficulty. "I asked the manager. He said to have a nice night."

"Well, certainly he didn't imply that you would have that nice night here!"

"Well, er, no. So anyway, we set up our display faster than we thought, then the guys wanted to hit the bars, but I said I had a friend to see, and here I am."

"That doesn't add up, Craig. It's eleven. When did you finish that display?"

"About five. But then we hung out by the hotel pool, then hit their buffet. I had to take a taxi to rent my car, and it took me over an hour to get down here, me being unfamiliar. I finally found that Hogan place, and they said to try here. But of course I went right by it and had to backtrack. But speaking of bars, can we do a tour?"

"Thanks, but I can't, Craig. I went sailing today with friends, and I'm super tired. Tomorrow, though, we're invited for a yacht jaunt. It's a big Sheffield!"

"You, tired? That's your excuse? Not to push my precarious position but you aren't so welcoming. You're being awfully catty. Is... Is something going, like, on?"

"Oh, all right! I'm expecting a friend! This one halfway decent guy asked me out! He might be here any minute! It's just this one time!"

"Sailing today with friends. It looked like just one to me. You on top of him!"

"That was all staged for my next book. But that was just the first sail."

"Oh, I saw that video too, that rowboat. So... So wh-where do I stand?"

"Nothing's changed! I make it a quick outing with this Buck, who I actually don't like, no big deal! Then tomorrow, when I was actually expecting you, we run down to Cocojo and wait for our friends to pick us up in their big sailing yacht! We can have a great time, Craig! It will, ahem, be an overnight cruise!"

"This sounds stupid, but okay, I guess I can fit into your schedule, then."

"My schedule! You just said you were at the trade show! Nice to fit me in!"

"If I stick around and meet this guy, I'll know him on the boat tomorrow!"

"He won't be there, and try appreciating this sail voyage I set up, for us."

He finally left, and Beatense staggered and guiltily fell into the vinyl chair.

Buck made his deliveries with a vacant and foolish grin. He made his last stop at midnight. Should he go see her now? Nah, who was he kidding? Being so beautiful, she wouldn't waste her time with him. She did make a few leading remarks, but she was just being friendly. This time, at least.

Tomorrow could be a whole different story. That *Do I know you* bit. But he was used to that by now, except this girl did treat him like a human being.

Still, it was factually too late to pay any calls. Buck drove home whistling.

Beatense wondered about the knock on the door at one. She didn't hear a car pull in, so it wasn't Buck, and her plans with Kit weren't until Sunday. She arose naked from her bed and opened the door. Her dream come true!

"Hey, come on in! Boy, am I glad to see you! Oh, Kit! Tan! Ing!"

Lights on, curtain open, they sat cross-legged on the big bed, facing each other. Kit stuck out quite big. Panting Beatense held with both hands, as they conversed.

"So I hope you don't mind the lights on, Kit. We're working on my next book and they will want photos of us two fucking. I can get you a cut, maybe thirty thousand."

He throbbed. "Do... Do all your partners get that much?"

"No, but that Sim and Elgin should. Tan as you. I better tell Darcy Books about them. Anyway, I have an idea for another book, where I teach kids all about sex!"

Smiling excitedly, Beatense lay back and put him in. Cameras caught them; the girl proudly realized she had the skill, strength and stamina for legendary play.

22

SATURDAY AM 10K

An hour after Kit left Beatense awoke and threw off her sheet and got up and sat at the lighted dressing table. She reflected on her night as she admired herself. She was a streak of dark chocolate, and her wonderful body was concisely strong.

She kept on staring, then got up and answered the knocking at the door. Young Jesse. *Now what the hell.* His buckskin shorts inspired a luminous glow in his black tan, and his barbell boy muscles shined. Yes, they could have been twins.

Incestial twins preferably.

"Oh! So, heh heh, you are here! Well, how did it go, Beatense?"

"Yes, Jesse, hi, I'm here. Despite my nudity enter. How did what go?"

He flopped back in the vinyl chair. His tan clashed with the mud green.

"What do you mean? I expected to see his... A car... I wouldn't of knocked if it was here. Anyway, what happened?"

She sat on the bed, slouching in a sharp curve. "He didn't make it."

"He what? But you... He... Why is your mirror already lit up like that?"

"You're seriously asking that? You of all people? Anyway, I made a real idiot of myself laying it on so thickly, only to have him too dense to get the message! Like pushing midnight I thought, stupidly, Well, he will be here any minute. Later, pushing twelve-thirty I thought, Well, he's on his way. By one I ran out of Wells."

"Something probably happened! Let me find out!"

"No! I laid it out quite plainly and he didn't get it. I'm highly insulted."

Jesse held his forehead, panting at the enormity of this catastrophe.

She didn't mention Kit. "I went up to Butler's last night to buy my new shirt even. But I'm just glad I didn't spend a lot on it! Then I would be really mad!"

"Yeah. Whew! This level of anger I can halfway handle."

"Anyway, today I sail with my friend Craig, hopefully, and tomorrow I get sun with Kitanning all afternoon. Which, I might add, is all set without me dropping all these hints that fell flat!" --/-- "Well, you don't have to yell at me about it."

"I'm not yelling!" --/-- "But you have plans with Kitanning? Good for you!"

"Good for him, isn't it? But I do admit, Kit came by at one and we fucked."

"What? Then what are you mad about?" --/-- "It's the principle of the thing."

Jesse made all kinds of faces as he interpreted this. "Yeah, ohhhhkay!"

"And before he came Craig came by last night, and I dumbly I kicked him out, me thinking Buck was coming. But thinking about it later I realized it worked out for the best, because if I did let Craig stay, it wudda been awkward when Kit showed up. So that's the trouble with my being all bendy, brown and bony, I'm in demand."

"Tell me about it. But look, this day is already getting complicating. Like, that sailing with Craig Whoever, can you hold off on that awhile? Because like I said, this morning you'll be running in the 10K. It starts at seven, and then we got to work out this Lorraine and Virginia rental thing after that."

"How long will it take? I want to get sun until we or I sail. What's a 10K?"

"I told you, it's a six mile run, the Mad Emerald, up into Madeline and back. The police already blocked off the Highway. That's why they do it so early, so it doesn't affect traffic. Can you give it a try, I hope? You can run it naked."

"Oh, good. But a try? I won at track, casually. Are you going to be in it?"

"Duh. And Shean. And then after we talk to Lorraine and Virginia, who might be in the run, how about if we grab the horses?"

"Jesse, are you serious? I thought I would have to fakely befriend you for weeks before I could take advantage of that!"

"We can canter along the surf down to Cocojo, and then you can dump me!"

The girl saw a huge conflict. "Hold it, foxtrot! Cocojo! Craig and I were going to meet Bondy there for the sailing! To repeat, if I ever see him again."

"Aside from that, this is even better. I leave you off there and lead Spec back. Meanwhile, I can go and raise Med Studs on the ship-to-shore up at the police to tell them to expect you around ten. With or without this Craig."

"Probably without. But I did see a radio down in the cabin, Jesse. I was out on her yesterday, being so invited everywhere. But yeah, that will work out. I can leave a note on the door for Craig. But I can run this 10K nude?"

"Yes, probably. It is wide open. By tradition it was a thong topless thing, but this year they're trying nudity. That way they get huge crowds watching."

"Beasts and super beasts. But can I trust you about the nudity?"

"We have to go the committee table and clear it with them. You could bring your thong piece if they say no. Oh, part of the deal is a free T-shirt, but most girls pick them up when they finish. They run as naked as possible."

"Smart idea. I hate running carrying stuff. I don't even bring water."

She was eager to run bare, to show off her iron rust tan. She could handle any size crowd dressed that way, but the only stickler was that the run might be routed along stupid residential streets, away from the beach area. But if she stayed in with other runners she might escape detection. Like at Gilmore Valley.

She looked in her mirror. Her heart pounded. She couldn't believe herself.

"You're sure this is okay. That Madeline is kind of residentially."

"So is Preston. There could be millions of nudes, with Main open now."

"Let me rub in some oil first. This will be good publicity for my books. But damn, my oil is running low. What I really need is a gallon. Do they sell it that way, Jesse?"

"At Hendrick Farmer's Exchange, on Barnet. But come on, hurry!"

She polished her tan to a high shine and put on her shoes and Nakee. The girl waved over to her double-taking landlord as she loped by with Jesse. But she did briefly distract him from his other interest, a thinned, rather dark brown teen-age boy patrolling the Highway northward with long blond shags aflutter on his racing bike.

His delta dagger backside was arched to his rippled belly, and his thin arms were held out before him like struts. His slimmed thighs were stretched, and his extremely long, rippling yellow hair lightly tickled upon his seared back. His hair was too long for him to be Shanty or Keter, but their resemblance to each other was close.

The proud athlete's fleeting impact was uplifting, affirming all the wonders of the human invention in its youth, but Beatense wished she didn't see that beautiful boy.

"That was my brother, Shean!" Jesse cried, his clear voice full with pride.

"That was…" Beatense was deeply impressed. "That was your brother?"

Waist flexing, she jogged at Jesse's side toward the start of the run, up by Tower Bicycles. She was targeted for whoops from the guys on their way to the race, either as runners or lowly spectators. Protected by the crowd, anonymous from the sheer numbers, they called and wise-cracked to the girls, whose sport and sun regimens made them magnificent. Indeed, many girls did flaunt the no-thong approach, but for this "special" fund raising event this flagrancy was permitted to attract more runners. Thrilled by her own flagrancy, Beatense was still taken aback at the mob as she and Jesse slowed to a necessary walk. She saw Honey Brown in shorts and T-shirt.

And as the crowds got thicker, the echoing PA speakers excited her.

Attention runners! Water will be provided out on the course by our esteemed volunteers! Please thank them and heed their directives for a safe and fun run!

Used to her Book Girl fame, Beatense was unrattled as the admirers turned her way. Her browning shined so dark in the hazy sun even those not annihilated flatly stared out of curiosity. But most were annihilated. Her gold belly chain glinted upon her tan as it held to her flexing, slinking waist, and her dainty breasts, straining at the tight hold of the skin shaping them, turned every eye upon her.

She smiled as whoops and cheers rang out, and even humdrum middle aged or older people applauded as she went by, near naked. Some had come with faces set with disapproval; their moral numbers had been becoming the decreasing minority all too quickly, and the trouble was that these immoral practitioners all had fun, exciting lives of starving, tanning, dancing and active fucking. But when the hold-outs beheld Beatense they too joined in the noise, discarding all their hostility in worship.

Back in Arrolynn her effect on everyone was like an orchestra showing up at the high school of a dull backwater and thundering out powerful symphony classics. The people here were culturally far beyond that, but still they were taken by her stunning impudence. If this was just another day here or on the beach there would be some hesitation, but this festive occasion eroded all normal barriers.

Beatense welcomed the attention, even the videos in progress, because in being recognized as the Book Girl she would get higher sales, the latest title included.

Jostling through the crowd Beatense followed Jesse to the committee table. She said that she wished to make the run publically naked, but she did tie her Nake on in preparation for any refusal. The mayor was goggle eyed.

"M-Madeline might be touchy," he explained. "B-But the run will be open."

She opened out her arms and smiled down at herself in floating joy. Jesse rolled his eyes up, and then started as a news camera focused on the girl. She told the interviewer that yes, she was the Book Girl, and as the camera caught the flexions of her belly she laughed. The lens then aimed right at her breasts; it was beyond the capability of the cameraman to resist. But it was okayed at the control panel, for by now half the population knew of those apples. The girl smiled at all the attention, as ever she unconsciously worked her quivering muscles.

Runners, we'll be starting in twenty minutes! Take your positions now, and let's welcome Krinkles in her non-kini! Sign up and join her if you haven't yet!"

Beatense looked up from herself as she said, "Jesse, Krinkles is here!"

"You know her? We have to find her! We can run with her!"

For once in his avid life poor Jesse was invisible. People greeted him, but if they had further words the sight of Book Beatense cut them off. One friend he did talk to was the Ecstasy pill buyer, whom he called Lara. Although she looked as if she had lost weight during last night's presumably active hours, she could easily handle the most demanding sport challenges. She wore a Yarn-Kini thong, that made a pointed point of displaying her precisely tuned muscles.

Other girls like Honey demurely wore cotton shorts and the free T-shirts, but they were of high caliber, and their long and strong, crispy tan legs negated this modesty. This is the public crime of all skinny, sun crazed girls, teen-aged daughters included. With browned faces proudly smiling they excitedly laughed and joked.

Beatense crushed them, but no hard feelings, they ravingly admired her.

A happily humming, petite young lady walked up; she chastely wore a polo shirt and cotton shorts. Like the summer home mother she was exquisitely frail in a way that her wide green eyes and the fine poignancy of her looks illuminated a wise inner joy. She was light muscled and so sunny brown that like Scab she was translucently aglow. She radiated health in waves, with an expression of transcendent bliss.

Green Eyes joined her friends, and as a lover of freedom she stripped to a light, gauzy thong. One girl put her things into her backpack, and little Green Eyes, if not naked, quite looked naked. Technically of late she was legal, but her protective web of mesh weighed less than a cigaret's ashes. In this costume she was quite inspiring.

Runners! If you have not yet registered, do this now! Step to the tables to pick up your T-shirts and number placards! We thank another sponsor of this event, Big Don's Surf Hut in Stony Arbor! Stop in after the run for a free rental, today only! And to repeat, by order of the run committee we ask that all girls stay fully clothed! Not!

Cheers rang out, and several bikini girls laughed in guilty delight. They had likely competed in dozens of these runs, and the long miles ahead would be as nothing to their trained young selves, freed or not. Beatense was proud of her kinship with them.

The retina ripping tan Karen arrived. Tossing back her shaggy thick yellow hair, she wasn't in a bikini, but paradoxically her butt-cut shorts, four inches hem to hem, and her drastically hacked tank top fanned the real fires. She had hard muscle.

The breast-bridged top just showed those breasts and bared her shoulders in the interest of "ventilation," and it also mercilessly unveiled her sunken, dark baked belly. She lightly paced around in springy, vibrant steeled readiness, and with long, strong, charred legs gleaming, she shook back her yellow hair.

This was the terror nightmare fear for the heavier girls present, who were gamely going to try running today. They stared with envy. The bikini indulgers and with the exception of Beatense even the thongies they could handle, they were just out for a lark, but this proud genetic elitist was lethal. And to maintain some semblance of self respect, few guys dared to give Karen the satisfaction of admiring her crackling tan.

Except, they really had to. Hating themselves, they turned and turned again. But she did warrant this attention. Having been gifted with a tightly thin body, she had whipped herself with sun and exercise to complete the job. As a dazzling touch she had taped her placard's tear-tag to her slat-like shoulder.

Apparently she didn't plan on sweating, and it looked as if her toasted skin was about to burn up that little white strip. With frizzled eyebrows proudly set she proudly tossed back her proudly clashing yellow hair. Cameras clicked.

Runners, more info on the water! Tables are set up at the two mile and four mile points! Also raise your arms if you want to be sprayed by our volunteers!

Karen imperiously gazed upon her slight shoulder, then bounced to her toes and waved, to another athlete who was tawny brown. Her yellow hair was sport cut, and she flaunted the same breezy outfit Karen wore. The girl walked with shoulders held back in erect carriage, her twin breasts triumphantly proclaiming that she was animal untamed. Beatense saw the two girls lock their upheld hands.

Beatense was both glad and mad that these distractions deflected attention from her. She got in line with Jesse, and retying her shoe she saw Craig over at the next table. He took his number placard and shirt, and their eyes met. His head jolted, but his anger took precedence over the shock of her public Nakee and storming attention she kept getting from everyone. He could see that she was very well known.

"Well, I had a nice night once I found a *place to stay!* How was yours?"

"Perfect! I had sex! Hours of it! Didn't you go back to your hotel?"

Like everyone else he haggardly stared. He had never seen such a tan, and her trim, muscled body and thin limbs crushed him. Her fertile breasts were like apples, and her gold chained waist was almost painfully tuned in from her hips. Worse, the fine curves of her forehead gave her superior command.

"Oh, Craig, I'm one of many! So how come you didn't go back to the hotel?"

Jesse gaped blankly at this exchange. The next runner stepped around.

"Oh, sure, go back and tell the guys you kicked me out! As it is I'll have to invent some plausible lie. Anyway, so how did it go with your laughing boy visitor?"

"For your information, laughing boy didn't show up. Now *you* can laugh!"

Runners, doctors are on the course! If they tell you to stop, do that! This is for your protection, and we thank all the medical professionals for volunteering!

"No, actually I'm sorry it didn't work out for you, Beatense."

The girl blinked. Another runner stepped past this discussion, regretfully.

"Jesse, I want you to meet my *boyfriend*, Craig Hamiltyn. Craig?"

Joyously relieved as he was, Craig had never seen any boy so muscled.

"Hello, sir. Er, nice to meet you."

Polite, too. An amazing boy. "Hi, Jesse. You get a lot of sun too, I see."

They shook hands. Craig compared their hand colors. *Yeesh!*

Jesse announced that he saw his brother, and he hopped off into the mob.

"So… So you still consider me your boyfriend, Beatense? I'll grovel."

"I was so stupid kicking you out last night," the girl said, stepping aside for the next runner. "But if I let you stay I don't think I would be here now."

"Nor I. But I did kind of intrude inopportunely. Is that a word? Did I get a red squiggle? Anyway, in looking back it was inconsiderate of me to just drop in."

Runners! Note the time on the digital clock, courtesy of Madeline High! As you cross the starting line, for accuracy deduct that time from your ending time!

"Actually I was just being nice to that Buck, because of what Jesse said."

The next runner was a small, ivory skinned athlete in sleeveless tank top. Craig saw that she was concisely muscled, and her long, trim thighs swelled out in shapely firmness from her cotton shorts. She stood in wait with arms crossed and alert eyes narrowed in uncomplaining acceptance. Her ponytail hinted that she was diffident in attitude, dismissive toward her looks and willing to defer to others and patiently wait.

Beatense stepped up and paid her fee and filled in her app. The smiling old lady behind the table gave her a poly-paper placard, and a T-shirt.

"Now we can hold onto your shirt and card for you, Miss Book, until you finish the run. You can just carry the tear-tag in your hand. And welcome!"

"Yeah, thanks!" Beatense replied, as the other ladies beamed back at her.

She took her tear-tag, number **5761.** Craig's placard read **6282.**

Beatense signed her disclaimer, absolving all parties of legal responsibility. She and Craig stepped away as young Jesse returned with the bike cruising, hair fluttering sun champion she saw earlier. He rivaled Jesse in tan, almost ridiculously dark.

Runners! Twelve minutes! Please complete your registration! And stop in later at Academy Motors in your Mad Emerald T-shirt for an extra fifty bucks off! We just got word that the Book Girl just signed up! What's her secret? Running, of course, in the sun! Why not join her today? A trifling six miles!

Poetically thinned and muscled, he was hot walnutty slathered to a flashing, dry dark brown, that clashed with his spiral wisping, loose tousled yellow hair, all long and thick like Jesse's. Along with advancing the theme that blondies can and do make beautiful brownies, he also proved that bracelets do go with boys. At the time he had ten gold wire rings and bangles on one boned wrist. His waist was stretched almost as slim as Beatense's, nineteen inches. He was the boy version of Krinkles.

The light gold chain that hung about his long neck limply draped onto his knotty shoulders, and collarbones. He was a wonderful boy in a way that told of laughter, learning and love, and his clever face projected a skeptical yet engaging enthusiasm for life. He wore raggedy faded old blue jean cut-offs, just holding loose and rumply low to his light hips. He was another Keter, or Shanty. Deep deep brown.

The equally striking Jesse spoke up. "So, did Mr. Denton let you off for the run, Shean? Anyway, this is Beatense, the actual Book Girl, and Mr. Hamiltyn."

The shattering boy brown stepped back and marveled at Beatense with his eyes wide. No pretended indifference for psychological survival with him. But he had his own survival kit, his Richter scale tan, superb build and life excitement.

"Hello, sir! Hi, Beatense! Nice to meet you! Great tan! Killer Nakee!"

His voice was child-like high, with the rounded fullness of pampered quality.

Runners! Eight minutes now! Please start assembling at the starting line! And remember, this is a fun run! Any unnecessary roughness will forfeit you!

During this announcement Shean openly gazed upon himself in admiration, and Beatense in turn drilled his proud chest. Like with Kitanning and Sim, his chest, neck and shoulders gave an intense focus to his circus freak tan. The girl also admired his long, straight thighs, that the folded cuffs of his cut-offs held to snugly. This gave the shorts their hip riding buttful sag, first seen with Bobby decades ago. Also Shean had brown, finely laced legs, with that girl-like twist of sartorious muscle.

Beatense broke off her study. "Jesse, I just saw Krinkles! Go find her!"

"I hate to say it, Beatense, but no one will look at you with her around."

"That's exactly what I'm after. Craig, you should see her. A shocker."

As Jesse ran off Beatense assessed the kid-little young women anticipating this run. Like herself, each was proof of the law that the thicker a girl's hair, the tinier her arms and slimmer her legs. One keenly smiling tanner of college age was so thin in build she was like a lass of thirteen after a growth spurt, with muscle that showed the strain of work-outs every day. Perfect, like the Krinkles that Jesse returned with.

Craig did go into horrified shock as gladsome greetings were exchanged.

"I can run a little ways with you guys, but I do intend to win or top-ten place."

Shaking, Craig took some safety pins and pinned his placard onto his run shirt, covering up the splashy *9th ANNUAL MADDY EM 10K DASH* graphics. He changed into it, and looked around wondering what to do with his original shirt.

"I can run it over to my bike, sir!" Shean offered. "Hey, Jesse, give me your shirt, and get your shorts off. We can just carry the tear-tags too!"

Safely as a local Jesse stripped to nothing but shine, drawing bewildered stares. Drawing stares also, his still legal brother bounded away with the clothing items.

"Nice kids," said Craig, watching Jesse. He was doing springing hip-hops, trying out his courageous new freedom. "Everything is sir this and sir that."

"True, but I kinda get the impression that Jesse is taking over my life," Beatense said. "I just want to use his friendship until I can get on his horse for a gallop, but it might be more complicated than that. Because he's finding me new digs, too."

"New digs? A beach studio? Hold onto it! I might be renting it someday!"

"I have a beach studio," said Krinkles. "When I give it up I'll refer you!"

Runners! You got six minutes! Course volunteers, take your stations!

Beatense felt little nigglings of worry. She saw mad looking hard-head men, with mustaches and thick argumentative eyebrows. Their pale scraggly haired legs were corded with crude misshapen muscles. They nervously paced around in knee raising steps, and they inhaled and exhaled as they swung their stringy, black-haired arms around in limbering up. They were taking this run too seriously to notice Beatense or even wide-eyed Krinkles, who would show them all her butt as she broke the tape.

They didn't even notice the precious younger snips, who miraculously manage to be as adorably sweet as they're athletic and brown. With their careful morality they should know better than to spend those active nights, except in this world spending those nights is abetted as knowing better. They're the loving sharers, whose tender hearts are also open to pure and natural nudity as liberated on these shores.

One young lady talking with a gentleman was so diminuitive she was a child, but her T-shirt proclaimed *Army Ten Miler.* She was fresh and tautly tough. With each word of conversation her tinty tan face and blue eyes made warm new expressions. Her friend, a frail nude, owned a rippled belly and hung biceps like the keen smiler.

No notice from the bullet heads. They high stepped and swung their arms and twitched and breathed. But one athlete stood supremely apart, Sailor Sim. Beatense positively gasped at the baked in density of his abhorrent tan. He wore cotton shorts, trim cut to fit low to his slim hips. Of the older guys he alone really had a tan at all, much less of that power, with a light play of barbell muscle. Beatense caught his eye and gave a quick nod toward Craig. He nodded back. *Gotcha.*

"Craig?" Thankfully he didn't seem to catch this interplay. "I'm a little iffy about running in this crowd. Before a crowd, yes, but not in one."

"It'll actually help you along as your competitive side kicks in. You'll see."

"Don't mention any competition. Compared to Army Shirt there I'm squat."

Four minutes and counting, runners! Four minutes! If you have urinary concerns attend to them now! Today's Tote A Toys are donated by Blue Valley Rentals. They are sanitized with floral scented aerosols to guarantee that all use will be a pleasant and enjoyable interlude! Why not make some memories? Stop in now!

So that's what Adalyn was talking about, Beatense thought, looking over at the blue poly housings lined up by Butler's. Their flimsy doors double slammed.

Two minutes to go, runners! If you're going to wimp out, excuse yourself now!

All eyes turned as the unusually hot baked young Shean rejoined his party. The slender lad was so effulgently deep brown he matched Sim, with darker nuances.

We thank you again for your participation! There will be Industrex spring water, Isotope Farms yogurt and Vend-O-Fresh muffins for you when you return!

"They didn't mention cookies," Shean said. "Not healthy enough!"

"Too shittin full of damn additives," said Craig, and the dear boys laughed.

Beatense was in no mood for jokes now, but then Craig said to her, "Good luck, kid. Just pace yourself and you'll ace out Krinkles." That girl forced a smile.

The runners began surging forward. Beatense hyper-ventilated as the humanity jammed together. She felt a tingle as Krinkles bumped against her.

One minute, runners! Stay on the streets! No sidewalks! Forty seconds!

The gun went off. At first everyone was so tight packed they could only shuffle. Beatense fretted as she stumbled ahead. Then she had room and fell into a hesitant lope. She, Craig and the boys crossed the starting line. The big stop clock showed 00:00:41.08. After six miles they would see this clock again.

Six miles! That's impossible! Beatense thought, as Krinkles leaped ahead.

Actually it was 6.21 miles, Shean said something about kilometers. In any case Krinkles would hit that distance long before her friends. Meanwhile the...

Boy was dazzling. If she could stay back of him Beatense could run all day. The packed caterpillar of runners opened up, and the girl sprang into a faster pace. Her thin legs swung easily, another advantage of being willowy thin.

A wide swath of hundreds of bobbing heads was already way up by Holiday Hill. Cheering, but lazy, spectators lined the sidewalks, all beneath contempt. Beatense looked upon them as refuse, even as the faster runners shot ahead.

"Craig!" She saw bare Keter, a quick glance. "Look at how far they are already, those runners up ahead there by the Holiday Hill bluff! How did they do that?"

"I don't get it either. They were right at the starting line, so that gives them forty seconds on us, but that doesn't explain it. How are you doing?"

"Don't ask me that now! We just started! We gotta catch up to Krinks!"

The boys laughed. Beatense guessed that the two thought she was new at this and so they paced themselves to her. She ran faster, and having her tan her blood heat took over. The slower runners plodding slowly along before her were in her way and she actually had to *pass* them! *Come on, you boobs! Move aside!*

Craig, Jesse and Shean were impatiently skipping past the slower runners, too. Without the leisure to look Beatense's Nakee was only a slight distraction as the mob participants jostled and fought for position. Faster runners bounded past Puppet and her friends, and so they too were despised obstacles. The shoes roared.

They passed the picnic park's Main Beach entrance, and Beatense gave a quick look at her springing legs. They were already flushed from her effort, with a sweaty fresh gleam. Her nicely swelled thighs slimmed delicately down to her knees.

Each muscle alternatingly had one of two assignments, one, to pull her forward or two, thrust her ahead. Like in track, as they traded jobs back and forth, they writhed under her tan like angry snakes. Her rope-like waist also flexed as her chain loosely flopped in patterns that no algorithms could predict.

Beatense eased ahead, and Holiday Hill cut off the view of the ocean, and the wind. People were popping out from the curb and getting videos, not just of her.

With bracelets jinkling, she waved, but then veered into the pack to hide.

They were now out of Emeraldeye proper, and two bare tanners ran lightly by to loud cheers. Black sweated. Beatense stared. One was Summer! Bare, and that tan? As for Beatense herself, her also running 99% nude in public was a gorgeous dream, and it made her lighter on her feet. More savages ran indecently by. The girl watched them, resenting her slower speed on account of Craig, who stupidly already seemed to be laboring. Meanwhile with thighs swelled the libertine girls passed her and her group with long backs arched, driving their proudly firmed breasts ahead.

Craig had his own distractions; he was now just back of Beatense, watching her tan, slim legs, unaware that she was facing a difficulty. All of a sudden she was just one more beach girl running along. Another dark tan girl ran by, bare in her thong or total lack, it was hard to tell, while Beatense had no retaliation. For the present she was as obscene as she dared get. But Craig didn't pick up on these thoughts.

Beatense's thick, multi-hued hair tossed at her upward-widened, hot black back. Her stretched waist was unnaturally slimmed, as embellished by its shaped muscles. These tightened and slackened in coordination with her long spine's flanking lumbars as she sprang along. The radical heat of her tan darkened with her effort, so that the gold lurking within glowed in blurred luxuriance. But here she was running slow.

Craig was blind-sided. He edged beside her, to get her out of direct vision.

"Oh, hi again!" She raised her arms. "Just trying to catch a breeze!"

They entered Madeline, and as they ran toward the first mile marker more thong wearing girls (if modest) sprang on ahead. Cameras clicked for them, Beatense too, and as a flustered official called out numbers the spectators raggedly cheered.

"7:25... 7:30... Let's go, run... Whoa! R-Runners! 7:45..."

Beatense made a face. "Craig, what's he yelling all those numbers for?"

"That's our time for one mile, Beatense. How ya doing? Cool enough?"

"Sure! I'm ventilated! Plus we can deduct that forty seconds!"

"Forty-one seconds," said Jesse, doing his own study of the runners.

The field had spread out, but the runners were still so close together none of the lazy spectators could cross the road. Beatense caught their attention, and she felt proud to be a part of this great machine, as her own wee steps added to the driving thunder of the hundreds of other footfalls. The compelling effect of this noise drove everyone along faster than if they were running alone. They had to keep charging ahead no matter how tired they might be either now or later, because that demanding sense of participation made slowing up unthinkable.

Also there was the fleeting but satisfying fun of hunting down the slower runners. Their nervously turning heads showed their fear of those feet coming up from behind; however they were too fatigued to keep ahead. Though partly slowed up by Craig, Beatense and the boys romped by these struggling fading laggards one by one in an endless procession. But sadly they weren't exempt from also getting blown by, which was cruelly irksome. Especially since the Highway up through this part of Madeline was boringly lined on both sides with houses in back of the spectators. As Beatense recalled from her bus ride, the beach sights were all in Stony Arbor or Emeraldeye.

The course took the runners past modest homes that actually could be listed at a million dollars. There was a safe prosperity, a sense of orderly serenity here, but the field was thinner now, and the topless and naked girls were in full view. They ran by lawnchairs that the residents here were watching from.

Back of the houses, a tall cliff loomed, as if the foothills had been cut off with an axe. Beatense gave the cliff a look but she was more concerned about surviving all this insanity. Torrey and Tenacity danced lightly up beside her. Torrey, just in those four inch white shorts, carried her *MAD DASH* shirt, and Tenacity was in a thong.

"Hey, Beat, where ya been lately?" said Torrey. She gave a second look. "Boy, your tan rocks! The Book Girl rides again! And Krinkles is naked!"

"Hi, guys! Yeah, I'm in all innocence! But isn't Sienna running with you?"

"Way ahead. I think she might place. Krinkles too of course. And how ya doing, Jesse? Is this your brother Shean? Nice to at long last meet you!"

Though beautiful himself Shean babbled. "Nice to… Nice…"

Torrey was like the sun, even with all the severe competition.

"This is my boyfriend, Craig, you guys! Craig, meet Torrey and Tenacity!"

"Hi, Craig. We heard all about you! I guess you'll be sailing today, hah?"

Now Craig was brain dead. No girl could be this beautiful, and sweet.

"H-Hi, Torrey. Y-Yeah, nice to m-meet… You, too, er, T-Tennis City."

Tenacity, with her trademark glasses perched on her nose, laughed at that, while the temporary visitors floated ahead into the less crowded field.

"You know some pretty nice people," said Craig, impressed.

"Yeah, they welcomed me right off. Friends are easy to make down here."

If you're attractive, Craig thought, getting his mind off that speedy Krinkles.

Beatense gave Craig a puffing overview of the events since she got to town, and guilelessly told of Elgin, Roke and Zapo. She blithely told of mating with her four Evader friends. He smiled wanly. Her report of this was a blow, even though he saw the video. She told of meeting Adalyn, she related the Sim event, and included the Chet episode when she and Adalyn sailed on Med Studs. But Craig wasn't told of all her exploits; she wisely left out Kitanning because that wasn't just a fun little fling.

Shean loped just ahead. He was having such an easy time his first sweat flashed off. He and Jesse could have easily whipped off six minute miles, passing the gently waving palm trees, but the boys were content to stick with Craig and Beatense. They called out hi to their friends they saw, including surf hero boys and surfer girls.

Craig noted that unlike him these pretty and skinny show-off kids were dazzlingly salt browned and tensile muscled. They laughed and shoved each other in play.

Not all the young women in the race were shattering tan. Many were just tawny gold kissed, but their eager, boned tight faces indicated that they openly delighted in their lovely looks and starved builds. But one girl with surf ratty hair and carved-soap muscles was so richly hot saturated, she looked greasy to the touch. She had a self conscious, half ironic smile. Like the other beach girls, she was pushing her freedom with impunity. But then Green Eyes, with her own fanatical, now totally exposed tan, scampered by seemingly without this pushy aggression. Craig choked.

"That was Absinthe," said Shean, dancing around backwards, glancing over his fine shoulder as he kept running. "The resident Holiday Hill nude."

"Lately everyone's nude. But Holiday Hill, Jesse, speaking of…"

"Don't worry, I'm working on it!"

Foam cups of water were handed out at Mile 2. Long tables were set up and the volunteers held the water out as the runners veered in to grab them. The times came in here at around at a so-slow sixteen minutes. Beatense found that drinking while running was tricky. She kept choking, but she did manage to lift her arms for an oil hosing. She held her breath as the light mist glossed her steroids tan with a sparkly shine, and the spectators cheered the re-energized girl.

It got tougher for Craig, as his legs ached and his lungs never seemed to catch enough breath. Oil wetted Beatense sprang along at his side, and she waved to the police holding up traffic. Several volunteers were flagging everyone over to the right side of the street, for the imminent return of the faster runners over to the left.

Up the street, they were coming as a storm. Beatense pointed this out to Craig, but he only grunted as he struggled to maintain pace.

At just two miles he was just trying to keep from collapsing. But all runners face stretches like this. The experienced ones await a second wind. Yeah.

"Boy, Craig, I really needed that oil spraying! Probably just mineral oil!"

"Y-Yeah. You… We're pretty… S-Sweaty… M-Me, too."

The first returning runners shot by as if from cannons, the grim bullet heads first. As white and stringy as they were, they could run unbelievably. But their breathing could be heard over all other noise, a hoarse, shagging rasp.

Following the front runners a whole mob, the bare Krinkles in front, began pelting by like a swarm of angry bees. Their apparent speed was doubled by the opposing directions, for a demoralizing effect. Not used to long distances Beatense felt herself decline. She didn't have the dreaded side ache, but her expensive shoes were ever harder to move. When she had started out her long legs leaped her ahead, but now unlike the flitting Krinkie, despite inflicting her tan she was getting sluggish.

Plus, with the real speeders still coming from the other way this stupid third mile seemed impossibly long. She had center-lined county roads many times back in her surveying days, and she knew exactly how long a mile was. They had measured out this third mile wrong, just using a car odometer, probably, or using a ruler on a map.

But exactly where did the oncoming runners turn around? They didn't just come out of nowhere. Especially Krinkles. Where was that wretched Mile 3?

Beatense labored along, thudding her shoes with a dull regularity. She numbly saw the sadistically tan Kitanning fly by, with a flash baked angel beside him. Then came the fairy sprite mother and her worshipping, lovely tan sons. Their easy speed was a lead hammer blow. But Beatense felt a little revived as she saw the runners ahead ponderously turn to the right. This had to mean something.

Yes, it had to be the halfway point, the turn-around at last! The mob turned onto Seneca Street and passed by Mile 3, unmarked and unattended as it was.

Not enough volunteers, those lazy swine! Oh sure, watch TV instead!

Beatense tiredly gazed at the Palisade cliffs that the race had turned toward, that loomed over this part of Madeline, majestically oblivious to the agony below. Then to her crippling horror she saw that the fast runners ahead were turning northward onto the parallel side street, away from town! *What is this?* As she and friends turned the corner onto Lagstar she peered ahead. It looked like they were taking this way just a couple blocks, where the race turned back left to the Highway. Well, of course! This was how they turned the run back south! The loud, constant applause of the running shoes eventually swung left onto Chestnut in a great sweeping arc.

"That's it, runners! Three miles! 24:50! 24:55! Let's go, half way! 25:05!"

"Three miles! Now? You guys, that can't be right! I thought we hit three miles back when we turned onto that Snicker Street!"

Craig had to smile at the scandalized little face of this bad girl, but he had similar thoughts. He hated these 10Ks; the only pleasure they had for him was crossing the distant finish line and then trading the horror stories. It was funny how he could recall every detail, just as his friends could. How they laughed.

Well, I'm not laughing now.

They made the turn back onto the Coastal Highway, heading south at last. The runners were tiredly maintaining position, no hot-dogging. Beatense was stunned to see runners still turning onto Seneca further down, a massive avalanche. *Wow, we're way ahead of them! They're that far back?*

This gave Craig a fleeting lift. "Boy, I can't believe we're that far ahead!"

"I bet we still have runners just making Holiday Hill," said the now sweat shined, muscle boy Shean. "I'll run ahead and give you a progress report!"

"I'll come too!" cried the also black shined Jesse. "See you guys!"

The two shot off, lifting to their toes. Beatense and Craig reached Seneca, and they felt like the privileged elite in watching the oncoming runners. Beatense cut over so they could see her. It was a great boost to see them react to her, but in humbling truth many runners of heavier build were now reaching the finish line.

And many other runners continued to pass easily by. A teen-aged gypsy girl in shorts and short-cropped camisole top sprang by. She was smoothly dusky in color, and so perfectly small (like Absinthe) she was like a doll. Desperate for distraction everyone gave her a look. With her wide almond eyes and pink tongue showing her concentration, the girl was ravishingly preoccupied with her effortless running.

Seeing her, Beatense decided she was lesbian. The only guys worth her notice were tanners, and thin like tinkertoys. Russ, Keter, Elgin, Sim, Kit, Shanty, Shean.

Speaking of, the popular mascots, that boy and Jesse, came flying back.

"The last runners are another block down!" Shean called as he ran up.

"Yeah, they're cleaning up the cups by Mile 2!" Jesse added.

Craig looked away from the flying Beatense to the now lighter field coming their way. The laggard runners still stumbling northward took very little notice of Beatense or the other bare runners; their only concern was deciding when to hit the wall. Now and then runners did stagger in a shaky hobble to the sidewalk.

They slunk away, defeated and beaten after having run just this far. This gave Beatense new life as she watched these quitters hang their heads.

"Mile 4, runners! You're looking... Whoa! W-We got water! Grab!"

For Craig this was the killer stretch, that long run to Mile 5. That upcoming last Mile 6 wouldn't be so bad, because step by slow step it was the last one. Beatense raised her arms for a spraying, Jesse also. People called out to the boy, they knew him, and as he ran by he unleashed a smile that explained his popularity.

Commander Hamiltyn watched the gauges with growing concern.

Manifold vacuum falling again on engines 1 and 3, sir! -/- Well, damn it, do something about it! -/- It's the carburetors, sir, they're clogging! We have to clean them! -/- Ames, peel your eyes! Where's that damn air base? We should be over it by now! -/- We are over it, sir, but with the fog and rain... -/- Sir, we're dropping! Engine 2 is overheating again! -/- Captain, Death Peak dead ahead!

Respectfully recommend hard left rudder, if you please, sir! -/- Oh, well, if you insist, but we must follow procedure here! Always radio headquarters first! -/- Nothing but static!

Craig's bomber sagged on as he wondered, *Is that damn Mile 5 marked or not?* It probably wasn't, this being the forgotten back haul. He couldn't even use Mile 1 for reference, it was taken down, and traffic was coming along as the police let the local residents in. But by now few cared about this or that mile, like at the start of the race, when everybody was hyped up. Besides, there stood Holiday Hill ahead, a landmark no one could miss. By now Craig hated the sight of all these dull houses with their asshole driveways so evenly spaced out. It took all of his strength just to run by one, but he had dozens to go yet. It all depended on if they had passed that Mile 5.

Well, of course they did. *But what's that table doing there?*

"That's it, runners, Mile 5! Whoa, it's the Book Girl! Only one last mile!"

Craig gave Beatense an irritated look. She was using this run for exhibition only. Clowning with the boys, and pushing and shoving them, she ran with her nips thrust ahead. Her oily film shined in the hot sun, giving her tan extra depth. Craig himself was a wet mess, purple patchy and dripping. It wasn't fair that these all beach girls even sweated perfectly. Beatense was pointing to the cliffs with raised thin arm, and their individual muscles were precisely knit together. She was teasing those beautiful boys, almost as if she was a kid herself. But she had a reason to be thrilled. She had flicked off this grueling race brilliantly, but she had recalled her desert and surveying runs. This was nothing compared to them. She was a natural.

Now what's going on up… Oh, no! No!

Craig saw to his horror that the line ahead was turning to the right off the Coastal Highway, a diabolical trick thrown in to get the full six miles. Beatense and the boys, unaffected by the effort so far, swung easily into the turn, passing the few spectators that remained. This street, Pickle Paradise or some shit, ran right down to the north flank of the big Hill, and Craig could see the distant runners turning left back to the Highway, thank God. If there was one, this was proof.

"Hey, Craig, what did you think of Torrey? Nice girl, hah? Like me!"

"H-H-Hah? Who?" His face was mottled; it had weird contractions.

Beatense carefully began slowing up. She held her side in theatrical agony.

"You okay?" said Shean, whose blond hair was airborne, wisping his shoulders.

The girl's fake slower pace partly revived Craig. His blood took the oxygen from his desperately heaving lungs and carried it to his screaming muscles, and there was almost enough to go around. Also a stirring of cool wind brought new strength.

But unfortunately as they got in closer to the north side of Holiday Hill the breeze was cut off, but that only meant they would be back on the Highway some day soon. Another half mile at most, even with that two-tenths teaser.

The great, limping caterpillar turned left onto Gresham. As Craig made the swing he glanced back and saw hundreds of runners still coming. That was a lift. Straight ahead were the Palisade cliffs. Top heavy, waving palms stood before the heights.

At least *they* were getting some wind, and finally the blessed turn back onto the Highway. They broke out past Holiday Hill and the sea breezes returned. The street was lined along both sides with cheering waving crowds, while plastic stadium horns were hooting. Craig felt like weeping. He made it. A firetruck siren pealed out.

"That's it, heroes! Mile 6! A thousand feet to go! You're gonna do it!"

Craig made a final dash for the line. Pompom girls, who easily finished long ago, waved and cheered him on. Beatense and the boys scrambled to catch up. As they crossed the line the event clock read **00:46:01:31.** The attendants were tearing the tear-strips off from those wearing the placards.

"Good job, you made it! Great! N-Next!" Beatense handed over her tear-tag and the volunteer who saw everything that day shook. "You… Y-You…"

Craig peeled up his shirt to wipe his face as he stumbled out of the way.

"Oh! I… I can't believe… I made it. That run was… A killer."

"Oh, wasn't it, though?" said Beatense agreeably. Her trembling legs buzzed in bewildered relief. She felt dizzy, exhilarated. As far as she knew she never actually ran six miles before. "Anyway, now we can go sailing, Craig!"

He gave her an anguished look. "I… I'm sorry, I have to get back to the trade show, Beatense. As it is I… I had to call in to do this run."

"But weren't you set up for us spending the day? Sailing?"

"I tried, and anyway it looked like, after… You know."

"Shucks. Well, it's my fault. Our reunion last night flopped, thanks to me."

Jesse said, "Anyway, I thought you wanted to drop sailing with Bondy."

"Well, she doesn't know that yet! And shut up, Jesse," Beatense added.

They went over to the mobbed snack tables. Beatense grabbed two bottles of spring water, and cracking one open she gave it to Craig. Her black tan drew stares, but she no longer was the big star, not with all the total nudes in the crowd, including Krinkles. This girl spotted Beatense and hopped over. Craig fell in love.

She was just so tender it was hard to believe she placed in the top ten.

They exchanged remarks, Krinks flew very lightly off and Beatense said, "But how long will your trade show last, anyway?"

"Oh, until three, then we have to pack up. I mean, if I had known…"

"I know, I know." She opened her own bottle and drank with hand on hip.

"Well, we can wait until five, then. That is if you even want to see me."

"How about this angle?" said Jesse. "Why not leave a little after lunch?"

"Jesse, get Craig's shirt. Craig and I will thoughtfully discuss that point."

"And you better get your shorts, Jesse," said Shean. "Come on."

The boys ran off with worried looks over their slim, dark tan shoulders.

"That will really help if you can get off at noon, Craig."

"I... I can't. We were real busy yesterday. And then we have to load the truck. Those display panels are easy to set up but hell to take down."

"Me, I'll be on a yacht or galloping bareback along the surf! Jealous?"

Jesse came back with his buckskin shorts. Shean had Craig's other shirt. Cameras turned on the boy as he said, "Well, what did you decide?"

"The show. I'm going riding with you, Jesse. Horses. Craig, when or if you get back to town, go right to Main Beach, College Alley. Can you make it by five?"

He agreed and the two hugged and Craig wandered off into the crowd.

"I got to get to work myself," said Shean. "Nice meeting you, Beatense."

They locked raised hands and Shean ran off. The girl turned to Jesse.

"Okay, next on the agenda is our seeing Lorraine and Virginia. Okay?"

Jesse showed uncertainty. "Er, they might not be there, exactly."

"What? You said you were going to set that up! Last night you were!"

"I couldn't find them! We can maybe catch them at the cabin if we run!"

"No, call me at my motel, but if I don't hear from you then I'll be on Main."

Jesse wanly agreed to this and ran off. Beatense, watching him with misgiving, went back to her sign-up table to retrieve her race placard and shirt. The ladies were full of congratulations, and the girl smiled and ran for her motel.

The backed-up cars moved slowly by, and Beatense looked down admiring herself as she carried her shirt just so, so that the drivers would see she was a runner. But they didn't care to see her just then, nor any of the other surfer girls, whom they saw too often. They were held up as the traffic was routed through the last detour, and although it was Saturday many had jobs to get to. As she neared her motel the Nakee Beatense saw the two bare sisters turn down Bastian. She ran to Mr. Cheevy, who was watering the flowers in the wooden planter box that formed the base of the faded corner sign. Her vibrantly tan tensions gleamed and her waist uncannily flexed.

"Oh," he croaked, staring. "Oh! My dear, did you run this m-morning?"

"Yeah, hi! A 10K! Six miles! I didn't quit once!"

"You... You r-ran like th-that?"

"Yeah, but I'm not as famous anymore. Krinkles and other girls ran nude!"

"That *child?* Oh, tell me, little miss, h-how is your sunning going?"

A dumb question. She was espresso dark, with a snow scrubbed glow.

"Great, but I need to buy more oil and add the cocoa butter I got last night."

"Yes. But I, er, didn't see your friend this morning, that, er, Craig."

"Oh, he didn't stay, he just said he was in town. He ran with us. Okay, bye!"

23

GARDEN CENTER

Panting, Mr. Cheevy distractedly sprayed the sidewalk as Beatense ran to her door. She went in and stepped in for a shower, leaving the curtain opened, and she watched herself in the big mirror as she soaped her long, emaciated thighs. Her legs deserved this care, they ran her six miles, but as she worked the suds she reveled in her entire self. The shower had its purpose, her skin was readied for the day's sun, and her heart pounded as she toweled her hair with arms raised and apples lifted.

She stooped down to dry the wet floor, a simple household task that, performed bare by this girl, had a disarming appeal.

Of course, the phone never rang. Not expecting any horseback ride or Spanish Inquistion now, Beatense fingered globs of the waxy cocoa butter into her bottle of oil and gave the bottle a shake. No result, the butter needed warming up.

She picked up her as neglected, lime green *Psycho Sunner* T-shirt, long cut, and her sheet and oil bottle and stepped out the door. Still in her Nake, cowardly. It was past nine, half the day was already gone, or so it seemed to this early riser.

As Beatense crossed the horn honking Highway it occurred to her that lifeguard Curt knew Buck, and she certainly didn't care to see him after last night's debacle, as fortunate as it was. But then a parachute sailed by out over the ocean, and she ran down the steps to the beach with legs like pistons.

"Hi, Curt! Look at those!"

The vain girl actually diverted attention from herself by pointing out to sea at the parachutes in tow behind speedboats. Each had a tiny passenger dangling.

"Hi, Beatense. A little late today? And look at what?"

"Oh, the sisters are back. They did the 10K. But those parachutes! Wow!"

"You ran it too? But yeah, they do that weekends."

"Yes, I did. Anyway, I got to town last Sunday afternoon and I never saw any of this. Just the planes pulling those advertising banners! Like that one, see?"

"Very observant. No, they quit if there's no takers. Now watch over there."

She looked and saw a fellow all tackled up, standing with a sodden bedraggled parachute lying on the sand behind him. There was a sudden loud burst of whistles and a waving of red flags, and he started to run to water's edge as the mother boat picked up speed. Suddenly he was jerked aloft, so fast he kept running.

He continued to gain altitude as the boat curved northward.

"Wow! I want to do that!"

"It's thirty dollars."

"For that? Thirty dollars?"

"Yeah, but for us it's a royal pain. We're always running out to get this shit idiot disentangled if he lands in the drink. I'm glad it's just on weekends."

The girl watched as a rectangular parachute was skillfully hooked in right over the beach, that was in full roar today. The wind held it in hovering suspense twenty feet up, and then with more important whistles and flags, the operation was apparently run by gypsies, the boat eased the passenger down to a gentle bump.

"Wow, is that slick! I was wondering about the landing part!"

"They have a nice wind for that today. That helps me."

"I would be halfway tempted to try one of those parachutes if some great guy was to lend me the money. Someone who was supposed to help me buy a surfboard."

He stared. She had a waist like a kid and an astronomically dark tan. Its golden velour glow shined through its rust cherry bake. Plus, she was cute.

"Aren't... Aren't you at all self... Self conscious?"

"About what? Being topless? Oh, yeah, with girls in the 10K nude."

"Wish I saw that. But with your muscles and tan you aren't self conscious?"

"I thought we were talking about me buying a surfboard? But speaking about me being self conscious, I *was* a little running in that 10K this morning. We ran along all these residential streets up in Madeline. It was fun how shocked everyone was! But what could they do about it? We outnumbered the police a hundred to one!"

"Oh, yeah! I heard them announce nude was okay. How did you do?"

"I had to hold myself back. My friend, you know, he kind of struggled. If it was just me running I would have tried for the first ten to cross the line. I either would have succeeded sickeningly, like Krinkles, or at Mile 3 collapse."

"It's hard to place. You have to start right at the line and keep position."

"Oh, really. Anyway, right now I'm on my way to Main. Bye."

Encumbered by her Nakee the girl hopped on her way, and pursuant to her deep held convictions she felt at home on the beach; it was her world. Most people feel a sense of peace on the shore, until they catch sight of its thin, tan and bare younger denizens. Beatense was one of these. The present heat filled her with contentment and excitement, while her circus freak tan and agile body assaulted those less gifted here at the time. They felt their inadequacies in a thousand ways.

On the shore at the time there were also intellectually insightful women with that patiently wise detachment of the analytical observer, who easily manage to own killer bone and blood. They know better but like women of lesser ilk, they can exploit this cruelly, and indulge in tanning, dancing, flaunting and mating for that transcending fulfillment. Then, scholarly glasses on, they engage in their school studies or work in abstract calculus, biochemistry or gaussian physics.

Spared this achievement level for now, but of advanced education nonetheless, Beatense saw the first of the many airplane towed advertising banners, the first string of silent pelicans flying in search, and the first military helicopter buffeting by. Wow! What a place! There was always so much going on! She saw her old friend, Hoggy Lodges, where all this adventure began. She did it six times that night. Why not?

Beatense thought of seeing if Kit was on lifeguard duty at the Breeze, to confirm their meeting tomorrow. Just as she recalled that Craig was in town, creating an icky conflict, she was stopped short by the loud shriek of a whistle.

A rope lying on the sand just two yards away leaped up to waist height, and a parachute rider was coming toward her at a run. As he was pulled up into the air she had to duck to avoid his feet as they flew by. She laughed.

"Hey, young lady want to ride?" one of the flag wavers said. "Very fun."

"Isn't it a bit obvious I'm not carrying any money?"

"You hang around draw big crowd, we let young chica go free."

Beatense showed her disgust and ran on, and drew near the tropical huts of the Breeze Hotel beach. She didn't see Kit in this crowded area, but certainly everyone saw her. However, she wasn't the sensation of old; refreshingly there were at least twenty nude young women here, whose colors ranged from milky pale to wheat crust bread brown. A couple girls were walking casually over toward the Barbarrosa Hut, and one tan girl, with her legs making a flying M, lay buttered on a massage table as the attendant worked her. If anyone was a candidate for upsetting the preachy old moralists, it was she. With girls of this caliber in full dedication to their sensual lives, they could no longer warn that this was the road to ruin.

That ruination gave beautiful lives. Beatense was thrilled to see the girl yell and squirm as she was rubbed; like herself she heralded those new freedoms, that would only get worse. People just had to accept it. Active sex! Public nudity!

With this kind thought the girl ran for the steps that led up to the pool deck.

Startling the others, she hopped up to the terrace, which was enclosed from the just awful tropical breezes with glass panels. But Beatense saw the reason.

It was ten degrees hotter up here, which was a vital consideration for the many tanners surrounding the pool on their cushioned lounges. Here the colors were more aggressive, ranging from pretzel brown to very dark brown.

Beatense worried that if these girls intended to bake out all day, they could catch up to her own radical tan, that was whirling the heads of the serving staff bringing drinks to the somnolent bitch girls. Of a pristine purity going back to when humanity was at its newest and freshest, they were starved thin and classically chiseled.

As the attendants kept them rubbed with oil or spritzed with quinine spray, they made no acknowledgement. In fact they were concentrating so deeply, it was quite possible that weren't even reflecting on the previous night's bed violence.

This was a jaw dropper to Beatense; until now she thought that her renown Book Girl status conferred upon her the Depravity Trophy. Two slinky lesbians on a double wide lounge played together, while two lovely youngsters noisily did the act.

However the politics and open minded values of the hotel's guests insured total acceptance. They also readily accepted the no-top Beatense, even though her belly chain, tan and muscle put her in the magnificently aggressive slut camp.

She went by a scorched tan, oil soaked skinny miss who was lying naked on her front on a cot, and as Beatense paced slowly by she raised her head with a smile.

It was as if she was gratified to have yet another witness of her degenerately gorgeous life. She lay her head back down with a joyous groan. Beatense saw her spray bottle stand alone on the cement with no swim pieces in sight. This meant she walked the halls to or from her $600 room uncompromisingly nude.

Beatense and Kit spotted each other at the same time, and she walked over to him nervously. Being so extremely dark brown, like Shean, he was alive with healthy infusions of rays, truly a child of the sun. Only younger kids tended to burn that dark, while the older boys like Bobby and Jhardon had to settle for the average kill attack. Kitanning still had that youthful skill, and unlike most of his age peers, he was finely knitted in build, with a girl's smooth complexion. He confirmed Beatense's status as a lesbian. He hopped down from his lifeguard perch. His small feet hit upon the deck with a just audible thud. Sadly, his trim, loosely held cotton shorts didn't slip from his delicate hips, but a half inch of white line did become exposed.

"B-Beatense? Hi!"

"H-Hi, K-Kit." The girl all but gasped as the perfect youth radiated his hot roasted fury of over-baked brown. "Thanks for the beautiful fuck. I, er, saw you in the 10K."

"Oh, yeah, I ran it with Tamdyn. She's the one over there on the lounge."

"Oh, she smiled at me. But how did your tan get that day-glow shine?"

"Carnauba wax. I got it at Hendrick's, on Barnet. Their lifestyle aisle."

He smiled at this rhyme, but Kit felt his eyeballs bulge. The girl didn't need any wax; she had a glistening, natural sheen (worse with lard or cocoa butter).

A nearby young tanner was sensually oiling her belly, in open sight.

"Boy, they sure have the right morals here. Just do what you want!"

"The big hotels fought for that in the courts, pool-deck nudity. Tamdyn and her uncle each own half this spread. She was a real crusader to get that ruling."

"To her credit. She owns this place? But she looked at me so friendly!"

"That's her. She set it up, if you're top cut you get hallway, even lobby freedom throughout the hotel, bars and restaurants too. With the beachway and beach open too, being careful girls are naked the whole time they're in town."

"I noticed. I also noticed that there seem to be limitations on who is what."

"No actual restrictions, but if you're fat it's better politics to stay decent."

"It seems to be better politics for them to stay out of town altogether."

"Yeah, that's a problem Tamdyn has, enforcing dress codes on them."

Beatense saw her flip over, and she turned to pull the back of her lounge up to angle herself right into the sun. But for all her heroic effort she was just middling hot coffee dark. Still, with her build and running this place she was shattering.

"But even if she does own half of this pig sty, can she just go around in it nude? Doesn't that offend any of the paying guests? And was she naked in the 10K?"

"Yes, that was her. She never wears nothing. Hey, Tamdyn! Get over here!"

She hopped over, lithe like an otter. She was slim and lightly muscled, and she had a dreamy smile, as if she was spoiled and raved over all her life but knew to be thankful. Her unexpectedly friendly, wide smiling face made Beatense want her.

"Hi! It's the Book Girl! You're all over the FieldNet too! What an honor!"

"Shut up. I'm the one who's honored. Boy, I should stay here instead!"

"So where are you staying? If you stay here I can give you comps!"

Kit was observing the dynamics at work here. The rivals could face each other without fear or threat, their being so matched in power. It was actually a treat for them to converse without all the nervous shaking and stuttering.

"No thanks, I don't want to cut and run from Mr. Cheevy for a better deal."

Tamdyn wonderingly shook her head. "You're too ethical, Beatense."

"No, the Hideaway is a middle class dump, but it's been just as homey as Hogan was. Hey, if you hired me there, I would jump at it."

"You work here and I'll pay thirty-six thousand. If you only sang."

"I do sing! I have a contract even and I'm charting! Mercaphony Records!"

"Perfect. But I have a housekeeper who has to take her kid in to the doctor so I have to fill in for her, cleaning rooms. And so let's talk later, Beatense!"

They shook hands and Tamdyn ran into the building. Her amber blond hair fell in wavy ripples down her long, obnoxiously tan back.

"Monkey HP shit, just like that I'm hired? Thirty-six thousand?"

"Yeah, and she's filling in for Janet, naked, so she won't get docked."

"Good, but I gotta get going! I might be riding horseback with that Jesse!"

"Yeah, I got to get back up on my highchair anyway. So let's meet about one. I lifeguard again tomorrow morning. It's a waste, my sitting here useless, but Tamdyn insists I give the place that tropical ambience."

Beatense happily went on her way. As she left the Breeze beach she suddenly was covered by a shadow. *A cloud?* She looked up and saw a parachute just over her, and she dove out of the way of its passenger. The gypsies wrestled to deflate the huge, billowing canopy, and another gypsy pulled the protesting girl to her feet.

"Hey, didn't you hear whistles? Be careful, watch you step!"

"Me be careful! You know, there are quality people walking this beach!"

The reply was only a loud blast of whistles as another brave smiling tourist was launched. The poor fellow got just up twenty feet when his towboat abruptly stopped short. He fell into the shallows, and just as he staggered to his feet his chute floated down on him and a wave hit him. A crewman splashing out to him was felled by the next wave, while the poor kicking victim was unceremoniously rolled into shore in his tangled wet wrap.

"What's the matter, can't he take a joke?" Beatense said to her gypsy.

He laughed and ran over, and the girl went on to Main's surfing beach. This hosted few families because swimming was restricted. Singles abounded but this wasn't the actual College Alley. Beatense unrolled her sheet only to find her T-shirt. *Now what did I bring along this for?* She lay back propped on her elbows with knees up, while she watched the surfers. She saw the teen-age Gabriel with his board.

As torch tanned as he was in his trim, white sailing shorts, and as elegantly fine and pretty as he was, Beatense rightly assumed that he was as superb in his surfing prowess as he was befittingly toughened with perfection muscle. His long, blond hair fell in stray, girl-like tangles to complete his tourist terrifying image. Her kind of guy.

Indeed he seemed to openly worship himself, as he gazed on his chest and belly lineas. Contrasting his chest, it was sunken in like he never ate. The feminine boy dropped his shorts, exposing a bikini, and a pale, flabby tourist took his picture.

Beatense was also on camera. The boy raced out into the shallows and flopped onto his surfboard. As he battled out against the sea his chest and hips bridged his belly, so that a sliver of daylight showed in the curve beneath. The sun flashed upon his dried tan back, until he bucked an oncoming breaker that sloshed over him.

He kept paddling on without pause, and he joined the other surfer heroes out at sea. In my 1976 opinion many of them seemed far too young to be left to their own devices a hundred yards offshore, especially here today. The surf was rough, unlike where Beatense learned. Cocojo was known for hodad beginner waves.

But these kids rocketed in toward shore on their boards in a nonstop invasion. Young girls also joined in these attacks. They were steely slimmed, salty tanned and taut acrobat muscled, with belly ripples, but ever dainty with their touching smiles.

Gabriel sat his board to the waves, watching out to sea. Beatense saw what he and the others looked for, she knew this from her own surfing, that tell-tale black line. The kids turned their boards toward shore and raced ahead of the rising swell as it chased them. A massive top heaved itself up, and the surfer kids as one sprang to their feet and caught its rolling curl and rode the thunderer in.

Gabriel embellished his moves by working hip-snaps to his moves, as he flicked and danced his tiny craft like a zephyr. He landed and headed back out, the same arrogant, hot tan kid I as a fat blob saw at Laguna in 1976.

Beatense saw Gabriel turn to catch the next breaker. He began skimming across it, but he fell into the turbulent white. His board shot straight up, and the youth was helplessly flailed into shore, with ankle tied board following. As he headed back out a brutally tan young girl knelt down beside Beatense. She wasn't one of today's surfer girls, but she looked to be a beach world veteran.

She was a doe-like little sand wisp, incongruously supple and hard in build, who was so richly rays endrenched she quite vibrated. Like many tanners here she was rich dark while still showing that warm saturated tropics brown. She had earnestly troubled eyes, large and sad, and long, straight, silken hair. Some of the sun blond strands fell lightly upon her bony shoulders. Her stretched muscles were shaped so that she quivered with tensions. A natural athlete.

"Are you Beatrice?" the Apparition said, softly and shyly.

"Er, the actual name is Beatense. But who are you?"

"Tammy. I'm… I'm Jesse's brother Shean's girlfriend." She said this as if she memorized it, and the precious child paused as if to make sure she got it right. "Yeah! So anyway, Jesse told me to look for you, Beatrice. You and me and him, plus Lorraine and Virginia, are going sailing now on the catamaran!"

"We are? I mean, Lorraine and Virginia? And you too?"

"Well, if that's okay, Beatrice." --/-- Beatense let that go.

"Tammy, I'm sorry but I'm not going. I already sailed yesterday. Twice."

"In a catamaran?" I mean, on one?"

"Well, no. First a sporty little scow, and then an actual sailing yacht. It's all over the FieldNet by now. Even this present conversation."

"Bea… Beatense, you have to try this. It's better than skiing!"

"Okay, I'll go on your recommendation. You seem very knowledgeable."

The Beach Being looked down and blinked her beseeching, wide eyes, as if she was embarrassed at this high praise. Studying her shimmery tan, lesbian Beatense had an urge to just grab her. As diaphanously fragile and Krinkly tender as this sweet young sprite was, she went infinitely beyond the realm of normal earthly beauty.

She was a Visitor, sent to be an example. The definition of ethereal.

"Like, it took me a long time finding you," the little sandpiper said softly, shaking aside the stray gold that had fallen over her eyes. "Jesse just said I would know you when I saw you. I started way up by Holiday Hill!"

"Oh, sorry, I was on my way to College Alley but ended up here instead. So did you go around asking all the girls on who they were all over the place?"

"No! Jesse just said to look for the girl with the darkest tan, besides his!"

"Not just me. But nice to get recognition. But I think you got our plans all wrong, kid, because Jesse said I was supposed to meet those girls and then go riding!"

"Oh, here's what happened! Jesse talked to them, and they said they did want to meet you, and then we went to the police to use their boat radio, and he explained to this other girl on the radio that he was taking you sailing today because it would be a crime to waste this wind. He said that right there at the police station!"

Beatense had to smile at the look on the poor kid's face. "Yes, that was a foolish risk," she said gravely. "If they locked both of up they would say Jesse already made his one legal call when he radioed Bondy. That other girl."

"I never thought of that!"

"So, sailing then. And thanks for taking care of that. I certainly didn't want Bondy to get mad at me if I didn't show up. I mean, that radio girl on the boat."

"That's okay, Beatense. And yeah, he did talk to someone named Bondy!"

Beatense began staring at this captivating nymph. Her black, oil smeared tummy was drawn tightly in to her curved posture, and its muscles were precisely defined. There was a troubling long plunge of bare skin from her reposing navel down to the child's handprint thong. Actually she seemed far too sweet for such effrontery.

Her nubile blooms were kissed with wee triangles of baby's breath gauze, which clearly showed her protruding nippets. Talk about criminal, how could her parents let her out the door in such a thing? Of course, many girls wore less. A cursory glance around confirmed the freedoms here in non self conscious play.

"What are you looking at, Beatense?"

Oops, caught! "Oh, that bikini of yours. Sometimes a beach girl just has to cut herself a little slack and wear something modest instead of being always nude. Now what about this sailing? I don't see a boat. How does that work out?"

"Oh, well, first we have to go to the garden center to get the key to the boat from Jesse's brother Shean, and then we come back down to the boat."

"Oh, ugly him? I ran with him and Jesse in the 10K this... Er, what's wrong?"

Beatense saw her beguiling friend rub at her elbow.

"Oh, my dumb new implant itches." --/-- "New implant? What for?"

"They're supposed to protect you five years, but with me so active Mama took me to the clinic for a new one last week, after just four years. It still itches."

"Four years?" Even her head was whirling. "How... How old are you?"

"Fifteen. Don't you have an implant, Beatense?"

"Yes, but I was told mine's good for at least ten years. I got it when I was barely thirteen. But if you've been at it since just eleven, it shows that you kids here know how to live. No degradation of character? No road to ruin?"

"Why would I have them?"

"Oh, some people like me have silly, outmoded ideas. So, let's get going."

Too late. Gabriel dropped his board upon the sand, and as monarch of the beach he shook back his long hair, then, biceps tightened he clasped his hands out before him, and he expanded his deep chest and drew in his rippled, concave curved belly. He was lightning bolt browned, and the sun shimmered upon him with its glare.

Beatense couldn't bear to look away from that sight. But girls, same effect.

The girls crossed Main to and then up to the promenade. Beatense felt insecure about the situation before her, that of walking in the city proper Nakee topless. She could put on her T-shirt, but did Krinkles not run that 10K nude? Meanwhile, Tammy seemed relaxed about the upcoming trek, but of course, she was local in a two piece thong. They got to the Highway and Tammy stepped along in her Buttercup bikini, tenderly unashamed and blissfully unaware of the bulging eyes, the tire screeches or the signposts walked into that she exerted. Beatense too. The cameras, good haul.

The girls went south along the Highway and turned east up Barnet. Barnet was a busy retail street full of coffee shops, nail spas and health food stores. This was a second visit for Beatense, but she was now a walking scandal as she made her way through the shoppers and strollers, including parents with curious kids.

As Barnet continued inland a forbidding stretch of apartments and homes. began. Beatense stayed topless for a couple uneasy blocks, but then the girls were too far beyond the beach's sphere of influence for her to keep up her brave foray.

She tiredly put on her green *Psycho Sunner* T-shirt, just long enough to hide her Nakee. Of course young Tammy was still walking as nude in her Buttercup, and the horns and tires kept up their noise.

After a few blocks the two got to the busy Sunset Del Camino and turned south. They went into a commercial district that managed to avoid business with the tourists. On a side street Beatense even saw a collection of crutchy bars and old shitty hotels, and she was reminded of home by the decrepit detritus loitering there. Stepping her spindly, rusted legs along, the girl saw a sign, Beachcomber Garden Center, down in the next block, and she braced herself for her second close encounter with Shean.

"Hey! Hi, guys!" Shean called in surprise as the girls entered the lot. He paused from his shoveling gravel. "Great sun, hah? Even I'm getting results!"

He was proudly skinny and black shined with sweat, famed talents of his, and his old, rumply jean cut-offs rode even lower to his hips, showing his butted split.

And like Bobby the snug fitting cuffs held to his slimmed thighs, baring the last possible sixteenth inch. And he was burned so dark brown, the hues and tints of his nuclear tan swarmed in a punishing attack. He too had a long waist.

"Hey, Tammy! What are you two doing way up here?"

The poor girl was panting. Beatense too. "H-Hi, Shean. I... I forget!"

"Oh, come on! There had to be some reason. Nice shirt, Beatense! But if you take it off, I won't tell!"

The named girl laughed politely. She was staring at Shean.

He was a stand-out among stand-outs, and he slammed home the striking tracery of his features with a feminine, crowning accolade of long, loosely curled yellow hair. His dreamy wide blue eyes guilelessly portrayed a happy but perplexed amazement toward the wondrous wide world. But with the jaunty set of his expressive eyebrows one also might see an insightful, all-wise knowing. This magical child was the most ravishing boy anyone had ever seen. Selected long locks tickled all the way down his scapula curved, seared back. He was thin.

"Anyway, Tammy, what's up? You two should be baking out!"

"We need the key to the boat, Shean. We're taking Beatense sailing."

"Oh for Pete's sake, can't you wait until four? Then I can go!"

"But Lorraine and Virginia are coming. They're expecting us!"

Dancing on tiptoes, the goldeny dark browned apparition worked his fingers into the slit front pocket of his faded blue jeans shorts, and he pulled out the key at last. The electric lad spun the key-ring on his finger, an effort that seemed to involve every pretty muscle. He was burned to a crispy rich intensity, Beatense noted.

"Isn't he beautiful?" her friend said as she caught the tossed key.

"Tammy, watch it," the exalted boy said in a gruff, secretly pleased aside.

It was true that this sixteen year old boy was happily in love with himself, but he managed to pull off his baldly self congratulatory opinion in a winning way that didn't threaten anyone. After all, his self absorbed obsession wasn't too terribly misplaced, and he certainly welcomed all admirers. Boys like this abounded in the 1970s.

"Gosh, I wish I could go with you, there's a great wind today." He looked at the cheap plastic used-car lot pennants fluttering from their wires. "If it's this windy way inland like this, out at sea it would be gorgeous!"

"Oh, why don't you come with us, Shean?" cried Tammy plaintively. "I don't see why you're shoveling this dumb old gravel anyway!"

"Me either," the spectacle conceded, holding the shovel with his biceps bursting. His boned wrists held a clinky collection of gold ring bracelets. "You see, Mr. Denton thinks I'm drawing business out here. Which I... Oop, here's a suspect. He spotted me as he drove by. Watch this!"

A car going by slowed abruptly down and hesitantly pulled in. The driver, a pale, suit wearing family father, had eyes only for Shean as he got out. In this town for the locals, beach girls were secondary refuse. Shaking, staring, his breath huffing, like Dean Appleton, he pretended great interest in the potted shrubs.

"Can I help you, sir?" said Shean, ambling over. "Those are on special!"

"Er, n-no. W-Well, I-I do n-need some, er, p-potting soil. One b-bag."

Shean warned that they had a two bag minimum and Bulging Eyes nodded. The boy happily hefted two twenty pounders and carried them with a flex-weaving of his long waist and a bulging of biceps and chest. He was a riot of muscle, and as he set the bags into the trunk even more muscles came into play. Extending his bracelets clinking thin arm, the glare baked whip of a boy shook back his cascade of hair and pointed toward the open fronted store.

"Pay inside, sir!" Shean watched him go. "He didn't even want them."

"He might have taken a statue," said Beatense, eyeing the stone fairies that back home were the closest match to her own looks.

Shean closed the trunk and the customer came out, along with the owner of the landscape center. Although not fat he had an abrupt pot belly, that made the legs of his limp flannel trousers baggily hang. The sleeves of his dirty white shirt were rolled over his elbows, exposing two pallid arms, his only concession to the blazing sun.

He wore a soiled rumpled vest that he had found at a charity thrift shop, and the mashed, grey felt hat tipped back on his head was bought in the same wild spending spree. His glasses had those severe, thin lenses used by bank foreclosure lawyers and mortgage cashiers.

Beatense dreaded the brewing storm between the sickly boss and the live brown athlete, but she did catch a fleeting, fond gleam in Mr. Denton's eye. The customer also gave a look, a last desperate look, as he got slowly in his car. Shean waved.

"And how is your gravel shoveling going, my boy?" the pale proprietor said, with thin lips cutting and cold.

"Great, Mr. Denton. I'm getting sun and I'm switching sides so my muscles work evenly. But it's real slow today, so I would just as soon take off to go sailing, sir."

Wide eyed Tammy covered her mouth.

"Does it show responsibility if one leaves because his work is unsuitable?"

"I knew he would get miffed, guys," Shean blurted out with a cheerful smile. "But unsuitable isn't what one meant, Mr. Denton. "At all. Not hardly!"

"You wish to leave this work to Knife, is what you foolishly dare to say?"

"He would rather do this instead of me anyway. So what about the sailing?"

"Oh, go if the sailing makes up for the hit in pay. Tomorrow, though, if you are still engaged here you and Knife will start in on the back shed roof. I will permit you two to work naked, police willing, but you will be wearing knee pads, I'm afraid, and so you might possibly get strap marks on those nice long legs."

"I can face that," Shean said without irony. "And thanks... Hey, Knife!"

Another tan youth approached, stepping his stealthy bare feet like a tribal brave. Perhaps nineteen, he was in faded, low-held butt-cut cut-offs like his friend wore. He was baked so flashing brown he shimmered, but he hunchily crossed his arms upon the taut hollow of his belly, as if somehow a chill was in the air. He had long, middle parted blond hair, and with his determined cheek bones his dissecting, cat-like green eyes were too deviously separated for one to catch both at once. He wore a knotted thong on one conductive wrist, and one on the opposite ankle. Pure savage.

Inspecting both boys, Beatense guessed that queer old Dent made up for his lack of young beauty by hiring anyone who had that, but with his liberal if not naked dress code they probably drove away more customers than they attracted. Shaped by their fine light muscles, the heated hides of the two proud boys preternaturally dark-brown glowed in the sun. Beatense started. H P Shit, this was that Red Dot ledge boy!

"I got those fucking shrubs done, hey," the explosive Knife said, still shivering.

"Fine, Knife. Get the gunnysacks and fill them with this gravel."

"Hey, I could have done that!" said Shean. "Sorry you have to do it, Knife!"

"I don't mind, hey," the boy said, ambiguously smiling with diverted eyes.

Knife misgivingly eyed Beatense as he turned his processing gaze to her. His canine eyeteeth were shifted out, adding carnal danger to his looks, and giving him a lurking, sullen defiance. Shean jammed his shovel into the pile of stones.

Mr. Denton absently gazed as the athlete hopped off. Tammy also watched, and Beatense was still troubled by Knife. Although as a fellow baker he seemed close to her in age he was definitely a generation younger, high school versus college.

"Knife, I remember you," said Beatense. "Tuesday afternoon, you were sitting on that Red Dot ledge, showing off that deadly blond-hair clashing tan to the traffic."

He flushed. "Yeah, hey. I think I saw you, too."

Shean ran back out. "Thanks again, sir! And next time you come, Knife."

The uncouth warrior looked down as if he was touched by this gesture. Beatense checked the yard statues again. One of the figures could have been the enigmatic Knife. The bare, long haired fairy boy sat perched with knee up.

"That's okay, hey," the living version said, flushing again.

"Oh, Shean, you can come after all!" little Tammy chirped.

Shean turned to the girls. "Okay, I got my bike, so I can quick cruise home and help Jesse rig the boat while you two run down. Okay? I need the key."

"You better plan on hiking down with us," said Beatense. "If I walk nude in those neighborhoods on the way back, no one will object to me with you along."

Laughing, Shean ran to the building and wheeled over his obviously $1200 bike. He pulled his rumply cut-offs up for a snug fit of the cuffs to his leaned thighs, and let the belt loops sag back down. He swung astride the bike, and with back arched he spun the pedal around to catch the toe clip. Golden locks aflutter he shot off with his latticed black belly curved to the curve of his boned black back.

Tammy gazed after him as he streaked away, horns honking. "Okay, now I can show you the way, Beatense," she said, as if her friend had specifically asked how to get from the garden center down to the Shattuck beach. "It's a long walk."

At this higher elevation the distant ocean could be seen through the building gaps in all its sparkling majesty. Sails were out crossing the seas, and the parachutes and advertising banners plying back and forth created a tapestry of adventure.

It occurred to the modest Beatense that if the ocean was in sight and they were going toward it, she could take off her *Psycho Sunner* T-shirt. After all, their direction showed their destination intent, unlike on Barnet heading east where she was taking chances to go topless as long as she did. With a quick tug she snapped the rag off.

24

MAIN BEACH CRUISE

Tammy untied her top for moral support. They headed west on Perdido. "I never did this before, Beatense! It feels weird! Can I really do this?"

A customer entering a hardware store gave the girls a foul look.

"Yes, everyone will just think this is for my new book. And we have our rights."

But for Beatense there were trade-offs. Having the shirt on did bring attention to her fresh browned, hippity-hoppity legs, and her useless college kid arms. When her shirt was on people had to guess if her exorbitant tan flowed from her face and limbs onto the rest of her, but now as she walked toward the Highway along Perdido Way they knew the nightmare truth. Her raging tan had a hot shine, that of soaking in so much sun it was reflecting it back out. Stretched to her muscles, her luxurious book selling tan was a living entity that raised the street's heat.

After the first block the street turned residential. Then retail again.

"Tammy, what is that up ahead, some kind of open air restaurant?"

"Yes, it's the Perdido Way Fish House. We're almost to the Highway."

The Highway. Not so evocative in name, but the gateway to adventure.

The girls stopped by the busy restaurant, with a table filled terrace shaded by an orange parachute canopy aglow from the sun. Beatense ignored the shocked stares bathing upon her and friend. As if on signal the near naked girls posed and flexed, flaunting muscle and tan. Tammy was a barbell girl too, happily committed, but like Beatense her muscles didn't bulge into strength until called upon.

But no one jumped to take photos; they all stayed seated. The girls sensed a certain hostility for whatever eccentric reason, and the reason was that these people were locals who felt that their pleasant little city wasn't on the ocean, but on the sea. They had a romantic reverence toward the wild winds and waves, so they resented these vain beach athletes who only saw the sand and surf.

Beatense had an idea and waved over a harried looking waiter.

"Hey, can we get a couple bottles of spring water? But we can't pay for it."

He shook. This bravely indecent child was so black tan she was a match for the Xanthica espresso he ground and brewed. Her legs were thin carved, and her belly hummed. Her shoulders had that set. He then noticed Tammy. Another one. A precious, doll-like face and she could bend iron bars. Both inhumanly tan.

"S-Sorry, without m-money I can just give you w-water in a glass."

She snaked her long chained waist, tipping her hips pointedly as her lankily sunk linea muscles seemed to vibrate. But her eyes were sadly wide.

"Okay, Tammy, it's no good to be published around here. Er, thanks anyway."

The waiter saw the busboy look at him like he was crazy.

"Wait! Wh-What kind?"

"Calypso Grotto," Beatense said, recalling an empty discard she saw.

He nodded and hurried off. This transaction irritated the other patrons, who were lunching in complacent peace until these beach brats came by. The waiter returned, and the younger sprite gave a clap as he handed over her bottle. The older girl twisted open hers and jauntily set hand to hip as she drank, displaying the hard flowing of her shoulder deltoids into the tricep and bicep muscles of her long arm. Her breasts joyously lifted. She gave back the empty bottle.

"Oh, thank you! I ran the 10K this morning and I'm still thirsty from it!"

"Q-Quite all right, miss. Are you... Are you the Book Girl?"

"Yes, and I'm with the future Book Girl."

The waiter watched the two kids walk away with waists sinuously weaving, as they kept on toward the heat shimmering Highway. Beatense ditched sheet and oil in her room. She kept her shirt. Tammy copied her untying bare.

The girls crossed the busy Highway to a chorus of shouts, car door fist bangings and horns honking. People almost got killed in the traffic as they ran to see. Tammy was new at this, but she saw how her friend ignored everyone.

They ran the steps down to the Bastian Beach, by the dark brown young sisters. They felt the street heat yield to the stiff sea breezes. A boisterous surf was working.

It filled the air with an anxious, unsettled roar that came in sweeping intervals.

"Ah, you nice hot chicks. No? A parachute ride, ladies? Cheap price?"

"No!" said Tammy to the gypsy, stamping her foot. "We're locals!"

They continued along the bursting surf. Looking ahead Beatense spotted Shean and Jesse working on the proud yellow catamaran she saw so often, by the little palm tree grove. The black heated boys, naked, waved.

"Hey, Tammy, nice and breezy, hah?" Jesse called out, as the two ran up. The younger boy was just in his clashing gold tummy chain. "Like it?"

"Yeah! All the way from Beatense's motel!"

Shean pushed Tammy back on the boat's deck and gave her a quick fucking as passersby watched.. The sky was crystalline blue; the sun blinding.

The kids parted. Beatense looked at the flimsy sailboat, then at the breakers as they socked in with a louder roar than usual. She began to feel uncertain about this excursion. But the wind's direction would keep the sail from blocking the sun.

"Uh, you guys, do you always launch in surf like this? It's kind of rough."

Shean took the mainsail from the sail bag and lay it onto the tramp-deck.

"It'll be okay once we get out past the surf. Nice, big swells out there."

"That I noticed, also. But… But like, how do we get from here to there?"

"That can get tricky," said Shean. "We almost capsized a hundred times!"

He stepped on the curved pontoon onto the tramp-deck. The poly coated canvas just dented to his weight. He clipped the halyard shackle to the head of the mainsail, and he raised the broad, color-banded spread one pull at a time as he fed the front edge of the sail, or leech, into the groove in the mast. Beatense watched, panting.

The wind caught the sail and it billowed out with an ominous, snapping rumble.

"Jesse, get the sheet run through the blocks," said Shean. "Hurry!"

"Are those dunes there yours, guys?" said Beatense, pointing at the palm shaded mounds that lay right out on the open beach. Just beyond them stood the luxuriant hedge of hibiscus, ohia and bougainvillaea guarding this wealthy stretch of property. "I mean, is this beach your actual property?"

"It's our frontage," said Jesse. He pulled the long sheet-rope complete with pulley from the sail bag and hopped with it onto the tramp-deck. "We're rich."

"Good. Me too. Now what about those two girls I'm supposed to meet?"

"We pick them up at Main," said Shean, grunting in his muscled effort to clip the halyard home at the base of the mast. "Jesse, get that sheet reeved!"

"Well, can't someone hold the boom still? It's swinging in the wind!"

The mainsail was still noisily pounding in the wind, giving even Beatense an evil foreboding. The boom was wildly jerking as Jesse set the coiled sheet rope onto the deck. The hot wind also buffeted everyone's shining dark skins.

Tammy stepped up and pulled the jib out of the sail bag. "Is Ned coming?"

"No, not today," said Jesse, as he began to run the sheet-rope through the pulley blocks. "He's playing ball with the guys, so that's good news for us."

"No kidding," said Tammy, and Beatense pictured a stooped, ugly horror.

Tammy ducked between the pontoons in front and began clipping the jib onto the forestay. Beatense, seeing what to do, caught the halyard and tugged the whipping sail up as Tammy worked. The boys looked at each other nodding their approval.

And they were gratified they could sail nude as usual instead of having to be all decent for this newcomer. And she did accept the sex, surprise surprise.

"Am I doing this right, Tammy?" Beatense kept an eye on Shean's long item.

"Yeah, but help hold the sail so it doesn't blow so much."

Sun flashing upon her Beatense complied as the strolling tourists stared. Shean tossed the lifejackets he had brought along into the sand mounds. "Who needs the fuckers, let's fly bareback." Tammy smiled as she tightened the jib halyard around its cleat, and now two sails were loudly snapping and cracking.

Beatense doubtfully assessed the delicate catamaran, but she had to admire the beast. Poised on its yellow, sixteen foot banana shaped pontoons, it looked ready to pounce, and the white poly trampoline deck was slung bow-string tight within the perimeter of its frame tubes. These were anodized black alloy, like the boom and tall thirty foot mast. The vinyl tramp-deck consisted of two length-wise panels separated by a three inch gap down its middle, criss-crossed with cord lacing. Stretched straps lay along both sides of this opening, with seeming little use.

The boat had no pretense of decoration, it was built for sailing only, but like the boys who would handle her it had a capable beauty in its basic design. Its dramatic, tall mainsail rose up in bold challenge as it rattled in the onshore wind, whipping the boom in concert, and the jib was also flutter cracking. The cat had two rudders, at the end of each pontoon. It was brutally sturdy in its construction, but presently the wind was driving the seas in a rage. The waves were trundling into shore in long lines.

From their long angle of approach the point of their impact shot along from north to south faster than a horse could gallop.

The boat was rigged. Four featherweight creatures would be handling it.

"Okay, the usual SOP," Shean said, still eight inches. "We'll push out when the wave at the time hits into shore, then we'll reach further out between waves." He took a bottle of tropical oil from the sail bag and began to shine it onto himself. His brass ring bracelets clinked. This glistening youth was stick slimmed and gloriously prune rum baked. "How does that sound to you, Jesse?"

The kid tried to hide his satisfaction at being deferred to. "Whatever." He started with the oil. "But if only we had another point or two on that wind."

Tammy took her turn with the oil. Apparently this was a ritual of sailing for these sensual sun worshippers, to make the voyage a steamy temp adventure. Beatense took the oil. It was a special blend for water sport. As applied the light oil ingredient would splash off in the wave action, but the grease would leave an all-day shine.

Beatense saw only a red blur. Panting, wanting it, she slopped the oil on.

Jesse put the bottle into the sail bag, along with the tossed aside tie-pieces and Beatense's T-shirt. He set the bag and a volleyball, snorkels and several bottles of spring water into the wire basket rack, that was mounted onto the deck's front frame tube and braced against the vee-strut below. With fluttering hair, Jesse finished the packing by tying everything in place with stretch cords.

Eight inch turned to Beatense. "The surf is roughest here close into the shore. If you go overboard just ride the surf back in. We'll come back for you."

The girl watched a parachute floating serenely by far out to sea, wondering why she felt so apprehensive. She was a skilled surf swimmer, and surf surfer.

"Beatense, you and Jesse pull the boat," said Shean, less stiff now.

Beatense and the younger boy hopped over and tugged at the front deck pylons, while Shean and Tammy pushed the stern frame-tube. In this way they worked the catamaran across the sand toward the thundering seas. A breaker slugged into shore, and in collapsing its racing tongue sloshed over everyone's ankles.

The boat became alive. It too was in its element.

"Okay, she's afloat, but not enough!" Shean called. "A little further!"

The sleek twin prows continued their progress toward the storm. With increasing fears, Beatense wondered about sailing on this glorified tabletop. It looked like pure punishment, not fun at all, and the incessant batting and whipping of the sails didn't reassure her. She pictured herself dead on the beach, tan faded.

"Okay, listen up!" Shean said. "After this next wave hits, hop on! Ready!"

The wave tore toward them like a waterfall, but like all waves, however violent, it collapsed onto the beach in a broad, moving field. Suddenly awash over her knees, Beatense flung herself onto the bucking deck, and Tammy dove on beside her. The flow reversed and the boat was afloat, tossing dangerously, mast waving.

The boys sprang aboard, and Jesse hauled at the sheet-line, taking up the slack. The rippling mainsail swung over and cracked out tight and full while Shean, working the rudders, headed them to the north. Unlike Med Studs this boat jumped ahead.

Tammy pulled home the jib, and as the wallowing cat plowed along just off shore they shot underway, with halyard clanging. Beatense, finding herself on that tabletop cowered on that surface, fearing the inexorable attack of the next wave.

Closer and closer it roared toward the boat, rearing ever higher, spilling over onto itself, white as snow, and loud as a jet taking off.

"Forward, everyone!" Shean, stiff again, called out. "To the bow! Quick!"

The craft shot along the front of the fast approaching top. Beatense scrabbled forward with the others and Shean swung the catamaran straight into the brutal fury. Contrary to the girl's fully justifiable terror and all sense of logic, that they would be engulfed, the pontoons punched up skyward. The breaker bashed in under the deck and pummeled up through the lacings like geysers. The kids roared with maddened glee as the gale tossed craft bucked and pitched forward over the crest with a lurching shake of the mast. A quiet sea-side vacation? Yeah.

The pontoons glided the calmer backside down as the bygone wave moved into the hapless shore. Shean pulled hard at the tiller bar, and the rudders swung the cat back around to its northern course. The sails filled again. Only a few yards out to sea were gained by the time the next wave rolled in.

As a veteran, Beatense took this one more calmly. "Shean! Let's go back!"

His long hair was a sodden mass. "Going back in would be worse! Sit tight!"

The storm assaulted them with yet another crash. But a little more progress was made in getting out to sea. Yet another bronco heaved itself up and hit, and in the following brief respite Shean, whose oil sparkled with countless water droplets, told Beatense to move between Tammy and Jesse on the port frame-tube for ballast.

Another slosh over the boat. Beatense held to one of the straps stretched along the mid-deck lacings. Not useless. As the wave moved on, she took her place.

Shean worked the boat back to heading north. They were at least fifty yards out. Under full sail the cat raced ahead, as in flight, and its angled, portentous approach toward the next breaker as it tumbled across their troubled flight path worried one tan owner deeply. Ever closer came that handshake of death. The girl who faced down this town naked kept waiting for Shean to turn and cut into it straight on.

Eyeing his hammer handle, he didn't. First catching the left pontoon and tipping them precariously sideways, the pitiless wave whipped into the exposed deck like an underwater volcano. In the stormy tumult Jesse, Shean and Tammy leaned out to balance the cat, that tossed like a dry leaf sucked up by a passing semi. And in that pandemonium Beatense was almost pitched off. But within seconds the craft blasted on unscathed. Then another wave slugged in, and as the lacings erupted from its flanking blow, the tall black mast spewed out swirling circles of dementia in the sky.

As they handled the speeding boat in this raging chaos Shean and Jesse had to work together. In light seas one boy could handle the cat, but now one beleaguered crewman was on the boom holding sheet rope, the other on the rudder stick.

The slicing, riding prows were sweeping the floating foam scuds under the tramp deck like a low level bombing run, and the rigging, reacting to the tons of conflicting stresses, sang out in a tuning-fork hum that filled the air from all directions.

The galloping speed was relentless. A strong wind swept in, and the left pontoon lifted. The frail banana skipjacked up and down as it flounced up spray in sheets. The kids felt energized with high voltage. The left pontoon rose from the racing seas and flew with the mast tilting. From the shifted weight the leeside right pontoon was half submerged, and it spewed up an arching stream. The kids whooped, and Beatense joined in. Tammy was right; this was huge.

That girl and the boys tucked their ankles under the near hiking strap, and leaned out backwards to balance the runaway cat. Their guest shoved her feet under the same strap, and straw hair flying she leaned out too, clutching to the frame-tube and shouting. The wind eased back. They pulled themselves back up, only to behold the distant Villa Miranda, a gorgeous tropics sight.

The Dillon Arms and old Hoggy came into view, and then the Breeze Hotel, home of the marooned Tamdyn and Kit, who probably had no idea of this crazy madness. Suddenly the Cliff Diving Rock appeared as a surf pounded wall, and the sails fell slack. But as the tall rock fell away, they cracked taut again.

The catamaran drove toward and through a fleet of kayaks like a mad bull. With the scattered boats for reference, Beatense was thrilled by the high flight of their own craft. It flew by at a dizzying, powered velocity as the kayakers frantically paddled to get out of the way. They yelled and shook their fists, but Shean just flashed a dental smile, as the tuning fork hum continued.

"Hey, Shean! We got a problem!" said Jesse. Actually shouted.

"Well if you're talking about the lifejackets, if we capsize swim into shore without one! Otherwise we don't have anything to worry about!"

"No, it's Lorraine! She isn't beachy! We can't sail naked if she's with us!"

"You never said that about her," said Beatense. "What's that Virginia like?"

"Body builder browner than shit. But Shean, we have those poly tie bikinis in the sailbag. We can get them on quick once we land!" Jesse said this hopefully.

They moved beyond the surfers to Main Beach proper. The steady singing hum chronicled the battle of the sails and stays against wind and wave. The left pontoon lifted and the kids hiked out again. Beatense felt her muscles wring in protest despite her stiff build. The quadricep cords of her tall girl thighs were curved from the strain, and her jutting hipbones distributed the stresses.

Her small breasts gave her a boy-like fighting trim. She too was a body builder.

The initiate felt a frenzy swarm into every nerve of her steeled being. It was like sex, which she always wanted but now far worse. Braced out flying over the waves, her heart pounded. Finally being so thin, and strong and shit brown, had a use.

Jesse yelled to her. "Grab that dogbone!" He had a knee cocked jauntily up, so his weight was levered on just one long leg, and his belly striations were tight. "That white handle! Take the load off them abs!"

The boy lived for this. He had pulled the thick sheet-rope to his hardened chest with biceps bulged, while the golden filigree of his encircling chain was almost lost against his black satined belly. Beatense admired her own chain, as she grabbed at the plastic grip handle that Jesse pointed out.

It was held at the end of an otherwise non-functional cable that was pulled down along the shroud by a stretch cord. What a help for her lineas! As the whitecaps streamed by under her whipcord self, she marveled at the unladylike swelling of her own biceps. In a classical sense her tan was unladylike, too. But it made life fun.

"We have to head in now!" yelled Shean above the roar, as Main Beach flew by. The wooded Holiday Hill bluff, at the end of the crowded beach, was drawing up fast. "Let out the sheet, Jesse! Beatense, ready on your ballast assignment!"

"Let's keep going!" Jesse shouted. "Up to Madeline!"

"We have to pick up those women! Spill the wind, Jesse! That's an order!"

The boy eased the main out and the boat fell back down to level flight, still swiftly gliding. They sat back in, but Shean stuck to their northward course, veering out to clear the Holiday beach rocks. The surf beaten promontory cliffs followed in sweeping succession, and Madeline emerged as the forested dune was rounded. The distant marina appeared, along with the full northern coast.

"Okay, wake up everyone! We have to come about!"

"That means we turn around, Beatense!" said Tammy.

"I know! I spent all yesterday sailing! I even got in a fuck! Two fucks!"

That's just what Shean wanted to hear as he called, "Ready about!"

He pushed the tiller bar away from him, turning the craft out to sea and into the wind. The sails fell limp and began rumbling, while the halted cat wallowed drunkenly in the riding swells. The freed boom swung back and forth in indecision as the boat continued to hesitatingly turn. The waves rocked it.

"Hold that jib, Tammy!" Shean cried, as the craft slowly turned. "Okay, you guys! Hold it… Hold it…" The jib held to its original left side made the wind back-draft it, prodding the sluggish pontoons around. At Shean's urgent shout Tammy jerked her starboard sheet free from the left jam-cleat as the boat aimed south.

Everyone scrambled over to the opposite side of the deck. Jesse hauled away on the main-sheet as Tammy hauled the jib. Both sails quickly tightened again and the boat started back south. Emeraldeye reappeared as Holiday Hill was rounded.

Shean headed them out at an angle. "Okay, jib left, Tammy!" he called, as they drew opposite the northern end of Main by Holiday Hill, a place Beatense recalled as being peaceful, quiet. They were two hundred yards out. "We'll run straight in!"

"What, right into shore?" said Beatense. "Someone answer me!"

As Shean targeted shore Jesse let out the main sheet. The boom swung over to starboard, and Tammy hauled the jib over to port. In this way both "whiskered" sails would draw as the cat ran before the wind, that now spanked in from the stern.

The boat jumped in a dead run toward the embattled beach.

"Shean! Are you crazy?" Beatense cried, seeing a disastrous finale.

Shean pointed back. Beatense saw the difficulty. A big wave was chasing after them. Further down the beach it was festooned with surfers.

"Hang on, everybody! If we can stay ahead of that dude we'll drive right up onto the sand! You girls! Get back to the left side! Crowd back! Hurry!"

They dove for the far side of the tramp-deck. Beatense kicked her feet under the hiking strap and spun her head back and forth. The rising wall of water behind them was potentially a threat, but that very solid landfall was coming up fast, only seconds away. The boat seemed to float on air as it cruised, then it began lurching as if one pontoon and then the other was grabbed by a giant tentacle.

The chasing wave heaved itself up just back of the boat, and thundered onto the deck in a roar like a dump truck unloading bricks. Geysers shot up through the deck lacings. In that assault Beatense expected death at any time, but suddenly the boat floated lightly onto shore on the flow of the breaking wave.

Shean cocked the rudders up as the pontoons furrowed the sand and stopped.

"Quick!" he yelled, never one to shut up. "Get her around into the wind!"

Beatense could not move, then saw her ankles held under the strap. Oh.

They sprang off and manhandled the catamaran around, facing it into wind and water. Then they pulled it back from the surf's reach. By now Beatense felt as if wild adventure was a normal part of life, so upon returning to dull, dry land she didn't quite realize there would be no further orders. Poised, she stood ready.

"Relax, Beatense," Shean said. "We're here! And you didn't do half bad."

"She did really good!" Tammy added.

"Yeah, besides a good bareback gallop, *Jesse*, that was the thrill of my life!"

As the people on the beach gathered to watch, Jesse handed out plastic packets from the sail bag. Beatense opened hers and removed a papery poly tie piece, good for non-swim use only. She tied it on and was thankful it had the same minimal fit as her Nakee or crochet. Plus, thoughtfully, it was white. *I'm practically black!*

"Why do you happen to be carrying these?" the girl said, observing how she and Tammy now wore the same antiseptic, health inspection team uniform.

"I had to land once at that fancy Picard Hotel up the coast," said Shean. "I was totally nude and walked right into a wedding reception. Fun but not fun."

It was hopeless for the two stiffened boys to tie the bikinis on, they stayed bare.

It being Saturday, Emmy Main was at capacity. The activity had paused as the catamaran dramatically landed. Tammy faced everyone with quiet poise. She had been nurtured on the liberties of her rich enclave, and besides she did have her poly bikini on. Still, her nips stuck forward. She and Beatense were proud expressions of muscle and sun, like all salty thin surfer girls on this beach that day.

Jesse put the sail bag back as two college women sitting nearby stood up and ambled over. One Beatense assumed was Virginia, because she was beachy, while the other, who was cavern-like in her paleness, had to be the nudo-phobic Lorraine. She had plenty of nudes around to offend her. A younger girl was even having sex.

"Cool arrival," Virginia said, elaborating no further than that.

"Well, here they are, Beatense," Jesse said, with hand placed. "That truthsome toothsome who I worked so hard to get you to meet, Lorraine and Virginia."

The two modestly wore T-shirts and shorts, and so just now Beatense felt at risk. One could make the case that her breasts were obnoxiously displayed.

"Er, hi," she said, grinning. "My T-shirt wasn't handy for this meeting."

"This is a beach," Virginia said, making no effort to be too sociable. There are certain superior faced, glasses-aggressive girls with leaned features, who don't have a natural tendency to smile. With their small lenses set upon their noses they're ever interpreting who and what they see. They are moodily detached, and sport muscled. Even holding doctorates they animalize themselves. Virginia was one of these. "So anyway, hot bod. You're the Book Girl?"

"No more. Anyone here can outsell me. By far. So, hi, guys."

"H-Hello, B-Beatense," Lorraine said distractedly, now that she got a look at this girl. She was quite unprepared for this tan drenched creature, who was the kind it takes time for a person to recover from. As their victims try to regain control, they might turn a corner and confront yet another sunbeam of staggering brilliance.

It's a lifelong struggle for the dumpy and plain. I did my part to comfort them. The question is, how can the drabs handle those twisty waists, that are such flexing long conduits of tightened muscle? And as thinned as their arms are, the set of their bony shoulders, along with the opposing bulk of triceps to biceps gives them an assured strong carriage. Lorraine had to face it; dark baked Beatense was one of these.

"You... That's... Quite the t-tan," she said, wondering if she would answer.

"Thanks, er, Lorraine, but just my tan rates mentioning?"

"I can only work on one crisis at a time. I'll get to that waist of yours later."

"It's a wasted waist," said Virginia, who had bragging points too.

Beatense met her match in her; she exuded a turbulent volcanic power that was subordinated to her cerebral poise, as exemplified by her glasses. Her small lenses exerted her high intellect in an influencing way. Tenacity quietly projected the same acumen, that of confidently charging into any argument, but she was retiring, without Virginia's firmed character. The latter was the type who, if she wasn't greeted by her perfection in the mirror, she would feel half dead.

But still, back of those lenses her eyes did impart the ironic humor of a wise and fun companion, once she accepted the friendship. And her dusky edged voice could be that of a loyal chum. But she had another difficult clash with one's equilibrium, and this was her forceful bearing. She carried this with a natural instinct; just as anyone with trained muscles like hers, that were elastically tuned, would.

She was a hunting animal. She had a deep brown polishing that glowed with rich sun, and her amber hair was blown back from her forehead and tossed back of her ears in impatient abandon. But the finely bleached hairs of her thin arms told of an artistic nature, so this at least meshed with her pea vine build.

"So, Jesse says you want to stay with us for just a week?" the girl said.

"I can't help it. I got tickets to return home next Saturday, I think."

"Can't you change them? I mean, yes, we would like to have you, but you might just want to stay where you are and save the trouble of moving."

"One backpack is trouble? And I can pay. Is a couple hundred a night okay?"

Lorraine started. "That... That would be acceptable," she said.

Virginia half laughed. "We don't want to hit you that bad. Make it a hundred."

"Can we discuss this in the boat?" said Shean. "We're wasting wind."

"Hold it!" said Virginia. She began pulling off her T-shirt. Like Beatense's it was vivid green, and as she lifted it, it bared her starved belly. "Ah, life!"

Lorraine was morbidly kicked. Beatense's tan also blasted her, and edifying her sensual bomb attack her thick auburn hair was surfer sun blond drenched. She had shaped muscle but this was actually cute, the sports nut kid, and her upturned nose was kindergarten sweet. She was small but tall, with commanding eyes.

"Lorraine, we want to be ethical," said Virginia. She had finished taking off her *Drag Queen* T-shirt and there were her breasts. She got out of her shorts, revealing to an appreciative Beatense an aggressive string bared and hardened body, de rigueur thin. "We'll take you free." Her tan hit the eye, enhancing the sleek tensions of her bendy athletic lines. She took the ownership of her rabidly provocative hide as her right. Like with all beach girls, it sustained, fulfilled and suffused her. She wouldn't be the same girl if she wasn't carved. "So, deal?"

Beatense was surprised by this offer. "Yes! This is wonderful! Thank you!"

"Fine, let's go," said Shean, apprehensively watching a lifeguard work toward them through the crowd. After all, he was nude. "All negotiations, underway."

Lorraine smiled at his typical male impatience. Beatense was annoyed that she had plain, iron colored hair and dull white skin, and although she wasn't quite plump her corners were rounded. She also wore glasses, that made her look bookish, but they seemed to cross her eyes slightly. This myopic effect was actually endearing.

She got off her T-shirt and shorts, exposing a purple atrocity of a one-piece tank. These were the ugly suits that the 1970 sun rebels flung aside in favor of the cheerily offending strings. Beatense shuddered; her suit was right out of Arrolynn.

"Now look, it's no bikini, but ain't I got a seductive allure in this thing?"

The approaching lifeguard stepped up. "Okay, Shack, we warned you about this a hundred times! You know boats are off limits here!"

Shean's eyes widened. "Ed, the rental boats all land here all the time! And the Holiday Hill beach is engulfed! Take a look!"

Ed saw the surf leap up as it hit the offshore rocks. He shrugged.

"Us two had to detour down through the trees to get here," said Virginia.

Ed gave her a closer look. "Stilkey? Are... Are you, er, t-tanner?"

"I'm cleaning pools for Candor Rentals. They say I can work the singles building naked if no one complains. That job just bakes me. But I defer to Beatense here."

"Oh, er, uh huh." Ed turned to Beatense, slowly, with elaborate indifference. "That... That t-tan is unreal, m-miss. You're... You're the B-Book Girl, right? They have you all over the Field. Your 10K videos have 20,000 views."

"For which I don't get paid. Even the sex videos aren't paying me!"

"I feel your pain. Now get this crate out of here," the rescuer insisted.

"We are just leaving, Ed," said Shean. "We just landed here to pick up Lorraine and Virginia. Jesse! Grab their things and stuff them in! We have to go!"

Jesse pulled out the sail bag. Virginia gave him her and Lorraine's cast-offs, and after thought, untied nude. Jesse shoved all this and the poly tie bikinis into the bag. The naked Shean and Beatense stood by the boat, ready to push it back out.

"Well, we're set," said Shean. "So come on, let's..." A blond girl of fourteen, so browned deep saturated she had a gold rich gleam, (El Paso, 1986) smiled at Shean as she stepped by. She wore white cotton shorts and a blue T-shirt, and her healthy tan, wholesome face and skeletal lines told of tennis, volleyball, marching band or the cheerleading squad, and the fond spoiling of her parents. "...Go." Lorraine laughed, despite never having the same effect on anyone. "Effy! Come on sailing with us!"

Naked in seconds she hopped over, placketed belly flexing. Ed joined in pushing out the boat. The kids sprang aboard and started bucking the surf. Beatense was ready this time. She saw that the damper-on-things Lorraine felt insecure about this, and that gave her extra courage. But the battle here was worse than with the first foray, because they had to first tack out through the swimmers. They all swam out of the way wisely enough, but too slowly, so Shean had to fall off again and again.

It was great fun for everyone to have this boat sail by, but the lifeguards lined the shore blowing their whistles and shouting. Shean finally found an open channel and turned northward away from Main, just as they broke free of the surf.

They hove to a half mile out. The boat gently rolled in the swells, sails rumbling. Charmed by this nautical perspective, Beatense turned away from Effy, who like that Honey Brown had an honest, non-forced, sun-loving tan, and gazed over the waters toward the buildings and palm trees ranged along the distant shore. They formed an almost surreal panorama. Back of the parachutes in flight stood the hazy foothills. A Sheffield trilled grandly by with white sails set. Another plane flew by, just overhead. And far out across the bright green waters, a big passenger liner swept by.

The warm winds were drying everyone but the sun deprived Lorraine to a salted, dark coppery shine. Virginia breathed deeply and shook back her hair.

"Boy, I would sure hate to be dinking with a pool right now," she said.

"Dinking with a pool?" said Beatense. "As a job? What's involved?"

"Faking it. They don't need cleaning. Defer to Lorraine who has a real job."

The two girls laughed, indicating a deep friendship since childhood. Beatense felt friendlier toward Lorraine. Shean turned southward and Jesse set the towering main just tight enough to get the catamaran drifting at steerage speed.

"Didn't you have any pools to do this afternoon, Virginia?" Beatense said.

"No, not on Saturday. I can't drag my hose around the one time the pools are in use. I do have a morning job I better make up, me in the 10K."

"Me too!" said Beatense. "Jesse, why didn't you talk to Virginia then?"

"Okay, places everyone," said Shean. "Beatense, take the jib from Tammy."

"Gotcha! Shean, tell me when to haul her tight!"

"Not me. Virginia is master now. Take over the tiller and sheet, Virginia."

Effy's eyes sparkled excitedly. She was cute, unlike Beatense at sixteen.

Virginia moved to the stern. "Thanks, Shean. Get ready for some G's. Grab on, Lorraine! And Effy, is it? There's no room here with us, lay yourself on the deck!"

Jesse and Effy lay together on the off-wind side of the deck, out of the way of the legs. Shean got in with Lorraine, Tammy and Beatense, who sat in the front corner, feet under the strap. She was proud she could contribute to this demanding sport.

She looked at her tan new friends, who were so certain and assured. They had muscles just for the thrill of using them. Despite her analytical glasses Virginia truly exemplified this. She didn't let them keep her from a wild life of sun baking and rule breaking. She was proof of the fervent need for sensual vanity.

The slight, keenly muscled girl glanced up at the sail. "Okay, let's stomp."

Lorraine secretly wished they would just keep rolling along. The girls on the lines hauled them in, and as the speed picked up the slicing pontoons spread out twin vee furrows of accelerating, rolling foam once again.

"Keep your eye on that sail, Beatense!" Jesse yelled, lifting his pretty head as the catamaran's speed increased and the disembodied tuning fork hum returned. "When the trailing edge flutters you're losing air! Pull her tighter!"

"I know how to sail! And I take my orders from Virginia!"

That unimpressionable sailor was in a curved, sunk belly slouch as she worked rudders and line. The catamaran was asserting its authority over the bounding main once again, and the spray lashed in all directions. The spurts coming up through the lacings pelted the feet of the five on the rail like ice cubes.

The pontoons were riding their way through the oncoming seas at a hot dizzying clip, conveying the driven velocity of a horizontal waterfall, and this was all Virginia. Beatense was impressed by her jaunty skill, just as she envied this predator as she battled wind and wave. Bare in vulgar freedom, Virginia had the raging forces of the sea in her skillful control, and there was almost an unseemly power to her thin armed mastery of them. Her tan was salt splashed.

Their southerly flight was cutting far out across the open sea of the curved coast. Sailing north to Holiday Hill they kept closer to shore, so they almost grazed the Cliff Diving Rock. But now that prominence looked lost against the buildings along shore, and the foothills beyond. Their speed was blazing.

"Shouldn't we be tipping?" Jesse yelled over the roar.

"Yeah!" the starved Shean shouted, greasily aglow, blond hair aflutter. He was stiffened, as long as a sheet of paper is wide. "Get some air under that pontoon!"

For Lorraine's reassurance Virginia was willing to keep a stodgier pace, but she saw another catamaran fly neatly by up on a single pontoon. The girl was slight, but her face, muscles and tan warned of a militant streak. She hauled on the rope as a new gust swept in, and the pontoon lifted. Prone Jesse reaching over Effy caught at the hiking strap, and he hooked his leg over to safely catch that strap. The three tan girls hiked out to balance the sail's pull. Shean and the anxious Lorraine stayed up.

The wind increased and Shean hung out. No one said anything to Lorraine as she stayed put; they knew if the boat tipped more survival would prompt her. The right pontoon flew upwards for minutes at a time, and just touched as it glided back down before resuming flight. Beatense used her strap tucked feet and the fighting tensions of the jib-sheet to cantilever herself out over the heaving seas.

She saw a military helicopter fly by, she saw dozens of other boats, and she was black browned, bony and bared, and very bed battled. And for all this adventure she had spent maybe two thousand dollars so far. *My life is beautiful. I'm beautiful.*

25

EROTIC PASSAGE

Amidst the spray everyone was all splashed wet. A stiffer gust swept in so that Lorraine leaned out using the dogbone. The boat was flying along at a roller coaster speed, as it tipped and tossed. In their flight the kids caught up to and passed other slower sailboats, one full of clothed non-sensuals. The tight, academically advanced Virginia dismissed them as so many insects. But a mile further on the breeze fell, and the catamaran eased down to a pedestrian speed and everyone levered back up.

As the catamaran had smacked along Lorraine had a longing envy for the svelte summer sirens surrounding her. Not until now did she yearn so deeply for being thin and tan. Not only for the night benefits, but for forever being a child, if one cared to, and for the simple delight in life it gave. These brown, proudly skinny girls and boys laughed in celebration of their bonied builds and resulting abilities.

"Well, I can say this," said Beatense, "that little dash there sure beat yesterday!"

"Yesterday, too?" said Lorraine, with a helpless look at those fresh peaches.

"Yes, first sailing with Sim, and then I sailed on this Med Studs with Bondy, if you know of her. It was this big yacht-like sailboat, so it didn't go nearly as fast."

From the action of the other sailboats the wind would be quiet for awhile, so Virginia unhooked her feet. "Lorraine, you want to take over?"

"Oh, let's get to Boulder Beach first," said Shean, dreading any beginner's delay. "We should keep moving. You're up for the trip back, Lorraine."

They were a mile out, Beatense saw that they were passing by Cocojo. The haloed dunes beckoned, and the beach had a good crowd. At least a dozen boats were moored offshore or pulled up. The girl wanted to land there. She would love to have her flaky friends see her on this sporty catamaran.

"What kind of place is this Boulder Beach?" she asked.

"It's hard to get to," said Shean. "There is a path but it goes down the cliff."

"Hey, Beatense," said Jesse, groggily lifting his head, looking over Effy. "I think I got you doing the rentals, up at the skateboard park. But Art might require a top."

"Good, thanks, Jesse, I can check that out. But Tamdyn is giving me $36,000 to work at the Breeze. Singing, I think. I'll see which job I like best."

"Which job you like?" said Lorraine. "You don't care about the money?"

"Oh, maybe, but all I need in life can fit in a backpack. Except my skin."

"The sun is of no use to me," said Lorraine, "but I wouldn't want to be inside on days like this. But all you obsessed tanners, you're out on the beach every day. No one is compulsive about staying inside, but oh boy, do the babes ever hit the sand to lay out. And they never get enough sun, even when they can't get any darker."

"It's just that we need the sun," said Beatense angrily. "It's our gasoline!"

"Okay, you get brown, but so what? What does that do for you?"

"It makes life possible," said Virginia. She paused. "At least for me."

Tammy turned her head. "And me. Are we still moving? The wind died."

"Ominous signs of a brewing storm," said Jesse.

Beatense looked back in toward Cocojo. Even from out here she could see its crowd. Lookout Mountain loomed over the forested hills and sandy bluffs.

"I wish Craig came with us, speaking about being stuck inside. He's at that trade show now, and he should have just told them to... What, Tammy?"

"My father is at that trade show!"

"Hey, I think I saw him last night. Jesse, was that him?"

"Yeah. We were playing tennis. And then that Kettner showed up."

"That other kid, yeah. So anyway, Craig whom I met on the train is at that trade show now too. A trade show, on a day like this!"

The winds swept back. Cocojo's rocky south shore glided by at lashing speeds. The catamaran flew by Le Tournepier town, that stood atop a tall sea-side cliff. The uncombably out-of-control pile's Beatense said to sail in close to this sheer rock, but Shean told that the surf would smash them into it like tomatoes. Lorraine, nervously, asked all that tumbled hair how she picked Emeraldeye for her visit. Working the jib, eyeing her spindly legs, the beach blonded, beanbag bellied, bamboo built and bitch blacked body believer looked up. Formed cheeks, wide placed, processing eyes.

"Hah? Oh, it was this advice letter, in *Chez Health*. Me being me, vidi veni."

Beatense was winding up her story as they arrived at Boulder Beach.

"Yeah, but you're no lez," said Virginia. "You get along with guys, thin or not."

"Hey, Shean and I better take over!" said Jesse, looking up. "Tammy, you better take the jib! Whisker it out opposite the main!"

The new watch took over. The cat was turned east toward shore in a dead run. The acceleration of flying before the wind was like a cliff-side free-fall.

"Okay, lez or not, you hear a knock at the door," said Virginia probingly, as if the flying catamaran wasn't careening wildly, and as if the tall mast wasn't drawing those erratic circles in the sky once again. "And you think it's Kit."

Virginia was referring to the tail end of Beatense's account.

"No! Him, I wish. I thought it was Buck, but it was Craig. I acted all edgy, he got suspicious and he took off. But I still had Buck in reserve, or so I thought."

"What you did," said Virginia, "is you suckered for lower grade product."

Jesse didn't care to have his friend referred to that way, but she was right.

"All was not lost. Kit did come by and we got in a long, really good fuck."

Lorraine blanched. A wave loomed up back of the boat. Beatense grabbed the frame tube, but it was too thick for a good grip. She felt like she was riding boxcars again as the leaping boat pounced toward shore. The mounting wave began spilling over on itself in a roaring cascade. It caught the boat, and Beatense gulped in air as she was flung off, and she was engulfed in a swirling storm, helplessly rolling in the deep thrashing froth, so indomitable moments ago, but now a bag of sticks.

The famed girl hit the sea floor again and again. Slammed into shore, she was pummeled across the sand as the sluicing flow continued to deluge past her. She wiggled like a worm as the torrent turned and the backwash swept over her in a loud flood. At last she was left alone. She got to her hands and knees coughing.

She blearily looked around and saw the others, except the ever unflappable Virginia, in the same dreary fix. Lorraine was a wriggling lump of purple. They crawled further onto shore to escape the next wave. The boat catamaran was on its side, the picture of calamity. The sail bag lay on the sand. Only smiling Effy was standing.

Shean staggered to his feet. "Is everyone here?" he called out.

Beatense raised her hand. The kids straggled together and hefted the boat back up. They were on a powder sand beach enclosed by a tall, sheltering cliff. Shean led the charge as they ran in to get off the sand. They had a splashing war and came out, and they saw they weren't alone here after all.

A small young woman approached them. She was like a twin sister of Tammy in being so slight and fiercely tan, except she had fake looking waves of blond hair, and her bony, fine face also looked fake, it was so flawlessly formed. Her blue eyes had that up-tipped look of intent scrutiny. She wore a thong, it was a line of quarter coins held with rhinestone laced strings. Lorraine noted that she was real dark brown.

"Hey! Hi!" she called out in a raspy shriek, that hinted she was all heart, but perhaps low in academics and social order. The voice had the habit of reflecting all that. "I saw your boat crash! Are you okay? You look like you are! You're gorgeous! I'm all alone here today! Glad to have the eye candy!"

Seeing how her friends goggled her, Beatense resented this cheerleader.

"Yes, we are that," she said, coldly. "That... That is some, er, bikini."

"What, this? It's my work uniform! I'm a dancer down at Crazy Jocko's!"

Lorraine also resented her. "How did you get here?" she demanded.

"On my sailboard!" the amazon screeched. "I flew up from Tooky Zozo! I tie my top around the wishbone and take off! But boy, you're all so tan, and you, gal, should join us at the club!" She was addressing Beatense. "You would get us all huge big tips!" She turned to Lorraine with unwelcomed interest. "But you, you got a ways to go! But today's sun will catch you up!"

"Yes," Lorraine said, forced yet again to envy beautiful undeserved tan.

Suddenly this excursion wasn't turning out well for her. Everyone, and now this Suzy Slapstick were gloriously athletic. The dancer's well meaning energy was hard to take. Even the boys looked askance at each other as she hollered.

But Tammy was hooked. "You surf sailed here?" she said in awe.

"Yeah! It almost beats sex! Come on! I got a Dactyl! I race! People think us dancers are just sluts, but we all work to keep in shape! Me, I do board sailing!"

"Go ahead, Tammy," said Shean, gaping. "W-We'll get s-set up here."

"Yeah, okay!" The child was beside herself that this experienced older woman actually targeted her for familiarity. "I'll be back to lay out!"

"That's what I was doing!" the board bird shrieked. "My poor old skin is ready to jump ship! I'm Courtlyn! I know, it sounds all prim and proper, but I'm dang wild!"

Effy was enthralled also. Non active herself, she admired those who were.

"Hey, you got any water? I can't bring any on the Dac!"

"Yeah, if you can tell us the time," said Shean wearily. "Jesse, get her one."

"Read the sun!" said Courtlyn. "It's Two oh oh! Prime time! Wooo!"

Jesse skipped over and returned with a quart bottle. Courtlyn opened and drank it, panting like a kid when she finished. Virginia drank the rest of the bottle into her own taut tummy and gave the empty bottle back to Jesse.

"Boy, thanks for the water! I only drink spring! So who are you all?"

As they told their names Courtlyn happily nodded to everyone but Lorraine, who received a warm, moist eyes smile from those blazing blue eyes. Lorraine grudgingly warmed up to her; Beach Women always ignored her. Busily talking, Courtlyn and Tammy made their way across the lonely beach. The older sand nymph waved back eagerly as the girls disappeared behind a house sized rock.

"Her hips were ten inches wide," Lorraine lamented. "That's almost criminal. No girl should be built like that! And her waist is as slim as yours, Beatense."

"Yeah, almost it was. But is it already almost two? We're wasting sun!"

"I'll get out the tarp," said Jesse. "It's good sailcloth canvas. Huge!"

"Yeah, hurry," said Virginia. "Prime time is nothing you want to waste."

Lorraine smiled wanly as the sailors emptied the hamper. Beatense, whom she had pinned some hope on for being a friend, helped to lay out the canvas spread.

She looked up at the sun, judging it. Virginia fell back upon the cloth with limbs starred out. Her pelvics protruded and her rib ledged belly had a long, starved curve. Lorraine woefully realized that with these sun nuts, hot ultraviolet was the agenda. She felt left out in her swimsuit. Also sex was imminent.

Jesse saved the day. "Hey, Lorraine, want to go down and look for shells?"

They left and Virginia flipped onto her front. "I need oil," she said.

"I can do that!" said Shean, kneeling down and reaching for the bottle.

Beatense grabbed it, wanting to get her hands on the sleek girl as much as she wanted to keep Shean's off. She kneeled astride Virginia's legs and squirted a line onto her iridescently browned skin. The girl groaned as Beatense slimed the oil in.

Shaking to the touch, she massaged Virginia's shoulders and long back, and her formed little rump. Virginia, brown with glasses, grunted and squirmed.

Beatense sat back. "Okay, I'm exploring," she said. "Be right back, guys."

Getting a look even from beach veteran Shean, the girl started after Tammy and friend through various gigantic boulders. Effy ran to catch up. They eventually found the two in a tucked away cove. The letter opener sailboard lay off to the side.

Tammy's friend was a true tanner, glowingly rich polished. Like Virginia she also wore glasses, but hers were uniquely ugly with thick lenses and bookish black rims. They quite diminished her, but gave an almost sad pathos. She looked happily up.

"Oh, guys, hi! Join me and Tammy for some hot rays and secret girl talk!"

Tammy gazed absently, in transports. And Beatense had to like this crazy girl. How she was so outgoing was an imponderable of life. She was a brilliant athlete; her slimmed muscles were shaped for tough capability and lanky grace.

"Effy can, but I was just doing some looking around, Courtlyn. Exploring."

"Yeah, do it! But wow, what tans you got! I only look so dark because I'm blond! Most normal people can't handle that combination! But you two are awesome!"

Beatense decided this girl was a rare gem. She said goodbye and went on, Effy coming with. With hearts rivaling the surf they entered a garden of rocky spires and came to an inlet cove, a perfect retreat for real sun worship. The girls kneeled in the shallows, letting the ripples wash over her twist-muscled thighs. The water was pool blue, and their dark tans clashed with it and the white sand beneath the sparkly limpid surface. Hand in hand the girls waded out to a rock that formed a hollow.

The sun flashed in with a fierce intensity, reflecting from the rock with triple heat. Beatense sat frog-legged, leaning back on her hands so her taut belly was slung. Its satin skinned lineas flexed as she breathed. Effy's eyes popped. The Book Girl!

"Beatense? I saw all your videos. What's sex like, anyway?"

"I play up to the cameras, Effy, but really it's just glorified tickling. But somehow sex affects your whole body. My first time was scary but I do recommend it for you. On the other hand, if you have things going, sadly sex will distract you from them."

"Yeah, my friends, all they do is lay out and fuck. They want me to do it too."

"Shanty the corn seller can help you. I can set that up, even pay his fee."

Effy sighed. With the sun as their companion they wandered the secluded cove, south into a maze of boulders. The girls came to a wider beach. A classic old cabin cruiser lay offshore, wallowing in the swells. They went on to the end of the clearing, where the cliff swung in as it walled off this end of the beach. Coming around a tall rock they she saw a blond, tight thinned young woman. She was so Creation Dawn exquisite, she was both fairy and flower. Her skin was gold tawny, as if the sun had only a friendly love for her, and for one of such a detailed delicate build she was lean muscled. Wearing a string thong, she sported a long, slim waist, and her fresh breast petals were proudly bared. Her sun fluttering tresses heralded her as a rebellious princess stubbornly on her own, a theme that her noble forehead, her regarding blue eyes and radiant purity forcefully exerted.

Although her face showed a quiet melancholy, she had that command that all sensuals project, that of insight, demanding expectation and natural authority.

It would seem that her stately mind and finely tuned assembly made her inclined toward certain actions, or perhaps an unyielding pride and an ethereal character kept her chastely guided. Hopefully not. The girls stepped closer.

Beatense said, "Hi! We didn't mean to intrude. Do you belong to that boat?"

"No, our bikes are way on top of the cliff." A tuned voice that could give orders. Again the vocal cords knew their job. "But you two are so awfully tan. I envy you."

"It takes work," Beatense went on. "For me anyway. Effy here is a natural."

"My son too, but he still works at it. Let's walk as we talk, and join him, atop that ledge." She pointed. "Poor Skye is up there now, wasting his life away on a towel."

"You're a mother? But you're so... So small! And... And beautiful!"

"Thank you. My son is fourteen, I'm twice that. I'm Moria. You're very beautiful, too. You actually look famil... Are you the Book Girl?"

"Did you see me on the news or the FieldNet?"

"The Field. We never watch TV. But sometimes I wish my poor Skye did. I think he might have you beat. Come see what I mean. He's an all-dayer."

"Me too. And I'm Beatense, by the way. But you're that old, seriously?"

"Not quite old yet. But my declining years are drawing nigh. Come on."

They came to the cliff and climbed up a rocky series of hand and foot holds to a broad shimmering ledge. A striking bare boy rose from his towel. He had that prized skill to bake in a tan with breathtaking ease and speed, and he was excruciatingly deeply brown. The boy had thick, long, sun lightened hair, and a reflective face.

His muscles were all out of character with his artistic intellect, and he looked too polite and sensitive to be so obscenely dense tan. The results he presented required hours of the most cruel dedication. The tan by accident Effy had eyes wide.

It was difficult to focus on him, the vibrant depths of his enriched tan tricked the eye, creating a blurry, halo-like shine of gold shimmers. His slightest moves enlivened his skin with vital, shifting shadings. He had a carved chest and hung biceps. All his muscles hummed. He was drenched very extra dark brown. Beatense, eyes wide. I saw kids like this, no lie. Beatense could only think that Kit or Sim was his father.

"Hey, I'm Skye," he said, smiling ruefully, as if his baking embarrassed him. His compliant vocal cords gave a firm lilting fulness. "Mom, she has a freak tan too! So why do you always nag me about mine?"

"See what I mean?" said Moria. "He doesn't know what being a kid is."

He smiled, but this seemed to be a sore point. "Mom, give it up. Anyway, if you're staying, you can use my towel. I actually tan faster on the bare, hot rock."

This was really a very nice boy, and both visitors were taken by him. Beatense knew what motivated him, she was obsessed herself at twelve. She didn't intend for her and Effy to stay, but she didn't want to hurt Skye's feelings even incidentally by declining his offer of the towel. The glare of the rock sizzled into him.

Suddenly the boy's eyes lit up. "You're the Book Girl! I watched your videos!"

"Yeah, they're filming me even now. Neat name, by the way. I like it, Skye."

"It's a lame name. Mom was a free love hippy when she hit that on me." Moria playfully gave him a shove. She worshipped him. "But do you want the towel? I don't need it." Panting, Effy replied by lying back on it, opened. The time had come.

"Ahem, let's swim, Beatense," said Moria. "Make it special, you two. Skye?"

The boy got on the shaking girl and went deep. Moria and friend watched, then dove off the ledge into the emerald pool twelve feet below, that was guarded by tall sentinel rocks. They knifed side by side into the placid surface, and turned and burst back up amid millions of bubbles. They loosely embraced in a weightless ballet.

"Those two have it beautiful, Beatense. As beautiful as that dive of yours."

"Thanks. I did diving in swim class. But my tummy is still up there!"

Moria laughed. "What there is of it. Let's play with the fish."

The girls pulled themselves down into a silvery school, that made no attempt to escape; they were used to these pesky humans. Beatense could out-swim everyone underwater, but had to surface. With her next breath she rejoined Moria, still under.

This glowing interlude was mystical. They swam around the bay inlet rocks over toward the cabin cruiser. They treaded water. The wide mahogany transom loomed over them. First one chrome exhaust port submerged, then the other, as the boat wallowed. The gold leaf lettering on the rising and falling stern spelled out the name

EROTIC PASSAGE

Four boaters came out of the cabin, holding drinks. "Come on aboard!"

"I can't," said Beatense. "I would love to but I can't leave my friend Effy."

"Go ahead, I can send her here," said Moria. "If they're finished," she added.

Beatense held and kissed Moria, who then flashed back around the point.

"She swims fast. Come on up. Easy there, that ladder can be slippery!"

"Tell me about it," said Beatense as she climbed up and in. "Hey, once Effy gets here can you take us down to that beach? My friends must be worried by now."

"Of course, but that's one heck of a tan! Funny you don't boil the water!"

One of the ladies, they were all middle aged, said, "I might kill you, young lady."

Beatense was so tan, so hard she inspired fear. It was a surprise that she was so unreserved in her conversation, limited as it was so far. She was shriek roasted with rays. She opened the offered beer and saw all three swimming toward the boat.

"Oh, it was a dream!" Effy raved as she climbed the ladder. "It just felt so good!"

The boaters smiled but they were hardly ready for Skye, gentle of mind but shock tan. That gentle mind didn't stop him from skillfully playing the girl, awakening her.

Everyone settled in on the white vinyl settee as one fellow fired up the diesel and hit a lever to haul in the anchor. Effy asked for beer and mother and son had wine.

"Don Edwards," said their host, spinning the wheel. "Where ya heading?"

"Us two, that cove inlet," said Beatense, as the boat got underway. "Sorry about the trouble." Stiff Skye smiled awkwardly. Effy held to him. "We could just run it."

"No prob. Kids, I would say to go below, but this will just be a two minute trip."

"That cove inlet is just around the rocks to the north. Might be shallow."

"It's the Book Girl!" one of the wives called out. "My word, what an honor!"

"Sorry, but Moria here is the real royalty, obviously manor born. Right?"

The Erotic pushed out to open sea with diesel rumbling; it was in no hurry.

"No, but a fine life that I made even better by having Skye. Folks, meet my son. Skye?" The boy sighed and waved. "Anyway, after college I ended up in insurance, claim entry, health. It was supposed to be temporary but I'm still at it. I have a pretty decent R/A but I sit away from the others so I can concentrate. Too much talk."

Beatense and Moira were openly admired. Erotic Passage idled north, passing varied rock formations, and then entered Courtlyn's cove. Beatense said thanks and good bye and the two dove in and swam ashore. Bare Tammy was out bashing the Dactyl. The boat swung around to take Moria and Skye back. Beatense waved. As the cabin cruiser swung out of sight Shean and Courtlyn fucked in the shallows. Effy watched, observing how Courtlyn was hooking her hips up for all eight.

Tammy sliced in right by shore, and with sail rattling she spun the board around abd re-grabbed the wishbone. She rifled off, brilliantly knifing the waves. Relentless Shean got Courtlyn yelling. Finally the shore birds returned to their original beach.

Virginia was searing her butt-bumped backside on the white canvas sheet. She was incandescently browned without being dark, and if her strident tan was as deeply healthy as it looked, she would be forever young. She rose to her elbows.

"Am I the only one sensibly getting this gorgeous sun today?"

"Sun!" said Effy. "I got it today! Me! Wait until my friends hear, and my Mom!"

"Break it to her easy," Beatense said, warmly smiling. "Where's the other two?"

Virginia luxuriously stretched. "Jesse came back to get the snorkels and masks. Lorraine's idea, if you can believe it. She's just kind of putting up with events today."

"Out of her depth," said Beatense, hiding her contempt. She sat leaning back on her hands with knees up. Shean gulped. "On the other hand, us beachables, we're admired for all the wrong superficial reasons. Talking to that Moria, I see that now."

"What's that?" Courtlyn screeched. "Until you're an exotic dancer you don't know shit about being admired for all the wrong superficial reasons!"

"That's sad in your case," said Beatense. "You're way better than that."

"Thanks, but not hardly sad! When I dance I give it everything I got! We all do! Then we do the drinks! I can get two hundred in tips! But the training is fierce. They want us to just tear the customers apart. I can make these wiggly moves you would think are impossible! I can leave a quart of sweat on the floor!"

"It sounds beautiful," said Beatense. "I got a few moves myself."

"We could sure use you! I can show you how we rile everyone up!"

"Me and my friend Knife do that too," said Shean. "We ride our bikes up into the city just in our bikinis, and all oiled up we hit our our tans at the shoppers and office workers, and boy, do we get the reactions! It's hilarious! We can't stop laughing."

"Shit, we can use you too," said Courtlyn. "If you don't mind gay acts."

The other two returned. Lorraine was relieved that everyone was having a quiet discussion instead of romping and squirming with the oil bottle, or worse.

"You shoulda seen it!" said Jesse. "We saw caves and even an octopus!"

"Not many shells, though," laughed Lorraine, setting several on the tarp.

"Oh, the tourists grab them all up!" Courtlyn yelled. "Them fuckers come right at dawn! It's shaded here then, otherwise they wouldn't come near the place!"

Tammy raced by on the Dactyl, working her whip waist like a whip. She skidded into a landing, grinding the skegs, and dropping the sail she ran over, half black.

"Oh, that was excellent, Courtlyn! Your Dactyl can do anything! Thanks!"

"Hey, no problem! But come on, we're going to lay out some more now!"

Everyone but Lorraine, who lay in the mainsail's shade on the tramp-deck, hit the canvas tarp. Virginia lay with elbows out, calmly gazing across the sand with glasses nose set. With her tan already sharply deep, she was roasting it mercilessly. Not as dark as Beatense, but like Effy good and solid. But the session lasted just an hour.

Courtlyn put on a dancing clinic. Facing away, she snaked her long back, and as she turned slowly round the sight of her breasts was fatal. Humming one of the bar tunes, she jiggled her light hips as her slim waist sinuously flexed. Then with a thigh stuck out, the sweat baked girl snapped her spine-dangled hips, working them in an orgy of wicked angles. She was just beginning; even Beatense felt her heart race.

Courtlyn wave rippled her spine vertically downward, working in rank invitation, along with possessed side to side moves. Her sensual efforts were maddening.

"Okay, girls, your turn!" she shrieked, still whipping her hips out of control.

Lorraine declined. Beatense had learned much of this from Lesta at camp, but Tammy, Effy and Virginia did get into it as Courtlyn fussed over them, bending them from pose to pose so that their painfully slinky moves flowed like oil. Watching them closely as they wormed, writhed and wriggled, as if beset with frenzied spasms of hot need, Lorraine took on a fear of them. What she saw at clubs didn't compare.

Suddenly everyone realized they were losing the wind. The crewmen of the cat quickly picked up and packed up and pushed out, and Courtlyn floated her Dactyl. Her sail had just enough draw. Her farewell screeches easily carried.

Beatense took the helm, stick and rope both. This took surprising effort, even in these light airs, and she felt her muscles protest. But at the same time the opposing strain of her famine thighs lent them a swelled definition, and her biceps were bulged into tennis balls. Even her apple breasts seemed to respond. Out at sea, away from the hot glare, like Effy's and Tammy's her tan shined as a dense berry brown.

Lorraine had grave doubts about Beatense moving in with them. She feared that the girl didn't seem to have that cute college girl, self effacing whimsy. Her crackling tan just lunged at her, and despite her slight teen body she burst with power, and her small but fertile breasts burst with health. The sailing exertion affected her belly; its ripples visibly worked. Its starved concave sunk turned its tan to a horror black.

Even with her own driven tan, Virginia shrugged off her formidable arsenal, as if it was a tolerated annoyance. But with her great sensual power Beatense took herself very seriously. This self focus can be a handicap, especially in selecting friends.

"Beatense, you're really good at that," Lorraine said, hoping for an answer.

"Yes, Lorraine, if you tried it you would see that it's possibly easy for you."

"Yeah, with wind that barely fills the sail, she says it's easy," said Jesse.

"But how can you just walk around naked like that?" Lorraine persisted.

"It's legal, but even if it wasn't like back home I would still do it. Why not, it's fun. Same with sex," the girl added pointedly. "Effy, it's a good way to stay thin!"

Not the answer she wanted. The tall cliffs marking the approach of Le Tournepier loomed. Sitting in a slattern slouch, Puppet, working rudder and rope, slowly veered closer in as the winds shifted erratically in confronting the egg smasher.

The cliff dropped lower, to where the Traders Neon Factory bar was perched, with its palm leaf roofed balconies precariously bolted to the rock. These were connected with covered step-ways. Beatense worked their way through the spread of moored boats. Those on board waved. The town had no beach; it sat atop a cliff, but a surf filled pool enclosure had been built out from the cliff, accessible by countless steps. It was charming to visit this foreign shore, even with that concrete building in sight.

"I do that big building's pool," said Virginia, pointing, then eyeing herself.

"Oh yeah," said the steersman. "This Sailor Sim guy I sailed with yesterday from Cocojo in his little yellow boat said he lives there. Good place for me, lots of sun!"

It seemed that Lorraine was getting a lot of reminders of her tanning prowess.

26

TONY THE CRUDE

But she said, "S-Sailing? Wh-What kind of sailing?"

"Both. We fucked. Effy, welcome to your new life. Anyway he laid right by us at Cocojo, so I invited myself out on a cruise. He just has the most hellish tan. But that didn't help him with this one Karen on Main the other day. She cut him dead."

"I know who you mean," said Virginia. "He lays there by the pool all day. He keeps staring at me, when he thinks I'm not looking, but it's so obvious. I would do a little inviting myself if he acted half normal. Maybe next time I will."

"Yeah, he was good, but I did all the work, I top hopped him. Of course a boat came and got a video of us, for my next book I think. This new one will be different, instead of professional photographers they're soliciting amateurs and paying them for any photos they use. They actually even get me brushing my teeth. But Jesse, what about this brother of yours? Why did you say you're glad he wasn't coming along?"

"He's kind of mental, like brain damaged, whatever, so he always complains. Life is against him." Sitting astride her legs he began to oil Effy's back. "Hey, lay still!"

"Worst of all, his friends are starting to find him difficult," Shean added, as the girl groaned. "They do put up with him, but he's such a constant whiner. Like say you're golfing, the fifth hole, and he wants to quit. You can send him back alone, which he won't do, or you try and play out the nine. Or three, you quit too. It sucks either way, and it isn't just golf. He always gets the smallest piece of cake, the wrong side of the back seat, or bread that's too dry for his sandwich or not enough ice cubes."

"But if you don't bring him along, boy do you hear about that," Jesse added, still rubbing Effy. "So you better include him, or real trouble. And the funny thing is, he's half smart in school." With that Jesse re-arranged Effy and went into her.

Everyone but Lorraine watched approvingly. Struggling, Effy smiled radiantly.

"And we're rich," Shean went on, proud of his brother. "If Ned only saw the great life he has. And Natalie likes him, but she doesn't count, being just a girl."

Despite twinges of pain the brown stick helped, hooking her hips up for a strong, yelling reaction. Lorraine was upset by this vulgar imposition, but she could tell from Shean's strained voice that the subject of Ned worried him. She was touched by the boy's empathy for his sad brother. But with his star-like looks he didn't seem like the type to have concerns. And although his being so gracefully slender at sixteen years wasn't unique, the studied carelessness of his various positions or standing postures proclaimed to all that this thinned boy was protectively proud of his bike-like build. In getting sun he had few equals, so that was the final crushing blow to his admirers.

It was well known that unless he was showing himself off in his boy bikini or as a nude, he flaunted his beloved old blue jean cut-offs all summer long, which were so raggedly soft faded and loosely indefinite in their staying on him. But as precariously as they held to his slim hips, and as abruptly long as he was in his shooting up in escape from their low slung belt loops, their edging onto his long thighs was minimal. The boy had cuffed the torn-off down-tubes so short, that his burned-darkness painted every millimeter of his stretch slimmed legs. Butt-cuts.

"Well, if I see him I'll be careful," Beatense said. Effy got off Jesse, all corrupted. "But it is sad." They left the Le Tournepier anchorage and came to Cocojo.

Beatense swung in right close to shore and let out the mainsail, to drift in a slow run along shore. The sun cultists waved from their tent city as the boat gently rocked by. Overlooking the purple plum, they keenly admired the indecents.

Lorraine knew they weren't looking at her. But then their focus made a switch as the people on shore saw the black cherry nude hand the helm over to her.

"Just ease her along, Lorraine," they heard her say. "And Effy, you total slut!"

The new steersman eyed Beatense's belly. "Aren't you ever hungry?" she said.

"Huh? No, at least not now. I guess I shudda eaten earlier. Why do…"

Beatense then saw a grinning, fat creep, possibly last night's tennis voyeur, who watched them glide by while stuffing himself with yellow popcorn. Angered, Beatense turned her petals full at him, flexing her shoulders. I froze. Yes, this was me, in those sad years of 1976 and 77. The boat continued to sail by Sorel.

Lorraine began to angle out from the shore to clear the end of the pier. She was the definitely odd man out in this proud little group. Still, she was handling the boat okay, but at their angle they needed another twenty feet to clear the end of the pier; they had to come about. Cheap fools at the rail above irritatingly watched.

"Get ready to come about," said Lorraine, with a worried look up at the thick under timbers of the pier. Fishing lines hung down. "O... Okay! Now!"

The rudders didn't work, not enough wind and the long pontoons had a stabilizing effect. Beatense jumped off as Shean dove over to take the helm. He pulled on the tiller repeatedly to swing the boat. Beatense flashed to the left pontoon's prow, and she took hold of the forestay, tugging it as she swam.

This made the difference. The boat cleared the massive log pilings by ten feet. Beatense launched herself aboard as the patchy wind caught the sail and completed the come-about. The audience cheered with two reasons, for the stopgap maneuver itself, and they all thought they were friends with the beach beauties by now, and they called and waved. Human nature, they wanted the affirmation of these perfects.

Shean, still at the helm, tiredly waved back, and the others fakely smiled.

"They really wanted us to crash," Beatense said, with a sly wink at Lorraine.

She appreciated that. "Thanks for saving the day. That was quick thinking."

"No think... Hey, I was supposed to meet Craig!" They came about, going north now. "I forgot about that! What time is it? I said for him to find me on Main at five!"

"I think it would be six by now," said Virginia, watching as the pier fell away.

"Six! But we're not even close yet! Get me up to Main, you guys, fast!"

"He'll never make Main by five," said Shean. "They will probably go for a drink, traffic downtown will be heavy, all those wrong turns, getting lost."

"So relax," said Jesse. "Even if he is there now, do you think he's bored?"

"Let's stop in at the house," said Shean, as the Oxhead dunes began a slow progression. Beatense saw the airy child and her lovely sons playing soccer on the summer home sand. The Amherst girl was playing too. Lorraine endured wretched envy for these magnificent creatures. And there sat Book Girl. Shean went on, "We can get the car and move Beatense out of the motel, then head up to the cabin."

"But really, I I have to get to Main! Craig is there and he's expecting me!"

"You told him you were going sailing," said Jesse, watching the soccer.

"Just who is this guy?" said Virginia. "Is he moving in too?"

"No! He's from Maher Ridge. Way inland. I met him on the train coming down, to remind you. He came down for this trade show. Didn't I say all this?"

"It was all kind of garbled," said Jesse. You kept backtracking. Pathetic."

A gentle wave glided the catamaran neatly in upon landing, and it was left sitting upon a shimmering tabletop of wet sand. The crew pulled the boat up, and a tourist couple stopped to watch. Beatense saw them turn to her in full stare, but she had no time for these low eaters, other than to gaze at them out of bland curiosity. Hot tan, shaped muscles, taut belly, these were essentials. Effy looked at them also.

"Well, see you, Beat," said Jesse. "I'm taking off on Windfire for a ride."

"Later," said Shean, as the lost looking couple turned their cnfused stares to the younger boy, then the older boy. "You have to help de-rig the cat."

"Not us," said Virginia. "Lorraine and I are hoofing it back. Coming, Effy?"

"Yeah, and thanks a lot!" said Lorraine, with misgiving, as Effy hopped over.

"I thought you two wanted a ride!" said Shean.

"I need to walk," said Virginia. "All bent over on that boat all day."

"And I don't need moving by car!" said Beatense. "*This* is what I packed!"

"You must have a toothbrush," said Shean. "No, really, the car is faster."

"Well, after our sailing adventure I can't really argue with you."

Lorraine and Virginia stood over by the palm mounds and watched as the sails were lowered. The tourist couple kept watch too, and Beatense helped bare Tammy unclip the jib from the forestay. Bare herself, she snaked her waist quite effectively, and she elaborately played her thin arms for the tourists. She helped Shean fold the mainsail, actually by just holding to the pointy head and stepping to keep position.

The late sun was baking across the powdery sand into her. Her bleachy shaggy hair was fly-away dried. Effy eyed her array of muscle with wondering admiration.

"Tayammy, Ah'm stale nawt hangruh!" muscle girl hollered, watching her breasts and arms, as Shean stepped toward her in rolling up the lengthwise folded sail.

"Me, either," the dreamy-eyed girl said, somehow catching the meaning.

Beatense let go the sail and Shean stuffed it into the sail-bag. Jesse looped the ropes for packing and Tammy began folding the jib. Virginia sprang over to help, to show the hated tourists she was sea worthy. Lorraine picked up the mound guarded lifejackets, and Beatense squirmed into her green T-shirt with stick arms raised.

With a haughty look at the tourists the girl pulled it down over her taut, steel tan belly, then saw that she had instead put on Virginia's *Drag Queen*.

She opened out her arms and smiled in contrived wonder.

"Aohhh! Lewk, Vuhjeenyah! Ah aaaaxadantly poot awn yaa shett!"

"Aohh, yeww fecking beetch!" Virginia replied, joining in the act, distorting her lips in horror. "Thayen Ah keen poot ahn yaaa tah-shatt!"

Beatense shallowly laughed. Shean rolled his eyes up and he picked up the sail bag. Tammy took the lifejackets from Lorraine, and Jesse got the hamper items together. Bare legged Beatense jauntily rested the boom on her shoulder.

"Well, hurry her home, Shean," said Lorraine. "And thanks!" *I guess.*

"Gaff ahh prapuhtee!" ordered Jesse, pointing the bumbling tourists away.

Shean gestured helplessly to the couple, in apology for the weird behavior. But as the two shuffled off, they actually felt validated by the play acting. In their experience the beautiful young people of the world never lowered themselves to acknowledge their presence, even to keep up minimum courtesy. The cruelty of the young rich boy was especially redeeming, but that girl made their day. And that blond young thing.

Lorraine and Virginia (in the Psycho) and the clothes forgetting Effy said good-bye and started for the distant Main. The older two were friends since first grade, despite their difference. But Lorraine feared Beatense would not be as amenable. This was correct. She wouldn't have agreed to the move if she knew about plain Lorraine.

"So, let's have you meet Dad now, Beatense," said Jesse.

She held her arm protectively. "Hold it! This is getting too complicated!"

"A handshake and we're on our way. No conversation necessary."

"Oh, okay. Vuhjeenyah!" she called. "Lewk foh ah gah wayen ahh syoot!"

Virginia turned and waved in acknowledgment. She would look for Craig.

Beatense turned back to her friends. "Sheet! Ah haope thaa fahnd heem!"

"You can cut that out now," said Shean, laughing. "Tammy, what's wrong?"

"Mama wants me home now, Shean!" She dropped the lifejackets. "I forgot, with Dad working at the expo I was supposed to mow the lawn!"

The boy held the child in his thin arms, looking like a tribal chieftain's son as he asserted his mastery over her with physical crudity. The savage girl looked as if she would be all too eager to acquiesce, especially with her stark lack of costume.

Beatense didn't want her taking off, and tried to stall her.

"Tammy, I'm glad I got to know you today. You're already a best friend."

The baby felt weak, unsure of her footing. Her face glowed as if alighted within. Beatense regretted coming out with such a remark just to delay meeting this father. Well, she did mean it. She set down the boom and gave Tammy a hug.

"Bye, Beatense. You're my best friend... What, Shean?"

"Hang the lifejackets on the boom, Tammy, so Beatense can carry them."

Beatense hefted the boom back up and Tammy shoved the lifejackets on. She scampered away down the beach like a little bare fairy, a flashing sparkle. The party stepped by the stray little dunes and went through a gap in the hedge of lush tropical blossoms edging the beach. Entering this sanctum Beatense paused in surprise.

She expected to see some chrome and cedar showcase, with those bold, jutting angles and ten foot tall slot windows. But through the scattered trees what she saw instead was little more than a shack. It was a shack, a junk steal-it-yourself shipping crate and scrap lumber hut. In fact the add-on rooms sticking out like afterthoughts were crawling room only. Their windows were just two feet off the ground. They were just open jigsaw cuts with or without glass.

"What's wrong?" said Shean. "Come on."

"You mean you have the nerve to sit there and say that's your house?"

rt>rt>rt>rt>>rt>rt>rt>rt>rt>rt>rt>>rt>rt>rt>rt>rt>rt>rt>rt>>rt>>rt>

"We're standing," said Jesse. "But we stuck everything into the barn."

She saw the barn, and its paddock. It lay off to the right, across the sparse, needle grassed yard, and the horses did have tonier accommodations at that. They had a cozy little log structure that was big enough for four stalls, and grain and tack rooms.

A good supply of hay bales could be kept up in the low loft. Windfire and another horse were out in the split rail paddock. Windfire spun around and whinnied at his Jesse, and the boy dropped his things and ran over to pet him.

"Quite the devotion," said Beatense. "But whose horse is the other one?"

"Ned's," said Shean. "Specterrific. Spec. I don't have a horse, myself."

Beatense almost ran over to pet the horses too, but she had the boom. But she instinctively liked this place. Tropical breezes were wafting in from the sparkling surf, and the bright sun was verdantly subdued by the leafy canopy.

"Gosh, I wasn't expecting any place like this, you two, but it's a lot more fitting for kids as natural as you two are. But how did you get zoning?"

"We're hidden back here. And we're gypsy. The libs love us."

Jesse returned and they went on to the ramshackle house that was set about twenty yards back. They set down the gear by the door and went in the kitchen.

"Dad, we're back!" Shean yelled. He reached behind Beatense to give the crooked screen door she lightly closed a loud slam. "Hey, we need the car!"

"Shut up, I not hear a word you say!" came the muffled response.

Let's get going, thought Beatense. Shean hefted himself back up onto the white enameled steel counter and peeled a banana. A violently yellow banana, held by a violently brown naked boy. Who was invitingly stiffened, continuing the habit.

The kitchen was walled with rough, grey aged barnboard planks. A cheap, steel legged dinette table stood in the middle of the varnished wood floor, and mismatched vinyl padded chairs were set carelessly around it. Overhead a four tube fluorescent light clung to the low ceiling, that was obscured by a big fishing net that was bumped down in squares from a gridwork of grey lath strips.

The cupboards were originally medicine cabinets, salvaged, providing mirrors for these openly vain boys. Shean opened one with a screech and he carefully critiqued himself in it. The steel counter he sat upon probably came from a rural clinic.

On the opposite wall a small apartment type stove and refrigerator also gleamed white, and between them, under the limply curtained window, that had no pane at the time, a big enamel sink stood on four plumbing pipes. All this junkyard plunder gave the impression of a carefree, primitive life here in the tropics.

The crudely cut windows didn't even have screens, and so the terrarium of leaves, flowers and fronds suspended just outside seemed to flow indoors upon the fragrant breezes. Beatense also noted that the spectacularly vivid coloration of sun carried in by the beautiful, long haired boys also conveyed that mystical islands theme.

Now both were long stiffened, apparently ingrained habit. The girl looked out the window at the close end of the medicine chests and she saw a swimming pool across a neatly mowed lawn of bright green grass. The chaise lounges and wheeled reflector panels parked out on the concrete deck made her shake.

She gave a last longing look and sat at the table, resting her arms on it.

"You guys *are* rich, having a pool. I would love to lay out there, under oil."

With head ducked to clear the netting, Mr. Shattuck came lurching into the room. Despite all apprehensions Beatense was hardly prepared for what she saw. He was mean, big and mean, a rogue bear. He wasn't remotely like his two delicate sons, he was surly and crafty looking or even brutal.

His straight, black hair was greased back with tonic, hopefully, and his face was bluntly malevolent. His arms were coarsely thick. He was wearing one of those fool palm splashed vacation shirts (*give me a break*), and pea green walking shorts.

Altogether these only exacerbated his faded gypsy swarthiness. Actually he had the lifeless, dull look of never any sun. With her own rays pampered tan warming the room, Beatense was horrified. She held her arm protectively.

This *father* crashed down onto a chair. With belligerent toothpick rolling in his pulpy lips he glowered at Shean, then at Jesse, and finally with a bit of a start at the visitor. He seemed to enjoy the silence that fell. Lowering her small arm back down, the skinny beach twit felt bereft for her new young friends. What an outrage, for such fine, illustrious boys to be stuck with this crudely suspicious ugly bar-bruiser for their supposed father. She awaited the inevitable explosion.

"The car you want. Is that it?"

"Yeah, big time, Dad!" replied Shean brightly, being quite brave in the face of this hostility. "We need to pick up Beatense's things at the Hideaway and run her up to Lorraine and Virginia's cabin on Holiday Hill. Oh, sorry, this is the town's newest arrival, Beatense Colwell, the Book Girl, and this is our Dad, Tony!"

Tony, what else, thought Beatense, half raising her arm again as she warily eyed the boorish looking brawler before her. She didn't offer to shake.

"Hello," the brawler said curtly, flicking his eyes to her, with a microscopic jolt.

For all her strap-like strength Beatense felt a tad vulnerable before this foul lout. But it might have been possible that in spite of his repellent face he was full of bubbly warmth and outgoing cheer. The party guy full of laughs. *Yeah, right.*

"Nice meeting you," Beatense replied. "But look, I don't really need a ride. I can handle the move. So see you later! Thanks for..." She began to get up.

"Sit down," the father said. "We give you ride."

"But I don't want a ride!" said Beatense hotly, raising her thin toasty arm again.

Jesse gave her a look as if to say, Be Careful, and fell into a chair. Sagging against the table with pretty head propped, he drummed his fingers on the table.

"So, you the young lady Jesse met in your room last night," Tony said, giving her more unwelcome attention. "And you run big race this morning. You tired, you get a ride. After you bring her things over, Shean, are you coming back to help clean the stalls, for once being useful around here?"

"I don't know, the mood you're in. And they're not my horses."

The fingers stopped in mid-drum.

"Oh, so we have a wise guy, a wise guy who is now grounded for a week."

"I can't be grounded! I have a job! And what's wrong with you, anyway?"

Fingers still poised, Jesse watched these proceedings with bated breath.

"That's what I want to know," said Beatense. "What's the deal? I'm not mad yet, and you don't want to see me mad." She bulged out her biceps.

The boys stared. The father hunched himself forward, slumping, burying his yes acne scarred and beefy face in his meaty hands.

"Ned had another fight with Shannon today," he said, shaking his head, "and it might be it this time with his friends. If I could just *hit* someone, you know? If there was some one or some thing I could fight! But this, I don't know what to do!"

He looked mournfully up. "Look, Miss Coldwell, I sorry to act like ass, but you all had happy fun today but my poor baby Ned at the end of his rope. This could be his new life now, no friends. It is nice to meet you, this dive could use a little class, but I occupied with this badly now."

"Those fuckers," said Jesse. "But I can see how it would happen."

"Gosh, I understand, Mr. Shattuck, and I'm really sorry about Ned."

"Agh, it always happen. The kid's mental, not right, his circuits go wacko, and he says things he doesn't mean. The boys can take it wrong."

Shean hopped down. "I'll ask him if I can go surfing with him tomorrow."

"Thanks, kid. He worships you. I worship you." Shean stepped out. "Well, Miss Coldwell, shall we retire to the living room? To our conversation pit?"

"Sorry, I have to meet someone, regretfully. And it's Colwell, without a D."

She was so brown, just so brown, his eardrums roared. At the present her legs were out of sight beneath the table, damn it. But they had to be small, and long and joyously fresh. Tony also noted her T-shirt, and her breasts that stuck out like apples. And here in person, the Book Girl. Destructively beautiful. Wide placed eyes.

"Conversation pit," said Jesse. "Dad, don't you mean conversation *pits?*"

He turned to Beatense. "The kid has a point there, I got the sofa reverse bidding. They started at fifty and worked down. I got it for thirty-four."

"That'th thirty-four thenth," said Jesse. "Dad'th worth thix hundred thouthand and our thuppothed thofa lookth like it was thtabbed with a thiththorth. Thadithically."

Tony reached across the table and gave his littlest son a playful slap.

"Ow! What was that for?" --/-- "I tell you not to blab our money! A week of bad trading and it's back to picking! How many others you tell, you big mouth?"

"No one, Dad! This last hour, I mean. During the 10K, I think just ten or so."

He looked up, seeking help. "Yes, Miss Colwell, I'm sorry to involve you with our family Ned problem. You don't even know him."

Beatense imagined a buck toothed deformity with a repellant twisted face.

"We did like tell her about him, Dad," muttered the adorably pouting Jesse, who incidentally was still bare, into the palm of his hand. "To warn her."

Tony took out a pack of cigarets and held it out to Beatense. "Want one?"

"Sure! We call them fags up north, but down here that exact term hurts too many feelings." She took the offered cigaret, a non-filter Brenton.

Tony lit his cigaret and he held his lighter over to Beatense.

"Thanks, but where did Shean go? I really have to get going."

"Pitiful," intoned Jesse. "Dad won't marry anyone who's always in a hurry."

It was Tony's turn to cough. "Don't you have stalls to clean?"

Jesse got up. "Me, two days in a row? But I better stow the boat gear.first. You should see her laying out naked, Dad. And dancing. Well, bye!"

The boy went outside and Tony smiled cheesily. "I wasn't imagining that."

"I should apologize, exposing your sons to that, but I am a naturist."

He trembled. "Oh, are you? But yes, miss, I can give my wonderful freeloaders anything they want, short of a real house, you noticed. I might get a park home, a double loft model. Depends on zoning. But my baby Ned is always so unhappy. He does have friends, and they do try to include him, but sometimes they start to argue. Ned goes too far with it. I don't know what to do!"

Shean came back. "He's okay now, we're set for surfing, if it's up."

"I can tell you one thing that's up," said Jesse, leaning in the window.

"Get to those stalls! And thanks, Shean. I couldn't quite reassure him."

Beatense finished her cigarette and flicked the butt out the window.

"Oh, I'm sorry! I'm not at home!" she said. "But it doesn't have a filter."

Jesse came back in. Radiantly tan, he slouched down onto a chair, and radiant Shean got back up on the counter, also slouched. These brothers were blinding, any interior space was fair game for them to suffuse with rays of gold. But as she admired them, Beatense wondered about this Ned.

From what she knew of the imbeciles all too often seen up in Arrolynn, compared with the fine and proudly alert youngsters here, intellect is a major if not the factor in how one's looks turn out. The mentally deprived all look alike because their minds are also dully alike, while the brilliant kids of this world were all dazzlingly unique.

But as Ned walked in he dashed this theory.

With sport spikes clacking, in spiffy baseball uniform he looked like the regiment mascot. Beatense positively gaped; Ned was the cutest most precious boy she ever saw. He was a veritable sapling shoot of youthful proportions, and he was deeply enbathed with all the sun's love. He was a delicate baby, and the long, black lashes of his tenderly serious dark eyes were self-importantly straight.

How unfathomed the depths of those eyes would be, as the boy narrowed them in the sun. And his surf blonded hair, loosely parted to one side, was a luxuriant, spilly thick mass of coppery gold. But he was unaware of all this.

With little neck set he looked gloomily around. He reminded Beatense of a baby duckling. A very put-upon puppy duckling, with those amazing eyelashes.

"Jesse, take care of the horses now. You go help, Ned. Every day I have to tell you kids to get at those stalls. I even have to do it myself half the time."

"Phooey!" said Ned glumly. "Jesse didn't help me yesterday!"

"I did them in the morning, alone, and then you did them in the afternoon. So don't say I didn't do my fair share, Ned. We should just do our own horses."

"Our own horses," said Beatense. "Happily, I'm in that club too."

Shean coughed. "Say, Ned, this is Beatense. She might be starting a job up at Cement tomorrow, at the rental counter, but she doesn't know squat about any of the boards and all the different trucks and their specs. I tried telling her about it but I get all confused. You're the expert. Can she borrow any of your magazines so she can get up to speed on the equipment and the different tricks?"

Ned's opinion of this unwelcome intruder rose in just those few seconds.

"I guess," he said grudgingly, and he left the room with a quickening step.

"Not half bad, Shean," said Tony, and Jesse nodded in grateful agreement.

Beatense didn't see a win here, so she was puzzled as Shean stretched out on the counter in luxurious self congratulation. These deep brown, vulpine boys, Jesse and Shean, for all their killer attributes, were very sensitive toward their troubled brother.

This was a family of solid bedrock love.

Ned came back with a stack of magazines, that spilled out over the table.

"This one's the best," he said, pointing out *Unbored Boards.*

"Yeah, thanks, Ned. This will help. But you know, I bought myself a skateboard yesterday. Could I come over here for some lessons maybe?"

"I guess," Ned said, as if lending the magazines was more than enough. "Except our pool is full. We better do it at the park."

"Your pool is full. What's that got to do with it?"

"You need the pool for verticals!" the boy said, as if this was obvious.

"Oh, of course. But one thing I noticed about that Cemented place was all these idiot boys hanging around there. You might agree, this town has too many boys in it, actually, and not enough friendly, smiling and smart girls."

"It does not! It has too many smiling and *stupid* girls!"

Beatense world-wearily sighed. "Well, we can discuss that later. But you know, back where I'm from, whenever too many boys are around, us girls would steal scrap lumber from a house being built and we would build a fort. Plus we always put a sign on it that says *No Girls...* I mean, *No Boys Aloud!*

"So then when we were camping out in it we didn't have to worry about any idiot boys bugging us. Smart idea, hah?" Tony saw the wheels turn in Ned's head as he glared at her. "Probably if you guys tried to build a fort you would keep hitting your thumbs with the hammer. Or if you built a tree fort and accidently kicked the ladder down, you would be stuck up there crying all night." --/-- "We would not!"

Tony saw Ned ponder this idea more attentively.

He loved the girl for her back handed suggestion, but once he saw her legs he would have all other thoughts concerning her. For her to just appear in his home like this was a development he was still trying to deal with. She had a ferocity.

Meanwhile though, an unsuspecting woodpile lay in wait for a nocturnal raid by eager teen-age boys, whispering to each other to keep quiet, flashlights off.

"Well, bye," said Ned. "Nice to meet you." The boy moved for the door.

"Hold it," said Tony. "Where the hell do you think you're going?"

"To talk to Shannon!"

"You change the hell out of that uniform first, and then get to the stalls."

"Oh, all right!" said Ned. He scuffed his heel and stepped from the room.

"I get a reprieve," said Jesse. "But I'm almost as old as they are. I can get in on that fort too, you know. I know where there's a good construction scrap pile."

"Miss Beatense, I very grateful to you. Nice thinking."

"Thanks, but I need that ride. I might still have a misguided boyfriend waiting for me." She stood and there were her legs. "Shean, let's haul."

Her prune fudge tan bounced off the walls. Her tee-hidden breasts lifted.

Tony began rigidly shaking, trying to hide it but his popped open eyes gave him away. With a fixed grin he pulled a towel off the rack.

With troubled control he said, "And use this to get that grease off you before you get in car, Shean. I don't want you fucking up the only decent furniture we have."

"Dad, this is my natural shine!" the boy protested, as he gazed upon his thin arm. Like Beatense, he was very dark rusted brown. "I get it from the sun!"

"I don't know how you do it, kid, even tobacco bows to you. You too, miss."

"Well, your reward for that compliment is…" The shirt, off. Tony choked.

He saw the extreme slimness of her waist. Her breathtaking tan legs were long, but only as big around as a child's. Her thinned thighs looked like tightly inter-woven ropes, inhumanly sun baked. She was very small, but exorbitantly shaped with tuned muscle. With her being so diminuitive and acutely hot dark brown, Tony would have aged decades if he was with the sailing party. Her belly was sunk.

As he shook hands with this *smiling* young woman, he tried to keep from openly sweating. Her grip was firm and strong; her veined bicep bulged. Deep eyes.

"Nice to meet you, sir. If I see more of your boys I'll see more of you."

"You have to, miss, when you bring back Ned's books, heh heh."

Beatense laughed at the baldness of his invitation. Shean had stepped out and returned wearing his cut-offs. The beautiful two stepped out. Trembling helplessly, the father watched out the window. The kids walked toward the pool then cut to the left through a gap in the hedge of holly bordering its far end.

"You shouldn't have popped that on Dad, going naked like that."

"I'm all over the Field, so what's the b-big... Deal..." There the luxury car stood poised, a magnificent deep rose maroon Camelback Espriado. "Wow, this is the car we're going in? You guys... You guys *are* shittin rich!"

"Yeah, but impressive or not it's actually quite... Shannon! My man!"

A narrow boy came up the drive, stepping barefoot without a flinch in spite of the crushed flower pot paving. As a coastal, his pure skin was gloriously infused with rich vitamin D, and this was especially true for those long, pretty legs. Not a show-off, he bared only his limbs with trim cotton shorts and yellow T-shirt. Real long blond hair.

His summer glory tan had a hot shine, but it was his politely earnest looks that impressed people. Real long blond hair and inquisitive features.

"H-Hi, Shean," he said. His eyebrows reflected wary discomfort, from the fight, presumably. He had exotic, upward angled eyes, with irises lifted, like Beatense's, a poignant effect. "Is... Is Ned around?"

"Yeah, Shannon, he is, but he's kind of mad at you, you know."

"He's... He's mad?" Shannon said, taking hope. That he could handle.

"Yeah, even though it was all his fault, again. Shannon, this is Beatense."

"Hello," the boy said, solemnly nodding. "Are you..."

"Yes, I am. But yeah, Ned is hopping mad. He's plotting revenge."

"Oh, he is not!" said Shean. "But look, Shan, all these fights of Ned's have been more and more embarrassing for me and Jesse. So just cut him off."

He stumbled backwards, mouth agape. "What... What a traitor you are!"

Beatense saw that Shannon idolized him. Shean with his job, money, looks and drivers license, and Shean with his killer tan, Shean with his Tammy, even doing her, and others, and Shean with his breezy, condescending authority.

This was a mortal blow. Beatense was just as shocked.

"It's time to be realistic about this, Shannon. Just go home and forget the whole thing. Unbelievably, Ned's even talking about building a fort! A fort!"

"Huh? A *fort?* Really? Er, bye. Nice meeting you." He turned, back length hair. Cut through the hedge and apparently saw Ned. "Hey, fuck, you're building a fort?"

"Shean! That was brilliant!"

"That bought another week, is all. And good idea, the fort. Nice kid, though, hah? They're worth a billion. Here, I'll let you in. We have to get going."

The girl was waiting for this, getting into that heavy car. Its landau roof padding matched the ruby maroon body, and it was that massive type of motor vehicle whose two hundred pound doors swing out in five foot arcs. The long, wide coach reeked of overstated elegance and gorgeously grossly gauche prestige. Whatever its setting it could not be overlooked. The financial district solidness and sporty flair of its swept sculptured lines portrayed fabulous wealth. Paid 5000 for my 77. The thin Shean hefted the bank vault door open, expertly stepping aside so he didn't crack his shin.

Provincial Beatense stared wonderingly at the royal ruby carpeting. The cars in Arrolynn had plain black rubber matting. And the floor in front was flat, no bump, both in front of the seat and where it slanted up under the hundred pound dash.

The car had no transmission hump! The dark cherry dashboard was a refined, massive sweep from side to side, whose twin tiered design gave it a vast depth in extending to the windshield. Its interior lights softly aglow, the ruby red leather of the baronial upholstery shimmered with a muted wax shine.

The car's transport function was nothing more than an added extra.

Shean leaned in and carelessly dumped the books in back. Beatense sat within the automobile, legs wrapped in her arms, and she felt the tuffeted leather cradle her as if with dozens of tiny pillows. Shean closed the door with a great thunk of finality, and Beatense turned from eyeing her belly and studied its equipage.

27

PIZZA AGAIN

She gave a glance to her thirsting, stuck out hips, then back to the door. Its upper half was padded with leather, and a panel of mottled wood with an ornate grab handle was emplaced here. The door's kick panel was faced with more ruby carpet. The girl touched at the wood door panel, that had a delicate knurled pattern.

And there was a swath of similar crosshatched detail across the wide, curved dash, punctuated with four chromed ventilation louvers. Beatense, absently rubbing at her hip bump, rubbed at the wood; it had an odd feel.

"Plastic," said Shean, getting in. He seemed even thinner. "Urethane."

He saw her pink split sitting casually opened, and his heart pounded. Just a foot away, maybe two, and she was black skinny naked. Shean adjusted the mirror, with his ring bracelets jinkling more than usual, and he pulled his seatbelt and buckled it.

Beatense never saw these in Arrolynn, but she did know of them from the camp vehicles. Shean watched her tough little arm reach over as she snapped her buckle. He pulled down the armrest between the seats. As with the fancier cars of Arrolynn, the girl liked this feature. She placed her elbow on it out at a wide angle, because of the width of her seat. Shean's seat was equally wide.

Beatense wondered, How could such a stalk skinny boy, like herself, handle this brute? How could he negotiate it with that runway of a hood out before them? Its wreathed medallion hood ornament was ten feet away! Shean turned the key and the muffled sound of the starter was followed with an audible trembling. Beatense cocked her ear. *It's running?* The boy touched at the switches on his door and the windows shot down. Then he showed Beatense how to adjust her seat.

With a whirring of hidden little motors Shean's one third of the leather seat tilted back, and Beatense tried hers. Her seat tipped back, and this continued until she felt like she was being swallowed. Her legs fell open, into the readied position, and she studied the floral brocade headliner. Shean studied her. Meticulous, methodical.

Beatense reached her thin, sun polished arm back to the switch and ran her seat back up, with her legs still propped. The stick girl shook back her gold washed hair.

"Boy, this is some car! You could almost sleep in this seat!"

He shook; sleep wasn't all that came to mind. He actually felt her presence. He shaded his eyes to test this. Yes. Heart pounding, he shifted the lever to D. The car began to roll, as the LR78 radials popped and cracked the terra cotta gravel. The boy touched his pretty toes to the gas pedal, that had a white rubber emblem, and the clawing front wheels shot the opera coach out the driveway, past the hedge.

This was all new for Beatense, even with her wealth. The cars she knew were dumpy and rounded, and their fenders bulged out from the body. All their glass was flat, and the windshields were split to angle the panes. There might be an extra touch, like the grey grip ropes across the back of the front seat, where an ashtray was often located, or there could be little cranks for the side vent windows, but the cars shook with sublinal vibrations and the engines were noisy even at idle.

But what magic they had, with their huge interiors, and their felty, stuffy essence of Motolene smells. And while traveling at night what was cozier than the soft yellowed glow of the gauges and their steady pointers? And the way those radios whistled as the distant stations faded out and other stations garbled in. Their red lighted tuning markers liquidly babbled across the Mars Rocket numerals as a new station was found. And in the garages where these machines awaited travel, the lingering exhaust fumes permeated the air with those evocative smells of miles gone by.

But it seemed that here in Xanthallado, as showy and advanced as the cars were, they were sterilized of romance and intrigue, and they provoked only misguided envy and false pride. But with its eighteen inch suspension coils the Espriado rode like a ship. Elegant Shean, whose toasty tan vividly glowed against his purple leather seat, was working the wheel with fine relaxed hand as he tooled along the wandering and wooded Bolingbroke Trail. Beatense had never before known of such V8 automotive power and impetus. As their hushed theater glided by the extravagant show-place homes of this exclusive enclave, she wondered how this bare youth beside her could handle this plush motorcar so effortlessly.

But with the vibrant lusterance of his warm, harsh dark skin, Shean was a proper fixture for this noble phaeton coach. Heat thinned, starve thinned, he looked as if he had almost no room for food within his muscle latticed empty belly. And slouched as he was, the belt loops of his jean cut-offs lay far down from his black surrounded navel, and his stretched thighs also looked black in the car's smoked glass lighting.

His tumbling, tickling spills of long blond hair amplified his heavy darkness. And with his many bracelets hanging to his thin arm, he was also the picture of the proudly vain gypsy boy that he truly was, a merciless reminder to everyone common of their distasteful imperfections. Beatense understood this. Lorraine worried her.

They reached the stop sign at the busy Highway, and the sudden appearance of convenience stores, motels, restaurants, surf shops, bank branches and numberless passing traffic lay in jarring contrast to the tropical glade lying behind the kids. They had to wait for a break. Beatense folded down her visor and a mirror lighted up.

Shean drew in his breath. "Hey, uh, care to see the P-Palisades?"

"Even the mirror is fancy. But P-Palisades? What's that? Oh, those cliffs?"

His heart pounded. Once they were up there maybe this beautiful, tan girl would realize that nectaring with a tan boy would be lovely magic. He spotted an opening, and whirling the two and a half ton pavement crusher out with a flourish, he gunned it up to speed. Beatense was pressed back in her seat.

"Exactly. There's like this narrow little road that cuts off Trenton and goes to the top of them. And the view is thunderous. It's… It's real lonely up there."

She set her feet on the floor. "How, ahem, lonely do you mean, Shean?"

He panted. "Lonely enough now, but they'll build condos up there someday."

The Highway slowly swung left, curving toward the sea. They were drawing toward the motel from the south. Beatense wasn't familiar with this stretch.

"Anyway, for now Knife lives up there, under this rock ledge. It's just him and the outside. He's just real tough. He and I ride into the city to show our tans."

"You said that. Let me go with sometime. I can try that stunt naked."

"Is… Is th-that your motel there?" He had to change the subject.

They pulled into the Hideaway. The two hopped out and entered the office. Mr. Cheevy was sitting at the computer, struggling over new entries. He looked up with startled perplexity and clumsily stood. Shean was stunned that the girl just walked in naked, but he too had an effect on the elderly proprietor.

"Hello, m-my f-favorite little guest. Y-You had a visitor. And, hell… Hello, young man. You… You seem to do very well in the sun. You… You are quite exorbitantly suntan and you have so much hair. Beautiful blond locks."

Shean coughed. "Er, uh, yeah. Thanks." --/-- "Well who was my visitor?"

"Your friend, Mr. Hamiltyn. It was very collegial to see him again. I told him that you would be returning, and he'll be back. Oh, and by the way…"

"Shean, we can't go up to those Palisades after all! Craig's here!"

"And Miss Colwell, your father called earlier with an ugent message."

"What? What!" --/-- "A run on the bank. You lost all your money."

"Oh, you had me scared there for a minute. But Mr. Cheevy, I hate to say it but I have to check out! I'm moving up Holiday Hill! Did he say when he's returning?"

"He went to look for you on the beach, he said. But… But you're leaving?"

"The beach! Shean, this is all your fault, making us so late!"

"You're the one who wanted to walk instead of getting a ride!"

"Both of you must get plenty of exercise," said Mr. Cheevy, shaking. "I see you riding by on your bike every day, son. I recognize you from your tan."

"W-Well, y-yes, I do ride my bike, and surf. But I get tan from my job too."

"Ah, yes, I admire you thin young people, who have such a youthful love of sun, and delighting in yourselves and freedoms we had no idea of."

Beatense caught Shean's eye. Her friend was a bit dotty.

"You beautiful beings of brown should always get all the sun you can."

"Fine," said Beatense, losing her patience. "I wish Craig just waited here!"

"I'll give him your new address, so when he returns he can find you."

"Shean! Do you know Lorraine and Virginia's address? Tell him it!"

"I don't know their address! As it is I hardly knew them before!"

"Oh, great! Neither one of you has the slightest shred of competence!"

Mr. Cheevy basked in the glow of the girl's rage. He and Shean laughed.

"Well, anyway, I'm moving out of this old fleabag, so give me a refund for unused occupancy, Mr. Cheevy, since I paid in advance through the week."

"Sorry, my baby, on short notice I can do that only if I rent your room tonight."

"But I won't even be here! I should have stayed at a quality place!"

"Just leave the key on the table, child. Now step back so I can see you."

Rusty black Beatense sighed and stepped back, showing her chained belly and snaking waist, her hipbones and with leg stuck out, her well-used split.

"There, your last look, you pervert!" Mr. Cheevy, and Shean, shook.

With a final farewell the two stepped out, glad to escape.

A tourist husband stared in shock; his wife in horror. Both youngsters destroyed any complacency they pleasantly had. And the girl knew by now that a look at her or from her could change lives. She unlocked her door, Shean felt faint.

A bed! They stepped in and Beatense got her backpack. She packed in a few books, among them *Dynamo Farm*, and other items.

"I wouldn't move if this place had a pool! You guys are so lucky."

Beatense took a motel towel from the bathroom.

"Y-You're not stealing that, are you?"

"Borrowing it. I didn't like that leather on my bare skin. Okay, take this."

The boy gazed happily down, noting how the lowering sun gave his skin a baked warmth as he stepped outside. His life was full of fun surprises like this. Beatense picked up her inline skates and skateboard and turned back.

"Good bye, little room. How I've changed since visiting you, freedom-wise."

She tossed her things into the car and went back and got her painting.

Shean reached in and pushed a button inside the glove compartment. The girl watched the trunk pop open unruffled, ready for anything with this beast by now. She retrieved her skates and skateboard and set them in, and with a play of splendid muscle Shean set her backpack in and gave the lid a downward tap. It sucked itself shut with a tiny click. That Beatense noted.

She opened the door and laid her borrowed towel on the seat. A noise.

"Hi, Beatense. Can we talk?"

She jumped. "Craig! Am I ever glad to see you! I'm so late getting back!"

He shook. The wispy girl shined extra, extra dark brown. Night camo.

"S-So am I. We had to wait for a loading dock for our truck to back in. That took an eternity, and we didn't escape until five. I didn't get to town here until six, all the traffic. I met your landlord and looked for you down on the beach. I felt like a fool in this suit. He said to look for the darkest ever tan."

"Well! So he noticed! But I was sailing! I never did make Main, Craig."

"So I gathered. You did say you might go sailing."

"Yeah, but not that jaunt. I'm sorry about this whole mess, Craig! I ended up sailing with Shean here, who you might know, on his catamaran. We sailed with my roommates, my new ones. I won't be staying here anymore, by the way. I'm up on Holiday Hill now! Just a great place. The day is just too hard to explain! As you noticed I didn't even have time to get anything on!"

Craig noticed, but glanced at Shean. By now the boy felt a bit awkward with this fellow in his suit standing before him, representing the real world of day to day work and responsibility. So although he normally craved this interest, for once he felt too boyishly boned slender, and unlike 99% of his life he wished he had a shirt on.

"Well, look, Beatense, I got a flight home tomorrow at two. My question is, and I don't mean this to invite myself anywhere, but where do I stay tonight?"

"Take my room here! I was just moving out. Technically it's still mine!"

"Okay I'll go sign in. Where can I look you up once I get my face on?"

Shean gave the tangled directions. Beatense smiled; gosh, it worked out after all! Craig looked at Beatense, as did a distant camera, he could only mouth dry air.

In spite of her beach burned darkness, her muscle-tightened skin was sweet and fresh. Her chained waist was long and lean, and her firm, youthful little apples burst exuberantly forth. The parking lot glare clashed with the naked girl's rust black tan.

"Are you... Are you sure y-you want to see me later, Beatense?"

"Oh, Craig! I was worried all day about finding you again!"

"She was, sir. It's all we heard out of her."

Craig floated to the office and turned to wave. Beatense waved and sprang into the car. She sat and importantly rested her arm on the door. Her belly was gauntly curved, Shean noted as he got in, and rippled. Trembling, he started the car.

"So, are we going to that Palisades place now?"

Shean looked. "Are you crazy? It looks like you got him lined up!"

"But it might be a good place for he and I to, er, like, check out?"

They went on to turn up Trenton, just across from Holiday Hill. This street was ratty, featuring a repair shop and machine shop, and a forlorn collection of dented old house trailers. Rusting junk lay in the yards, including old bent-up bicycles, a couple axles, old mattress springs, oil drums and a half inflated beach ball. This was also where the foothills moved in. Shean slowed up as he drove by a riding stable further along to the right. Four young girls came ambling out bareback along the dusty road entering the ranch. Oddly, they were in T-shirts and shorts.

They looked summery tan and tiny atop their ever accommodating pets.

"They got miles of trails to ride," said Shean. The girls, who raced to a clattering gallop along the shoulder, charged past the slower car and ran ahead and started up the long climb into the hills. "Okay, we turn here. Hang on."

Trenton Street ended in a gulch closed off with a quarry, but Shean didn't go this far. He hooked left onto a narrow roadway, that climbed upward in a steep incline. They entered a natural chasm of two walls of rock, so close the car's big doors could just be cracked open. The sudden shade was cool and deep.

Shean worked the wheel, intent in concentration as he tried to peer ahead of the curves that unwound before them. The speedometer was just above zero.

"We have to go slow," Shean said. "In case another car is coming down."

"I'm changing my mind about this. This is too slow. Let's turn around."

"We can't until we get to the top." --/-- "Then back down."

The sheer rock faces along both sides sloped into tall angled banks, and the sun returned with heat concentrated. Shean pressed ahead a little faster, even though the path itself remained just as narrow. And five minutes later they came back upon the four horseback riders, trotting down from the heights. Apparently the now-bared kids had ridden hard to make this circuit so fast, leaving clothes behind in their haste.

"They probably took the shortcut," said Shean, as he halted.

They climbed out their windows and faced the girls. Despite their blue and blond genetics their lives of dusty trail heat had deep browned them. Their thoroughbreds chuffed and stamped, and lowered their heads searching for grass. Beatense sprang over and petted the horses and rubbed their ears.

"What? You're blocking the road!" one girl whined, with a look of anguish.

"Well, we'll just turn around, Sheila," another perfected athlete said.

"I think you can get by us," said Shean, staring.

"You're awfully dark. Are you that Book Girl?" another baked child said.

"Yes, but I seem to be losing my thunder just lately."

"Balilaika is tanner than you," another girl said. "She isn't with us today."

"Should we try going around them?" the fourth girl said.

"It's too steep, Millicent! We can go back up to the little nook and wait."

The primeval creatures said goodbye and rattled back up the road.

The two continued the trip and passed the girls in their off-set. They finally broke out from the confined passage, and Shean gunned ahead over the flats and stopped. They got out and sat by the cliff's edge, and Shean ditched his cut-offs. They gazed out toward the distant sea. The hot wind was stiff, the blue sky was without limit. The sun was still high over the sea despite the late hour. Beyond the waving palms and Madeline rooftops the rolling surf was ranged out like strings of white yarn that broke into flowing fields of foam. The sailboats were countless. The marina was vast.

"Shean! I should have laid up here all this week instead! What a view!"

"Yeah, you could try and look at something besides yourself. But there's Holiday Hill, and the Cliff Diving Rock and the skateboard park, and the Breeze Hotel. You can see the whole stretch down past Sorel. There's Boulder Beach of recent memory."

"Oh, yeah! But anyway, this one Karen lives in that pink building by the Breeze there. She's a tanning fanatic even worse than me. She ran the 10K this morning."

"I know of her and saw her." Shean sighed. "But anyway, there's the view."

"Oh, duh. But you say that Knife lives up here? Where? Like in a tent?"

"He lives under a ledge. His parents are old and crabby, so he lit out."

Shean was eight inched. The girl on a knee swung her leg over and sat him in.

"What are ya doing? Ten minutes ago we were just talking to your boyfriend!"

"This has nothing to do with being faithful or unfairthful. Remember Courtlyn?"

"That's different! Tammy and I have an understanding!" He changed his mind.

Shean got on top and worked, until came the clatter of hooves. A darkly sweat tanned boy galloped toward them. He skidded to a dramatic side-to-side stop on the rock, to the glorious workings of his glorious muscles. He reined in his stallion. Bare like the girls, he was disturbingly beautiful, with a heavy thatch of yellow straw.

"Wow, the Book Girl! Hi, sorry to interrupt! But did you see the girls up here?"

"Five minutes ago, Cimarron, heading down. Naked. Even Millicent."

"Shit, they took the quarry pass! Yeah, Mill finally got sensible! Really fucks!"

Beatense approved of Cimarron's approval. His magnificent freedom was jarring. His muscles sang; the liquid sun poured upon his heated skin. Tuned ripples.

"Can I ride him?" said Beatense, as she and Shean separated.

His pealing laughter was clear and bright. "You'll never get up on Venture! He's sixteen hands!" He jumped down, quite a drop for him. "Okay, try it."

Beatense sprang up easily and, belly curved, found her seat. This told the steed she was a rider. She nudged Venture off at a rocky gallop, reining him at a showy angle. She flew across the open flats, flexing to the horse's bounding strides.

She felt him in her blood, as her hips moved with him. She pulled him round in a flying turn and recklessly raced him back. She also skidded him to a stop.

"Wow, decent horse!" the panting girl said. Legs gripping, she reached and patted Venture on the neck. The low sun gave a sharp insistence to her color. Still mounted, she went back to her lanky slouch. "But my legs stink now."

"Not with Venture. He sweats clean. Hey, you are the Book Girl, right?"

"Let's get this straight, I was wrongly picked. But thanks for the ride."

She hopped down. She gave the reins over to Cimarron and he vaulted up onto his horse. With a play of extravagant muscle he reined him around and shot off with stones flying. Hair fluttering, tan flashing, he bolted down the chasm road.

Shean had a new respect for her. "S-So you r-ride, hah?"

"Horses too, yes. I shouldn't have run him on all this rock, but he was shod with pads. Hey, we better go, Shean. Good thing he came by! I was almost unfaithful!"

The two got in and threaded back down the canyon. They turned on Trenton and then the Highway, and Shean gunned up Ringdon Walk and searched out the cabin. He stopped and the girls burst outside.

"Where have you been?" the slight but kinetic Virginia demanded.

"We went up the Palisades," the still bare Beatense said, hopping out of the car and grabbing the magazines in back. "Maybe we shouldn't have."

"Like duh," said Virginia, watching as the neighbors materialized. She was in Beatense's *Psycho Sunner* T-shirt, so presumably that girl was the attraction. "I guess it doesn't matter, but we started wondering, is all. So come on in!"

"Yeah! My new home! Oh, hey, did like Craig come by at all?"

"No," said Virginia. "Would we even recognize him?"

"Shean, he must have fed me a line! That was at least an hour ago, and he was just coming from the Hideaway! Are you two sure he didn't come here?"

"No one came knocking," said Virginia, "but I would say no."

"Well, let's go in," said Lorraine, gazing at Shean. "You boy, get her stuff."

Bare Shean got her backpack, Virginia the skate items, Lorraine the ugly picture. They went into the cabin set in the whispering pines. Beatense stopped.

Was it the rough log rafters that caught her heart? Was it the check printed café curtains, or that gas grate stove with the porcelain knobs? Was it the three barrack beds with their grey army blankets, or the dressers thickly coated with paint? Was it the old refrigerator with its rounded corners and Gambles emblem? Was it the chain hung wagon wheel overhead, with the miniature harbor lights around its rim?

Or was it the dumpy old sofa and lumpy old armchairs, or the cast iron stove with the split cordwood neatly stacked beside it? Was it the gun rack, with rifles?

The only modern touches were a stereo and TV on a low table, plus an old desk with a laptop, and a microwave. Still naked, standing just in the door, Beatense was caught by a lucky camera. She entered and set down the magazines.

"You guys, this is beautiful! You don't know how all this rustic charm affects me! It's better than Hoganforth, which is tough to beat!"

This gratified Lorraine, but there she was, nothing on. "So, you're staying?"

"I have to! Craig took my room at the motel, I hope."

"It got so late we ordered a pizza," said Virginia. "It'll come any time."

"I gotta go," said Shean, also still naked. "Thanks for coming sailing."

"Thank you!" everyone said as one, highly embarrassed by his *reminder.*

Shean took off in the swanky car. Beatense looked around the room again. She was a nice kid, really, but her state of dress showed conflicting personality traits.

"Yeah, the beds are out in the open, no bedroom," said Virginia. "These old ratty cabins were never meant for us promiscuous sluts. The Hill was this medical retreat over sixty years ago, and all these cabins were built as housekeeping units."

"Funny they call it Holiday Hill, then. So which bed is mine?"

"The middle one," said Lorraine. "We just cleared our junk off it."

"That pizza is sure slow," said Virginia, watching Beatense check herself in the mirror. Actually she leaned on the dresser and stared. "You… Okay?"

"Yeah, but… Pizza! We can't have pizza! What if that Buck delivers it?"

"You'll be in the tub," said Lorraine. "You have to get that grease off."

"Grease! That's all washed off!" Quoting Shean, "This is my natural shine!"

"It… Is? Anyway when you finish I'll be in to help you with your hair."

"I don't need any help with my… Is that the bathroom there?" Radiating a non greasy shine, Beatense pointed to the closet enclosure in the back corner, whose right wall was tactlessly set right by the kitchen sink. "Pretty handy."

"Isn't it," said Lorraine, blinded by her. "Now hurry. Yell if you want me."

Beatense didn't want her, but she solemnly nodded and stepped in.

She closed the door and Lorraine collapsed on the sofa. "She seems okay, but she's just this muscled engine of sex. I mean you can just see her simmering with it, the way she just walks in naked. I hope she doesn't being *friends* over."

"I might bother you with that myself. So, going in to help her, hah?"

Lorraine had stood. "And I'm going to bother her."

She went to the door and knocked. "Beatense, can I come in?"

"Now? Well, let me step into the tub and demurely pull the curtain first! Okay!"

The bathroom Lorraine stepped into was stuck in back when the resort closed the central latrines. It was paneled with those vertical car-siding strips with the rounded grooves. The interior was painted shiny white, and the glass lensed light fixture over the medicine cabinet was doubled in its brightness as a consequence. The sink was supported by two chrome pipes, and it featured separate faucets. The ancient toilet had a porcelain flush handle, and the cast iron bathtub stood upon eagle claw feet.

A slim black figure within reached a thinned arm and started the water. "Ow! That's hot!"

"Oh, I just rinsed out my swimsuit. It took a *lot* of water. Sorry."

"Ah, that's better." The plug clanked shut and the old tub began to noisily fill. "Gosh, I wonder where Craig is. He said he just had to put on his face."

"He said that?" said Lorraine. --/-- "Hey! There's no soap! Lorraine!"

She tried steadying her voice. "We... Us two, we started to use this herbal bath powder instead. I can p-pour some in for y-you."

Beatense sat leaning back on her elbows with knees up. "Okay."

Lorraine opened the curtain. The child gazed at her unquestioningly. She looked like and was a small carving of oiled walnut. The girl splashed the rising water onto herself, flexing her ripples. Shaking, Lorraine gritted her teeth and tipped the box.

The powder spilled out and creamy rich suds began to billow up around the black tan girl. Her chain and navel disappeared, and the water made temporary little islands of her protruding hips. No wonder she was so sexual. Wow!

"Boy, that feels good, Lorraine. I did get really burned today. Deeply."

"Y-Yes," Lorraine said, watching as the rising froth reached her petals.

"When I do get a burn it makes me look a lot darker than I really am."

Lorraine gave her a washcloth, and the girl washed herself with gusto.

"I'll use the shower for my hair." She stood, and the suds slipped from her, leaving smears of foamy bubbles. "Hey, Lorraine, I'm as white as you! Ha ha!"

She liked guys, she really did. But with the exception of Kit, who spent his life in cotton shorts or jean cut-offs, most guys didn't project to her in a meaningful way, like all the skinny beach girls in town did. It was their extreme confidence that got her.

Beatense aimed the hot spray onto herself, chasing the sudsy foam off. She stepped around in circles as stray droplets flew out onto the floor. She dunked her head under the flow and blindly reached for the shampoo.

"I better close the curtain for this, Lorraine."

"Yeah, m-maybe you better. But wait." She opened the drain. "Okay."

But the girl left the curtain open. She left the water running as she worked in the shampoo. Thick wet globs of foam slid down her, and the spray danced on her wet, charred tan, continuing to splash the wrinkly linoleum floor. Finally with a stern look she turned off the water, and stepped gingerly out onto the towel Lorraine laid on the floor. Lorraine wrapped the elfin sunbug in another towel.

"Ohhhh, poor baby. You're so cold after all that nice, hot sun today."

Beatense scowled in a little pout, sensing this was expected. "I just hope Craig makes it! Shean and me were fucking but we got interrupted, so it's up to Craig now, unless Shean's stupid directions got him all bungled up! All these miserable turns!"

Lorraine paused in wiping off the mirror. *Fucking!* "Don't worry, he'll find us."

"I should have gone right with him into that office! Except for you, Lorraine, he's my only chance for sex tonight. I had Shean deep in but then this boy rides up!"

Beatense let the towel fall artlessly away as she began drying herself. Physically drained, Lorraine sagged into the corner and watched. With her long jaw the child's facial profile reached eagerly forward, as if for socially engaging. This was conflicted by her upturned nose, which made her look as if she was tenderly on her guard.

She worked the towel, and the taut resilience of her stretchy muscles was cruelly evident as she played it on her skin. Her forearm tensions were embellished by her sliding and clinking gold bracelets. This wild sunbug's baked skin tore at Lorraine.

Shaking, she sprayed the suds down the drain. As Beatense bent over to finish drying her hair, and the floor, her friend stared at her neatly arched back with its little spinal bumps, and the correspondingly arched belly.

"Lorraine, you bitch! Be careful! I just dried the floor!"

She had accidentally strayed the spray. The tan little fawn straightened up, all starchy polished to a deepened burley burn, near black in this light. She sat upon the toilet. Her paired thighs looked very long. She sat forward in a tightly curved slouch, resting her chin on her hand, and with a little frown she went.

"Okay, just sit there, brat, and I'll back brush your hair."

Lorraine ran the drier over the surf beached tips of her friend's auburn hair. She fingered the locks and teased the brush inward, for a ratty fall over the girl's jointed, coat hanger shoulders. They were bony and knotted with muscle.

"You're just so thin. You have thicker hair than your smallness justifies."

"Shut up, Lorraine!" She turned and gave her a little slap on the head.

Lorraine was thrilled. She kissed the girl's shoulder, all burnished with bake and already smelling of sun. Beatense contemplated her with serious eyes.

"There, you're perfect. Now tell me what to get for you to wear, baby."

"Wear! Are you out of your mind? Oh, get me Virginia's *Drag Queen.*"

"How's it going in there?" said Virginia, when Lorraine staggered out.

"Unless she and I share my bed she has to go, Virginia. I can't take it."

Beatense stepped out. Her luminous, sternum separated breasts hummed with energy. Lorraine shook, panting. Virginia saw what she meant.

A car was heard pulling up. "Well, finally Craig is here!" said Beatense.
Virginia looked out the door and held her forehead. "It's fucking Buck."
"Buck! Don't let him in here!"

But he already was at the door. Supposedly being a friend he had to be asked in. Virginia met him, grinning, glad she was decent for this encounter.

"Virginia, hi! Got your Wagon Wheel!"

"Thanks, Buck. Er, how's things? Er, come… Come on in, heh heh."

The deliveryman stepped in and Beatense stiffened with resentment.

"Hi, Lorraine. And B-Beatense, er, wh-what a surprise to f-find you here!"

She fell into an armchair, legs pointedly opened. "Well, yes, here I am."

Trouble. Most pizzas went to women who thought him a clumsy boob, and now this. Feeling the after-effects of being crushed by a rhinoceros, a daily employment hazard of zoology interns, he set the insulated carrier down in despair.

"Er, d-did you g-get lots of s-sun today? Y-You look like you d-did."

Lanky long Beatense looked upon her bony shoulder in hate. "Some, yes. I'm a strong supporter of full public nudity. One benefit, us beachies attract sex easily."

From outward appearances nothing was wrong. He laughed as he took the tens, and thanked Virginia when she held up her hand, refusing the change.

He unzipped the carrier and pulled out the box with a hearty smile.

"Well, see you later. Eat enjoyfully! Er, bye, ev-everyone."

No reply from her. He retreated in black defeat. *What happened?*

The other two stood open mouthed, glaring.

"What? I told you all day that I'm justifiably mad at him!"

"See if you can get your room back," said Virginia. "There's the phone."

Beatense panicked. "You… You mean you're kicking me out?"

She leaped up to run out after Buck, but as he drove off she sagged against the door. Then she bolted out and chased after the Burroughs. Her roommates took off after her. The bare girl ran track star fast but not fast enough. Several neighbors walking by stopped to look at this girl standing alone, her face bereft. Her friends joined her, one of them adding to the other's swarm of sun.

"I tried, you guys! He didn't see me! He doesn't have a rearview mirror!"

"You seem to keep a running count of those," said Virginia. "Come on."

They returned and went in and sat at the greasy box. That typical smell filled the cabin, but following her debacle Beatense didn't feel like eating that very pizza that caused all the trouble. Also she wanted to save her appetite in case Craig ever did come to take her out, as unlikely as that was. She lifted out a wedge.

"Before I eat this, I want you guys to know I want to apologize to Buck."

"You have your chance," said Lorraine, turning. "He just came back."

There came the sound of an approaching car stopping. Beatense hopped over, and saw instead her missing trade show friend. "Craig!" The fellow tiredly got out of his car. "I thought you wised up and left town!" Roommates watching, the child-like nude sprang out to him on her spindly, long rusty brown legs. "What happened?"

"Your... Your old room was already taken, Beatense, just as I went in. But I got back in where I stayed last night, the Skiff down in Naomsnon."

"What? But... Well, come on in, first. These are my new roommates!"

Introductions were made. Lorraine was overawed. He was no partying student, but a professional who was established and succeeding. On the other hand Virginia wasn't about to concede interest quite so easily, but did smile in welcome.

They went in and sat down to the pizza set out on the coffee table.

"Eat it up, Craig," said Virginia. "We ordered a sixteen inch monster."

"Thanks, but I was hoping to take young Beatense to the Tropic Grille uptown. That is if the lady agrees to change out of that particular spectacular lenticular."

"What vernacular. You just tell me where you were all this time, you cad!"

"I said, Naomsnon. Stupid name. It took me two hours to get down there and back. I'm sorry. But Beatense, I got you a refund, your room being taken."

"Great! Thanks! And that explains it. Let's eat pizza, Craig. Sorry about my nudity. It's full time! So try and get used to it. My roommates did!"

"I thought you were bad enough topless. But... I'm o-o-open minded."

Beatense ate two slices and fell back, stuffed.

"What, that's all?" said Lorraine. "But look here, Beatense, we better come to an understanding. I can't have you just sitting around naked here!"

28

DANCING BINGE

My dress code will stay out of this discussion," Beatense said. "I mean, like Shean walked in here naked too but you didn't say anything to him."

The child was twitching and wriggling as she said this, and Lorraine thought that her incredible body trapped her into behavior she otherwise wouldn't have. And the trouble was, the way she happily paraded herself, she incited others. Was there not more to life than the act? Would all this catch up to her someday? Never.

Privately Craig had similar thoughts. Whatever her state of dress her beautiful tan was a violent imposition. It assaulted the eye and refused to be ignored. It dominated one's mind relentlessly. A girl that tan was a wild menace, forcing all kinds of injurious reactions in people, because of the self dedication required to get that way.

She was actually just as tan back on the Queen Of Steel, but then she carried a regal dignity that reassured people. Now she was an unrepentant slut. He saw the videos, that hostel and sailboat one, the dancing lessons and others.

Beatense continued. "So anyway, back home girls have to be very careful about staying in line. I did not, but I was an accepted exception. I laid out in the sun nude and let everybody know I fucked. I ended up making tens of thousands of dollars, because even though they couldn't live in freedom themselves, with my explicitly hot books they could artistically see what it was like. Well, the money disappeared in a bank run today, but my goal since I was twelve was getting the word out, if you have the right body to just unleash yourself no matter how damaging it can be to people."

Craig thought of the tan rabid teen-age kids back in his hometown, where the health clubs had special rooms for the younger bodybuilders. It was all part of an insidious campaign to give every advantage to the sensual, while leaving those less endowed behind. Beatense all too obviously was a believer in this.

"Well keep in mind, Beatense, there's a social contract where we do have limits," said Lorraine. "There's a fabric of personal control that keeps families and society overall functioning and progressing. You can't buck this forever even if just now you seem to be getting away with it. I admit, I have the perspective of not being a player, but yes, I and most people are on the right track in the long run."

"The long run is getting old," said Beatense, "which I will not do, as evident."

"Yeah, Lorraine, personal control, be considerate, nyaa nyaa nyaa," Virginia said, vibrating herself "But are we up to checking out a club or two on Barnet? Beatense, we can put those dancing moves Courtlyn taught us to good social contract use."

"I did learn a few tricks, but I was doing most of that starting back at camp."

"So I understand," Craig said, sweating. "Virginia, are there bars nearby?"

"Dozens. Bum For Sun is a dive right on the Highway and it has this patio deck overlooking the beach. I would recommend that for starters."

"Yeah at thirteen," said Beatense, "I learned a lot. Everyone helped me along."

"It worked out for you,: said Lorraine. "But Beatense, getting anything on?"

"Lorraine, I don't want an argument. I'm going like this. I did it before."

"I think looking at your wardrobe might be a good idea," urged Craig.

"Some wardrobe. Virginia, what are you doing? I insist on going naked!"

Virginia opened her closet and held out a little frock made of T-shirt knit, cut so short it was indeed a long T-shirt. It had nipped short sleeves, and a wide, open neck cut that looped deeply down for that *This Cannot Be* look.

"My Student Teacher, it's called. I wore this to class just after spring break, much to the disapproval of my chattering feminist sisters. But my belief is, just shit the so called traditional values with everything you have. Interested, kid?"

"Thanks, but I got me a dress worse than that, this Grape Stomper. I got it at the Strings N Things. And I do have my bargain bin gel jobbies for shoes."

"No, these big, clunky black ones." Virginia held them up. "Maid's Day Off, is what they're called. The heels are wedge cut for an unsteady walk."

"We have the same things in Arrolynn! But not with that kind of heel."

"Do you need help changing?" said Lorraine brightly.

For some reason women who weren't hot animals took to Beatense. Trinket, Ida, Chubbo, Molly and now Lorraine. The girl nodded her toward the bathroom.

Buck made it back to Pasta-Rama despite his headache and bile filled gut.

Did he misjudge the situation, thinking that he and Beatense were special friends? Did she not greet him happily last night, and did she not follow him out to his car? Maybe that's when the axe fell. The back seat was piled up full with test equipment, old handbooks and numbing semi-conductor catalogs. Plus he had an old CPU, an oscilloscope and his tool box. Junk that lively girls hated. And that missing rearview mirror didn't help. His old Burroughs was a clunker.

So what happened? How could it fall apart so deadly fast? Should he let a few days go by and hopefully rebuild their friendship? Good idea, except with her being here on vacation time was short. Right now she didn't seem to have any boyfriend at all, but if she did she would be far less interested in any stupid friendship with him. If only she didn't get so tan, it was like waving a red flag. She was far beyond being merely desirable. And yet she seemed to like him!

Buck went up to the counter. "Hi, Monica, anything else?"

"Yeah, Buck, one for the Hideaway and one on Chalcedney."

No! Not that! He didn't want to go near the motel. Instead of being filled with joyous, laughing memories, now it was a black hole of horrid, ghastly pain. He drove there as if he was on his way to his execution. Actually, death would be preferable.

He knocked on the door, three over from Beatense's old room, not the same one, thanks to the gods, and he handed the belligerent frat boy the box.

It didn't help for him to see wild Karen with her rat's nest of tumbled blond hair, like Beatense's, lying ready on the bed. She was always turning up. Buck grinned at the cheap tip as the door closed in his face. Always that.

He casually sauntered down to Mr. Cheevy's office. He was just going to say hi. Nothing wrong with that. And if he wasn't in, why, could he help that? The door was left open. Mr. Cheevy didn't care for air conditioning. Buck went in and paused, panting, and reached over the counter for the card file. With hands shaking he flipped through the cards. *Please, don't be in the compu... Ahh!*

NAME Colwell, Beatense Ann EMPLOYMENT Student, and surveyor ADDRESS 906 Sarnia Street Apt 6C, Arrolynn 11, Clar. PHONE (27) Dul-8829 PURPOSE of VISIT Get *shittin* tan and fuck!

Buck put the tin box back and he wobbled back to his car shaking. He lowered himself to reptilian depths, and for what? He learned a few things that he could have picked up by just knowing her better. Actually he learned more than he cared to, but he did know of her legs-open play. And what if Mr. Cheevy caught him?

Buck, what are you doing? You pervert! I'm calling the police! I'm telling her all about this! She'll be very angry! The police! The police!

Ann. He never would guess that as her middle name. Such a basic, unadorned grouping of letters, that of a studious young lady in a drab, buttoned sweater, standing on the corner on some chilly fall evening with arms intently crossed, awaiting a bus. But in a way its work-first, levelheaded simplicity said more about that tan rabid nut than even she knew. Not that it mattered now. *Shittin tan. And fuck.*

Probably every hot girl said that, Buck chuckled desolately. Then acted.

Lorraine marveled at how unguardedly her attraction to their new roommate was accepted by her. She even held the door and waved her into the bathroom. The tan child, with her wispy, see-thru dress hung on her shoulder, openly admired herself in the mirror. Undeniably she was beautiful: Bone and blood.

The light over the medicine cabinet was on, she looked very brown. This mirror was far smaller than her dressing table one at the motel, but the room's shiny white paint made her dark skin smoke with seared intensity. She was like a car that was in the hot sun all day, then radiated its heat into early evening. As she gazed at herself her friend reverently floated the skimpy, leg baring little shift upon her.

Her slim waist drew the gauze closely in, and the risky cut of the dress gave her exposed front a sensual sophistication. It just held to the shoulders, and her gaunt collarbones were those of an initiate wasting away from learning all about her body. The wide, deep cut just grazed upon the girl's apple breasts, but they were separated enough to just give her nips safe coverage. But either profile view was a terror.

Beatense felt her heart pound, and she gazed into her idolizing friend's eyes, the young bride seeking reassurance from her mother. Her large, probing dark eyes were troubled. The girls grabbed and kissed for long minutes.

"You're the only one who understands me," Beatense said, panting.

"N-No, w-we all understand you. You thrive on being just so beautiful."

Later the thriver sat twitching within her scanty outfit, while Virginia was all slut in her Student Teacher. Both animals were bursting with bone and bake.

Lorraine came out of the bathroom in her polo shirt and chino pants. Craig smiled politely but quickly stared at the other two again.

"Well, sh-should w-we head out now, girls? We can take my rental."

"Cool. We usually walk down," said Virginia. "What did they give you?"

They piled into Craig's rented Eclaire Custom, an econo box. They voted to go cruising first, it was too early for the bars, and they took the busy Coastal Highway all the way down through Turtle Rock, Tucumzozo and Le Tournepier.

The bars were packed; Craig had to park two blocks away. As the party came to the notorious Bum For Sun, the pounding music from within gave even Beatense the flip-flops, despite her hitting the oil camp club at thirteen, and her Sails West jaunt.

With her lankily curved poise, she had the wobbly, knees-bent strides of a trim young career girl proudly on the job, She felt excited about the dancing coming up. Just so they allowed nudity, not that she needed it to tempt Craig.

"Hey, Marty," Virginia said to the bouncer. "Any kind of crowd tonight?"

"Hey, hi, V-Virginia, Lorraine. Not bad. Them two with you? I need ID."

"What's ID?" Beatense demanded. She noticed the fellow's stare.

"Y-Your drivers license. Or passport. Is... Is th-that tan real?"

"With the week I put into it, yes. But I don't have my license with me!"

"I can't let you in, then. Sorry."

"She's the Book Girl," said Lorraine, proudly.

This would make history here. "I... I can let you in. But keep that on."

They went into the darkened bar area. "Hey, neat place!" said Beatense.

Except for the loud music, Bum For Sun wasn't neat at all. The sticky floor had a collection of tottery old tables and cheap vinyl padded chairs, all grubby. But the bar welcomed all comers, so along with the crowd of students, beachers and weekend tourists, there were even actual job holders present. With this casual clientele Craig was noticed right away in his sport coat, but it was Beatense's and Virginia's breezy dresses that got the attention. Craig grandly offered his friends the shaky chairs, and Beatense sat down and nodded to the bass beat. All eyes turned upon her.

Her tan looked black, yes, her being the Book Girl.

"Craig!" She had to yell. "He said to keep my dress on! That means..."

"Yes, it means they strip here! But cool your jets, at least for now!"

"I did spend a lot on this dress! Hey, I know them guys! Hi, Ted! John!"

The four Evaders smiled in surprise, overjoyed that this famous girl who let them take her one by one, publically recognized them. It seemed that she was crucially far darker than they recalled, even considering the dim, smoky lighting. Her baked front was well bared, as the dress fit to her slim starved self. The guys would have joined her, but she was With. They waved and the kid waved back, clinking her bracelets.

"I bet this dive isn't quite your style, hah, Craig?" Virginia shouted, laughing as the sales rep loosened his tie. "We can do better on Barnet if you want."

"No, this place brings back old memories! What will you all have!?"

Beatense thought of that Hoganforth Lodge party. "Beer!" she said.

Craig went to the bar and got a foam sliding pitcher of bock beer.

The DJ started up another thunderous song, and his cocky remarks gave anyone blind the impression that the floor was packed. But shortly more disco animals stepped through the tables to the floor. Beatense curiously watched as the girls, many nude and magnificent tan athletes, began writhing and shaking.

"That's so beautiful, isn't it?! But hey, Virginia! Let me get us some cigs!"

Carefully studied, Beatense wobbled on her tippy heels and skinny stretchy legs over to the cigaret machine, counting her change. She put in the quarters, with wrist cocked, so that her bangles hung just so. "Four bucks! That's pure extortion!"

She returned to the table and got a dollar more from Virginia. She wanted coins but Virginia explained that paper worked too, it could roll right into the machine.

She ended up going over with the girl, and the room temperature went up ten degrees. Beatense watched the dollar go in and slide back out and go in again and slide back out as Virginia manipulated it. Finally it took.

"Like we're a couple of counterfeiters," Beatense complained.

The girls tripped back to the table and lit up their Roycetons, and Craig set the glasses in a line and filled them from the pitcher. Beatense chugged her glass down, and dribbled what was left between her breasts. Staring, Craig refilled her glass.

Anyone waiting for the girl to dance had to keep waiting. She had the dumb habit of smoking those miserable cigarets and yakking with gestures and pouring herself more beer. Craig was hoping the whole evening would go like this.

He saw the smiling, thin beach girls dancing nude, and he surmised that this was how the species was perpetuated, by driving their watchers quietly mad, so that they vent their needs with anyone available, anyone. Even their wives.

Craig overheard Lorraine say, "It's almost a form of crime!"

"What's a form of crime?!"

"That dancing of theirs! They're practically turning themselves inside out!"

"It's just their pre-celebrating a long active night!" said Virginia.

Beatense felt her split throb in need. She learned as Puppet what dancing could do, both to herself and those watching. But Virginia suggested they go on to Barnet, and they got up and left. The four boaters looked at each other and followed.

Beatense still wore her dress as they traipsed the sidewalk, but since it could be lightly twisted into the thickness of a garden hose, it was extremely sheer. A good investment. They entered the Plastique Palm.

The Plastique was a tonier place, in that nudity prevailed because the clientele here had a college level appreciation of ethereal aesthetics. Craig saw hot browned aristocrats of impeccable quality dancing, talking together and sitting at the tall tables, all naked. There were even a few teen-age nudes. One bone thin maiden was all oily bared and sparkled with glitter. It turned out she was one of the waitresses, the fast Krinkles. Krinkles! She greeted Craig and took his sweating order for four whiskies. Beatense was delighted; she hopped up and kissed her friend, to applause.

Then she pulled Craig off his stool and led him over to the dance floor, and room was quickly made. The girl began working herself in the sultry moves she learned at camp, with Courtlyn's spinal enhancements tossed in. Her nearly nonexistent dress was just as enticing as if she was nude. With witnesses and the booming music and laser lights coming from all directions, and with her 8 x 4 inch waist and opened front, her wild moves came to her instinctively, and she radiated a wide smiling but bestial display of wanting a very, very educational night.

Watching her need for wholesome academic achievement, Virginia tossed aside her Student Teacher and grabbed Calder, and as they danced the girls tried to outdo each other. But sadly for Virginia and the others on the floor, Beatense's waist was extremely flexible, and her snapping, swiveling and tipping hips acted like they were possessed. Dress torn off, splashed with sweat, she wormed and squirmed in sexual abandon, under the beam of an aimed spotlight. The girls turned their efforts toward each other. As ignored, the embarrassed guys stepped away as the girls unleashed their energy in a blood riot of lesbian seduction. The other nudes joined the two in a breakdown of all that is right and good. The set, where the songs flowed from one to another in ever increasing power, finally ended, and the proud girls hopped back to their not fully welcoming friends. Split open, Virginia sat with the four boating guys.

"Sorry, Craig!" said Beatense over the noise "I'm glad you're still here!"

"I couldn't let this whiskey go to waste!" Craig replied with a slight edge.

Talking with her friends, Virginia began twitching uncontrollably, and she grabbed Calder and danced with him again. Dale diplomatically asked Lorraine to dance, and Beatense gave a wink of thanks. Spotlight on her, she and Craig went again.

She danced more sedately this time, but even though she managed to calm her hips down, her full, surf bleached hair and thin limbs still had a hypnotic effect. The guys who didn't have to pretend indifference stared rigidly, and began to get drunk.

Virginia stole the show; it was like she was made of clinically insane rubber. Here was her chance to warm up a bed, any bed. Her next dance was with John, and Beatense took on Ted. Craig danced with Lorraine, whom he was starting to think of as preferable. Beatense of famed, gifted face was a carnivore. Working to overheat the many cameras, with legs set just so she ravaged all morals with torrid flexings.

"So I'm thinking of continuing in accounting, Craig, but it's so corporate!" said Lorraine, shouting over the music as she danced, while watching Beatense.

"I'm corporate myself, I guess, but where I am it's basically paternalistic!"

"What does that mean, anyway!?" --/-- "I'll tell you what it means! They'll check over my room charges to make sure I was unaccompanied, and so the guys usually sneak their friends in at the motel's back parking lot door!"

"I guess I'm not in favor of either one, but they watch you that close!?"

"And then on the train here's this prim and proper young maiden with a nice tan, but now look at her. I thought she had this proud reserve, but not quite."

"Oh, give her a break! She loves sex but especially loves attracting it!"

Writhing, Beatense danced with Craig again. She explained her getting sex with the four guys. "Yes, you saw that video, but that's just it! It's all for my new book!"

Craig nodded curtly. "Speaking of, you say lost all your money in a bank run?"

"Oh, yes, but I didn't need it. Look at my life! What do I need money for?"

Virginia danced with the boaters in rotation, then all four together. Finally saying her goodbyes she left with them, leaving her dress. Lorraine was grateful she wasn't going to bring them home; just one friend was terrible. Virginia was a devoted friend, but she just would not show consideration. She threw herself and screamed.

Beatense stutter-stepped her long, bared legs in a swarm of bizarre moves. She wasn't alone. Thrilled with their thin builds and wild tans, the other beach girls were shimmying themselves in rapture heat, a scene of loose abandon. The brown Karen whip-flung her slimmed waist in weaving ripples. Eyes half closed, mouth pouty, she raised her clasped hands and tipped back her intelligent head in panting ecstasy.

Krinkles joined in, and fell into a primitive jungle rhythm, dangling crookedly and leaning back sideways as she counter-twisted her slat shoulders to her pelvic action like a bicycle handlebars. It was a very lanky and disjointed enacting; her limbs had minds of their own. Oddly, Craig accepted her moves but not Beatense's.

Another young lady might have been a physicist, and from the skeptical set of her irreverent blue eyes she seemed above all this. But she spent the day in coldly calculated sun worship, a surprise for her friends, and she was volcanically alive with browned burn. She wore cute butted, leggy tight jeans riven with thready holes, and seemingly to the "Go for it!" urging of her friends, a back baring hanky halter of mesh gold, tied with strings about her neck and across her baked back.

With a bemused but engaged look she danced her need for a regrettable night, which would of course advance her scientific inquiries. This was a perfect excuse, it turned a cheap fling into explorative research. The misguided scholar was working toward widening her horizons, in search of cosmic awe. Five cameras saw it all.

Craig danced with Lorraine again, and Beatense took on her old bus driver, the banana-oil-shined Kathy. The kids were delighted at their reunion. Beatense moved ever faster in celebration, hot lashing her limber self as her slim hips dangled loosely from her snaking waist. The books, the videos didn't compare. Unaware of those watching, the cameras, she was in her own world, because the songs were merged together from one to the next with increasing intensity. Craig danced with her again.

After a few more songs the two sat down. Craig signaled for two refills.

The girl downed her drink, happily panting. "Wow, Craig! Am I pumped!"

"Er, uh, should we head out now?" he said. "I... I can drop you off."

"What!? Drop me off!? Nice try! We can drop Lorraine off!"

Lorraine said she could walk back; carrying Virginia's dress she left with her Hill friends. Cameras watching, Beatense left with Craig with her dress hung over her shoulder. The girl of sweat shined tan twitched all the way down to the Skiff Motel.

They entered the room, up along the balcony overlooking the parking lot.

"Before we go to sleep, Beatense, I think we should watch the news."

"Sleep? News? Are you crazy? You can't put me off that easy!"

Beatense was like five pythons. Craig struggled with the fighting kid. And a kid she was, a mere child struggling in fear, her pretty wee muscles working against his.

29

MALL TRIP

Wake up, honey. It's morning."

Yes, honey. But he had grave doubts about her, she had taken to his loving with frightened innocence, just so darn small, unable to bear the ecstasy.

"Mmmmphh? Wh-What?" Her voice was husky. "Oh, sex. Not… Again!"

"No, it's six-thirty. W-We have to get going before they see you here."

She sat groggily up, cross-legged with ingénue's split opened. And now he could get another look at that waist, that had worked in such wailing turmoil.

"Before they see me here! Craig, you snuck me in, but that's only because neither one of us wanted to waste the time going to the office last night!"

"I understand that, but the problem is, if I have an overnight friend listed on the charges here, I would be nailed at work."

Her mouth fell open. "But they know about me! You said you told them that you stayed with me Friday night!" Her rich tan shined from the infusions. "You told them that so they wouldn't think that we had a tiff! And this is on your own tab anyway!"

"It-It is on my tab, Beatense, heh heh, b-but they'll be reimbursing me."

"But that show was over yesterday afternoon! You're on your own now! So give me use your phone. I have to call my Pop. Then we can *sneak* out."

She dialed home. "Hey, Pop, hi, me. What about this bank run?" **--/--** "I tried gatting in line but they rans outta money!" **--/--** "Well darn, but thanks for trying. The trouble is I have to wait on the advance for my new book." **--/--** "Meredith did tuck away 100,000 into a security account for you." **--/--** "Sign it all over to charity, Pop."

She folded the phone and gave it back, shrugging at her misfortune.

"Thanks. Obviously since you're sneaking me out of here I couldn't use the room phone. By the way, you were super last night. Just what I was always looking for but not quite getting. I think I lost weight. I'm almost hungry."

"It was all you. We can stop somewhere. But, going like that? Let's run for it."

"Craig, I'm a mess. I have to take a shower. And look, I do want to show on the charges. Even this fleabag has a right to know who's on the premises."

He had standards, He didn't want to go down to the wise-guy clerk and cheesily admit to his guest party, especially if the nude party joined him in the office with hair disheveled, radiating that sex enlivened tan and bonier loss of weight.

"Well, this is the spot I'm in. This morning I have to see this one contact from the show, and that being business related I have to submit last night's charges."

"You're going to go see someone? Now? How long will that take?"

"Maybe just an hour." He was in a minefield. "I n-need your... Help."

"But they'll know you had a girl in here! This bed looks like a war zone!"

"Good point. You just hop in the shower, kid, and I'm going to try and steal some clean sheets from the maid's cart."

"You're such an incurable romantic. But what good is that going to do?"

He saw that she was dangerously close to realizing that if he didn't put her on the charges, she would just be a cheap throw-away. Also he had to put a stop to her increasingly suspicious questions.

"Yeah, what am I thinking? An undisturbed bed would look just as suspect. So, let's us two go down to the office. You get in the shower, honey, while I see if I got in any messages. This place does have hi-fi. Maybe that guy called it off."

"It being Sunday, yeah! Join me when you're done with your messages."

Craig turned on his laptop, the first time since last evening. He checked on Today's Beach Girls and was stunned to see Beatense at both bars last night. There were also video clips of Virginia and Krinkles, who was just so trustingly innocent looking, but she danced up a storm. This upset his ideas of what was appropriate for well adjusted young ladies deeply. If she put on a little frock this morning, everyone would say, Oh, what a charming treasure, so sweet, so active.

Craig had almost thirty unread messages, as he checked them they all gave him high fives, even the doughty old vice president of sales. "Next time you go on a trip I come with, my boy! To keep you out of trouble!" Another e-mail, the airline had set him up with an earlier flight if he wanted to take it instead.

"Craig? Come on!"

With reservations he joined her in the shower. "Hey, hun. Guess what?"

"What? Come on, soap me!"

"That guy called off the meeting, that's the good news, but the bad news is I'm set up for an earlier flight, at ten. But the more good news is, at work they know about you and I got all these congratulations!"

"I'm the one who should be congratulated. Hey, I can go on the charges!"

"Exactly. Geez, you're beautiful. Here, come on, step out onto the towel."

With both dripping they stepped from the shower and dried off. Craig left a tenner on the table and they stepped out on the balcony. Below, in the parking lot confined by the U-shaped building, yawning travelers were packing their cars.

Beatense, of course, got their attention. She carried her rolled up dress in hand. They took the gritty, pebbly cement steps down to the parking lot and crossed to the office. Beatense shook back her volumes of drying hair. Cameras everywhere.

"Well, you'll probably show up again in Today's Beach Girls," said Craig.

The guy in the office, as soon as he saw who they had as a guest last night, tore up the tab. He too took a photo, and Craig saw the USB cable. Great.

"Gee, thanks for giving us that break!" said Beatense. "Nice place here!"

Once they were heading north in Craig's Eclaire Custom Beatense asked for his phone, and with feet crudely propped on the dash she re-called her father.

"Well, it's nice thinking of yer old Pop, wastings my time with another call!"

"Pop, listen to me, I changed my mind, keep fifty for yourself. Okay, bye!"

Tears stung his eyes, but he said, "Wait, I gots some news for you, darter! The railroad people called to say they found this big sinkhole doing track repair, gotta build a trestle. They thinks you'll be gittin yerself another week, at least!"

"I saw that track work! But look, call Mr. Morley about me doing another record!"

"I got Flora in yer badroom, darter! We got too much going for all that!"

She closed the phone. "That son of a gun! Wow! Hey, I have to run yet!"

"How… How many irons in the fire do you have?"

"My latest book and music, for all the good they're doing. I lost a quarter million in that bank run. I wish I was set up for pay for play with my videos."

"Er, yes. Should we stop for a bite? But we better use the drive-thru."

"No, you got that flight. And I'm never hungry." --/-- "I noticed."

"This new book, I should have stipulated no sex. The other pictures of me beach and street naked are valuable for teaching perfection, but all that sex is overdoing it."

Craig agreed. A bus ran beside them and the passengers looked down and saw her. The girl felt chargrined to be seen bare in this cheap econo car. If she was in the big Espriado she would have loved it. She rubbed her jutting hip, wondering how her skin stretched over it without hurting. She saw that in daylight her tan was still very dark brown, with a fresh, recent-sex glow of crushed gold. The tensions of her sunk starved belly made it look sore, and after the last night it was sore.

Looking up she saw Kit's apartment building. Le Tournepier.

"You know, Tamdyn who owns the Breeze Hotel offered me a job, the exact nature of which I don't know. Because she said she could use me as a singer, except I'm not familiar with the music down here. I could never sing that stuff they were playing last night, even with 36 thousand as the incentive."

"That's just short of what I make! But yeah, they could have you do torchy old romance songs. Most hotels are full of golden-agers, you know."

"Not this one. They were fucking right on the pool deck, even kids, and Tamdyn the the owner goes naked all over. But I guess we love each other, hah."

He swerved, someone honked. "Are... Are you serious?" *Hopefully not.*

"I'm very serious." She truly meant that, but with stipulations. She had that meeting with Kit... Horrors! She had to get rid of this guy! "When is that flight going home? We better scoot! But wait, what about sailing with Bondy?"

She added that just to increase Craig's sense of urgency.

"I can't do that even with my original flight time! Yeah, I better move it. The trouble is I'm not real good at what I do, and I have to work extra off the clock just to stay in stride. I-I'm not a big success, Beatense."

She took his hand. "Do whatever works, Craig. But for next weekend, can you get a better car? This isn't even up to Johnny Lucke's standards!"

Laughing, they entered Emeraldeye; Beatense was in home turf. She slouched down so she could admire her twin softballs and taut black belly.

"Wait a minute, next weekend? You want me back?" **--/--** "Like, I did get myself one more week. You really have to try that sailing. Boat sailing, I mean!"

They turned up Ringdon and drove through the woded settlement. They entered the cabin hand in hand, beaming foolishly, being such lovers, and saw Lorraine..

"Craig, hi! And Beatense, you're back! You're back!"

"Hi, Lorraine. Sorry to bug out on you last night. Is Virginia back yet?"

"In the bathroom. I think she lost five pounds, and she has that pool to catch up with. But anyway, I was delighted to have the place to myself last night."

"Well, as worn out as I am I have to go for a run, Lore the Bore. Where are my shoes? Did I leave them back at the motel?"

Virginia came out of the bathroom. "Hey, hi. Your shoes? Under the bed."

Craig was confronted with two browned nudes. He had to get out of there.

"Look, I better catch my flight. They moved it up."

"Have some coffee, Craig," said Lorraine. "We have the good stuff, private blend for Hendrick's. Virginia, get out some of that dry bread for toast."

Beatense was tying on her shoes. "Okay, you guys. You eat, I run."

She and Craig hugged and kissed good-bye and she was out the door.

Sunday morning. The musty old hut was filled with the smells and sounds of the coffee pot gurgling on the iron grate stove. Misted by the leafy boughs, the early sun streamed in through the windows, through which came a distant, muffled roar of surf. Craig sat down with the girls for coffee and cream, and boxed donuts.

"Don't read the label," said Virginia, with tan simmering. "Sixty ingredients."

"This is good coffee. You almost match it, Virginia."

"I always tanned easy. But anyway, Lorraine, let's us push the three beds together so we can sleep like lesbians should. Craig, how did the kid do?"

"I'm kind of wondering how I did. She encouraged me along beautifully."

Beatense ran toward the noise of the surf, otherwise she would have gotten lost. She managed to astonish a dozen or so Hill residents even though they all were familiar with Absinthe's casual habits. She came to the sand path heading down to the Holiday Hill beach when she saw her mistake. She should have run toward Ringdon instead, so she would be on actual pavement. She gamely ran down the sand path, turning from one ramp to the other and came to the beach.

She ran by the sandy mounds and then cut across Main's expanse to get to the Beach Walk. The sand made the running difficult, and she fought to run as lightly as possible for the payment-hopeful cameras watching her progress. Finally she got onto the Walk and she whipped up to a full sprint, dashing by everyone naked.

Sleepy tourists were emerging from their lodgings, but the Walk was mostly busy with the usual athletes. The airplane banners were already in tow. Hot day ahead.

Beatense was a familiar fixture; the locals took pride in letting her run by without disturbing her with stares, whoops and cheers. The girl ran the Breeze frontage and flitted on to Hoganforth. There she turned onto Smoot and got back to the Highway, and headed north back toward Holiday Hill. She wanted a short run so she could hit the sun early and also possibly catch Craig before he left.

But he was already ready to go. "Gotta run, you guys. Thanks for the acid etch. Be back next week. Nice talking to you last night, Lorraine." --/-- "Same, dude."

Craig turned north out from Ringdon as Beatense approached it. He waved but she didn't see. The kid found that Ringdon was a tough go. She burst into the cabin, and Lorraine gasped. Heat waves radiated from the tan, sweaty athlete. And being beautiful, it seemed unfair that all that was invested in one person.

"Craig's car is gone! Did he go already? Well then, the sun now."

"Me, work," said Lorraine. "At the Mad Com College."

"And I got that catch-up pool to do," said Virginia. "But I'll get sun too."

The girl looked in her mirror. "Hey, I'm getting pretty blond!"

"True, but what are all these skateboard magazines here?" Lorraine said.

"Ned lent them to me, Jesse's brother. If I read them I'll be reasonably ready for my interview at that Cemented skate park place."

"Are you awful sure you want to work there?" said Lorraine. "Those rattlesnakes beat up anyone who strays in there, tourist kids especially. It can be brutal."

"Oh, speaking of brutal," said Virginia, "At the pool I'm calling around to get us a party tonight. It'll be a buy-in, five bucks each. You okay with that, Beatense?"

"Yeah! If I can be naked. But Virginia, about this party, can you try calling Buck for it? The poor guy, I still owe him an apology."

"That's decent of you. He's not worth it but I can call him."

There was a sound of approaching hooves, that stopped. The girls turned as an ebony tan boy stepped in the door just far enough to give the wide eyed pony he led by the reins a peek inside. Ever the free spirit, Jesse was wearing a bevy of bracelets, and a string of white incisors. His long, reddish tinged black hair fell in pretty loops over his shoulders. He hit the girls with the impact of a cement mixer.

"Hi, bitches! With nudity legal now look what I'm not wearing!"

"Yes, but that's as far as that mule is coming in here," said Virginia. She stepped over and made a half reach for the broom. "Hey, Win. Donut?"

Beatense sprang over and petted him, and she also gave him a donut.

"Hey, old Windfire, I'm finally meeting you! But Jesse, you cripple, I got to know about this skateboard thing. When is that interview?"

"Oh, any time. I can come by to pick you up."

"The hell." She continued to pet Windfire. "I'll be baking down on Main."

"Well, you better get right down there. Shean is orunning over to the mall for new inflatable lifejackets, and he's coming by to pick you up, so you better run!"

"It's open on Sunday? But yeah, I better scat anyway. It's getting late."

The tan boy stumbled forward as his horse gave him his nose.

"Win, quit shoving me! You got slobber all over my back!"

Lorraine jumped for the damp dish towel. "Hold still." She rubbed Jesse's crispy back, shaking, then eyed his belly. "Don't those tensed-up abs ever feel sore?"

"Mine do," said Beatense. "For various reasons."

"For the interview," said Jesse, "plan to be back from the mall by ten."

"Ten! The day will be half shot by then! Where's my bed sheet?"

Jesse pushed Windfire out by his nose and sprang up and on, and the kid tanner shot off at a gallop before he was seated. Lorraine wistfully watched him go.

Shean pulled up minutes later in the flashy big Esp. The lad came in the cabin in just his old four-inch jean cut-offs, but he did have a blue and green striped polo shirt hung over his bony browned shoulder. With bracelets, gold neck chain and long fall of blond curls, the boy was almost as day-wrecking dark as Jesse.

He was the soul and breath of summer. Humanity as it was meant to be.

Beatense stared, open mouthed. "I… I'll be right w-with you, Shean."

Her mind changed, the girl hopped over to her dresser with hair aflutter. She put on her shorts, an equally a narrow band, and found her rubber shoes.

"Okay, guys, I guess I'm shaking."

"You're… You're going to the mall like that?" said Lorraine.

"Why not? I can't be beachy all the time! Lorraine, I wonder about you."

"You, er, might carry along a shirt," said Shean, wide-eyed. "A T-shirt."

She got her peach colored tank top out and with a switchblade no one knew she had, she hacked it off to a ten inch hang. She then she saw her Aunt Clara shocker with its three inch webbing and put that on. Ned was in back of the fancy car.

He didn't react to her; many of the young women and girls of Bolingbroke Trail lived as sun obsessed nudes. As tender as the boy was, wearing a T-shirt and cuffed jean cut-offs, he looked like a beautiful child prince in his coach.

"Hi, Ned," said Beatense, getting in. "So how come *you're* coming along?"

"To get door hinges for the fort!" the boy said, as if this was plainly obvious. "And we better hurry because the other guys are starting to build it already!"

"No prob there," said Shean. "I got work. What are your plans, Beatense?"

"Main baking, so tromp it. Oh, thanks for lending me the magazines, Ned."

"You're not welcome," the reportedly troubled boy replied grudgingly.

"What are you making this trip for, Shean? And isn't there a hardware store right down on Barnet Street? I mean for Ned's hinges."

"It's on Brand Avenue, but pretty close guess. But I want to look into those fancy inflatable lifejackets. The ones we got were too bulky to take along."

"Yeah, Beatense!" said Ned, and the girl thought, *I see what they mean.*

They left for the vast Black Canyon Mall up in Cardiff. This was Beatense's first venture northward since getting to town, besides the 10K. As they rode the Coastal Highway through Madeline and then Stony Arbor, she recalled her bus ride a week ago. Back then she was intimidated by this exotic new world of surf and palm trees, and especially by those sidewalk girls. Now she ruled.

Up at the north end of Stony Arbor they tunneled under the singing tires of the expressway. They turned left and followed the stodgy car just ahead of them up the entry ramp as Shean swung his head back and forth in trying to knife into traffic.

Beatense only saw that they were in the shade of the foothills.

"This is the first shade I've seen since coming here, Shean."

"What?! Damn you! Go! Hurry!"

"Me, hurry? You're the one who's driving. Anyway, I said..."

"I heard what you said! Come on, pop! Get a move... Ah, hang on!"

The sedate sedan stopped to await an opening, but Shean wrenched by him.

His brown skin was shined with sweat as he panted from the stress.

"Old people should walk," Beatense said, inspecting her braceleted stick-like arm as the high speed flow adjusted to the Camelback's lordly intrusion.

They stayed on the expressway and so they ran along the back of the hotels facing Cardiff Shores. This spared Beatense the sight of the bared beachgoers frolicking in the sun, the idea of which was deeply frustrating to her just now.

"Come on, Shean, step on it, I said! I want to get out in that sun!"

"You'll be back by ten! Relax! Quit tangling and untangling those legs!"

"Yes, but I want to buy me a chase lounge, but not if it takes all day!"

Shean clenched the wheel and breathed with tension. "Well, here's another little detour, tonight. We were going to the Gulliver's restaurant on the Wharf, and Dad wants you to come. You say no? Okay, fine."

"I didn't say no! But I'll be tied up with Kit today if we ever get back!"

Ned listened to this shouting girl, highly bothered by her noise.

Shean thought she would be impressed by the green sign heralding their turn onto Suspect Boulevard, and by the train of signs heralding the cities of West Swallwood and Bentley Hills. But she only peevishly kept working her thin undeserved thighs, still burned black despite the overnight sun deprivation. Actually she was intrigued, these sights were right out of her magazines, but she felt impatient. They turned into the huge mall parking lot and Beatense eyed the distant glamorous building doubtfully.

Shean slowed down as a woman began nervously backing out of a place.

"Come on, lady!" Beatense urged. "Your cheap-o-matic clunk can go faster than that! Ah, there she finally goes! Quick, Shean! Move it! Find a place closer in!"

"There never are any!" Shean replied, as he parked with bangles jankling.

They got out and ran for the big inviting entryway. Beatense was ravaged by the sizzly, dried baking of Ned's classically slim legs. He was in fact remarkably tan, and under his T-shirt he had exemplary muscles. And he was cute.

And crazed to campaign his own tan in the fabled Bentley Hills, Shean left off his shirt. Once inside the shirtless boy left for the Riggers Boat Works, and Ned and the Clara wearing Beatense wandered off for the Staven's Any And All Store.

As she and the boy hurried along Beatense was amazed by the trendy shops and boutiques that resided in this prestigious fortress. But she also bag carrying tourists untouched by sun, and indifferent in build, and disliked by the clerks. They turned to stare at the reddish blond, black limbed surfer in her sensational outfit.

Then Beatense saw a slender young woman with blond hair and eager blue eyes, proudly strutting along in her T-shirt and jeans. She had that tawny golden skin that quickly responds to sun, and she had that cute look of being important and popular, and of being on her own with a fun job in this tropical realm. She walked along with back flexed, signaling that she was a modern liberated girl who wanted it.

Then a skinny, barefoot young woman in halter top and cut-offs walked by. Her fragile, wide eyes told of the peace she had in being so excitingly brown. Her light, fine, teen-like body was exquisite in its boned muscle detail. She was a determined sun lover, and her stepping child-like legs reflected her mad, mad devotion.

The cameras, hardly believing the Book Girl was present, were torn. Because the other girl's long, sleek thigh muscles moved in supple, coordinated tensions as she paced along, joyously glowing. This Bone and Blood child, the green eyed Absinthe, smiled as if in recognition at Ned, who was whistling a tune.

"Now that is a beautiful girl, Ned, like me. Plus she runs. Remember that."

"I don't have to!" --/-- "And stop that whistling! You're embarrassing me!"

"Well you're embarrassing me!"

A pack of arrogant surf boys in white butt-cuts approached. They were shirtless and luxuriously rays embaked. One lad in particular, who had piles of blond hair and uncannily devoid blue eyes, was a factory of tan, burned royally black. He was gifted with lovely muscles despite his thin build. Poetical. Cameras got him too.

He walked along with the attitude of a god, openly studying his held-out arm and also his belly and chest. His friends reverently allowed this, and he steadily returned the many gulping stares aimed upon him by the shoppers. His skin looked wet oiled, but actually its shine came from its coppery depths. He came here just to show off.

Beatense saw that the old people were devastated by these sightings. She and Ned got to the big Any And All store, that before going bankrupt sold everything from bridal gowns to smelly tires. The store's fluorescents gave both kids a rich heat.

In hardware, Ned looked at the hinges, and the girl handled the tools and loudly disapproved of their prices, and she had to quick grab at the level she tried balancing on her finger. Ned sighed in disgust. Several helpful clerks moved in, drawn by her breasts that kept flitting into view, and her fame.

She argued with them, and warned Ned to be careful, then dropped a six pound pipe wrench with a jarring clatter that cracked the tile. She tried juggling screwdrivers bu they fell also. Ned sighed. They went to the patio shop and after long debate she bought a beach cot that disassembled into a cloth bag. She also found an academic pair of reading glasses so she could imitate Virginia's bratty and brainy look.

The kids started for the Riggers store, but they met the still shirtless Shean at the food court. He was worried to see that Ned was coldly scowling. Shean had a bag from *Bentley Bons,* and they sat at a table by the fish filled aquarium pool.

"Eat up," Shean said, shaking as he opened the bag. "I got work, I said."

"So?" said the fudge baked Beatense, blinking at the huge cinnamon roll that he gave her. Everyone stared, walking slowly. "I'm overdue for a hot lay-out."

"Oh, brother," Ned said with eyes set, as he globbed butter on his pastry.

Shean looked at him closely. He almost seemed half... Content?

And Shean saw that Beatense's eyes were dancing all over Ned. The boy didn't seem to notice, but he had a spark to his look. If he was acting more like usual he would be whining that he didn't like cinnamon rolls; he wanted ice cream, etc etc.

The girl slouched down and ate her roll with gusto. Nearby a tan young lady was wiping off the tables. She saw the kids and smiled. She was lovely in a sturdy, boy faced way, and as if she knew she was beautiful throughout, she beamed with purest joy. She had warm dark eyes and plentiful honey amber tresses, which were tousled back to reveal her conscientious, noble forehead. The cameras turned to her.

Carrying various discard items, the girl walked with swinging strides and a slight backward tilt, which reflected her confidence. And all she did was clean tables! She asked an older couple if they had finished, with a crackly edged voice that had a lack of any inflection, like a little child's. Beatense was dethroned again.

Shean kept pressing for speed even as he turned on the slow Coastal Highway. His shirtless courage at the mall was a nice success, so he wanted to get at that roof job in the hot sun. He would wear his bikini, even if allowed nudity. His tanning skill addicted him to that sport and put him in competition with others with the same bent. That kid in the white shorts back at the mall was life-changing, but Shean felt that he himself could still bake darker. As soon as he got to that roof, he and that brother in sun Knife would roast unmercifully in those gorgeous, shingle reflected rays.

"Damn tourists!" Shean yelled at the car ahead. "Come on, hurry it up!"

Beatense expressed a similar sentiment, then turned to look back at Ned.

"Ned, I hate to say it, but in the store I noticed your butt is too big."

Shean forgot his sun-deprived desperation. He felt like he was punched in the stomach. Gripping the wheel, he hyper-ventilated. Did she forget all their talk about his touchy condition? He sat tensed, dreading the reaction.

But Ned jerked his head up eagerly. "Your butt is too big!"

"And be more polite! Such sloppy manners. Personally, I'm disgusted."

"You're disgusting, all right!"

Shean looked back in the mirror, turning it. Ned's bright eyes sparkled.

"Ned, try and face facts. You're so nutty you make fruitcake look rational."

"You *are* a fruitcake!"

"That statement is baseless. If you want my esteem, make changes now in your calculatory conduct, cooperative collegiality, courtesy and comportment!"

"Oh, yeah! The way you dropped all those tools at the store!"

Shean saw to his relief that Ned was thrilled to make this accusation, but he did wonder about that tool incident.

"Perhaps I did, accidently, but at least I didn't shoplift. Unlike you!"

"Come on, Beatense, I think you can do better than that," Shean said sotto voce, sharing a conspiratorial wink with the girl, who tried to hide her smile.

"Hah, you stole everything! And you argued with that lady at check out!"

His little neck was set in righteous indignation.

"Merely to make sure she didn't overcharge me for my cot!" She looked out her window. "But hey, Ned, look! What's all that blue stuff up there?"

"What blue stuff?" the boy replied sourly, rolling up his eyes.

"Can't you see it? It's all over the place up there!"

"Oh, you mean, like... The *skyyyyy!*?"

"Oh, so that's the sky. Well, I hope it doesn't fall down and hit me on the head."

"Yeah! I hope so too!"

Shean saw that Ned looked very troubled, staring with eyes bulging.

She wasn't through. "Ned, do you have any manifest regrets in your stupid life, besides being... How shall I say it, such a shrimp?"

"Yeah! You! And you're the shrimp!"

The girl looked back at him with questioning disapproval. Shean laughed.

He got Beatense back by a reasonable 10:30, but she was quite insane about all the sun already wasted. Shean followed her as she sprang into the cabin.

"What do you want? I'm not in the mood for chitchat just now! I'm warning you, Shean, I'm not going to be sociable having endured your slow driving!"

"I know you're in a hurry. So am I, work. But how did you know Ned would take your teasing okay? He seemed to half like it." --/-- "One look and I knew."

"He must like you, for some peculiar reason. But look, I got this for you."

"Another cinnamon roll? No thanks. I shudda bought... Whoa!" It was a pink cropped T-shirt, ribbed for a close fit, that bore the legend, *CHOCAHOLIC.* "Wow, thanks! Is that excellent! I assume this is correct for all occasions."

"Try it for Gulliver's tonight. Okay, gotta go. Roofwork, in my boy bikini!"

Shean left. As the piney breezes wafted in with the muffled roar of surf, the girl gathered her things. With heart pounding, she rolled her sheet up inside the cot bag and also added her slop oil, spring water and legalizing Nakee.

She took a deep breath. After all, lying nude right among the tourists would be a drastic step. But she had to advance the right of all hot blooded girls to aggressively tan in flagrant dedication, wherever. On impulse she put on the glasses. She left and started for the beach path through the cursed trees, shocking the neighbors.

Virginia had finished her first pool by 9:30. She had to ride fast to her next stop, which just needed a chlorine check, but then she had to make the calls for the party that night. She needed the swelled up, old directory for the pay phone, which was illogically set on the shady side of the utility shed. With a sadly frustrated gaze at the hot cement she looked up Buck's number, that wasn't in her contacts.

She lay on her towel naked, of course, and made her first call, of five.

"Meg? Oh, Nut. Vagina. Party time, our place. Someone's got to take on these cultural affairs. You can meet our new roo... Yeah, the Book Girl. She's all right. Can you like get the word out? I can't make twenty calls on this battery. Thanks!"

When she finished her next pool, Virginia saw two bared girls come out from the building and they lay right in sight of the other users. Beautiful.

Buck had been sitting at his desk with his *Appliedl Rectifiers* textbook lying open, but he only wrung his hands in helpless despair as he tried to come to grips with how Beatense was so hostile the last evening.

When I made the delivery Friday night she was all over me! So I half think that we're special friends, but then at the cabin last night she blows me off! Why did she turn so hostile? Did she suspect that I love her? How else does she think guys are supposed to react to her? In my case I would dodge traffic to rescue her dropped sunglasses. So why can't she accept my worship? Secure in her position why can't she be half agreeable to this poor, affable boob who happens to adore her?

And yes, I am a boob fool, but I do have this one comfort, I'm out of the running. And to be perfectly honest, it's good this happened now, before my hopes got all built up thinking we were friends. Who was I kidding, anyway?

30

INTERVIEW

The second big flub of his life, Buck left for a walk just before the phone rang, while Beatense was running for the ramp-like sand path. As she jogged through the cabins she saw two bony girls in string bikinis washing their car. Like Dryden Page 2 they were slopped with soapy suds as they happily worked their sponges and hose. Beatense could just make them out; until she looked over her new glasses.

They seemed to recognize her and cheerily waved.

Beatense came to the sand path, caressed by the sea winds. It was still early enough that the sun didn't yet angle in on the path. The shaded sand felt cool to her feet as she hopped down the incline. She felt iffy about her upcoming full exposure, not in College Alley but right in with the tourists. Down on the Holiday beach the surf was light, the sand lay dry. Beatense came out by the sand mounds on Main, and peering again over her glasses, she saw two tanners lying bare, hidden from curious eyes. Beatense almost joined them, but this would offend no one.

Coming out on Main she was a jolt to the shell searchers, but her authoritative baking conferred artistic status, and her nose set glasses gave academic legitimacy. With her myopic persona the nude conveyed a caring insight and understanding; she was above reproach. Wildly sensual despite her advanced collegiate character, she was an untamed student of brown. The deploying Book Girl.

Main was so expansive that its pre-noon visitors were scattered in the shimmery haze. The girl's glasses made everyone indistinct. Over the blurry sands Beatense saw scattered figures in the glare, lugging their things. Except for the light surf it was preternaturally quiet, and as she scampered by the various parties, their voices softly carried, even in remarking about her.

Watching for Kit, the girl angled her way across the wide beach, aiming for the tourist haven between the Alley and the Breeze. She carried her cot bag on her shoulder, and her bangles slid down her thin toasted arm, as her legs marched her along. The drowsy tourists, drowsy no longer, recognizing her, watched her wander into their midst. Finding a spot, she set down her bag.

Everyone stared, this was an unexpected intrusion. One tourist son was a pretty fourteen years, with thick, long blond hair, and a glorious, neighbor killing tan. He seemed sweetly unspoiled, full of love and laughter. A young Keter. He smiled as Beatense struggled with assembling her cot. He wore jean cut-offs that were snugly cuffed to his thighs, and rumply sagged to his hips. Giving him a look the naked girl eyed the sun and set her cot just so, and laid her fluttering sheet upon it. The close proximity of the others annoyed her, but with a deep breath she got out her oil.

"Oh, wow! Hey, Mom, look at that! She's the Book Girl!"

"Boyd, you've seen enough. You find Todd and go swimming."

"I wonder how she strayed over here," said the laughing, gulping father.

Beatense heard other remarks. Her neighbors stared as she sat on the cot and opened her oil. Her live, boy-like muscles felt sore from her lively night, even with all her activity lately. She squirted out her oil and smeared it on.

Young Boyd bent moved in for a smiling closer look. His interest troubled the intruder, but she lay on her front on the cot and, trembling with high excitement, began tanning publically bare in this off-limits area. Breasts pressed out, she began her hot bake right among these people. She knew she was unwelcome, but concluded that she was morally correct. Along with many others the lifeguards came patrolling by to check on the misplaced tanner. With their expertise they could normally catch all the details with quick glances. Not now. She was dark brown, the cameras noticed.

The College Alley dudes lacked that face saving skill of one look only. As word spread they began traipsing over from their distant blankets, scuffing their feet in the sand to establish the required slow pace well in advance. With eyes full upon the rust blacked little nymph, they straggled by her, staring in undisguised horror.

Buck dejectedly strolled the Beachway, while the skating or running girls dodged by, laughing at him. Karen came happily by topless, proudly tossing her yellow hair. She seemed to have a crusade in progress to show off the most shattering tan ever seen on Main, but as Buck gazed across the sands he saw her nemesis lying on a beach lounge, right in the crowd of tourists. He was too far from her to tell for sure, but what she had on for a bikini wasn't quite visible.

Shaking violently, he had to get a look. *Naked? There?*

As the sun soaked in the heat dizzied Beatense. She was extravagantly but very legally displayed. Looking serenely about, but with heart pounding, she saw the mob that encircled her blurred as a mass. The various sounds of the shore carried to her. Her head swam from the heat, but she was alert enough to feel the collective collapse into terror of the nearby dumpy housewives. Obscene, and she actively fucked.

This particular rays devotee was not only charred extra dark upon her sheet, but the sun had smoothed her lustrous tan into sleek tightness. Also the flanking of her lazily curved vertebrae by her taut strung lumbars grooved her spine with an espresso sheathed furrow. Embellishing that stretched flow were her delicate shoulder blades, and her dainty, shaped butt. Her long, intricately slimmed legs also had that graceful flow. Her waist was just eight inches wide, her hips, eleven.

The slopped-on oil sizzled the rays deep into her, shining her wet black. With her bumped butt, sleek waist and widening back her offended auditors stared. She lay in repose, heart pounding. Buck panted as the girl twisted and looked back at herself, and she saw that juncture of tight waist to tight hips. Her coconut lobes and thinned legs were wet with oil, like her back. Despite all the people nearby Buck gaped in a catatonic seizure, his every fiber ripped into raw shreds. *It's her! It's her!*

The reckless young tanner rose to her elbows, poking up her shoulders and idly waving her feet. Truly this was the greatest triumph of her long sunning career.

With her exposure limited only by her chain and oil, she lay prone again.

Boyd came over and fogged her with ice water from his spray bottle. As a thin dedicated seeker of beautiful truth she yelled and shook. Without acknowledging the boy she lay back down, with all the ordinances misguidedly giving this freedom.

Head abuzz, she woke at noon. She drank water, propped upon her elbow to tip back her head. Droplets ran down her reverse arched back. The heat was stiff, she felt groggy and detached from reality, in response to her lens hazy vision and bravely disturbing circumstances. It was in a heart warming way fulfilling.

Beatense flipped over. Her hipbones abruptly jutted as the mob, including the returned Buck, stared upon the black tan child. Her gold bangles jankled on her stick arms as she slopped on more oil. Her peaches wriggled like rubber to her careless caress. She set her heels to display her wholesomely utilized split, but simply, why could she not do this? No one challenged her.

Well, it remained to be seen if the police would respond.

The tourists and few locals saw that she looked black dark in that dancing glare, belaboring her starvation. Her blasted heat was baked sharply in, being surfacy rich yet deep. Her hips stuck out gauntly, and her sunken, rib ledged belly invited playing like a violin. The gold chain lay glinting upon it, wetted by her oil.

Her pinks poked like fingertips. To the sun addled eye she did look black, a result of the glare and her oily shine, but truly she was just a vibrant rich brown. The heat cradled her slim, writhing form as her sweat washed through the oil.

Nudity in College Alley, a dynamite situation but controllable. But within the tourist enclave, where people came from all kinds of backgrounds, the nude girl was pushing too far, and so the rescuer two-way radios started buzzing.

"*Talk to the Book Girl, Mort*," the radios rasped. "*Tell her to get legal.*"

Two lifeguards walked over, full of reluctant dread. They shook.

"Excuse us, miss, hate to b-bother you, but you m-might want to get legal."

With a wicked flash of taut, snaking muscle she rose to a kneeling position. The glasses notwithstanding, she sat dull eyed, the typical hard tanner who bakes in the sun all day, preparing for later struggle. The lifeguards, and the nearby Buck, saw how the black of her long, tensioned thighs reflected the white of her sheet, and how their quadricep muscles were pulled into taut curves. Her glinting belly chain was loosely hung to her eighteen inch waist. But it was her all-business glasses and the bored eyes back of them that subjugated.

The spokesman took a breath. "D-Did y-you hear me? Get decent!"

The second lifeguard courageously spoke. "Y-You see, miss, heh heh, you don't really belong over here. Th-This is the tourist part."

"I ran six miles topless all over town but I can't freely tan on a nude beach?"

One of the tourist husbands came over. He had short, peppery grey hair, a good catch-all description if you have writer's block, and the reddish, lined face of an avid back woods hiker. With his rugged but scholarly mien he had the keenly appraising look of genuine interest. In his mid-fifties, yet nonetheless one could guess he was a cross country skier, and he rode a mountain bike, in the actual mountains.

He had that open minded, and pleasantly eccentric, look of a guy who likes to try gadgets and read up on things. But his composure was unsettled when he saw the girl's face. She had an ethereal, bone carved urgency.

"Er, hello there, boys. I'm Dr. Kip Hiller, and I wonder if there's any way you can forego disturbing this young lady. She takes her sun seriously, like I do restoring my Atwater or downloading jazz. She isn't bothering anyone."

The second rescuer turned to him. "Thank you, sir, but we were just saying this isn't the right part of the beach for getting sun that seriously."

"You two seem to be on the wrong page. The wrong part of the beach here is full of people who came to town just to see the nudity. Not me, of course."

"I happen to be an activist who enjoys extreme sexual orgasms," said Beatense, not real helpfully. "These people have all seen my videos, or bought my books."

"So, it's not a problem then," Dr. Hiller persisted. "And medically speaking, boys, she does help the circulation. Even my *eyesight's* improved, heh heh."

Another lifeguard came chasing over, and he almost tripped over his own feet as he caught sight of Beatense, whose slouchy posture curved her belly in. "G-Got a problem, dudes. We got that Karen riding hard over in the Alley, and I mean she's yelling. It could blow wide open, worse than this!"

The lifeguards warned Beatense to be careful and left. Kip shook his head.

"Well, that's that. And miss, that is one meretricious tan. Name's Kip."

"Hi, er, Kip. I'm Book Girl Beatense." The lawless one shook his hand, as he noted her perfect expression of muscle. "Thanks for standing in for me."

"Not at all. And just a hint, I think you can relax. They won't be back."

"Well, I am legal." The girl thought she saw Buck some ways off. But the glasses made this uncertain. "Can... Can you give me my water there?"

Dr. Hiller handed her the bottle, and poised with little arm raised she drank out of the container, a little act that also drew the eye to her flat belly. She lay back again, and re-set her heels in explicit display. Dr. Hiller left shaking. Even his liberal values had reservations with that explosive wet pink invitation.

There are the free spirits who are so avidly sensual people openly honor them. They emanate, live and breathe untamed sexual skills and thirst. Tanner Beatense knew too well that she had this status. Darcy Publishers picked the right girl.

And so the migration of voyeurs continued. Their throbbing bloodshot eyes tore into her fertile breasts and glinting belly chain. What possessed her to make such a spectacle of herself? *That dark!* One victim got too close, a dirty vague blob. Was it that popcorn eater? The girl propped up on her elbows, an action that sunk her belly further as her small breasts out-shifted, and she used the insightful authority of her glasses to stare him off in sputtering shame. She lay black back again, at peace.

Karen calmed down, the rescuers later returned, to get a well deserved look. At two bare Jesse came trotting up on Windfire, following the meandering path used by the outlaw's admirers. The lingering, catatonic Buck quietly exited. Jesse reined his proud little pony to a halt and flipped off, posed like an acrobat.

"Ta daaa!" the publically stiffened boy sang out. "Wow, I saw you a mile off!"

She rose to her elbows. "Jesse, hi. It's not time for that interview, is it?"

"Yeah, and go like that! Wow! Nude right in tourist Main!"

"Do you have to belabor the obvious? Everyone can see my condition."

He shrugged, pretending indifference, while, the nearby tourists marveled at this tropic lad's arrival on his golden maned, russet palomino. Their already high respect for the troublesome girl rose immeasurably. She slung on her Nakee and took apart her cot and put it in the bag.

Jesse stared. "Shean s-said you g-got a chase lounge. G-Good move!"

"It's actually a sand cot. Hey, can we first do a loop so I can find Kit?"

"Oh, he's in the Alley. Leave the bed. No one will steal a ten dollar item." She re-set her glasses. "I paid fifteen, but I can risk leaving it."

Beatense glanced over at Kip inquiringly; he nodded. Jesse sprang up onto his horse, and the girl backed off and did a vaulting run over Win's rump. This caused quite a sensation. The kids scatted off, at an easy canter. As they slowed up to ride through College Alley, amidst whoops and cheers the showy little horse was aimed through to the cement wall over by the skateboard park.

Beatense wondered how much of this applause was because they were bare, or because they were riding his pretty little horse. Windfire clop-clopped up the ramp.

The kids flipped down, and Jesse hung the reins over the iron pipe fence. They entered the park and crossed the concrete over toward Art's umbrella table. Making history Beatense felt awkward, for a gang of fiercely tan teen and pre-teen athletes in helmets and pads watched them with knowing smiles.

Cemented Passion was a municipal facility that wasn't making it. Public works made a mistake in assuming it would be a tourist attraction, and so it was set up for admissions and rental fees. But no one told this to the kids as mentioned, who had season passes, and they had the habit of snaking any tourist kid venturing in.

The Passion was a hang-out for the local veterans, so there was little gate. The clientele was an uncertain union of athletic gods, boys and girls, who were all tanned, tuned and talented radicals, along with pale skinhead punkers who wore baggy, ratty clothes, and who lacked showy muscle. They were actually equally accomplished as skaters, but they purposely had no star power. Back in the glory days of movies, legend and song, the skate parks attracted paying tourists, but the songs faded.

Art managed the Passion, much to his regret, it was a form of banishment, but he realized he was lucky to have even this job. He hated the beach and its smiling, tan surfer girls, especially since what he made was far less than what they got from their parents for their "living expenses." He lived in a skuzzy trailer on Trenton well within hearing of the quarry's day and night blasting, and bulldozers, and dump trucks.

He got up from his wobbly lounge with an old rumpled fishing hat perched on his scraggly hair. Its dreary sportiness tiredly confirmed his lined, washed-up detective fatigue. He was wearing cheap tire shop pants and a tropical vacation shirt that was putridly drab. Like the punkers he was flat pale. He wore a perpetually worried look, as if he could never relax because of his money and ex troubles.

"Okay, Shattuck, what," he said by way of greeting. *That damn Book Girl.*

"Art, hi, this is Beatense. You know, she's the woman I said could run the rental counter yesterday. She has a degree in inventory management."

"How about a degree in stopping the inventory from disappearing? Such as it is. And I can handle the rentals in this snake pit myself."

"That isn't what you said yesterday!"

"I didn't say anything yesterday. You did all the talking."

"The hell! You said you would think about it!"

"I did think about it, but I got ten year old terrorists laughing at the outdated junk here, which means I don't need anyone's help to just let it sit there."

"Look, Beatense can help you get more business! The tourists especially!"

With this invitation he perused the girl. *He might have a point.* But she was the type to call in sick to fuck her live-in, or lay out and then fuck.

"Maybe, but Accounting uptown is watching every... Oh, cut that out!"

Jesse's eyes became very large, and he sagged his pretty head down.

"Look, Book, I can't hire anybody just to happy up this brat. Parks and Rec is on my ass enough as it is. Can I offer a beer, though, as a consolation?"

During this discussion several lethal browned young renegades moved in to rate Beatense, and their muttered asides made her feel uneasy. They sported elbow and knee pads, their badges of courage, and their helmets were cocked smartly back on their shaggy heads. Her fame didn't impress them. No one did.

"Er, yes. A beer, you say? A single serving? I... Well, okay. I guess."

"Relax. Don't strain yourself with too much gratitude."

"Art, you can at least try her out!" Jesse persisted. "It's only for a week!"

He looked at her sharply. "What? You can only work for a week?"

Grinning: "Well, heh heh, it doesn't make any difference now, does it?"

Art shook his head and led the two over to the main shed, that was open back of the rental counter. They walked through this shaded space, set up with metal shelves full of unused equipment, which looked abused nonetheless. Beatense followed the two into Art's airless little office. The one fluorescent tube garishly shined upon the beach nudes taped to the corrugated zinc walls. Beatense saw herself.

Art opened the noisy refrigerator. Its cord was patched with duct tape.

"It's not fancy, but it's home. Light? Draft? Bock? Pilsner? Malt liquor?"

"None for me, Art." He was agreeably taken aback at her gesture, right off using his name. "I don't want to be a party to your drinking on the job."

"Cola? Grape soda? Strawberry? Orange? I hate orange pop, myself."

"The orange, if it's in a glass bottle."

"You would have to go back decades for that. I wish I could hire you."

"But you can, Art," said Jesse, taking his cola. "She's available!"

"Well, I wasn't aware of that, miss. I'm, heh heh, available myself."

"Sorry, I just go for losers with aimless lives of perpetual disappointment."

"Honestly, I can't help you on that one. You better raise your standards."

The girl sagged on the table laughing. She asked for root beer and Art took out actual beer. The door opened, and a remarkably fine bred boy stepped in.

With innocent curly hair he was in trim, neon orange shorts that severely clashed with his rich dark browning, and in turn his lush tan and cleanly shaped muscles were at odds with his aura of perceptive contemplation. His anxious expression gave his doubting-all intellect an urgently evocative pathos.

"Can... Can I use your phone, Art? My battery ran down."

"Is that the best excuse you can think of? Here she is, look at her."

"I'm actually here to look at you, Art," the boy said, with a smile.

Beatense laughed and Art familiarly yelled at the intruder to get out, and the sad boy left. Beatense recalled him as one of the sidewalk hawks she saw Thursday. From her own habits she guessed that his bereft expression was borne of long mirror studies, trying varied mental states and settling on one that looked like he was facing impending tragedy. This does wonders for lovely looks.

"That Oliver is the worst of the tribe," said Art. "He goes for the victims older and heavier. He can get them down twitching in five seconds."

"Me too," said Beatense. "Although I last did that back at camp."

"Yeah, that raid. Now where did I put my whip for these punks?"

They stepped back out onto the heat waving deck, and Beatense gratified Art by offering a friendly hand. She and Jesse headed over to the entry, through a smirking gauntlet of boredly curious outlaws. Young Oliver watched, as he did standing pedal pivots on his chromed stunt bike. He then dropped the front tire down with a bounce and he attacked these ten foot tall opposing ramps. With lurid flashes of his savage tan, and with precise interplays of striking muscle, the boy flung his bike from ramp to ramp, until he broke free and popped aerial flips, snaking around midair to dive back down. Beatense was open mouthed.

"Look at that kid go, Jesse! Dork killer or not, that's amazing!"

"Oh, I do that, too. But let's get out of here. They're fixing to kill *us.*"

Beatense didn't doubt it. She was grateful for her tan, it conferred authority. But Jesse was at a disadvantage, being a good boy. Out on the promenade he shooed away the wide eyed kids who were petting the sleepy Windfire.

The boy untied him and led him over to the access ramp. Skaters and runners went by them. Parents pushed strollers. Sightseers ambled. Everyone gawked.

"Let's run down and grab Spec and us two go riding, Beatense."

"Jesse, I can't! It's almost two-thirty!" The girl looked out over the College Alley area. "Kit is waiting for me to get sun with him! Plus more again, I hope."

"You can be late for that. We just ride down to Cocojo, along the surf."

"You shit eating little pig, tempting me like that! Okay, there and back!"

Jesse leaped upon his pony, and Windfire snuffled and stepped and tossed his head. Beatense bellied herself on. From this higher vantage point she gave another look over the beach, but even Kit was apparently hidden in the mob.

Jesse rode down the ramp, as his pony's hooves clopped hollowly in that classic way. They worked their way back to the cot bag and Beatense hopped down and gave it to Jesse. Everybody longingly watched. The girl was a spectacle all along, but her equine skills were unbearable. They recalled those high gallop book photos.

Young Boyd, who planned to display his sickening tan back home, and was now iron baking it deeper, stood up and watched as the two waved and scatted off. Half mad, Buck watched the thong bared little whip from a safe distance.

The riders hacked at a canter along the light surf. They came to the catamaran and rode right through the gap in the tropical foliage into the shack enclave. They left Windfire at the trough in the paddock and went in the cabin.

"Dad? Ned? Shean? Hello? Anybody here? Can we take Spec?" Jesse turned to Beatense. "There, now your riding him is legal. *We asked.*"

As they stepped back out the girl ran for the pool and dove in. She swam down into the bright blue deep and slowly rotated above the drain. Jesse was worried; she stayed down a long time. She burst to the surface and vaulted out and ran over with Jesse ran for the paddock. The girl introduced herself to Ned's horse, Specteriffic.

Jesse didn't go into the tackroom, hinting they would be riding without bridle and reins, nor halters with lead-ropes as reins. This would be real riding, two animals on two animals, with a grab of mane for control.

Even with glasses Beatense was a savage. She led Spec out of the corral. The poor little horse, what did he think as he followed this wild girl, looking upon her long, leaned back? Its widening up to the capable breadth of her hinged, bony shoulders warned that she would ride him hard, for she walked with a sure, waist snaky swing of her hips, which left the carriage of her head steadily unaffected.

She had strong surety in her bendy build, and in the worried Spec's equine vision her tan shined black, and it flashed to her aggressive muscles. He curiously sniffed. The girl had that alien smell that his young master often carried, neither human nor otherwise natural. Pool chlorine.

Jesse hopped onto Windfire, and Beatense gave Spec a quick pat of control and also sprang aboard. Spec just felt ninety-six pounds instead of her normal hundred, because she had spent the night in heavy rapture. Also, all she had eaten so far that day was a long forgotten cinnamon bun. Her rippled belly had a starved curve.

"Jesse, where did you put my things? Not just on the kitchen counter."

"In my room, if you can call *that* a room. Hold Win while I get the gate."

Beatense leaned over and caught Windfire's mane. That fluid shift in her weight reassured Spec that she was a rider. Jesse hopped off and swung the gate shut and sprang back on. Windfire made little mincing steps, snorting and tossing.

The girl easily rode to Spec, holding him with her long legs as he stutter stepped nervously. Heart pounding, was she ready for this, bareback especially.

"A word of warning, we will have to hand gallop through Sorel, so if you don't do that level of riding we'll stop at the border out of caution and turn back."

She eyed her thin black arms and thighs. "I'll wait for you down in Cocojo."

Moments later the girl was loping southward on her sturdy little steed, alongside her beautiful and bare friend. In stricter moral climes doubting suspicions could arise concerning their ultimate plans, but here she was flying along the rolling surf, just as depicted in countless travel brochures, except unlike their riders she was skinny and naked. As the envious people the kids passed by stared, she tossed back her hair.

31

JUNGLE RIDE

Beatense was riding Spec at the same crooked angle she had ridden enture, for a stirring, showy effect. With hair tossing she rose and fell into a light, flexing slouch. All the while she thoughtfully reminded herself that she was brown and bare, but of course, Spec made it all possible, and it was his show.

Spec was a honey, eager and responsive. Beatense could tell he accepted their teamwork., but Windfire also interested her. For all his stallion bravado he was just a big baby. He was a palomino, if one was to just by his blond mane, tail and forelock, but the rest of his coat was dark gold. This was a stunning show horse effect.

He was a nice size for Jesse, big enough for when he got older, but not big enough to be a threat to his devoted young master if he ever went bonkers. A blowing candy wrapper was often the perfect excuse.

As the hot wind shined the kids with sweat, they loped along the summer homes. Collapsing waves raced in under the horses, and their hooves dashed up thrilling sheets of spray. The dainty, teen-age looking mother, who by now had burned battle cry brown, a jolt to Beatense, paused from her sand soccer sport with her pretty sons and waved. The boys waved too.

Jesse knew of them as Judge Croftly's daughter and grandsons, back for their annual summer get-away. He ruefully reflected that yet again they looked like walnut carvings. From their high breeding and love of sport these beautiful, airy boys were superbly muscled. The mother, he didn't care to think about.

Yes, she was a happy person who thought life was beautiful, but hit her with car payment struggles, rent in arrears or a shit job, and see what she thinks then. But at least for the present the clothing budget for her and her sons wasn't a factor.

Jesse and Beatense ran by the tumbled Oxhead dunes, as seagulls reeled and skreeled above. This beach was private, outsiders weren't welcome, but the residents waved. Obviously, dressed as the riders weren't (their tie thongs left behind), and as tan as they were, they met all requirements. They galloped into the crowded Sorel, causing these confused, simple low-lifes much sudden consternation, turning to each other with pulpy lips working. This was dangerous territory for nudity.

But Beatense spotted her friend. "Jerry! Jesse, stop! Jerry, hi!" She broke her speed and trotted neatly over to the rescuer and stopped. "Hey, podner!"

He was staggered. "W-Wow, I-look at you! H-Hi, Beatense!"

"Hi, Jerr! You better call the police again! This is one place I'm illegal!"

He didn't tell her that the Book Girl had been cleared. A crowd gathered; these kids were like space aliens, spellbinding to behold. Me, same reaction.

Jerry gaped at this lightly thinned warrior, who was seared to a glisteny espresso brown. There was nothing legal about her, even with the unexpected glasses. His breath shook. Yesterday the catamaran, and now *bareback!*

"Y-Yeah, th-that's illegal, all-all right. B-Both of y-you are quite a s-sight."

The girl smiled shyly and cast her eyes down. "Oh, Jerry."

"Hey, he won't kick, will he? I can get closer?"

She shook back her hair and petted Spec's neck.

"Sure you can, silly! Spec is sweet!"

He stepped up and patted the cute horse. "Actually, I've done roping in my day, Beatense. Hey there, you fat little pony." He turned back. "I'm giving you two safe passage. But remember, I asked if we could, er, see each other?"

She sagged lankily back, propped on one hand and absently toying with her mop with the other. Her jutty hips flexed her split into Jerry's shocked view. Her slack sunk belly also zeroed in. Ripple etched, its tight curve seemed to hum. Her nectarines burst with fertility. She was whipped by the glare to a grotesque tan, but even worse, her face had an all-knowing focus. No videos from the Skiff, but good audibles.

"Yes, but I hope you would be very dangerous for my inexperience! But you say we have a pass? Meaning we can be nude? Jesse! We're legal!"

He normally overlooked raw sensual impact. As a lifeguard he didn't pay special attention to the occasional caliber surfers coming here. But his pulse defibrillated as this bareback brownist patted at her gold chained belly with a delicate, shy smile.

She sat back up. Her back was curved, hooking her hips just so, and setting the knees-bent hang of her legs. Her light body was indeed naked and lashed with sun. He turned again to her breasts. Yes, those audibles. She was screaming.

Jerry's troubled question was, *How much effort do these babes think they have to enforce to get themselves bedded? How much tan do they need?* Many surf women of the boned echelon, this child especially, made The Physical their very lives.

These musings took seconds, he was a rescuer, after all. But in that role who would he rescue first? This girl, or some tub? Unethically, he would get Beatense.

"Today only. But will next Friday work? H-How c-can I get hold of you?"

"Holiday Hill. And Friday will work out! My father said I can stay another week!" Looking upon him, she momentarily let Spec have his way, and noticing this, he playfully danced around. She held to him, swaying and flexing her waist as her hair tossed. "B18, I think. I'll... I'll be free... For that... That whole night."

Jesse had stayed back. He didn't care to be recognized by any staffers on this beach. He was the most magnificent creature the folk gathered here ever saw. With his exquisite face, sideshow tan and remarkably long, curly hair, he was celestial.

Jesse watched as the supernatural grabbed at her horse's mane and turned him around, leaning with the effort. She scatted over to rejoin the boy. Shined with hot sweat, long waist flexing, she gave the rescuer a bracelets clinking wave and the two show-stoppers jogged off through a long corridor of admirers, cameras included.

"Beatense, besides him, how many guys are you stringing along?"

"Let's see, there's Craig, Kit, Jerry, Sailor Sim, Zapo, and possibly Buck."

"Sailor who? And Buck, really?"

"Sim. Real tan. You must know of him. And I think I saw Buck today, over on Main. But I'm not mad at him any more. My shortest grudge."

The kids entered Cocojo. Just past the NO LIFEGUARD sign a child-like young mother lay bare with her toddler son, who happily squealed and pointed at them. Beatense thought this effrontery stole some of her thunder. Factually she was in Cocojo proper, but she was blatantly within total sight of everyone in the south end of Sorel. And because this brave girl was just freshly golden, her obvious motive was, rather than working her tan, it was showing off her divine little body.

"How can she do that, Jesse?" Beatense ironically demanded, as the boy patted his mother's firmed little butt. The very picture of nature rightfully having its way, the girl reached and ruffled his hair. "Two inches over the line!"

Jesse was getting impatient. "Big bummer," he said, riding to his also impatient pony as he stepped in place. "So anyway, race ya down to the rocks!"

"I can't see with these glasses!"

Beatense could look over them but she needed an excuse to ride slower.

Jesse abruptly pulled Windfire around and gave him a nudge with his heels. The horse bolted off like a shot, leaving Spec behind. Beatense squeezed with her legs and a volcano erupted beneath her. Spec went into full extension as he pounded in pursuit. Beatense moved to his furious speed.

The gallop. In a blur the rear hooves come forward and dig as the front pair pull through their transitional arc. Now it's time for those back legs to launch horse and rider ahead, while the front legs extend for the next lunge. Conveniently both the front and back legs are the same length, but a precarious rocking does persist, especially when all hooves are lifted. Despite riding bareback, Beatense had total mastery over this motion, even as her crazed horse worked the uneven sand.

This is the passion of all riders, to recklessly fly atop swift horses, with an endless distance beckoning before them. Beatense goaded little Spec to ever higher speeds, using her hips, as the hot wind caressed her wild tan.

Her tough, thin arms, stretched out before her, she temporarily disregarded.

The beach was busy, the sun culturists were back. They all watched. They saw the shallows splash up beneath those flying hooves, then as dry sand was crossed it was kicked up in powdery clouds. They saw the girl's tossing hair spill over her slim shoulders for an instant before being whisked away. It seemed she was a mere wisp atop that beast, her bare profile was that slim, and she was rust burned dark brown.

As the spent waves sizzled across her horse's flight path, one detail bothered the girl as she rocketed along, not always able to see. It was all those idiots in her way, strolling the shore as she pounded toward them. She used Spec's pricked ears as a sort of gunsight, aiming, but she whooped in warning. The cameras followed her.

Up in the Alley girls got tan to get sex, or they used sex to justify tan. But Cocojo was a haven for those who just got tan. For her efforts Beatense had an excuse, her books, but for most devotees the adventure of discovering their ability turns into self imposed ordeals they feel iffy or defensive about. So they seek Cocojo's solitude.

That solitude was ending fast. The boulder wall at the southern end of the lonely shore was closing in. As the horses drew near Beatense kind of had the question, Would Spec recognize the barrier and stop? Jesse pounded up to the wall first, and he rode to the jolting chaos beneath him as Windfire wisely skipped to a halt.

Beatense charged up seconds later, and Spec hit her with the same berserk riot. This answered her question, but she floated off and ingloriously fell to the sand.

Spec looked down at her with a bewildered little face. Jesse hopped down. "Beginner shit," he said, helping her up. "You were as slow as sludge, then you go and fall off! Here, let's let them roll."

Beatense got up and looked herself over. She was unhurt, but she was dusted with powdery sand stuck all over to her sweat. The horses snuffled and pawed and investigated, and finally sagged down and rolled on their backs and wriggled in the sand, waggling their legs. They awkwardly heaved themselves back up and like wet dogs shook off the sand in curtains. They traipsed into the surf and their riders ran in after them. They sprang onto the horses and romped in the frothy waves.

Beatense already knew that riding a crazed bronco could be somewhat amusing. Splashing through the warm shallows, she and Jesse tried pulling each other off their horses, and they traded mounts a dozen times as they fought.

They staggered ashore and were greeted by the toasted-to-a-shine Sienna. She wasn't blackety dark, but her tan was a dense, old penny brown, giving her deep saturation. She weighed just more than Beatense, all of it extra muscle.

"Forget it, Sienna," Jesse said, as the horses ambled off toward the shimmering dunes. "I refuse to let you ride him!"

"I knew you would be an ass about this, Shuck. Let me take Spec, then."

"No way, Sienna," said Beatense, admiring her friend's tough, glossy burn.

The sun was champagne crisp, the sky a crystalline blue. Despite her own cruel tan and surf girl avowal Beatense was sickened at the sight of Sienna. To just hand Spec over to her was unthinkable. Practically criminal.

"Colwell, you're so fuck bitch dark I didn't recognize you. And glasses? Copying old Tenacity, hah? Anyway, shitty way to greet an old friend, J Boy, saying you can't lend me out your foundered mule. All you liberals believe in equity and inclusion, but you get a chance to help the little guy and you come up with all these fuck excuses. Look at me, I can hardly make myself decent. I spring from the dunes to raid picnics, just so I can survive one more day. Yet you *dare* to deny me the most basic right, that of personal travel to the welfare office! Well, don't say yes now, it's too late!"

"I was just going to agree, Sienna, but you said it's too late."

"*But,* I have a medical need. My legs are too sunburned for me to walk."

"I better ride with her, Jesse, to pick her up if she falls off, that sunburn."

"You cunts! You can't take over my horses! It isn't fair!"

"Aww, Jesse, it is fair, it's economic justice. Share the wealth. Right, Beat?"

"Yeah! Come on, Jesse, you're helping to avoid that 10% class warfare!"

"Oh, all right!" the boy said, slumping. "But what am I going to do?"

"Torrey's here," said Sienna. "Back in the bowl, banana oil. Give… A look."

"Naked too, I suppose," said Beatense. "Why, just like us!"

"Let me warn you about something, Beatie. It don't prove shit to be nude and/or topless naked. Nude today, nursing home irrelevance tomorrow. That's why Jesse's letting us take the horses; in his heart he pities us broken down old bitches."

"I'm more worried about his reaction to this global warming, myself."

Jesse whistled the horses over, and snorting and kicking they pounded up. Sienna flipped up on Windfire, and Beatense flipped up on Spec. She lay back on her elbows with legs dangling. Sienna grabbed Windfire's mane and jumped off at a hot gallop. Beatense was left in mid-air as Spec also left. Furious, she quite publically ran after him. A hundred yards off Sienna dug Windfire to a sliding stop, riding his haunches. Beatense caught up and quite publically sprang on Spec, who had dutifully stopped. Sienna pointed toward Sorel and thundered off in a blur. There was a crowd today; Beatense quite publically followed, whooping. Yes, money, who needs it?

As if born on horseback, Sienna had a knack for it. But Beatense did too; she raced Spec ahead at a hot run. Her belly chain flopped on her slim waist.

Sienna tore right up to the Sorel boundary and skipped Windfire down to a quick stop in the soft sand. She made him rear and hop ahead in that stance.

Ripples painfully flexing, Beatense wrenched Spec's mane and plowed him into a sideways leaning stop. Several college men who were kicking around a soccer ball openly stared, and the natural little mother also looked.

"Not bad, Beat, but you fucking got to speed up! See you, losers!"

Sienna blasted off and Beatense quickly caught up and galloped alongside her. With eyes ablaze the girls flew down to the distant south rock, flying by the many sun cultists upon the sand that day. They whipped around and charged off back toward Sorel whooping all the way. They pulled their stallions into dramatic calf roping stops far past the invisible border line, defying Park Law, and brown Beatense trotted Spec lightly by a low income family gathering. Shaking back her tumbled tossing hair, the wild naked child dissected them with her scholar's lenses.

She spun her pony around and the intruders blasted south back through Cocojo. This was all very disconcerting for the others on the beach, especially with the wicked tan hides the girls flaunted, They knew how worrying the sound of their approaching hooves might be. They avoided any sunbathers who were obvious pros, but people who didn't fit in here were terrorized.

The hated furies whooped like savages as they bore down on their fool victims. Beatense saw Popcorn Fats again, and she galloped toward him as he ran. He cried out as she tackled him just like at the oldie camp. She washed his filth contact off in the surf and ran back to Spec, who was getting used to this errant passenger.

She hopped aboard and the girls continued rioting around, then fell to a lope.

Sienna wasn't much affected by their attacks, but black Beatense fiercely panted, not used to high action at ninety-eight. Her running sweat dripped off her feet, taking her surf bath with it. The girls raced back through the dunes to the bowl, where they spotted the torched tan Torrey, who was in an oil bake against a dune.

Out of character, she was one bare ethereal of many other solitude seekers.

Jesse sat watching her and the others. "Hey, Torrey, the socialists."

She hopped up. "Beatense, hi! Wow, you two sure have the right idea!"

Beatense, gasping, sagging with belly curved, eyed Torrey's spring water.

"This... This is more work than the 10K," she complained. "Even sex."

"So, Torrey, if old Starry isn't here she must of got work," said Sienna.

"Yes, picking grapes. In this heat! Beatense! Look at that tan!"

"They say dark colors absorb heat and now I believe it. But you're deadly!"

"You noticed! No, I laid out by our shack yesterday, after the 10K! Summer and Tenacity are there now, but I just felt like the beach today. It's funny, I felt it in my bones to come here, just as if the bones even know what a beach is!"

"Ah, yes," said Sienna, caring little what bones knew or didn't know. "Okay, bake up, Torr. Jesse wants you. We were just heading into the woods."

"We were?" said Beatense. "Torrey, can I have a slug of that water?"

"Not until the horses drink, Beat," said Sienna. "You know that. Come on!"

Beatense thought that as she lay dying, the last image before her burning eyes would be the condensation-covered, half frozen bottle of water on Torrey's big white sheet. She doubtfully waved goodbye and followed Sienna on a winding quick gallop through the sandy hills. They charged out into Sorel's far south parking lot with hooves clopping. The girls trotted through the parked cars toward the open sand.

They pounced out onto the beach and ran to and across the border at a ripping clip. They slowed to a lope southward along the dunes. Sienna signaled a stop.

"Had enough, kid?" she asked, panting exuberantly, gleaming darkly.

Beatense sagged, bracing herself on Spec's withers. "I wanted that water."

"Hey, me too! But don't you see, kid? Guys can't run around half wild like us, it would look stupid, but us girls can get away with it. Don't ya love it?"

The girls cantered along the line of the dunes, then turned and scatted up a rise. Beatense paused at the top to look out at the glorious, hazy beach. The two sprang down the backside, heading inland through the dune wasteland. Beatense glanced down at her breasts. They were still tumescently firm despite her thirst. If they held water, like a camel's hump, she didn't feel any less thirsty.

The girl pointed toward the tall ramparts of sand looming before them.

"Hey, if we have to go up that slope to get to the woods, it's kind of steep!"

"Just lean forward and grip with those long, killer thighs of yours, kid."

They hacked on through the blanketing heat and started their assault up the tall slope toward the line of trees. The horses chugged upward in leaping bounds, and working in partnership with him, Beatense held to Spec's mane. Her tough muscles, especially her sunken abdominals, flexing in tensed concert with her horse's jumping, unleashed her needy coital fluids. The girls stormed the summit and suddenly found themselves under a shadowy canopy of boughs.

The temperature fell twenty degrees. The girls let the horses nibble at the sparse grass, while they gazed across the undulating yellow mounds toward the wavy green sparkling sea. The sky was bright, tough for any tanners stuck inside.

"Wow, what a painting that would make, Sienna!"

"Or screen-savers. Old office dipwads point to them and say, 'That's where I'm going when I retire.' Like shit! Oh, can you see those parachutes back up in Em?"

She leaned out and looked. "Not with these gla... Okay, yeah. Why?"

"Nothing but those fucking tourists ride them, office dipwads. Okay, ride."

The fiercely demure Sienna turned her horse and led the way back through the ferns and flowers of the conservatory forest. Beatense half expected to hear those taunting jungle bird calls as they riffled through the glossy dark leaves that spilled out over their trail. The roofing trees hushed out all sound but the steady pace of the muffled hooves and the occasional horsey snort. As they ran deeper into the woods the path grew wider. Beatense trusted Spec implicitly, he knew the way.

The quick turns along the path added thrilling moments of wild chaos as the girls clung on through the changes in speed and lead. And suddenly they came charging out into an open glen with a small rainwater pond. A picnic was underway at its near edge. The intruders pulled back as the startled party lurched clumsily up. The uncouth primitives stepped their horses over to them, showing dangerous hate.

The hunters saw that they were oh so concerned humanists, who resented their brave arrival. The depleted-of-all-health men and women were all "casually" clothed, and the two hellions were fearful of their deprived color. As the PhD vegans warily watched, the warriors sat sunk belly slouched, white only in eyes and teeth as they exuded deep vitamin D. Beatense's glasses added to the image; despite her obscene nudity and baked hide she read and studied. She raised her thin arm protectively.

"You get out of here," said Sienna, pointing. "You're trespassing."

"I hardly think so," the party's pale, bearded and already facially lined spokesman said. "For your information this is our Government's land."

Sienna snorted at that, and the carnivores ambled their weary horses over to the little pond and let them drink. Beatense's desperation raged worse. She hopped off and ran over and grabbed a bottle of water. "Hey!" the spokesman cried, as she ran back and tossed it up to Sienna. With breasts heaving her friend chugged the whole bottle. Beatense was enraged. *That rat!* She sprang back and took another bottle, and the world worrier grabbed her arm.

With a whip-like flexing the slippery savage twisted free, then in a stance on one foot she put her other foot into his chest. The others stared in terror as he fell. The naked girl jumped back on her horse. The girls shot off, heading toward that strange shaped hill, Lookout Mountain, that towered up like an old volcano.

The path started up the steep flank of the hill, and the girls leaned forward. With this slower pace Beatense drank of her water. The path wandered up more sharply, and she lay close, hugging Spec's neck. The trees were smaller here, struggling old growth, and the hillside was littered with boulders and fallen trunks. Minutes later the girls reached the open hot sky of the sawed-off summit, of broken stone slabs.

Dried old bushes clawed upward from the cracks, and stray patches of saw grass grew in the wider cracks. This lofty retreat was closed in by the treetops reaching up from the hillside, and also by tall rocks that jutted up like snaggled teeth. Beatense eyed the rays heated flagstones of this atrium greedily.

She was crazed to hot bake here. Sienna hopped off Windfire and spanked him off. Spec left too, and his rider was briefly airborne again by his quick exit. She just broke her fall to the rock and leaned back on her hands.

"Beat, I didn't know you had it in you, dropping that T/A. Still thirsty?"

She lay panting, a delicate fairy, rubbing at her leg. "Yes, in fact I am! And now I'm probably in trouble with the police over a bottle of water! Two bottles!"

"Shit, you're gorgeous. That was beautiful, your abusing him like that."

"Yes, but I need water! That one pint didn't do it!" The slight girl's muscles writhed as she hopped to her feet. A thin girl of bone and blood, she was shined black wet. "Sienna, what if that dipwad rats on me? He even has witnesses!"

"No way. He grabbed you, and you were smaller. And those cunt women, who believes anything they say? Piss! I should have did some kicking too."

Sienna stepped over to one of the rimrock edifices and muscled aside a flat stone at its base. She pulled out water in a plastic gallon jug.

Running with sweat, Beatense started. "Sienna, that's water! Give me it!"

The wildcat didn't comply. Holding with both hands she drank with great, shaking swallows. It was all Beatense could do to keep from attacking her too. Finally she grabbed the jug away and downed a quart. Sienna reached back into the crypt and she took out a big bottle of extra virgin olive oil.

Beatense wobbled, blinking blearily. "Oil, too? Fuck, am I going to bake."

"Right on, Little Miss Prissy. You missed Thursday up here, if you recall."

She already thought of that. "Yeah but I got those boaters to gang fuck me."

Beatense splashed precious handfuls of water to get the horse sweat off her legs. Sienna scrambled up the rimrock, and Beatense climbed up after her. She suddenly found herself before a steep cliff. She gazed out over the jungle forest, that was a convoluted carpet of fluttering dark leaves. The dunes and mighty ocean lay beyond, blurrily dotted with sailboats spread out over miles.

Sienna was below her, on a ledge. "Hey, you coming? Get down here!"

"Catch me if I fall!" The girl scaled down one scary hold at a time down to the precarious perch. She dropped the last couple feet. "Here we lay out?"

"Yeah. I brought the oil. Did you bring the water? Shit, no." Sienna sprang up and retrieved the water within ten seconds. "Okay, lay back, kid."

This wasn't so easy. There was a drifting breeze, but the rock was sharply hot. Sienna solved that by pulling a bed sheet out of another hidden crypt. She lay it out and Beatense excitedly sprawled back on it, split open. Sienna sat astride her.

"Hey! Ease up there! This rock is hard!"

Sienna grimly oiled the girl. Beatense squirmed to her rough handling. Sienna kneaded her sleek muscles and apple breasts with discerning scrutiny. She did her jutting hips. Finishing with a deep finger squiggling, she let Beatense apply her.

This girl observed that both starved sprites glistened unnaturally, as if they were other worldly. But they both had a long history of that, sex too, since childhood.

"Total seclusion," said Sienna. "We can queer some more."

"We can do that anywhere. But hey, it's after the fact but is that water okay?"

"Yeah. Jesse runs water up here every few days, for any of us laying out."

"Someday I'm laying up here with... Oh, no!" The girl sat abruptly up. "I have to go, Sienna! I got a guy waiting for me! Kitanning, up on Main Beach!"

"See, now you got him. Now he thinks he's a lower priority. Good move."

"He is *not* a lower priority! He's as tan as Jesse, and me, and even though he's college-aged, or because, he's a stickboy. Like Shean!"

"Whoa, I might approve of him. In fact, I know who you mean. He fucks?"

"Ahem, yes, but that's the problem, because so do I. Starting at age twelve I've been on a tanning rip, that really fired up when I was at the surveying camp in the Geode Desert that next summer. Being inexperienced, despite all the photos in my magazines I was hardly prepared when Milky hit so deep into me. I was half insane. But I liked it, just shaking for fuck, so Lesta set me up with ten years. Years later I'm still wholesomely rabid, especially being so hot skinny, but I'm way overdoing it. You almost have to envy my one roommate Lorraine, being unbeachy she's inert."

"Overdoing it? And what roommate? I thought you were in that dive motel."

"A nice motel, but now I moved in with these girls up on Holiday Hill."

"Holiday Hill! Then you'll be right in with all those weenie college brats!"

"*Whom*... I'll be meeting tonight. We're having a party. Wanna come?"

"I could never make it. No car. But let's blast in the rays now, okay?"

"But we're going to queer, aren't we, like me and Krinkles?" --/-- "After."

The nudes lay in bake. Beatense's eyes rolled up in ecstasy. They put in two hours, then wrestled in explorative squirming play. Later like flitting deer the girls ran the trails down. They found the horses in the grassy clearing by the pond.

The two mounted and chased off in a game of jungle tag, that tore them through flower and fern. The broad leaves clawed at the savages as they shot through, but their oiled shines prevented the hated scratches. At one point Sienna fell back out of sight, and Beatense galloped ahead and flung herself up onto an overhanging limb.

Seconds later Sienna shot by, and Beatense flipped down. Feet barely touching she flew the other way. She hid in a ferny thicket, thrilled by her camouflage tan. She finally realized that Sienna wasn't coming, and ran for the dunes. Her friend galloped up from behind and leaped off and took her down. They wrestled again, working their hard muscles in play. Beatense was overawed by Sienna, she had a strap tough body of scent and sun like her own. They were both real dark brown.

Sienna pinned her and picked a blossom and sprinkled its pink petals onto her friend's writhing, black tan abdomen. Beatense tried to toss the petals off, but the oil stuck them. Her sunken belly stuck her hips and rib ledge out sharply.

"Beat, look at this study in contrasts. Sweet, soft and pink, versus salt, hard and brown. Me too, we're blood sisters." She licked in. "Now we're married."

Beatense felt like she was just learning what she could do with her beautiful self. The girls sprang for the horses and tore through the trees at a hard run, and dove the tall sand bank down without pause. They streaked through the blast oven dunes and broke out onto the beach. They galloped along the surf in a floating glide, and Jesse had to flag the sweating, whooping phantoms down three times to halt them.

32

WILD RIDE HOME

You grass eating owl molesters! We have to get to that restaurant!"

"Jesse, who eats at four, anyway?" said Beatense, as a crowd gathered.

"Four! It's got to be six by now! Sienna, I need that horse," Jesse added.

Sienna complied by hopping down off Windfire, and Jesse flipped on.

"See ya tonight, Senny," Beatense said, as her horse stutter stepped, flexing her waist. "The party, if you can grab a car. Follow the music!"

"No prob. Okay, thanks, J Boy, for lending us the guys, slow as they were."

Heart pounding, Beatense watched as her friend ran for the dunes.

Sienna's taking off left a silence, but it was one of suspense. Knowing what was coming, the restless horses nervously pranced. Their riders nudged them and they catapulted off, northward along the beach. Nothing impassions both horse and rider like open space such as this, and Beatense niggled Spec for ever higher speeds.

The kids crossed into Sorel and recklessly cycloned through the scattered beach visitors, as the lifeguards leaped down from their towers with whistles pealing. Seems the day passes had expired. Looking over her glasses Beatense saw a party of men wearing suits, escapees from some seminar, and she bore down on them whooping. Everyone watched in horror but the volcanically tan girl, noted as being so bony she looked starved, veered by them within inches.

The renegades finished off Sorel at speeds that shot wide eyed terror through its visitors, and they whipped by the Oxhead dunes and the summer homes. Here three of the teen-age looking mother's four sons were gathering driftwood. The boy of ten and his delicate young mother carried a grey log. It was devoid of life, but like the others the two radiated life and all the wonders life could do.

The oldest boy was on a blanket coupling with the sun fanatic Amherst girl. The lovely mother and her lovely sons, all bare, were celebrating life by being vitally thin and healthy brown. The airy sun believers waved at the riders, and Beatense pulled up. She gave a shaky hair tossing wave, and took off again.

A certain yellow catamaran rollicked by, and then the Bastian Street beach a few blocks later. Sweated ripples flexing, bare Beatense gave Curt and the two sisters a wave. The race now turned serious. The girl used her hips to drive Spec on, working him impatiently, and at a fierce cost in pain to her thighs she gripped him tightly.

She tore the Windemere beach like a whirlwind, as everybody hurried out of the way. Jesse also tore along the beach like a fury as he took the lead. The Hog, Villa Miranda and Dillon Arms careened by, and the kids became ever more urgent as they shot the Breeze Hotel cabana huts.

The all-over toasty Tamdyn, raking the kelp, waved. Beatense waved back, but Jesse was inching further ahead. She dreaded losing this race all because she was riding a slower horse, because she would still look chicken. But she saw that Main didn't have any open pathways, even at this later hour, so as they raced out into its crowded expanse she eased Spec down. Ever since Bastian cameras followed her. Within minutes anyone with a phone could watch her, including a certain Craig.

Jesse chased ahead to the foot of Holiday Hill, that loomed at Main's north end. Beatense, aware of the stricken stares upon her, goaded her horse into a pounding finale. The beach was less crowded up here. Jesse fought to halt his horse before plowing into the mounds. The girls who were hidden in there sprang up.

Beatense pulled Spec's mane back and shifted her negligible weight, and broke Spec into a powdery slide with forelegs planted. She popped off of him in a springing dismount and stumbled to a stop, oiled sweat flashing. What hath evolution wrought.

"Where did you learn to ride like that?" demanded Jesse.

"I have a horse myself! You saw my videos! Here, wait!"

Bare Beatense petted Spec, and the girl joined the others nearby in admiring the resplendent hair-down-his-back boy, knowing she caught looks herself. Jesse spun Windfire around and took off with Spec. The girl ran the hook over to the Holiday Hill's little beach and splashed in to get Spec's sweat off her legs. She waded back.

A girl came running down the sand path in a braking jog. In shorts and a T-shirt, her skin just had a dusky ivory tint. No sunner, but her dark eyes had a satisfied set. She was child-like thin and boy-child muscled, and her pinned-back dark hair showed her fine, cornered forehead. The happiest of friends with her small pedigreed body.

Beatense thought, *Pride In White. It is possible.* She ran up the sand path ramps and sprinted the trails through the trees. But, as she came to the first of the cabins, drawing surprised stares, she felt a little edgy being naked, and it didn't help that she didn't quite know how to find her cabin. The path, now a roadway, reached a sandy intersection, and the greasy girl paused to read the old wooden sign.

She was at the West Loop, with bungalows C1 - C8 off to her left, and C9 - C11 straight ahead, and addresses C12 - C20 to the right. Nothing about the North Loop. The girl attracted the attention of a student working on his car.

She showed the wobbling fellow how to use the tire iron to lever his alternator to tighten the belt. He noticed she was quivering with excitement. Beatense left and chose to keep on straight. As she ran the dusty road she came to a willowy young woman who didn't have that beach image, in that she had on a trim little office blazer and skirt. Her delicately assembled forehead was angled back, and it was burned to a more deeply flushed gold than the rest of her bony, tested fortitude face.

Her blue eyes were analytically narrowed and wise, and her thin lips would bring her exquisite teeth into play with every magical expression. Indeed, even now each facial muscle, taut under her tawny complexion, was involved with her forceful eyes. Her lank blond hair had stray wisps, that gave her forehead a purposeful look.

Beatense continued toward her, a bare twit living for beach, bake and bed, but the career achiever disarmingly smiled at her.

It wasn't a smile of, "Ah, caught you!" It was purely friendly. Taken aback, but with insecurities bravely reassured, Beatense also smiled.

She ran on and saw a familiar but blurry face. "Kenny, hi! Remember me?"

The sleepy youth, tan in butt-cut jean cut-offs, reacted noticeably to her impact.

"Hi, uh…" His breath huffed. "Oh, are you ever… Are you ever t-tan."

"Thanks, but I'm lost! How do I find that miserable north loop from here? I moved in with Lorraine and Virginia!"

"So you're their new roommate? Cool! I… I can take you there!"

"Permission granted. You see, I'm being taken out to eat soon, Kenny, and I'm all covered with oil, and road dust too, and I'm naked! Just look at me!"

"Well… If-If you insist."

Kenny felt embarrassed as he escorted this wild shameless foundling, but she felt legitimized by him. She noisily recounted her day, with gestures, so the residents could see she had a friend up here. Besides, she was trying to make points, the boy was tanner than she remembered. Actually drenched. A likely candidate for bedding.

The showy Kenny stumbled along, trying to recall her name.

"…Then we played tag in the woods after that, Kenny. Until just today that was a part of Cocojo I didn't even know about. What a paradise!"

They came to another intersection and turned left, toward the elusive North Loop. Residents continued to abound. They were either walking the roadways or sitting out on their stoops. These included sun crisped beach girls laughingly talking with their friends. Greatly to their credit they seemed unimpressed by their own brilliance, as if they still remembered being hopscotch and piano playing kids.

Beatense saw her cozy little cabin, North Loop B18, at last. "Thanks for the help, Kenny. Oh, would you be coming to our party later? I need a friend."

He glanced at her hardened shoulders. "Y-Yeah, I'm c-coming, Bernice."

"Bernice! Kenny, Beatense is bad enough! Okay, bye!"

She hopped over to her cabin and burst in. "Hi, guys!"

Her roommates bulged their eyes. She had the same effect as a locomotive in a classroom. The girls lurched uncertainly up from the sofa.

"H-H-Hi," they responded. Even Virginia, who was perfect, was rattled.

The doe girl was confronted by a stooped old man whose old suit fit baggily. He looked as if he grimly despised any and all pleasures, and this Mr. Denton look-alike was now dedicated to spreading this doctrine every way he could.

"Beat," said starved Virginia, sizzling in shorts and tie-top, "this is Setticase, our slumlord. He wants you to sign a statement that you're here as a renter."

Glasses set, she held her arm protectively. "I refuse! I'm here as a guest!"

Mr. Setticase eyed the Beach Girl's severe lack of costume balefully.

"You're Colwell? Asked Cheevy about you. You seem a favorable risk."

"A favorable risk! I could buy this whole loop! How dare you imply I'm a risk!"

Lorraine proudly saw the old landlord gulp as the girl angrily stared, flashing with bake. That and her shaped muscles, that belly, were too explosive even for him.

Beatense turned to Virginia. "How did he even know about me?"

"Don't look at me. These landlords have a secret grapevine."

"Well, that means Mr. Cheevy told on me! Unless it's some kind of law!"

"Exactly that, young lady," said Mr. Setticase, eyeing her boy-like muscles.

The girl removed her glasses and signed the paper, and the villain left.

"Where did you get those glasses?" said Lorraine. "Are they ever cute!"

"Forget that! I have to hit the tub! The Shattucks invited me out to eat!"

Lorraine hopped into the bathroom, anticipating another shaking session. As she ran the water to get it warm Beatense came in and closed the door.

"If you think you're watching me again, forget it, Lorraine!"

She was standing in front of the white enameled door. Exuding the richest shades of the tanning spectrum, she had an intensely blurred gleam.

"Well, young lady, it's not just me watching, with you running around naked."

"I couldn't help it! Me and Jesse went riding and my stuff is at their house!"

"You went horseback riding? Really?"

"Yeah, with Jesse and then Sienna. She took over Jesse's horse, Windfire."

"Well, whatever. But let me know if you need anything, honey."

"You can hand in my Aunt Clara and jeans when I pound the wall."

The suntan girl stepped in the tub and swished soapy cold water all over herself. She stepped out and dried herself. Lorraine came in with the clothes.

"You bitch lesbian, Lorraine! I didn't hit the wall yet! Get out of here!"

Lorraine watched Beatense's thin arms as she struggled into her tight jeans with their three inch zipper, and she put on the Aunt Clara, with its 3 inch webbing.

"There! Now where's my…"

Lorraine stared. "There, what! You can't go like that! To a restaurant?"

"I wore it to that mall this morning, successfully. What's the big deal?"

"Well, this Jesse's father, who I think is a little iffy inviting you to dinner like this in the first place, might *object?* And where is he taking you?"

"Let's see, Shean said it's this place called… Gulver's."

"Gulliver's? Well, maybe that's okay. It's a fun place. It's out on the amusement pier up in Madeline, by the marina. I think you can be risky there, being casual."

Beatense scrubbed in a light coating of oil with her towel, and then just in case Gulliver's had funny hold-over ideas, she added her belly chain and ring bangles. For shoes she put on her 10K veterans. Looking over her business-like glasses she was sorting through Ned's magazines when the big Espriado pulled up.

"Beatense, your *limo* is here," Virginia announced, looking twice. *Wow!*

"See if we can come," Lorraine said, thrown in as a joke.

"He might not even be buying for me, so I'm bringing a few hundred."

"Just be careful," said Lorraine. "No bending over or sudden turning."

She stepped outside. The sight of the big Espriado gave her pause. The leisure suited Tony got out with a cigar in hand. He shook. A bullet would have less impact. Her long, weaving waist looked slimmer, and in this leafy filtered light she looked hell fire black. Her messy piled hair was turning surfer blond. But that lacy top, it looked like it would be worn over a black dress at a funeral. Definitely not alone.

It loosely hung from her breasts. Her kid's jeans, tight as sweat.

"H-Hello, y-young lady," he stammered. "N-Nice, er, uh, glasses."

"H-Hi, Tony. Er, I hope this is okay. I'm sort of counting on being recognized as the Book Girl, so people will wonder why I'm so modest in this stifling outfit."

"No, th-that's f-fine. You… You wear glasses?"

Her nerve drove him to madness. This was completely out of line, but from what he saw in the FieldNet, even nude she was popularly accepted. She was inhumanly dark brown, with golden glints. Who would protest that? *But still…*

"Reading glasses, I got for my father. But I think I might keep them."

"She can't come!" said Ned from the back seat.

Her dark eyes snapped to life. "Well, you're in a bad mood, I see, Ned!"

"Well, who said you could ride my horse? And you're in a bad mood!"

The moody girl slid in beside the electrified Shean, and she looked back at Ned accusingly. She saw that Jesse wore a bibbed pair of painter's pants done in raw cotton, that fit to him exactly. He had no shirt under the shoulder straps. As usual for him he shined elegantly dark. Also notably tan, Ned wore jean cut-offs and a T-shirt, and his tender face was furiously disapproving.

Tony got in beside her, getting a full profile view of her delectable breasts, and, looking at her tight, leg separating jeans, he thunked the bank vault shut.

"Ned, keep quiet back there, if I may kindly ask. I need tranquility."

He warningly rumbled in his breath through his tonsils. "You keep quiet!"

Shean laughed at his father's surprised look. A big surprise. Happy Ned.

If this had any connection to her rank sun smell they all should have been happy. Despite her recent shower she reeked of bacon and brown sugar.

"Head… Head to the Wharf, wiseguy," Tony said to Shean. "Hold it, what about your friends, Bea… I mean, Miss Colwell? Do they want to come?"

"They might be tired. They worked today. I would say no. Let them rest."

Tony turned to the two girls who had eagerly come to the door. The smaller one was sunny hot. Her glasses also gave a discerning, no-nonsense effect.

"You two get in." Tony got out. "I'm Jesse's father, Tony." He shook with them and they happily gave their names. "Unless you have other plans."

"Lorraine does," said Virginia. "See you later, my dear friend. Good bye."

"I'm coming too!" said Lorraine as the girls squeezed into the back seat.

"Ohhh, no!" said Ned bleakly, and he fussed as he moved over.

Sunny hot Virginia pointed to her athletically scanty outfit. "Is this okay?"

Lorraine was safely in a *Madeline Comm Coll* polo shirt, and pocket pants. Tony assured the girls that, compared to Beatense, who had slid down to press her knees against the dash so she could admire her belly chain, they were fine.

"Beatense, if you catch any static," said Virginia ironically, "I don't know you."

"I'm in jeans! Repeat, jeans! If my lungs were in my legs I would suffocate!"

"Do that," said Shean, looking upon himself. He was smashingly shirtless in his peach linen sport coat with its sleeves pushed up. His loose, low holding pants were made of limp curtain cotton. "Can we go? No last second potty runs?"

Shean drove off. He had to make a wide loop because the car couldn't be turned around. Beatense's belly ripples were tightly working with the swerves moves of the car, as Shean swung the curving drive. Beatense pushed back her hair with bracelets jangling. Tony next to her saw that her slight body was all lankily connected, bone to bone and muscle to muscle. She didn't have one ounce of fat. She quivered with a tuned efficiency. Her hair fell in abundance. Hunger shaped her face.

"Hey, Ned, how's the shed building going? Can I come help?"

"No! It's in a secret hide-out and you can't find it! Anyway, it's a fort!"

"You just watch me find that shed, young man! I can bring some girls."

"No! No girls allowed!" Ned yelled, and everyone smiled to each other.

They turned north onto the Coastal Highway, toward Madeline.

"Dad, Beatense laid nude right in with the tourists today," Jesse blurted out. "On a chase lounge in full sight on Main Beach!"

She grinned cheesily, as Tony felt himself catch on fire.

"That's *shayz* lounge. And actually it's more cot-like. I was surrounded."

Virginia had exhibited that day her own public nudity. Her sport athletic self got so easily tan, as a kid she thrilled friends, relatives, neighbors, everyone.

They parked and walked over toward the entry gateway of the holiday outing pier. Now they would see the famed Book Girl in action, even as nearly decent. Beatense stepped away from the others, and walked through the puttering tourists in open sight. The people here had heard of her, they read about her, they saw the photos and the endless videos, but they had no preparation for the girl herself.

True, she was in jeans, but her Aunt Clara effrontery was explosive. With a wide smile she projected a simmering joyous excitement, from her crazy day of horseback terrorizing. Her abundant bush-like hair was turning blond, and some people saw the progressive lightening of her hair as they viewed her photos day by day. This told of her importance; everyone knew hour by hour what she was up to.

The restaurant was right on the big pier, at the very end. The place was one of several attractions, including snack concessions and rigged carnival games. Torrey had her art set up. As the sounds of shooting gallery reports, sirens, slot machines and glad cries filled the air, Beatense and Jesse ran over to her.

"Torrey! Hi!" Beatense called. "Boy, you sure got here fast! Any sales?"

"Hi, guys! I came straight here! And yeah, I better paint more up! Anyway, how goes it with Bookie Wookie? Notice how everyone is stopping to look at you? If you stick around, Beatense, in that lace yoke, they might also notice my pictures!"

But Torrey herself was also a big draw. She was in a cropped yellow T-shirt and trim, cuffed white shorts. With the reaching radiance of her blond hair and wide blue eyes, Tony, who didn't know her, saw that her toasty tan had that golden tinted glow that most Beach Girls can only try for. She was also muscled, but not in a way that would detract from her sweet appeal. She was almost boy faced, but her real assets lay in her intellect and refined blood. With eyes dreamy she was intoxicating.

The others came over. "Oh, Shean, hi!"

He couldn't believe she remembered him from the run Saturday morning.

"H-Hi, T-Torrey. S-So you sell this stuff right along, hah?" he said cleverly.

"I can't keep up. I should do you in that 10K! It would sell way fast! And Jesse, stop out by our shack, both of you, and pose for me!"

The two defibrillated, but even babies, toddlers and infants responded to this girl. As a contender herself, Beatense introduced her foolishly smiling friends, and Lorraine forgot Beatense existed.

"I, er, might b-buy one of these m-myself," said Tony, by way of openers.

"Why, that would be great, sir! Er, Tony. This one here is of Beatense."

"What?" She studied the crudely splotched globs of burnt umber. *It is?*

"Okay, sixty dollars, is it? Are... Are you sure that's enough, miss?"

"Sixty dollars is blatant robbery. I only need four hundred a month to live on. A certain *proud* roommate adds one hundred more. Oh, Beatense, Sienna says before you rode nude today, you hit the tourists nude! I wish I joined you!"

Tony gaped at the girl's sunken, flexing belly. These body builders.

A tourist couple stepped hesitantly up. "You really did these paintings?" said the husband, to the personably smiling artist. "They're... They're quite n-nice."

"See ya, Torrey! And thanks again for my painting the other night! Bye!"

Torrey assured everyone she *loved* meeting them. The family floated on.

"Y-You knew her, too, Shean?" said Tony, as the party moved on.

"We ran with her for two minutes in the 10K, and she remembered me!"

"So... So, how did you know her, Beatense?" Tony went doggedly on.

"I met her at Cocojo with her roommates. They're all sun believers."

"How unusual," said Tony, as another believing specimen approached.

This jean cut-offs and camisole (embroidered *Let's Fuck!*) bared beach girl came striding brightly along with her parents, who were obviously humdrum. She had that thin self-assured build, and messages sizzled as she caught Tony's eye. Contrary to the usual tourist malady of burning red, she flashed real brown. Her homely parents beamed with pride as everyone turned to gaze upon this exquisite player. Her nips stuck out into the cloth of her belly shirt without shame. She had delicate knob knees, a nice touch for her slim, smartly stepping thighs. She gave a smile to her father.

Tony, ears roaring, was already under stress from Beatense, Virginia and Torrey as he led his party into the restaurant, which was really a fast food place with a plate dinner menu. They went over to the bustling counter. Despite the bulging eyes and sudden silence, Hurricane Beatense casually read the lighted menu board.

"Oh, I go first? I'll have the chili, please. Medium size with chopped onions."

Tony was used to being around jaw droppers; his beautiful sons caused people to nudge each other wherever they went. But this was different.

He said, "Chili? Beatense, there's a whole menu there!"

"If you don't have one of their chocolate malts, you die," said dietary Virginia.

She was in a novel position; in her recent life usually she caused the uproar.

"Okay, a small chocolate malt, please, and thanks."

"A *small* one?" said Jesse, as the noise level began to inch back up.

"Ned, why not go wait in the car for us." --/-- "You go wait in the car!"

The others placed their orders, for meals or baskets, and they went to a six seat booth. Beatense joined in getting their drinks, and also helped Shean get the straws and napkins, and little cups of ketchup.

"Hey, that ketchup pump is pretty slick! They didn't have these at Burger Spa!"

This was said amongst forty-five stares. Shean nodded uneasily. He was a little embarrassed, because her fame and her noticed slim waist and just hidden breasts suddenly made him also very noticed. He was glad to sit down.

"So how does this work, do they bring us the food or do we have to go back for it? Ned, for Pete's sake, wipe that irritating smile off your face."

"You're the one who's irritating!"

"They bring it," said Tony, noticing the first-time-ever spark in Ned's eyes.

"This is quite the restaurant, I must say. Ned, I saw a sign saying boys fourteen years old can't eat here, so you better exit, my friend."

"Oh, yeah! Like I'm your friend!"

That reply brought out happy laughter. Tony was impressed at how she handled his troubled son. She charged right in with her comments and he actually accepted them with alacrity. He was glowing with eager excitement.

"Baskets! Why do they put the food in stupid baskets?" said Beatense, as Ned rolled up his eyes in disgust. "Are they wicker baskets, with a carry handle?"

The windows overlooked the marina. Beatense gave Ned a disapproving look, then she gazed out over the many boats. She couldn't see old Med Studs, but there were so many slips and so many masts it was just one of hundreds. Somewhere in there the Erotic Passage also lurked. It was a scene of huge prosperity, so that the entrances to the slip docks were security locked.

"Wow, quite a spread out there. That one boat looks like a converted tug."

"It was probably built from a kit," said Tony. "Years ago I used to work on those fishing charters further over, working it into the picking seasons."

"Picking? You mean like produce? Because this girl I know, either Summer or Staranne, works at picking. Jesse, you know her, she lives with Torrey."

"Yeah yeah, but where's the food?"

The atmosphere became more relaxed because people were making the effort to accept this girl as an ordinary state of affairs. Of course anyone walking by did give a look, but to just stare was bad form.

"Hi, got your food here!" the waitress said as she set down the trays.

Shean and Jesse felt weak, they had their eyes on this one. She was beachy tan, tall and blond headed, and her blue eyes had a probing and proud irreverence. She had on a white uniform shirt that had its short sleeves cuffed up to bare the pretty biceps of her capable arms, and her cuffed shorts made a lovely show of her long, mahogany polished legs. Her shorts were actually a little tight for those thighs, giving them a driving, sleek power. Tony guessed her weight at one hundred-ten pounds, more appropriate than the weedy Beatense. Virginia had similar trained muscle but in a much smaller but equally sunned package.

With her lowly chili Beatense looked at the abundance of the others in dismay.

"Gee, those hamburgers don't look so bad. Ned, give me yours."

"No! Go get your own!" --/-- "Okay, be right back!"

"Hold it," said Tony, not caring to have her parade through the place. "You can have one of mine. Here's your chili, and this is your *small* malt."

"Too small. Ned, let kindness be your guide and trade with me." --/-- "No!"

He glared at her fiercely, not knowing how glad everyone was to see that.

"I can get you another hamburger, Beatense" said Lorraine. "No one will pay any attention to me. And do you want a bigger malt?"

"No, Ned will just steal it from me. Or pour it on my head."

"Hey! Good idea!"

That brought a gale of laughter. Beatense looked upon Ned with contempt.

As Virginia picked up her hamburger the play of her light arms caused their tan to shift in shading, with the tensions working in opposition. Beatense was nearly too far gone for that effect, Tony noted, except for possibly that waist of hers.

Beatense turned to the frowning Ned, who was actually a cute boy. His coppery blond hair was thick, and like his brothers his skin delighted in sun.

"Ned, thanks for letting me ride your horse today, but he rides so slow!"

"You ride slow!"

Tony caught that double entendre, but to his relief the wanton girl did not.

"Tony, Ned's favorite saying is, Nothing ventured, nothing gained."

"It is not!"

"That's your favorite saying, Ned?" said Tony, going along with this.

"No!" --/-- "Then why do you keep saying it?" --/-- "I don't keep saying it!"

Tony saw a gleam in his son's eyes. Far from hurting him, those cutting remarks enlivened him. Now he could worship her with free rein.

Slurping noisily, angering Ned, Beatense started on her chili. She decided that it along with her malt was enough. She gave Tony back his hamburger.

"Oh, say, guys, I forgot to mention, I talked to my father this morning, and he said I can stay another week. They were doing this track repair up at Maher Ridge, where Craig is from, and they discovered a big sinkhole that could have caved in. So they changed my ticket for after they're working on that. Ned, be quiet."

"You're the one who's doing all the talking!"

"Well, then, we do expect rent for that second week," said Virginia.

"I can pay for a month. It's worth it. With all the noisy activity and planes and helicopters flying by, it just seems that adventure is in the very air."

Tony and Shean looked at each other, as Lorraine and Virginia also looked. In those few words she captured it. Now what words could capture her?

"I can stay here indefinitely, actually, because Tamdyn at the Breeze Hotel offered me thirty-six thousand, for job unspecified. Ned, quit that insane blubbering!"

"You're the one who's blubbering!"

"Honestly, I would go with that job," said Tony. "That Tamdyn is pulling the hotel out of a financial sinkhole, speaking of, and if anyone knows the price of towels by the dozen or in lots of a hundred, it's her. But she could use help."

"She wanted to know if I sing. I do, but I don't know the songs down here. If I faked them, not knowing all those subtle little nuances, I would be a total flop."

"No kidding," said a certain boy coldly.

"Look, Ned, they surgically removed my extra finger. You can't even tell."

"Yeah, they also removed your extra head! Too bad they picked the wrong one!"

Beatense endured the laughter. "You know, I once had this crazy dream."

"I'm not too big on dreams, girl," said Tony. "I speak for all of us."

"Well, wait until you hear this one! You see, I dreamed about this peninsula that stuck out to sea, and it had all these cobblestone streets and housekeeping cottages and cozy little inns. There were all these craft and gift and art shops, too. Out at the very end of the peninsula they had an old stone lighthouse that was combined with a nautical museum and post office. People traveled hundreds... What, Ned."

"Boy, what a stupid dream!"

"Shutteth uppeth. People traveled hundreds of miles to stay there and they ate at all these charming little dining nooks. Elderly folk would sit at their easels and paint seascapes, or they painted old sailors fixing their nets and sails."

"Beatense, that isn't so funny," said Lorraine. "Nice imagery though."

"What color did they paint the sailors?" said Ned. "Purple?"

"Shut up, fool. So anyway," said Beatense, "I was walking..."

"Are you sure you don't want this hamburger?" said Tony.

"Mr. Shattuck, we really appreciate your treating us," said Lorraine. "I mean, we're just tag-alongs with the Beatense invite."

"It's always fun to come here." said Virginia. "For the wharf itself, too."

Beatense clenched her teeth. "So there I was, in my dream, walking..."

"I don't want to hear your stupid old dream," said Ned, with neck set.

Tony realized that he wanted this girl's friendship badly.

"Okay, you were walking toward..." he prompted, causing eye-rolls.

"Not toward! I was just walking! I saw those buildings out on the peninsula in the dawn sun's misty haze. I thought, I bet this must be a dream, you don't see that in real life! But I could see every detail so clearly!"

Tony shook his head. "Beatense, really..."

"This place should have a salad bar," said Jesse.

"Jesse, let her finish her exciting dream," said Lorraine. "It might pick up."

"Lorraine, I'm only trying to lift you out of the boredom of your dreary existence by telling a funny story that you can repeat to others for their amusement."

"If I do repeat it, it will be in a padded cell."

"Ha ha. So I keep walking, and there's this retail plaza that includes a bakery."

"A bakery," said Virginia. "What about the cozy little nooks you mentioned?"

"Okay, there might have been a little redundant market saturation. So anyway, I think, If this is a dream, wouldn't I be able to control what happens in it?"

"Boy, that was a funny dream," said Jesse, giving Lorraine a droll look.

"So I think, That bakery is closed now, let's see if I can open it. And, *ding!* The lights go on and these ladies are inside slicing and wrapping bread.

"So these people waiting outside do a double-take and think, Oh, so they're open now, and they go over to it, but just as this one guy reaches for the door and pulls on it, *ding!* The bakery is closed again, no ladies and the lights are out."

"Well, that is a story worth repeating," said Virginia, with a strained look.

"The guy was pulling on the door just at that exact time, only to find it locked with the lights out, so he had the cheesiest grin as they all edged away from him. Like, What are you doing, trying to go in there when the place is obviously closed? Never mind that they all thought it was open, too."

Beatense sucked on her malt, that had warmed up enough for the straw.

"So like, then what happened?" said Virginia, actually now interested.

"The next details are a teensy bit unclear, I'm afraid, but I do recall that he made such a fool of himself, I thought I better re-open the place to restore his dignity."

She took another prolonged pull on her straw.

"Does... Does it go on from there?" said Tony.

"Well, it's just a repeat. *Ding!* The lights go back on, the ladies are slicing bread, and everybody kind of looks at each other and shuffle in. Which is exactly when I decided that the store is closed after all! And, *ding!* The lights go back out, and the ladies slicing bread disappear, and there they are, locked in the dark wondering what happened! And they were trapped."

"They weren't the only ones," said Ned.

"I agree. Let's haul out of here!" said Beatense, and she began to rise.

"Hold it, wrap this up quick and then we'll go," said Tony. "And by the way, are any of you up for pie?" --/-- "So they were trapped..." prompted Lorraine.

"Yes. So I go by the other stores and I see these romantic lovers running toward each other. 'Hank, Hank!' and 'Mary, Mary!' But just as old Hank opens his arms to sweep her up, she disappears, in point of fact she never existed.

"'You should have seen his shocked look when he grabbed for the thin air and stumbled from the expectation of her weight. So he looks around at everybody with bewildered guilt. They all thought he was wacko, of course. Like you, Ned."

"Like you!"

"So I go on and laughed evilly at these people, who jumped back because they realized I had this power. Then I go into like this business meeting in this restaurant, where these suit types are all sitting there self importantly muttering. This one guy is the moderator and he starts talking, and I see this floor lamp behind him. I decide to make it taller, and *ding!* The shade rises a couple feet. The talk starts back up, and I raise it again! Now the muttering gets louder, the speaker is looking at everybody, at which time I raise the lamp right up through the ceiling, and sunshine beams in!

"It even lights up the floating dust. The speaker turns to look, so just then I bring the lamp back down to its original height. Now, he isn't sure that he saw that hole in the ceiling or not, so he just kept staring up at it in front of all these guys. He looks back around with this embarrassed smile, because by now of course no one cares to own up that they saw it go through the ceiling either! That's when I woke up!"

"Okay, very funny," said Shean, laughing with the others. "Let's try the pie."

They got up and went to the dessert bar, where a sun loving, brown loving young lady was proudly slicing the steamy plump pies. The blond tendrils curled before her ears gave her pert face a lovely delicate warmth, and the way facial bones influence character, her cheeks indicated a very sensitive intelligence. Her short sleeved crisp white shirt gave her thin arms a warm, sun kissed appeal, and her trim butt-bumping slacks showed how tall and slight she was. With eyes dreamily closed she bent over and sniffed at the brownies with a little nose. Like her slacks this posture also called attention to her refined lines. The vignette of her sniffing the cake was so touching even Virginia smiled, but Tony saw that she bore an implant scar. But instead of that diminishing her sensible personality, her need of protection showed just how happily determined she was to celebrate all that life had to offer. She loved sex. Why not?

Tony coughed. "Heh heh, wh-what kind of pies do you have, miss?"

She straightened up, cutely flushed with embarrassment.

"Er, we're featuring cream pies tonight, sir! But we always have berry pies!"

They returned to the table. Beatense tucked into her cherry pie. She gazed out the window right, again looking over Madeline boatyard. She saw a big, mahogany sterned cabin cruiser like Erotic Passage on its way out to sea, and first one chrome pipe, then the other burbled underwater as it lazily rolled. She saw boaters carrying picnic baskets and nautical gear strolling the wide expanse of piers and catwalks out to their slips. The gulls wheeled in circles.

An employee of the marina, a teen-aged youth who just wore cotton duck shorts, came walking by with a push-broom on his shoulder, and he carried a suds filled pail. His gloriously slender form and his limbs were burned to a depthful shiny brown, like that of Elgin, Kit, Sailor Sim and the pie girl. He greeted everyone with wide smiles.

"It isn't fair, Tony," Beatense stated. "That kid out there can prance around in just shorts, and show off his tan to the world, but if a girl is out there in shorts, with top, mind you, people read all this sex into it. And so that's what happens, the honest love of sun turns into attracting sex. But to be honest, I am active. And it's all okay."

"Mr. Denton lets me and Knife just wear our boy bikinis," said Shean.

"You make mistake bringing that up," said Tony. "From now on you try and wear something decent, Knife or no Knife, permission or no permission."

"But Mr. Denton doesn't mind! I even wait on customers in my Cove Boy!"

He rolled his eyes. He was actually proud that Jesse and Shean were such avid tanorexics; they got him accepted in a neighborhood that otherwise might have been huffy toward a pack of gypsies. The ravishing looks of all three kids was a factor too, and they were horse lovers. That apparently counted for a lot in their neighborhood.

It was sort of an In, like skiing and sailing.

"I used to work those boats, Beatense," said Tony, referring to the flying bridge charter craft that abounded. "I was just a trained monkey, I had to grin all day and be as inconspicuous as possible."

"You already said that. You worked it in with your picking."

"Yeah, but that's how we eventually got rich," said Jesse. "I can tell how."

"No!" said Tony. "It's a longer story than that boring dream we just heard."

Beatense laughed. "At least Ned liked my dream." --/-- "I... Did... Not!"

Tony saw how hard the boy had to work at keeping his stern expression.

"Like I was saying, I have no complaints except for having Ned around."

Frowning with distaste, she carefully took a bite of her pie. "Ahhh! Delicious."

"I was just thinking how horrible it is to have you around!"

"Impossible. But hey, Ned, my butt itches. Will you scratch it for me?"

"No!" --/-- "Why not? I would certainly scratch your butt."

"Probably you scratch lots of butts," Ned replied, pleased by the laughter.

Beatense finished eating. She rested back, then felt in her pocket.

"Oh oh! I'm missing my ten dollars! Ned, freeze!" --/-- "I didn't take it."

"Tony, you should give your sons far higher allowances so they aren't tempted to steal wrongfully from honest people like me!" --/-- "I didn't take it!"

"She does have a point there," said Jesse. "Allowance-wise."

"But why did you take it, Ned? The way you shoplift everything, like at the store this morning, is money necessary? But say, egg nose, this might surprise you, but I just found out that only a few people think I'm a buck toothed nobody."

"Yeah, that does surprise me," Ned conceded, arousing more laughter.

But Tony felt the moody, sun saturated power of her cheeks-chiseled face.

"Good one, Ned," said Virginia with a bemused look, courtesy of her nose placed little glasses and steady eyes. "Tony, thanks again. This was great."

Looking across the room Beatense saw a familiar face.

"Excuse me," she said as she stood. "By cracky, there's someone I know!"

Wiping her chin, she sprang up and skipped over with her Clara bib aflutter.

"Hello, Ida, do you recognize me? It's me, Beatense, from the train."

"Well, if it isn't my skinny little dandelion!" Ida said as she got up. The lady now took in her throbbing tan. "Oh my... Oh my word."

Mr. Cornhill, who, despite his famed stuffiness, was a fair judge of the desert oil interns, favored this girl with a very surprised look as he also stood.

"Is… Isn't she b-beautiful, Herbert? Our famous little Puppet!"

She snapped off her Clara. "I must be famous if even you know about it!"

She shook hands with the drilling engineer, who stared in horror. Ida, who was a hardened veteran of worshipping young tanners, had an idea that set her at a huge, enviable advantage to everyone else here, who couldn't invite her.

"But baby, I want to hear what you've been up to," she said. "You're just so darn *brown!* I wonder… Heh heh, I wonder if we could g-get together t-tomorrow."

"That would be difficult, Ida. I'm really pushing my tanning. But wait, if you're staying in one of those Cardiff Shores hotels, that I have to see!"

The lady couldn't reply; the girl snapped and sizzled with burning sun. And then the friends were joined by a boy. This kid was right out of Ida's desert.

"Oh, Ida, this is Jesse, and Jesse, this is Ida. And this is Dr. Herb, her hub. Jesse, me and Ida were old desert campers and Steelers together!"

"Steelers!" --/-- "The Queen Of Steel. The train we rode here, eons ago!"

33

THE PARTY

Beatense got the details and the two quick hugged and the kids returned.

"That Lighthouse Hotel up in Stony Arbor is pretty Hitsy-Witsy," said Jesse. "But if you like zapping out old people, boy, that's the place. Shean would love it."

"Yeah, him walking in on that wedding naked at that Pickwick hotel."

Tony saw the girl's smile, after first noting her lack of a top. Every eye was upon her, and in response Shean removed his peach coat. People gasped.

"Nice try, Shean. You guys, that was Ida, who I met on the train."

"You mean she didn't run the other way?" Ned growled.

Everyone laughed, yet again, and Lorraine never saw such a smug look.

Shean had an edge over Beatense; the fluorescent lighting gave him that vibrato glow. But as they stepped out of the restaurant the girl regained her supremacy. On the way home she slid down with her feet propped on the dash again, and Tony saw the muscles of her belly work with the car's moves again. Breasts too.

Virginia asked Tony if he could stop by Short Drug for picking up the beer half barrel. Tony, Virginia, Lorraine, Shean and Jesse saw the stupefied reactions of the clerks and customers as they beheld Beatense. They couldn't believe she could just walk into the store like that. Virginia took honors too. She was just in her tie-top and shorts, and her tan was still coming in from that hot day. She inflicted a self satisfied look that came naturally with her inquisitive glasses. But it was Beatense's upwardly twin-peached escape from her low-cut jeans that seemed to interest people.

The lighting of this place rendered her black, she observed.

They ended up hefting the barrel into the trunk, with pump and ice tub, and they tied the trunk lid down with coarse jute twine as provided. The boys grabbed at the flimsy plastic cups and happily set them atop their pretty heads like hats.

Such dear, good boys, Beatense thought, as she found her cot bag.

"Ned! Get that cup off your shrunken head! You're contaminating it!"

"Well, Shean and Jesse are doing the same thing!"

"But they washed their hair just last winter! And where's my ten dollars at?"

"I didn't take it!"

What's her secret? Tony wondered. Not one civil word to the poor kid!

Tony and Shean lugged in the beer as it sat in the thick poly ice tub. Ned brought the tube-bag of cups in, per Beatense order, and the poor kid looked so woebegone performing this duty that she also insisted he bring in the ice.

"Why should I have to do this? It isn't fair!"

"We can discuss your shameful attitude later, Ned, which stinks!"

The girls thanked Tony and he left with Shean and Ned. Jesse stayed.

He watched Beatense set her painting off her dresser, to expose the mirror. She studied herself as if the image was a person she was in love with.

"Hey, that's a Torrey," he said, recognizing the globby painting.

"Oh, that solves that mystery!" said Virginia. "Now, pour in the ice, Jesse."

"The hell! I can't handle any ice! My hands!"

But he began opening the bags. Virginia strolled over to the utility shed to throw the breaker for the colorful plastic shaded party lights strung through the aged trees. Beatense, with a saddened look at how little of the butter oil she had left in her bottle, began oiling her skin to freshen it up. Lorraine descended on her.

"What do you think you're doing?"

"Getting ready for the party! Lorraine, can you pick me up some of that Omega stuff at Hendrick's tomorrow? Make it a quart. No, wait, a pint of Omega and a pint of coconut. But right now I need a towel to rub this in."

"Why don't you do that in the bathroom?"

"With that stupid medicine cabinet mirror?"

"You could dry paint at ten feet with that tan," said Jesse. "Mine too."

Virginia threw the switch and stepped back out and looked down the lane. It was still too early for the lanterns to show yet, but they did come on. She ran back to the cabin, looking down at her brown, child-like legs. Returning to the cabin she stripped nude, as did Beatense, and she oiled her friend's back.

Across town Buck knew nothing of brown, except as a color for paper bags and human filth. In defeat he clambered down the metal roofed stairs from his dreary flat for dinner in the bar. The Lucky Dollar was a den of losers in a world of winners. The beaten regulars here knew nothing of healthy self. They morbidly sat drinking and playing dice on even brilliant days. The sensual young women and their free spirited lives of beautiful, sun heated pleasure were alien to them. They feared their looks of horror, whenever they encountered each other.

Back at the cabin Jesse strolled over with beer and cigaret in hand.

"Okay, I'm corrupted now, you two."

"Oh, poor dear," said Lorraine. "Absinthe will probably be naked too."

"Oh, Jesse, go find Buck and get him up here," said Beatense.

He brightened up. "Sure! But it might be awhile. I don't have my bike."

Jesse stripped bare and lit off. Beatense hoped he found Buck, she needed a friend in case Kenny didn't come, or Sienna. As the popular Puppet she knew about parties, and she had the Hoganforth refresher. Everyone straggled in, and once they pumped their beer they stood around talking. The rocking stereo was ignored, but the silence between songs was always noticed. Virginia turned on their carriage styled, cobweb filled porch light, so some of the party overflowed outside.

Beatense stayed in. Everyone was curious about this famed Book Girl, and she was surrounded by admiring fans, who weren't terribly offended by her hot tan naked presentation. Despite her being so impossibly perfect they found her to be disarming and funny. She said that pie girl was the one they should have published. "By far."

Beatense kept Lorraine by her side, so that she got attention too. But then she saw friends and joined them. Virginia held court with the four boating guys, and the ever bare Absinthe joked and laughed in the middle of a group outside.

Absinthe caught the bemused attention of two skeletal, lanky girls, who with their hacked-at scrappy hair and nose rings, had cutely smug, irreverent looks. Both were grudgingly tawny golden, as if they had no need of tan to achieve self worth. These were Nut and Meg, who as twin sisters were so in love that they often matched each other in speech and movement. As if on signal they shucked off their clothes, then being commited lesbians went in to scope the Book Girl. Holding her beer, Beatense radiated the cruel power of her black tan, her whip-like waist, and her tight, starved belly. She had a cascade of salt dried, surf yellowed hair. The twins coveted.

The beach girls present were terrors, too, but for most of them one had to use some imagination with them. They wore T-shirts and shorts, or airy light frocks or tie tops with tea towel sarongs. All flashing with exorbitant tan, they had that precise boniness caused by their really hating to eat. Live, pure muscle.

But Holiday Hill had its share of ordinary, sun phobic girls too, and if they were leery of being out of place here, their interest in seeing the Book Girl precluded any hesitation. Also many of the guys, disinclined to get tan, weren't the type to get very tremendously noticed. Lorraine found a happy, chattering home with this group.

Karen entered, wearing the same outfit she wore for the 10K, including those slit soccer shorts and short cut tank top. She had just come from a run. The effect was like an axe splitting a log. She too had a tan still coming in from the day's sun, and it roiled the air like heat waves. The stunning girl flaunted her tuned muscles.

Beatense went over to her. Karen, aka Sylphire, was a blinding beam of deeply enriched sun, but she was also somehow known for her healthy, sturdy smile, that of the hardworking athlete who always credits her teammates and coach.

"Hey, Karen, is it? Can I introduce myself? I'm Beatense the Book Girl and you stole those two guys from me a couple days ago, Will and Gene."

"Oh, yeah! The three of us went to the Jammers bar and found a friend of mine and we all ended up at my place! It was, shall we say, an active night!"

"Great! Because I'm a strong believer in talents not going to waste."

"Well, that brings up a slight point. You come out of the blue with your bitchy tan and turn the whole town inside out. I wish it was one of us long suffering locals who took that initiative. You come in as an outsider with no history here, and it's like some rich cunt from Burgundy Hills buys a $5 charity raffle ticket, and takes the $1000 gift certificate home with her. That is to say, I'm actually with you all the way, but some girls here feel a little upstaged."

"I agree, since coming to town I have seen dozens of girls who outdo me. But at age twelve was I sitting there inside playing with dolls or playing records? No, I was tanning up on our building rooftop. Plus I was a public criminal of nudity. Then out at the desert surveying camp I upped the ante, at thirteen, mind you, where I willingly exerted myself with good fuck. I admit I was crazed for it, and that must be what the publishing agent saw in me when I was back from camp the second time."

"He saw you fucking?"

"No, but with the desert tan I had the implications were there. I still don't know what he was doing up there in Arrolynn, but the result was I ended up making over three hundred thousand in book sales." She flexed herself. "See why?"

She didn't mention that her earnings were cut by the bank failure.

"Boy, if I pass Qualifyings Tuesday I'll be lifeguarding down at Sorel, making just twenty an hour, all wrapped up in a one piece. Wish I had your life!"

"Hey, talk to Jerry, I think he can arrange a bikini for you down there."

"Yeah! I'm going to be coached on the written test by him, I think, tomorrow after work at his place. I better see him at the park tomorrow and remind him!"

The rivals parted and Beatense kicked into star mode, where she seemed more interested in everyone's talking to her rather than her talking to them. She had an easy, relaxed smile that looked like she was drawing a reason to live from everyone, and this even won over Karen's resentfully envying doubters.

Beatense was radiating sizzly electromagnetic waves throughout the cabin, while the guys talking with her were almost already pale office schnocks. A girl came over and joined them. In tight jeans and classic cotton shirt open four buttons down, and with the sleeves rolled to her elbows, showing the shapely flow of her forearms, she stood aristocratically willowed in build, and she had impeccably boned, gentle looks.

In the cabin's dim lighting she was just so brown, a shifting saturation of hot burn that shined with rich golden glints.

"Hi, you're Beatense? I'm Flammchen, the Hill slut. No, I wish!"

"Flammchen? A name worse than mine? Nice tan. Good honest effort!"

"No, I lay in the sun in the mounds just two or three hours every day and that's it. If I ever actually laid out all day dogs would howl and babies cry. Back in my teen years I used to lay out all day because I got such shocker results, which seemed so crucially important then, but now I'm surviving with other diversions."

"Fine, but just two hours a day? And you have a tan like that?"

"It's a family thing. Hit or miss, though. I have cousins who hate me. So these days I just go for that artsy/nutty look of healthy self indulgence."

Beatense saw Canterbury enter the cabin. Her wave to her wasn't seen.

"I wish I could settle for just nutty. But I'm like a factory, steel sheet in one door, stampings out the other. If I cut off the flow in, like the punch presses I just stop. I think if you look at that new arrival over there, Canterbury's another addict."

She was slim and severely tanned, and she wore a bikini tie-top and fringed and faded cut-offs. These gave her long, stretch-muscled thighs an extra depth of rich brown. She had that blank look of sultry disapproval, and as she walked the cords of her long and leaned middle flexed. Her belly had a tautly defined linea crease, while the deltoids of her slimmed shoulders stood out in boned splendor. Her hung biceps had a capable swelling, and their opposing triceps had a rugged work-out bulk.

The girl studied her surroundings with distaste, as the tendons of her long regal neck coordinated the slow turning of her set-just-so noble head.

She sported a white key tube hung from her neck.

Cup held, she stood with steeled legs flexed, haughtily gazing upon her hard shoulder as the eyes bulged. Her surf tan was so hot saturated, like Flammchen she projected over one hundred varying shades as she moved. All vied for attention in a translucently golden blurred, iridescent glow. She had the attitude of a professional tanner, one who despised the non-tanners of the world.

"Hi, I know you!" Beatense said as came over. "I'm Beatense! I met you on the bus when you got on up at Cardiff Shores last Monday! You were laying out nude in total public! Boy, what a shock! But I caught up! You're Canterbury!"

Her mouth dropped open. "Hi, I wondered who you were, waving at me when I came in. I was a Netty star until you hit town. You're very transformed. And look at that hair! Before you were kind of dark reddish, but you're getting really blond."

"On the outer surface mostly, but thanks for noticing! I was talking to Flammchen in the shirt there, about tannability." Beatense's other friend returned. "Hey, if you want blond hair, Canty, I defer you to Karen here!" said Beatense nobly.

Canterbury had little interest in a rival's hair. Beatense saw the difficulty.

"At least, if you're wearing a lifeguard one-piece your hair will get sun!"

"You're a lifeguard?" said Canterbury, now accepting the hopeful rescuer. "First Aid certified for heavy surf rescue? I did that summers back in college. It was awful, we had to sit in those stupid fiberglass enclosures up on stilts."

"They don't have those down at Sorel, but maybe you can help me. Before I'm hired I got this one pre-qualifying written to take first. Is it hard? I'm supposed to be coached on that tomorrow evening. Then I'll be tested for surf rescue."

"No prob," said Canterbury. "If they want you, and they will, you're in."

Like Canterbury herself, this rescuer to-be didn't particularly fit the image of the dedicated guardian scanning the seas for anyone in trouble. With her surfer shagged yellow hair and white frizzled eyebrows, that warned that this sand sunner was too mercenary for such selfless heroics, because they don't bleach out that pale without fanatical sun and self worship. But of all the surf hots in the cabin, Beatense included, only Flammchen had that commanding poise that acted to subjugate others, because she was quite artless while still carrying great pride.

As all the talk bragged on an older girl entered the cabin, and she stared at the violently roasted surf girls in smiling wonder. Perhaps late twenties aged, her firmed features of expression had that homey and pleasant familiarity with artist easels and book discussions. Her face was pale, but her arms were tinty golden.

She wore slimming faded jeans with those inner suede inserts of a horse trainer. Her T-shirt just cleared her belt loops, peeking her flat belly, and this was her only threat to her warm friend-for-life appeal. Her light pretty arms had a formed muscle flowing, as if she was still the tree climbing trouble-maker. She had bright blue eyes, that told of responsible character. She seemed the type who would rather stay home and keep her parents company than go out just to get out. Her ash brown hair was tousled in readiness for any occasion, from tents and canoes to recitals or banquets. She had a careful, practical quality that told she would always be a daughter, niece, companion or employee of treasured worth. She wrote letters full of smiles.

"I'm Caroline," she said to Beatense, laughing. "You're tanner in real life!"

Beatense saw that this girl frankly, openly admired her. She was a rare find, she wouldn't hold back her compliments, even if it lessened her own position.

"Yes, I'm Beatense, Caroline. I'm here on vacation, down from Arrolynn. While I was gone my bank had a run and I'm almost broke, but I'm tan, yes."

The fellows turned their heads back and forth. Beatense was a decent kid even though she was so immeasurably tan, but Caroline had the real grit.

"You're from Arrolynn?" a spokesman cut in. "I can't believe that."

"Okay, try me. I've fed mountains of sopping laundry through the wringer rollers, watching so my fingers don't get crushed, then lugged the clothes up to the roof to hang them out to dry. I also dragged our rugs up to the roof to beat the dust out of them, and I carried the coal scuttle up from the cellar at dawn to get the stove going. Plus I can knead the dough for ten loaves of bread in two shakes, and we don't have microwaves, computers or air conditioning."

"Well, my first years I used a manual typewriter at work," said Caroline, "until we finally figured out how to get away from carbons. So I paid my dues."

"You don't half know what dues are," argued Beatense. "Did you know that our TVs are only black and white? And our phones are wired to the wall?"

"But you made it through very beautifully," said Caroline, smiling with the friendly attitude of selflessly admiring a friend's new car or huge windfall.

"There you are, roomie! I didn't know you came inside!"

It was the competent career miss Beatense had met on the roadway earlier, the actually on-the-job dressed young lady with the lank blond hair who smiled at her in welcoming acceptance. But she was in camisole and butt-cut shorts now, a useless, skinny thing, who with her golden tawny tan wasn't half as practical looking as before.

Caroline laughed. "I'm just checking out your competition, Kellye."

"Hey, I know you!" this Kellye said. "I saw you on the path earlier!"

"Yeah, I saw you! You were dressed for some kind of career job."

"Well you just affirmed my existence!" said Kellye. "But what of Caroline?"

"Oh, she's way above us. Whatever I say doesn't add or detract."

The girls laughed. Two miles to the south Ned and his friends were in his room doing a lips-to-arm rectal recital with a battery tape recorder, singly or altogether. The naughty boys were helpless with laughter, and Tony, overhearing their antics, shook his head. The change in Ned the last couple of days, happy at last.

"Kell, Beatense here is from Arrolynn," said Caroline. "Do you believe it?"

"I would never guess that! And do you get that tan up there, too?"

"No, the latitude is bad. I need a real heat wave to get the dogs barking."

"What would that be like?" said Caroline. "Getting so tan you smoke."

"And look at that waist!" said Kellye. "Like mine is too, of course." Indeed. A slight and very impish looking girl, also a mad tanner, very, came over.

"Are you Beatense? Viturna told me to look for you here. I'm Bitsy."

"You're Bitsy! Oh, boy! Look where I am now because of you! My hero!"

"If I knew of your getting so tan I never would have wrote in!"

"Well, you got your points. And that Cocojo, it's a gorgeous paradise!"

Bitsy, in tie-top and shorts, laughed. The talk went on in this party that was nicely lively, even if it was on a Sunday night with class or work the next day.

"I can be so careless here! I even rode along the surf naked!"

"That must have been glorious," said Caroline. "I dream of that."

"You dream of it? But you live here. Why not just do it?"

"I keep Tapioca at Bunker Ridge. It's a show barn, hunters and jumpers."

Beatense did think that Caroline had that classy persona of one riding to fences. She wanted to discuss this, but then Kitanning entered. He was in a too-small, short sleeved shirt of heavy white cotton. This was unbuttoned to bare his blackety chest and belly. And with his frayed, thigh tight jeans riding to his hips, the slim boy stood proudly tall. But his royalty status wasn't resented.

"Hey, Care, Flamm, Bits and Holl, I have to talk to Kit there. Stay here!"

Beatense felt a tad unsure as she approached Kit. The shrunken size of his food service shirt forced it to hang fully open, so he almost leaped out from it.

"H-Hi, there, Kit."

"Oh, hi, Beatense. Nice to see you, finally. I kind of looked for you, *today.*"

"Yeah, I ended up riding with Jesse to Cocojo. I'm sorry about that."

"If you knew I was going to be on Main how come you didn't look for me?"

"You could have looked for me! And then I had this interview..."

"Don't explain. But I got off from the restaurant tonight, giving up big tips."

"Well, getting the sun you *obviously* did today nicely compensated you."

"Well, I guess this whole thing is a little unfortunate. Nice, er, outfit."

The girl was left with mouth open, but then she saw the shirtless Kenny come in, filling the ugly grey void that opened before her. She rejoined her friends and Kenny came over, gaping so openly at the girls that Caroline, Bitsy, Flammchen and Kellye, impressed by his beautiful tan, thought he was a wee bit youthfully clumsy.

"Hi, B-Beatense. How... How you doing?" She stared. *Monkey HP!*

"Great. But boy, did you get sun today! I'm sorry about wearing what I was today, Kenny, if that bothered you. But I'm way more civilized now."

"Y-Yeah. B-But you beat out th-that one Troubadour babe... Over by Kit."

The girls turned. Canterbury, and Karen, with Kit. To Beatense, it seemed their tans gained in power, matching Kenny, even as she helplessly watched.

"That's... That's Canterbury, Kenny. Not Troubadour, but Cardiff Shores. I saw her when I first came to town, on the bus. So what did you do today?"

"Basically I laid out." Left unsaid, *Just for you.* The girl noticed again his all day effort tan, nicely burned in. "Did you... Did you lay out at all?"

"Yes, on the wrong beach, as it happened. I rode Ned's horse Spec with Jesse down to Cocojo, and then I rode with Sienna, if you know her."

"N-No." *That belly.* "But I never... I never saw anyone so... So tan!"

"It's a family thing. Some blood heritage thingie, but it's hit or miss."

Flammchen laughed at the plagiarism. As the talk went on Beatense hoped to sleep over with Kenny, and fuck. He had wide, shy, adorable eyes and scruffy hair.

And important too, chiseled teeth. They gave him a quality family pedigree. He was brown and thin in that youthy healthy way where people wink at each other.

Beatense didn't want to scare him off, so she went into an ingénue act of gulping nervousness even though she was known to be quite aggressive. Even more trembling and nervous was Lorraine, who had somehow succeeded Canterbury and Karen in talking to the mighty Kit. Her eyes were wide as one would expect, but the boy just seemed to open up to her in frank conversation.

Beatense continued talking with Kenny, obliquely dropping tender hints. She saw that Lorraine was alone. She excused herself and sidled over to her.

"Hey, roommate? Like, what's happening?"

"Trevor and I are going for a walk! He's outside right now!"

"Is he. But don't keep him waiting. I know from experience he hates that."

"I have to duck in the bathroom. Go hang onto him for me!"

Beatense went back to Kenny. "Be right back. A matter of diplomacy."

With that the girl went out and confronted Trevor.

"Look, you ass, if you're hitting on Lorraine just to get back at me, I kill."

His young face looked startled. "No! We just got to talking, and she seems to be my type. She isn't all hypered up with that beach girl mindset of tan, tan, tan."

"But you're tan, tan, tan yourself. You must just deep bake, worse than me."

"I do deep bake. Kenny does too but he isn't militant like me. So that makes me atypical with normal guys, an all-day tanning self fanatical outlier."

"Or a gay suspect. Except I know you're not. Me, I'm a lesbian. Okay, I do see where you're at now, Lorraine is different like you're different. You're a couple."

Kit gave an embarrassed smile and Beatense embraced him.

He wasn't invited, but for these beer parties no invites needed, and so Buck, who Jesse somehow missed, decided to try it. He was walking up from his car wondering about his chances, when to his horror he saw the very girl step from the cabin and hug Kit. His world became a swirling, black hell vortex. He took a last disbelieving look, like a doomed sailor who stares up at the distant silvery surface. He stumbled back to his dented car, with the merry glow of the party lanterns lighting his path. He heard laughter, music. He sagged against the car and tried to find the will to open the door.

It had to happen, Kitanning is her lover. That fling in her motel room, no fling.

"Hey, Buck, aren't you going in? You should see that... That Book Girl!"

"Hah? Oh, yeah, Allen, I heard of her. I... Er... Got a delivery."

Kit. It was inevitable that those two would get together again, after that night.

Beatense met Lorraine as she came out. The two went their separate ways, one more happily than the other. Absinthe was still sitting cross-legged on the stoop, naked, delighting several fellows. Her vibrant tan glowed against the grey wood, and her skeptically intelligent face was radiant. Whom would she fuck? All three?

Beatense rejoined Kenny, but his trouble was, everyone had to talk to the famous star. She was all too delighted with their close attention. Kenny lost heart as the girl turned from fellow to fellow, eyes aglow. Then the miracle, she turned to him.

"Kenny, I'm not going to let that shit tan go to waste. I want to join up with you."

34

CARDIFF SHORES

A small, work-out built athlete wearing crisp little glasses joined the party. She burst with hot brown and muscle, with unkempt boy-cut hair. She had a clever, boy's face with bone-carved character, and it seemed her glasses gave her a mischievous spark. Her looks told of blood-lines going back to the era of isolated forest villages, of bonfire dancing accompanied by primitive instruments, of maidenly conjoining per tribal ritual, and running down deer barefoot and killing them with steel. All this was eons behind her now, but she had that residual toughness, where aged trees and eternal streams still heated her steaming blood. The guys greeted her as Armitage.

In response her wide, engaging smile formed dimples. Naked Krinkles who came with her was also noticed. Their social tenure was cut short, the party broke up with Monday's class or jobs. Canterbury left with the boaters, and Absinthe left with her porch friends. Kenny watched Beatense, Krinkles, Virginia, Bitsy and Armitage push the beds together. Their combined power scared him off and he said good-bye. Her heart pounding at the lesbian prospect awaiting, Beatense gave him a relieved hug.

The girls wrestled wildly, and the cameras at the door moved right inside.

At dawn, after running Krinkles home and Bitsy back to the Hog, Beatense sat at the table and counted out her rent. Virginia also sat bare before the open door.

Beatense waved to a camera. "Okay, here's ten fifties. My rent."

"Not enough," said Virginia, taking the bills anyway. "But what I'm wondering is if letting Armitage keep the deposit for taking the barrel back was too generous."

"She was a dream, so no. Bitsy was too. But we did make a profit, didn't we?"

"Yeah, we had a good turn-out. Fifty bucks, we cleared. But talk about dreams, Lorraine, you had Kit all night? Him?"

"Yes. We went out to the ledges. He was saying that this nudity revolution went against his grain, but he was thinking of sunning bare in the mounds."

"That must have been a very engrossing conversation," said Beatense.

"So, we got to the ledges and Kit got naked. You can imagine my turmoil."

"I thought he was against nudity," said Beatense, recalling his white butt.

"He is. But he said he was cooling down his burn in the night breezes."

"Aha, an exception to the rule," said Virginia. "Okay, then what?"

"Well he was stiff and against my better judgment I took hold."

"How far did you go with taking hold?"

"It was how far he went, you mean. Look, I'm not on anyone's short list up here, but he led me led me back to his cabin. It was just so beautiful. An hour, at least."

"After a little coaching Kenny might work out," said Beatense. "I gotta try him."

"HP Shit," said Virginia. "Like, I can't complain but I shudda gone with him."

"You, see, I'm pudgy," said Lorraine. "It was all him. I almost feel guilty."

"Don't," said Virginia. "I mean no one is as obsessed as I am for tan perfection, where I risk getting arrested and/or fired by doing my pools nude, but most guys just don't go for that radical tan approach, Lorraine. Kit is one of few."

"He told me he isn't into that beach mindset," said Beatense. "Unlike Sim."

"But he works at tan and knows the mental process," said Lorraine. "So he must have at least some mutual respect for girls who are equally dedicated."

"More dedicated," said Virginia. "How was he this morning?"

"We laid in bed together and just talked. Then we did it again."

"I don't want to hear about it," Beatense said. "But that topic aside, for me this is going to be a shitful day. I can't see Ida until noon, because she's seeing the dentist. We didn't have a dentist at the oil camp. So there I sit all morning, because if I start baking it will be torture to cut it off just to have weak tea and dry crumpets, in some stifling and stuffy hotel coffee shop full of old people."

"It does sound hideous," said Virginia, aglow. "Where is she staying at?"

"The Lighthouse up in Rocky Arbor. No, I mean Stony Arbor."

"You fool! That place is knocking right at the door of Cardiff Shores! Get in your sun there and visit your friend for an hour and then head right back!"

"Yeah, I can give my tan a rest break! Excellent idea! Except, how would I get there? That's kind of far. I guess I could skate it. Yeah, I can do that easy!"

"You can't skate it," said Virginia. "Madeline doesn't have a bike path."

"Well, I don't want to run it because if the police chase after me, my being a little too naked, I can't get anywhere on foot. I need speed."

"We can discuss your options," said Virginia. "But I have to ask you two to keep quiet about any recent beddings of mine, last night included. I have a boyfriend; he does road work. On bad days he rakes at the steaming asphalt behind the paving machine. But on good days he rakes gravel, just in his cut-offs, so even Kit would be sickened. So don't mess things up with him by blabbing when he ever comes here."

"Like these track crew guys I saw," said Beatense. "Anyone got a phone?"

"Use mine," said Virginia. "But for getting up to Arbor try renting a bike."

"Good idea. I'll shoot up to Cardiff and get in a good bake, then see Ida for one hour, only, and then return to Cardiff or ride back and bake Main at my discretion."

"Yeah, you and your discretion," said Lorraine, happily staring. *So thin!*

She called home. "Me and Florrie was just leaving! So make it fast, darter!"

It was fast. Beatense left the cabin in her running shoes and Virginia's cut-offs.

This girl prized her fresh brown legs, whose each delicate muscle showed, so she trimmed her cut-offs so short they were just a butt-peeking four inches hem to hem. She had also washed the shorts with bleach, which faded them and left a fuzzy white fringe of threads all around, giving a darker look to her nimble long legs.

As she ran, Beatense couldn't take her eyes off her own long tan legs, that were maybe too slim for their shapely length. Cameras watching, she hit the Highway and ran down to Tower Bikes, where the 10K started, and she entered the open door.

She saw the bikes on display and her heart pounded. For her nothing stirred the blood like brand new bikes all lined up and set to go. There was also a collection of surfboards, just enough so they could say they sold them.

The mechanic came out from behind the back counter and recognized her as the Book Girl. The slimness of her waist wasn't lost on him, but it was those quivering, bare, out-shifted breasts that got him. Plus her tan splatted him.

"We-We're not... We're n-not open y-yet, miss. I was just cleaning up."

She inspected her arm haughtily, then inspected the propped-open door.

"Oh, I see. Not open." She pointed to a rack of skis. "What are those?"

"You don't *know?* Skis. We show them year around. Er, we open at nine."

"I saw skis now and then in my magazines, come to think. But it sounds stupid to just slide around on the snow like that, doesn't it?"

"Well, here, miss, I'll pop in this demo and you can judge for yourself how stupid skiing is." The video played. "Is that... Is that tan real? That's... It's incredible."

"That skiing looks fun. But yes, people say I look darker than in the Field photos. I'm already in this morning, if you dare look. But today I'm meekly in these cut-offs. Hey, is that Rocky Arbor picky about going nude up there? I would rather go free if I could. I seem to have clearance for Madeline, based on the 10K Saturday."

"It's Stony Arbor, and yes, picky. But are you just here to ask that?"

"No. I want to rent a bike."

"None available. The tourists snap them right up. I just have clunkers."

"What tourists can you fucking mean? It's Monday, they're all back at their mops and shovels! Look at all these bikes! Can't you rent me one of them?"

"I can only sell you one. I recommend it, actually. You're one hell of an athlete, and I tell you what, I'll set you up with bike and board for a thousand."

"Make it two. I'll pick up the surfboard on the way home." She pulled a wad of hundreds from her pocket and counted out 20. "Okay, set me up. What kind of bike should I buy?. I don't want any of your clunkers, I'm warning you. And by the way I know how to surf, but I want a nice easy board that I can get better on."

"I got just the right one for you. Used, but excellent shape. Six-six, twenty-four wide. Now do you want a mountain bike? A racing bike?"

"Racing. Something fast so I can shoot through Stony Arbor topless and not get caught. Oh, and I need a carrier for carrying my towel and a bottle... Oh, hell! I was going to buy more coconut oil at that Hendrick's!"

"They're just around the corner and up Barnet. Why don't I set up your bike while you run your errand? You can go in there top... Top... Less."

She had removed her shorts to her Nakee. "Okay, show me what bike I should get. This friend Shean has a Cruise-Acc. He said it cost $2000 and looks it."

"He bought it here. The Nemrac is just $800 but almost the same. Its Chambord group-set is just forty grams heavier than the pro-rated Cantigny. You can compete with the Chamby in the local races but you won't necessarily place."

"Let me take a look. I already paid you two thousand. I might go three."

"No. You're getting way too much bike as it is. Go with the Nemrac."

"My Pop this morning said I'm back up up to sixty. But okay, the cheapie."

Shaking he set up the Nemrac Beatense picked out in the repair stand. The girl was dazzled by the intricate precision of its derailleurs. Also the thinness of the tires crazed her; they were like a good cigar in size. Kenny was way bigger.

"Boy, these bikes are built better than I am, and that's saying a lot."

Eric turned the pedals and the rear wheels spun around in a humming blur. He clicked through the gears, *chit-chit, chit-chit, chit-chit!*

Beatense couldn't get any words out. Tears ran down her cheeks.

"You seem impressed. Only a few of my customers are. But I need to get your inseam and arm lengths, Beatense, so I can set up your fighter while you run over to Hendrick's. Why do you keep looking at the door?"

"If you were a tanner you would know why. How did you know my name?"

"Everyone knows your name. Even without your being the Book Girl."

She took back 900. "Tip, $100. Now get down to business."

"Yes, but it's quite the honor having you here. You're all over old Netty."

"Half the women in town are. I don't know why I'm so great, besides my full effort tan and fucking skills. So let me run to the store now, old chap. Chappie whappie."

She ran out the door and was almost knocked over by the direct sun heat. What a day to waste by going on some visit. She ran the corner onto Barnet and went on to Hendrick's Farmer's Exchange, a glorified grocery store. Every head turned as she entered, but actually other near-nudes were present.

They were all stately Staceys, of impecaable breeding. Yes, barewear here was the new reality for this beach land. Beatense saw a stack of beach towels and took one, and she found the supplement aisle. Here, vitamins, minerals, diet accelerants, essential oil extractions, herbs and protein powder, etc, were on generous display.

There were over 20 feet of shelves on both sides of the aisle filled with these body better items. This was why the people of Xanthallado were so genetically superior to the Arrolynn misfits, their obsessed, fanatical self care.

Beatense selected a pint bottle of coconut oil, Olli vitamins with the label fraught with macro and micro anti-oxidants, and a pint bottle of Omega 3-6-9. This was a prized find; it healed sunburn as fast as it came in, or at least that's what the article said that the girl read long ago. She handed over a hundred dollar bill and waved off the $15 change. Just outside she slopped on the Omega. As she ran back she took out another hundred and gave it to an elderly homeless gentleman who was trying to cling to his dignity. Five cameras caught this. Darcy was overwhelmed.

Oil wetted, she re-entered the bike shop and her Nemrac was all set to go.

"What's that?" she said of the bent-tube contraptions on the handlebars.

"Power aero bars. I can take them off if you don't want them, because you can't get to your brakes as fast with your elbows propped in. But boy can you go."

"I'll take them. And thanks, Eric, is it? This is great! That seat looks a tad high, though. I need your counter a sec." She rolled her bottles and shorts into her towel. She placed this on the carrier rack with the stretch cords Eric provided. She saw the frame mounted water bottles. "So what about the surfboard?"

Shaking, he stepped over. "This one here." It was neon lime green. "It will work best for you down at Cocojo, but Main has this submerged reef that's a little tough for hodads; the waves do funny things. It's a little wider but that will give better stability, and flotation. Meanwhile, th-that's one heck of an oil shine you got."

Eyes bulged, Eric went on to explain that he took off the toe clip pedals and gave her basic rat traps instead. This gave her a credit. He applied this to the little tool pouch under the seat, onto which he put on a fluid seepage sock. The glossy girl put her vitamins in the pouch, joining a spare tube and basic tools.

"Riding this bike will be as good as a long bake. What are those, gloves?"

"Purely for image. They will set off those thin arms and bony wrists nicely while giving you a pro look. See, they're fingerless, with padded leather palms and an open back, with a crochet knit for ventilation. More ventilation. My compliments."

"Ah, crochet. But what's that black tube thing there under the frame?"

"Your air pump. Also we have free air out in back. Now feel that rubber."

She tried to squeeze the front tire but it was as hard as a rock. "Wow!"

"Yeah, wow. A hundred and ten pounds. Keep it there, for speed."

Beatense tugged on her biking gloves. They did gave a nice boned set to her wrists. Oil flashing, she put on the spiffy ducktail styled helmet, with visor.

"Okay, miss, now let me deduct your Tan Girl discount."

"Do you really seriously have a Tan Girl discount? Because I qualify!"

"Just barely, or very barely. With discount it all comes to $1800, with the board. I can take off the old wax and get it all re-waxed and textured for you."

"Thanks! I don't know anything about any old wax, but thanks."

"It will help your feet keep a good grip on the otherwise slippery deck."

In Nakee and helmet, the girl gave back two bills and she proudly wheeled her spiffy Zheupeau Nemrac outside. She leaned it over and raised her leg to mount the racer because the cloth covered seat was set so high. It was a sliver of hard leather that widened out to just three inches. It promised a painful ride.

"Okay, thanks, Eric! This is built like a watch! I'll give her a test ride!"

"It's fine. You just get on it and go, Beatense. I need peace and quiet."

She paused in setting foot to pedal and laughed, gratifying Eric hugely.

"Hold it," he said. "Let me hold you upright while I check your posture."

Her foot was on the pedal, ready to push off. Eric held the bike upright and the near naked savage assumed the racing posture, back arched, belly curved and her arms rod straight. He saw that her alignment was correct. He shoved her off.

She twisted back and gave a wave. "See you later, you extortionist!"

"You have to come back! To pick up your surfboard!"

As she picked up speed past the parked cars along the Highway, Beatense was shocked at the responsive ease of motion this bike had. She felt an acceleration and impetus that was almost frightening, as she shot ahead ever faster. Her alloy fighter even kept up with traffic! But this was easy. Seeing her the cars slowed up to keep pace with her, wandering and almost colliding. Horns honked, and dudes whooped encouragement to the lustrous oily girl, stick built and psychopathically dark brown.

Those power bars were tempting. Biceps bulged, Beatense set her elbows into them, and gripping with gloved hands her chin led the way. Riding in this precarious, actually perilous way, her sweat shined back lay street parallel. She shot on up the Highway past Holiday Hill and entered Madeline, passing the old 10K sights.

Her heart pounded; she wasn't too sure she was cleared as topless here. She went a couple blocks and came to a red light. She had to stop! She backpedaled, but realized, not coaster brakes, handbrakes. She quickly raised herself up and grabbed for them, and she squeezed her speed down.

The athlete girl getting into the sport truck parked there paused and smiled, as if she rode herself and knew the problems. Showing her arms, legs and shoulders in a light shift, her tan shifted in depth with her fluidic moves. She was tawny and strong, and her arms had a pleasing gymnastic tightness. Her surfer yellow hair was tousled back to reveal an assertive forehead, but her arresting, driving blue eyes seemed to have a wry humor toward the heat stress everybody faced that day. She got in and started the truck, the light changed, and shifting she zipped off.

Beatense thought she would try low gear for taking off, but the lever didn't move. *What the...* She labored off in high gear, thinking of taking the bike back. Obviously defective. But as she got to speed she pulled the lever back again and the derailleur jigged up to the granny gear. *Aha! I have to be pedaling!* But the gear was too low, she clicked the lever a couple clicks back. *Perfect.* Elbows back into the bar cups.

I should have asked more... She saw a police car, his lights went on. *Shit.* She rolled to the curb, braking. *I guess it had to happen.* The officer got out and let the cars go by and then came over. Several pedestrians stopped to check her out.

"S-Sorry, miss, I d-don't know about Emeraldeye, but here girls must wear tops. I have to have to write you a citation. Do you have a top with you?"

"Just shorts. And hey, I've been trying to get those Emmy Eye police to write me up for a week now. They just look the other way, or try to. It's actually nice to know that laws are still actually being enforced. I appreciate it."

He furtively looked right and left. "Parker Trace starts just a couple blocks up by the marina. Get yourself up there and you should get through okay."

Beatense let the bike tip to the side so she could get her foot on the ground. As she got off she saw that the bike lacked a kickstand. "Could you like hold this?" The officer shook as she undid the bungee cords and got out $50 for the fine from her shorts. She redid the bungee cords, her bike one piece of paper lighter.

"Of course paying the fine clears me. No double jeopardy if I stay topless."

"True, but I was letting you off! And this fine here won't cut it in Arbor."

Beatense laughed and took off, still in third, but she quickly shifted up to seventh. Using her suicidal elbow bars she again rode parallel to the ground, but with a slight arch. Going thirty-five she felt like a shark racing toward a swimmer in this position.

She loved her bike. With its trim frame it had a resilient ride, and despite the tire pressure it glided right over any bumps. And as she headed northward she was ever more amazed at how fast her meteor could fly. It was actually a part of her, especially since she and the bike had similar builds, as *lubricated.* Chin forward she hit forty.

The bike girl cruised on through Madeline, and she came to the stoplight by the marina, where the policeman said the bike-path started. When the light turned she spun over to the opposite corner and waited for the green here. She saw a sign that helpfully pointed over to the bike-path, and three racer bikes came flying out from it.

As a rider herself the sight excited Beatense. The light changed and she crossed into the marina parking lot. From here the walkways, slips and mooring docks spread out in a vast network. The tan dock boy was guiding a boat down one of the launching ramps, while the nervous driver backed his trailer crookedly. Beatense slowed to a near stop to watch, creeping her bike forward as she kept it upright.

The heat glared into the angelic brown boy as he called out and signaled. Like Keter he had a child's voice and thick hair. He saw the boat safely afloat, and he turned and happily faced Beatense with both 12 gauge barrels. His chest, shoulders and rippled belly focused his beautiful baked tan. Darcy used these photos.

Beatense winked and shot off. She came to the bike path, that ran back of the beach here, past a long line of condominiums and apartments, Marina Dell Bay. The girl clawed her racer to a stop and set her foot down. Time for water. She reached down with gloved hand and swung one of the bottles up, and with professional impatience she pulled it open with her teeth. A bulky fellow riding a mountain bike rolled past her, and he stopped and looked back with a grin.

"What time is it?" said Beatense, sweaty now, showing her annoyance.

"It-It's, er, 9:15, miss," the biker replied, glancing at his clunky sport watch. "Heh heh, you're the Book Girl! You must have just bought that bike!"

"I'm renting with option to buy. So, no congratulations necessary yet."

She dropped her bottle back into its rack and took off by him, and she glided back up to a quick, crisp speed. The sparsely used beach here was a wide world of sand, overlooked by the condo buildings. A sixteen year old youth swung onto the path on his skateboard, with thin body curved to the effort. Just in his hips-held butt-cut blue jean cut-offs, he too was burned to a thrilling satiny brown.

A younger boy also in cut-offs walked by carrying a sadistic looking spear gun. Though tender faced he was tan all out of reason, another radiant escapee from the shoe polish factory. He openly gazed upon his chest and ripples.

Besides these two this Marina Dell path had few other walkers, bikers or skaters along its beach sweep. This was a residential area, and along the right the path was terraced into a long line of cement steps that ran along the snazzy condominium and apartment buildings. Many of these were tourist rentals. There were the occasional realty signs, and one would expect to pay two million for a timeshare.

These buildings were set in explosions of tropical foliage, with stretches of exotic flowers, trees and shrubs decorating the quiet scene. But there were no boutiques, cantinas or beachside bars. No one carried surfboards, and there weren't any surfer hopefuls out at sea. But this was Xanthallado, where people woke up every morning with that expectant air of adventure. Beatense untied her Nake and got going again.

The girl became caught up in a cadence that gunned her along in a dead smooth flight. The pavement under her spinning front tire flowed by in a thirty mph blur.

Her Nake hung by its strings from her teeth, so that an older woman gave her a stern look. Beatense almost kicked her in going by. With her oil wet with sweat she admired a biker as he approached, a slender, gloriously tan boy of fourteen.

He was in faded, low sagging jean cut-offs, that, like the other two boys, he had cuffed up to show all of his pretty, dark tan legs. His tously yellow hair emerged from his helmet and tickled upon his boned shoulders. He had the lovely face of a delicate twelve year old girl carefully raised. The cameras had to work fast. Darcy began to think of a bigger book, full of Beatense's encounters. Quarter million advance.

Ten yards behind and perhaps deliberately following, was another rider drenched with brown, Sailor Sim. Although Beatense figured he was rather older, I was just as graceful in my lines as the boy ahead. Like him I also wore jean cut-offs, while my long flashing back curved my belly into a leaned arch over my own race bike.

His, my, shimmering tan blasted out with a sickening impact, even as non-oiled.

He gave Beatense a glance, but apparently he saw her as just one beach girl out of hundreds. She quick stopped to look back at the sailor's back, and she saw him and the mountain biker pass by each other in opposite directions. What a contrast!

The one was earnest, solid and pale, repelling Beatense again as he rode by her, smiling hopefully, while Sim was a sensual sunbeam of slim proportions. Fifty yards further along he slowed to break off his chase, and after brief hesitation he turned to ride back. His mouth fell open as he rode up. Stopping, he seemed to brace himself for a situation that was highly embarrassing to him. But no problem, she smiled.

"Hey, Sim! It took you that long to figure out who I was, even after we fucked?"

"H-Hi, B-Beatense. I… I w-was just riding b-by and thought I recognized you."

Beatense couldn't process how guys like this could legally go shirtless. His bony shoulders were slats, and the sag of his butt-cut cut-offs along with his hot tan was a criminal conspiracy. Nonetheless Sim stared into Beatense's tight black belly for the second time in his life, in agony. He saw that she was publically naked.

"Yeah, I'm on my new racer! Like yours! So, you're off today again, hah?"

"I'm working nights. I got my towel and I plan lay out. Th-That is a nice b-bike."

"Way better than nice, b-b-but thanks. I was just going to see my friend on it."

He now looked at her oil-rubbed breasts. "Wh-What friend is that?"

She was too dumb to toy with him. "This lady I got to know on the train. But darn, working nights as you do I won't be able to see you, as in, tonight?"

"Maybe I c-can get off tonight, if I call in by noon." He pulled a watch from out of his slit pocket. "But wh-where do you live, Beatense? Can I... I come b-by?"

"Yeah! Holiday Hill! North Loop, B18. We can sail. Deep water and deep me!"

"Y-Yeah, I'll... I'll see if I c-can get off. I think those dB motor tests can wait."

"Sure! But don't leave me hanging. That's unpopular around here."

Sim did not seize on his unexpected victory. Instead of persuading this girl to forget her visit plans, after parting remarks he pivoted his bike around and continued south. Beatense went on her way, and a small, preoccupied young miss cut out onto the path ahead of her. Although she was tearing her trail bike along as fast as she could, panting heavily, precious legs working, Beatense easily passed her.

Her T-shirt bared arms and cut-offs bared legs were fresh expressions of muscle and warm tan, but her worried face (she had an upturned nose, and her wet red lips were held open as if she faced tragedy) was too worried then to notice.

But nude Beatense did notice her own long limbs, and her Nemrac was a perfect match for them. With its alloy micrometer derailleurs and titanium sprockets the bike was a jewel of lightweight precision, and its sparkling, wet looking paint, its spiffy drop handlebars and shift levers also added to its showy flair.

Gosh, the freedom she had! Here she was racing along bravely illegal, while not quite believing her propelled velocity, as she pedaled against the live resistance of the forged cranks. The bike path continued on past a sign heralding Stony Arbor, where the Highway swung in and the path became its sidewalk. This seaside town seemed cozier than Emerald, and the Highway traffic puttered slowly along.

And so Beatense, going slower herself, took in the salty zest of tourist serenity in the air. But her riding black nude in the town proper was an act of savage disregard and she knew it. It was so beautiful she released sexual fluids. The drivers had no time to get a look, and there was no way for them to go around the block. Also the passengers gave difficulty; they had to pretend not to notice, even as they shook. One car was full of surfer dudes, who banged the doors and leaned out yelling.

Beatense found the Lighthouse Inn, in fact she just rode toward the beacon itself, and she pulled up to its covered front entrance and left her bike. She entered the modestly fancy lobby, and removing her helmet she went to the desk still naked, but the girl on duty also raped the sleepy ambiance of the place.

She had boy-cut hair and was hardened, thinned, and suntan slammed. She wasn't typical of the typical beach girls of Xanthallado; she unapologetically lived as a wild sensual. She was in shorts and a light halter top, whose short cropped length made a revealing point of her smoking taut tensed middle. Her nipped breasts were set apart and like Beatense's stuck out like fists.

Her icy blue-green eyes pushed critically out from their small, almond openings. With their stunning effect, few guests would register any complaints.

Beatense blinked. "Hi, I'm, er, looking for Ida Cornhill, to visit her."

"Her? Well, she'll be back at noon, she said. She's at the dentist."

"Oh, that's right! Every time I'm a public nude I forget those little details."

"I recognize you as the Book Girl, and really great videos, I can say, otherwise I would tell you to get decent. Boy, that is an unbelievable tan." An older couple came into the lobby. "Hey, you Hagens, look at her. A work of art and loves sex."

Contrary to Beatense's expectation they turned in worshipful admiration. A phone camera was taken out and Beatense and clerk smiled for twelve photos. Finally they left and sent the images to Darcy. There was just no way for them to choose.

"Those will be all over the Field. I'm a big fan of you myself, your barebacking."

"And surfing. Well, when Ida gets back tell her I'll be back down from Cardiff."

Beatense left and continued along the Highway, as she wondered how to find the Cardiff beach. She knew the Highway ended at a ramp that led to the expressway. She could hear the rubber already. Would she just come to a dead end?

A harried bus driver struggled with the lazy traffic. He gave Beatense a longing look. That girl, who saw that the driver was not Kathy, caused most of the slow-up. There were three reactions to her: Paralyzed shock, a smiling shake of the head, or indifference. For the first case the interest wasn't all animal attraction, part of it was disbelief. For the new tourists especially, they had never seen anyone so tan. It was worse for the locals, the clerks in the stifling shops or stores who saw her floating by. Most of these people had nothing to do with the world of beach, it was just there.

But they still had to face the onslaught of vain sun worshippers, Beatense as the libertine Book Girl especially. She rode by Stony Arbor's cheesy Welcome To Town billboard, framed with painted wood, and went on toward the singing-tires overpass. Every startled driver seeing her from that elevation estimated the time it would take to cut back from the next exit to try another look. But the idea had to be dropped. At some point one must take control. The fee driven photographers were also stymied.

She's perfect, JT. Doesn't mind the cameras and attracts superb specimens.

Beatense saw a sign pointing the way to the Cardiff beach, which actually was in direct sight. The girl went into shock herself. It was so vast that the biggest crowds were scattered. Riding toward the bikes approaching her, she followed the winding access path and took this alongside the parking lot toward the beach. She rode past the multiple rows of parked cars, all heat waving. She got to the last line of cars, where the trail turned along the hot sand toward the distant pavilion.

Then she saw Canterbury Biscotti lying in bare bake on her surfboard.

Beatense called over. "Canty! I knew I would find you here! Can I join you? I just rode here on my new twelve hundred dollar bike, plus accessories!"

Canterbury rose to her elbows and imperiously regarded this intruder.

"Hi, er, Beatense! Yes, do join me! What, er, kind did you get?"

"A Zheup!" She wheeled her rig toward her friend over the smooth sand, leaving meandering grooves from the tires. She held the bike with one hand and undid her stretch cords and set her rolled towel down on the sand. Canterbury, sweating upon her surfboard with her boned shoulders poked up, grimly gazed upon her belly. She hated company while sunbathing, too much talk. But the new arrival was a pro.

"Boy, is it great here!" Off came helmet and shoes. "This sand is dazzling!"

She lowered the bike on its side and lay out her towel. Canterbury observed that she was street naked, and she had ridden at least from Emmy that way. This took staggering courage. The cameras saw her dive onto her towel and happily squirm.

Canterbury studied her. In the divine miracle of the skinny girl's form her firmed little butt curved into the narrow and chain-decorated small of her hot back, that in turn curved smoothly up and over her aesthetic shoulder blades. Her biceps and triceps were pleasingly swelled, and her tough shoulder deltoids were knotted.

With her weight on them her breasts were pressed out.

"Wait! I want sun on my front!" she said, and she flipped onto her back.

"Not that I would quite accept the competition, Beatense, but I think this beach is where you should have been laying out all this time. You would be even darker."

"Yeah. I mean, I'm all over the FieldNet. So you know my Cocojo romps!"

"Yes, you made being nude politely accepted, right in crowds, wherever."

Canterbury watched as the girl re-oiled herself. "What is that stuff?"

"Borage omega 3-6-9. I'm trying it out. Maybe I shudda got me lard oil instead. But boy, this sand is so intense you can tan from all directions as you walk. Too bad I have to leave at noon. Maybe later." She flung out her limbs. "Ahh!"

As a tan worshipper, who would normally be very self involved, Canterbury found her hard to take. The girl's hips stuck out like her own, and her chain decorated, rust blacked belly was a flat stretch of discipline that lay gauntly below her stark ribs.

Canterbury saw that in spite of her height she was fetchingly small, with a smile prompting upturned nose. But in repose her looks and explosive hair gave quite a different impression, that of an erotically demanding combatant. And that seemed to be the case. Her bone starved face exerted a sacred force of brave character, while her sprawled exposure did nothing to change that impression.

"So, you surf. Me too. I bought a board myself. I pick it up later today. But I see you got your towel laying on it. Doesn't that shit up the wax?"

"It messes up the towel but it's great for the wax. It gives a perfect texture."

Beatense looked around, as usual with heart pounding. Even with the sidewalk wiyjin ten feet the girls were secluded. She excitedly wriggled and opened her legs.

As the occasional staring person or persons walked by on sidewalk or sand she knew they could only stare in helpless defeat. This gave her joy.

She gazed at the shimmering cars. On this Monday the vast, blazing sands lay partly deserted. Blood roaring, the bony girl contemplated a family walking just by on the sidewalk. The father grinned weakly at his wife. He was in a bad spot and didn't think the remaining day here would be any calmer. First these two girls, and now he faced hundreds more, all splendid, dancing and fucking athletes.

Sim rode by, with tan flashing. Spotting the girls, he stopped further along and walked his bike back casually, as if looking for a likely spot. Even with his impact Canterbury didn't like his dumb glasses, they made him look too Mod Cool, and she stared him off. Maybe that was a mistake. She awoke Beatense after two hours.

Recklessly bare the sprite ran bounding for the slope-hidden shore. She sprang the edged slope down and everyone stared in shock. It wasn't her nudity, there were plenty of examples. It was her black baking and gnawed-from-within build. She dove in and swam off her sweat and most of the oil. She emerged from the light surf and walked by her helpless audience. It seems they had the Sorel disapproval; their old beach of long ago past had betrayed them by letting these bitches flaunt themselves before all with bar-dance excited cruelty. But for their kids they would stay away.

Getting the occasional resentful look Beatense re-oiled herself and rubbed it with her towel to a dramatic shine, then got on her shoes and helmet and packed her kit. She hated leaving here; it seemed she did burn real dark. With her oil-lubricated sex anatomy sliding her seat cover from side to side, giving slimy wet ticklings, she got to the bike path leading back to Arbor and gazed back at Cardiff Shores longingly.

But wait, she couldn't leave without giving that busy boulevard and the ritzy hotels along it a good educational walk. Just like she saw coming to town!

Beatense flew through the parking lot out to the Harbor sidewalk and she turned onto it. Riding through the brave girls walking here bare despite the traffic, Beatense shot to the north end of the Cardiff beach, where by law the freedoms ended. At least this is where the happy girls all turned around.

Heart aflutter, Beatense got off her bike and walked it back southward, joining in this wicked parade of exhibitionists as a fellow nude. It was fun to shock the drivers and their passengers. And it was fun being a part of this hot stroll, and to return the proud smiles of these brilliantly tan saltines, many of whom walked here thong nude or all nude all day long. Beatense felt content, justice at last.

She walked to the south end of the pavement and turned back to the park entry drive. She got on her bike and rode back into the parking lot. She aimed for the pavilion building through the baking heat of this broad concrete expanse.

The girl got on the sidewalk and rode by Sim, who lay bare with limbs starred out on his towel. However, she didn't know it was him; she just knew it would take her a week to get over that tan. She bent forward and set her elbows in the suicide cups and raced back toward the Lighthouse, right with the traffic.

Beatense was again at risk riding back to the hotel, because Stony Arbor wasn't yet inviting to public street nudity. She almost wished she could be half normal within her blackety tan and at least wear her Nakee. As she slowed down the tourists and shoppers along the busy sidewalk stared in disbelief or angrily looked away.

Beatense had an inspired idea, whereby at the end of the block she stopped and got off her bike and walked it along the sidewalk, naked right through all the people.

It was thrilling, that killer instinct of obnoxious display, but her thrill went too far.

"Hold it right there, miss." --/-- "Oh, is there a problem, officer?"

A crowd quickly gathered. Her nips poked out further in response.

"Yes, there's a problem. We got enough on you to take you in."

"I hardly think walking my bike along the sidewalk is an arresting offense."

"Don't be cute. You're in violation of the local statutes for public decency."

"But I'm not decent, I'm indecent! Well, not totally, I am wearing oil."

The girl used her eyes, those eyes that could seek out and expose every deeply held secret, the most anxious of insecurities, all with a probing focus made the victim feel as if she was arranging the most humiliating punishment. Actually with her lifted irises her dark eyes always looked that way, but now they meant it.

"Er, uh, if... If you h-have any clothes with you, you b-better get them on."

"I legally refuse. I happen to be a professional tanner who wishes to display the ultimate in daring. Besides, I have to build up the inventory of photos for my book."

"That Book Girl dodge isn't going to work with me. That's a $100 fine!"

"Boy, we're going to have to reward you, sir! Me getting ticketed for public nudity here will make a great series of photos! I'm going to insist on it to the editors!"

The crowd swung to her side on that, so as the encounter ended the scofflaw got back on her bike and made her escape, using the aero bars for speed. At the end of the block she cut back onto the road proper and, back flashing, shot on to the hotel.

She walked her bike into the lobby, radiating her obscene tan shamelessly.

35

LIGHT HOUSE

T here you are!" said Tandra, at the desk. "I'll call your... Your friend."

Beatense set her bike against a pillar and paced around the lobby. The sun was brilliant; she hated to waste it for even this short time. Ida, wearing Capri slacks and a poplin shirt, came out of the hallway with a smile. She wasn't terribly nonplussed by Puppet's oil shined lack of clothing. The two grabbed.

"Ida, here I..." She stepped back. "Hey, you're actually wearing an outfit!"

"Yes. Surprised? I am. But just look at your... Er... Outfit!"

Beatense smiled. "I try. But you look great, yourself. How are the teeth?"

"Better. I go to the dentist down here because the drills are faster than the old string and pulley kind you know all about. But come on to the room, baby."

As the two went by the hot wild Tandra looked at the bike wheeling girl as if she was surprised she would even know someone like Ida, much less befriend her.

The two friends walked down the mini-chandelier lighted and wainscoted hallway and entered the room. It had an old charm, so that on a rainy day the wildcat would have loved sitting in the armchair with a book, and tea and toast. In some ways she was half normal. She plopped down on the sofa and set her feet on the coffee table.

"Ahh, feel that A/C!" she cried, with insincere delight.

"Are you planning on staying?" said Ida. "Let's go out by the pool."

She sprang up. "Are you sure, Ida? It's hot out today, you mean old hag."

She laughed. "I know all about you sun bugs. In here you stay ten minutes at most. Out by the pool, maybe I get you for an hour. Come on."

"Can I leave the bike here? Don't answer. I am anyway."

She removed her towel wrapped oil bottles from the carrier.

The Lighthouse had a broad pool terrace that overlooked the sea. It had rows of umbrella tables and wooden lounges, now sparsely occupied. The ladies crossed to other side of the pool. They sat by a table, with Ida in the shade of the umbrella and her friend targeting the early afternoon sun. An older couple was sitting just ten feet away. The small but tall girl's careless nudity was a bit disconcerting, tut tut.

Ida smugly caught their stressed look. The girl she was with was beautiful, with boned character and devious, eager eyes. Her helmet and gloves set her off as one of life's best. She was torridly dark brown, and her surf bleached blond hair was hugely unkempt, proclaiming to the cameras her conceited sex-and-self loving youth.

Beatense unrolled her towel and lay it on a chair, and she sat sprawled on it, a paradox of slack relaxation and hungered tensions. Her limber posture showed how trim her often-exercised waist was, that formed a taut oval four by eight inches.

"Would you like a bit of lunch, dear?" Ida said, happily staring.

"Lunch? Gosh, Ida, as you can see I never eat lunch, but yes, thanks!"

The eyes of the other couple bulged with a yearning envy. How could this girl be so appealing and unaffected? Her face just shined upon her old friend.

"You got so blond, just like at camp. A beautiful clash with your tan."

"Yeah, my tan, that has made me thousands. I'm just getting dark enough where babies cry and dogs howl. And all my sex is getting me there too."

"Oh, you naughty kid. Back at camp the last place you would be found was your own bed. Of course I'm joking but you even did do it once by the pool!"

"Yeah, but the drawback is, Ida, it never leaves you alone. Ever since I was just twelve I've been a tanning maniac, and then I discovered sex. I mean it is great fun, but you want it around the clock, you never can get a break. And until the run on the bank I was worth over three hundfed thousand dollars, all because of my talents."

"Those books are beautiful, and I've been watching your videos, dear."

"Well be prepared, Ida, this evening you'll be seeing yourself. See that guy over there? He's taking us. Also the hotel will sell the security footage for one thousand. Tandra at the desk will aim the cameras with remote control and get a cut. People want to watch me even without sex, because I'm bendy and brown."

"And beautiful, child."

Ida studied the slimmed knitting of the girl's long legs. Each muscle of her thighs was twisted into place with shapely, and cutely youthful, intricacy.

"What are you looking at? My nudity? Sorry. A funny habit of mine. But Ida, this will be a short visit. It's nice visiting you but I do need a good bake."

Ida almost swooned. "You… You can do that if you want. I can read."

"Thanks. I owe my back three hours, for which I will stay naked, you know."

"Honey, out in that desert I see it all. So… So g-go ahead."

Nonetheless, her blood roared. Nothing is as thrilling for skinny young tanners as forcing their toasty hides upon any misfits, young, middle-aged or old. Beatense had been mercilessly doing this all week. The couple at the other table sat straight up and they glanced at each other nervously.

Beatense trembled. To give her friend a chance to change her mind she started with her athlete shoes. She reached down with bracelets clinking and untied them. Her bent over posture gave her belly a tight inward suck, and the arching of her long, leaned back raised her spine in little bumps. She set her shoes onto the table with a dull, metallic clunk. Ida saw how tiny they were. The gloves next. Their fingerless style added that professional racing flair. With bangles jinkling she worked them off. They were too tight, she had to tug the finger openings past her knuckles. The girl gave an uncertain look, and set her jaunty helmet on the table. She slouched down in her chair with pulsating split open. It dribbled lubricating fluids.

"There now. Except if I'm going to do my back I'll need one of those chaise lounges. But I can do my front for awhile like this. You're sure this is okay."

Ida wasn't so sure. "You... You had a run on the bank?"

"Yeah. But they got in big orders and I'm back up to sixty thousand."

Ida's breathing huffed. The wealthy savage shined dark rusty brown.

She critically gazed upon her slung belly and jutting hips. Here she was nude in the most inappropriate of circumstances. She set her heels fully wide.

"Don't worry on my account, Ida. I'm legal. Tell all those old people."

That didn't sit well. Best to get lunch over with and get rid of her. The girl even began squirming, which was carrying this too far. This was awful.

"Beatense, this isn't going to work. You got me where I can't breathe."

The other couple stopped breathing, too, with their eyes riveted upon the lanky, slouchy girl. Her belly was sagged in a curve from the suspension of her spine, so it laid tightly gaunted between her navel and sharply starved hips.

The heat roiled off her ravenous, burnt cherry blacking, that shimmered with a multi-depth gold. Her tumescent nectarines bulged, thrusting her nips out.

Then, competition. A young woman in a bikini came over. She blandly looked at the nearby older couple and stopped just in front of them. She had a flash baked, sports annealed body of about one hundred-twenty pounds, and as she lay upon her towel her bikini turned out to be a thong. Her hard, T-stringed bulging lobes vulgarly gleamed. The couple stared nervously; it was obvious that her crude intrusion was meant for them. Smirking, she untied her top and her long tanned back glared sleek and bare. Beatense gave her a concerned look.

"How do you like that? This is my territory. Or is she a guest here."

"She... She might be, but I w-wouldn't know."

A gasp came from the nearby table. The girl turned over, and she lay upon her back brazenly topless. This was an act of appalling disregard, and then as the real kicker the girl untied bare. Her breasts were milky white, adding to the jackhammer effect, for she was bravely venturing into new turf. She sat up and put a disc in her player, and her grapefruit breasts stuck proudly out from her. She rested back again and the older couple got up with a hurried scrape of their chairs.

They crossed to the far side of the terrace. A fine old gentleman in a white safari jacket and explorer helmet stopped by the miscreant.

"Miss, my apologies, but would you like a privacy screen?"

She raised to her elbows, an action that opened her breasts well outward. "No, I prefer tanning in the natural open sun." She lay back again with eyes closed.

"Very good," the nonplussed steward said at this offhand dismissal.

He then turned to the other nude by Mrs. Cornhill, expecting no better luck.

"We need to order lunch, Tifton," said Ida hurriedly. "Is a waiter available?"

"I would be happy to assist you, my lady. And what will we have?"

"The Lighthouse Specialty Kasimer salad and turkey sandwich for myself, with a pitcher of with lemonade mixed with iced tea. Beatense?"

"Cottage cheese and peach half, and graham crackers with hot fudge. Like me!"

Tifton would have to send young Simmons down the street for that one. "Ahem, we will ready your request for you, miss. Thank you." He bowed and withdrew.

"So, can you tell me what else happened, while we wait? Anything much?"

"Lots! I don't know how I worked it all in. Surfing, fucking, sailing, barebacking. I did have a good night with Craig, but he wasn't the only one. By far. I lezzed, too!"

She began her account by starting with Cardiff Shores, then old Hoganforth, but interrupted her saga. "Wait a minute, what was Mr. Cornhill doing down here?"

"The Company sent him here to do research on exotic formations."

"Well, for that he cudda studied me, back at camp. Everyone studied me."

"I was half afraid he would study you. Anyway, he called to tell Operations that they hit this unusual anticline dome, and they told him to await the helicopter to bring him in for consultation." --/-- "Boy, good service."

"Well, it comes a couple times a week. It's the intern and mail shuttle."

"Us campers just got that bus. A yellow schoolbus with all the gauges on red."

"But back to my travels, while he was gone I went north to check on our renters and take care of other things. That's how we met on the train."

A young lady in white polo shirt and shorts walked by. In her twenties, she had yellow hair, a nutty flushed face, and blue eyes, that all together told she got a kick out of life. She spotted Beatense and started outright laughing, as if the only reasonable reaction to her extravagant lush tan was that. The musical quality of her lilting voice told of an upper middle class happiness that enabled her to also laugh at herself.

She had a healthy tan of her own and was deceptively thin.

"I'm… I'm sorry! Oh! Ha ha! It's just that… That tan can't be real!"

Beatense chuckled, but she didn't care for this humor. The lovely loved girl sat nearby with a book, with brown legs stretched contentedly out. Somehow they were deeper in tan than her face and arms. Off came shirt and shorts. Brown all over.

"Look at that! But yeah, the train. That was a year ago, Tidy Idy. So I talked with my father and he said I'll be getting another week because that track crew we saw came across this sinkhole they have to fill. So anyway, that night Zapo came over."

Her tale trudged on with no detail overlooked, so that even Ida's doting interest flagged. As Beatense described Cocojo with indefatigable accuracy, the girl saw she wasn't getting proper sun. It was coming from the right, so the rays were tragically hitting at an off angle. She reset her chair with a clunk.

A father playing ball with his toddler son in the wading pond came into her view. The father kept glancing toward her, and he threw their ball this way and that, but always so the girl was in sight. He had a way of being very casual as he focused on her a few seconds at a time. The boy ineptly tried to catch the ball at another throw, but it bounced away and rolled toward Beatense. The girl coldly watched the father approach hesitantly and then pick it up.

His jaw dropped at her flexing, sunken baked belly, with gold chain. "S-Sorry."

Beatense held her thin arm protectively, staring at him in affected horror, but she saw the little son look at her quizzically. Changing tactics, she laughed shaking her head, as if to say, That's the way the cookie crumbles. He was mollified, but even as nude the laughing lass was safer territory, and she got his further attention.

A stuffy looking, silver tray bearing waiter came and set the food out on the table, and he made his own study of this split-celebrating slut sprawled in her chair.

The girl spotted her broken graham crackers and fudge.

"Oh, wow! You guys came through! Try it yourself sometime!"

She set her chair by the table, and sat with knee at chin level. Bending forward, she rested her head on her hand like a spoiled kid. Her long tumbling dry hair tickled upon her rich, fine leather as she dug at the food with pouty indifference.

With a bulge of veined, trained biceps she drank right from the pitcher, held with both hands. Some tea splashed upon her. She showed her teeth in rage.

Ida didn't know what hit her. "What's the matter? D-Don't you like it?"

"Of course I like it, you fool. I'm just playing to character. People expect it."

But there were few expectant people in the nearby area. The natural tanner, the girl with the book, also very natural, and the father and son. But she kept up the act.

"This tastes like shit. Get that Tiptoe over here. There! Get him, Ida!"

She waved him over, dreading the confrontation but more fearful of the girl.

"Yes, my lady?"

"Hey, Tiff!" Her eyes. "This graham concoction was great! I would even guess there's some cream mixed in, to give it that decadence. Add this to the menu!"

He stumbled away, estimating that this high would last into next week.

"It seems that you can make or break people, Beatense. You have a gift."

"Oh, yes yes. So then we went to the Bum For Sun, right on the beach. But we never went out on the deck. We went to this Plastic Palm. I danced naked."

"Yes, Herbert and I once went to the club for a drink and we watched you there."

"Yeah, they taught me these wicked dance moves, to rev up sex. But really they corrupted me, beyond return. For me fucking is like another beautiful dimension."

Beatense finished her graham craclers and began on the cottage cheese. When she finished she turned her chair back into the sun. The girl resumed her saga that went on to the mall expedition and her chaise incident.

"I wish you could have seen people's reactions, Ida, even if I was just doing my front. I mean… She started up. "HP Shit! My front! I meant to do my back! I forgot all about it! I have to get that lounge over here!"

There were two lounge types on the pool deck, the old time wooden ones with canvas slings, and metal tube ones with bands of thick white vinyl. This is what she dragged over, with that steel tube on concrete chattery scraping.

Beatense set it at a predictive angle to account for the sun's passage overhead, and she raised the back to 45°. She lay her towel on the poly straps and in turn lay on the towel, with her back bent backwards to aim it into the sun.

"Can you oil my back, Ida? Use that Omega stuff, very thick."

"I would love to, but look, it's $40. Why is it so expensive?"

"I read about it in one of my magazines, it heals your burn into tan."

"Your burn, you mean. You just hold still."

The girl groaned as Ida's shaking hands worked her with the slippery oil.

Beatense continued with her story, but she truly felt that this diminished the sun's power, because she wasn't concentrating every neuron on it.

"Yes, dear, but could you pick it up? It'll be dark in six hours."

"Well, I was just saying I hope I see him tonight, but he's a little odd. Like that Kit has this superior attitude, but Sim acts like he's defensive about getting so tan."

"Send him out to the Gurney. Plenty of boys with that curse out there."

"I noticed. I was in a couple ahem parties with those survey boys."

"You were the life of the camp. But who's Kit again?"

Ida realized her mistake too late. Beatense told of all the Kit run-ins with glacial momentum, so finally Ida said, "Yes, yes, he swam out after you."

"Well to fast forward he came to my motel room late Friday night and boy did we fuck." Ida wished she had a better vocabulary. Beatense continued, then said, "So, were there any gaps in my story? Otherwise that wraps it up, here I am."

As she had told her story, various gentlemen got up to "stretch their legs." They tried to saunter casually by but they could not. They all stopped to ogle her even as they felt the shame of being watched by everyone knowingly. And the waiter stared clearing the table. At least he had an excuse to be there.

Beatense tuned out in concentrating on the sun and a skinny collegiate girl came hurtling clumsily out onto the terrace on in-line skates. Her wild gestures, her T-shirt and shorts, and her peeking tongue as she floundered about had an appeal that had everyone fondly smiling. And they could watch this tan girl guilt free.

She battled around the pool a couple times waving and wobbling, but despite her apparent tenderness, she was steeled like a track athlete and her slim thighs were woven with muscle as if for gripping barrels. With a last heroic effort she rolled up to a smiling lady and grabbed the table beside her in stopping.

"I did it, Mom! I did it!" she cried, panting heavily.

Her loud yelling invited everyone to turn to each other with a chuckle. But then the girl artlessly stripped to a tie-thong and settled back on a lounge. This should have spoiled her charm, but her edgy state did seem quite blameless. If she entertained a friend all night, working her sunk tummy, even this wouldn't defile her tender image.

Oblivious to her, Beatense awoke after a couple hours and she dove into the pool and swam like a black shark. She lunged up incredibly and took hold of the diving board. Her biceps bulged as she pulled herself up and on. She dove in down to the drain and prowled the bottom to the shallow end. She flashed out and spring jogged around the pool and rejoined Ida. Still wet she got her things rolled up into her towel, and got on her shoes and helmet. She sighed happily.

"Great day! But I better get going, Ida. I have to pick up my surfboard."

"Yes. Your bike is in the room, remember. And it's a marvel."

Drawing stares the two crossed over and re-entered the building. Just in her wet tan, Beatense walked the hallway as a smiling sun enthusiast, refusing to even place her hand for anyone in the hall. The two watched the news and had cold pop and nachos with chunky salsa. These weren't new to Beatense, but she ate half a pound.

"So what do you think, Ida, of my fucking? Me, I take the intellectual approach to what's happening to me, so I don't go into full orbit. Kids should do sex too, and they do, but of course in being younger the analytical aspect escapes them. Being heavy can be a detriment too. I can't imagine chubby girls getting all the mindful benefits."

"So it's okay to be promiscuous if you're thin, but not if you're fat?" --/-- "Yup!"

Beatense borrowed Ida's phone and called home. "You won't recognize me, old man, my hair's totally blond now. But hey, this hotel offered me mucho money. With that I might just stay here, Pop." --/-- "Ye ain't got no need for that, brat! Mr. Morley deposited 80,000 today!" --/-- "Oh, then screw the job." --/-- "Darcy says they got a quarter million ready for your new book. They just need a few more days of photos."

Ida was wide-eyed. Money like that! Beatense worked on her gloves. She put back on her helmet, and Ida joined her as she wheeled her Nemrac out to the fancy lobby. They went out and Puppet gave Ida a hug. Her friend felt her heated skin.

The girl swung her leg over and caught the pedal and took off with a wave. Her black tan belly was tightly hooked to the curve of her arched back.

Beatense's blood throbbed. Her impact might have exceeded that of girls with sensible attitudes, but without exception they too crave showing themselves to best effect. It's war out there and Beatense was a terror. The cars going by had drivers within who had been stuck at desks or punch presses all day, so her dark tan was a cruel trick to play on them. But for all their grief her victims, once back home, had to act normal. It would take days for them to recover. For the plain heavy women there was sick envy that left them shaking. Beatense knew this and thrived on it.

Her slimmed thighs, whose stretched assembly of muscles had curves of driving strength from her pedal action, would have been the targeted distraction if she wore shirt and shorts. The fact is, slender girls wear shorts everywhere, even though long tan legs can cause extreme stress and turbulence all by themselves.

Beatense, aware of the fearful looks of those beholding her, was relieved to get back on the Dell Bay path, where she wasn't out of place, even as naked. She went slow, because the beach and by extension its sidewalk had gotten busy with surfers, sunners and swimmers. And now it was her turn to get trampled. She spotted these cute, sun blasted young surf boys, one of whom matched Beatense's shagged pile of yellow hair. Like his friends he just wore a Cove Boy tie-bikini, and like them he was salt burned to a shiny dark tan. Each of his fresh muscles was an embellishment; he either worked out or he was a natural, but unlike that Oliver, who was also inspired in build, this athlete was a laughing, eager boy. His eyes had a friendly sparkle.

Beatense stopped. As they stared at her she gazed back at these fine boasting boys, because of how they exemplified the joyous wonders of this tropical land.

A surf browned young woman came toward them. She was just in her twenties, but her cheekbone focused, intelligent face had such a dewy bloom of tan purity, she could have been teen-age. She had complex blue eyes, that were warm and tender one moment and coldly cutting in their analysis in the next. The effect was ravishing, even intimidating, as these two forces worked in constant opposition.

Pacing along in her sport maillot with volleyball held under a lovely arm, she was the archetypal beautiful young woman that all beautiful young ladies must compare themselves to. In an older era she would be the adored countess who, in her golden gown at the Summer Cotillion, would radiate all that is becomingly sweet and dear in those damsels learning to carry themselves with confident and graceful poise.

Beatense didn't know about any of this; being sensual from age twelve she was forthrightly rather vulgar as a consequence. This girl was different.

She joined the boys, who happily greeted her, and Beatense realized it was her persuasive smile. Persuasive, in that she invited people to share her live joy. One could guess she was wealthy, a poor enough reward but the best the world could do. Her sun streaky, amber hair fell loose to her shoulders, and with her nut complexion clashing with it one had to think, she was no accident of evolution genetics. She had that sleek maillot on, that showed how dazzling tan and tight she was, but it was the deep insight of her structured face that got the worship.

"Sandy, hi!" one boy yelled. "Volleyball, hah? Is that why the one-piece?"

"Yes, we play really hard!" Her voice was warmly subdued but eagerly inflected, that of a cared-for young treasure just discovering the bright new world. "But the real reason is I'm heading over to Mom's now, and she doesn't know about my thong!"

"It's being topless she doesn't know about," said another remarkable boy.

Sandy's eyes snapped enchantingly. "I want her to think I'm reformed!"

The kids laughed aloud, as if this was very funny, and then the nearby nude had Sandy's wondering attention. Beatense actually felt out of place. By riding her pedal she kicked her bike over to the water bubbler a few yards away.

The entourage of impressed boys stepped for a closer look, but the spell binding Sandy was secure enough in her honored perfection to stay back and simply smile in benevolent admiration toward this irredeemable beach goddess.

"Hey, it's the Book Girl!" cried a shepherd youth statue in sheen aged bronze, to everyone in the area. "Nice, er, swimsuit!"

"Like how can you just ride naked?" said the mop-top. His dried straw engulfing intensified his smoking, espresso heat. "On the beach, yes, but biking?"

"I almost got busted back on Newport Street. So I am like pushing things."

"Hey, that's Stony! You're in Madeline now! You have safe conduct!"

"But I almost got busted here, too, down by the marina. Okay, gotta go!"

She and Sandy caught their eyes. At last, each was equally matched. In a wise flash of inspiration the boys thought it best to discretely move on as the two girls faced each other, drilling into each other's souls. The girls laughed, a draw, and Beatense smiled. One boy, looked back to the enchanting Sandy.

"Nice running into you, Baggy! But next time wear something breezy!"

"*Byy-yyy-yyee!*" she called back in three prolonged syllables. "And I will!"

The boys cheered. It was a bit disappointing for Beatense to hear that she would sully her image with string or thong. The girl seemed to be of a better cut than that.

As she pondered this Sailor Sim came riding down from Stony, with his freakish, life wrecking tan drawing huge stares, and he wavered to a stop.

If he was able to resist either of the surf girls singly, he couldn't resist both. But Beatense saw he didn't see or recognize her, his look was elsewhere. She resented his inflicting his dangerous tan on Sandy. It would belittle the girl to call her innocent, even though she looked just that, but she had an aristocratic character that should have sheltered her from this seminal ostentation. Sim was heat wave shimmering.

Caught in this turmoil Sandy processed the threat the sailor inflicted by worriedly blinking at him, with just the slightest swallow. But signals were exchanged.

To give the guy credit, he did redeem himself by ignoring the far more sensual alternative, as if there was some captivating essence about this divine creature that transcended carnal appeal. He flexed out his chest, that widened upward from his leaned waist, giving a capable set of shoulders. He had a fine definition of muscle, and his belly had a drawn-in curve from his slack, bike leaned posture. He had a proudly dramatic impact, which was a point of great concern to Beatense. Despite his need for glasses he was a slimmed shaft of deeply untamed brown, slender and tight and lean. He was hosed with sweaty oil. Me, ages ago, facing same.

Stricken, the princess blushed and gazed down. Perhaps the sailor's power and the potential threat he presented were agreeable to her. She gave a last quavering look and hopped up the adjoining line of steps to the street. Sandy got into a clunky little car and drove distractedly off. The temperature fell to ninety.

Now it was Beatense's turn. Sim was startled as he recognized her at last.

"Oh, h-hi, B-Beatense! I... I... W-We, heh heh, m-meet again."

"Yes, but surely I'm more noticeable than waiting room artwork, Sim."

"Delayed reaction. It took me awhile to raise my eyes above your legs! I, er, did try calling in earlier, about later."

"Earlier later about what. Tonight, you mean? And what did they say?"

"It depends on if these motors come in that need testing right away."

"It's almost six now, past quitting time. You better call back in darn quick." She was unsure about this encounter. Was she lowering herself with him?

"Well, first I need change. Do you have any? There's a phone here."

"No cell on you? But it's too late to call now, isn't it?"

"Oh, no. We have a second shift. Well, see you later, I hope. I better call."

Sailor Boy left and he caught up to the young surfers. He gave them a look in wheeling by them, competitors sizing each other up. These proud boys were full of joking banter. Anyone could openly admire these young barbell athletes.

But just then Beatense wished that Sim ignored them. The damn fag.

To him, she was just one of many, and as he wobbled to a stop to openly admire the boys she realized he was altogether unsuitable. But he was light and thin. He was no sturdy yeoman pulling on the spokes of his wagon wheel to free it from the mud. Like that barrel-built guy with the watch. Sim's fine lineage was above all that.

Beatense waited before going on. She rode fast, even at the risk of passing Sim up. She came to the marina and glided through its busy parking lot, and she saw the popular dock boy attending to some savagely brown boys and girls with water skiing gear. Waiting at the ramp was their snazzy towboat, that must have cost $60,000.

Beatense stopped at Tower, where Eric decided that he would have to bring her board over himself because there was no way she could carry it on her wobbly race bike. The bare girl gave her address and rode back the short distance north. Then at the foot of Holiday Hill, back arched, she geared down for the steep Ringdon Walk.

36

NEW IMPLANT

Beatense couldn't blame Sim for confronting Sandy, whose sweet appeal was the very essence of her being. Her healthy surf tan was in bloom, so that her brown face and sky blue eyes looked as if they were in conflict. And she had that tender, abashed pride that comes from within, rather than the mercenary pride that feeds on the reactions from without. But apparently all it took was someone's worship for her to blossom ravishingly. This was her special gift to mankind, for those weary souls who are uplifted by celestial young ethereals.

Honest pride, strictly rationed out to a select few. Beatense had a tight pride that she awoke with every morning. It whispered to her all day. It wasn't a pride borne of comparison with the less capable or poorly attractive, but that was a factor.

She made friends with her lessers, but with the understanding that she was the superior product. People sensed that she gained some kind of benefit in talking with them, as if she had some need that they could fulfill, however unlikely it seemed.

The manager of her motel, in his decline, felt this keenly. And yet she could take sun and strenuous athletics that were lethal.

"So, a biking helmet," Lorraine observed, as Beatense entered the cabin with her hair falling over her knotted child's shoulders. "You bought one?"

"Yeah. It's one good thing that happened today."

"Wh-What do you m-mean?"

Beatense plopped down on the sofa and she set aside her helmet, then began to work off her gloves with hard biceps ashine.

"I buy the bike, fun transaction, and on the way to see Ida I go naked. Also fun. Then I run into that one Sim I sailed with. I ask him to come by here tonight, quite generous on my part, and he agrees. Then he goes and rides off! So I finally get to the hotel only to find Ida is at the dentist. So I go on to Cardiff Shores to get in a hot bake and run into Canterbury. She was at our party last night. Gorgeous two hour session, then I walked my bike nude by the hotels, and that was gorgeous. So then I laid out still naked with Ida out by the pool with all those old people, way gorgeous. Then I walked my bike on the sidewalk in Arbor by these stores, still naked."

"Naked? On that busy sidewalk? You bitch! Publically naked?"

She took off her shoes. "Rather. So then I'm heading home and I run into this Sandy girl, who has this wholesome, love-of-sun tan that everyone delights in, as an extra plus to her heartwarming friendly appeal. I can take her as a rival, bow to the best, seriously, but Sim rides up, and looking at her he doesn't even know I'm on the planet. And by the way to remind you I was at that point still naked."

"And you're still naked. All day, you were?"

"Er, yes. So she leaves and now he does deign to notice me. So anyway, I ask him if he got tonight off per his earlier promise and he gets all evasive about it. He forgot. Now you take Kit, he's actually darker but he isn't all weird."

"Terrible. But speaking of bikes, can I see it? What did you get?"

"A really fast one. A twelve speed! It's so light even you can hold it out at arm's length! Some hi-tech alloy, Flyaswati. The tires are like thick ropes!"

They stepped out and Lorraine admired the machine, not expecting an advanced state of the art racer like this. Somehow this exotic Zheupeau personified Beatense. Her own bike was a basic three-speed, that went tick-tick-tick as she pedaled. Even Virginia's snazzy ten-speed looked utilitarian in comparison, until she was on it.

But the trend was toward all-terrain bikes, so this was a bit anachronistic.

Racing bikes, how us thin actives loved them, we could fly right with traffic to the beach and smugly publicize our obnoxious hides at the same time. Once on a rural road this older couple stopped me to ask directions, and get a longing look.

"Beatense, h-how much was this?"

"Fourteen hundred, I think. I bought a surfboard too. And look, here it is!"

Eric pulled up in his SUV hybrid, and with a calm look at the Book Girl he got out and stood on the running board and took her surfboard off the roof rack.

"Wow! Thanks, Eric! Nice vee-hickle! And boy, did this bike scream!"

The news that the Book Girl bought a surfboard was already spreading all over Holiday Hill, and the first photos of the delivery were posted to the FieldNet.

"Yes, for the money you bought the best, Beatense. Now this is cold water wax, so keep it covered while you're not surfing or else it will get soupy."

Lorraine was dazzled by the sleek little watercraft leaning against the vee-hickle, and Beatense's knowing how to use it confirmed her goddess status.

"So, Eric, doing anything tonight? I'm feeling really twitchy, again."

"M-M-Maybe I can swing b-by later, but we're open until n-nine tonight."

She took him in her arms and kissed him meaningfully.

"Riding that bike was an erotic experience, but you can't ride it at night!"

Shaking, he got in his truck and raced back to the store with its Back Soon sign. Did he dare go back? Would she remember her invitation?

Beatense brought the bike inside and Lorraine carried the surfboard. It had that curiously grubby touch. They fell back onto the sofa.

Lorraine sighed. "I should give you Kit back. He was here earlier. He burned in sun all day, and he's getting into the nude habit too. Unbelievable."

"I can work the kicks off with him and then do Eric while you do Kit."

"Good plan. But speaking of, do you think you need a new implant?"

"No, I got my implant just turning thirteen and it's good for ten years."

"Oh, that young. But they say they're safe for ten years, but I doubt it."

"Hmm, if I'm doing Kit and Eric tonight, and then maybe Sim, I could be at risk, I guess. You know, even that dessert girl last night had an implant and it just seemed like it made her all the more precious, contrary to all good-versus-bad girl logic."

"It's not contrary at all. She especially deserves beauty in her life."

"I was just saying, you ignorant cunt!"

Beatense, who had spent all day in intense sun worship, and the rest of the time riding her Zheupeau out in the drought heat, got in the shower while Lorraine called Strings N Things to see if it would be open later. She also called the clinic to get her friend's file started. In the background she heard a clamor of sweet young voices. "Me next, me next! I can't wait to fuck!" Lorraine warmly smiled.

Beatense came out from the bathroom, and her dark tan had the starchy shine it always did after a soapy scrub. Her belly chain tickled her ripples.

Virginia came home wearing the outfit she had left in, her work bikini. She wore only it for traffic purposes, so she took it off now. It had been her habit to bedevil anyone in the cabin with her nudity well before Beatense came along.

As she admired the bike and board she sizzled with her own high baking.

"Absolutely gorgeous. That gear-set is just 4 inches in diameter."

"Is that good?" was the comment, seen and heard by the cameras.

"Well, you need strong legs. Let's compare thighs. Lorraine, measure us."

"Wait a minute, Beatense," that girl said as she worked the tape measure. "You invited that Eric over but I thought you were also set up with that Sim!"

"Shit, that's right. Five inches diameter each. Now let's compare our waists."

Virginia put on a six inch tube skirt and tie top, and Beatense added nothing to her brown skin for a demure look. The three girls walked down into town. The Highway and its sidewalk were busy, and as they jostled through the staring tourists Beatense updated her friends on the Sim run-in. When she told of his ugly building down in Le Tournepier, Virginia said she knew of him; very unguy-like he was always getting sun by the pool, and he was there Sunday.

He pretended disinterest, but as she handled the skimmer and scrubbed the coaming tiles he kept stealing urgent looks.

"Yeah, it's like he feels guilty about it, Nin, or corrupted. And I had to initiate our having sex out in his boat. I top-hopped him only because of the cramped quarters."

"If he comes by tonight I can dispatch him," said Virginia, with glasses set.

The girls went into the Studio Tropique, which had evening hours because it was closed Sunday. Beatense felt edgy, back home beauty shops were the realm of the ghastly rolled curls. The practitioner was clearly cut out for a better life; she had the fine, cornered forehead, exquisite arms and shore life tan of a pedigree upbringing.

Her hair was loosely done up in a haphazard bun. Lorraine introduced Beatense as the appointee, and Book Girl, and she gave a misgiving smile, the look she would give to a friend who said she was going camping with six guys and a case of beer.

Patiently, she explained that the client's needs went beyond just a basic pruning; she would get the full Sauvage treatment. The bare girl sat in the chrome and vinyl chair in a low, belly hooking slouch, but Stel made her sit up. The doubting girl was fitted with a poly hood perforated with holes. Skillful arms at play, Stel used a little hook to pull various locks out through the holes, and she wiped them with metallic gel. This was an accent to Beatense's extreme surfer bleaching. Watching herself in the mirror the girl admired the clash her hair and tan inflicted. Fluids were secreted.

Naked Beatense was lowered back over the sink and the formula was rinsed out. The wisely competent Stel then brushed out her fly-away hair with a drier and gave it a careful snipping to remove some of the rattier bulk.

The girls looked up from their magazines and had a shock, Beatense was radically transformed. Stel had worked in thin pencil braids and hanging leather thongs with beaded ends. The vibrant blond as accented with the silvered green tinting added to the rampant chaos. Sauvage, yes.

"I should charge you extra for squirting on that towel I laid on your chair."

Beatense was carrying a roll of bills and gave Stel $100. They went on to Strings. Tess was upset that despite her advice Beatense had burned herself royally black. Also she disliked her explosive hair. The girl wasn't in the mood to add to her sparse wardrobe, but along with an opened mesh pink sweater she did buy a classic cotton office shirt with a collar so big around, it slid off her shoulder. She wore it one-button full open. The girls went on to the sex clinic, an old converted store-front.

The place abounded with smiling, shining girls patiently waiting, some with proud parents. It was a measure of their sophistication that even disturbingly younger girls were here, but like their active friends they were so tanxotically fine, their pre-teen or early teen lack of years wasn't a preventative in taking this important step.

As they nervously sighed, facing their painful incisions, they exchanged amusing remarks with their doting parents. A few girls were here on the sly and one child's mother had an ashen look, as if she had no idea that little Priscilla needed surgery. The girl's mercenary intention would alarm older people, but like the other kids in wait she still had a winsome, grandparent hugging tenderness.

Whatever their actions as enabled, they would continue as homework doers, dog walkers, book readers, piano players and parent adorers. This society had accepted their carnal play, so that the beautiful youngsters could freely explore the wonders of their bodies. Indeed, the posters on display showed children enjoined.

Drawing puzzled looks both for her age and bared tan, Beatense studied a photo line-up of pretty boys, including Shanty, with silken hair and tans aglow. These were the Helpers, who were paid by the clinic to assist the nervous first-timers.

"You two, this is a racket here!" Beatense whispered in a rage. "Look how young these kids are! I'm all for modern freedoms, but not until you're ready!"

"Here, let's sit down, Beatense," said Lorraine. "You're here for you, not them."

She did sit down and carelessly opened a *Liberty In Love* magazine.

"This beats my books," she laughed. --/-- "When I opened my birthday card and saw that implant date and time, I wept," said Virginia. "Just in sixth grade!"

A twelve year old wearing a skirt like Virginia's paced back and forth in her crisp accessory jacket and clunky shoes. The knees bending action was clumsy, and was perhaps a contribution to her aggressively muscled legs. With their classic form, the skirt's minimal length was appropriate, with thrilled visiting relatives approval.

This particular child, as a sensually aggressive sun worshipper, her tan looked dynamited in, and she had the typical resigned expression that comes with facing a temporary inconvenient pain in exchange for many years of greater benefit.

But she had all of the sweet charm of her age, and her cutely immature features showed an advanced knowledge, that was normally years beyond her ken.

The nurse back of the poster decorated counter stood. "Constance?" The skirt girl turned and stepped over, swaying with the wobbles of her shoes. "Hello and welcome, Constance! Will you need any explanation or counseling first?"

"No." She waved her hand. "I had all that in school. And I am on pills."

The girl's smiley-faced mother joined them. "Yes, a year ago I came upon her having intercourse with fourteen year old Justin, and knew not to disturb her! I later discussed it with her, and we agreed she should stick with sleep-overs at first, with friends! But my baby is beyond those parties, so she needs more than just pills!"

The girl sighed and the nurse laughed. "Okay, Constance, no more pills!"

Giving Beatense a last assessing look, working her sizzling legs the girl followed the nurse through the door back of the counter. As Beatense shook her head in fond approval another girl came out from back, smiling with other-wordly joy.

She was a radiant fifteen, and her muscles were stretched taut by her athletic thinness. She had the eyes aglow that proclaimed she was beloved and precious, a daughter of steady, diligent and becoming character. But sadly she was fashionably slutty in her shrunken, belly baring camisole and a butt-cut short black skirt.

She was ecstatically tan, possibly from marching band practice, track meets and tennis matches. She looked like she should know better than to add this other sport, but she gazed upon her bandage with grateful tears in her eyes. Her foolish, flannel shirted father with an office loving, deprived grey face stepped over and hugged her.

"Layton, I'm really proud of you. You have always been so responsible!"

"Yes! Now I can super sustain, Dad! Tonight I break my Prudent Miss in!"

"Prudent, your implant and you! We won't expect you home until morning!"

Beatense was impressed. Like the other kids in quiet wait the cherished Layton was highest pedigree. Another girl, entering with her mother, was a frail fourteen, all dusky tan. Dreamily happy, perhaps she esteemed herself even more wonderingly than her slimmed mother, a capable go-getter who seemingly did pottery or stage sets or paintings. Just that artistically perceptive look, that of a sought after teacher.

To the receptionist, "Hello. Alden and I think that Tawnsun here should get more active, so she will be fully skilled as she seeks partners of adult length."

"Yes, it's best if kids gain experience at the unpoiled ages. Hey, Tawn!"

"Lorraine, I like to see this. Back at surveying camp I learned real fast, after we disco danced. This gay taught me, just cosmic. Next day Lesta helped me get my implant. The nurse was all smiles, she said my slight build gave me extra sensitivity, so long play could be traumatic. It wasn't, and I had no idea sex was supposed to be bad. So for these kids it's beautiful they can indulge in it, in guiltless freedom."

"You just said something smart! But that's why this outreach is so helpful."

They went over to the nurse that had returned. She was petite and fine, and sun kissed. Her steady, clear cut eyes were both mischievous and solemn. Her boy-like face and business-like forearms showed she took her job seriously. And thereby she gave the clinic's promiscuous outcomes unassailable moral credibility.

Now that was a deadly betrayal. With her cultured looks and professional mien, like Beatense's nurse at survey camp, she would reassure the young fearful girls and their parents. The catch was, if she had any hesitations about children as clients, by extension she might also hesitate to treat their older sisters. Many surveys showed kids were getting very active, so better to just quash one's silly doubts and work the kids through, they would fuck anyway, and also keep up the clinic's funding.

"Yes, Beatense Colwell? The Book Girl, hi! Your waiver is all set for you to sign. These services are free, but we do need your ID Tracking card."

"But I'm from Arrolynn! We don't have those up there!"

"Well, we can assign you one. This is also done with our clients who, ahem, are somewhat too young to be employed yet. Here, we're on line." The nurse sat at the laptop and Beatense watched. "There, it was that simple!"

"Good, thanks. But I should explain, I do have an implant already, I got it back when I just turned thirteen. It's a tenner, so I only have seven years on it, but I'm getting all kinds of all-night hard sex lately I thought I better re-up it. Is that okay?"

"Oh, yes, that is very wise, especially for when an orgasm can go two hours!"

Beatense watched the knife cut in, flinching only as the implant was inserted.

"Thanks, really glad to get that done. But how long will this one last? The one you just took out was a tenner, doctor, but I'm here after just seven years."

"Yes, Jenny said that. They under-rate their life to prevent any inconvenience."

Once the three returned to the cabin Beatense left just in her new shirt (fluttering unbuttoned) for the Shattucks to show them her new bike. First she stopped by the Hideaway and walked her Zheupeau right into the dumpy office.

"Hey, Cheevo, it's shy and retiring me!" She took off her helmet and shook back her newly ravaged hair. "How's the old fleabag doing? Any more pesky lawsuits?"

The old manager blinked. Who... It was Beatense! Her hair was tempest blown as usual, and her knotted thong necklace closely encircled her long neck. With shirt hung open, grazing her nips, she radiated a sensual driving power. Her loose rolled sleeves showed a bandage by her elbow. That got his notice too. *My God.*

"Beatense! How wonderful to see you! And goodness, look at your hair!"

"Yeah! I got it all ripped up! But didn't you notice my bike? I suppose not."

"Yes, indeed, I noticed. Why, it's lovely. Just lovely!"

Look at the chain on that waist! If you can call that *a waist!*

The girl stood proudly astride the craft, holding to the handlebars with pro forma gloved hands, so that her shining forearms were pleasingly tensed. Her sunken belly sang of starvation. Her felt her rusty black hide's energy as she reached to hug him.

She paused in putting her helmet back on. "Mr. Cheevy! Lovely? A *bike?*"

"I... I meant you, my baby." --/-- "I agree, we can sleep again, but not now!"

He watched the baked girl back out the door and catch her pedal, curving herself to eye her foot. Her long tan thighs were steely with muscled swellings. She rode to the corner and stood ready on her pedals, then with a break in traffic she shot off.

She thought of Virginia getting cut at twelve, or even eleven. How sensible! And as a special child she likely had countless cute boys in deep over the years, the rat!

37

SHATTUCK VISIT

Beatense rode on to the shack and went right in the open door into the kitchen.

She found all three boys, who were conducting a surfboard waxing clinic. This she knew all about. They were in the first step of the process, getting the old wax off. The evening was hot, the sweat filmed, sun fiend boys met the eye with shades of prune toffee, prune toffee and caramel toffee. They were just in their short cuffed blue jean cut-offs, loosely held to their light hips. Their ragged shorts were so riddled with frayed holes they were safe for home wear only. Of course, the boys wore them everywhere. Jesse also wore a string of teeth and feathers in his hair. The thin, sun drenched gypsies didn't notice the intruder as she removed her helmet. Ned saw her first and he looked at her coldly.

"Get out of here, Beatense," he ordered.

"Beatense!" Jesse shouted. He saw the bandage. *Didn't she have one?* "You got a... A p-perm!"

"Wow, Sickening City," said Shean reverently. "Them braids are a killer."

"Well, me too. Hey, Ned, how's it going, pal?" --/-- "Horrible!" --/-- "Horrible? Is that all day or just since I got here?" --/-- "Just since you got here!"

She gave him a dirty look. "Oh well, do you still have a kiss for me?"

"No!" --/-- "Some day you'll regret that. You guys wanna see my new bike?" Shean saw the bandage. He wobbled. The boys scrambled outside.

"Wow!" Jesse yelled. "You got an actual Zheup! With airflow bars!"

"Good choice, Beat!" Shean said happily, head still whirling. "Can I try it?"

The girl sighed with eyes rolled up and the tanner got on with a swing of brown long leg, and as he rode the cement walk he hung his thinned arm down and shifted. There was a series of snapping clicks and a clunking of chain.

Vibrant Shean, who looked as dark as Jesse and Beatense in the early dusk, and in full sun was just two shades lighter, returned and neatly stopped.

He gripped the brake levers as he stood astride the race bike, making a show of his biceps. His thin thigh, cocked up as it was on the raised pedal, like his shaggy blond hair it shined in the glow of the porch light, as did his swimmer's chest and neatly rippled belly.

"Beautiful action," he whispered, also obviously but correctly referring to himself.

"I agree," said Beatense. "Ned, you disgust me. Just go back inside."

"You just go away!" Ned fiercely replied, but his brothers had seen the light leap into his eyes when she first walked in. "Now!"

"Beatense, this is a semi-pro racing bike. Amazing piece of engineering."

"That's why I bought it. Ned, you can watch us others talk but stay silent."

Jesse and Shean laughed at Ned's scandalized look.

"At least it isn't a girl kind," said the boy as they piled back into the cabin.

The girl hung her shirt on the back of a chair becoming nude, as usual, and Tony turned off his computer and entered the kitchen. He was stunned to see Beatense, thinking that the restaurant jaunt would be it. Her piles of blond kissed tendrils made her a forest divinity. Her tan shined as she stood, with her snaky chained belly.

Living in a town full of beach girls, Tony had recurring cardiac bouts.

"Wh-Why B-Beatense, hello. You… You had your, er… Hair d-done."

"Hey, Tone, yeah. Thanks again for the chili last night. And hey, I saw my friend Ida up at Stony Arbor today. I'm glad we picked that exact restaurant."

"So… So you came over here, how?"

"My new bike. I'm on that thing going forty and the two of us become one."

He felt an anvil fall on his chest. He gaped in stricken horror, such a tan should have been illegal to achieve and especially display. Stretched as a sheath over her tuned muscles, her lush baking had a reverberating, deeply golden gleam. She was burned to a rusty enriched, very dark brown. That yellow hair with the metallic wisps clashed with her shrieking, catatonic tan. And some girls use sun block.

They all went out again, Ned fussing, and Tony admired both beautiful, precision machines. Beatense just didn't know how to quit. They went back in and Jesse and Ned fell onto the rickety chairs. Standing, Shean scraped the old wax on his board. The loose, low embrace of his cut-offs burst his slim, chest widened self upward in glorious, sun annealed escape from his hip slung belt loops. He too was brown. He wetted his rag with mineral spirits and lightly rubbed at the remaining wax.

"Easy there, you can take the paint off," said naked Beatense, as Ned glared.

"How do you know so much? And it's not painted, it's lammed over."

"I surf too. I even got a board today, a used Kestrel, at Tower. Eric set me up."

"So… So you surf?" said Tony, eyes bulging, as lead pellets filled his stomach. "But what is all this? What the hell is going on with these surfboards?"

"We're slapping our slabs, Dad," said Jesse. "You had to ask that?"

"I kill, then ask. And your hair looks g-great that way (he huffed), girl."

"Thanks, but blame it on Erin. She thought I should tone down the blond, and so she metallized all these tangles to give a clashy look. But now this one Sandy that I saw today, her hair is all blond and likely to stay that way. And real tan."

"Sandy?" said Jesse, looking up. "Sandy Bagel? Where was that at?"

"A truly lovely... Sandy Bagel? What a... What a dumb name!"

"Sandy Bay, actually," said Shean. "So, heh heh, where did you see her?"

"Oh, just anywhere. On that beach bike path up past the marina. By these Dell Bay condos in that Stony Arbor. Oh, wait, it was Madeline."

Beatense sensed that it was a mistake to bring the subject up.

"A girl like that is one in a million," Tony said. "You did see her."

"Yes! I saw her! She and her namesake food made the news!"

"Exactly where was it?" said Jesse, trying again. "Any landmarks?"

"Being so upstaged I didn't think to check out the metes and bounds!"

"Speaking of distractions," said Tony, as Jesse dimmed the room by hopping his luminous tan out the door. "I see you're not a drag queen again today."

"No! What is a drag queen, anyway?"

"It's a guy who wears women's clothes," said Shean.

"It's a what? Tony, did you seriously think I was one of them?"

"Yes." That implant bandage terrified him. "Yes, I did. At first."

Jesse came back in with a bike lock. "You'll be needing this."

"I have one. Didn't you see the bracket for it?"

"How could he miss it?" said Tony. "Ned, get Beatense some ice cream."

The boy recoiled. "Do I have to?" --/-- "Yes! Move!"

Ned sighed terribly, looking sadly tragic, as he struggled to his feet with moaning effort. Beatense told him to hurry as he almost fell over from his limping.

Tony shook his head. "Okay, clear off the table... What, Ned?"

"Beatense has to get out of here!"

"I agree. Shean, could this be your surfboard? Kindly have the courtesy to set it elsewhere. Do that in loving obedience, my son. I have a map to show you."

Shean lovingly obeyed, and Ned brought over a large plastic margarine tub full of ice cream. He set it down with cold civility. "Here!"

"Thank you, Ned. I haven't eaten since... Since those nachos with Ida."

As she started on the fudge ripple Beatense told about her day.

How can an implant make a girl even more beautiful, Tony wondered.

"So anyway I walked my bike nude by the hotels. It was fun."

"Oh, you bitch!" said Shean. "Me and Knife should do that. Play gay!"

"Yeah, take Ned and leave him there. Ned, where's my ten dollars?"

"I didn't take your ten dollars!" --/-- "What a lie. Give it to me, with no questions asked." --/-- "You won't be able to anyway, with your teeth missing!"

Blubbering her lips foolishly, Beatense said, "Vuv-vuv, vuv-vuv, vuff!"

Shean, Jesse and Tony laughed. Ned tried to hide his sparkling delight.

Throat lumping, Tony took a rolled up paper tube from the counter.

"J-Jesse, open… Open this chart here."

The youngest boy stood and he unrolled what looked like a tourist souvenir map. He and Shean looked at it blankly, as Beatense continued with the ice cream.

Ned gave her a stern look. She glared back at him.

"Well? Are you that overwhelmed by this? What you think?"

"What I think?" said Jesse Andrew Jay. "It neat!"

"Neat, hell. Are you too wasted to know what this is? It's a treasure map!"

"Gee, great, Dad," said the oldest, Garydak Timothy Shean, wearily. "But it looks like you bought it from out of the trunk of someone's car in the shitty part of town."

The boys sat down, noisily collapsing into their chairs.

"Oh, Mr. Armchair Comedy Night has spoken! You dipshits! This could be worth millions! It tells where you can pan for gold!"

"Hey, it's on my side of the table!" Peter Christopher Ned objected.

"Oh, sorry," said Shean, shifting it. The thin sun worshipper braced himself. "Father dear," he said tiredly, with his startling child's voice, "this is fake."

"The wisdom of our resident leisure artist, clearing me right up on this."

Jesse stood up from his study of the map. "Shean! This might be legit!"

"That's what I try to tell you! If you just listen!"

Beatense looked up from the map. "Ned, will you just give me five dollars, to half pay me back for the money you stole?"

"No!" He was oblivious to her violent impact. "And I didn't take it!"

"Okay, listen up, meatbags," said Tony. "Gary got my Timlin sell order mixed up and he sold the wrong stock, Tolnaftate Petro, which tripled from two to six a share. Meanwhile this prospector gives him this map to settle his account in arrears."

"How about two dollars?" --/-- "No!"

"So Gary gives the map to me, to shut me up."

"Would you consider one dollar, for closure?" --/-- "No!"

"But Dad, that's illegal!" said Jesse. "A broker can't make good like that!"

"Penny stocks over the counter, he can. So, the map could be legit, unless that miner was some kind of donkey-leading coot, hah?"

"Highly unlikely," said Shean, coolly gazing upon his decorative arms.

"Fifty cents." --/-- "No!"

"Shean! Can't you see? This is Geode! Gold or no gold, let's go there!"

"Negitude, no. I have a job, remember? And it's a desert. I surf and sail."

"How about a sanitarily wrapped tongue depressor, you ignorant fool?"

"I don't have one! An you're the one who's ignorant!"

"I'll go, Dad!" Jesse announced. "I wouldn't mind exploring Geode!"

"Agh, you just want to lay in the sun. You black now. What color next?"

"I'm not even half black!" the chieftain boy protested. He opened out his arms, letting his audience admire the satined inter-playings of his taut rippled belly and the exerting power of his capable chest. "I'm not nearly as bad as I get when the trade winds bring in that super humidity!"

"You shut up about super humidity," Tony replied to his son.

Jesse's white incisor necklace, and the hawk feathers tucked into his long hair, gave the wily youth a savage look. Ever aware of her own head splitting cruelty, still Beatense positively gawked.

"I can come," she said. "Jesse and I can run wild out in that desert!"

"You better not come!" said Ned.

"I agree," said Tony. The thought of her in the desert sun scared him.

"But speaking of Geode," the tanner said, "Ida lives at this big oil camp out there. I went there myself at thirteen for surveying camp. The kids are all real desert rats. They live sweat naked in their electric tans, boys and girls both, and they run across the flats for miles, or ride dirt bikes or horses. They're as tough as hickory switches, I too. They called me Puppet, and I went naked like them, unless I put on my extra long T-shirt to to visit these older couples. But they all said to take it off. My friend Geddy and her parents, I was naked with them and got Geddy to join me. It was like a small city, lots of oil wells, and even a refinery and cracking tower to make our own gas.

"I was poked open right away so Lesta took me in to get an implant. I was rabid but my Pop didn't mind. Just earlier I got a new one at that clinic. But those young girls there, they looked so innocent you wonder how they even thought to prep up for sex. And it's really unfair, unlike with the plains, beautiful looks, lives and nights."

Tony made a loud sigh. How much of this was Ned catching on to?

"Come on, Shean!" Jesse pleaded. "I'm desperate! Think of it, for once in our lives, blasting sun that can actually kill us! We can make the *Barnet Gab!*"

"Sun," Shean said flatly. "I get too much of that here." His tan had a living, pure translucence, enriching its baked cacao shine. The thinly braceletted youth of sixteen summers clasped his hands out before him, flexing his chest. "I'm just real brown."

Tony was impressed by his assessment but he gave him the finger.

"What was that for?"

"Beatense can't come!" --/-- "I can too come, purple pee."

"You too damn arrogant, Shean. The idea is to search for my gold bricks, so no rotisserating for neither one of you. For each ingot I pay you a dollar."

"A dollar!" said Ned. "Nathan's dad pays him two dollars!"

Tony blinked. "You tell Nathan he'll get three from me."

"Well, then we should get three dollars!"

"Three, five, ten... Just bring them in, you silly, funny guys, you."

"I thought we were panning for the gold," said Shean.

Beatense was giving Ned a cold disapproving look. "Mr. Shattuck, will you please ask this son of yours to act halfway intelligent? Like me?"

"Ned, Beatense asks that you act half intelligent, like her."

"That should be no problem," Ned growled dryly.

Concerning the matter of how persons so proudly vain could divert their attention from themselves, however justified their interest, the self obsessed Jesse and Shean burst out laughing. Ned smugly looked at the fuming Beatense.

"Oh, hey, Beatense," Jesse said, "I finally got you a job, running this drink stand! Old Kelliher hired you sight unseen! After I said who you were."

"Oh, he's seen me all right. I hope I'm worth the pay. And thanks, Jesse."

The girl gave the stormy Ned a superior look.

"Let's get back to searching for my gold," said Tony. Jesse and Shean sat down, falling upon their chairs, as if trying to break them. "You guys take a weekend and check out this map. Then we get serious later if you find anything."

"Okay, okay!" said Shean. "But how are we supposed to get around there?" The heaven-sent lad looked upon his arm, again, as he pointed. "See? It's all rivers!"

"The map follows the rivers, so take the catamaran. And Jesse, I forbid you to get too comotoast in that sun. Little enough of you as it is."

"Just one detail, my going is contingent on Beatense's going."

All eyes turned upon her. Not easy, with her looks, bone build and hurtful tan.

"B-Beatense, c-can you sp-spare us a couple days n-next weekend?"

"I can't. Not with my trip home coming up. But I might get another week."

"Check on that," said Jesse. "Dad, should we take the metal detector?"

"If the gold is there, it's there. It is foolish to bring such a gadget along."

"We could always use it to find someone else's gold," said Shean drolly.

"I use it to twist around your neck. Okay, so the trip is on?"

"That trip is," said Jesse. "Plus I think we should head up for some skiing."

"What in hell? You're talking about skiing? In summer? Does that vacuum you call a brain need a lube job? Get serious, child."

"I am serious! They got twenty feet of snow this winter! We could take Beatense up to the condo and actually ski! We need some reason to be rich!"

"Now, that is something else to carefully consider. How about it, girl?"

"Leave me out of this! But for once Jesse could be right. I overheard Tammy's father tell him about it at the tennis courts Friday night."

"Well, that's convincing enough," said Tony. "Jesse, check out the ski reports. Shean, you call Gold Camp to get us our condo, and call the airlines!"

"I'm just glad Beatense isn't going skiing with us," said Ned.

"Well, I could go..."

"I'll call the Ski Hot Line, Dad!" said Jesse. "And look at the web site!"

"Good! Plus get on line and check out the weather up north! And no lies."

"I might consider it, guys. My skin could use a rest."

"Shean, get Knife to handle the horses, and ride them. Ned, ask your friends if they were up there lately. They can tell you if conditions are any good or not."

"Okay, but just so Beatense doesn't come!"

"It's just that this all came up so suddenly."

"We should get out the skis for waxing and filing, too!" said Shean.

"Start right away," said Tony. "And see if Tammy and Natalie can come."

"I think Tammy can make it," said Shean. "Or else. But Ned, you better find out about Natalie. Remember to ask her now."

Beatense stood. "Well, I better head home now while it's still half light. I want to scare the tourists with my nudity. Have fun on the ski trip, if you ever make it."

The boys went to get up but Tony signaled them to stay put. Beatense went out waving farewell and they called goodbye. Tony followed her.

"Tony, what are you up to? I thought you were arranging this ski trip! 'Call the newspaper! Call the condo! Get the Hot Ski Line!' It sounds to me so stupid!"

Confronted by her moody, cheeks-chiseled face in the evening gloom, he felt his breath taken away. Her bleached hair had a particular radiance, while her published brown skin sizzled in the overworked porch light's glow, slugging him in the gut.

"It's... It's Ned. He wants you along so bad. Can't you come, little miss?"

"I don't know how to ski, Tony! Plus I don't have all that junk you need, the skis themselves and those big clunky boots! Of course, my inlines are just as big. Shit, I haven't skated in days! No wonder I'm getting so flabby! See, I can pinch an inch!"

He saw. "We can set you up. Girl, I beg you. I never saw poor Ned so happy. Peeking in his room he was always so sad in his sleep, but now he's smiling. Thank you so much for bringing my son back to... Where... Where you going?"

She paused. "Skiing!" She then hopped her butt back into the kitchen.

38

LONGLEAD-UP EVENING

Hey, scumbags! I'm coming!"

Tony heard cheers as he followed her. He saw the change that came over Ned, although the boy did try to hide it by looking disgusted. The girl turned to him as she donned her helmet, with baked little breasts lifting just so.

"Oh, Ned, thanks again for letting me ride Spec yesterday, pokey as he is."

"He is not pokey!"

"Hah! It's so obvious how slow you ride him." **--/--** "You ride slow!"

Tony was glad that point was cleared up.

The trip details were argued, then Shean and Jesse stripped and ran with bared Beatense as she left for home. Night had fallen, the headlights caught the kids and their friend. The car horns tooted in greeting. Out at the intersection Beatense said goodbye and raced north. The drivers paced their cars to her as they stared. The girl hoped to also ride that Eric. By devoting herself to body beautiful, her life was a joy. She got off her bike and still bared walked it through the sidewalk tourist crowds. The visitors just new to town were horrified, even with the other nudes stepping along.

Over the Lucky Bar Dollar Buck sat on his smelly couch, nursing his decision to never see Beatense again. The sight of her would be too painful in being deprived of her good will. But he was entitled to one last secret look. He had to be careful. If he was seen by her or her roommates, or worse, by her and Kit, pointing and jeering, it would be disastrous, especially if caught on those bastard cameras. Speaking of...

"A ski trip now?" said Lorraine. "Beatense, you lead such a magical life!"

She got off her bike. "It would be lots more magic if I was going with KitKat!"

The named boy laughed. A fervent show-off at heart, he had shyly come to the open door in white butt-cuts, and now he sat sprawled on the sofa in extremely lanky leisure. Agog with his shimmering presence, the girls couldn't take their eyes off this hardened gleam of sun. He had the day off, but he spent it by the Breeze pool. The hotel owner, the lovely tan Tamdyn, gave him a flimsy boy bikini. She made him tie it right on and lay bare beside him by the pool. This was all day.

Her session didn't help hotel operations, she was supposed to be filling in for the head of housekeeping who was doing inventory. Before her lay-out Tamdyn made a call to replace a maid whose boy was sick, instead of subbing herself as usual.

When she finally hopped out by the pool to lay by Kit the guests smiled fondly.

Kit, oblivious to her company beyond their easy friendship, used lanolin butter to bake his darkest tan ever. Very nice with his stretchy lines, the roommates thought.

"Throw him a T-shirt, someone," said Virginia. "Then I might put one on."

She was just in her thong, justified by the cabin's trapped heat. All over town the self admirers were similarly dressed or undressed. And it was more convenient.

Lorraine panted as Beatense collapsed onto the sofa and took off gloves, shoes and helmet. Earlier as she entered the cabin nude, the incandescent lighting, along with a dash of monitor and TV, gave her wild tan luminous new depths. Her muscles had their usual stretched shine. Her waist, four by eight, soon to exercise smaller.

"Boy, I can say this," she said, "I might finally be getting used to all the freedoms down here. Shean and Jesse ran naked out to the Highway with me, then Shean ran off to spend the night with Tammy, right at her house! And I should add I was totally freed all day. So what's the use of being employed and responsible, accountable and productive if you can just live for pleasure instead?"

"Work means you can go it on your own," said Virginia, with a flickering interest. "Me, I clean pools so I get the income and pleasure both, useless as the job is."

"Hmm, good point. But you have crude brutes by the thousands working in shitty factories, packing plants or mines, just so us ungrateful sluts can fuck and relax in fun lives that offend them. To be fair they should role change us now and then."

"You said this before," said Lorraine. "And aren't you due for a switch?"

"Who, me? I just did a role change! I was a surveyor two weeks ago! And that reminds me, including travel time I'll be a surveyor again in another two weeks."

"Beatense, no! You have to stay!" wailed Lorraine. "You can't leave me!"

"So treasure these moments with me, Rainy," the vagrant said, taking out a cold Orange Grotto from the refrigerator. "But all I do is depress you, me so tan, naked and oh-so fulfilled. And cute. I bet if I work my implant tonight you will die."

"It would be the sweetest death I could think of."

Beatense stepped to the door. With bicep bulged she raised the bottle to take a swallow, but Virginia made a pithy remark and head tipped back she laughed. Buck was hidden behind the woodpile. He froze as the girl had come to the door, but she didn't see him. He saw the bike just inside the door. From the video he knew it was hers. The camera caught her telling its price, $1400, just as her surfboard arrived.

It wasn't fair, her beautiful life compared to his life of shit. And when he first came and watched, he didn't quite recognize her because of her re-done hair. It had been wildly styled, and with her brutal tan it was lethal. And she spent all day naked, per all the photos. She was doing splendidly, and her laugh was one of a confident, gaining life. He saw those beach skinnies pull in to the Redi Quik in their $60,000 SUVs and stride in, grab muffins and coffee, slide their cards, and stride out. Plenty of money. And with Beatense, her royalties were reportedly in the hundreds of thousands!

Worse, that sight of Kit inside filled his stomach with blood, and the thought of he and Beatense at play hit him like a fist. But other than to stare at the brown boy, and why not, she kept her hands off. That was a hope. Buck took a last drowning sailor look and cut back to the other drive, tripping over the tangled dead branches.

He got in his car with his heart burning. As Buck turned onto the Highway two vehicles swung the turn and started up the drive, a racy, two-seater Tapadero and a Bushwhacker with surfboards on the roof-rack. The one he saw in the video!

He felt a bear claw grip at his heart, but laughed it off. At least with Kit as her boyfriend he didn't have to worry about other guys. But it bothered him that he didn't have a decent car to compete with.

"Just so you know, Beatense," said Virginia, as she took a bottle of Resch's beer out of the refrigerator, "Chris is coming by for a visit, so you two will have to clear out for a night or two, so we can get touchy-feely. He's getting as tan as you, Kit, road building. He e-mailed me pictures of himself at work. I hit the rafters."

"Let's try to time that with my upcoming ski trip, Virginia," said Beatense. "Or else the alternative is for me to go to the Hideaway, with some friend, I hope."

Virginia bumped the refrigerator door shut. "Oh, Kit, do you want one?"

"Is there another spring water? Tamdyn says you get darker on water."

"You know, Beatense, we could stay in a motel together," said Lorraine.

"Yeah, two girls, two beds."

Lorraine laughed. "Nice try. But… Who… Who's out there?"

They had heard the busy engine of a sporty car pull up out in front, followed by a quick squeak of its brakes. Then, another car? Beatense stepped to the door. She saw a little red sports car, a Tapadero, and the person emerging from it was Sim. And there was Eric's truck. *Oh no! Oh no!*

"Sim? Hey! Hi! You actually got off, hah? Call in sick? Er, welcome!"

"Hi, er, Beatense? Is that you? You had your hair... You l-look great!"

Eric walked up also, looking confused and bothered.

"I... I g-guess there was a misunderstanding," he stammered.

"Oh no there wasn't," said Virginia, who had stepped to the door. Lorraine came also. "I can snatch victory from the jaws of defeat for you. You're staying."

"This is Eric," said Beatense. "He sold me my bike and also just caught me two timing. Eric, I apologize. But Virginia would love a ride in your truck."

"I think I might at that. That is..."

Eric was no idiot. This Virginia was a walking forest fire, a wonderful catch.

"L-Let's roll. B-But can you throw something on?"

"For how long? But yeah, let me..."

"Wait! And this is Sim, everyone," said Beatense. "Who I mentioned."

Virginia said, "Sim? Oh, say, I clean your pool, down at Francis Gorham."

"Oh, I th-thought I r-recognized you. Y-Yeah, hi."

Sim didn't seem too elated by this revelation. Virginia sprang in and sprang out again in her breezy Student Teacher. She shook hands with Eric, widely smiling, and he was impressed by her glasses. They gave her a look of careful discrimination for all situations. Making polite good-byes the two hopped into Eric's truck and drove off.

And now here was Sim.

All doubts fled, Beatense saw he was wondrously presented. He wore a pink vacation shirt with splotchy yellow flowers, that was a little shrunken for him. It was opened in a chest baring vee. And he wore size 31 white jeans that fit so tight the muscles of his long, thinned thighs showed. In one more dim porch light he looked horrifically baked. But the main attraction was that spiffy car. I had one too.

Sauvage hair aflutter, Beatense was all over the vehicle in her admiration.

"Oh, Sim, sorry about the confusion. But what a car! Is that ever slick!"

"Thanks! Er, g-great outfit. B-But you say I'm still welcome?"

The Eric incident unnerved him, but the small girl was all smiles.

"Of course! This is terrific! How did you find the place?"

"Y-You... You... You told me your... Your address."

"Oh, you're the one I told? Whew, I can't let that out to just anyone!"

She was dazzled by his proud display. Gone was that lonely outcast, forlornly showing off his impressive but suspect tan in the tropics heat. He sparkled with live social energy. Beatense turned, only to find Lorraine behind her.

"Er, this is Sim, Lorraine, who I sailed with down at Cocojo Friday! Oop, that's whom. Anyway, Sim, this is Lorraine! And oh, here's Kit! He's my true lover."

Kit sized Sim up. The two were instant natural rivals.

Sim turned pale. "Oh... I'm, uh, sorry," he faltered. "I d-didn't know."

"No such luck!" Beatense laughed. "See?"

As if on cue Kit put his thin arm around the astonished Lorraine, his first act of companionable affection. Sim was saved from additional embarrassment.

"Er, hi, nice to meet you all. But Beatense, is my being here okay?"

The other two withdrew inside and pretended to do everything but listen.

"I invited you! And after being naked today I deeply need male attention!"

"Well, you have mine. But like, b-busy at all? Want to go for a spin?"

"In that? Wow! An actual two-seater! A roadster! I could die!"

"But are you s-saying y-yes?" He suddenly wanted her desperately.

"Of course! Come on in while I get something clubbier on!"

Sim didn't care to chitchat with these strangers, especially this tanner Kit.

"Guys, I'll just be in the bathroom. Bore Sim with your usual banal blab!"

Lorraine opened the refrigerator. "Want a spring water, Sim?"

"That would be f-fine, thanks."

Lorraine then joined Beatense in the bathroom as she studied the mirror.

"Beatense, just what do you have in mind, young lady?"

"My Grape Stomper, is what I have in mind. Can you get it for me?"

"Beatense, I just don't advise this. All evening all we heard out of you was how weird he was. Even that sailing sounded weird, if you ask me."

"That was not weird! It was... It was beautiful."

"Yes, but... Wh-What are y-you doing?"

The bare girl began crisply buffing her coconut oil into her gold glinting tan with a towel, reducing her rank sun smell. With a foot placed on the spout as she continued her toasted thigh shined very long. Lorraine shook.

"I'm getting ready! Now get my clothes or I will!"

Lorraine stumbled out. The others looked at her expectantly as she groped her way across the room to the closet. She was in a blur, her ears were roaring.

"Lorraine, are you okay?" said Kit.

"Y-Yeah. But Sim, j-just prepare yourself. Better yet let me have her."

Lorraine brought the dress and the girl eagerly floated the Grape on. This outfit gave her tan intense power in the porch-light competing bathroom light. Lorraine did her dilated warm eyes. It was hard to look into them, they held great power.

"Basically I'm a child, Lorraine. I never did m-mem-menser... Or whatever, and seriously, I don't do my legs yet, and no pubicals. But I can do whatever it takes."

They came out, the others started. Beatense's risky dress gave her cream jugs a live presence, and their lifted fullness gave their tan a hazy patina glow. The short frock's soft gauze gave her rusty hot, near-black tan a fashionable elegance. The slimmed flow of her arms matched the slimmed flow of her extremely bared legs.

Her somber dark eyes were lined, enlarging them with a softly forceful power, but only a rat needing a nest could like her hair. Sim had sailed with this girl in his boat, and he saw her naked that day, but he had no preparation for this. The open gash of her dress bared her stark collarbones, most of her breasts, and her rippled belly.

Looking outwardly calm, Sim shook in horror at her showing.

"H-Hey, g-great outfit, B-Beatense."

She studied her arm and jingled its bracelets. "Thanks. Oh, just wait."

Bondy had warned that the real excitement of staying with a new friend was the possible danger. She stepped to her dresser, with painting, as her hair long fluttered down her back, like a rippling flag carried over her shoulder.

She checked her mirror and secretly slipped her switchblade into her wallet case and tucked it under her arm. The pressure of holding it bulged her bicep, somehow giving a more sensual impression than all the rest.

"Thanks for the help, Lorraine. I... I d-don't know if I'll be back."

That "if" was a message to Sim. She was simmering with erotic needs, but her cooperation wasn't a given. He held the car door open as the black cat slipped into the low seat of his sports buggy. Her posture slackly slung her taut belly, and her bared thighs were long enough to reach her knees all the way to the dash.

As Sim stumbled around the car she pulled her seatbelt over, but any possible dangers were of other natures. She had her knife for the one, and she was highly primed for the other. Indeed the way she still tingled from her tanning that day, she needed the other. And it was all so easy if one was beautiful!

Hot bake all day, get in a friend's car and go! Innocence itself, and fun!

Sim, who could hardly handle his keys, got in beside her and, shaking, he ripped the little engine to thrumbling life. He popped up the headlights and he drove off. He swung the north loop around to avoid making an inglorious Y-turn, while one excited girl bounced in her race-car seat as the tuned springs flexed to the road's bumps.

Her flimsy dress fluttered. Her breasts were open to sight.

"W-We won't b-be going far, B-Beatense," Sim said, even shakier.

The twitching girl was dressed as if she expected a thousand dollar spree.

"Won't be going far! You can drive me all night in this nifty little car!"

He dreaded the spot he got himself into. No way he could make her cry out. But sitting beside him she widely smiled. Either she was just friendly, or expected heat.

Speaking of, "D-Did you g-get a lot of sun today? Y-You look like you did."
They turned down Ringdon with a swing of the headlights on the trees.

"Yeah, I was naked all day, plus rode my new bike. Did I say it was new?"

"Yes, but nowadays people keep their bikes up so well they all look new."

"Nowadays. What do you mean, nowadays?"

"Well, it's just that bikes weren't taken so seriously twenty years ago." To his horror he realized he was in a minefield. His age. "Er, nice night, hah?"

"Yeah! But Sim, I'll sure keep my bike up. It cost fourteen hundred dollars!"

page number at top left and author name at top center

"Oh, a used tourist rental, hah?" Sim said, and they laughed.

They turned onto the Coastal Highway, and the girl was importantly shot along in the showy little rig. Although she had taken a shower that evening, leaving a flowery scent, and then rubbed herself with the oil, her bacon sun scent now reeked through it. Her muscles gave her skin additional shine.

"Will... Will you be okay in that outfit, Beatense? It can get chilly out."

"Chilly, muggy and tepid, words I hate. But I'm okay. You can warm me up!"

The girl sat restlessly twitching, as her skinny self flexed to the gear shifting and suspension movements. She rested back her head, baring her refined neck, and she listened to the mid engine's revving reactions to Sim's shifting. He was quick to vary his speed, usually up, and also to change lanes. He did signal.

Except for the passenger, the above account does reflect my history.

The fast car excited Beatense, the neon gauge lights and the shift tunnel dividing their jet cockpit impressed her deeply. Also the bright cosmopolitan lights of the busy Highway dazzled her as the humming little engine (unlike Craig's rental) spun the two along. She did intend to stay with her friend, as a way of topping off this ride.

They flew past Sorel, Cocojo and Turtle Rock, and kept on to Le Tournepier.

"I don't think I should come home all late and wake Lorraine up, hah, Sim?" He froze. "So let's try to get back by midnight, about."

He unfroze. He was actually the moral type to tread carefully. Except, he did act an older woman for several months. He started off-season pale with her, then his tan came in with spring, and his sleeping really got active.

"Y-Yeah, sure. There's this one club built on this seaside cliff. Traders."

"Yeah, I saw it from three different sailboats!" --/-- "Do you ever rest?"

Kit was put on the spot with the kidnapping of Beatense, and Virginia before that. He hintingly motioned his head toward the door, but the practical Lorraine first locked Beatense's bike. As if impatient he grabbed and led the gasping girl to his lair.

Lorraine weakly protested as he pulled her in. At the time Shean was flying with Tammy, and further south, on a picnic blanket in the dunes, a brown summer home youth was taking a brown summer home maiden to all new levels of being. Life!

"Er, Beatense, I-I'm sorry I overlooked you earlier today. I keep running into that one volleyball girl as if it's fore-ordained or something."

"Pre-ordained. I should apologize also. I have a boyfriend on the side. You saw him at the 10K. Not tan at all and a mature build. Why is this car so steery?"

"Rack and pinion. Plus everyone's driving like assholes tonight. As usual."

They rocketed on and reached Traders, but Beatense wanted fuck instead.

Sim helped the girl as he watched the hesitant action of her slimmed legs as she got out. She set her dress to partial decency, and the two crossed the parking lot.

The light breezes wafted the upon Beatense's bare skin.

Monday was an off night, but Beatense was taken by the tropic ambiance of the grass roofed hang-out. The place was built out of timbers and planks, and it featured cantilevered balconies overlooking the night sea. The girl minutely moved to the soft music as she waited while Sim went over to the bar. The dozen patrons in the place watched her, aghast. Her dress gave a profile view of her plumped but small petals, and its stark whiteness avidly enriched her blackety tan. Everyone stared, reeling, as the sensational sunners took their wine out to the adjoining balcony.

The wary friends watched the white-curled surf tumble in.

"Wow, is this cool! We must be two hundred feet up, Sim!"

"We might be. The other balconies go way down the cliff."

The single overhead tube of yellow neon gave her skin an all new shine.

"It's so beautiful here! And that's why I have to be brown, so I fit in with all things beautiful. The sun is beautiful too, and I bake it in deeply to identify my very with it."

"You... You are real, real tan. And y-you're b-beautiful yourself. Actually you're remarkable. Just this incredible build, like spring steel struts."

She smiled guiltily but proudly. "The publishers thought that too."

"Good point. Is the wine any good? It's a local vintage, Alhambra Cellars."

"Wine makes me too tired, Sim. I'm sorry. Let's have root beer instead."

"Yeah, okay. I'll take the bottle home, even though it *is* yeasty rotgut."

They poured out their glasses. The wine fell away in globs and splattered on the shingles below. Sim took off his flowery shirt, getting his friend's approval, and went back in to the bar as a stretch of muscle. The patrons waited expectantly, hoping to see the other explosion come in also. It would be far too obvious going out on that wretched balcony. One has his pride.

Beatense took off her dress and felt ecstatically bare. Sim returned with the root beer and his head did a little jolt. *Fucking naked!*

"Er, uh, th-they looked at m-me k-kind of funny, but here... Here it is."

"Thanks. I hope it cools me down. The sun was real hot today!"

"Yeah, forget about getting sun on those humid days, but today was perfect."

"Exactlly! But isn't it fun, Sim, we're both professional tanners. I'm far too gone myself, but there's something to be said for that nutty, healthy, college girl brown."

"I overdo it too. My working nights will be the end of me. I get six hours of sun every day. And I don't know how I do it; I never seem to really sleep. Or eat."

"So you're a sleepless anorexic too! Plus you show yourself off. Last night us lesbians debated that, if you should show yourself off all out even if it upsets people. We agreed one must. Sim, what do you think of sexually active young kids?"

He shook. "It... It depends on how active. Even young girls get implants."

"Yes, I just got a new one at the clinic. Full of smiling cute kids. My first one I got at thirteen, at that surveying camp. Sex was so overpowering I fucked every chance. But being black whip naked, what was I supposed to do, read magazines?

"So once we raided this camp of oldie duffs. This fleabag was running, as if he could escape, yeah right, so we galloped up beside him and I leaped off and tackled him. I don't think he ever got back up!" --/-- "Y-You... Killed him?" --/-- "Maybe."

"Mr. Elkor saw me in the video and asked me to stay the night. I said no, I was booked up. Why not by the pool the next day? He hesitated, that being pedophile public. Little Katrinka came with. Me just shaking I got him deep. He went easy at first, as if me being little made me all delicate, so I said, "You saw me take that guy down! Go!" So he got rough. Kat was just eleven but he got her rough too. People took videos, they went all over the Net. The raid videos too. Helped sell my book."

"S-So there is a happy ending. W-Was that old guy the only one you attacked?"

"No, me and Geddy headed off an old guy running away from these boys."

Sim shook, but his flagrant bakings also did severe damage. He actually wanted people to hate their lives, even bad enough to crawl in a hole.

They stepped back in. The patrons awaiting them got more than they hoped for. The couple took one of those tall tables, and the nude perched on her stool with one foot hooked on the rung, while her other leg swung free in extension.

Sim couldn't take his eyes off her corded black belly. Her arms too, with those unmistakable, defined tensions under the skin, that ingénues have at their peril. It's hard for them to convey that frail femininity if they're taut thinned.

At the time the girl Sim was with was gazing about, wearing as she was her provocative lack of outfit. Her eyes looked out of focus as if to show bland boredom, typical of all conceited and spoiled career women, who are so exotically and erotically hot, and live and love it. The girl held court like a proud but woefully ill-prepared little heiress. She looked hatefully about and shook back her dried, straw-like hair.

It was an act but Sim thought she was getting tired of him.

"I-I g-guess it's kind of slow here tonight, B-Beatense. No m-music even."

"It's shit here. But do you know much about computers, Sim?"

"Enough to get by. Actually when we got the first computer at work we had to sign up to use it, and it didn't even have a hard drive. Flexy discs."

She laughed, but suddenly frowned. "Just... Just how old are you, Sim?"

He rubbed his forehead, huffing. "Kind of like... R-Real old."

"Twenty-five? I can accept that. But I would guess you at my age."

He sagged. "I'm... I'm in my m-mid... Thirties, B-Beatense."

"You're... You... You're like thirty-five? Print near as old as gorgeous Elgin."

He looked stricken. "S-Sorry to mislead you. We can go, if you w-want."

"You almost look like Elgin. Uncanny. I'm sorry, but I do want to leave, but not because of your age. This dive is all full of junk now. Let's try again Friday night?"

"You... You mean... Really? Yeah, great! And let's get out of here!"

They went out to the car as each wondered what was next. Their agreeing to see each other again gave them both an out for not going further onow, but it also acted to legitimize their getting more *acquainted* because of the possibility of a relationship in the near future. Why wait anyway? The coast breezes of the tropical night breathed with sex magic. The distant surf rumbled, and the air had a balmy, liquid essence.

Sim held the door and yet again stared in shock at the nude's long, bared legs as they negotiated getting their owner into her seat. He got in and fumbled the Tapadero to a start. With a screech they whipped out into the street.

"Well, sorry, Beatense, but the other clubs won't have beach crowds, either. It's not Torch Night. I guess I'll just run you *home* then, hah?"

"Sure. Where's it at?"

"Why, it's back... Oh, my home? Oh, uh, sure, w-we can go there!"

Sim asked and she told about being the Book Girl. "My skin got me rich!"

Sim panted. They threaded their way along the meandering streets that lay upon the foothill slope. The lights of the city below spread out wider and wider. At last Sim swung into the parking lot of his grimly forbidding, ten story building.

It was built of poured concrete, raw and grey, and the iron bars on the balconies looked like so many cages. The Francis Gorham was post-modern function-first. A rent machine. But Beatense noticed the balconies.

"Boy, those ledges would be handy for sun worshipping, now that you mention it. Just step out and there you are! I should rent here myself!"

"Yeah, do! But the sun doesn't really slant in until eleven. So I can actually get errands done like any normal person. Even get a capuccino."

They got out and went in the neglected lobby, complete with a pin-up board full of junk for sale and notices of subletting. A couple guys seeing the girl went coronary. The two took the elevator up to the eighth floor. This was a self-service push button type. Beatense was used to elevators as run by uniformed attendants, who at each stop opened and closed the crisscrossed brass gate with white gloves. This elevator had a fluorescent light fixture with the plastic panel broken in half. The tile floor was gritty. The interior was painted in a muddy beige scribbled with ball point pens.

The friends went down a hallway carpeted with orange commercial crap, that was stained beyond hope and spotted with dirty gum wads and cigaret burns. Beatense began to have doubts, but these quickly vanished. Sim opened his door and the girl beheld the magnificent panorama through the ten foot wide patio door, that he always left open. She hopped through the darkened room out onto the balcony.

"Wow, just look at that view! You can see for miles up here!"

Sim stripped to a boy bikini, that he poked out so far he took it off, and he joined her. He was gratified by her reaction. Not all visitors noticed the world beyond. The balcony seemed suspended in outer space over the countless fixed or moving lights, close in and out yonder. Out at sea a brightly lighted cruise ship made passage. Its progress could be marked by its slow movement off beyond the glowing buildings.

"That blackness beyond is the Teramasion Sea, Beatense. See the boats?"

"Yeah! Little ones, plus that ocean liner! It's like a city it's so big!"

The nude was quite impressed. From this vantage point she actually felt the vital ferment of this sensual land's energy. She felt intoxicated, and she was overjoyed to see Sim seven inches naked. *Oh boy!* But she warily accepted his embrace.

By then Tammy was entering her third crisis, and her sweet cooing moans were turning to stricken cries that carried to the neighbors. Her parents warmly smiled.

And Lorraine's savage was assisting her. Hidden in the summer home dunes the Amherst girl, notorious for her all day sun worship, was flying with a boy known for his own tan. Life! And Virginia was getting to know Eric better.

Beatense didn't know of these vignettes, but she felt the power of the view before her. The way of the tropics, where all things possible actually occur!

Elsewhere in Sim's building there came a knock at a door, a sharp rapping.

"Who could that be?" the lifeguard Jerry said aloud, looking at the door.

The knocking persisted. He sighed and got up. He opened the door into the dank hallway. It was the aspiring lifeguard. She wore a light, skimpy dress, pale blue, the optimum color for publicizing a tan. And the cheerful slut had evidently spent all day and actually all week blasting hers in. She had a toasted density of golden burned brown. Her eyebrows were frizzled to a white blond.

"M-Miss S-Silva? Wh-What are y-you d-doing here?"

"Hi, Jerry. Remember? I was supposed to come here for my coaching."

"Oh, that's right! I forgot! But... But it's kind of late to cover it all now."

"I had my interview with the park superintendent, Mr. Holderton. He said I would need to review the CPR chapter, because they can't hire me if I fail the test!"

He pulled her in. "Y-Yeah, okay, uh, sure!" He started sweating. "B-But I gotta get my laundry out of the dryer. Stay h-here, I'll b-be right back!"

"Sure, but don't fold it. I got my pen and notebook, Jerry, all set to go."

Karen stepped out onto the balcony. A couple stood on another nearby balcony. The trembling Sim still held his friend. Feeling restless, the girl's sensual need was humming at high tension. She was long, lean, lanky and bony, so she was tensed all times anyway. She moved closer into her friend's shaking hold. She wanted him.

"Sim, look at th-that car d-down there, moving so slow. I b-bet he's lost."

"H-He m-must be delivering a pizza. I s-see that all the time, with all these streets so confusing. Heh heh. B-But B-Beatense, uh, c-can you stay over?"

She caught herself on the rail. "I... I d-don't know. Y-Yeah, I think."

Jerry paced within the slow elevator. At last, *bing!* He sprang out. He found the quivering bare Karen lying back on her elbows on his bed, with a knee invitingly up. She was a live feast of baked rays, taut as violin strings. Perhaps ta little too sure of herself, she smiled. She sat up cross-legged, in a curved sunk-belly slouch.

She could have been a child of just twelve. Her shagged ripples of sun blonded hair caressed upon her small but firmed shoulders. All her muscles were precisely shaped. She was browned to a beautiful screeching that had no apologies.

"Hi! That was a quick trip! What are you going to coach me on first?"

Some girls have an animal side to their beings, a wild force that was deep in play for Karen now. If this was three decades earlier she would belong the garden club, taking her seed catalog and shy suggestions to the meetings. But she would simmer with yearning needs, while wondering what was wrong with her. But in present times this animal spirit has no restraint, and coiled within lurks the primitive beast.

When the beast strikes, even sensible and studious young ladies will shamefully degrade themselve, breaking down at last as their souls are bared.

It little helps that there are only single witnesses of their ragged defeat. The final, abject surrenders will bring tears, but better that than weak social club tea.

Sim and friend stepped back in from the balcony. Just within but over to the side was a folding sofa, that was opened flat to make a bed covered with just a sheet. It faced out toward the shimmering city, that filled the room with twilight. The trembling Sim folded back the sheet, exposing another. He turned on his purple radiation light and the two sat facing each other.

The girl exclaimed at the lamp's dim but vivid glow. She saw that her own and Sim's tans were black, and her gold belly chain gleamed against her flexing sunken belly ripples, ready to work. The sheets glowed unnaturally white. Panting, blood thundering, Beatense leaned back on her hands and opened her legs.

"Th-That b-breeze is just f-feels so good, Sim, even inside here."

"Y-Yes. Well, I guess w-we b-better call it a n-night then, hah? It's getting late. Wanna, like, er, turn in?"

"Yeah!" She turned. "But look at that picture, Sim. Who is that, you at fifteen? That boy is just incredibly tan. Wow! Like... Like you!"

It was a framed black and white photograph, enlarged to poster size, of a naked, thinned and stiffened teen-age boy holding a surfboard. He was bursting with light muscle and he was black tan, with shiny dry highlights and stray sea water droplets. His long, thick hair was bleached blond with lingering dark streaks. An evil face.

"Last summer, down at Cocojo. It sounds queer, but he was just so steeled that I had to take his picture. He didn't like it, as you can see in his expression."

"Some expression. But magnificent." She took hold of Sim's own stiffness. Then another distraction. "Sim, what are all those on the chair there?"

He turned. "Oh, my bikinis. I washed them earlier. They're drying now."

"Oh." *That many?* "And what are all those bottles on that table?"

"Different kinds of accelerator oil. That tall one I used down at East Bluff Sunk. Yucca. I baked all day and slept in the dunes, and laid out the whole next day. The red one I used for this one prairie camp-outing, and that Solar Slave I used down at The Landings of the Geode Desert. I laid out there naked for a week and burned painfully black. I hurt for a week. I have pictures to prove it."

"Like Keter. Pictures of yourself? Well, why not? But who, er, took you?"

"I used shutter delay. I picked the best ones for posters of myself, like that wild surfer. But I keep them rolled up. I mean, I got myself to look at."

The girl saw four shirts hanging in the closet. These, the bottles of oil, a stereo, his bikinis and several bracelets were all he seemed to own. Plus that car. But her ideal was a guy as tan manic as herself, like Elgin or Kit, except Sim took it too far. She did see a computer, reassuring her that he had at least one other interest.

Karen was bathed with sweat, and she wiggled and writhed like a pinned python. Nearby neighbors closed their balcony doors, as her cries of triumph floated out into the quiescent night. The two friends smiled. Sim raised his hand, be right back, and ducked into the bathroom. Beatense thought, *This guy is either Elgin or his brother!*

Karen's cries had fine, rounded, top quality tones. Later Beatense's did too.

39

POOL SIDE SUN

A bare black figure and a bare white figure left one cabin and strolled over to another. There was no one to see, but suspense excited their hearts. At the second cabin the one roughly embraced the other. He carried her in and lay her in bed with another girl, whose friend had a Bushwhacker parked outside until an hour ago.

The black figure slipped away into the dim light of dawn. The paperboy saw him. He was equally naked and black in the gloom. He had thick, shaggy blond hair and refined muscles that were as beautiful to behold as his hard face. He had come from Bolingbroke Trail, and one day a year ago down at Cocojo he was annoyed by this queer taking his photo. But the guy had his respect, obviously an all-out tanner.

An elfin child lay on her front, grunting as her friend rubbed the smoothed hide of her long, widening back. She yelped as he held her small waist. She had that fresh, luminous skin that is so responsive to soft touch and cool breezes. She too looked black, in this apartment that faced away from the rising sun. Normally in full sun with cameras watching she shined with an intense, copper glinting very very dark brown.

Her bare friend's long, slim laced thighs, poised on each side of her, also shined black. He caught her sunny scent, akin to turbinado sugar and breakfast bacon. The girl, resting from her five orgasms, gazed out upon the throbbing view of the city and the sea beyond. She wriggled Sim off and sat cross legged with chained belly starve curved. She picked up the pictures, of him, sitting on her two books, *Fourteen* on top.

Sim took his tape measure off his bed stand and wrapped its clinking metal band around the sprite's charred middle. Beatense took the nearby water bottle, and with little arm cocked and head tipped back, she downed it in a gulp. Her chain and tape moved to her sunk belly. She tossed the bottle aside. Sim read eighteen inches.

Her thighs were sixteen, for a firmed diameter like a CD. She took the tape.

"Seven inches! No wonder I yelled!" --/-- "Well your waist is impossible!"

"As long as we're in the praise mode, these pictures are criminal, Sim. You *should* tan all out. And add your own book to mine there. Oh, and thanks for my screams."

He smiled, he got some credit at last. "I should get p-pictures of you."

"Hey, cool! While you're at work I can ultra bake all day to prep up!" She looked at him. "C-Can… We go again, Sim? To keep me in practice for my next book?"

He sweated. "N-No. I m-mean, I g-got to get in to w-work, B-Beatense."

My lady friend, we began January, me white but slight, and stiff. Dozens of times, we always woke in time to fuck again before going to our respective jobs. By May I was wild deep brown. Sim also deeply brown. Heart pounding, girl held. He worked in, she excitedly cried. A gay a block away with televideo always aimed got them.

A shower. Sim delighted in her, as he delighted in himself. Like the girl he was bony thin and sudsy dark tan, and like her he was shameless in self worship. They dried off and Beatense hung her dress on her shoulder. It was pushing eight as they hit the elevator. A career type new to his job (that's why he lived in this student hole) stared at the iridescent sex machine. Naked. Bony thin. Blond hair stray wild.

They climbed into the little red cockpit and joined the early work torrent.

"You should button that shirt up, going into work. That chest is a weapon."

"I just work in the lab, it's okay. Working nights I just wear a bikini."

"Cool! But Sim, you seemed kind of antsy about work, before we re-fucked."

"Well, I am running late. Oh, hey, get sun today at Cocojo, for the photos."

"Hey, I said before at the Hogan this real tan older guy Elgin looked like you."

"Yeah, that will be me in ten or so years. Kind of a time warp."

Her head whirled. "Yeah, th-that is a time… Warp." *What the… This is nuts!*

The peppy little engine sped them along with a gutsy vroom. They arrived at the cabin and Sim hopped out. Ready for work, he wore the same floral shirt of the night before, fully open, and the white, leggy jeans. Beatense saw, as slouched low in his seat, his blacked belly had the same starving that her own did. He helped her out.

"Like last night you weren't half bad at sixty, Sim, but be sure and rest up today."

He comically staggered. "Yeah! Us geriatrics and our iron poor blood!"

"Oh, hey," Virginia said laconically, as they stepped in the cabin. Both girls were tough willow wisps of muscle. "So, you spent the night? Cool. Eric took off already. We agreed to keep meeting. And Sim, if you're tired of that car I can take it."

After making noncommittal remarks to the roommates, already quite late and not sure of his prospects once at work, Sim got in his envied car and took worriedly off.

"News, Beatense," Lorraine said. "Kit says Tamdyn needs a concierge."

"A what? Lorraine, I can't, I'm not staying that long. So anyway, old as he was Sim got me hot last night." She opened a box of donuts. "How did Eric go, Ginny?"

"We went for drinks, did some dancing, and I got it hot, too. A definite repeat."

Dining on milk and donuts Beatense recalled her night. "We went to that Traders and then went to his apartment. His balcony looks over the city with all those lights, and he's long as my arm, but…" She told of the bikinis and bottles, and time warp.

"Everybody in this book is from all different times," said Virginia. "In fact you're a composite, Beatense, you have no real life counterpart. Oh, virtual Jesse called."

"No, he's a phantom. Thanks for the donuts. But what did he call about?"

"He called about this job, which reminds me, I better run. I got four pools today, including Sim's, whatever decade he is. If he makes any moves I got dibs."

"No, he's on days today, maybe all week. No *sailing* until this evening."

"Talk about sailing," said Lorraine, "Kit was just real attentive. I got it hot, too."

The naked composite hung up her barely worn dress. The phone rang, Jesse.

"What's this about my job, Jesse? Is this just an excuse to see me?"

"We might be able to catch Mr. Kelliher now. Can you get over here?"

"Why the detour? I can run down to that drink stand in two seconds!"

"I was thinking of taking the horses." --/-- "Good idea! Okay, wait up!"

She tied on her running shoes and lit out, resuming her rule as the Book Girl. Her gold chain tossed around her slim, flexing waist as she ran, heading toward the sand path to get down to the Hill beach. She attracted her usual stares. Already she was hitting the publishers. Beatense planned to run by the drink stand on the ocean front walk to see what that illusion Mr. Kelliher looked like. She turned onto Main and ran across the sand, which took far more effort than paving, toward the access ramp.

She ran up the incline to the beach front walk and loped by the drink stand, but it was closed up. Well, later with ghostly Jesse then. She ran down to the Hogg lodge and recalling its mirage memories she cut by it to the Highway on Smoot.

The same pandemonium: Tire screeches, near misses, pedestrians colliding and shouts. People sitting at the restaurant patio tables jumped up to watch her run by. The girl watched her reflection in the store windows and saw that she did indeed look awfully naked. In one window Beatense thought she saw Buck's old Burroughs chug slowly by, and as she looked she saw it was him. She waved, just as a truck moved between. Then, as she ran on he came by again from the other way. She didn't see him in time; she missed another chance.

At this point Beatense realized she should have been showing off her new bike, and she wondered if it was stolen because she should have seen it this morning now that she thought about it. She turned back and ran worriedly faster and at last got to Ringdon. Few people ever ran this flat out but she did, right up the hill. She then ran the confusing loops and finally burst into the cabin. She saw her bike.

"Lorraine, what the hell! My bike wasn't here this morning!"

"We hid it in the tub because none of us would be home last night. It was locked and we locked the door but you can break in with a credit card."

"Thanks, good thinking. But while I'm here I better call my Pop."

She got through. "Yeah, Pop, me, Beatense. Hey, I need your permission. This nice family invited me along on a ski trip Is that okay with you?"

"You must really wants to go, darter! You didn't ask about your account with the bank! They got you a new advance of two hundred and fifty thousand!"

"That's nice but I don't need any old money, Pop. All I need is being brown and skinny for a fabulous life. That includes our surveying, you old sodden drunk."

"Agh, get on with you, darter! If you don't want it I'll takes it!"

"Sorry, I closed out your power of attorney. And I am going skiing! Bye!"

Beatense in Nake rode her brakes down the long Ringdon Walk and turned onto the Highway, where she cut through the picnic park to the Sea Walk. Her spokes twinkled in the sun as she rode by the drink stand. It was opened now, but she didn't see the owner, his being behind the cart opening boxes. Despite the high pedestrian numbers on the path the girl used her suicide bars, so that her parallel set made her long waist look even smaller for those watching from their lodging or condo residence balconies. Meanwhile there were collision risks and Beatense had to go into evasive action. She was inexcusably delayed in her ride, the tourists were all along the path. They stopped abruptly in her way to gawk, unlike the locals, who knew the time-warp composite as a familiar sight. If they gave a second look, it was her new bike.

She didn't know that the wiser bikers stayed off the Beachway because the stray sand on the pavement got into the gears and chain. Beatense turned again at Smoot and got to the Highway She came to the turn into the world where the paperboy and friends lived in freedom, and she shot in along ritzy Bolingbroke Trail. She rode the crushed terra cotta of the Shattuck driveway, and Jesse met her by the cabin.

He was in trim, white duck shorts, that warmed up his dark tan horridly. They fit low to his hips, barely holding. His chest was proudly bulked, and his drawn in belly looked painfully rippled. For such a baby faced kid his muscles were world class.

"Oh, shit, Jesse! Can't you ever wear a shirt? I was all calm until now!"

"Well, good morning to you, too! You're not much better. Nice, er, shirt."

"Shut up. Where is everyone? The car is gone. And where's Ned?"

"Shan came by for him to go to their shed. Shean is biking uptown with Knife, a show-off bikini run. But we have to rip. Mr. Kelliher is setting up the cart right now. I spotted him down on the beach with the binoculars."

"I don't know who you saw but when I rode by he wasn't there."

"Hey, I saw you! He was digging through the boxes behind the trailer."

"Well, shit! But let's get this over with because I have to get sun today!"

He dropped his shorts. "It's early yet. Park your cheap bike and let's ride."

They got on the sleepy steeds and broke out through the bordering tropic hedge onto the beach. They galloped along the lightly breaking surf. They raced past old Hoggy and the Breeze, giving a java jolt to the wading shell searchers. They led the horses up the ramp. The petite, deep brown Absinthe, perched on the railing as she sang in welcome to the sun, wore blossoms in her hair. Looking like a forest nymph who ventured out into civilization, she waved. But she wasn't the only nude on that railing. Flammchen sat there too, dog-howling toasted and skeletal. The two riders stopped their horses to both stare and exchange coastal paradise greetings.

Bruce Kelliher was coarse, vulgar and beefy, with little concern for his curly body hair. His stained sleeveless undershirt showed him in all his fat, ugly, repelling, cigar smoking sophistication. From his shrugging sneer at Beatense it seemed he was all too used to beach girls, and it also seemed he was elaborately unimpressed by her famous tan, at the moment bared. With her chained belly flexing the stick Beatense, worth a quarter million, held her arm protectively as he crudely appraised her.

"So, you're the one, hah? You're in. When I call you start. Try clothes."

"That... That's the interview? And will I be trained at all? And let's just make it clear right now, no top. I'm the Book Girl and I wear or don't wear what I want."

"Whatever. Tuffy can fill you in. She ain't here yet. You want a tour?"

Beatense looked through the narrow door into the five by eight wagon. Oranges, lemons, peaches and bananas sat in small baskets on the counter, along with a juice pulping blender and other apparatus. "Nah, it looks pretty straightforward."

The urbane drink baron rolled his eyes up at this display of blithe ignorance. He was pleasantly startled that the girl laughed out loud. "Laugh if you must, but don't think I'm giving you this cake spot. I might start you down at Naomsnon or Zozo."

"I hope I work out, sir. I have cameras on me already so I have to make good."

The two got free drinks and sat with them on the bordering back ledge. Absinthe and Flammchen now stood against the railing pipe, and gazing out to sea, they were sublimely unaffected, even as the clumsy tourists stared. Then the girls sprang over the rail to the sand below and ran for the sea, through a flock of seagulls.

"Okay, are you done, Bea... Oh oh, we have to stay here a little longer."

Beatense saw why. An elegantly slim young lady in pencil leg jeans and a chest and forearm baring rib knit top, petted the horses and stepped to the stand. She had looping rampant hair, and the dusky tint of primed fluids. With her cheek points and lightly curved nose her face was so sensually attuned she probably felt self conscious about her sultry erotic voltage. But her inquiring dark eyes and fine eyebrows had an engaging delicacy. She was bone tight and blood hot. A BBB self deifier.

"Excuse me, sir," she said with a properly urbane voice. "Are you open?"

"By that you're inquiring if I'm conducting business?" Bruce got his second laugh that day, this one from a true model. "What do you want, anyway?"

"Peaches and Cream. I just got to town. What a beautiful beach."

Jesse hopped up. "I can show you around! Take Spec here!"

"Jesse, I got to get my bike!" said Beatense. "And shoes. Think for once!"

"Those are your horses? And are two you ever tan! And if you're the Book Girl, you're my first celebrity!" She paid for her drink. "Thank you, sir."

She left, swaying in that graceful, elongated S curved way that very few women naturally or affectedly present. After a caring long look Jesse deemed it was time for them to ride back. They cantered down to the hotel beach and Jesse waited with the horses by the cabanas while Beatense hopped up to the pool deck.

"Hey, Tamdyn, I won't be needing the singing or concierge job, to let you know."

"You wouldn't have to sing or do anything. Just be here. Think about it."

Beatense ran back down to the beach. The two scatted off southward, and they reached the summer homes. A big moored cabin cruiser lay offshore. The soccer playing mother and her lovely sons, all quite naked, waved as the two flew by.

Beatense waved back, holding onto Spec's mane with her left hand as her black tan belly flexed. She continually glanced down to study this. Sorel was a threat, but after his long night Jerry was in a kind forgiving mood toward bared tanners and their radical habits. He gave a wave. Sweat shined, Beatense rode over close to Jesse.

"Did you see that? He gave us a pass! Old Sorel is liberating up!"

The libertines galloped down to the tumbled rock wall at the south end of Cocojo and skidded and chuffed to a stop. Those in the area ambled over, casually.

"Let's just canter back, Jesse. My spinal cartilage is all squished!"

"Yeah, you are getting hunchbacked. I'm ashamed to be seen with you."

She coldly ignored that. They started back at a hacking gait that regretfully gave everybody time to deploy their cameras. The heat was blazing, and as they pulled up to the mother and her adorably famed sons they were every square inch wet.

"Moust eenspahreeng. A moust chahming spayctacle eendeed!"

Anyone watching or taking photos would think this was from a child just fourteen. She was deprivation thinned, and in that way of tan she seemed even thinner.

"Yeah, Maum, we should hahve ahh hauses heah," said one of the sons.

Jesse did a double-take. *That's the mother?* Then he recalled, Judge Croftley's daughter and her nauseating pretty boys, here every summer, unfailingly polite.

"We kin luke eento eet." She turned to the panting riders. "We need anothah foh soccah, if eyether of yew cayah to join us. Mutiny eesn't daown yate."

"Nah, I'm heading for a certain pool to get some sun," said Beatense.

"Yew? I thoht Ah was myking prohgress unteel yew cyme cahntering bah!"

The boys laughed and the interlopers jogged their horses on, mainly to get away from that tedious elitist accent. They rode on into the Shattuck yard and led the guys into the barn. Beatense helped brush them down, thinking sun, sun, sun.

"Jesse, I'm going to be using your pool, but I don't want company."

"That's okay, I'm taking the cat back down to Jo. I don't want company either."

"Well, I walked into that one. Hoisted by my own petard."

Beatense went in toward the house and the pool beyond. She saw various bikes by the house. Ned's friends were here, and just then the boys came out.

Ned showed his disgust. "Oh, no! Get out of here, Beatense!"

Shannon had described her to the other boys, but Kildy, Jeremy, Kelly and Jads weren't prepared for this girl. It wasn't her athletic thinness, nor her legendary tan or Nakee, around here these were commodities, but it was her kid-like face.

"Hey, Shan!" That confirmed it, a kid. "I thought you were up at the shed!"

Beatense was impressed by these boys, who were slender, real deep brown and disarmingly cute. Their personalities were universally endearing, but with their fine, recklessly enchanting looks, splendid muscles and shining, never-cut hair they were, Ned too, magical beings. That's what correct addresses do.

"We had to wait for Doofus," said one dazzling boy, with a nod toward another of the dazzling boys. "His work-out coach came and he had to do a session."

These two boys were introduced as Jads and Kelly. Kelly was the barbell client. His butt-cut jean cut-offs and cropped-off white T-shirt amplified his ultra dark suntan, and his wide-placed, wide blue eyes made him look sheltered from all the evils of the world. Despite his slight build each muscle was detailed. His spine lengthed spill of blond hair rippled fell, for a princely, embellishing effect. The other two boys, Jeremy and Kildy, also caused self-doubting anxiety in their beholders with lesser attributes.

"Oh, so you're heading to the shed now? I'll go with!"

"No!" Ned yelled. "No girls allowed! And it's a fort!"

The other angels didn't quite share Ned's sentiment. In fact their bright tan faces brightened even more at her suggestion. But in their having more insight than many adults they pretended to agree with Ned. Also, having spent most of their own lives nude, their sisters too, the boys accepted Beatense's little patch automatically.

"Yeah, lady," Kildy chirped up. "Go build your own shed!"

"Yeah, but don't expect us to help," added Jeremy. "Go have a tea party."

"You'll rat on where the fort is," accused Kelly, with an enchanting smile.

Beatense slumped. "Well, goll, you guys, if I'm not wanted I'll just leave."

"Oh, all right!" said Ned harshly, secretly gladdened. "Come on!"

The kids, Ned excepted, admired Beatense's fancy rig, and helmet, then took off their T-shirts for the upcoming ride. They looked as if they were genetically ordained for their pampered tropical lives. Kelly, fine in his lines, presented leaned muscles tightly clad by his velvety skin. Baked to a far richer brown than his friends, he owned an uncannily long, slim waist, and thick blond hair all the way down his back.

The boys got on their bikes, awkwardly clutching their tools, and started off along Bolingbroke. They crossed the Highway and rode on to the residential Talbot Street, pausing the neighbors in startled admiration as they patrolled up toward the foothills. They came to Del Camino, and Beatense could just see the garden center.

Shean wasn't there now, Jesse explained earlier that he and Knife had ridden up into the city to rattle the sidewalk crowds. This under a haze that obscured the sun. Beatense knew that hazy skies give the ultimate tanning effect. The kids began their now steeper climb toward the rocky fastness. The houses ended, then the street.

The boys on trail bikes chased ahead along the arroyo that snaked on up into the heights. Beatense joined Kildy and Kelly in shoulder carrying their thin-tired race bikes. They rounded a bend and came upon the "fort," a deck of planks laid across a dry wash-out gully, with a bare framework of 2 x 4s forming the outer walls. A row of half inch boards were already nailed in place to start the siding. Beatense saw this was a glorious place to bake, with a spectacular view. Like the Palisades and Sim's apartment the ocean and every rooftop could be seen.

The boys anxiously looked for any signs of intruders. Once reassured no one messed things up, they stripped and explained to Beatense what the fort would look like once it was complete. The point of pride was the escape hatch in case of sieges, and a stone fire-pit. Then came an energetic discussion of the need for a window for shooting out, and finally the work of pounding in more stolen nails began.

Young Kelly carried a long plank with his chest and biceps in annihilating flexion. His belly had the same gorgeous effect. Then as the hammers continued to echo in the hills, the boy gazed down at himself reverently. The pounding stopped.

"Kelly, give us a break!" Jeremy said. "You can love yourself later!"

"He's just *now* noticing his beeyooteeful tan?" said Jads.

"Come on, you guys, this is my livlihood! Unlike you dirtballs I'm a star!"

Like Kit and Sim/Elgin, Kelly was openly a serious body beautiful self worshipper. He wore a gold necklace chain that draped over his collarbones onto his living chest, and in the dry heat of the gulch he was so confrontationally dark brown, even Jesse had taken note of his inspired presentation. Encountering him, people gasped.

"Hey, Kelly, how… How did you get that sickening tan?" Beatense said.

The normally agreeable lad looked down at himself with knowing-better distaste, gazing upon his precise belly ripples, then he contemplated his shoulder.

"I'm on the South Coast Youth Trick Ski Team. We have to be tan."

The hammer pounding along with occasional lusty swearing resumed.

"Oh, so that's how you're a star. Trick skiing? On snow? Flips and all?"

"Well, water skiing flips. I wear a boy bikini for my costume."

"You ski in public shows just in a bikini? Of course, I should talk."

"Performing is okay. But waiting to go on with the crowd right there watching sucks. We learned how to handle it, we just look back at everyone like they're shit."

"*You* should talk. But your tan has all these nuances. It just swarms."

"Well, you're really unreal. We need a PA girl to announce the different acts and beg for donations. Come on and find out about it. You can see the cup skating."

Beatense agreed to this, wondering what cup skating was.

"Ned! Ned? Yoo hoo! Working on your shed, hah? Hi, there!"

"Hi!" the boy replied gruffly, as he continued his pounding. The boys smiled.

"Ned, I hate to say it but I really see a grim outlook for your future."

"Well I see a grim outlook for your future!"

"Why? Because something bad might happen?"

"Because something bad will happen!" The boys laughed.

"I noticed, Ned, that everytime I tell you how ignorant you are, you get all mad."

"What else do you expect?" said Jeremy. --/-- "Alvin, Ned and I are having a serious discussion here, and he doesn't want you butting in." --/-- "I'm not Alvin, I'm Jeremy!" --/-- "Oh, did you change your name just now?" --/-- "No, I was always Jeremy!" --/-- "Then who's Alvin?" --/-- "I don't know who Alvin is! I never heard of him!" --/-- "Well, he must be someone!" --/-- Ned rolled his eyes up.

The boys laughed and the hammers rang out again, echoing. Beatense eyed the gravelly, sun dried dirt banks and scrubby trees. Good tanning place.

"Hey, Ned, how about if I read you guys some poems?" --/-- "No!!"

"Well, instead I can read the phone book. Oh hey, you guys, speaking of, I just read that fourteen is the age when boys all begin to realize how stupid they are."

Everyone automatically turned to watch Ned's disagreeing reaction.

"Seriously, Ned, did you ever consider attending slow learner school?"

"No! But tell me what it's like!"

If the kids were here to work on the fort they forgot all about it.

"Based on that remark, Ned, I don't know if you're half smart or half stupid."

"Well, I can tell you what you are! Half stupid!" --/-- "Do do dah dah do do."

Jeremy laughed so hard he fell to the ground. The other boys staggered.

"Ned, I figured out a way you can get some extra money. All you do is go to the bank and roll the guard up in the rug, then you can take all the money you want."

He looked at his friends. "Oh, yeah, that is a good way to get extra money."

She felt herself baking as she stood. "Yeah, Ned, remember it was my idea."

"Yeah, your share will be two cents!"

"I knew a boy who was way more generous than you, Ned. Someone way better than you. He was kind, considerate, well behaved, thoughtful and just so obedient."

Ned rolled his eyes up. Thrilled for him, the boys were wide-eyed incredulous.

Beatense said, "To change the subject, Ned, just as a warning, the last boy who tried to hit me... Oh, hey, he might be getting out of the hospital any day now!"

"Oh, hey, you might be getting IN the hospital any day now!"

Her face saddened. "Yes. No one seems to like me very much anymore."

"No one ever did like you!"

She clicked her tongue and made a horrible face with coughs of protest. Eyes shining, Ned watched as his friends elected to resume laughing.

"Ned, I don't care if you like me or not, but I do want you to respect me."

He snorted.

Beatense picked up her bike. "I'm going now. I just hope I don't get lost."

"What?" said lifted-irises Shannon, pointing. "Just take the same street!"

"Or better yet, just get lost!" Ned suggested kindly, eyes snapping.

"Oh, when it's time for your nap, Ned, you can just go lay there in the dirt."

"You can just go play there in the dirt!"

Laughter pealed out yet again. The girl untied bare and carried her Zheup back out, and heart pounding she hit the Talbot hill using her suicide bars. She stopped at the busy Del Camino, and long thighs swelling, she fought her bike back up to speed. Naked, she had to stop again at the Highway. Almost drunk with her daring freedom she shot the Highway northward all the way up to Holiday Hill. She flew so fast she could occupy the actual traffic lane, with horns honking. She secreted fluids.

She turned back. Smiling with joy she rode Bolingbroke, admiring the avant garde houses, but she liked the old wealth summer homes better. Running with hot sweat, she came to the shack and saw the big Espriado; Tony had returned.

Not in Nakee, she rapped on the greyed board wall beside the open door. Tony yelled from inside. "Beatense! C-Come in!"

She strolled in and collapsed onto a chair in the ninety degree kitchen. She took her helmet off. Its rakish lines matched her careless personality.

"Hi, Tony. I was just up with the kids at the shed. They got a good start."

The sleek girl's dark, bared tan was a monstrous imposition. Her breasts, her opened legs and sinuously ever-flexing belly were obnoxiously indecent.

Tony was hit by a truck. "Y-Yeah, it's all th-those kids t-talk about."

She went to the sink and got the water going. --/-- "Water in the fridge."

"No, my split was oozing from excitement, riding naked." She rinsed clean. "So, can I ask a favor? I wish to bake out nude today by your pool. Okay?"

"N-Nude?" He felt every artery in his brain burst. "R-Right in t-town here?"

"Tony, be reasonable. I rode here like this all over town from the fort."

He stared at the bony child. "Girl, t-topless if you must, b-but not nude."

"Tony, I won't be bothering you at all. A girl practices the piano, no big deal, but she works on her tan or likes sexual intercourse, and it's this huge moral breakdown. People should be realistic. At the clinic last night half the girls there were polite and shy, of the quality that rides their bikes to the library, or helps in the garden or helps fold the laundry, and works on their book reports or science projects, or plays in the band or school sports, like tennis or golf. So why can't they indulge in sex? I started working at sex at just thirteen, and that fucking taught me how beautiful life can be."

Tony agreed, naked. With trained muscles in play the girl aimed the lounge into the sun, with the back at a half angle. Tony carried out an icy pitcher of lemonade, a beach towel, a tub of melted margarine and a paint brush. The tanner sat upon the lounge with a light twisting of her snake-leaned waist, and with her legs opened.

Tony's blood roared. He saw the videos. Her antics were violent.

She held up the brush. "What's this for? You want me to be useful?"

"N-No. The… The b-boys use it for spreading on the m-margarine."

"Margarine! Tony! If I'm going to get results I insist on butter! Or lard!"

"Jesse said margarine w-works b-best. Its trans fatty acids."

"Okay. It sounds like he knows what he's talking about. Oleo, we call it, but it comes white and we have to squeeze the bag to mix the yellow color in. Okay, it's getting late, I better make a start of it. Oh, can you get me a mirror?"

"A… A m-mirror?"

"So I can look at my progress. And wheel over those reflector panels."

These were Shean's idea, that cost Tony $800. They were frameworks of steel tubing on casters, with silvered polycarbonate panels at an angle. As he set them the girl's effect on him was like jumping into ice water, he couldn't breathe.

He thought he was used to the tan beach girls, but he shook at the sight of those pert little apples and her ever flexing ripples. No wonder her books sold.

"Boy, these will really concentrate the rays! Okay, thanks, please depart."

Tony staggered away. Discouraged by the late hour, with heart pounding the girl nonetheless stirred the brush in the yellow slime and slopped it on wet. Her nips and hips sharply poked. Her hungered belly was tightened to the snapping point, but still had a caved-in sag as she lay back. In the glare of the panels.

This was to be a day of deep sensual concern, that all beautiful self worshippers thrive on. At two hours Beatense would be satiated. In the high heat glare she was slop oiled to a wet black shine. She pushed back her hair with greasy hands, and with belly sunk and heels propped she writhed herself into an obscene sun drenching.

Her eyes rolled up. Brain dead again that day, courtesy of Sim and Sun.

Tony, coming back into the kitchen later for a can of beer, saw the binoculars on the counter. *How did they get there?* After troubled tortured internal debate he tried spying on her, but the panels were in the way. *Not smart, Tony.* But he did see that she regained consciousness. With cold disapproval she hatefully patted at the oil on her slack belly. She blandly watched the jingling of her bracelets and the lay of her chain on her twitching, work stressed ripples. The leaned muscle of her slim carved shoulders reacted also. With a bulge of biceps she held the pitcher with both hands and put a full quart down. Several ice cubes fell in escape, sliding down her front.

The girl's heart pounded as the meter reader came pushing through a gap in the hedge, coming out onto the deck. Now she had a victim, a fool in a servitude uniform. He saw the black tan girl gaze at him. He stumbled over to the house as she turned her long neck impassively in watching. One eye was set in bemused study, and the other was narrowed just slightly, as if wary of this low creature. Shaking, he took his pitiful readings and wobbled over to the greasy, squirming snake.

"S-Sorry to d-disturb you, miss!" he said, as a pathetic excuse to look.

With thin, bracelets-hung wrist cocked and bony shoulders hinged, she scoodled the oil dripping brush between her bare apples. She painted the oil down her black front, right onto her chain and split. The oil filled her navel and slid off right and left.

Her roasted tan hit her observer like a hammer, but it was that belly chain that strangled him. He clenched his teeth to keep from grabbing her. She ignored him as he gaped in stricken horror.

"You're... You're the Book Girl!" he stuttered, still staring.

It was comforting to Beatense that if she objected to his staring, and she did, she could call for the police to apprehend him. If she had a phone. She had to get one! Just for filthy situations like this! An innocent girl tries to work on her tan and look what happens, all these ignorant subhumans come crawling by!

Tony came out. "You read the meter, now leave. Girl, are you okay?"

"No, I feel violated!" The intruder slunk away. "That shit stared at me!"

"Okay, but I'm not calling any police. I kind of feel for him, myself."

"Tony, what nonsense! A girl working on her tan while therapeutically resting her muscles after a night of extremely active sex, and you feel sorry for him!"

For some reason he loved that response. "Okay, if you need anything yell."

When she hit three broiling hours she sprang to her feet and picked up the fancy chrome barbells. She worked her curls, bulging her biceps into tennis balls. She did side-leans and side-twists, efforts that strained her ripples. She finished her session with presses and squat-thrusts, as her thigh muscles appeared individually. It felt good to get back at it, especially naked and oil shined black. The binoculars watched.

But her pride and self satisfaction were temporal. Beatense had to realize what she really was, an insignificant hundred pounds of bone and meat. Truly, a person is too frail to really last, he or she just isn't durable. But somehow skinny girls easily outlive their cars built of heavy iron and steel. But by age forty it can be all over.

Except, these days girls were running and working out and reading labels. They were rabidly taking care of themselves, plus they were enjoying an exercise that was forbidden decades ago, that swarmed their perfect selves with restorative freshening hormones. This sport was a point of pride for these tan athletes, and society honored their dedication. They would not get old. With these smug thoughts Beatense reset her lounge and panels to correct for the sun's progression.

Tony got tired holding the binoculars. As she lay back again with eyes closed he studied her red blacked shine, with an agonized, shaking shock. In that blinding hot deep glare she was grilled to a rusted charcoal bronze, that luridly flashed. Her belly chain sizzled. He saw her separated, out-turned cream jugs. Despite their petite size they had a healthy fullness. Her shoulders were bony stark and her hipbones could slice bread. And he knew from the Net that, including this morning's blurry telephoto video, that she repeatedly put her split to energetic and unrestrained use.

This girl was steeled, so the fluid tensions of her muscles amplified the hot shining of her wetted skin. She had a tuned timbre borne of feline resilience. Her sunk, rib ledged belly lay depletedly parallel to her curved spine, cupping the sun.

Her stretched trunk was curved to connect her rib-set to her poking hips. The flagrantly aimed poise of her bared breasts playfully taunted her paralyzed observer. Her carved, braised face had the hauteur of an insatiable aggressor of self, who must be and will be willowy thin and darkest shit brown, and insatiably fuck active.

Tony could stand it no longer; he brought out another pitcher of lemonade.

She awoke. "Tony! Get away from me!" Squirming, she held a wet oiled black stick over her pulsating apples. "You can't just sneak up on me like that!"

"I… I b-brought m-more lemonade, B-Beatense." *Her split!*

"Fine, but let me finish the first gallon first! Now spray me with that water!"

"I guess I can take orders at my own house. Get that arm away."

She protested but complied. She was complying with a lot of things lately.

He fogged the cool spray mist on her and she shook. The oil and water weren't compatible, she became sparkled with hundreds of silvery beads.

"There," she said, as if she did the spraying herself. "Now I'm prepped."

She closed her eyes in dismissal. Her host slunk away cursing her.

Later the bare little Tammy came tip-toeing out into the blast oven as if she was entering a sanctum. Beatense, holding the dripping brush, waved her over.

"Oh, Tammy, er, nice swimsuit! Can you join me? I'm getting some rays!"

"H-Hi, Beatense," the slim slip said shyly. "Are you *ever* getting rays!"

"Except, I have to do my back now. Move that panel and grab a lounge!"

Tammy moved the panel and dragged over a chaise. Its tubular legs made that characteristic grating, ringing sound on the concrete. Sweat shined, the girl lay back right on the white vinyl straps and, like Beatense, opened her legs.

"No towel? Well, good idea, actually. Your sweat can drip right through."

"Yes. But how long were you out here? Hours, I bet, you're so black!"

"Just since eleven, so it's three hours doing my front. I better turn over."

Tammy dunked the brush into the margarine and calmly painted herself. She lay back in glistening glory with her abdomen starve-sunken to match her friend's.

"Are you excited about the ski trip, Beatense? I'm going too!"

"Hah? Good, I'm glad, but I forgot all about it." She turned over, flexing herself adversely on the angled back. She groaned as Tammy buttered her long, furrowed, espresso hued backside. "Thanks, kid." She then fell asleep.

Down on the catamaran tramp-deck catamaran the wheels began turning for the upcoming ski trip. Beautiful Shean, just in coconut oil, was talking to the travel agent on the cellular. Tony was leaning against the mast having a cigaret.

"I see, but that would get us in at one AM, Merrilee. Isn't there…"

"Shean, shouldn't you be writing this down?"

"Dad, *shhshh!* Okay, there's one landing at eight. How much is that?"

"Shean, let me talk to her. You'll just botch this up."

"Five hundred each? Boy, that is steep. Wait, I'll have to ask my Dad."

Tony nodded. Beatense was coming, so what's a few thousand?

As Shean plowed on with the booking details a tawny young lady in a T-shirt and painted-tight jeans rode up on Spec. She had slanted, wide almond eyes.

"Natalie!" said Tony, getting off the boat. Her limbs, thin but tightened. "It's good you show up! Head up to the fort at a gallop and get Ned!"

"Sure thing, Tony! But what's this all about?"

"Our flight for the ski trip leaves at six this af… This evening!"

40

WILD RIDE HOME

Oh, that ski trip I wasn't invited on, you mean?"

"You were invited! Didn't Ned mention it? But can you come with us now?"

"No! Ned did tell me, but I got band camp! And I'll go get him!"

Natalie shot through the hedge and Spec was heard to gallop off.

Shean finally hung up, realizing he could have done this on the laptop.

"Shean, call Tracy at Gold Camp to see if we can get our own condo at this short notice. And where's Jesse? Is he still sailing?"

"On his sailboard. Oh, he's in sight! I'll swim out and get him. Sit tight."

"Hold it, I not want you drownding naked. Get the megaphone."

Bare Shean ran for the shack while Tony called the condo office. Then out at the pool the two somnolent girls heard a metallic version of Shean's voice.

Jesse! Get your buttski in here! We got a plane to catch! Hurry it up!

"What's that about?" said Beatense groggily, noting her black arms.

"I don't know," said Tammy petulantly, "but they woke me up!"

Beatense lay back down to continue baking. Shortly thereafter Jesse and Shean came out to the pool-deck, noting the greasy leaned sleekness of the two somnolent girls. They were wet shined, and their brown skins were luxuriously appliquéd to the taut flow of their muscles. Nothing is as decadently elegant as small and thin women lying bare upon their fronts as they wickedly bake their tans, with backs widening up from their slim waists to their slat shoulders. The reverse bend of their backs shaped their buttered butts like twin coconuts. Both were very sexually active.

Bare Jesse quietly poured the last of the lemonade on the girls.

"*Aghhh!* Jesse, you miserable creep!" Beatense screamed, recoiling.

Tammy sat up coughing with her eyes squeezed shut. "*Ohhh!* That's cold!"

"Shit bite, are you two ever dark!" said Shean. "That's disgusting!"

"Okay, what's going on?" said Beatense. "Why this interruption?!"

"Our flight is in two hours, at six," said Shean. "So we have to run."

"That ski trip is now? But I have plans! And my back needs another hour!"

"You'll live. And forget the plans. Ride home, like that, and pack!"

Beatense dove into the pool. Shean and Tammy followed, but Jesse stood at the edge, and as the others riotously splashed he urged them to hurry.

"Come on, you guys! We have a lot to do! We got a plane to catch!"

Beatense shot out of the pool, and started to dry herself off.

"Wait! I can't go! I said I have plans for later! Sailing!"

"What sailing is that?" said Jesse. "Shean! We better get the ski rack on!"

"It's in control," said Shean, as he and Tammy got out. "If we fucking hurry!"

"I said I can't go," said Beatense. "I have to get down to Cocojo."

"The hell!" said Shean. "We already bought your ticket! Get riding!"

"Not your bike, Beatense," said Jesse. "Ride Windfire! It'll be faster!"

"Good idea. I guess I can give up on this sun and just forget all my plans."

"Gee, you show such eagerness. Hey, I can ride your bike home for you."

"Shean, I'm showing eagerness! I love sliding down hills! And good idea."

The girl started as Ned and Natalie rode out onto the pool deck. Natalie was on Ned's bike, that she had ridden, and Ned was on Spec. Beatense admired Natalie as the others productively argued about who should do what. The girl smiled back, with a shrugging, conspiratorial wink and dismounted. *So this is Ned's girlfriend. Wow!*

"Hi! You must be Beatense! I'm Natalie! You're famous! Awesome tan!"

Shean was discussing the logistics. "Jesse, yes, we can buy her skis up at the mountain, but if Tammy has skis Beatense can use, she should use them!"

"Hi, Natalie. Thanks. Nice to meet you. Are you coming on this trip too?"

"But the prices are so low now! Tower is practically giving them away!"

The young girl had the pure, classic features that foretold urgent beauty as she matured, and her wide, dark eyes had a mischievous, clever brightness that warned everyone that she knew this all too well. But their angled placement also gave her eyes a vulnerable look, as if the unpleasant realities of life wouldn't register with her if they were too distressing. She was rather pale for this tropical beach world, but her tawny complexion would be intoxicating to behold in winter climes.

"No, band camp," Natalie said. "But while you're all gone I can ride Spec!"

"She might need bigger boots than mine," said Tammy.

"Way bigger!" said Ned, seeing Beatense as a huge bother on this trip.

Natalie, widely smiling with her hands in her back pockets, laughed.

Tony joined them, and they went to the paddock. Jesse led Windfire out and the bare girl flipped onto him. As she rode to him, the wild steed snorted and skittered in circles. She tried to control him, with her snaking, gold chained belly curved to the effort, but Windfire only stutter stepped backwards.

The girl's hair flew in all directions, adding to stylist Stel's assiduous efforts.

"Okay, bring along my *STUFF!*" Windfire had bucked. "Shean, get that gate open! Instantly!" Windfire bucked again, and reared. "Some horse, Jesse!"

The lushly verdant shade made her flashing tan look extravagantly darker, but it was this flyweight's angry yelling for the gate that paralyzed Tony, again.

"Should... Should you be riding bareback?" he shouted, over the tumult.

"It's just a couple miles, and the weekend is over! Fewer tourists! Shean, go easy on my bike! One gear at a time! And take Windemere and the Beachway!"

Jesse swung open the gate and Windfire erupted out of the paddock.

Tony tore his bulged eyes from the sweat filmed rider and pulled the hedge gap wider. Beatense, trusting that all would go well on this ride, swung Windfire around to aim for the hole. Tammy hopped over and gave Win a whack. The stallion did a few more kicks and bolted out through the hedge and leaped out onto the beach.

He capered again, scattering several wide eyed strollers, but the waist waving girl just wrenched him around and rode to him. In the chaos she saw Honey Brown naked on her own stallion, dazzling princely white. The girls eyed each other in challenge.

The horses catapulted off and pelted up the beach in runaway, pounding hooves gallops. Racing beside Honey Beatense held onto Win's mane with thiin arms lightly flexed. Sensing the rivalry he tore ahead, making it hard for Beatense to control this demented beast. But pressed for time, and with the other's fool idea to beat her, she needed the highest speed. She worked her hips to goad her horse on in a reckless rampage. Rising and falling to his stride, she felt a part of him, especially in oil only.

Their speeds were terrifying, and the trees along this first stretch of beach blurred by in a torrent. Beatense dreaded falling off, that Honey was a magnificent rider, but she would just hop to her feet and run the rest of the way. She whooped out the triumph of her wild blood. The hot wind fanned the girls, and they flew along the surf like hot streaks of cocoa buttered lightning. The tourists along the beach watched in fear. The girls hit the Bastian Street beach and Beatense reined Windfire down to a dancing stop. She gave the startled Curt a wave. In fair play Honey had also halted. Glistening with oily sweat, the savages rode to their horses as they turned in circles.

"Hi, Curt! How's it going?" Beatense called out with ripples flexing.

The rescuer gasped. As she turned he saw her concaved belly's slim profile.

"B-Beatense?" He mouthed dry air. "Y-You..."

"Yeah, it's me! Ain't seen ya awhile! On a mission! Got to get home fast!"

The girls nudged their horses and shot off again. Further along two fellows yelled and hooted. Beatense collected Windfire and jumped him over a driftwood log. She careened on, giving more eye to her leaned, butter oiled arms and sunken belly than the road ahead. Her chain and bracelets loosely tossed. Her thighs gripping back of Windfire's withers, she worked him into a racehorse gallop. But Honey kept up.

It was amusing to Beatense that she, weighing a hundred pounds, could control this stallion weighing six hundred. As strong as she thought she was, and for all her abandon, she knew that any stray litter blowing across her path could spook her ride, and she could quickly part company with him. The zephyr reacted to this by bravely niggling Windfire with her heels, and his strides became leaps. Honey kept up.

They flew by the Villa Miranda and Dillon Arms, and the hot wind, that caressed their wet bellies and disproportionately stretched thighs, excited the girls deeply. This Windemere stretch of beach wasn't crowded; it was fronted with apartments, condos and private homes. The girls flew at full tilt past the Hoganforth Lodge and then the Breeze complex arrived. Beatense slowed up, targeting the velvet rope fence of the exclusive hotel enclave. Honey slowed too, wondering what the other had in mind.

Beatense planned to jump the rope and run through the palm cabanas pell-mell, but in her approach she saw this would just get some idiot killed. Instead she turned and, leading her enemy on, tore along the surf, as the horses kicked up spray.

The guests cheered, and the girls thundered on past Karen's pink stucco building. This stood atop the concrete retaining wall, along with hotels, motels, beer dens and cutesy-cute boutiques. This was the start of the surfing beach, sparsely populated.

The girls slowed to a trot to rest the snorting horses, posting with just the grip of their knees. Beatense's fine nose was raised in regal superiority. The girls rode into College Alley and kicked into a canter, taking that open stretch between the blankets and waves. The lifeguards cleared their path of the few stragglers with whistles and shouts. Only belatedly they saw that Honey's partner in crime wasn't Jesse but the Book Girl, who slapped fives with the other and ran out onto Holiday Hill's beach.

She charged her horse up the shady, switch-backed sand path and galloped the trails. The residents along here jumped aside. Where the cabins began she slowed to a lope and rocked easily along, angling Windfire crookedly for a showy effect. She pulled up at the sight of Flammchen, walking along with tall, stately grace in shorts and T-shirt. It was quite obvious that the slim, proud girl had spent the day soaking in the sun, despite her modest look and outlook.

"Flamm, we both had the right idea today! Sun and more sun!"

"Yes, I was down with Absinthe, in the mounds. Oh, bye!"

Beatense had shot off. She came to the cabin and sprang off. Lorraine, thinking that the hoof beats heralded Jesse, stepped outside. She saw an elfin, black tan girl pet the horse with a play of her frail shoulder blades.

She gave the pony a swat and sent him flying home. She turned.

"Oh, hi, Lorraine. Say, I have to hurry. They're coming to get me for the ski trip. I need a shower, horse smell, you see. So can you get the water going?"

Lorraine found her voice. "Oh. Oh, yeah. A shower, good idea. But…"

"But what?" The kid sprang into the cabin, whirling her head in search. "No time for a shower now, come to think, except for my legs! Find my backpack!"

"You need a shower, kid. You stink of micro-wave popcorn."

She smelled her arm. "That's my margarine! Even after swimming!"

Lorraine wrestled the protesting animal into the bathroom. She began to doubt the wisdom of her living there. Beatense quickly sloshed the cold spray on herself with a soapy wash cloth and got out and grabbed the towel. The girl scrubbed herself to a brassy, starchy shine. She came out and faced Lorraine who had her backpack on the bed, and stated what she would wear for the trip, nothing as usual.

"You better... Oh, say, I forgot, you got this letter from Buck."

"What?" She tore open the rumpled envelope, complete with weird stains.

> **Dear Beatense,**
> **I am writing this to say that I can never**
> **see you again. For some reason you don't**
> **seem to like me even though I LOVE you in**
> **many ways! It is too painful for me to be**
> **reminded of you just thinking of you much**
> **less even just getting a glimpse...**

"Yes, read on," said Lorraine.

She mumbled her way through the rest of the screed. "Fuck him! Me all naked as a black tanned wild sexual activist, and I have to feel sorry for the shit!"

"I agree, but no nudity, kid. You'll be in a crowded airport, and plane."

"I guess I can ease up a little. I can wear my long neglected crochet patch."

"No, wear your new pink sweater and jeans. You really have to, Beatense."

She put on her patch and sweater. This was open-mesh knitted from pink cotton string, with dime-sized holes. Lorraine approved. Shean, panting in sweaty tan only, came bursting into the cabin with Beatense's bike, followed by the sound of a car's stopping, and a quick toot of the Espriado's tuned horns. But bare legged Beatense gave bare Shean a hug, then checked her bike for damage as if there was no hurry.

Getting out of the car, Tony gaped at the child who sprang from the cabin. She wore a pink, open necked sweater of nip-showing breezy mesh, that was in effect a subsitute dress. It brazenly left her corded thighs and chest bare to the air. While Shean frantically pulled on his clothes she hopped to the car.

"Hi, Tony! Hey, guys! Hi, Tammy! And Kelly, what are you doing along?"

"They're dropping me off up at the marina," the boy said. "We got practice."

He got out of the back to let her in. He was back to wearing his jean cut-offs, and the long hours of hazy sun up in the gulch had dark baked the beautiful, slim waisted athlete with a far deeper Flammchen-like bake. A sereptitious camera caught him.

Beatense looked in. "Oh, no, Ned! I didn't know they were taking you along!"

"I didn't know they were taking you along!" --/-- "Tony, tell him to get out."

Shean finished his costume change and he opened the trunk for Lorraine as she doubtfully hauled out Beatense's backpack. Skiing? In this heat?

"So how are you getting back, Kelly? We're on our way to the airport!"

"Oh, I'll just run it. Speaking of, I hear you run." --/-- "I squeeze it in."

Beatense hugged Lorraine and got in. "Move over, will ya, Ned? Yeesh!"

The boy snorted and set his neck, but it was evident he was quite pleased.

Jesse, over by the far window, squeezed closer to it. He wore his white cotton shorts and his now hot cropped 10K T-shirt. The boy was ravishing, his long looping hair made him an enchanting god, but he knew this in a benevolent way.

Kelly got in, and his close proximity upset Beatense. Like her own, his browned thighs were slimly curved with tensed strength. Used to the stares of his fans, he laughed at the girl's perplexity. Tammy was sitting in the middle up front.

Like Beatense's ventilation sweater, the breezy mesh of the child's string knitted, vanilla hued little frock all too flamboyantly showed her hot tan. As Shean got in to drive, Beatense hitched herself forward, and she happily noted that Tammy's long legs were also breathtakingly bared, for the benefit of any airport voyeurs.

Lorraine stuck her head in. "Bye, kid. Have fun, but hurry home."

"Look at the dress she has on, Lorraine! I had the right idea all along!"

"You had a right idea?" said Ned coldly, with laughter following.

Shean drove off. Beatense turned back and waved to her roommate. Except for Tony, of course, she was happily esconced among choicely brilliant human beings

"Shean, how did your ride uptown go with Knife?" --/-- "It was fun! We hit that Yesler Street plaza and laid in the sun there right in the middle of everyone!"

"That's mean," said Tammy. "But you were just in your bikinis? Cool!"

"When aren't they?" Tony muttered. "Shean, step on it, will you?"

"Here, watch this, Beatense." As Shean drove the loops Kelly held his browned arms straight out. Like Stel's, Natalie's, Absinthe's and Peachy Cream's, his refined limbs had a shapely flow of tight muscle. "Here I am holding the tow rope."

"Or holding back those admiring fans," said Beatense, as she stared.

"We had to hold some gays off," said Shean, with a wan smile at his father.

"And now I have to pull the slack in fast," Kelly continued. With bulged bicep he held the phantom bar to his chest with his left hand, and he entwined his right arm around the "rope" as he caught it. The play of his muscles was riveting, and the fine ripples of his belly perceptibly tightened. "And now, letting out the slack, I can hit my hot flips. I can coach you on that. If you do our PA you should know all our tricks."

"If you don't mind teaching me. I don't want anyone else coaching me."

They had turned onto the Highway and were heading north into Madeline, and Beatense saw the Palisades. Traffic was slow. Beatense was enough of a native now where rush hours in the tropics had lost their charm. She looked at Ned.

"Oh, Ned, your doctor said your brain is 60% water, 30% fat and 10% stupidity."

"Your brain is 100% stupidity!" Ned retorted, to bellering laughter.

They were still smiling when Shean turned off from the Highway at the Wharf and he stopped up at the north end of the marina, by the boat launch.

"Thanks for the ride!" said Kelly, as he got out in one fluid, trained motion.

Beatense saw cute boys and girls lifting their skis, ropes, marker buoys and their other equipment from a truck. Kelly fit right in, these bikini sport athletes were almost celestial, raisin baked and hard muscled. People ambling over from the nearby wharf stopped by to watch, disguising their envy and shock.

A boy of ten was juggling chrome weights. Two other tanners, back to back and splash oiled, were limbering themselves up by tugging against each other with linked hands. One long haired child had a Jesse-like tan. He wore a capri bikini and a gold chain about his neck. Holding his trick skis, he indeed looked on the passersby as if they were fecal. An ethereal little surfer girl with crystal blue eyes intently guided the tow boat down the launching ramp. She seemed very proud of this honor, the one kid here who was still a kid. Then Beatense saw the cup skating Kelly mentioned.

Two lines of plastic cups spaced a foot apart lay separated by four feet, and two young girls in polo shirts and waist-slimming cargo pants were dancing through them on blade skates. The way their springy legs were going zip-zip-zip as they spun out pirouettes made it seem almost impossible that they didn't knock any cups over.

Their troubled observer thought, *And I can hardly stay on my feet.*

As the car moved on Beatense wondered about this trip. It would deprive her of crucial sun, but there were conflicting theories on this. One says get all the sun you can, six hours a day at least, decline even fun invitations, while the other says take a break now and then, so when you get back at it, you catch the skin by surprise.

Another concern was that she was traveling with these albeit friendly people she hardly knew. If she was addicted to skiing, then yes, she would set aside any logical reservations and join in. But she never skied before, and it looked stupid, so the only real reason she was going was Ned. He sat scowling but his eyes shined.

41

AIRPORT

Tony, Ned foolishly went pee-pee on the floor back here."

"Ned, not foolishly!" *That girl, what next?* **--/--** "I did not!"

"Oh, Ned, yuck!" said Jesse, smiling at his brother's stormy look.

"The one day he doesn't wear his rubber diapers and look what happens."

"You wear steel diapers!" **--/--** Beatense said, "Jesse, there is snow, right?"

"In the mountains a thousand miles northwest from here, yes, Beatense. It's the altitude, plus over twenty feet of snow this winter." **--/--** "Yeah, Beatense!"

"I wish that Ned would be silent," Beatense said, angering the boy deeply, if his expression was any hint, and she slouched down as the luxury car shot along.

This was the same highway she had come into town on the bus. But today the vulgar people in the other cars, who didn't realize that jets could solve these pesky climate problems, were pointing at their ski rack and laughing. However one had to agree, it did seem like a lot to ask, to go from this heat to actual snow.

Beatense's sweater was ventilated, and that marvelous air conditioning was on at full tilt, but she could still feel the lovely heat outside right through the car's roof.

And meanwhile, tensions were building. Jets were flying in at their famously low altitudes toward the runway, as if they were aiming to strafe the rooftops, trees and cars of the local district by the airport, Little Wittlee. The startled Beatense wanted to duck as the shadows thundered by just overhead.

"Now what?" Shean suddenly shouted. "Are all these cars slowing down for the airport exit? Come on, you dip bags, let's crank the speed! Hurry!"

Beatense hitched herself forward. "What's wrong, is there a slowdown?"

He laughed bitterly. "Yeah, a slowdown. Come on, you organisms, move!"

"Shean, watch your language!" said Tammy, turning to him, mouth open.

Tony lit a cigar. "There might be an accident. Show concern."

"An accident! What right do they have for an accident now of all times!"

The line of cars was inching along. Beatense eyed the big green sign marking the airport exit as it drew near. The sense of dragging was heightened by the cars still shooting by in the lanes just to the left. But per the speedometer, that was a rotating horizontal drum with a fixed indicator line, they were going about five miles per hour, progress, and per the clock they had a good hour to get aboard. And then the cars slunk over onto the exit ramp proper, and the distant terminal building.

The ramp curved and widened out to four lanes, and of these, the two right ones sped ahead under green signs that read **Terminal Drop-Off** and **Terminal Pick-Up**. The left **Long Term** lanes still managed to be shittily backed up as the cars crawled toward the distant parking ramp, that was as big as a factory.

Beatense saw the ticket barricade arms rising and falling as the cars crept through like giant confused snails. For this she was missing tonight with Sim!

"You just watch," wailed Shean, "they'll close it as soon as we get there, the rotten pigs! They should just wave us through free when it gets so tied up!"

"But that wouldn't be fair to the people who had to pay to get in before us!" said Tammy, in all earnestness, and Beatense decided she was a fine person.

"Took you long enough, Shean," said Jesse, as they reached the gate.

Shean shot his window down and took the ticket from the gray clock box. The gate paused maddeningly and then jerked awkwardly up, and with the open road ahead Shean pounced ahead into the huge eight level ramp.

Beatense was wide eyed as the car raced through this grey concrete structure of decks, pillars and half walls. The ramp was tier upon tier, all crammed with countless parked cars lurking in the cavern semi-darkness. Every horn was honking, and the near-miss swervings didn't rate a blink. Up another incline, down another row, but the would-be skiers had nothing but smug rows of taillights to greet them. Worse yet, the travelers lifting luggage out of their opened trunks, the ones who had infuriatingly just beaten the Shattuck party, the drooling filthy smug maggots.

"Come on!" Shean shouted, working the wheel. "Can't any of these cars ever leave? And why don't they just tow these cars out of here if they stay too long?"

"Then the truck would be blocking us," said Tony, wishing he drove instead.

"Shean, I saw a spot in the next row!" said Jesse. --/-- "Lucky for you!"

The Espriado rocketed ahead and screeched around to the next row. The back seat passengers slid together on the waxy red leather as the distant hood ornament veered drunkenly, like the gun-sight of a doomed cockpit. Another car approached the same stall. Shean hit the headlights and he bore down on the enemy.

He rapidly worked the by now fatigued wheel with the heel of his hand and rudely took possession. Crookedly. He re-parked the beast and killed the engine. The big five foot doors were eased open so they just touched the adjoining cars. After the air conditioning the heat was stultifying, but no one noticed.

"Shean, run ahead and print out our boarding passes! Then hurry back!"

The beautiful tanner, dressed in his soft peach colored linen sport coat, a brown chest showing white office shirt and faded tight jeans, didn't need persuasion. He ran off at a sprint. As he rounded the far corner with full blond hair aflutter, Beatense felt his urgency. If nothing else she had to call Sim and explain.

Tremendous noises boomed out everywhere, from the ear-splitting shrieks of the taxiing jets and the quaking roars of those taking off over yonder. The low clearance cement decks of the parking ramp seemed to shake, echo and amplify these sounds, giving Beatense an uneasy keen excitement. Despite the sun she was missing.

The trunk was opened. Tammy's boots were set on the pavement and Beatense took off her gel shoes and stepped into them as everyone watched expectantly.

"Way too big, but they'll work." --/-- "No, we get you new ones," said Tony.

Jesse took a trim white yachting blazer out of the trunk and exchanged it for his runner's T-shirt. He put the coat on open fronted over his cuffed white shorts.

Tammy was equally electrifying. Her dress made no attempt whatsoever to even partly conceal her shiny long legs. Long legged also, due to her sweater, Beatense hefted Shean's snazzy skis to her bare shoulder and she imitated the mirror-lensed Jesse's cosmopolitan aplomb as he strode importantly along.

Tony regretted dispatching Shean to retrieve the passes. For speed the boy had just taken his sport bag, leaving all the other luggage for them to carry. But he was an impressive sight as he dashed off, the finely handsome rich boy. He was actually a nice kid, always polite, a dream son. And Beatense was teasing a very exasperated Ned at the moment, and no one overhearing this banter would guess that indeed the girl was glamorous. Certainly Ned didn't seem to think so.

Their clumsy staggering took them to the garage elevator, and Tony nudged the button with his elbow. The party shuffled in and when the door slid back open, they saw a glass walled sky-walk that led over to the terminal building. Beatense looked down at the dozens of taxis, cars and buses that were jammed below in the drive-up lanes. Even the train station back home was never this busy.

Shean came bursting into the sky-walk at the far end, running toward his family. Watching the heads turn, Beatense wished she had an excuse to run here, to show everyone here that she too had important affairs to attend to. But she had the quiet satisfaction of knowing she would be recognizied as Miss Book.

"Got the passes, guys! Here, give me something to carry! And we better rev up the agenda up, we have to get our skis checked in!"

At the end of the sky-walk they entered the largest interior space Beatense ever saw. End to end it measured a good six hundred feet, and the free span ceiling was forty feet high. The plate glass windows that faced out to the taxi and bus lanes were equally tall, and their dark smoky tint reduced the sunlight to an unnatural dimness.

There was a scene of constant motion as everyone came and went. The ticket counters were ranged along the opposite wall, and long lines snaked out from them. Bustling sounds both near and far filled the air, but everyone took it in stride.

Shean led them to the Ryd-Air counter that had the shortest line, but as always happens the stout woman at the counter at the time, whose puffy hands that were resting upon the tall counter were stuffed with tickets and documents, held everyone else up. She seemed to be arguing with the agent.

Beatense looked over to the next line and espied a small young woman in youth sized farmer overalls with shoulder straps, under which was a pink T-shirt. She was taking the noises, crowds and travel uncertainties calmly, and indeed she was leafing through *With It Women*. She had regal, fairy princess looks, and her widely curved eyebrows showed that she was competent, conscientious and collected. Despite her extra-effort tan she was silky blond and her smoothed skin was dewy fresh, and from the capable bulge of her little biceps it was obvious she worked out. She shoved her bag absently forward with her foot as her line moved. *And I'm the Book Girl. Yeah.*

They finally got to the counter and set their skis and gear on the steel luggage shelf. The harried agents attached tags to the items, and they were set back onto a conveyor, where they were shunted away through black rubber flaps.

While they waited Tony had looked at the boarding passes.

"Shean, our seats are all over the plane! Don't we want to sit together?" He turned to the agent. "Look, man, we have to get our seats together."

"Oh, they can do that at the gate, sir. But it might be a little tight."

"Well let's hurry, then!" said Shean. "We have a plane to catch!"

Tony looked up at the blurry monitors displaying arrivals and departures. "Shean, our plane is late. It isn't even on the ground yet."

Beatense, spotted the En Route notation on the screen.

"I don't understand why it has to be late!" the girl exclaimed.

Ned, in faded, tight shaped jeans and a sport jersey, eyed her critically.

Getting rid of their junk helped. The prospective skiers strolled along the broad windows toward the Red Ribbon concourse, and Beatense looked out over the apron area. Huge airliners were taxiing by, and the turbine whine of their engines carried right through the glass. Dozens of jetliners were parked by the gateways, and service and fuel trucks raced back and forth. Baggage conveyors driven by ear cupped drivers also raced by. As soon as an airliner pulled in, the trucks immediately fell upon it, including squat tow vehicles and a luggage train.

The party reached the Red speed walk, a sort of horizontal escalator, and they stepped on it and began their first hundred yard glide. Beatense was impressed by this, and would have made some comment, but she saw a sensually proud and bone stretched tanner in amazingly tight jeans coming from the other way with aristocratic indifference, and so she kept her mouth shut.

"Tony? Can we stop? I want to look at the planes!"

"Wait until we get to our gate, Beatense. We can't just stop this, you know."

"Well, look, it's ending just ahead there. Shut up, Ned. What's a gate?"

"That's a gate," Tony said, pointing to one of the many boarding areas.

The gate he indicated was a sad collection of sparsely filled seats, where a lone agent stood behind a counter. A passenger offered his ticket to him. A digital sign identified the destination, Amberton. This humdrum scene was wildly incongruous to the darkly business-like windshield of the jetliner just outside the big window.

"Our gate is 23A, so we got quite a shit-load to go yet."

When the Shattucks got to their gate Beatense looked for their plane. Not in yet. She joined the others at the counter to get their seats changed.

"Wow, all you need are these little slips of paper to get on a plane, right?"

"Those little slips of paper cost us plenty," said Tony. "Jesse, get over here. Where did Tammy go? Ned, stay with Beatense." --/-- "Do I have to?"

Tony finally got to the counter, and happily saw that its agent happened to be a precious little girl. Somehow she didn't look up to the job.

She was tawny faced, but her arms were deeply hued. Her only ornament was a fine gold chain set to the joint of her wrist. It neatly embellished the fine shape of her delectable forearm, that complemented the second pretty bicep pair seen that hour.

"Look, er, Raya, hate to bother you, but can all of us sit together? We made the reservations over the phone and didn't know what we were getting."

She looked stricken, but remembering to be brave she gamely smiled.

"Oh! I wish I could help you, but I can just sit you in threes!"

Tony and Beatense too felt protective toward this ineffectual child, who obviously had been hired because somebody in human resources felt the same way. Frail and fluttery in looks, she trusted people to be nice. And they were. They were.

"That would be fine. I realize it's short notice."

Raya mouthed dry air in adorable panic and looked at her monitor, hoping for a miracle. "Oh, sir, we have a whole row open! But it's just five across! Sorry, one of you will have to split up!" --/-- "Set me up next to Ned," said Beatense.

"No!" the boy responded, although without his being quite aware of it he was hoping for exactly that seating situation. "Don't put her next to me!"

"I get to sit next to Shean," said Tammy.

"Here, Beatense," said Jesse, "take the window seat and I'll sit by you."

She agreed. Jesse's élan made him a lord. As they walked the concourse she saw how everyone had admired that smart young jet-setter, at her expense. Veteran fliers know there is always at least one boy like him in any airport, an elite pampered boy with uncut long hair who reeks of moneyed superiority. These pretty boys are so above and sophisticatedly self assured, they wouldn't look out of place with drink and cigarette in hand. In Jesse's case his taut formed belly ripples, bared by his opened coat, were further proof of his elitist quality. Under their shirts all the privileged boys here today had muscle, and they were also kissed with the socially elevating nautical tans borne of their pampered lives, and isotopes.

"Hold it, Jesse," said Tony. "You have to be our floater."

"Okay!" the boy agreed, and he abandoned Beatense to quickly glide over to an aspiring model and friend. "Hi! Do you two need someone to sit with?"

"Oh, no. We're just waiting for someone," the girl said, smiling.

Jesse hopped back. "Well, I tried. Just give me anywhere, miss."

The new passes were issued, and the party went to the seating area. Beatense was excited she had a window seat, just back of the wing, and Ned would be to her right. He indicated little enthusiasm. Tammy had the aisle seat across from Shean, while Tony had the other window seat. But the plane itself wasn't in yet.

Tammy sat down. "Shean, we can hold hands across the aisle!"

"Nuts! I have to sit next to Beatense!" said Ned coldly, in trying to hide his extreme satisfaction. "You just better leave me alone!" --/-- "I plan to kiss you, Ned."

"Settle down you two," said Tony. "Jesse, where will you be sitting at?"

"Up towards the front. Probably with a couple of right wing yahoos."

"Tony, just now for no reason Ned hit me in the jaw so hard I can barely talk!"

"Well Ned, you should have hit her a little harder," said Tony, meaning it.

"Thanks for your concern. But I'm going to call home. Be right back."

Before Tony could get his out, Beatense ran back out to the corridor. Payphones were still in place, luckily. As she dug out some change, a rich boy walked by. Twelve years old, he had emotional, moist red lips, the black lashes of sheltered tenderness and hollowed cheeks. Distancing himself from sun he was milken pale of skin.

His randomly tuffeted, long black hair marked his extreme societal and wealthy privilege. Despite his favored-few life and lordly persona he wore old, torn and faded jeans, and an ordinary white school shirt.

Beatense watched after him as she absently dialed her number.

"Lorraine, hi! Well, here I am waiting for my flight!"

"Great, but Sim was here looking for you. Virginia, turn that down!"

"Oh, no! Lorraine, what did you tell him? We were going to go sailing!"

"It's what he told us, is what you might be more interested in. They canned him. He forgot that this morning he had his progress review, and he came in late for that. Then they said he should have come in last night to test these motors because the vendor wanted word on them. Anyway, he's in a real bind."

"Shucks, well I can give him a thousand. If he asks. Okay, bye!"

Beatense returned as their jet came wheeling in. All eyes upon her, she ran to watch as the long, windowed fuselage slowly turned and haltingly rolled in. Its stern mounted jet turbines were visibly spinning, and its broad wings and swept back T-tail exemplified that word, "Flight." As the jet drew in, an airman below signaled it into position with orange batons, and the pilots behind the low, dark windshield watched. The engines were cut and whistled down, and the box-like structure out by their gate rolled up snug against the plane's rounded side. Shean joined the girl.

"Boy, they're sure serious about ventilation here. Look at that ductwork!"

"Duct? That's no duct! That's the jetway, for boarding the plane!"

The other agent got on the mike. *Gud ayftanoon, lydies and jaynts, Flaght 298 haze arrahved. Ayz soon as the depahting paysengers ahh awl stayped ohf wee kin begayn bohding foh the cohntinueeng flaght to Cahloose. Thynk yew.*

As the arriving passengers ambled out from the jetway, Beatense saw a tan and dark eyed girl standing nearby. "Ah yew wau-king?" she said in the same odd accent to the tall but still overawed fellow she apparently had struck up a conversation with. She had a live, crackly voice. The blushing, flustered fellow mumbled a reply.

But the girl looked fun. She wore tight jeans and an old white sweat shirt. One would suspect from her clothes that she had some menial job that kept her poor, but her struggles with life's inequities added to her appeal immensely. Bondi 87.

The tanner hitched her backpack to her shoulder and she shook hands with the trembling fellow. He regretfully went to the gate across the way, and waved.

She familiarly turned to Beatense. "Jest me rawton luke, ahh guying ane ohpceet draykshuns! These bleddy jates! Nayvuh to see heem agyne!"

Beatense smiled at the sweatshirt girl and she turned to the passengers as they continued out of the jetway. They didn't seem awfully impressed with the experience they had just finished. Some turned to Beatense with the usual recognition surprise. Tammy and the boys caught stricken looks, too.

Yoh ataynshun, please, we'll staht bohding naow foh the cohnteenueeng flaght to Cahloose. Lates avv yew meuve oop naow, the fahst grewp.

Beatense rejoined her party as the tender little child of an agent (can't quite recall when I saw her) pulled aside that symbol of civil order, the velvet rope.

42

BOARDING PASS

Beatense grabbed Tony. "Thank you, thank you, thank you!"

"Beatense, you silly girl, you're not even on the plane yet."

"And she's not getting on the plane, either," Ned warned, coldly.

But minutes later Beatense handed her boarding pass to the fearful little girl and then strode into the jetway tunnel, paneled with putty dull laminate. The blond haired willow stick ahead of her just had a canvas ammo pack hung to her shoulder for her luggage. Beatense already had seen her tiredly severe blue eyes, that clashed with her brown face. And along with her tight, faded jeans she wore a waffle-knit thermal undershirt, whose pushed up sleeves showed her clashy forearms. *Aced out again.*

The bunching passengers in the plane's foyer gave Beatense the chance to notice how the entry door was curved to the thick aluminum fuselage.

She showed her boarding pass to the stewardess, whose hypnotic, shallow-set dark eyes daunted her. They were made penetrating by the firm, fine prominence of her carved cheekbones, and her dark, wisteria garlanded hair fell in soft, wispy loops. Her nutty complexion was that of summer afternoons out on the tennis court, but her most potent weapons were her delicately small lips and teeth, that minutely, fleetingly inter-played with those daunting expressions her wiltingly moody eyes inflicted.

Beatense knew greatness when she saw it; she was an exiled countess.

"Hello," the emigre said, glancing at her ticket. "Uhhh, you'll be seated in the back cabin. Joann is waiting to help you. Welcome aboard. Book Girl? Hate your legs."

"Me too. They take lots of work. Ned, show your ticket, idiot!" --/-- "I am!"

She turned to look at the cockpit through the narrow door to the left. The pilots, who were joking as they went through their pre-flight, saw her interest and nodded in permission. The girl stepped in and danced her eyes over the gauges and controls. Shean, fearing that she was barging in, wearily sighed behind her.

"Wow! How do you guys know what to do, all these gauges! Shean, look!"

"Well, it's not really all that confusing, miss," said the first officer.

Shean, surprised that Beatense actually got a response, moved beside her.

The pilot pointed up at the switch laden panels just above the seats. There was little headroom. "These are just switches here. Cabin lights, landing lights, wing lights, servos and remote fire extinguishers. We don't even have to look."

"That's reassuring," said Shean dryly. "What are those levers for? Jesse!"

"Well, I want to see!" the boy said, and he squeezed in.

"On the console here? Well, these rev the engines, this one handles the landing gear and these set the flaps. These hit the thrust reversers, for braking."

Beatense looked at the control stick bowties, atop their pivoting pedestals.

"Okay, but not much for steering wheels, hah? What cheapness!"

"An automotive steering wheel would block the gauges, miss."

"You guys get the hell out of there," said Tony. "Shean, let Ned see."

Shean stepped out and Ned moved shyly in and solemnly regarded the cockpit. Beatense stooped down. It seemed to her that as far forward as the low windshield was over the shrouded instrument panel, it would be tough for the pilots to see ahead through it. It reminded her of the tiny cowl plate on old Neptune, decades ago.

The pilot turned. "What are you looking at, miss?"

"Your windshield doesn't give much of a view from where you're sitting."

"The only view we actually need is in landing, miss. But I'm warning you, get to your seats. If you're caught here we'll all be sequestered."

"That's the word! Oh, and why did that boarding agent talk so funny?"

"They all talk that way in Waverley, miss. Now scram!"

"Come on, Beatense!" Ned ordered, and the kids shuffled out.

The boarding continued. The three brothers headed back, but the sweatshirt girl was approaching the foyer, and Beatense stayed forward.

"Wayll, haylo! Wayll, ee goht me addrayce and phaohn noombah!"

"Bloody pushy of him," said Beatense, smiling at her energetic voice.

"Nah. Een ayapohts ya wauks fahst. Ee deed, Ah mane!"

The two went on by the galley, where food carts were being wrestled in from the elevated body of the catering truck outside. They entered the First Class cabin, and. Beatense met yet another nemesis. A self importantly browned, child-thin nymph sat sprawled, so that one slim, sun toasted leg quite blocked the aisle. Her stray auburn hair fell so that it enigmatically obscured her left eye, but both her eyes had a sleepy half droop, as if she was complacently self satisfied. Her rich, sunny sheen roiled off from her in visible waves, and her silky little shift hung from her hot carved shoulders with two light strings. She boldly returned the helpless stares of her lessers as they stepped themselves and luggage over her long, placed leg. No one protested.

"Ah knaow the tahp," Beatense's new friend said, as they entered the long tourist class cabin. "She pohps intah hah ayraobeecs clahss een hah tohnga, and eef enny chap geevs hah a lewk, she geets eem toosed aout."

"I would be naked, myself," said Beatense. "Oh, this is your seat? Bye!"

"Nyme's Meggie! Gud skeeng!" --/-- "I'm Beatense, and thanks!"

They shook, nice strong hands, and Meg, who didn't recognize her, sat down.

Beatense pushed on, assured that she was top royalty here. Everyone seemed honored that she was sharing their flight. The jet's interior was a long, softly lighted tunnel done in beige ivory. The seats, set in threes to the right and twos to the left, were covered in jade, autumn rust or magenta fabrics. The seats all had wide eyes, and those bounty hunting cameras, fixed upon the famous Book Girl. It seemed that she was bared within her loosely hung pink sweater, with nips sticking right out.

The jolted gentlemen, expecting a dull magazine paging interlude, now anxiously awaited the end of the flight, in hopes of seeing her baked face, and legs, again.

The matronly women feared her, but her being a star oddly helped.

The boarding progress was slow, because once people reached their seats their impatience mellowed, and they dreamily stowed their luggage in the overhead bins. The long, twin lines of the lockers gave Beatense an idea of just how long this plane was, far longer than Sabbatical Quest. It was hard to imagine it could actually fly.

The girl went by Jesse, who was forlornly resigned to sitting by a business suit working on his laptop. His woebegone look was adorable as he smiled wanly at her, with seatbelt snugged just below his dark tan ripples.

According to her boarding pass and Tammy's getting up to let her in, this was Beatense's row. She opened the luggage compartment and stuck in her backpack, and the passengers behind who wouldn't see her go by watched closely.

Tony, who had endured this girl grilling under oil by his pool, felt faint. The girl wormed her way in past the protesting Ned and flexed herself into her seat. She felt rather squeezed, at least compared to the space on the train, but she could stick her feet under the seat in front of her. Also there was a little tray table that opened down out of its back, a feature that the Queen seats didn't have. But compared to the train the windows were small, just eight by ten inches.

Beatense turned the latch and pulled down her table.

"You're not supposed to have that down now!" Ned said, angered. She folded it back up so she could keep an eye on her legs. "And buckle your seatbelt!"

"Yeah, in a sec, bubble butt. But hey! What's this button on my armrest?"

"Don't you know anything?" --/-- "That's for reclining your seat, Beatense," said Tammy, who was presiding in her ingenuously scanty, tatted lace frock. "But you have to keep it up now." --/-- "Yeah, Beatense!"

The girl glared back at Ned. She reached up and turned her reading light on with a little click. She also swiveled her vent nozzle, and this seemed to displease Ned.

"Ned, how do you roll down this here window?" --/-- "Oh, brother!"

"Boy, I had the weirdest dream last night." --/-- "Not again!"

"I wonder where Jesse wound up," said Tony from across the aisle.

"By that girl with the sticking out leg, up in that First Class, Tony."

"He's sitting there? But I didn't see an empty..." He stopped, not caring to let on that he had paid any special attention. "Where is he really?"

"Ten rows up. These jets sure are long. There must be thirty rows, total."

"At least," said Shean. "There's no dignity in us being crammed in together like pigs just because we're cheap. Hey, what are we renting if we land, Dad?"

"If we luck out and make it, an Illuminati mini-van with a ski-rack, not cheap."

Beatense looked out her window and watched the luggage conveyor speed the suitcases, skis and skiboots up into the plane's belly. She heard an occasional clunk underfoot as the items were hurriedly tossed in and stored below. Then came louder clunks as the lockers below were shut. The conveyor truck backed away, and as it drove off the catering truck swung away and followed. The last few passengers took their seats and a stewardess came along checking the seatbelts. A silence fell, as a muted, whirring hum began, like a vacuum cleaner a couple rooms over.

As it wound up higher in pitch it grew more insistent. A second humming started up at the original low pitch, causing a trembling vibration, and finally the third engine joined the warm-up chorus. The overhead speakers hummed.

Good afternoon, fellow travelers. First Officer Banks here welcoming you aboard the continuing Flight 298 to Curlewis. The Book Girl inspected our cockpit and gave her okay. Beatense felt a lurch. They were moving backwards! *We are off schedule by forty minutes, but we will land on time. Now please pay attention to Rachelle and Joann as they explain the the safety precautions on your seat-back cards.*

The backward roll stopped. After a pause the engine three-pack revved up to a turbine drone, easing the jet slowly forward. It turned, sweeping out a new view, and began taxiing at a walking speed. The long fuselage jiggled and shook in wobbling vibrations as the jet airliner jogged purposefully along, and as its high pressure tires responded to the uneven pavement. These were reflected in the light flexings of the swept-back wings. Beatense gave Ned a dirty look, then turned back to watch.

The concourse building scrolled slowly but steadily by, as the swarming activity around the docked planes continued, and as other jets came and went.

Beatense even saw an old Constellation. Noble Airlines.

The stewardess, whom Beatense guessed was Joann, stood in the aisle, and as the speakers detailed how one buckles a seatbelt, Joann demonstrated this with her own miniature belt she held up. She clicked together the buckles with a flourish, then the girl showed how to put on the oxygen masks, "...just in case air cabin pressure should fall." She pointed out the emergency exits over the wings with a wave in their general direction, and she held up a safety card. By now she was hopelessly out of sync with the speakers, and she began to laugh.

...and now your hostess will show you the safety feature card.

Joann bowed to applause. The jet trundled on, and every hundred yards or so it made a pivoting turn. Gazing out at the wide acres of concrete and heat dried grass, Beatense guessed the horrible truth, they were lost. The plane groaned to a stop.

Well, ladies and gentlemen, we arrived at the runway, and they say we're fifth in sequence for take-off. Update your wills and we'll be on our way shortly.

At that the pilot reached and rattled the cockpit door shut, which had been open. The engines wound up and pushed the jet just ahead and then wound back down. There suddenly came a huge roar, and Beatense saw a plane rocket by over on the next strip of pavement. Presently their own plane shoved ahead again, as a distant plane took off at a steep angle, with curls of black smoke trailing behind.

Then another jet shot by on the nearby runway. Beatense got impatient.

"Well, I do declare, Ned, this certainly isn't helping our lateness situation!"

"Oh, yeah, like you know all about it." --/-- "Actually I do, watermelon head."

The plane eased ahead once more, and it sounded as if the engines were tired of winding so portently up, only to be immediately cut back. Another plane shot by. At last their own plane moved ahead and ponderously turned, and the entire two mile length of the take-off runway swept into view. The plane pivoted into one last turn and stopped with the tri-pack of engines humming. Beatense saw a sign, **RUNWAY 07**

Their plane was aimed straight down the highway, like an arrow in a drawn back bow. The engines were held at a low RPM, waiting in suspense for the clearance to take off. The terminal building and hangars shimmered in the hazy smog. Beyond them, the tall hillside of Little Wittlee and Tankers Rill.

The speakers, quietly: *Crew, prepare for take-off.*

"Ned? I fear for my personal safety. Can I hold your hand?" --/-- "No!"

A sudden wallop came from behind, as the jet turbines roared up to full blasting rage. They rocketed the plane down the runway in a wild blur of acceleration. The aircraft was rocking and shaking, and buzzing vibrations were heard as the massive stresses shuddered through the airframe, and as the heavy lurching and thumping of the runaway plane grew increasingly urgent. The wings flexed as the pavement shot by beneath them. The jet aircraft continued to stagecoach along, as if this whole trip would be on the ground after all. Suddenly there came a sinking lurch as if they had run off the edge of a steep cliff, and the ground fell quickly away.

Beatense sank in her seat. "You guys, look, we just took off!"

"Whoopee ding," Ned rejoined. But his eyes showed life.

"Wait, what was that noise?" --/-- She had heard a grinding, clunking thunk somewhere beneath the floor. "They just folded up the wheels," said Tammy.

"Yeah, everybody knows that," said Ned coldly, glad for this explanation.

Beatense glared at him, just to stay in practice. The turbines now had a driving, surging whine as they fought upward for altitude. The mighty metropolis of Cardiff lay stretched out below, and the girl gazed down in wonder upon its vast expanse.

Beyond lay the fabulous sea, and its sweeping waves were ranged out like white windrows. *Magnificent.* As they lofted up through a gauzy layer of cirrus Beatense wept. The jet made a long, banking turn toward the northwest, as the trio of engines faithfully purred them along.

"Beatense, what's wrong?" said Tammy. --/-- "She's a crybaby!"

The PA speakers hummed. *Good afternoon, passengers, this is Captain Jack welcoming you aboard Flight 298 to Curlewis. In another minute off will go those seatbelt lights. We'll reach an altitude of 36,000 feet, and we'll be veering away from the coastline below to the northwest, for an on-time arrival."*

Tony quietly showed Shean Beatense's bareback video on his phone. Someone had spliced the segments together to make one long shot. Then the Sim episode.

The girl herself settled back. She turned to her disapproving seat-mate.

"Ned, I got a nice story for you. There once was this foolish boy of fourteen who wouldn't listen to girls who were older and smarter than him, so you can just imagine what awful miserable things happened to him because he didn't pay attention to their wisely educated advice. So you just let that be a lesson to you, young man."

Tony, straining to hear her words, struggled to hold in his laughter as Ned looked disgusted at this enlightening story and its valuable teaching.

"I can tell you a story about a girl who gets her nose punched!"

"You guys quit it!" Tammy pleaded, but she did see Ned's contented look.

"Tell Ned to quit it," said the instigator, and she turned to her window.

Clouds. Beatense gazed out at the enchanting, secret worlds tucked deeply away in those billowing white bursts. The clouds drifted by in a lazy succession, as if their plane was going ten miles an hour instead of six hundred. And each cloud was very different from all others. They had wide, yawning caverns that invited one to explore far, far in, and others had forbidding chasms hundreds of feet deep. But Beatense wearied of this vapory realm, and she reclined her seat and looked up at her swivel mounted air vent and the reading light. She reached up and turned on Ned's light.

"Hey!" --/-- "Hey, what? Say, Ned, you don't think I'm ugly, do you?"

"Oh! Nooooooo!" said the boy, his wide eyes looking very worried.

"Good, because I would rather be stupid than ugly." --/-- "Yeah, well, you got no problem there!" --/-- "I beg your pardon, Ned, but do I like detect a note of sarcasm in that comment?" --/-- "I beg your pardon, yeah, you do detect a note of sarcasm!"

She glared at him. She noticed what a lullaby the pervasive rushing of air out of her window was, like a forest waterfall, that muffled all the conversation into indistinct murmurs. And the jet lightly tossed in the air, a wonderful sensation.

"Shean, go find where that Jesse ended up," said Tony, in a detached voice from another world. "And Ned, get up, I want to talk to Miss Colwell there."

"Gladly!" --/-- "Ned, I heard that, and I'm very disturbed."

"You're disturbed, all right!" The boy got up and took his father's seat.

"Tammy, watch your feet," said Tony, playfully kicking at the tiny things. He sat beside Beatense. "Hi, young lady, heh heh. Glad you could join us."

"Well, this skiing will give my skin a rest. And my legs aren't fading yet."

It wasn't what he wanted to hear, but she was right about her legs. If it was just their tan he could take it, but they were so slimly laced with tight muscle that anyone beholding them could only think of her rapture as she held to her lover with them.

And Tony saw how irreverently the girl was slouched. That ability to so slackly relax was an additional bonus to her skinny damsel frame. But now it was her elbow set arm that caught his eye. Bared with the fall of her sleeve, there was the slim stick that was her forearm. Her upturned nose stretched her jawline almost an extra inch, so that it conveyed decisive assertion. The fine boned curve of her burnished forehead showed that as an elitist she expected deference.

"Tony, I'm sorry I gave you and that meter guy that naked abuse today."

"We deserved it. But do you like skiing so far?" --/-- "With you along, yes."

"Dad?" It was the noticeable Shean. "He's up with this one business guy."

"Yeah, thanks. Sit back down. I'll be back over in a minute."

"Shean is so beautiful it's frightening, Tony. And tell Ned I like him."

Tony turned. "Ned, isn't that great news? This young lady likes you."

"It is not great news!" --/-- "You hear that, girl? He doesn't think it's great."

"Well, I might have been a little mean to him." --/-- "A little mean!"

"By the way, that's an incredible sweater you have on. Just long enough."

"Oh, I'm thong patch legal. But that girl up in first class is real competition. How can she just sit there like that? I thought I had nerve until an hour ago."

He gulped, recalling that smoking leg he saw while just trying to get to his seat.

That hot baked skin was so stretch smoothed over those long runner's thighs, she was a fright. But Beatense's legs were slimmer. And her waist? *Better not go there.*

"So, ahem, what possesses you to lay in the sun like that?"

"Us long, lean and lanky girls just have it wired in. At some point years ago we decided that we just wanted to bother people. That killer instinct thrill of obnoxious display, where everyone says, *This Can Not Be.* And I say, we all say, go bite! And that also applies to our discovering sex as wholesome fun. Of course this just turned us all into active sluts, but all those stodgy people reassured themselves by thinking, *Well, in time they'll see their errors and get back to the old morals.* But instead even their sweet, cherished young daughters eagerly strip naked for all night fuck."

"Kids too, is one doubt I have," said Tony. "But when they can go to the clinic on the sly (if they have to) and get surgery, what's to stop them?"

"Yeah, when I was at that desert surveying camp as a kid, I wasn't stopped from fucking, and I had totally no scruples about it. You get that rare girl who will not get involved, but once her friends set her up, she's hooked. For me, a sex party got me going. So this intern Lesta helped me get an implant. I broke it in fast."

"Speaking of fast." Tony played her the Windfire video on his phone.

"Wow, that sure volumized my hair! Am I gorgeous! I was that tan?"

The slowly approaching stewardesses stopped by their row with a rattly serving cart bedecked with cans and bottles. Rachelle asked, "Anything to drink?"

Tony got coffee, and Tammy asked for root beer. Beatense got Agri-Cola.

There was an announcement of "Oh-kay!" by Rachelle for all of the cabin to hear and the cart lurched on, helped by Joann. Although she was tinty pale, her skin had a bright appeal, and her wide forehead just begged for a sailor hat as worn at a jaunty angle. She was descended of aristocratic lineage, but what tore at the heart was the poignant legacy of distress in her presently sparkling dark eyes.

"Well, there's a pale girl for you, Tony. Now if she was to really bake, what might motivate her? She couldn't be after that nutty nature look, she's too much a city girl. Nor would she do it out of willful rebellion, either, just to rattle people, nor from all-out sensual aggression. But these comes a time when you have to pamper yourself. And being light and tight, us fine blooded girls get sun out of sacred self worship, and we just live to soak up the sun. Us tan seekers indulge in hot, deep nudity, and if we're college or working singles still at home, right out in parent or neighbor sight. It's just so beautiful to lay there hour by hour, wasting all that time just to luxuriate all brown."

"I indulge like that," said Tammy, as Flight 298 continued along. "I go all day!"

Tony took a last look as the tight Beatense regally gazed out her window. Along with the tangled thickness of her surfer hair, it was distinctly three colors, blond gold, metallic amber and red auburn, as it showed her head's noble shape. And but for her nose and chin it formed a privacy sanctum, where one would hesitate to disturb her.

Tony got up. "Move your stubby legs, Tammy. Ned, I want my seat back."

His eyes fleetingly gleamed. "Why can't I stay here?!"

Beatense exchanged dirty looks with the boy as he sat by her again with a sigh.

"Tammy, how do you think I'll do with this skiing?" she said right past him.

"If you can surf and gallop bareback, you can ski, Beatense."

"She's too clumsy!" --/-- "Yeah, good, because I actually did surf."

Beatense, studying her legs, saw the map pocket tucked behind her table. She pulled out the motion bag, complete with metal closure tabs. "What's this for?"

"Put that back!" --/-- "That's the barf bag," said Tammy.

"Barf bag? You mean like puking up the contents of one's stomach?"

Ned began to lower himself in his seat. He rubbed his forehead.

"Yeah, Beatense, in case you get airsick!" --/-- "Air can make you sick?"

Tammy widened her eyes in exasperation. "Beatense!"

The flight continued. Beatense had a huge one hundred mile shoving match over the armrest between herself and the boy. This contest was waged in grim, teeth clenched silence with eyes fixed straight ahead. Tony, seeing this going on, smiled and shook his head. This girl highly exasperated his poor son.

Only when the stewardesses came by with the food cart did the fight stop.

"Hold it," Beatense said, "how much does this cost? And Ned needs a bib."

"It's priced right in the ticket, miss. Here you go. No bibs! Oh-kay!"

Beatense opened down her table and eyed her airline kitchen meal. She would need it; she didn't eat since the donuts, and she had that hard sex with Sim all night.

"Ned, go to the bathroom and warsh your hands. This instant!"

"They're clean!" the boy protested, turning his hands for inspection.

"You can use your Wash Wipe towel, Beatense," said Tammy.

The girl picked up the little packet. "Oh, I heard about these!" Ned rolled up his troubled eyes. "Wow, is that ever funky! No sink needed! And sanitary! Wow!"

Even Tammy looked bothered, as Ned breathed heavily in disapproval.

Beatense opened her butter and globbed it onto her roll in one good smear. Ned was going to do it the same way but pointedly used his plastic knife. The girl took inventory. First, the roll, and a small salad in a plastic tub with a peel-off top. There was also a one ounce container filled with ranch mustard. The 6x8 inch oblong plate had a slice of corned beef rolled around boiled cabbage, plus there was a pile of pilaf rice. There was also a packet of garlic crackers from some grubby caterer that was trying win customers by providing its savory product free to the airlines. For dessert there was a slice of cranberry cake with butter sauce.

Altogether the girl had a decent but skimpy meal before her sun indulged self.

She tucked in, *accidentally* elbowing Ned with each sanctimonious bite. Despite his angry irritated scowling the boy was highly pleased. But he finally objected.

"Dad! Beatense keeps on poking me!" --/-- "Stop that this instant, girl!"

Eight seconds went by in relative peace, and then… "Dad, she did it again!"

She blew Schesky Bros garlic cracker crumbs at the beleaguered boy.

"Hey! Cut it out!"

Once the skimpy but decent food was handed out the attendants went back up front and began retrieving the empty trays. Beatense hurried, the antics stopped.

"That food was just so great!" she said as she handed her tray to the susceptible Joann, holding her arm against Ned's face. --/-- "Hey!" --/-- "It was eggs-quisite."

"Please don't eggs-aggerate." --/-- "Eggs-zactly."

The stewardesses went on (Oh-kay!) and Beatense squirmed restlessly.

"Ned, wipe that mouth of yours! And your hair is all messed up!"

She squiddled her fingers on the boy's pretty head. Ned tried retaliating but their struggle rattled their tables. They sat guiltily still for a minute, glaring their embittered accusations, and then Beatense tried patting Ned's arm.

He jerked it away. "Dad!"

Tony saw the girl quietly page through her magazine that she took from the seat pocket. "Look, Ned, that's you," she said, pointing to a monkey. --/-- "That's you!"

Tony felt his eyes sting. The change in Ned these past few days was far beyond his wildest hopeless hopes. Life was suddenly agreeable to him.

"Oh, Ned, my dream! Well, not now, I better tell about this other thing first." Ned indicated little interest but the girl began. "This is what seriously happened to me once. Okay? Like once I was surveying with my father, you know?" --/-- "Oh, brother."

"We hiked into this forest. Now you see, I'm woodsy, I can eke out a living grubbing for roots and berries, but that isn't germane to this story. So anyway, I came to this tall hill, and guess what. At the foot of it I discovered this cave."

"Big deal." --/-- "I decided to explore it and I crawled in on my tummy, but then it got too dark so I stopped. It was a darn good thing, because there was a drop-off."

"There was?" --/-- "I dropped this rock and it never hit." --/-- "Wow!"

"I scrambled backwards to get out, but my foot bumped into something, and the rocks caved in and trapped me inside. Not to be theatrical, but I was doomed."

"Well, you did get out, I see!" --/-- "Yeah, ruin the ending! Anyway, I saw this dim light over on the other side of the drop-off, that even in the darkness I could tell that it wasn't that wide." --/-- "Where was the light coming from?"

"Just wait, will ya? So I crouched down and leaped across the chasm."

"You... You did?" --/-- "I had no choice, Ned. Being trapped I faced sure death either way. But the only trouble was, in that darkness I misjudged the distance and I landed with my legs dangling over the edge." --/-- "Then what?"

"I grabbed this one rock but it broke loose, and as it fell I heard it bouncing from side to side down the shaft." --/-- "Oh! Weren't you scared?"

"No. Mostly I was mad because it was a great day to get sun, with that certain balminess where a girl like me can find a hidden spot and really soak it in."

Ned accepted this at face value, and Tony, listening in, knew all about that.

"Well, I found this crack and dug my fingers into it and pulled myself up in a human triumph of brave determination to get sun another day. So I crawled up this narrow passage towards the light, which slowly got brighter and brighter, and I escaped from the cave, my tanning dreams fulfilled." --/-- "Boy, lucky thing!"

"Except, I was way up on this ledge on a sheer cliff, with no way down."

"You were?"

"Just listen, will you? The ledge was too small to lay in the sun, so I yelled for my Pop. He finally came by and called for a helicopter, and there it came."

"Really?"

"Hey, my Pop spared no expense. It had this rope ladder, that I leaped out at to grab it. But the ladder swung away and I missed it. But luckily it swang back and I caught it at the very end. I began climbing the ladder but just my luck I saw this one part where the ropes were frayed. I kept climbing up to the helicopter, but then the left rope broke, leaving me dangling hundreds of feet up by only the last strand. I paused to reflect on my life and decided that by spending it tanning I lived wisely."

"You did not."

"I started shinnying up to get above the break, but just as I got hold of the good rope the bottom part broke off. But sadly my feet got tangled up in it so I had all that extra weight to carry. Lucky I was light. You know, it's more than just looks."

"Didn't your hands get tired?"

"A little, but what was worse was that the dangling rope caught in a tree. I quick kicked my shoes off. Anyway, we were flying over a big woods, and finally I saw a town come up where we could finally land." --/-- "It's about time!"

"We headed over to this park where all these kids were playing badmitten. But spitefully they didn't let us land until they finished their game."

He digested that. "Beatense!" --/-- "What, Ned?" --/-- "Oh! Goll!"

"What, Ned, what?" --/-- "You made that whole thing up!"

"No, I didn't! I swear with all my acclaimed integrity that it's the truth!"

As Ned scowled, Tony and Shean turned to each other. Both were relieved that Ned was ultimately astute enough to see through that wild story.

"But how long did the game last?" asked the poor trusting Tammy.

"As long as it's going to take me to go to the bathroom. Let me out, ugly."

The girl found that the aisle of a gliding airliner was easier to walk than that of a speeding train, but there was a floaty sensation. There were two biffies facing each other across the aisle at the far back. Back in this close space it was relatively dark, and the curved ceiling was angled down to the rear exit door. Also, from the leverage effect the plane's flight movements were magnified, and with the nearby engines the ambient noise was rather a roar. The girl stepped into the port side restroom, that was shaped into confining closeness by the narrowing down of the tail. The left engine was only inches away, and its penetrating turbine grind filled the compartment.

Now bare, the girl lingered just long enough to eye her legs.

She nakedly returned, and standing narrowed she took down her backpack and traded her sweater for her belly baring swirl shirt and but-cuts, that she put on.

The plane began its Curlewis approach, a long, hundred mile glide, and for this the engines were cut back. The reduced noise brought a clarity to all other sounds, and conversations were overheard. The second round of drinks and avalanche supply of Schesky Bros Garlic-Ettes added to the conviviality. Jesse came by for his own B/R use. The nice boy waved to family and friends. Beatense waved back, but just then the waffle knit also went by, so it looked like she was waving to her.

Down, down, down the jet continued its descent. The gridwork of fields and roads thousands of feet below grew ever larger while even smaller features were clarified. Dry meandering creek beds were interspersed with huddled farm buildings.

And even small towns slowly swept into view. These fit entirely within Beatense's window. They looked terribly exposed and vulnerable from up here. She then saw a broad panel fold down along the back of the wing. This deploying of the flaps slowed the plane down markedly as it also pitched its nose up, and also caused the craft to buck and side-wind. The plane made a long curving turn as the PA came on.

Attention, we are now in approach into Curlewis, please return to your seats, the seatbelt light is on. Please fold your tables in and raise your seats fully upright.

"Ned, being such a hunchback, ask if you can keep your seat back." *--/--* "No!"

The jet was low enough that the individual trees of a woods could be picked out. Beatense could even count the cows on the dairy farms. They dropped ever lower. They were getting close to the city, as they flew just over a highway with various lone businesses spaced along the road. There were grain elevators, a feed mill, then an implement dealership and a truck stop. An isolated suburb with a dozen homes.

Farther on a construction site with machines and dirt piles lay sprawled. Beyond this residential areas with schools and stores lay like a carpet. The jet lowered, and rooftops by the hundreds glided silently by. They crossed over a narrow street lined with restaurants and shopping plazas. Off in the distance tall buildings towered.

A heavy clunking sound filled the plane and it bucked again. It was much lower now. Real low! And fast! They glided over a highway. More stores, more rooftops, more trees, cars in the driveways, someone on a bike. A shopping mall appeared, momentarily, then was gone. Warehouses and trucking terminals. Mountains in the distance. Bare ground, occasional weeds. Fifty feet, thirty, ten now, just ten!

Pavement, the runway. The plane's shadow raced the plane itself. The wide sweep of the wings was tilting right and left as the pilot sought a touchdown for the landing gear. With their sound reflected and amplified by the runway below, the jets were whistling, and big painted numbers flew by under the plane. The blue marker lights and signs along the blurred runway also told of their reckless speed.

The plane made a sudden, last sinking drop. The wheels hit and hit hard, as the speeding jet was staggered by a hundred tons of hurtling impact. The passengers were shaken in their seats, and a violent roaring came from behind as the clamshell thrust reversers were actuated. Convulsive vibrations shook the airframe, while the plane's massive deceleration leaned everybody forward. The thundering continued, and at last the decelerating plane quieted and and turned off the runway.

With jets quietly whirring the long excursion to the Curlewis terminal began.

Beatense gave Ned a quick kiss. *Ppsbpbsps! Hack cack!*

Rachelle came on the horn. *We just arrived at Curlewis. The local time is a punctual 7:20, the temperature an unseasonal 56 degrees. On behalf of Ryd-Air we thank you for flying with us today. Have a nice evening, get ready to exit the plane.*

The ride to the gate continued and Beatense watched as this new world out her window unfolded. She felt like a mariner who had been at sea for a year. The plane made a last turn as directed by a crewman outside with flashlights, and it nudged into the terminal. The passengers erupted from their seats the instant the engines were cut. Those back of Miss Book stared upon her.sunk black belly as they shuffled by.

She actually smiled. The overhead luggage compartments were spilled open as one, and the half crouches of those waiting to get into the aisle were almost comical. Tammy jumped right up, and Ned and Beatense also stood. The passengers ahead of her finally got their chance, but they had no preparation for this swirl shirt sighting.

The slow trudge up the long aisle began. The forlorn Joann and emigre Rachelle stood by the cockpit saying goodbye. Jesse was waiting in the gate area. Beatense saw Meg and fell in with her for the concourse trek. The aisle blocking Anntique was just ahead, wobbling along on her long, shiny baked legs, as if with knees of rubber.

"Yew bleddy Xanth wims daon't knaow whane tew slack back."

"Surely you're not pointing the accusing finger at me." *--/--* "Aoh, nevah!"

Beatense laughed. The main terminal ahead featured a line of restaurants and stores opposite the ticket and car rental counters. They gave Jesse an idea.

"Hey, Dad, let's find that one ski shop! We can set Beatense up right now!"

Beatense gave Ned an eyelid sagging, splibble lipped look. He responded.

"Good thinking. I was wondering how we could work that in. I can get the van while you're doing that. Ned, quit sticking your tongue out at Beatense."

"Well, she was sticking her tongue out at me!"

"Ned, I was licking my lips." --/-- "Oh, sure!"

Beatense then saw that Meg had a surprise. Her airport friend appeared.

"Wayll! Yew bleddy fool! Whayah the bleddy hayl deed yew coom from?"

A look at Beatense "I... I w-went over and got my ticket r-reworked."

"Wayl, Ah'm note shah Ah lahks yew thayat mooch, boot eef yew steys ovah at mah plyce tewnaght theyah waun't be enny spayah bayd, aynd no saofah!"

They happily left, and Beatense knew envy. She felt deprived, going from bed to bed like Puppet just for the intercourse. Then ahead she saw the skinny Waffle Knit, who apparently had no one to greet her, and come to think, no one had seen her off. Now an ugly woman could console herself, It's my looks, but this stem-built browner had no comforting reason for being alone in the world. Being too good for everyone didn't cut it. She likely bar danced up lots of sex, her nakedly tan aerobics would be irresistible, but after a heated night she and her mate would part without a word. But back at camp the extremely active Puppet enjoined over a hundred times, then years later Beatense had dismissed most of her Hoggie partners, and that Roke.

They entered the ski shop. **SPORT PORT,** its sign said, **Mates Rates.** All winter gear was 60% off. Shean and Jesse whooped aloud as they saw the prices.

"Naow heah ya gao, miss, these bohds heah will dew ya raght, and the prahce is raght. Mesaylf, wauking heah, Ah've bean whyting a yeeah foe thees prahces."

The boys fixed the girl up with serious gear. No cheap package, she wound up with a flashy pair of Whiz skis with Marlowe bindings. Her Head Crusher boots, used by experts. Beatense went along with the purchase, but it seemed like a lot to spend just to slide over the snow. But despite her doubts, in her new ski outfit (or bibs), as she held her radical skis in the crook of her arm, turning the daisy wheel of ski poles, this was one time she had no idea of the figure she cut. She used her own money.

She got out of the bibs, re-exposing her nervy swirl shirt and conduit waist.

43

NO SPAYAH BAYD

At last, out at the rental lot they loaded their futuristic Illuminati van, with its sleek polymer lines and huge swept back windshield. Beatense said it looked like an anteater, and Ned replied that she looked like an anteater, etc, etc.

No one paid attention anymore to their nonstop exchanges of criticism.

As they got in and drove out Beatense assumed they would merge right out onto an expressway, that would quickly head them toward the mountains. But instead they got buried in miserably cluttered little side streets, where every light turned red. The grim world outside their van was forbidding, even by Arrolynn standards. They went by a gloomy old factory, that according to its rusting sign produced steel stampings, and it looked like a horrible place to work.

John Galt Pattern Works

The dirty building was built of corrugated tin, with green fiberglass windows that were tilted uselessly open. The plant lay across from a dreary neighborhood of squalid stucco cottages, with institutional, zinc framed windows. These drab bungalows had little tiled roofs over their stoops, and carports walled in with more green fiberglass panels. The sparse and forlorn front yards were edged with ozone yellowed shrubs and bushes. The shit houses were so close together the neighbors could hear each other squeezing out their toothpaste.

They drove by the Parra Sav U Rite. This was the aged kind of supermarket that was a modern marvel fifty years ago, but now its white painted stucco walls would shame an army base exchange. The broad four by six foot windows were sectioned into smaller sections with that popular zinc framing. Garish

482

posters were taped up in the windows, telling of fabulous savings on dates, collards and kohlrabi, and over the open twin doorway was posted an obscure sign that had the simple message,

M I X E D B U S I N E S S

The next block was devoted to more small stores, that included a green grocer, fish monger and chemist. One business delivered barbecued ribs on motor scooters, with three parked, and a sullen looking shoe repair shop held its proprietor more securely than any prison. In the next block an aging factory's corrugated iron contruction was painted in fading dirty primer red (which went well with its ubiquitous green windows), and it produced power line tower assemblies.

"Hey, you guys, this can't be the fastest way! Don't you have a map?"

"This is the fastest way," said Shean wearily, watching the light turn red.

"You think you know everything," said Ned.

"Well, I am the smartest anteater around, by cracky."

It was hard to understand how her pestering could work.

The next block was devoted to lethal four story apartment buildings that were all half invitingly faced with putty colored cheap brick in front, but the warehouse sides of the lifeless buildings were either poured cement or cement blocks, unpainted.

"This place is pretty darn awful," said Beatense, with arm held protectively.

"Is it worse than Arrolynn?" said Jesse. --/-- "Way. Ned, stop crying."

They eventually left cheery Curlewis behind and the van started up the first of the mountain grades, and the snowy, sunset enflamed peaks reared up over the actual modern highway and the upward-winding canyons it climbed through. Most vehicles sported ski racks, and Beatense felt smug as her own pair shot along above her.

The girl peered out at the Burleigh Front Range, whose lighted ramparts loomed against the bright magenta skies. Tucked up among them, lonely towns bravely lay, old mining outposts that were descended upon in winter for their gas, uncertain food and/or blizzard-bound motels, and in summer for their sourdough charm.

Heavy semi trucks were chugging up the long grades, and fancy campers all too typically slugged along at a crawl. The Illuminati slowed down, but a flashy Rocker UTV truck passed them, driven by a smiling girl, and a rugged little pick-up Grit came following. This was driven by an outdoorsy fellow who looked like one of those thinker idealists, complete with obligatory flannel shirt and beard. His dog riding in the open back was probably named after a brand of baked beans.

A downhill stretch began, and Shean hit eighty as the van shot along through the curves. He caught up to and passed the Grit, then the Rocker.

The girl was widely smiling, apparently proud of her tan capability, off-road sport truck and transplanted new, adventure filled life. She had that confident, thin college girl outlook.

Her slim, tawny arms were held out before her as she quickly drove, and except for a few stray wisps, her blond hair was tucked up inside her baseball cap. At that she still managed to look finely bred; she had bone pointed cheeks and the curved nose and forehead of quality. She was cute, important and loved.

Shean strategically slowed down in front of her to force her to pass, but the Grit cruised by instead. Rocker Girl followed in a flash, and she went on to pass the Grit. This time Dedicated Earnest did look. Then, far down the grade, the Grit passed the Rocker back, and he exited off at Marshall.

"Well, that's the end of that epic romance," said Shean.

But the Rocker exited too. As their van took the overpass Tony reported that the two vehicles turned into the same gas station.

"You mean it's that easy out here?" said Beatense, envying her fun to come.

"You have to be halfway decent looking, though," said Jesse. "Sorry."

Beatense gave him a hit, cementing her bond with this family.

She saw a big green sign, announcing the upcoming County TV.

"Shean, we have to take that exit! Hurry!" --/-- "Why? How come?"

"Because then we can be on TV!" --/-- Ned's eyes rolled up on that one.

Impatient skiers in their irrational haste can often cause spontaneous slowdowns. The brakelights ahead began coming on and Shean slowed down with a sigh.

"Ned, calm down," said Beatense.

Further on light snow began covering the ground, and as the highway crossed an invisible line called the Continental Divide it lay far more deeply.

Night had fallen when Tony said, "Slow down for the exit." And Shean said, "Oh, gee, thanks for the tip. Jesse, you lucked out, there's tons of snow here!"

Beatense saw a great, vague mass off in the darkness over to the right, that was swept with broad white bands. She guessed this was the ski mountain, and all eyes were upon it. Moving lights were seen high up upon the towering face.

"Grooming the slopes," said Tammy. "Good. That means there is snow."

"Well, you can see the snow, can't you?" said Jesse, tired of the subject.

They exited, and Shean stopped down at the intersection. A crowded shuttle bus chugged by, with a side ski rack, and Shean turned and ambled down the long road toward the Hammersley ski village, that lay in the base area of the looming and now closer mountain. From this distance the town was a twinkling wonderland of many hundreds of lights, that shined on the snow covered roof tops blanketing the scene.

As she beheld this panorama, Beatense felt insecure. The people she was with knew where they were going, of course, but she wasn't familiar with the place herself.

They turned down the busy Chuckwagon Way, that had more pedestrians than vehicles. Hammersley Transit shuttle buses went dieseling back and forth, giving Beatense the uncertain feeling that comes when everyone else knows what they are doing and where they are going. Laughing, shouting girls and guys walked with each other right out in the snowy street, and kids chased ahead of their parents who tried calling them back. This was a world of comfort, wealth and serenity.

The skiers and other visitors strolled along the old time wooden sidewalks, and happy revelers swarmed into and out of the many eateries and saloons. All these replicated that charming, down-home-on-the-old-ranch or farm theme, and everyone was country friendly, judging from their toothy smiles and cowboy hats.

Shean parked across from the cavernous Hedlund Lodge. Jesse told Beatense that it housed the gondola loading operation, and the ticket and rental facilities, and also restaurants, clubs and stores. The girl nodded agreeably, but as a worried non skier in a strange new world it meant nothing to her.

She had far more interest in the big horse drawn hayride sleigh, packed full of joyous skiers, that jingled merrily by as free transit. *Ring-ring! Ring-ring! Ring-ring!* Then an actual stagecoach rolled by with high-stepping horses. With the light fall of snow it was a magical scene, and snow topped anything that was halfway stationary with huge marshmallows. As the others yelled over the snow surplus Beatense tried sharing in the excitement, but for once she had lost control of her situation.

"Dad! Dad! I told you there was snow! No one believed me!"

"My boy, you're not in the clear yet! That could be goat feathers!"

"Put her there, Jesse!" Shean shouted. "All forgiven! I can hardly wait!"

"Just so I don't have to ski with Beatense," said Ned coldly, getting a shove.

"I tell you what," said Tony. "Let's hop in and get the lift tickets right now!"

"Yeah! Good idea!" even Tammy, *Tammy*, yelled, as Beatense wanly smiled.

Her vain confidence was severely tested, life's way of getting her back.

The van might have been illegally parked, but as Beatense shivered they all ran and mobbed into the Hedlund building regardless. One of the six sales windows was open in the darkened lobby area, and a couple skiers were just walking away from it.

"Well-well-well, if it isn't the Shattuck deadheads!" said the girl on duty.

She presented a problem to Beatense, never had she seen a age twenty woman so thrilled with her existence as a splendid human being. She had an open, *perfect teeth* smile for her old friends, and her narrowed eyes may have looked that way from far north pedigree heritage, where the snow is blinding. She wore a tight necklace of beads about her long strong neck, and her rib knitted, open necked T-shirt revealed other necklaces of woven thongs and gold. Her blond hair fell in radiant ripples and spirals, and her lovely details of form included her marvelous slim arms. Like Waffle Knit, the Rocker girl and Peachy Cream she was kissed with shining tawny burn.

"Hi, Laurie!" said Tony. "This is Beatense. She's going to try some skiing."

For all her iron pride she did smile at her. "Hey, Book. Hate your tan."

"How did you know that's me?" -- /-- "Airport photos. But you changed outfits."

"At least she's in one," said Jesse. "But Lor, are our season tickets still good?"

"You guys, half price, but your famous friend is full price. Hey, Tam, Ned."

Laurie had to get more tickets, she walked with shoulders unmoving as her waist lightly swung. Nodding to the muffled cacophony of a remote dance band, Beatense stepped over to look at the big trail map mural painted right on the wall. The lift runs showed as thick black lines, and the slopes were wide white bands crisscrossing the twin peaks. The front one was called Mount Plymouth, and the taller one behind was Mount Molloy. The monstrosity of this mountain panorama overwhelmed her.

"What are you looking at, Beatense?" said Tammy, who joined her.

"Look at this! Where do you even start? How do you know where to go?"

"Oh, I got you this trail map, Beatense! Here!"

She opened it, and besides photo-session grinning ski instructors, she saw the same confusing jumble of slopes and trails, but she wisely nodded to Tammy. A mob of young tan kids came running in, all with expensive sweaters and lives, who made Beatense feel even more insecure. This was a world of exclusive pampered wealth that she had no idea of, where the privileged people played. Money seemed to be in the air itself, and though rich herself Beatense felt intimidated, out of her league.

"Well, we're set," said Tony, turning from the window. "Thanks, Laurie."

"Sure, Tony, thank *you!* And Jesse, just a friendly warning, the Ski Patrol will be laying for you. I told them to watch for an ugly kid with shifty eyes who falls a lot."

"Thanks, but with me, there is no Ski Patrol."

Except Beatense and Ned, everyone laughed. They returned to the van.

Away from that snooty, noisy lodge, Beatense felt better as she got back in the van. They drove on and got out at the Gold Camp lodging, and the shivering girl set her skis on her shoulder to carry them in. Her doubts left as she eyed their high tech graphics, and even the waxy red of the long poly bottoms had a sporty flair.

Also boosting her morale a little, she, they, would be staying in a jetset condo.

The cheapest ski condominiums are just studio rooms, often sleeping ten. They have just one bathroom, a kitchenette, patio doors that lead out onto a small balcony, rugged sofas that fold flat into double beds, and a fireplace. The Shattucks had a bigger lair because of their longer stays, and Tony had his own room. As he went in, Beatense was excited to see a tanning bed within, familiar from her magazines.

Shean and Tammy put it to use for high tension voltage once they were settled. Jesse built a fire, and soon its crackling sounds were added to the news on TV, the micro popcorn in progress, and the fans of the bed beyond the closed door.

"Used to be sex was for adults only, Beatense. All very mysterious, the kids discussed it secretly if they even knew about it at all. Now they took it over, so of course it's off limits to us. What gets me mad is how we just by law handed it over. Now what do us parental providers have that is ours and ours alone? Bill paying."

Jesse was lounging on one of the sofas. "The older generation speaks."

"Someday you will be the older generation. Not that you're concerned."

"Shit, no. But relax, they're not doing it."

"I know, son, and I apologize. They don't want to crack the plastic."

Tammy's cry rang out like a shot, then more cries. The two lovers emerged later hand in hand. Tammy smiled joyously shy, and Beatense felt her eyeballs strain at Shean, the boy who rode into the city to show off his tan. In his raggy cut-offs that all but sagged from his light hips, the same cut-offs he wore to wait on customers, this leaned streak of bake looked like a carving of heat shined dark chocolate. Tammy wore a lone pair of shorts roughly stitched together from buckskin scraps.

They knew what a stunning couple they made, so when Beatense went in to try a session she set the dial at "Mega Blast" to get even. She lay upon the acrylic surface with blood afire. As the long blue tubes pink-pink-pinked into action, she pulled the cover down and slept as the fans fought the increasing heat.

She didn't awaken until the powerful bulbs blinked off, and as the girl got up she was astounded at the sweat that puddled on the plastic surface. She put her swirl shirt and shorts back on and went out and fell beside Jesse on the sofa.

"Ah, this sofa is much better than the one Ned is on." --/-- "It is not!"

"How did it go in there?" said Jesse. "You smell like you really got hit."

"I do?" She sniffed at her arm. "Yeah! Talk about accelerated baking!"

Tony stared. Heat waves seemed to smoke from her.

"B-Beatense? I w-was wondering if you w-would like to go down with me to this hangout where I have some friends. Just to check it out."

She held her arm straight out to inspect it. "I would say no, but I am in the obligatory position of owing you for inviting me on this trip."

"Well, since you're so excited about it I won't feel guilty taking you. Shean, get decent and go get some ice cream for your siblings. Here's a tenner."

Shean took the money. "I can get service like this," he said.

"It is summer," said Jesse, as his brother carefully looked down at himself.

Beatense ducked into the bathroom and took her weapon tight jeans and chaste Aunt Clara out of her backpack. She got them on and stepped back out.

With the Aunt Clara resting to her firm breasts she shook back her blond jungle braided fall of thick, stray dried hair, tied with thongs. Tony stared, shaking.

"You... You can't go like that!" --/-- Arm held protectively. "I'm not naked!"

Even Ned saw she was rather the sensual animal. Her bared waist looked even smaller, because of her jeansed eleven inch hips. Tony had to agree to this, but he didn't want anyone to think he was showing her off.

"Well, get your shoes on and let's go. Shean, get that ice cream, and buy grub."

The two left and with Beatense shivering they walked the long swing down to the main village. Light snow was dusting down, and that, along with the old-time street lights and cozy shop windows, created a warm but of course fake holiday spell. The covered wooden sidewalks were crowded. Beatense drew stares. The two took the outside steps up to the second floor Monk Under and went into the clamorous den.

Tony was called over by some young patrons. "Hey, dude! Slide over!"

"Yeah, you owe us a round! Not that we're keeping track!"

Tony waved to his ski bum, shuttle driver, ski instructor, lift operator and service personnel friends, sitting at the tables that they shoved together. These thin young women who cleaned the rooms between bookings or worked the bars, restaurants or various shops. Their hair was milkmaid braided for that long necked competent look. Along with the others, they had no idea that they also invited over that tan babe.

Everyone wildly stared as the two approached.

"Hi, T-Tony. So you're b-back, hah?"

"Here for some skiing, are you, Tony? Can you... Like introduce us?"

This seemed like a delicate request to Tony. How could he explain this savage? Lavishly baked and bone thinned, she reeked of sophisticated, sexual power, sizzling and snapping. How would he even know such a woman? Her rippled, dark tan belly flexed like a snake. Her light chain held to her slim waist, and in turn her three-inch zipper jeans held ridiculously low to her child's hips. Her outshifted breasts were like peaches. Though child-like in her lines she had body builder muscle.

"I'm... I'm Mr. Shattuck's, uh, companion," she said blurted. "Er, h-hi."

Everyone except the upstaged girls answered with elaborate loudness.

"Hi! Hi!" And then, "You're the Book Girl!"

That made it okay, especially as the others in the bar had turned for a look. The actual famous girl herself! A collective sigh of acceptance arose as she sat down.

Beatense turned on her sacred eyes mood and was then friends with everybody. Even the overworked lodging maids felt that uplift. After all, she was a star, and it seemed that she was drawing upon them instead of them upon her. Everyone felt reassured, but in the bar's dim lighting her bared skin shined luxuriously silken black. Even as clothed she burst with elaborate tension. Her nips poked into her Clara, her collarbones jutted, and her wild hair was partially braid laced. She had biceps like tennis balls, but her evident thigh muscles were slight from the stretch of her legs.

"B-Boy, you're... You got da t-tan," Mark ventured, vulgarly staring.

"Thanks. My atomic genes make me a tanning natural. Plus I really work at it!"

"We know," said one fellow. "The Field. Sorry, but you are public."

"Yeah like that gallop this afternoon," said another. "Unbelievable."

The talk went back to snow conditions, a subject of great concern to these skiers and workers, especially so late in the season. Tony ordered two pitchers.

"S-So, d-do *you* ski, m-miss?" Brian asked, as the beer was poured.

"No. Up my way I never even heard of it. I'm worried I'll really flub it up."

"N-Not at all," said Wreck, surprised by this concession. "Y-You j-just relax and it will go okay. Just go down at an angle and carve your turns."

The others nodded in comradely agreement, but no one believed her protest of her skiing ability. Her athletic presence was overwhelming. The talk turned to her habits. They all had seen the videos of her running, blade skating, walking, surfing, and even biking naked. Even a telephoto camera on a rooftop a block away got her and Sim. She obviously loved sex, and this they understood. Ski village women were easy.

Then almost impossibly Beatense was upstaged. A tall, willowy girl, like Waffle Knit, joined them. Her flared cocktail dress was severely short. She had an elegant tan of baked caramel, and even though her sleek lines and slimmed limbs could halt a battleship, she had an ironic, self effacing smirk. She was sveltely graceful, but not naturally so. The ease of her moves told of long hard training. She wore a white cloth strip tied over her tight sun kissed bicep.

Her short-cut hair was impatiently thrown straight back, exposing her high, clean chiseled forehead. This spoke of a Tandra or Bondy like irreverence, with blue pertly alert. She had firmed features, those of a ruggedly dependable team player, and she sat with the back of her chair between her tan shined, live action legs. Her legs were appropriate for the building tensions in the place.

"Hi, guys. Hey, gals. Tony, welcome back!"

"Hi, McKinley," said Brian, with easy familiarity. "How's the rafting going?"

"Oh, the usual... Oh, hi, you're the Book Girl! Your tan is worse in real life. But anyway, Brian, it's the usual flat-landers. This one lady screamed as we entered Lantern Canyon." The guys laughed, they could relax with this girl.

"What did you do?" asked Wreck, his stare benignly accepted.

"We pulled in by Widow Warp and I told her to jump over onto that big rock, and said I would hike back later and rappel down the cliff and haul her out."

"I bet that shut her up." --/-- "Suddenly that raft looked much safer. When we finally got back I confided that I was scared myself the first time, and she tearfully thanked me." --/-- "Were you really scared?" Lloyd asked. *McKinley?*

"Most assuredly not, but I did get a twenty out of it. But hey, how did you happen to join us here in this dive? That is one bitching tan! Name's McKinley."

Beatense had no problem with this girl. She indeed did look strong enough to pull someone up a cliff, so why not admire her like everyone else, and make some points here? She saw girls all the time who beat her out. Pink T Shirt, Stel, Tiffany...

"Hi, I'm Beatense, McKinley. Tony's friend. You're really b-beautiful."

"Beautiful. *Ha!* I question the good of that. You too struggled with heavy grocery bags as you tried to shut the car door with your hip, and you too got gas standing in greasy puddles. You pay the same high rent and prices as everyone else too."

"That, and shoveling coal into the furnace at three AM," Beatense added.

"Uh, exactly. And your car payments are wretchedly high too. And if it's snowing or below zero there you sit scraping your windows to leave for class or job. No one says, 'Oh, you're so beautiful, let us subsidize you.' No, we meet with crude insults or gotcha indifference, and we labor in grinding obscurity while fatties hate us, when all we want is just one good, reassuring yell-out-loud fuck."

"No shit," said one of the maid girls, who was just so skinny. Luminous eyes.

McKinley's perceptions and indirect compliment toward Beatense explained her popularity. Everyone saw Beatense's admiration, and this raised her stock.

"But McKinley, your working to make your own way just makes you all the more beautiful, because it hones and toughens you. You develop character."

This remark was favorably received, but Beatense didn't notice; she saw Rocker Girl at the bar, or it was another girl who uncannily looked like her. But at these high altitudes there was a cookie-cutter look that all these sunny outdoor girls shared.

She was with Grit Guy, or someone who looked like him.

Beatense overheard the girl exclaim, "I've been up here over a year now!"

Grit beard-ishly and shotgun-ishly and downhome-ishly and dog owner-ishly and wood stove-ishly nodded, deciding this girl was no new-ish flat-lander.

The jukebox kicked back in and McKinley danced with Steve. She did a rocking, sideways twisting that was so fast her light dress kept swinging the wrong way, as it floated. She wasn't trying to show any overt erotic unleashing, her athletic prowess and long, steely legs were show-stoppers quite without mixing sex into it.

Besides, these guys were all old friends. Beatense was awed by her inspired performance, then Mark asked her out and she stepped uncertainly out to the floor. All the lift operators and lodge employees in the joint stared. Her spindly, jean sheathed legs and adolescent lines promised McKinley stiff competition.

She unleashed a whirlwind of terror, recalling her Puppet days. Tony was beside himself watching. At song end she returned to the table and took off her Aunt Clara. Thusly bared the hot tanned girl danced with Kevin, working her waist like a pinned python. As Tony condemned himself for even thinking such terrible thoughts, it did seem that Beatense also wanted a reassuring fuck.

When this riot ended he stood, only to see Lloyd take her. Smiling widely, the bendy baker went into twitchy contortions as she "expressed" herself. Steve took the surprised skinny maid out to the floor, and Tony clutched his head in grief.

"Tony, what's wrong? Are you okay?"

"Oh, Wreck. Yeah, I was just… Th-This altitude, and the cigarets…"

"Well, it's not bad enough for the smoke alarms, yet. Can she dance."

They returned to the table and Tony took her. After all, as her host he had some rights. She refused. He dragged her out, she twisting and yelling.

"Tony! You can't dance with me! Let me go, you creep! Help! You guys!"

"You dance with me or you find someone else to ski with tomorrow."

"Okay, but I plan to hit the tanning bed instead of skiing anyway!"

He was enraged, bringing her along was a stupid idea if not disastrous.

He had no preparation for this. She leaned back with one leg disjointedly stuck out, and she used that long limb to snap her hips in herky-jerk shakings of dire need. She clasped her hands high over her thrown-back head, showcasing her long neck and beseeching throat. She slinky swiveled her wild spine like discs stacked on a rubber band. Her waist hypnotically whipped, as her ripples sequentially tensed.

Lesta and Courtlyn once had a very observant student.

The songs all flowed together. Levitated by the music, Puppet's flexy spine gave her dangling hips and stepping legs lethal moves. Meanwhile in enticing Steve the demure little maid enacted her own demons, as the aristocratic Rocker Girl, all set to throw herself (wholesomely) over to old Grit, excitedly made her own moves.

Other pairings seemed to share the same goal. And this was just a bar for the locals; the flat-land tourists didn't even know about it. Finally everybody had to get going, thankfully there were jobs the next day, and the next. McKinley and Lloyd left together, and The Tan also left, just in her jeans, with Tony.

"Where did you learn to dance like that, Beatense? That was incredible!"

"I know! I want you to reassure me, Tony, with a good yell-out-loud fuck!"

He was spinning in a black cauldron of clawing fog. No, he just could not.

The two were halfway up the long swinging condo drive. It was late, few people were out, many windows were darkened. The white mountain loomed.

"Why did I have to drag you out onto that floor?"

"Oh, you played that perfectly! I was embarrassing you, but for you to grab and drag me like that, it was like for once I had a guy take charge with me."

"That… That was all an act?"

"Of course! I mean, there I was by the pool and you left me to my own devices. I thought, I gotta get this guy one way or another! So let's do it!"

They entered the building and silently rode the elevator up. They read the note taped to the door. Beatense was to sleep with Tammy. They went in and found the kids supposedly asleep. Tony gladly escaped to his room.

Beatense undressed and slipped in with Tammy. "Hi, kid. Wanna play?"

"Beatense, you don't have to lez with me, you know. Go in with Tony!"

"Shhh. The note said to sleep with you, and it wouldn't be right."

"Oh, bull. That note was just to… Oh, you wised up!" Beatense had left the bed and stepped away. "Hey, Shean! Hurry! I really want it!"

She went to Tony's door and stepped in. She sat upon the bed, sagging lankily back on her hand, knee up. The dunes girl's bony shoulder poked up and her wet black hide shimmered. Tony shook as she warily eyed him in the dim lamplight.

Half turning, writhing the muscles held by her gold chain, she coughed with slim bicep bulged. Tony shook. Her relaxed yet tensioned body was flexed like tempered steel, and her hips jutted. Tony shook. Her delectable little apples quivered, and her smoking sun residues gave her taut skin a lurid shine. There were other points of interest, including a pulsating split. Tony shook. Her hardened muscles were tough like cartilage, pulled tight under her greasy gleam. All this was incongruous with the child's shyly inviting smile lighting her bone hungered face. She fell back opening.

44

CABLE CAR

Beatense awoke early the next morning, and Tony closely nuzzled her. Her skin still had a stiff smell from the tanning bed and all-night exercise.

"Tony!" Sitting up, covering her mouth, with her bicep bulged, she coughed. She was black skinned. Her belly was curved in painfully. Her voice was husky. "Stop that! What t-time is it? Are we... Are we having more sex? I hope?"

What dainty little breasts! Look at that tan! Such thin arms!

"N-No. Not... Recommended. And the time? It's too early to get up."

Now cross-legged, she leaned back on her hands. Her hipbones stuck out. Eyes smoking, she squirmed her sunk-curved, rippled belly.

"What do you mean, not recommended? I'm not through yet!"

"I mean, if you knew anything about skiing, you would know what I mean."

"Well shit! Tony, for just any guy I wouldn't want more!"

She lay on her front propped on her elbows, feet waving in the air. Tony hyper ventilated. He rubbed her rich tan and she accepted this with a happy little wriggle and a smile of delight. She flipped back over with pink split readied.

"But what time is it? It looks like it's snowing out there, but it can't be!"

"Five, about. And that snow will make any skiing all the harder."

Holding closely they enjoined. They later awoke to the ruckus of the kids.

"Damn those kids of yours, Tony. Why are they making all that noise!"

"Making breakfast. But it's just six-thirty. They're jumping the gun."

The girl leaned over and brought up a vinyl clad barbell weight. She sat up and began flexing it with a sweet little bulge of bicep. Her flashing tan gave her trained fresh muscles a look immense power, which by now Tony knew was fact.

"Where did you find that weight?" **--/--** "Under the bed! Isn't it yours?"

"Damn it, this room is supposed to be locked when others rent it!"

"Yeah, your tanning bed would be a real draw. For me, anyway."

"When those tubes burn out the new ones come to $2000!"

"So the staff left this room unlocked? But we got a free weight!"

Her eyes had that look, again. "Er, uh, girl, we b-better get up now."

Instead they worked, and talked, as if this was a normal way to converse. *Agh!* "How come Natalie…" *Ohhh!* "Barely looked…" *Aghhhh!* "…Tan."

"Nat just gets enough color for a little character, is all. But you can tell with those snappy dark eyes she's always planning some disaster. Like you."

After the fucking Beatense put on Tony's old flannel shirt, that she swam in, and her friend put on his bathrobe that he took from the locked dresser drawer.

Meanwhile, Tammy and the boys were almost bursting as they made the pancakes and fried potatoes and hurriedly set the places at the breakfast bar. They were so excited they never even thought to argue. As the door opened the four kids suddenly rubbed at the glassware water spots.

Tony coughed. "Hi, kids. Er, you have breakfast ready. What a surprise!"

"Surprise," said Beatense. "I heard Ned banging around since six AM!"

Ned glared rebukingly in reply, but he was thrilled with her accusation.

"Did you two, er, sleep well?" said Shean cheesily.

"Let's set up our skiing roster now," said Tony, quietly changing the subject. "You and Tammy, Ned. Jesse, you and I. That leaves Shean and Beatense."

"But Dad!" Jesse said anxiously, like young Oliver looking bereft. "Isn't there like anyone else in particular you want to ski with?"

"Jesse, Miss Colwell needs lessons, and Shean is best for that."

They sought reassurance in this, and Shean was philosophical about it.

"So let's get going," said Tony. "They're running out the gondolas already."

They looked out the patio door. Across the wide base area and through the light falling snow, they saw a distant line of cable hung gondola cars that were feeding out one by one from the massive Hedlund Lodge. The pancakes were eaten hurriedly, without taste. After they finished Beatense felt like they were girding for battle as they got on their outfits and clumped on and buckled their ski boots.

Then the lift ticket ceremony. Beatense smiled proudly but a little uncertainly as she ran her wire loop through her zipper pull and folded the sticky label onto it. She popped on her mirrored sunglasses and got together her skis and poles.

They stumbled out to the elevator, walking clumsily in their stiffly buckled boots. They crowded in with their equipage and rode down. The door opened and they staggered outside, and they dropped their skis down with chinging clacks onto the snow and stepped into the bindings. Jesse impatiently sprang himself up on his poles and clomped his Slapshots up and down.

Sporting his trim $80 sweater, with its rad lightning bolt design and slalom elbow pads, the kid made an intimidating and distressing sight. His grenadier styled tights leaned his strut-like legs into springy weapons of motion, and his own metallic lenses warned that he was a combatant. Ned and Shean exerted the same look, but there was a professional danger with jetset Jess. The striking, walnut tan of his elitist mien exuded privileged blood at play. I saw kids like him on fifteen mountains.

But Beatense was proud of her own snazzy outfit. She, Tony and Tammy were wearing bibbed ski pants and sporty jackets, that flashed with dash too.

"Well, you're doing great already, Beatense," said Shean. "Don't think I'm being funny. Most beginners think they have to fall down just standing still. So, what we're going to do now is cross country ski over to the gondola lodge. That will get you all used to the action of your skis by the time we get there."

"Shean, what do you mean, gondola? That cable car thing?"

"Yeah, that. We're going to ride it to the top of the mountain."

"We are? Us? Wow, I though that was just for the big shots!"

"They even let us migrant farm workers ride it," said Tony. "Okay, are we all ready? Beatense, do you need a room key? In case you get separated?"

"Nah. I would just go in and spit on Ned's clothes." --/-- "You better not!"

Going first, Jesse charged across the hard pack parking drive, to the steep slope leading to the snow field below. Tony, Tammy, Ned and Jesse quick shot down this, leaving Shean and Beatense behind. He showed the girl how to sidetrack down, but within a few yards her skis got away from her. Now skiing, she felt a sudden rush of speed, but she glided safely down. The only awkwardness was that she kept going past where the others skidded to a stop. She slid on by them and slowed down and they chased after her.

"Beatense, that was excellent!" Shean raved.

"But I couldn't stop!" the girl wailed, which should have been a warning.

This broad area, that stretched out a quarter mile toward the distant viaage and lodge building, was actually the lower run-off flank of Mount Plymouth. This sloped gently from left to right, toward the base area village. This was connected by a road that swung back toward the condominiums in a long arc. This expanse was bounded at its far end by the Bomb City beginners slope, that had its own lift.

Shean watched as one more new skier started out across this field.

"Gosh, you seem naturally good at this, Beep! Most beginners would have fallen twenty times by now! Especially coming down from the parking lot!"

"Well, I can't see how you can fall backwards or forwards on these things."

"Oh, you can." --/-- "And let's not forget sideways. Ned, get away from me!"

Beatense felt exhilarated as she glided her skis upon the snow in extension of her robot-like walking steps, using her poles. This skiing was fun! No wonder everyone got so excited about it! And what exercise! She was using her every muscle just to stay up, because her skis, being so slippery, got away from her so easily.

But to just slide along on her skis was slow compared to the skating moves used by her friends and everyone else in sight, and so Beatense also tried that trick. She first pushed ahead on one ski and then the other, and she did glide faster. But her skis kept getting further and further apart, until no matter how she fought she couldn't get her ever widening stance back together again. Finally with legs out at full stretch she could only wobble and fall.

Shean pulled her up. "Try that going full tilt sometime. Be real careful."

Then as the girl dug in her poles for a good push, she found that her waxy racing skis did a splendid job of moving ahead. At the same time she would have preferred joining them in their travels, rather than being left suspended by her poles.

She fell, and although she thought she should have been able to get back up easily enough, it seemed that her skis kept sliding forward, and she couldn't hop ahead fast enough on her hand to catch up with them. She gave up.

Shean reassured her by ringing out with a cheery, good natured laugh.

"Try doing that at full tilt," he said, again, helping her up..

She began to wonder about this skiing. "Hopping on my hand like that?"

"It happens." --/-- "Come on, Shean, what can I do? I keep sliding ahead!"

"It's easier to get back up on an actual slope. Just get your feet centered under your weight before you try standing. Wedge your skis into the snow."

Beatense wondered if she would ever catch on to all these weird tricks as she chased after the others, who began to work up a low hill. Jesse muscled his way up the slope using skis and poles, then getting to the top he shouted various insults and dropped over the far side. Beatense chuffed upward using the gripping herringbone walk like the others. At the top the gradient fell away to the closer gondola lodge in a long, broad sweep. Hundreds of skiers dotted this terrain.

The girl started down, and just as back at the parking drive edge she let gravity take over. In fact gravity seemed even more eager to help this time, and Beatense watched in terror as she glided downhill ever faster. But Shean caught up to her and showed her how to snowplow. This angling of her ski tips toward each other helped. She made it to the crowded bottom of the slope still vertical.

"Well, that's that. I don't even mind not sun worshipping, doing this!"

"Good thing," said Tony, looking up at the falling snowflakes worriedly.

"If it wasn't snowing we could bikini ski," said Tammy. "It is summer."

"Well, let's not stress about that now," said Jesse. "Come on!"

He was impatient because the turf before them was mobbed with skiers heading toward the cable car lodge. Adding to the urgency the nearby parking ramp echoed loudly with car doors slamming and boots on the cement. Skiers marched out of the towering hotel with their skis, and as her party moved on Beatense felt panicky.

Gone was the relaxed pace of their isolated trek across the open snow, now she was caught up in a big chaotic flood of confident skiers who all felt happily at home. Her assets useless now, Beatense was alone in her beginner's hesitant shuffle.

And the way those colorful little gondola cars kept hatching out one by one from back of the lodge like giant eggs didn't reassure her, either. She stared after them as they rode up and got lost in the swirling snow, so tenuously suspended.

Her friends scrambled off, as if getting in line was the sole purpose of their trip, and the girl continued her slow grind. The so-called line was a packed mass of sardine humanity funneling in toward the open door of the cable car entrance. Everyone had their skis off, so Beatense stopped and pushed at her bindings with her poles, and she almost fell over from the shock of not having the heavy skis on anymore.

She saw other Whiz skis, but instead of proudly feeling like one of the gang, she felt foolish as a beginner to have her advanced equipment.

Then came Ned, sparing her searching for her friends in that thick hellish crowd. Many in the crowd recognized her, damn the videos of her dark tan dancing.

"Boy, are you ever slow!" Ned yelled. "Come on, hurry up!"

"I don't know about this skiing, Ned," the girl confided. "I might just go back and spend the day in the tanning bed and sitting by the fire reading trashy novels."

"No! Then one of us will always be a single! Hurry!"

With skis and poles sticking out as if to knock everyone over, the girl lurched over to the "line," chasing Ned toward the bigger mob ahead. More video voyeur stares.

"There you are! What kept you?" That was Shean, merrily laughing.

Everyone was laughing, anticipating the day's *fun*. Jesse talked with other lovely boys like himself, snooty young lords who also had brown faces, silkenly scruffy long hair and that air of conferred privilege. All but one splendid thin teen boy, who would be skiing in a bikini (the snow wetted his dark tan, while his frumpy non-skier parents waiting with him gazed with pride, their worship he accepted as a grim responsibilty) flaunted hi-tech racing outfits, with races-won award patches on their sporty sweater sleeves. Jesse wore several too. He introduced Beatense, and from their cultured breeding the boys politely smiled. They were thrilled for her: Her first time on skis.

As the line slowly digested itelf into the entrance Beatense felt nameless dreads. Her party moved within the doorway, where smiling attendants in cowboy hats were punching the lift tickets and repeating, "Yup, great new powder today!"

Beatense gave an uncertain smile as her ticket had its turn, and she followed the others over to the boarding operation. It was then that she noticed the complex drive apparatus for the cable cars, and she regretted her previous anxieties.

A massive framework of red enameled girders housed giant spinning gears, with some twelve feet in diameter. These were also painted red, but their six inch shafts and machined teeth had a silvery gleam. These sprockets were silently revolving amidst the racket roar of the gondola apparatus, the stumping ski boots and excited shouts of the crowd. And with the loud whirring of the large electric motors, the two inch cable itself was sheaving around the twenty foot Lazy Susan in the car loading area, as it fed in and then out of the open ends of the building.

Just under this speeding cable driving turntable a roller rail was curved around at the same radius, from which was hung a carousel of the carrier cabins. Small drive motors of the same industrial red were slowly moving these around the track, and as they moved by the lift operators waved the skiers over and helped them in the open doors of the pods. From here they turned toward the exit, where they were jerked up onto the thick transport cable speeding above, launching them into space. They shot off in a steady and endless march.

It was exciting for Beatense to behold this glorious sight, this great colossally orchestrated clockwork, and she was proud of her engineering studies.

"Six of us!" yelled Tony, pointing out who was with him.

"Okay, sir, step on over! The blue one coming up! Get your skis ready!"

The pounding roar almost drove Beatense mad. Skis held vertically she clumsily wobbled over to the boarding area, as their car glided slowly up. This was a small, rounded fiberglass cube, with wrap-around windows front and back. There was a square window in the door, with another one opposite. Her friends squeezed into the curved oval door, and an attendant took Beatense's skis and stuck them into the bracket beside the two by four foot door. She was told to keep her poles.

She set her heavy boot on the sill and stooped to get in the car, but since it was moving she hop-skipped a step. She tumbled in and fell gracelessly into everyone's laps. She heard yelling, and as she struggled to extricate herself with minimal loss of dignity, the attendant hauled her back out. He stuffed her back in, and closed and locked the door. Beatense sat with Jesse and Tammy.

Even with their small sizes on the forward facing bench it was a tight fit.

As she looked around guiltily someone said, "You sure are clumsy!"

"Everyone is wobbly in ski-boots at first," Shean said agreeably, as the little cabin continued to jiggle along its curving track. "Even I was. Yes, me!"

"Yeah, my legs felt like rubber fence posts, now that you mention it."

Poor Ned rolled his eyes up. The car ahead of them rocketed off into space, and moments later their own car rattled to a stop with a portent click.

"How come we stopped? Ned, explain this!" --/-- "Boy, are you stupid!"

"Watch that counter-weight!" said Jesse, wiping the fog off the window.

Beatense watched a red cast iron cylinder being drawn up by black pulley guided cables. It paused at the top of its travel, then fell. When it hit bottom life came to an end. Their claustrophobic car was jerked up onto the speeding main cable above, catapulting it off out of the lodge exit as if it was drop kicked. As a low rumble shook their suspended cabin, the girl turned and watched.

With the heavy black cable bisecting her view in its downward sweep, the lodge building, the crowd and the ski village fell quickly away in the flying snow.

"Oh, is that beautiful! That is just beautiful!" --/-- "Sit still!"

Beatense continued to watch until the snow obscured the view, just as the frigid treetops passed by below. Presently their suspended car shakingly clunked over the pulleys of the central support tower, that quickly fell away into the snowy haze, so this meant they were halfway up the great mountain.

Shean opened his trail map. "Listen up. For starters we'll hit Spillway, which is Intermediate. We could do an Easiest first, but you're beyond that."

"Maybe we should have taken Bomb City a few times," Tony reflected.

"So after Spillway," continued Shean, "we'll run Lift Alley over to the Ruby lift and take it up to Blood Cougar. We ski that down to the Emerald lift. See? That we take back up to the lodge, that we're coming up to now. Sound okay?"

"Yeah. It almost could be fun. Silence, Ned. Look, what's this Tuckville?"

"They call it that because skiers all drop into racing tucks on it as we come down off the mountain," said Jesse. "Actually it's an Easiest."

"Well, maybe I should ski there, then." --/-- "You ski where we tell you!"

"Hold it," said Tony. "We're coming into Gun Barrel Lodge now."

Beatense leaned forward to see, watching as the mountain top lodge glided down toward them. The gaping dark interior swallowed their car up, and as it dropped off from the high speed cable onto the slower rail, it bounced and swung.

A lift attendant quickly unlocked and opened their door and waved everyone out. Beatense extricated herself first from the moving gondola, and her friends followed. Scuttling in her clumsy boots, she grabbed her skis out of the rack and jittered out of the way as the next car arrived. Once again she felt like she was in a madhouse.

The hammermill roar of the gondola unloading operation unsettled her. And she had another new trick to learn, that of getting down the snowy wet cement steps that led out of the building in her wooden-like boots. No, again it was her legs that were wood, she had to take the steps one by one, holding to the 2x4 banister.

45

NIGHTMARE

This caution was justified, but she had to be careful not to hit some idiot with her skis, that were perched on her shoulder like a giant scissors.

Beatense lurched after Shean, as he went out into the crowded yard and halted. He dropped his skis down with a clatter and stepped into the bindings with good, solid clicks. The girl set her skis down more quietly. Propping herself with her poles, she chunked the skis on. She felt better, back in the saddle.

But still she looked around worriedly. The lodge area was amassed with skiers. Tony, Tammy, Jesse and Ned skied over and said their good byes.

"Good luck, Beat!" they variously shouted to the girl. "Burn some snow!"

"Let's meet back at the condo for lunch," said Shean.

"Forget it," said Tony. "No groceries. "Let's meet here at the Gun Barrel."

They all agreed to that, and the groups separated. It seemed to Beatense that despite his bulk and age, Tony was surprisingly graceful as he skated off with the others. Sliding along on her skis she chased after Shean as he threaded through the crowd. She caught up to him at the threshold of the Spillway slope, that was peopled with moving dots far down its broad, tree bordered length. Her face showed horror.

"We're going down that?" --/-- "It's easy. Watch the others for a minute."

In looking down the slope's snowfall-obscured runway length, Beatense saw that the near and distant skiers were swooping down it effortlessly, flitting back and forth like songbirds in love. Some skiers were moving awkwardly, but it did look easy.

"Shean, that does look fun! No wonder you guys came all this way!"

A large woman drew up to the precipice and, after she adjusted her goggles she dug in and bombed down at sixty miles an hour and cut through the lovebirds. It was the first time ever Beatense had been shown up by someone of that build.

"She wasn't even athletic, Shean! For me this will be a snap!"

"Yeah! So see that sign?" the boy said, pointing down toward a tiny yellow dot at least two hundred yards distant. "Stop there and wait for me, Beep."

The girl nodded impatiently and slid forward. *Finally!* She eased ahead over the edge, and she let the incline take her. For the first second she moved at a gentle speed. But for that second second she quickly went faster, and during the third second she went ballistic. She tried to force her skis into a snowplow, but only succeeded in crossing her tips. Eyes wide with terror, she pitched forward, her chin arriving at the scene first, and she rolled helplessly. She stopped, minus a ski and herself well tangled, and she eyed Shean guiltily as he drew up.

"Are you okay?" --/-- "Yeah, but I got going kind of fast."

"Well, just six more falls and you'll be at the bottom."

He recovered her ski and pulled Beatense to her feet. He cleaned off the bottom of her boot and helped her step on her ski. He sagged on his poles.

"I should have explained this to you before. If you prefer to go fast, all you do is head straight down the hill. Perhaps you already concluded that. If you want to be totally stopped you stand cross-wise on the hill. And if you want an average speed you aim at an angle down the hill. Does that make sense?"

Beatense watched the skiers fly by. No one was heading straight down. But some pampered rich kids rocketing by were awfully close. Kids again! Why not just turn the world over to them, the way they're so good at everything?

"But everyone is going fast no matter what angle, Shean!"

"That's because they're experienced. Are you experienced? Not yet."

She chose to ignore that. She saw another beginner crouching along in a stooped stance, and at his angle he was holding his speed to a crawl.

"Well, if he can do it I can do it. Okay, the sign!"

She shoved off with her poles and crabbed her skis across the hill at a slight angle, gliding smoothly along at a moderate speed. Shean sprang down to her.

"You got it, Beat! Perfect control!" --/-- "This is just so great, Shean!"

But the girl's fears quickly returned as the wooded edge of the slope came closer. She obviously wasn't supposed to ski into the trees, so she fell down.

"What did you do that for?" --/-- "I was heading into the trees!"

"Fine, just carve a turn and head back the other way. Never fall just to fall."

"Yes, I can see that that's a distinctly unpopular club around here."

Shean laughed, but he was the scared one now. Despite her planned fall in a flat area Beatense struggled getting back up. Her skis kept slipping ahead, but finally with belly muscles popping she wrenched herself up. But she saw to her horror she was still aimed at the trees. Shean hung his head and sighed.

The girl started to turn around, only to take off backwards down the slope.

Shean watched as her somersaulting fall unfolded, then he rejoined her.

"Gosh, I wish I could ski forwards as well as backwards!"

"You mean you're not hurt? That was an awesome fall." --/-- "Thanks."

Beatense stood without a hitch. "Hey, what happened? I'm actually up!"

"You did it right that time. Damn, is that snow getting worse?"

"No more than your typical summer blizzard."

Beatense wiped off her sunglasses and scoped out the next leg of her troubled descent. Presently she might reach the sign, with a little luck. She started out at a stupidly easy angle, and minutes later she nervously read **SLOW AREA** as she sailed by the sign. Slow indeed, the sign abiding skiers were blitzing by her in droves. She wobbled on, noting that the slope here was flatter. She swung a long slow turn back the other way. An actual turn back the other way.

"Beatense, that's perfect! I was just going to tell you to do that!"

She waved, but then saw that this flatter area was a deceptive intro to a steeper drop. In crossing the slope's broad width her speed was building up again.

She panicked and fell. Even worse, both skis popped off. Shean pounced down on her, grimly seeing the irony in the mocking sign. *Slow Area.*

"Look, Beatense, just stay up. You'll learn balance if you do, I promise."

"Oh, I'm imbalanced, you say? Gee, thanks for telling me that!"

"And look here, your skis came off! Crouch as you fall so they stay on!"

"Look, what was I supposed to do? I was building up too much speed!"

"In that case turn back uphill. Think about it, no one has skied uphill yet!"

"That's true, I guess." She saw a guy stop to stare, obviously wondering how she managed to be so inept. "But why does this hill have to be so steep?"

Shean tried a diplomatic approach, rigidly ignoring the dozens of skiers flying by whooping as if they had no concern at all for the less fortunate. "Yeah, they hit beginners with this right off the gondola. But we can find an Easiest. Here, get up. Let's get your skis on. But first get the snow off your boots. Like this."

He popped his binding and balanced with one pole, he scraped his boot bottom with the other, even though it already was clean. Beatense didn't see why she had to get the snow off her boots, but copying Shean she did the first one.

"Oh, you should have positioned your skis first. Don't put that foot down!"

Impersonating a construction crane with her leg boomed out behind her, the girl placed her skis nicely together. She also wiped the snow off the bindings.

Shean grudgingly approved. "That's fine. Hurry it up now."

She stood and glared at him. "You were the one who said to do this!"

"I'm sorry, I guess I just said that automatically. Instead make it snappy."

Standing on the slope Beatense discovered that the skis had to be set just so. Tipped sideways as they were, she couldn't turn her clumsy boot to align it in place. Instead of engaging, the binding of the ski just popped loose again. She bent down again and jammed the ski level, while Shean watched the other skiers continue by, reflecting on the superb mastery he could normally display.

Beatense had very little superb mastery to display. She lurched back up only to see a spoiled rich boy whose solemn staring face was a lush beacon of live brown in this world of white. Well, Shean's was too, but she was getting mad at him. And he had on his ski outfit. The boy was in butt-cut shorts, with back lengthed hair. He idly observed her as one would an insect, then as he dropped away backward he flicked around in a steep dive. The girl gazed after him, cursing her ineptitude.

She cautiously toed in her binding and far less cautiously shoved her heel down. The spring locked. The second ski would be harder, because in standing on the first ski there wasn't anything to prevent her from taking off down the hill on the idiot thing. She managed to clean off her other boot and tried nudging the ski on. It squiggled ahead despite the brake prongs. She jimmied ahead with her poles and tried again. She set in her toe and felt that reassuring click.

"Whew! That's a bitch!" --/-- "Your bindings might need tightening a little."

Maybe that would help. She took off, and Shean hung from his poles the eighty millionth time that day, waiting for the inevitable fall. When he finally looked she was still on her way, even getting to the slope's far side. *Well, that's better!*

But the girl was swinging her turn way too slow, prolonging her exposure to the maximum slope angle. Of course, she veered into the downhill trajectory. With gravity at free rein, she catapulted ahead in a fierce race with death. Viewed objectively, it seemed she was in as much terror of falling as she was in keeping going. Happily, a few seconds later the decision was settled for her.

Shean witnessed the spectacular flailing dive that slowly unfolded.

He rejoined the girl and helped her to her feet. She was actually smiling.

"I survived that earthquake! I thought I was a goner big time, Shean!"

"All unnecessary. I should have taught you how to make those turns."

"I made half of it okay. There, fetch my ski, will you?" --/-- "The trick is," Shean said as he cleaned her boot, "cutting your turns faster. You turn way too slow and wide, and that gives gravity its chance. The way to beat it is the stem turn."

"It better work," Beatense said, stepping on her ski. "Because to remind you I'm sacrificing tanning today, and this hasn't been a good substitute yet."

"The stem turn will fix that for you. It will get you down the mountain. Okay, by holding your weight to your downhill ski, you can ride your uphill ski over the snow as you're moving. So what you do is position it out ahead at an angle. Watch."

The boy as stationary moved his uphill ski ahead with the tail angled out, and the girl saw that its tip lay awkwardly ahead of the other. "Now you can either do this still moving, or you can stop and pre-set your ski, like I am now."

"But aren't you tippy like that?" Beatense said, watching as yet another chubbo shot by. "McKinley was right, a lot of good it does being beautiful!"

"McKinley, hah? So next you shift your weight onto the uphill ski, which is set for the upcoming turn, and you can carve it much faster. And dig those edges."

"That makes sense. But that fat lady wasn't going through all that!"

"She was connecting her turns, is all. So once you carved your turn, you set your floating ski that is now the uphill one down beside your downhill one!"

"Can you give me a demo, Shean? I think I know what you mean."

"Stay here. I'll sidetrack up a ways."

Beatense was taking hope as Shean made his hopping climb, but then a pack of expert young kids came hurtling down in racing tucks. As they flashed by one of the stars caught an edge and hit the deck. Although he lost a ski in a blizzard of flying snow, he rolled back to his feet like an acrobat. Riding his on ski he kicked himself over to his off ski, and he stamped it on and resumed flight.

Shean got moving and angled his uphill ski out and he shifted his weight over to it. He curved a quick and skidded to a nice, neat stop.

"Okay, you saw what I did, so now you try it."

"Okay, but I'll ski to the other side first. No need to hurry the next fall."

Shean watched every fool on the hill roar by with sickened envy. He wished he started Beatense on a beginner slope after all. He saw her cock her ski out and shift her weight to it too soon. She tripped over it, and fell, but she got going again before he could reach her. She wobbled out into Lift Alley.

"You almost had it, Beatense! Now head down to the Ruby lift!"

Beatense glided the slight incline of Lift Alley down, between the two mountains, and really, despite her many fearful doubts, it was fun to move along like this. As caught by the cameras she proudly looked around at her fellow skiers as she joined Shean at the end of the lift line. Being so self importantly dark tan of face, she drew haggard stares as the two worked through the line, alternatingly sliding their skis.

"Now you're doing great for a first timer, Beatense. You handled the Lift Alley run perfect. Now about these chairlifts, as soon as the chair swings around to pick up the skiers in line ahead of us, chase out and get in position and look over your shoulder. You'll have ten full seconds. And the next slope will be way easier."

The lift line consisted of a serpentine fence of yellow poly ropes. As the smiling skiers hurried along, turning again and again at the ends, they had multiple chances to eye this face carved Book Girl who was so intercourse-freshened snow peach dark.

They made the last turn and Shean pointed out how the skiers looked over their shoulders as the chairs as swung in, as they also took hold of the armrests. The couple in front of them skated into position, and when their chair swept by Shean slid ahead to the wait line. Beatense quickly followed, thinking of those ten seconds.

She looked back just as the seat bumped her, and she held the armrest and sat neatly back. Their chair shook over the guide rollers (skiers at their desks dream of those hurried little bumps) and they were on their way.

Copying Shean, the girl slid her poles under her legs and sighed.

"You boarded the lift just right, Beatense! This ride is seven minutes."

"So this is a chairlift! And I did get on it okay! But seven minutes, that long?"

Her gaze followed the twin cable lines that tracked up Mount Molloy. The distant chairs were tiny specks where they disappeared into the falling snow. Except for the squishy rubber hums of the spinning pulleys on the lift towers as they passed by, they were soundlessly gliding uphill. Also silent were the empty chairs on their way back down. The snowy trees hushed by, with more snow ever falling. The girl found it pleasant for this aerial tour to unfold before her.

"This skiing is a pivotal event in my life, Shean. It's a sport I can't do."

"Of course you can. You obviously have more skill than you think."

"That name got me, Spillway. I spilled, all right. What are we doing next?"

"Blood Cougar," Shean said, before the tamer Powder Puff occurred to him. "But look, just ignore the names! Just keep your wits about you and try not to fall. You'll learn tricks of balance only if you stay up and don't give up."

"I just wish I could stop. Everyone just seems to lean into their stopping."

"Exactly. And you need to work on that stem turn. You almost had it."

The cable pulled steeper and like me Beatense dreaded these implications. But she shut her eyes, lulled by the chair's swinging jiggles. She reopened her eyes and saw Wreck of Monk Under fame come wildly bashing down the narrow lift corridor's bumps. She was glad to see someone older than ten ski like that, but then as she turned to watch him continue down her heart almost stopped. From this perspective, because of the extreme steep drop of the path as it fell away, their suspended chair looked a hundred feet up. It looked, but wasn't. Still, it was unnerving.

"Shean, we're not skiing down this, are we?"

"Only if you insist. No, we're taking the long way around. It'll be easy."

"Oh, is Blood Cougar an Easiest? Good!"

"No, it isn't an Easiest. There aren't any Easiests up on Molloy."

"Molloy? You dip, that's the back mountain! I'm not ready for exploring any new territory! Spillway was tough but at least I knew where I was!"

"All you have to know is which way is down. Now listen up, when we get to the unloading ramp, angle your skis so they hit square onto it. Then once your skis hit let them slide along, and when you get to the down part just stand up."

Beatense watched the unloading platform quickly approach. It was built on stilts and included a little observation hut. She angled up her skis and they hit the ramp incline with a clunk. They clacked up onto the level part and slid along ominously. Shean stood and so she stood, nervously, and as their still moving chair nudged them toward the drop she saw what Shean had meant by the term "down part." There it lay, stretched down like a flight of stairs right at her feet.

Beatense frantically tried to snowplow down the slippery ramp, but halfway down she only managed to swirl around and fall. As she slid to a stop the next skiers started down, and they almost fell too as they veered by her. She tried to scrabble out of the way, but felt like she was made of wet mud. With her heavy skis she could only drag her legs, ineffectually twitching them. Then she...

Saw to her mortification that the chairlift was stopped, apparently all because of her, but at least in compensation for being contemptuously stared at by the pair of skiers waiting above she wouldn't be cut in half by them. Feeling two inches tall, she wriggled out of the way and Shean pulled her up. A couple other guys skied over.

"Are you okay?" one of them said, as full of "concern" as his friend.

"Yeah, but I felt so stupid," said Beatense guilelessly, as the two stared.

Shean proudly noted their surprise, in how this famous girl honestly confided her situation without denying her incompetence.

"D-Don't worry, that happens all the time," the other said. "Take care."

They skied off. The lift started again, slowly, with loud cable groans, and the flow of impatient skiers resumed. Shean saw their double-takes, as they saw that it was that amazing girl they remembered from the lift-line who caused all this trouble.

"Okay, after this don't try to snowplow those ramps, Beatense."

"I panicked, is all. All of a sudden, wham! Here was this steepness!"

But she realized she was being far too militantly grim about this. She had seen other skiers fall, yelling with hysterics, and the whole mountain was echoing with fake screams and happy cries of laughter. As she skied over with Shean to the head of Blood Cougar she contributed her own cute bimbo squeals.

But this momentary respite was only a prelude to the cruel horrors lying ahead and down. Blood Cougar was steep and also rough, as if they forgot to groom it the night before. Beatense either fell because she got going what she thought was too fast, or she fell before she even barely went fast. The faithful stem turn had long since been forgotten, the wavy bumps in the snow made it too hard to neatly set that angle.

But at least the girl learned how to fall without breaking off her skis, most of the time. All too often her kicking legs felt that sudden freedom as her skis broke away.

"Shean, what the hell is wrong with this damn ski? The stupid binding keeps on popping back at me! Why can't they make these things so they work!"

"You have snow on your stupid boot, that's why! Think about it!"

"Snow on my boot? Scrape it off for me! I can't bend my legs any more!"

Shean grabbed her foot and pulled it roughly up. "Look at this! If you don't care to scrape off your boots, at least keep them out of the snow!"

"Oh, you mean walk on my knees? Well, what if I ski on my knees too so I have less far to fall?" --/-- "Funny, I was just going to suggest that!"

"But do I let out just a half scream or a full scream, just to be *cute.*"

"Don't waste energy screaming. Just get down this damn mountain!"

Shean was done worrying about missing out on real skiing. The continuing snow obscured one's vision, and the wet snow had a sluggish, doughy quality.

At any time he saw other people's skis catch and go their own way, so that even experienced skiers seemed wearied of forcing their will into every turn.

Beatense started out with her skis cocked out at a width she thought would be stabilizing. For each traverse she cut across the slope at very sedate angles, then as she got toward the trees she turned level to stop. Then, propping herself with her poles, she walked her skis around to head back the other way.

At times this worked, but it was lifting the poles to turn the skis by them that was iffy, and gravity always had a way of sneaking in with its help at the most inopportune times. She usually took off like a shot, but she was philosophical; she could drop at least 100 feet before taking the next pre-emptive fall.

Usually her skis stayed on and she learned to get up aimed over the other way. She was happy skiing this way, since each fall brought her that much closer to slope end. But even with her easy angles the bumps in the snow caused her to veer into a steep descent and the inevitable disaster. At one point she lay inert in the snow, an insignificant lump of a refugee of bitter defeat. Shean skied over.

She looked up. "Look, I can't have you always solicitously hovering over me so full of pity and understanding! You're driving me crazy!"

"Believe me, I'm not hovering over you full of pity and understanding!"

"Okay, then just take off without me and let me quietly freeze to death."

"Oh, please don't talk of that! It's not cold enough! Try starving."

"I got a good start on that. Where are we at now? Hell Unlimited?"

"We're almost down to this one rock formation, which means we're halfway down this puppy. It's going to be much less steep now, I swear."

She got up. "Oh, if it's less steep I'll get further between falls."

"You have such a positive attitude. So here's the plan. Down at Lift Alley we will take Emerald back up to Gun Barrel. After lunch there's a nice Easiest we can take back down to the condo. You won't have any trouble with it."

"What's it called, Slaughterhouse Five?"

"Hey, good guess! It merges into Tuckville and goes all the way down."

"All these stupid names. They should name one after you, Nagging Jerk."

The girl started slowly down and actually made it to the tall rock formation without falling. In a sickening display of mastery a bared brown boy flicked off from the rock, and with a hair-floating fall of twenty feet he landed lightly on his skis. The baby face looked at Beatense blandly, then shot off. The girl, her turn to be shocked after her nude bike ride, hesitantly tracked around the slope's dogleg to the right. All too often she was given another chance to study Molloy's varying snow textures. She fell a wearying ten times to make Lift Alley. But this place was familiar, that helped.

Several slopes of both Mount Molloy and the back side of Plymouth swept into here, concentrating the skiers en masse. As Beatense slid down the alley dozens of skiers strafed by her, hurtling down Lift Alley toward their lift-lines, and dozens more were seen through the blowing snow on the slope ramparts above.

Beatense had been here before, she was an old hand, and the snow was better, being packed from all the traffic. She glided along after Shean down to the Emerald lift and got in line. She saw Rock Jump three rows over. Rippled hair to his tan butt. It was debilitating to see how so many kids here were such hot experts, naked or not.

"You people must be borderline psycho to like this stupid sport."

"It is not stupid. And you fell just eight times on lower Cougar."

"Ten. That jump off the rock shook me up. Anyway, what about that Easiest?"

"It's up by Gun Barrel. We'll find it after we eat. Chainsaw, it's called."

"Chainsaw? That's a confidence builder. And how can that kid ski naked?"

"He's probably worth three hundred thousand." --/-- "Well I'm worth that!"

The two took their chair uneventfully. Halfway up Beatense had a thought.

"Hey, Shean, if we were at the bottom of Plymouth there, why didn't we just ski Lift Alley around to the front of the mountain? Why all these detours?"

"Lift Alley is a saddle between the two mountains. We're still way up. It's too late now, but if you looked up to the left you would have seen Spillway."

That old friend. As their eight minute ride ended she viewed the unloading ramp worriedly. But she made it down and actually cut out of the way. Shean gave her a thumbs up and pointed to the lodge, that lay far downhill.

"Okay, we'll go in there and have lunch. Possibly we'll find the others."

Beatense looked down at the snow obscured lodge building. "No, just take me to that Easiest. I want to head down and hit that tanning bed now."

Shean very readily agreed and bombed down the lodge slope. Beatense dug in with a dull snowplow and followed. She got to Shean and he pointed out Chainsaw, that branched off to the right. They said good bye and Beatense started down, still plowing. This did work, Chainsaw was like a driveway, but the slope was so narrow she felt like she was dangerously in the way. And she felt too shaky to keep up her wedge stance, but without it her speed built up too much. She fell at intervals just to stop herself. Getting back up was hard, the slope was too low to push up off it.

Finally like me she resorted to poling herself down, alternating them step by step. She had a vertical drop of 500 yards to negotiate in this way, but flat out it was three miles. Two on Chainsaw, and raceway Tuckville had the last endless mile.

46

GUNTER INTERLUDE

$\mathbf{A}$n hour later Beatense reached this intersection, where the Garnet lift was loading. She saw an iron thinned young lady in cropped T-shirt and shorts, whose belly, limbs, face and long neck were buttery brown. She had that sure, wholesome look of honest pride, just held in check. Beatense was devastated. I too.

Buried in wretched defeat the girl kept heading down, still poling. Tuckville curved from bend to bend as it drifted down. By the time she got back to their building it was about three, and still snowing. Locked out, of course, she got off her skis and sat alone on the snow, watching countless happy skiers fly by and cut over toward the gondola lodge. A half hour later, the *need* of a bathroom.

"W-Well, wh-what are you d-doing out here all by yourself?"

Had to happen. Out of the corner of her eye Beatense had watched as this anal clown walked by carrying his skis before pausing at the door of the building and coming hesitantly back. She looked up, seeing a frat spoiled beer chugger who was obviously intent on striking up a "casual, oh by the way" chat.

She loudly sighed. *That tan, damn her!* "I'm locked out here all by myself."

He was shaking. "Well, ha ha, wh-why aren't you... You skiing then?"

Gee, why didn't I think of doing that? "I don't know how to ski, A, and B, I hate it too passionately to want to learn. Like curling. What time is it?"

"Three, I think. Er, d-do you want to c-come up for some hot chocolate?"

"Hot chocolate, also called *cocoa*." She rolled her eyes up as if seeking escape. "How most terribly quaint. With marshmallows? Oh, whoopy."

He felt incensed. "Okay, it's not that great, but you should come in anyway. You shouldn't just sit out here like this. Wh-What's your name? I'm-I'm Gunter."

"Hunter? You're asking me to come in with you with a name like that?"

"No, it's Gunter. But end of discussion! Have a nice day!"

He left her and Beatense jumped up. It was easy without her skis on!

"Gunter, wait!" He dubiously turned. "I'm sorry! Can I still join you?"

"Of-Of course! Sure! B-But… But wh-what's your name?"

"It's worse than yours and my skiing skill by far. I'm Beatense, and could I like make use of your bathroom, too? That's actually my ulterior motive, heh heh."

"That name! You're the Book Girl! But yeah, come on in! Bring your skis."

"My skis? Why?" *--/--* "You had a bad day, but at least you were trying."

Reassured by that (*He's right, I was trying*), Beatense grabbed up her gear and clattered with Gunter to the door. They went into the lobby.

"Are… Are y-you really th-that t-tan?" Gunter said, eyeing her shamelessly.

"Yeah. What do you think I am? An inveterate coffee drinker?"

Gunter fought to divert his gaze. Medically, he had to. He had hoped she would have said she used that instant tan or bodybuilder toner. But she was far too dark for that. Dark, she was horrific. He had seen her books and videos. She was beautiful, her face was honest and solid, with that bony structure of liking books, doing good deeds and sticking to every character building moral but one.

The elevator arrived with a ding and the two stepped in.

"You… You didn't get that tan naturally, did you?" He pushed his floor and the door closed. "I mean, you're j-j-just… Unbelievable."

"Gunter, this is just my face. I was going to slip out of this stupid ski outfit once in your condo, but maybe I better not." *--/--* "Oh, I th-think you can."

"Thanks, I appreciate it." The door opened and they stumped out.

"A Xanthallado tropic girl," said Gunter, as they stumped down the hall.

"Isn't this Xanthallado?" said Beatense, as they reached the third door.

"Are you kidding? This is Waverley!"

The girl's face registered this blunder, and Gunter laughed. He unlocked the door and let Beatense in. This condo was just like the Shattuck one in its layout. A cat wandered curiously over and the girl set her skis aside and stooped to pet it. Gunter saw that her hands were the lightly muscled and fine boned variety, best seen at the ends of jean jacket sleeves while handling a pick-up truck or a rifle.

"If she b-bothers you, just push her away. She does take hints. And sit d-down while I get the water going, Beatense, in the micro."

"Talk about water, first can I use the bathroom? Heh heh?"

He had stepped away but he could still could feel the force of her face.

"Er, yeah, go ahead. It's not too polluted. Puff! Stay here!"

"Hey, clever name. And I'll get out of this costume, too. But wait, shouldn't you be skiing still? I don't mean to hold you up from that great sport."

"No, I just came back to see if my parents left a message. I need a better phone. No bars. And the skiing today, that snow had a mind of its own."

"Tell me about it. Okay, be right back, old sport. My rescuer."

She clumped into the bathroom while Gunter nervously rattled through the lock cabinet looking for the mugs. He couldn't believe his luck. In spite of his carefree varsity boy looks he was shy and hard studying. Whenever he went out to the bars with his friends he was happy to just watch the cute college girls have fun dancing. That always gave him a lift, but this situation really did not.

Gripping the counter, he tried to keep from shaking. This verbal girl was the most beautiful creature he ever shared a hemisphere with, her upturned nose had that regal fineness, and her enlarged eyes, so steadily moody, were keenly alert.

She was small but tall, and within her ski outfit, taut.

The girl came back out. Her friend was out on the balcony. She kicked her removed ski-boots over to the hall door and took off her ski outfit and went out to join him. Skiers continued to fly by over on the Chainsaw slope, and the distant gondola was still sending up its pods. She leaned on the balcony, dark brown naked.

"Hey, Gunts. Wanna fuck?"

He went rigid. He was aware she was tan, of course, but her silky darkness was a thoroughly uncalled for, antagonizing shock. The brightness of her snow freshened face added to his trauma, as did the tough muscles lying under her electric browned hide. All this was bad enough, but that casual invitation!

Deepening the damage, her blond streaked, auburn dark hair was uncombably tousled thick and mini-braided, as it enframed her espresso cooked face with urgent sensuality. Her hips, nip poking breasts and collarbones stuck right out.

"What's the matter?" She shivered. "Come on, it's cold out here!"

"W-We're not going to just j-jump into this, y-you know."

She smiled. "I learned over the years that delayed gratification is best."

"Er, nice commendable ideals," Gunter managed, as he followed the bared girl in and slid the heavy door shut. "The water sh-should be ready s-soon."

"Sure, no problem!" she said as she fell back on the sofa, set right angles from the door. There were actually two sofas, companionably facing each other at the balcony door. She sat cross-legged, with pulpy split all too obvious. Her blackety tanned, whippety thinned self was laced with live, sleek muscle.

She looked out at the snow with a loud sigh. "*Ahhh!* Thanks for rescuing me!"

He had trouble understanding that this child was so open and friendly. He had seen the various photos, and she did smile for the cameras she was aware of, but he assumed this was just a fake set smile. He sat on the facing sofa.

"I... I almost d-didn't. I was afraid you would sh-shoot me down."

"Well, I did shoot you down! But I can make amends." She set her feet down and slid forward, legs open. "Okay, make it memorable!"

He shook. "I thought you wanted delayed gratification!"

She sat back cross-legged. "Okay, but you have to see where I'm coming from. Up on Plymouth there was this young lady not *quite* as tan as me, but with the same tall lanky lines. In her cropped T-shirt and shorts she was proudly delighted that she was so beachy tan attractive, and she's thrilled too at how her being attractive makes people so friendly. And she would be way more delighted at the time if her being so attractive got her a long, beautiful night of sex. Now me, I'm more mercenary toward sex; I just want deep working fuck, you know.

"If I can get that I'm rich right there. I told my Pop all I need is myself for a terrific life, plus my backpack with a few necessities, including a quart bottle of coconut oil. And my new bike. But then I come here and I see what money can really do besides buy food and shelter. My Pop updated me, the publishers say they have enough FieldNet photos to run a new book, and they have 200,000 in advance sales, and my advance will be a quarter million. Until this trip that kind of money was just some abstract number, but now I'm seeing wealth at its most powerful. And I can buy in."

"That kind of money would be no abstraction to me. And I can even ski."

"Oh, ha ha. Yeah, that's where I come up short. Just a horrible day."

"No shit. I'm an advanced intermediate, but I couldn't see more than five yards, and my skis kept catching in these soggy clumps of snow and heading off weirdly."

"That's what happened to me!" --/-- "And my skis just submarined into the snow and down I went." --/-- "I had that happen too! Up on Blood Cougar!"

"And did your skis keep catching funny in all these grooves and ruts?"

Her mouth fell open. *Uhh! Uhh!* "Plus they had all these idiot bumps!"

"And did you have to fight to stay up every minute?"

"No, I just let myself fall. But your micro just beeped, Gunter, old boy. You better check that water. And your messages. Thanks for letting me be naked."

He got up. "Thanks for reminding me, but the red light isn't blinking. I guess my parents are on their way. Say, I could just give you a beer."

"I'll have a cocoa, please. A single serving. No, make it a double."

Gunter opened the oven to a cloud of steam. He stuck his finger in one of the mugs and set another minute. He pried open the cocoa. He looked over to the girl. She was lightly shaking her thin arm, so that her bangles jingled as she inspected it. She was sitting in a low slouch, slackly curving her whip waist.

The oven dinged again and he stirred the cocoa into the hot milk. He carried the mugs over. The girl took hers, with a light bulge of bicep.

"Thanks, Gunter. How come that cabinet has a lock?"

"We own this condominium, and that's to keep the renters out."

"Oh, yeah, Tony said something about that!"

He was going to sit down but he stood stock still. "Tony? Tony Shattuck?"

"You know them? Yeah, I'm along as a friend of the family. Me being cute, they naturally invited me. Jesse isn't a bit jealous, my being as dark as him. Or Shean."

He sat down with his head spinning. *What kind of a friend of the family?*

She tried her cocoa. "Yow!" She fanned her tongue with a baked hand.

He sat down. "So, do you live down there in Emeraldeye now?"

"No, I'm actually from Arrolynn, and I'm going back."

"So how did you end up here with the Shattucks?"

"They wanted me along because of Ned. We kind of get along."

"You get along with him? *Him?* Would you mind repeating that? Because he can be perfectly pissy. You can't say anything right with him."

"I know. We argue all the time. I'm kind of like his volcano steam vent."

The girl picked up Puff. Her thin, dark rusted arms were those of a piano player, and they made a striking contrast to the cat's soft, ivory plumpness. Her conductive wrist was ever so neatly cocked as she tickled at his scruff.

"What do they mean by grooming the slopes, Gunter?"

"Hah? Er, well, it's a little hard to describe them, but they pull around these big, long cylinders made out of this corrugated metal..."

"Sure, like sections of culvert! I saw them up on the mountain."

The girl tipped back her head and fell asleep. Even then her fresh muscles were tensed in opposition to each other, like an ever-alert dancer's, and her stretched neck was just as intricately shaped in its flow as her thighs. No one is more admired than the skinny girl who energetically plays in rugged sports, but then later changes into a gown that transforms her into an elegant countess.

Presently the brown recluse awoke. She looked around in confusion.

"Gunter! I fell asleep! I... I didn't drool, did I?"

"A little, but it dried." --/-- "Whew! But what time is it?"

"Four. The mountain will close soon, but I would think your friends are back by now because the skiing was so shitty today. Wh-What are y-you doing?"

She slid down and opened her legs, invitingly but also unaffectedly even as her sunk belly squirmed. "Oh, sorry, I'm just so used to being naked, everywhere."

"Y-Yes, starting with those oil camp videos." --/-- "Oh, I started being naked age twelve, but there were no cameras to catch me, then. So you saw the vids, hah?"

He said he did, everyone did. The two drank their cocoa. Then the child got up and pulled her ski bibs on, put on her jacket and stepped into her boots.

"Hey, Grunty, hows about that old Monk tonight? You wanna at all?"

"Well, once my parents get here they'll want me to visit awhile. B-But sure! We could do that! The Monk is a local dive but I actually prefer it."

Smile widened, she put on her jacket and got her skis and poles. "This fool junk. Whoever invented skis should be shot. But stop on up at nine or so."

They went out to the elevator and quick kissed. The traveling cubicle came and the girl stumped in and pushed the button. Gunter watched the lights blink.

He almost heard her clumping boots as she stepped from the elevator.

He started back, thinking of the prospects of the night ahead, and her videos. He heard the phone ring, and he raced back in and grabbed it.

"Grunty, is that you?" --/-- "Yeah, Mump. Where are you calling from? Why *are* you calling?" --/-- "I'm calling from Antler. They closed Fanuel Pass." --/-- "Why, how come?" --/-- "It's been snowing all day, dear, so we can't go one." --/-- "Oh, where's Dad?" --/-- "The chain laws are in effect. He's getting a set on right now. We're fortunate they had any left. We have to go back down to Warner Park." *--/--* "Oh, but can't you go by way of Wiggle Worm Pass?" *--/--* "We're through driving today, Gunter. Besides, that's also closed." *--/--* "Shucks. But guess what, Mump! I got to know the Book Girl! She's up here with the Shattucks!"

"That naked tramp? Well, that doesn't sound promising, but that's nice."

"She's nothing like that." *--/--* "Well, be careful, though. But look, Gunter, the plows aren't keeping up. Have fun tonight, but don't tell me about it."

"Oh, yeah, like as if I'll luck out. Well, say hi to Dad. Bye!"

Hanging up, Gunter's heart pounded in earnest. *They aren't coming!*

The object of this excitement dragged her skis to the Shattuck door. As her new friend predicted, they were back. She could hear them yucking it up.

Fine, don't worry about the horrid time your guest had, or where she is!

Shean was talking. "I don't know, Dad, I try to help her and she gets mad!"

"I know, I know, I know. I'm too old for her anyway. But where is she now? You should have given her the key, Shean. She had to get in the door."

"Yeah, I'm surprised she didn't get the key from the office."

"I don't know how we can find her. I hope there's nothing to worry about."

Beatense thunked in like a robotoid, watched closely by a disapproving Ned. But he was as relieved as everyone else.

"What's this about your worrying about me? Ned, stop looking so foolish!"

Tony turned dead pale. "How… How long were you listening out there?"

Beatense leaned her skis against the coat pegs. "Relax. It all worked out. But Shean, I didn't like your commentary about my attitude."

"Who is good at skiing the first time? So I got impatient! So I saw you make the same mistakes a dozen times over! It would be like for you having this friend who insists on a movie at high noon. Wouldn't that grit your teeth?"

"Yeah, shit, I see what you mean. And never, ever repeat that example."

There was a big sigh of relief. Shean had wisely picked the best scenario for the situation, the only one that would work with her. Messing with her sun worship.

"She kept making the same mistakes?" said Jesse. "Boy, what a loser."

Ned glared at the girl as she joined the others in laughing.

"Anyway, Tony, I have to regretfully conclude that I hate skiing. And now I plan to hit the tanning bed for some attitude readjustment. And to get away from Ned."

"You can go get lost again!"

"Wait, me and Tammy got dibs on it," said Jesse, as the young girl nodded.

"You… You two? But…"

"It's okay, Beatense," said Tammy in little chirps. "Shean wants us to!"

"Whatever your foul intent, I get it first. But talk about dumb, leaving Gunter just now I didn't have to put my boots and ski outfit back on!" Tony felt a chill wind blow. "And there's old Ned, sitting in the corner blowing spit bubbles, as usual."

"You never stop blowing spit bubbles!" replied Ned, to laughter.

"So you ended up with Gunter," said Shean. "We'll have to look him up!"

"And his parents, whenever they get here." She got out of her bibs, showing her bare self. "And Tony, I hate to say it, but I will not be wearing this again."

He managed to smile despite her nudity and urgent fears concerning her visit.

"Don't burn it yet. But look, we plan to head over to the old Packsaddle for some grub in an hour, so get your butt into that tanning bed."

She saluted and hopped to the bedroom and closed the door.

Beatense hit the acrylic plastic surface, lying upon her front so she could admire her arms as she seared. Yes, as her magazines lectured, her thin body did give her fulfilling happiness, because, except for the skiing fiasco, it made all of her life's fun advantages possible. She could play at and take the punishment of sports and fuck, and no one could relax better than the long and lanky lass. Beatense relaxed.

Dial turned to max she burned In the equivalent of two hours of desert sun. Her excitement secreted fluids onto the hot plastic. Incredible unfair luxury. What a life! She reflected on what her father had said before, that they were going to put on the cover of the new book her flying to tackle that fat guy, as she leaped from Spec.

The girl finished her session and emerged in the pink union suit romper she had gotten at Strings. With the little white buttons opened down to show a deep vee of baked brown, her spindly limbs added to her black heat attack. But the kid still came off as fetching, inspite of her lion's mane of dried yellow hair, and showing bones.

47

PACKSADDLE

$\mathbf{A}$h, much better!" Beatense said. "And that skiing wasn't so bad. I did a lot better than Ned, anyway. Being so darn clumsy."

Tony saw the boy almost purr with contentment as he glared in answer.

"This whole place is culture shock, finance shock and self-worth shock for me. If I didn't have a new book coming out I would feel like two day old spit."

"You do anyway," said Ned.

This reply was missed by Jesse and Tammy, in the bed as the fans began again. The girl let fly a series of loud joyful squeals, and Shean benignly smiled. But Tony's reluctant belief that beautiful privileged youngsters could and should play in freedom was sorely tested. The kids emerged out of the bedroom, and clad in shiny costumes of coconut oil, they had sweated quite grotesquely dark.

They calmly regarded the sudden knocking at the door.

Their composure impressed Beatense deeply.

Gunter stuck his head in. "Hi, guys! Beatense told me you were here!"

Everyone yelled in loud welcome, and the two tanners capered naked, but Tony had a dread premonition as the intruder turned to a certain girl.

"Hi... Hi, B-Beatense." --/-- "Hey, Gunt, aren't you placating your parents?"

"Nah, they have to hole up down in Warner Park because of the snow."

Tony shook hands with him, sadly deciding that whatever the two did earlier was best left alone. He was too old for the silly twit anyway. Still, it was an irk.

"We were just heading down to the Packsaddle, Gunter," Tony said. "Er, want... You two degenerates get some clothes on! Want to come with?"

He agreed. As they were leaving the girl turned a stern face upon Ned.

"Ned, while we're gone, why not give a whirl with the vacuum cleaner?"

"Good idea!" Ned retorted, and a shocked Gunter saw the gleam in his eyes.

The party left the building and they sauntered along the sweeping curve of snow whitened road toward the ski village, and then as they reached it they noisily clumped upon the covered plank-walk, past the diamond-paned shop windows.

"Hurry it up, Ned! Sometimes the way you act so stupid, I can't think!"

"You don't know how to think!"

"That just proves it, it certainly is a waste of time being nice to you, Ned."

With neck set the boy drew in his breath over his tonsils in that disgustedly warning way. "Oh? How did you figure that out?"

Beatense threw her arms up, as if appealing to the heavens for justice.

The others laughed, but Ned's pest glared at him with frigid disapproval.

"You know, an excellent way to shut you up, Ned, is for you to donate your mouth to medical research. I can assist you with all the forms to fill out."

"We can donate your extra head!" Ned countered, but suffering as he was during this dispute with the girl, he was walking at her side as if glued.

"Here we are, so shut up," said Tony, with a wink at the bewildered Gunter.

The Packsaddle had a heavily beamed, rough logged construction, with old plank tables setting off the roaring fieldstone fireplace. The place was decorated with old bear traps, branding irons and shotguns, and chuck-wagon coffeepots. The restaurant was boisterous tonight as the rowdy skiing yahoos recounted the day's events. As a failed skier Beatense hated everybody here, and in particular she targeted the flannel and just-bought cowboy hat wearers for her wrath.

The hostess led their party over to a big round table. In fiction there's no waiting. Beatense drew more stares, cowpokes and dudes alike noticed her. She hoped to sit by Gunter, but instead ended up between Ned, who gave her an unwelcoming glare, and the also-noticed Tammy. With no more than some distant pancakes and cocoa that day, Beatense decided to tolerate this place. The waitress came.

She was honey cinnamon burned, and with her facial muscles as firmed in shape as the muscles of her taut slight form, she had that sports active look. In her case, skiing. She was as narrow as a reed rooted in loam earth. She had smartly assured dark eyes and long blond hair, and for a framing effect she had turned her hair softly out, just showing her ears. Her forehead was splayed with breeze tousled wisps. Those breezes of course came from her sports active high speed skiing.

She had on the classic black skirt, that was cut so short one first assumed she was wearing shorts. Her long, slim thighs were vibrantly steeled. She also wore a white dress shirt, and its rolled up sleeves bared her tan forearms. Her opened buttons indicated that she had a yen for avoiding support garments, but she did like to wear several caressing gold necklaces at a time. Over her shirt she also wore a brocade fronted gamblers vest, whose close, back buckled fit gave her the look of one who could get things done. She had packaging that said, "Neat Person Inside."

She hummed with live, sensual tensions.

Nanny told of the specials, and as a goodwill ambassador she patiently replied to the questions that were always repeated with these larger groups.

She rewarded the gloomy Ned with special attention. "Oh, perfect choice, sir! Our hamburgers are famous! And... You're the Book Girl! And you?"

"That Rib Crawl, please," said Beatense. "I probably will share half of it. Ned, do shut up. And how fast will this come? This is quite a crowd here."

"Pretty darn fast! We're corporate, we have a system. Okay, who's next?"

As they awaited the salads Beatense said, "Tony, I don't know about you or your family, even now. Ned, be quiet, I said. So tell me about who you are."

"I don't know how far back you want me to go," said Tony, happy for her interest, "but we used to be migrant pickers. During the off-season I worked the sport fishing boats. One day these two fellows gave me stock tips. Oil drilling penny stocks. You could get a thousand shares for four hundred dollars, fees included in the spread."

"This one friend, Staranne, does picking, Tony. She lives with Torrey."

"Yes, that artist Torrey. So we took the plunge and actually tripled our money, beginning an investment avalanche. I was one of the few investors who chained my stocks along and actually got rich, then got out. It was all a bubble."

"Yeah, like bubble headed Ned. Ned, I announce that you're not fourteen."

Gunter saw the kid's difficulty in showing indignation at her very presence.

"I am too!" --/-- "You're fifteen." --/-- Again Ned tried very hard not to look pleased. --/-- "Well he's almost fifteen, Beatense," placated Tammy, ever the diplomat. --/-- "Yeah, Beatense!"

Gunter worriedly watched as the girl left off her abuse as she received her plate. She included him in her general remarks, but didn't address him directly.

"Oh, Ned, congratulations! You just went five minutes without drooling!"

The pesky nag tucked into her barbecued ribs, a food unknown to her until camp. She had a full rack but gave away half. For dessert they had Gold Bar sundaes, an ice cream slab rolled up in a crepe and enrobed in a thick bed of whipped cream. These were laced with steaming dark chocolate as poured from a little silver jug. Beatense dispatched hers in forty seconds.

"Beatense, you can get another one," said Tony, as everyone laughed.

"I don't know, I have to watch it, really. Do you think I could be a model?"

"Ixnay," said Jesse. "You're too dark. You would have to whiten down."

"Yeah, that nutty nature health look, like Flammchen. But even for bikinis?"

"Especially bikinis," said Gunter. "They want to sell dreams or fantasies, but not outright inattainable impossibilities."

"Oh," Beatense said, not catching the indirect compliment. "Ned, silence."

"But I see really tan women in the catalogs or web sites," said Tammy.

"They throw them in so that guys look too," said Shean. "Or, ahem, so I hear."

"Yes. But really, I think my personality is more important than my looks."

"Well, you got a ways to go then," said Ned sourly, to laughter.

Beatense turned to him. "Ned, you stupidly don't know what we're talking about here, so kindly have the courtesy to excuse yourself from this discussion."

"I'll kindly have the courtesy to excuse you, period!"

People at the other tables looked to see what was so funny, again. Tony gave the hopeful model a cigarette to go with her coffee, and he had his own hopes that she would catch on to what a wonderful life she would have as his bride.

He had to have her. The age difference meant less and less to him.

"Beatense? Are you with us?" It was Gunter.

"Hah? Oh, yeah. I was just kind of thinking."

"Oh oh, everyone duck," said Tony, whereupon the girl kicked him.

"My, what a temper," he said, gratified. He stood. "Let's get."

"Wait, Ned poured his water in my lap, and it looks like I had an accident!"

"That's okay," said the accused boy coldly. "I went pee-pee in the backseat of the car. Remember?"

Everyone turned to see what was so funny, again, and bewilderedly joined in.

They wandered out and strolled through the busy village, stepping into any likely looking shops. In Hammer River Ski Works the boys checked out the skis, and as Beatense looked at the racing sweaters Tony offered her a bandanna.

"Tony, this is the best you can do? And Tammy, what are you doing?" The younger girl tied it to her so it hung just so. "Oh, thanks! But I do want one of these sweaters. It's funny how you can just tell they're ski sweaters, hah?"

"I thought you hated skiing, girl." --/-- "I don't hate the snooty skiing image. Oh, Ned, quit messing everything up!" --/-- "You quit messing everything up!"

Hear hear, thought Gunter, feeling like useless baggage. Like the others he saw how her romper had a diaper flap, held by two buttons as it openly sagged.

They puttered on to the Rocky Gulch Apothecary. Like other places in town it reeked of rustic charm outside, but inside it was just a regular store. The few patrons stared upon the lovely kids; it's the human condition to respond to any and all kinds of superiority. Certain cars too get this attention, and horses.

Jesse showed Beatense a bottle of Solero Bron. "See, it has tyrosine in it."

"Kerosene? Oh, yeah, just what I need."

"No, tyrosine. That's the tan protein in your skin. It gets you way darker."

"Ah, wisdom! Oh, Ned, look, here's soap! You might try using it sometime. But Jesse, you just put this gunk on and you automatically get tanner?"

"B-Beatense, what I saw of you before w-was dark enough," said Gunter.

"Let's go, you guys," said Tony. *How much did he see of her?*

The Solero was purchased, and Beatense rubbed some on her face.

"Well? Is it working?" --/-- "Give it another minute," said Tony. "Let's go."

Gunter finally got up his nerve. "Er, say, B-Beatense, do you still w-want to like try a couple b-bars tonight?"

She didn't quite care for that phraseology, that incriminating little mention of *still*, and she grinned. "Why, heh heh, did I say that? Well, maybe."

Tony froze. "Sure, go ahead, kids," he said gamely. "B-Be back by ten."

"Ten," said Beatense. "You are joking. Ned, stop that shoplifting!"

"No, he's not joking," said Jesse. "Dad, it isn't fair to let them go off alone!"

"Yeah, we should stick together," said Shean, seeing trouble ahead.

Tammy felt a jab. "Y-Yeah, Beatense. We were going to have popcorn!"

"After all I ate tonight? But how long *are* we going to be gone, Gunter?"

"Oh, we were just going to the Monk for a couple beers. Single servings."

"Sure, see you later," said Tony. "H-Have fun, you two. Watch the time."

Gunter and Beatense first walked, then they ran for the lodge square.

They chased the wooden steps up to the Monk. They found it nearly empty. A couple of washed up, purple nosed ski bums turned to look at them, sullenly.

"Well, it looks like we'll make Tony's curfew," said Gunter quietly.

"I didn't really want to come here anyway," Beatense announced at large. "I just mentioned this place because I came here with Tony last night." At that the bartender recognized her with a jolt. "And there are other, better bars, I bet. Me being worth a quarter million and shining all hot slathered deep suntan-suntan-suntan brown."

"Like our author on too many occasions," said Gunter as they stepped back out. "Anyway the Monk is just a bar for the locals and they hate all us weekend warriors. But I have an idea. How about if we try the hot tub over at the condominiums?"

"There? We can't go there! They'll see us! But wow, they have a hot tub?"

"Yeah, let's try it. But to get there we take Shindig out to Chuckwagon, and from there to Cowpoke, where it's just all motels. Your family won't go there."

From the balcony, Beatense gazed upon the busy square of stores, restaurants and boutiques, that were all part of the greater lodge village. She saw Shindig Alley, that was a sort of stroll-way lined with gift shops, wine bistros and comedy dens.

She agreed. The two raced down and crossed the square for the crowded alley. They hurried along through the ambling window shoppers and festive night-lifers as they anxiously looked at the oncoming faces. At the far end they halted to peek out along Chuckwagon. A jingling sleigh glided by. Beatense said, "Let's go on that!"

"We would be in plain sight! Come on! Cowpoke is just ahead!"

Watching for the Shattucks they ran across Chuckwagon and then ran the narrow street that lay opposite Shindig alley, between two hotels. At any moment Beatense expected hails of recognition, but they reached Cowpoke unscathed. The two turned and pressed on past a line of cozy log cabin motels half buried in snow. At the next corner they crossed that street at a touristy stroll to avert suspicion.

"Okay," said Gunter, "past the parking ramp we'll take Partridge Trail behind the Pear Tree Condos, and then cut down through the Ranch Hen Woods."

"Through a woods? Are you crazy? Gunter, I'm just in running shoes!"

They ran on and at the next corner they dropped back down to an innocent stroll, and Beatense bumbled like a lost tourist as she watched for the others.

Again they ran. "I know," Gunter said, as they ran by the Trading Post, complete with snow covered gas pumps. "Let's cut through the parking ramp!"

Beatense sighed, but followed Gunter down the iron edged cement steps leading into the big garage between Chuckwagon and Cowpoke. Gunter stuck his head out and gave the all-clear. They speed-walked the dank, grey avenue of parked vehicles and the strollers also taking this short-cut. Beatense looked around worriedly.

"Gunter, we're sitting ducks in here!" --/-- A fellow stared, wondering what crime movie dangers lurked. --/-- "But it's quicker! Hurry!"

Beatense inexplicably began to laugh. Her pace slowed down to a stagger and she sagged against a concrete pillar. Her peals rang out.

"What's so funny? And quiet it down! They might hear you outside!"

She took a step and then fell against a car.

"Ha ha ha! Gunt... Gunt, it's just that... Ha ha! It's just that until this afternoon we... We didn't even know each other, and now look at us!"

"Yeah, us being such conspirators. But look, we have to beat them back."

He was too stupid to see that this was a great overture on her part.

She managed to rejoin the chase. At the end of the garage they ran back out on Chuckwagon, and dashed to reach the Gold Camp buildings. As she ran Beatense turned to worriedly scan and admire the broad sweep of the brightly lit ski village.

But she realized that this brief stop would be in full sight of the Shattucks if they happened to be out on their balcony for any weird reason. They hurried by the parked vehicles, each with a ski rack. They ran to the door and into the lobby.

"Okay, just try to act natural," said Gunter. He punched the elevator button. "So far, so good." He saw her stricken face. "What's wrong?"

"Gunter, we can't just sit here in plain sight waiting for the elevator!"

The button light indicated the 4th floor. "The stairs! Good point! Come on!"

They jumped into the stairwell, that was black as a cavern when the door closed. Beatense swam her arms in front of her as she edged toward the first step. Gunter, with footfalls echoing, already reached the first landing.

"Gunter, why is it so dark? Wait for me!" --/-- "Shhh! They'll hear you!"

"Well they can just as easily hear you yelling!" Eyes bulging, she found the iron railing and started up step by step. "Where is this hot tub, anyway?"

"Ah, here you are." Gunter led her up the next half-flight. "The tub is behind the other building, but I have to get the key and my swimming suit."

"Forget the swim suit! Is it outside?" --/-- "No, it's in my luggage! Quick!"

"How many floors do we have to go up? And why is it so dark?"

"Two more floors and I don't know. One good thing, I can't see your suntan tan."

They clambered up the remaining steps with only the faint thin strips of light under the hallway doors to guide them. Gunter peeked cautiously out.

"What the--- We're on the fourth floor!"

"What? Did we go up too many stairs? It seemed like we did."

"We must have lost count, all your laughing." --/-- "I wasn't laughing here!"

He could just see her white teeth in the gloom. They went back down, and with stealthy steps they crept down the hall to Gunter's door.

He pulled out his keys. "If they catch us now we're cooked meat."

"Why would they be on this floor?" The elevator dinged. "Gunter, hurry!"

He got the door open and they stumbled in. They grabbed and hugged. Their dangerous adventure gave their kiss special meaning.

"You're so beautiful, Beatense. You're just so beautiful."

She looked at him with eyes wide. "Gunter, let's… Let's st-stay here."

It was a good, very good, idea, but the hot tub would be better.

"Beatense, wait here. I'll go get my suit on." --/-- "Oh, let's be naked!"

He went into the bedroom. That bed. *Almost, they could, actually.* But no, his parents had the habit of showing up unexpectedly: "We made it after all!"

"I thought you were changing to your swim trunks," Beatense said accusingly as her partner in crime came back out a minute later, carrying towels.

"On underneath. Okay, now comes the tricky part."

She hopefully decided to just let whatever happen, but as Gunter led her back to the stairwell she held him back. "Do we have to take these stairs again?"

"Especially now. Watch yourself. By the way, what are you wearing?"

"Isn't it obvious?" said Beatense, as they went in the stairwell. "This!"

They felt their way down. "I mean underneath," said Gunter.

"What does it matter? It's all coming off, Mr. Swimming Stupid Suit!"

Gunter gulped. Hand in hand the two fished their way down through the echoing darkness and Gunter cracked open the door.

"The basement! What's with these stairs tonight?" --/-- "Are you sure it's not the lobby? We went down three flights!" --/-- "Take a look at your lobby."

Beatense looked out and saw a row of washing machines. "Looks like a normal, average lobby to me. Come on, we're wasting time! I want yell-out-loud fuck!"

They reached the lobby and casually walked out to the parking lot.

"Wait, maybe they're back by now," said Gunter, pausing. He looked back up at the building. "Which windows are yours?"

"How should I know? We are up on five, though, not going by the stairs."

"That's yours up there." He pointed. "And they're not back yet, unless they're all huddling in the dark telling smutty jokes and yodeling."

"That sounds like them. Or, they're all in the hot tub laying for us."

"I never thought of that! But come on, we'll take our chances."

They held hands and ran for the neighboring building. They crept into the empty lobby and took the elevator (this time) just up to the second floor. They went out the back door of the building, that like the others was set on a slope so this was ground level. They followed the brick path over to the board fenced enclosure.

Gunter undid the padlock with the key. The hot tub deck was either redwood or cedar. With the snowy pine trees closed around the hidden enclosure, the place was nicely secluded, but balconies did overlook it. Gunter pulled off the cover.

"It's kind of dark here, isn't it?" said the girl, holding her arm protectively.

Gunter stepped over and shoved the breaker lever with a clunk and the glowing underwater lights and pumps came on. The heated water steamed in the cold.

"Wow! That's more like it! Gunter, that's... That's beautiful!"

Which is why I brought you here. "So are you. I knew you would like it."

She eagerly leaped from her romper and tossed it aside. Nude, surprisingly.

She was long, lanky and bendy, and her spindly thighs were stretched very long. Her bandanna just hung to her peach-like breasts. She was a perfect symphony of muscle, bone and brown, with sex athletics her proud specialty for eight years now. She had emaciated bony shoulders and her taut waist was whip slimmed, sinking her belly. She had a shiny hot tan, the sickening kind that radiates. Her starved, rippled belly's skin was tightly applied, and she had firmly hung, veined biceps.

Her braid-dangled, stray tousled thick hair was blond. With uncanny flexions she sat upon her towel on the ledge and lowered her kicking legs into the steamy water. Her belly was painfully curved to her tuned slouch. She looked up with a smile.

"Gunter, come on! This is gorgeous!" Leaning back, so that her tensioned belly sag flexed, the girl lowered herself into the swirling pool. "Ohhh! *Ohhhh!"*

Gunter fumbled off his clothes, and his fool swim trunks. He eased in, and the child sat right in his lap sideways, with her arm happily around him.

"There! What luxury! I'm so glad for my unchubby body, Gunter. It's made for this! Not skiing, of course, but this! And sex. I'm open to the possibility of a fuck!"

The water's filmy soapiness gave her tan vibrant succulence, all the deeper with the surrealistically lighted blue interior. With nips extended, her apples pulsated. Her waist snaked with excitement. Gunter panted. She sat astride him and took hold.

"Ah, big. But look, this water is so hot, the snowflakes are melting as they fall."

They looked. As they swirled down the swarming flakes were dizzying.

They didn't see the camera up on the balcony above them.

Gunter kissed her tendoned neck. The girl squirmed happily and she jiggled her long blackened thighs with excitement. Her joyful smile was wide.

He ran his hand down her curved spind bumped back. Eyes closed, she purred. He rubbed her belly, he felt its tight ripples lightly tense under its chain. Her long waist flexed. He placed his hand atop her long thighs and felt their steely curves. He nuzzled her hard carved shoulder and squeezed her wee tough bicep. She writhed as he lay his hand to her chest and felt her heart beat beneath her bandanna. She resat with him in.

She worked. "We should have gotten some wine, Gunter. I bet we passed by at least twenty Ye Olde Spirit Shoppes tonight." Her tan was scorched hot, in the neon light it wetly gleamed in its stretch over muscle and bone. "You know, to relax us."

They heard voices, the latch rattled and the gate creaked open. Beatense made no move toward modesty, and in fact continued to work. But she turned to see.

The intruders came around the shed. The woman was large, indeed fat, but she carried it well, and her eyes had a peppery spark of fun humor. Her diminutive, older husband had a sort of ironic, eyebrows-raised "Oh what next?" look, as if suspecting that somehow, at any moment, he would face ruin. Beatense turned around to face them and sat Gunter back in her as the two undressed to their modest swimsuits.

They introduced themselves as Elsa and Doug. The other two said their names.

"Oh, Dougie, for once the glossy promotional brochures do not mislead! This hot tub is just as the color photographs depicted it! Why, even the models, caught in the act, are here with their Minto-Dent smiles of welcome!"

"We are not in the act," said Beatense frostily. "He's just in me."

"Yeah, it sure beats the outhouse basement we stayed in last night."

"You... You cleaned up first before coming here," laughed Gunter.

Arm held protectively, Beatense delicately sniffed at the air.

"We had to or we couldn't have been seated at dinner," said Elsa. "Yes, we just came from a spacious, modern restaurant lavishly decorated with posters."

"Posters?" said Gunter, and the facing-away-from-him girl resumed moves.

"Posters," said Doug. "Two For One Corndogs! Skier Special! Taco Bash!"

"I assure you, each menu item was tastefully displayed, was it not, Doug."

"Yeah, plus for a pre-meal sampler you just lick the tabletop."

"I had the Rib Blow-Out at that Packsaddle place," said Beatense, now obvious in her efforts. "Ohhh! It... It was a lot of food but I stay skinny with all my exercise."

"I can see that," Elsa replied. "You think you can't gain weight. Take it from me, mosquito, once you say to yourself, I'll just have that fifth jelly donut, it's all over."

"Five donuts!" Pausing, she held her arm protectively again, horrified.

"Or corndogs," said Doug. He gave Elsa a pat. "She had those tonight."

"Skillfully prepared, with exotic spices not excluding the ever popular salt."

"Are you really that tan?" said Doug, with a low whistle.

"It's the lighting," said Elsa. "Pay no attention, as I am doing."

"I have extra tanning genes," Beatense explained, getting off. "Plus I'm a surfer. Free style. I'm an amazing athlete. You should see me ski. Totally out of control."

"But you're such a stick your clothes fell right off," Elsa chided. "But now us two recognize you as the Book Girl, an honor we shall treasure daintily."

Arm around Beatense Gunter quietly eased the patter around to where the couple was from, how was the skiing, etc. "Us, ski?" The kids finally got out and got their clothes on, and as the devoted couple got lovey, the two went out to the parking lot.

"Well, now what?" the girl said. "We might make that curfew yet."

"Not just yet. The clubs are busier now so let's check them out. We better cut across the lower slope back over to the tasteful village. With posters."

Beatense gazed out across the wide, white expanse that lay between them and Hedlund square. Bad enough on skis, worse in her untied shoes.

"Okay, but with all this skillfully prepared new snow you better carry me."

"Okay, hop up on my back, once we're down this stylish, modern hill."

They threaded between two cars and skidded down the slope from the parking lot to the snow field. The girl sprang up onto her friend's back and they began their long journey toward the village. This snow wasn't groomed, it was rough and clumpy, and Gunter lurched and struggled under his load.

"Gunter, can you not walk more steady? Just stay upright!"

"Well don't fight me by leaning against my steps like that!"

Their wobbly trek took them toward the towering hotel. oThey reached the tennis court retaining wall, and the girl hopped down. --/-- "We better head to the Monk, Beatense," said Gunter, "so if they see us we can say we were there all this time."

"Just keep stumbling like you were before and they'll believe you."

He suppressed his rage. The two cut around the big hotel back to Chuckwagon and ran back to Shindig, only to confront the Shattucks.

"Hey! Where are you two coming from?" Jesse yelled, the pesky little brat.

"Yeah, if you came from the Monk Under you would be coming the other way," Tony said, casually, as he hefted his bag of groceries to get a better grip.

"Oh, er, we t-took the long way around," Gunter babbled. "Heh heh."

"Yeah, up around by *Cowpoke*," said Beatense, shuddering at that name.

"Boy, how stupid," said Ned.

This was a handy diversion. "Ned, do let your superiors speak without your input. But didn't you guys go back to the building, like you said you were?"

"Well, the kids wanted to bowl a couple lines so I just stumbled around."

"I see," Beatense offered, vowing to de-complicate this life of hers.

Gunter felt equally insecure. Cheesily, "Heh heh, wh-what's in the b-bag?"

"Tomorrow's breakfast. Are you two coming back with us now?"

"Oh, we were just finding a club to finalize our riotous evening, heh heh."

"Plus we wanted to buy some Taco Bash posters," said Beatense.

48

CATCHING ON

Why don't I taco bash you," said Ned.

Beatense gave him a shove, just to show how guilt-free she was. They started back toward their building. As the eggshell interlude continued Gunter escaped to go ahead with the kids, and Beatense found herself all alone with Tony, much to her edgy regret. They passed the tennis courts, buried in snow, and to the left lay the parking ramp. Beatense knew these landmarks.

"Now why do those kids keep looking back at us?"

They were doing just that, even Ned. As if afraid to get too far ahead of the erstwhile lovebirds, they were idling along with furtive looks back. Gunter paused.

"I got a text, my parents," he said as the kids waited. "I better find out what it's about. I'm out of minutes. So, er, s-see you all tomorrow, I expect."

This was his set-up line, to see if *she* would protest his leaving. It failed, he left defeated. The kids almost collapsed with relief. Beatense did too.

"You kids take this bag and run along," said Tony, also on the upswing.

They chased away laughing and yelling. Tony and Beatense strolled slowly on, eventually entering Gold Camp's long parking drive. The condo buildings were lined along like disjointed boxcars. Half their windows were alight.

The two sat upon a lowered tailgate. Four worried pairs of eyes burned through the snowy darkness from a fifth floor balcony, and another pair burned in anguished vigil from one on the third. Later the two entered the building hand in hand, and the kids dove for their beds. The girl's hot tub indiscretion still made her uneasy.

Early the next morning the bare child Beatense got to her knees and looked out. "Hey, wow!" Her rippled belly and starkly poking hips were flexed forward, tightening her delicate butt and curving her spine. "It's sunny out, Tony! You should see the purple smoke rising up from that hotel and other chimneys! And the snow is so beautiful on the mountain! It's a wonderland out there!"

"Thanks for the welcome update. Now get back down here, pumpkinseed."

She took a last peek and cuddled back under the sheet. Her friend sniffed at her bacon and brown sugar sun smell, baked in permanently.

"Why do you always smell me? There is another activity, you know."

He burned his eyes upon her golden black shine and live muscle.

"More activity? But I have a serious question to ask you."

"What is this question? And what if I ski today, after all? Can I?"

"You want to? I thought yesterday dampened your interest."

"It did, but I don't want to be the only one in this whole town not skiing."

"Good point. So where exactly did you and Gunter go last night?"

She sat up. "That's a serious question? We just came from the hot tub."

"Hmm, I see. The boys stopped using the hot tub. It's bad for the skin."

She pushed back her all-out-of-proportion thick hair. "It... It is?"

"Yes. It tightens it at first, but then the skin gets all wrinkled."

"Oh, come on!" She looked way disgustedly. Her twin blooms pulsated.

Not having sex is good, but shit. Having sex is shit, but good (plagiarized). Tony's companion very very noisily took the shit route and then hit the bed. Meanwhile Tony wondered about that hot tub interlude that she so casually mentioned. He knew that Gunter wasn't quite the type, inexplicably his chaste behavior went back thirty years, but Beatense had a varied history in these matters.

Following a quick breakfast Beatense, who was in her crochet in anticipation of skiing topless, hung her lift ticket from her belly chain. The boys and Tammy were in bikinis, because temperatures were already in the 70s. The room was flashing from the beautiful, browned skin shines displayed by these healthy kids, Ned included.

Beatense was informed that the mountain had a ladies teen and older dress code until the last run, and so she tied on her old yellow top with its miniscule triangles.

"So anyway, Ned," she said as she started buckling on her boots, "stay here and guard the place today, will you? Oh, and get my skis, please."

"I don't have to, statue!" In his bikini the boy was every bit as resplendent as his brothers. The sun up at the fort had burned him thrillingly dark.

"You better wear more than that, lady," said Jesse. "You will be falling."

"You're right!" She tied her bandanna around her neck. "There!"

Bare in his Cove Boy, Shean approved. Tammy, a shocker herself in her string tied Buttercup pieces, wobbled as she stared at the thin, viburnum boy.

Jesse stepped out on the balcony and he began greasing himself with his Sleeky Slick carnauba wax. He scrubbed it with snow until he was polished to a high gloss darkness. He was counting on the wax to protect his bared black self both from the upper mountain cold and any high speed falls. Beatense watched as this young kid rubbed at the protesting ripples he had in his inventory.

"Hurry up out there, Jesse! Let's get going!" Shean yelled. His light frame was intended only to serve as a rack for the placement of his starvation formed muscles. Wisps of his blond hair tickled at his collarbones. "We have to ski as soon as we can before the sun starts melting the snow too much!"

"Boy, am I going to sicken the whities today!" Jesse said, coming back in.

Beatense, thinking of herself too, said, "Jesse, you look like a licorice whip."

"I'm that tan?" the boy said. He looked down at himself with his arms open. He looked like he had been splashed with oily, soapy water. "By jingo, I am!"

"You almost look fake," said Tony. "But I can't let you ski like that."

"Hah? What are you talking about?" The young tiger boy stood with his shining dark eyes warily defiant, and his long waist flexed with his stance, working his set of beautiful ripples. "I have to! I can't be the only rich kid not in a bikini!"

He liked being reminded of his hard fought wealth. "Okay, I guess."

Beatense went out on the balcony to also put on the carnauba. Committed as she was to hating skiing, still she wanted to get out there. It was quite warm.

Shean rolled his trail map into his neck-hung plastic key tube. "There! Not that I need the map, but I do need the accessory!" Tony rolled his eyes up.

Glossy Beatense saw Shean's white plastic tube hung upon his baked chest as she came back in. "It is warm out... Shean, do you ever quit? Anyway, I'm just doing Bomb City today. I just want to learn some rudiments, and get sun."

"Will... Will you want company?" said Shean, yesterday forgotten.

"I want to ski, not stare! I ask the skillfully tasteful Ned to join me." --/-- "No!"

As they moved toward the door Gunter came bursting in. "Ta dahhh!"

He was loudly greeted, but fakely, and the shiny Beatense had misgivings of her own. Having shared Tony's bed twice now, and still dizzy, she was his.

"So, are you heading out now?" Gunter said, smiling hopefully. He passed his gaze casually past the wet-look skeletal, but she diverted her gaze.

With this type of welcome even reasonably assured guys face terror. But then reprieve came, Beatense did smile. They stumped noisily out to the elevator. They were too many for one trip, so the kids went first, holding their skis. Once they were outside Tony took a photo of everyone. They looked at the LCD, and then he took Beatense alone. Smiling, she held her skis, wondering if this would be her last civil expression today. The LCD showed her waxed rich darkness and sunk belly.

Tony returned the camera to his belt pack, and everyone dove from the parking drive edge to the snow field below. Almost bare, Beatense made this drop with a skilled flexing. Along with her friends she glided toward the distant gondola lodge.

She felt proud to be part of the shouting migration of skiers that grew with each minute. Gunter was stunned by her flashing, black cherry tan.

They got to the crowded lodge area, with skiers in all kinds of swimwear, bikinis too, and even a few nudes. The gondola pods were carrying the skiers skyward, and with everyone anxious to get aboard the girl was the subject of just a few quick photos. The base area was a madhouse, but Beatense accepted this, guessing that with her tan and messy hair, people assumed she was a radical. But the broken necks were caused too by the mirror-lensed Jesse, by virtue of his thong bared, black waxed tan and acrobat muscles. Cameras turned on him and similar other rich kids.

Beatense, also taken, looked up at the towering hotel, of purple haze fame. She saw people waving to family and friends from its balconies. The girl was tempted to join her party in the gondola line, but she had far too many horrible memories from yesterday. Gunter offered to join her at Bomb City, but she said she wanted to be alone for this, to figure it out without all the helpful hints. Top now off, the skinny girl trekked through the staring skiers over to the distant Bomb City lift line.

"Single!" she called out in time honored fashion, but the startled lift operator just waved her over, half the chairs were swinging empty. She skied over and stood with hips set by the angle of her boots and held her chain up to get her ticket punched by the staring attendant. One skill she did learn previously was how to get on a chairlift. With top-holding hand reaching she sat neatly in place, on the cold slats. *Yikes!*

During her mile long excursion, with the seat slowly warming up and the massive white mountain roaring up before her, Beatense saw beginning skiers working their slow way down Bomb. *It's not just me!* The unloading ramp came; it was easy.

The snow was clean and hard, and no trees were waiting at the edge of the slope. Actually there was no edge; the hill was rounded side to side. Beatense surveyed the base ski village that lay surprisingly far below, as the lift continued to deliver whooping skiers. Despite her ineptitude she felt ready to join the ruckus. She was hopeless at skiing, but in looking around she saw she wasn't the only one. She saw a woman fall with a scream halfway down the lift ramp, but the others nearby (who had recently done far worse) just laughed. And Beatense saw a hunk dude with snow all over his jeans wobbling on his crossed skis. With a crying shout of panic he grabbed for the friend beside him. She screamed; they both went down. Beatense joined in the laughter.

"Miss? Could you help me get this ski on?"

Beatense turned and saw a brave older woman perched on one ski.

"My binder thing keeps… My word! I didn't know it was possible to… Why, you're the hot tub girl! Still with that tan! Anyway, my binder thing keeps popping open."

"Oh, you have snow on the bottom of your boot!" The girl clopped over and bent herself down beside the lady. "Okay, balance with your poles and lift it up." Useful even as a sensual, she rasped at the crusted snow with the point of her pole, brown hand at work. "There, now try it!" The ski clicked right on.

The woman was transformed. "Oh, that's… That's wonderful! I was worried I would have to go back down to the rental for another pair! Thank you!"

Beatense didn't tell how she picked up that bit of expertise. She smiled, and gingerly set a course across the top of the slope, in the direction of distant buildings, that lay across the wide snow field. She curved slowly around the other way on the City's gentle slope, without that horrid acceleration, heading back toward the lift. She actually skied right under it. To do this, to set a plan and follow it, redeemed her.

She ignored the crazed shouts from the lift as she glided under it and kept going with legs braced. There was a certain thrilling magic to that crisp *tch-tch-tch-tch-tch* sound of the snow under her skis. Her travel was in control and she could sweep out nice, smooth turns. But for the cold seats, sometimes things do work out.

She swerved another wide sweeping turn and swung around under the lift again, scanning the snow ahead. She saw a rough patch and decided to ski downhill of it. She did this, and her skis, instantly aware of her steeper lie, speeded her up. She gritted her teeth, and with waist flexing she swung around through the turn. This was hard, she headed straight downhill midway through her arc and her speed shot up.

But she held to her curving path, and as she made another trip under the chairlift she restored her safe angle. She stayed up but there had to be a better way. She came to the bottom of Bomb at last, but she couldn't stop herself except to snowplow past the lift. She charged back clomping her skis to the line, of admirers.

She read the lift operator's name tag. "Hi, Fred. No falls yet!"

"Oh, y-yeah. N-Nice going. And nice t-tan. Hey, are you the Book Girl?"

"Yeah! Is it okay if I ski topless like this? I saw nudes over by the gondola!"

"Here, make another run and I'll call in to ask. Step up, now!"

Beatense rode up as everyone stopped to watch her pass overhead. She slid down the ramp and glided to a smooth uphill stop. Up on the mountain she would be falling yet again, but here it was easy! She felt like weeping. The girl worked her way down with the same sweeping glide paths. Fred met her with the news that she could ski topless, if she didn't mind the videos.

"Heck no! Greedy Publishing needs all the footage they can get!"

Beatense made more flights down Bomb City, with each run a trial for some new technique. But nothing seemed to pull that magic string. Her turns still swung out far too wide and slow, and it was only the slope's forgiving angle plus her determination to avoid bruising her tan that kept her halfway vertical.

She had already learned that snowplowing was useless. It was hugely tiring and didn't work. No one else used it except incidentally, if already going slow. How did one control his speed? It was a puzzler. It looked as if the better skiers were somehow using their turning action to also brake their speed, by angling their skis and working their edges. But how *did* they turn?

Beatense watched the other skiers near and far, trying to unravel this, when she saw someone familiar. Who was that girl who, with her noble forehead and firmed cheeks, was so far beyond being beautiful to also be boy-like handsome? And then Beatense realized she saw her clearing tables back at the mall Sunday morning.

"Hey, I know you!" she called the short distance down to her. "Weren't you at the shopping mall Sunday morning, working in that food court place?"

"Yes, that was me!" the surprised girl replied in a wispy, child-like voice, with no inflection. But that untroubled timbre, along with her alert expression, was adorable. She wasn't afraid to admit to her lowly job. "Do I know you, though?"

"Only as a mess leaver," Beatense said, as she glided easily down to her. In her preoccupation she let her skis do the work. "I was with two ugly boys."

"I remember you! How can anyone forget that tan!"

"Beach battle damage. And now skiing. So how did you end up here?"

"My parents. I could never afford skiing, me being a student."

"Me either," said Beatense, not caring to admit to this sheltered ingénue how her particular trip was financed, in part. "This is costing us a dollar a minute, and here we sit." The girls laughed. "So what's your name?" Beatense went on.

She had to admire this girl's nut honey tan, her expressive facial complexity, her serenely accepting eyebrows and hair hiking-girl tousled.

"Renee. Boy, I never saw a tan like yours, er..."

"Beatense, and yes, I can coax a tan out of rain, but on skis I'm hopeless."

"Well, have you fallen yet today?"

"Why, no, come to think! But hey, do you know how to stop, Renee?"

"Sure. Just be patient. When the time comes you'll do it naturally."

"I hope so. But look, why are you futtsing around here on Bomb City?"

"I'm waiting for my brother. You can join us if you want... Book Girl!"

"Yes, it's me, but I would just hold you up. And speaking of I better go!"

She eased off. As her speed built up it happened, she made a turn. It was over before she knew it, but a come-about it was! Why, there was nothing to it! So stupid Shean was almost right! She just had to weight the downhill ski and cut the uphill ski around! She went faster. She angled her ski out, then carved it slickly around and stepped the other ski beside it in smooth succession.

She yelled, "I can ski, I can ski! Hey, you over there! I can ski!"

The startled older gentleman, who decided that somehow miraculously it was he that the girl was shouting at, smiled and waved, while seeming to envy her progress. And Renee, having heard the uproar, dropped down on her.

"What's the matter, Beatense?"

"Matter!" She glided off and sliced out a smooth little turn. "See? *I turned!*"

"Yes, that was perfect, but you're all bent over. Stand right up on your skis with shoulders straight and knees flexed, so you have more control."

"Seriously? I would think you would have less control. But, I can't argue."

She shoved off, standing straight with a slight flex. *More control? Perhaps!*

"Beatense, weight your tails!" Renee called in her crackly little voice. "Oh, I see Russ. Finally I can escape your tan. But weight your tails! Bye!"

Renee raced down, and Beatense erratically zigzagged after her, by connecting her turns. The hard won satisfaction of this was intoxicating.

She swung into the lift-line as a veteran, poles in one hand. "I just learned how to ski, Fred! I can do turns now! It's funny how easy it is, really."

"I did see, Beatense. But gosh, I guess I'll be losing you, then."

The empty chairs rattled by. "Hah? Whaddya mean?" --/-- "You'll be skiing the big hill now." --/-- "No! I want to ski here! Who needs any old mountain?"

This day was classic. The sun was bright; the air clean and brisk, even as the temperature inched slowly up. The snow was dazzling white, and in the blue above, the combed wisps of cloud were edged with ruffled feathers, that had a luminescent glow. The cable cars were plying overhead, and the ones hurrying upward on that great sweep of cable were packed with joyful skiers. Hoots and howls were heard from their opened windows. And presiding over all was the majestic mountain.

With her new skill Beatense now felt herself a part of this scene. She wasn't an interloper anymore. All us skiers had that same kind of day.

Beatense made more runs and began to chafe at the slow beginners glide of the chairlift. Before these tours were a welcome break, but now they were irksome.

After one such maddening ride she shot the ramp and cut sharply around like a fighter breaking formation. She strafed by some brave knock-kneed skiers, but then she braked herself down through a wandering series of turns.

No use kidding herself, she still couldn't stop. But she began trying faster speeds. She stopped to catch her breath and saw Shean riding a chair and gave him a yell.

The boy started in happy surprise. "Beatense! Stay right there!"

"Okay, but hurry it up! I'm not here to stand around for photos!"

Once at the top, his hair a golden cloud Shean sprang down to the girl, and dug into a glorious sliding stop. Beatense blinked at his shining muscles, dark tan aglow.

"Got anything in the progress department?" --/-- "Watch, King Biscuit!"

Shean saw the girl whip out a series of shuttles back and forth, with flowing turns linking them. Then as she neared the bottom of the slope she bombed the rest of the way down. She needed more work, her stopping technique consisted of dancing out all sorts of peculiar little circles, but overjoyed, Shean roared down after her and slashed to a snow (that clashed with his hide) throwing stop.

"Beep, you wasted degenerate! That was brilliant! Now for the mountain!"

"Shean, are you crazy? I can't do that! That's just for all you experts!"

"Come on, you just have to be up there, Beatense. It's to die for."

"I am suicidal. But wait, I thought Gunter was coming to get me instead!"

"Ah, yes." He didn't say how they all conspired to keep him in the party.

As the two started over for the tram entrance, Beatense gave her new friend a helpless shrug. He waved, and the devoted others in line did too. She waved back. Heading into the more experienced crowd, Beatense saw athlete girls in bikinis, with season passes hung from their necks. They confidently shined with muscle and full health. But she could scoff today. Waiting urgently, she didn't pay any attention to the lift machinery this time. She and Shean got into their own cubicle, and as they were launched a low rumble filled the air. The girl gazed down upon her good old Bomb City. Then, as the gigantic panorama slowly unfolded with their car's upward ascent, the buildings of the village fell away.

It was the most mystical and magical experience of her (and my) life.

Their cabin rattled over the central support tower pulleys, the halfway point. The girl surveyed the ski slope far below, and the tiny figures weaving down it cut up little puffs of snow behind them. The cabin drew closer to the slope below like a landing plane. It then trundled into the Gun Barrel gantry and fell to the slow rail. The attendant opened their door; they hopped out and grabbed their skis, top forgotten.

They clambered through the other skiers, and crochet patch Beatense studiously paused atop the cement steps to gaze upon the crowds of *fellow* skiers. The busy lodge area was an exciting place as skiers came out of the Gun Barrel or came down from the slopes. They were either stamping on their skis or taking them off, in a noisy chaos. Crochet patch Beatense, causing a silence, followed slender Shean through the throngs, carrying her skis and walking clumsily in her boots. Skinny girls have an electric, life changing effect, but this smiling girl wasn't aware of this. At least on this occasion she wasn't one of those rare orchids who, with theatrical affectaton, never seem to be happy. Not that this can be in any way criticized.

"Hey, Shean, where dem udders at?"

"Hah? Oh, who knows? It's a big mountain. But look at that view!"

She gave the scenery a glance as she cocked her bindings with her poles.

"Yes. But look, can we get going?"

Shean noted that this remark was in direct contrast to yesterday's endlessly dreary commentary. "I told you, we're heading for Sp... Spinn..."

48

SPINNAKER

He openly gaped. She was in a white T-shirt that was loosely tucked into her trim jean cut-offs, that were cuffed up to neatly show her longs, tan legs. In fact, the slim, curved muscle of her thighs caused the snug cuffs to ride up. She was one of those endearing college treasures with that cutely silly, trusting smile of being very cared for, along with a tautly shining tan that was also borne of few concerns. Her blond hair was full of frilly curls, each inspiring protective love. The joking males surrounding the appealing but silly girl called her Valerie.

"You guys! You're making me nervous! Shut up!"

Beatense could accept Shean's interest, but it puzzled her that he ignored the many bikini athletes. He finally took his map out from his accessory key tube.

"Okay, Beastie, we'll take Rowel down to the Sapphire lift." He looked again at those long, berry brown legs. "Then we take that up to Spinnaker. Okay?"

"Got it," Beatense said, watching as helpless Valerie haltingly edged over to the Spillway threshold. But her clumsiness was faked; with a jump she sprang down the slope in a magnificent dive. "Boy, look at her go!"

"Give yourself an hour," Shean said. "You have everything she has."

Gun Barrel stood atop a broad rise. Sweeping her wide turns Beatense followed Shean to the right, toward a narrow trail that cut through a woods. She got going too fast for her comfort, so she dug into a snowplow and lurched to a gangling stop by the trail marker sign. Shean swirled around backwards, making his own stop.

"I'm sorry, Shean," Beatense said, as skiers by the dozen raced by the two. A few slowed down to stare, not all at the shivering girl. "I got going too fast."

"No you didn't. This trail will be a nice, slow glide. Just relax and ride with it. It does not get steep and you won't go too fast."

She looked down the long avenue. "But it looks too narrow for my turns."

"You don't do turns here. Instead, lean your weight from ski to ski while you turn your tails out and dig them. Shift right, press left; shift left, press right."

She wished she was told this over at Bomb City, where she could practice it with less traffic. She bit her lip and poled herself into the trail, that was actually a slowly winding and snow packed ledge set in against the wooded mountainside.

As she joined the flying crowd she set her skis in a lightly angled plow, and shifting her weight regulated her speed. She even ran straight in stretches.

"Beatense! You're doing it!" Shean shouted, as he came after her.

The cold humidity filmed her. She dragged her poles, so their end rings jittered behind her. Ready to weep, she nodded to the boy as he cruised by her.

The trail was working its way around the eastern face of Mount Plymouth, as the view continually changed. The valley that lay far below was in full view, and actually forgetting her tan self momentarily, beyond the village the girl even saw the highway they rode into town. This was a serene reflection, but the other skiers flying by were turning Rowel into a human pinball machine.

"Shean, if I'm holding you up, just go on ahead." --/-- "No, this is fine. I should look at some of the scenery anyway." --/-- "Yeah. I saw that scenery."

She flew along. This was better than stepping through all those methodical stem turns. Previously she just had the interest of solving a puzzle, of getting down the hill without falling. But now that she was shooting along with her skid braking she had a sense of real velocity, too. Even woth her heavy boots she could feel the intricate surface of the moving snow as crisp little vibrations. *Tch-tch-tch-tch-tch-tch-tch-tch!!!*

"Start stopping for the turn up ahead, Beatense!"

She leaned harder, alternating right to left, to scrape her skis. Shean approved. They stopped at an overlook point. Beatense wiped the condensation off herself. At this point the trail swung left, and then went on to cross under a busy chairlift further along. From there the trail rounded a tree-filled valley rising up from the mountain's lower flank. Beyond this lay the valley of rolling hills.

"Nice view," said Beatense. "Boy, it's cold up here. Funny I'm sweating."

The skiers lingering nearby also considered this. The two moved on, and they approached the chairlift that crossed over the trail ahead. The last half mile of skiing transformed the girl. She skidded to a neat stop under the chairlift, not realizing she learned that vital trick just then. The shouts that normally came for exceptional girls were stilled. Word had gotten around, and now there she be. People hurriedly took photos as she gazed impassively back, with hips set.

Not intentionally, it was the angle of her boots. Her back had a lanky curve.

Shean, bare in his bikini, showed everyone the legendary baking he owned, that was unnaturally vibrant. The helpless skiers on the chairlift, carried away inexorably, had no chance of restoring calm that day. They turned to look back.

"Beatense," said the bikini boy, as the chairs continued their troubled ascent, "up ahead there's this shortcut and I'm taking it. It's an Expert so don't come with. Keep going on the trail here, and we'll meet again at the bottom."

She glanced down at her tensed belly. "I can probably handle it, Shean."

"Oh-h-h, no! It's really steep, and if you fall your tan will peel right off."

That convinced her. She clumped around and took off, digging in her poles with shoulder blades protruding. The two flew by the sapling trees edging their trail, and they came upon a wide avenue that fell steeply away to the right.

It had a very rough lie. Without stopping Shean sprang down this, and with poles and tan glinting in the sun he rocketed down this slope, bashing around, over and through the crowded dumplings of snow distorting its lie. The boy had a wild twisting grace and a precise, instant balance. Beatense realized that her mastery of Rowel counted for naught. Then two black tan racer kids, one a naked Tammy twin and the other a naked Jesse twin, both long haired and wealthy in looks, leaped upon her.

They came so fast they shot up sheets of snow as they ripped the turn into the steep drop. The light muscled pair pounced off airborne and viciously assaulted the steep drop with tans flashing, and their hair and season passes fluttering behind.

Beatense wondered if their skis ever made contact. Sickened, she pressed on down her complacent little trail. She passed by some wobbly beginners, but in the main she was in the way. Rowel was actually a roadway, that briefly interrupted the mountainside's steep tumble. The Ski Patrols, on course and wearing cowboy hats, gave her a startled wave. Smiling, she waved back. She wandered along another quarter mile, and coming around a long bend she saw the waiting Shean.

"You didn't fall, hah?" he said, as she drew up and neatly stopped.

A gang of skiers came bounding down the shortcut and swooped in hard leaning turns onto the slower trail and blasted off. They gave her abbreviated stares.

"The question is, did *you* fall? And did you see those two tan rich kids?"

"Yeah, for two seconds. They're worth a hundred million. Each."

"Yeah. But anyway, Shean, what are all those bumps?" She pointed up the hill.

The two pushed on. "They're moguls, caused by the action of the skis."

They curved the last bend, where their little wandering trail became a wide slope that fell away down to where two distant chairlifts were at work. One was the one they just skied under. Stopping, Beatense gazed down this steep incline doubtfully. Others skiers easily shuttled their turns, gliding back and forth.

"Okay, let's bomb this," said Shean. "This you can handle."

She stared in shock. "*What? Bomb it? Are you out of your mind?*"

"Two hundred yards, but you'll be down before you know it."

Shean hopped ahead and rode his skis down the slope in a smoothly rapid drop, making the bottom in seconds. He tore across the wide flats toward the lift shown on the map as the Sapphire. Beatense held up. If she made it, she could call herself a skier, but if she didn't, her fall would make the headlines. She willed herself to hit the edge. She dropped in exponential acceleration. The wind roared in her ears, and her famed sunk belly was left ten feet behind by her speed. Cameras caught her.

The snow ahead came leaping toward her in a blur. She had to fight the rough bounces of her wild, runaway skis. She was terrified, but it seemed that the end of this cascade was coming up to her just as fast as she was dropping toward it. Seconds later she zoomed out across the flats, and she didn't stop until she plowed up to the waiting Shean, close by the end of the lift-line.

"Hey, Shean, I actually made that puppy! I can ski like all you experts!"

He smiled and gave her a push. Openmouthed, she ingloriously fell.

"I told you not to fall so much!" --/-- "You ass! How dare you!"

The nearby skiers, watching with interest, tentatively chuckled. Shean gave her a hand and she flexed lightly up. Her smile reassured her audience.

The friends glided into line and started the roped zigzag. Minutes later the two looked over their shoulders and took their chair, and it bumped and rattled over the alignment pulleys. They went on to float up through an aspen forest of trees, and the aqua-yellow color of their leathery bark clashed with the pristine snow.

The hibernating quiet lay very deep, broken only by the soft rubbery squishings of the pulleys spinning under the cable on their tower mountings. Voices could also be heard as the other riders conversed, and there were faraway shouts.

"Shean, the way you live in the tropics, sun all year." --/-- "Nah, winter is foggy and rainy. We all fade and look <u>death</u> watch pale." [AP 6/18/2000]

As the ride continued the aspens gradually yielded to shivering evergreens, that were all enshrouded with diamond dust frosting. The high altitude sun was dazzling, and in certain areas the trees opened up into little glens, where the snow lay deep. Despite the far distance already traveled, the lift towers were still beyond counting in their voyage up the mountain. The chairs were being hushed unceasingly upward, in and out of the shadows, as the empty chairs came back down in a lonely parade.

A good sign, Beatense decided, comparing her dark tan legs to Shean's.

The Glorious Tour finally came to an end. Watched by a dozen skiers, Beatense cocked her skis up onto the lead ramp and rode the incline down with practiced skill. She cut sharply aside at the ramp bottom and flicked around backwards and slid to a hot girl stop. She didn't know she could or would do this, and would have argued if Shean suggested it, but in skiing even I enacted spontaneous creativity.

Just in crochet, and wax, she importantly clumped her skis, then smiled around at her witnesses. She had expected to find herself on a craggy peak up here, like in a coal company calendar, but instead this mountaintop was gently rounded. Yes, off in the great distance there were your classic pinnacles, but Molloy was really just an impressive bluff. And yet there was a zephyrous sense of summit pervading the rarefied air, and a spirit of adventure crackled among the skiers here.

Shean led Beatense along through the mountaintop wood, and within a hundred feet the powerful Spinnaker's broad threshold lay before them. This slope was over a hundred yards wide and three thousand long. The lone pines scattered along this immense length rendered a vast impression of distance. This was a wonderfully wide world of inviting white, and Beatense felt honored she could ski this magnificence.

Just in her few square inches she started down at a slow angle, heading for the rightward edge of the hill. Spinnaker was steep, she got going too fast, but just like back on Bomb she edged her downhill ski to slow down. It worked! This technique was effective on this packed powder surface. At a hundred feet she eased to a stop and set her ski for her turn. She hesitated, wondering if her teacher was watching.

No, he was in conversation with one of those fun, well adjusted and sport active athletes whose healthy brown glow can be seen a block away. Beatense pushed off with her poles and shifted over to her uphill ski. As soon as she veered into her turn there was an abrupt blaze of speed. She felt a thrill of paralyzing terror, but the girl fought through the long arc and got back to equilibrium. In the process she reversed her direction, her plan, of course, and now she needed a new landmark to aim for.

She saw a big snow covered pile of rock down yonder. It was a viable goal, and as Beatense glided toward it she looked uphill for Shean's approval. Still at it, but if she wanted any approbation the boy flying by her made her progress look comparatively clumsy. He was only ten, but his stance was aggressively poised for speed.

Slowing down by edging uphill, Beatense came toward the rocks where the dude had stopped, with wetly red lips rounded into a breathless O. Along with his racing tights he was sporting an hugely oversized jersey shirt, and the gold chain setting off the twin tendons of his little neck hinted that he adored himself. He was likely cocky enough to have collegiate friends. They would call him Ace.

Beatense, sailing by, saw that he wore an ugly pair of purple sunglasses, whose metallic glint gave the kid a contract killer look. They set off his spiky blond hair, that was cut to show his elfin ears. Overall he seemed to be the type who loudly protests his homework, but still does it. Ace lifted his shades for a better look at the tan girl teetering by, and made no secret of his interest. Beatense glared back at him. He shrugged, such a misguided woman, and he took off again. He jitterbugged through the mogul field that lay below like a sprite.

Facing these threatening hillocks, Beatense stopped as Shean joined her. "Hey, Beat! How's it going? This is your first actual skiing, here."

"I did okay but I'm worried about all those humps laying ahead."

"Just take them slow. Er, who was that kid? I think I know him."

"Ace, someone. But what about all these bumps, Shean? What can I do?"

"Oh, easy, just go between them." The boy waved to the lovely, slim girl he talked to before as she bounded toward them. The T-shirt and shorts wearing girl gracefully stopped. "Hey, Rindy Lee! This is Beatense, the Book Girl!"

Rindy Lee smiled, in that way that invited everyone into her heart. She was beautiful only to make people happy, to bring joy to friends and strangers alike. The girl exchanged Isn't The Snow Great Today remarks with Beatense, then skied on.

Shean gave an apologetic shrug and followed her. Beatense eased ahead and entered the mogul field, that the preceding two friends danced off in a twinkling. She tried following the downward diagonal gouge between the humps, but their descent was too steep. She stopped by skidding into a handy mogul, then pivoted and aimed up and over the next mogul. It was the only way to maintain a gradual angle, by establishing her own line of travel despite the contrary lay of the land. She continued down through the obstacles, nervously adjusting her skis second by second.

The ride of her life ensued as, with skis deep flexing, she jerked from crevice to bump, and all she could do for control was to frantically wedge against the humps.

Her angle didn't follow the lie of the moguls; she had to cut across their faces in succession, but her skis miraculously gripped at the snow. She came to a flat spot, an unexpected miracle, and she made a quick turn and headed back into the maw. Bouncing up and down, Beatense headed toward a tall, bare tree that stood starkly alone at mid-slope. She barely managed to stop by it, and was delighted to see she was already hundreds of yards below Spinnaker's gateway. Good.

For the rest of the mogul field the girl guessed that she might need twenty more turns. Wearily she shoved on and went back to snapping her spine and popping her knees. Her steady poised flexing was more skilled than she gave herself credit for, because the rank beginners were falling in terror all around.

She finally finished her shuttle diplomacy and emerged onto real snow.

She stopped by Shean. "Beep! You're doing great! You were brilliant!"

"I beg to differ. Those moguls are atrocious. I'm surprised I stayed up."

"You're a natural. But go on. Try your skid turns here. Not the stemming."

She worked a combination of tricks, depending on pomp and circumstance. If she came upon an audience, she went for the pomp, or the aggressive skid turns. But for circumstance, a steeper drop or rougher snow, she did her stem turns. The scattered trees were scenic, but they too were circumstance.

Turning above them might bring a full stop, while turning below them could cause out of control speeds. Shean stayed with the girl, and a mile down from the top his wide blue-green eyes suddenly widened more. "Beatense! Stop! I see the others!"

She cut her ski and veered in a button-hook to a stop. "Where are they?"

"Coming out of Muleskinner down there! Now quick, shoot down and wait by that middle stand of trees until I catch up with them! Then start down!"

Beatense took off for the little grove fifty yards below. She made this glide in a straight drop and dug into a side skidding, thigh burning snowplow to slow up, like a pro. This is what can happen when the instincts that know better take over.

The reunion took place. "Dad!" Jesse rang out, happily. "It's Shean!"

"Howdy, podners! Fucking nice day, ain't it!" --/-- "Shean!"

"Have you seen Beatense?" said Tony worriedly.

"She wasn't at Bomb City, so she must be out on the balcony by now."

"She does that," said Gunter, shaking at the thought of her in the hot tub.

"Hold it!" said Jesse. "That's her up there! I know those legs anywhere!"

The party beheld a skier descending in fast approach as she worked her turns in poetic rhapsody. Her stance was unconsciously perfect for controlled balance and speed regulation. It seemed that she was so eager to prove herself that her hesitant fears were banished. The eager athlete shifted her weight back to lift her tips as she skidded in to a stop.

"Beatense! Way to go!" everyone yelled in similar manner, except Ned.

"Hi, everybody! I think I caught on! Ned, aren't you sharing in my fun?"

"No!" the boy replied coldly, scowling, but his worship was obvious.

"But how did you learn so fast?" said Tony. "That's amazing!"

"I'm just letting the skis do the work! Ned, go ski into the woods."

Tony held her. She accepted this, and Gunter clenched his poles. *So that's how the cookie crumbles.* Not that this was a surprise, not after that tailgate interlude.

"Thank you for this ski trip, Tony. With that lovely view out your window so early this morning I knew this day would be special."

Gunter froze, not that he had any claim. Jesse thought it expedient to make some distracting noise, to show they weren't staring like hungry dogs.

"Beatense, somehow you turned Expert in just three hours! I'm impressed!"

"She skis stupid," Ned announced, and Beatense looked at him.

"Ned, do you just wish I would go away and leave you guys alone?"

From his bereft look it was obvious he had little hope for this deliverance.

Beatense sagged between her poles laughing. Although Tony was charmed by this little vignette, he, and the cameras, did notice the black flash of the girl's tan.

"It's time we eat," he said, as Ned continued to glare. "Gun Barrel, guys?"

Everyone whooped, but Gunter just forced a smile as he helplessly stared.

"Then after we eat let's do Aquarius!" said Shean. "Right out the door!"

"We saw that from the cable car!" said Beatense. She looked at Jesse.

The boy's fluorescent skin was catching the sunlight and forcing it to reflect only the healthiest deep shades of the spectrum. His sun fed proteins exuded strength and energy, and his bracelets, long hair and tooth necklace imparted a proudly splendid savagery. With his muscle pack he embodied life that was wild, beautiful and free.

"Yikes, Jess, my Pop's morning coffee is lighter than you are," the girl said, also reminding everyone of her own color. "And you're not even cold, I bet."

"Are you talking to me? Can't you see the tight definition my pecs and abs have from my shivering? And aren't your abs tighter? You're cold too."

She eyed her sunken belly. Gunter felt intimidated. In jeans and flannel shirt, he wasn't incuded in all this sun drenched talk. He gazed upon Shean's angelic stature and luxurious browning for the first time with real envy. Worse, the thin, long haired boys just wore bikinis, and stung the eye with their barbelled biceps and chests.

The party continued on down Spinnaker, that now fell away more steeply, giving Beatense trouble. Even addressing the most routine turns she swooped down and around at supersonic speeds, and she had to fight to slow back down. But the snow lay flat, there were no moguls, and in spite of her comparative pokiness, the others were content to jog along with her. Tammy shadowed her and tossed in tips. This advice was irritating, but Beatense also had her victories acclaimed by the girl.

Shean and Jesse lost patience and shot down out of sight, and Beatense saw how they handled their speed. With legs together they added serpentine motions to that lean and dig trick she learned on Rowel. The moguls returned, but with her golden chain tossing Beatense navigated them in a set stance that almost popped her thigh muscles out from her skin. The boys were waiting at the wide bend at Spinnaker's halfway point. Beatense and Gunter stopped together.

"That's okay, Gunter. Don't hold back on my account."

"No, this is fine, but look, do you have something going with Tony?"

"I guess you can say that, or so he seems to be hoping. Why do you ask?"

"Well, it seems that you've been ignoring me."

"Well, until now we never had a chance to not ignore each other. Like, until just now we were on different parts of the mountain. I wasn't even on the mountain, I was down on Bomb City. So that discards your concern, Gunter, near naked as I am."

That wasn't the answer he wanted but the two swept down together to rejoin the others. The boys challenged Gunter to a purely innocent race, and he jumped at this as an escape. Tammy went so far and stopped, leaving Beatense alone with Tony.

He cleared his throat. "B-Beatense, d-did you think about it?"

"Think about what? Your proposing to me this morning? Tony, I'm sorry but it can't be done. I'm not going to get into any love; I'm a way too enthused sexual.

"Plus, you can't ethically ask someone to marry you on a ski trip! In these fun circumstances I would say yes in two seconds if I relaxed my scruples!"

"Forget your so-called scruples. I would try to give you a wonderful life."

"I know you would. Just being here proves that. But I can't agree to anything, Tony, just because of our two nights together, that were surprisingly energetic."

A ways away Tammy watched this transaction worriedly. The two started down. Tammy raced ahead, joining the boys waiting anxiously by the Diamond lift.

"Tammy, what was going on up there?" Shean demanded.

"Oh, it's terrible, it looked like they were having a fight!" --/-- "What do you mean, a fight? Don't just babble!" --/-- "I'm not! And it sounds like you're blaming me!"

"You saw they were fighting and you just ski merrily off? That was smart!"

"But I was too far away!" --/-- "Well, I guess there was nothing you could do. I forgive you, Tammy." --/-- "You forgive me!"

Gunter was beginning to grasp the complexity of this situation.

"That's them!" said Jesse. "Her tan is faded and she's fatter but that's her!"

"She did gain ten pounds," pondered Shean. "Okay, this is a three-holer lift! We need to get those two together, with Ned! Jesse, you ride with Tammy and me. And just act natural! Sorry, Gunter, you're the seventh, but this is a crisis."

"Don't be. I'm doing Spinnaker again. See you guys after lunch!"

He skied over to the nearby Sapphire lift, glad to get away. Way glad.

The two in question arrived. Contrary to all the fears they were smiling.

"Thanks for waiting, guys," said Tony. "Beatense fell."

"Again?" said Shean. "So let's go up. Tammy? Jesse? Come on."

"These are three-seaters!" said Beatense. "I'm not taking the middle seat!"

"You sit where we damn well tell you," said Tony.

They moved into the Diamond line, that went up to Gun Barrel. Beatense got in with Ned and Tony as they took their chair. The kids behind strained to hear.

"Ned, I get the impression you think I'm a fool." --/-- "That's cuz you are a fool!"

"And maybe I'm a little skinny, but not very." --/-- "You're way skinny!"

"I highly don't think so, Ned. Why, just the other day I heard people say I'm not skinny." --/-- "Why, just the other day I heard people say you are skinny!"

Tony shok his head. They passed over the crowded Rowel, where Shean and Beatense had stopped before, completing a big circle. At the top, with a light flexing Beatense shot down the Diamond ramp. This was a little tricky because of the three unloading at once. The distant Gun Barrel Lodge stood atop a rise that lay across a wide valley. The massive building looked incongruous in this mountainous setting.

The skiers were all bombing down the drop, and they rose up the far slope to the lodge. Shean suggested that the waxed hot Beatense also bomb this.

"Yeah." Heart pounding, she jammed her poles. "Like hopping boxcars!"

Beatense let the others go ahead while she waited for a good straight shot. Her rusty black tan shimmered in the snowy glow, as the helpless stares bathed upon her. Cameras, too. Then, with blinding flashes of her panic-attack tan, the girl sprang off with her poles, hitting her skis onto the hard snow with a loud clack.

49

AQUARIUS

She dropped into a tight tuck. Everyone edged forward and watched.

Her hair generously fluttered upon her shoulders, and her nip waisted back.

This flight was steeper than the drop at the end of Rowel, and rougher. The girl's flexing skis did quick little hops off the bumps as she flew toward, up and over them. Her chain flopped. She reached terrifying speeds as the cold wind pressed against her. She considered ditching, but being nearly nude the sliding impact would scrape her crochet right off. She had painful damage concerns too, and fears of groveling in agony and making a worse spectacle of oneself.

But Beatense quickly reached the bottom, watched all the way, so now her uphill run quickly dissipated her speed as she drew up to the lodge. She tried to skate up her speed, but she finally halted just below where her party waited after their own stops. They all gave the expected congratulating remarks, but privately the girl felt lucky to survive that plunge. They skied over toward the lodge and took off their skis and stuck them in a snowbank, amidst hundreds of other colorful skis. Even in this crowd of elitists everyone stared at these illustrious kids.

They hobbled through the mob over to the lodge entrance in their clumsy boots, and Beatense's heart pounded. It seemed that eighteen inch waists weren't terribly short in supply, nor tans that could stop a train, and many girls were of an even higher caliber than herself, she noted, and looked almost naked in their thongs.

"They're going in there like *that?*" said Tony, wide eyed. --/-- "I hope they do," Beatense replied. "The cameras can get someone else for a change."

They reached the entrance of the lodge as Gunter pulled in. He never went up the Sapphire, he returned to the Diamond, and he now watched as

544

the family reached the door, and he saw Beatense in her crochet, actually invisible with its in-butt string.

All the ski boots thunking up and down the wooden steps within the building drummed like thunder, and the adjoining tram facilities added to the racket. A skier now, Beatense was proud of the contribution made by her own boots. She was very aware that her beautiful waxy tan, and hot build, and definitely her fame, caused the descending boots to pause, so that she did feel teensily conspicuous.

The family went into the Ye Olde Mainbrace Saloon, and cameras watching they were led by the skinnily vivacious hostess to a big table in the corner. In real life, of course, they would face an hour's wait only to be split up, and Beatense would have been told to get on a shirt. The broad windows by the table had the busy Garnet unloading ramp just outside. Distant mountains loomed in panoramic grandeur.

A camaraderie prevailed, where strangers could sit together if all the tables were taken. The skinnily vivacious hostess seated everyone. Tony, Shean and Jesse quietly studied her. She had a cornered forehead, reassuring people of her intelligent spark, as did her cheek points. As a skier, her skirt bared thighs were laced with muscle, but her pretty biceps only drew fond smiles. She was dusky in complexion, and she had a sensible but cute high-tassled ponytail. She walked with the springy, flexing step of crazily loving life. People found this charming.

"Your server will be right along!" she said, "way before those tans fade! Oh and you, miss, the manager recognized you, and the Mainbrace welcomes you!"

"Us too," Tony protested. "But can we do the buffet? Do you still have it?"

"No, sorry, that closes with the regular season. I wish we did have it!"

She left and Beatense watched the chairlift out the window, and saw Gunter go skulking by. The lucky waiter came over and greeted his old friends. He had heard that the Book Girl was with them and now here she was, right at his table! Her shiny tan and surfer's mini-braided hair were sensations. That wasn't all.

"I could use a beef sub but it isn't too big, is it? I can't do a foot long."

"It is a footer but you can give half to one of these hungry boys."

"Ned can take it, being so skinny," Beatense said, and the boy replied. Trying not to stare Toad sweated and battled through the other orders.

"Okay, folks, B-Becky will bring your grub. N-Nice seeing you again!"

Tony smiled and turning red cleared his throat. "Look, I have to tell you kids, I'm trying like hell to get Miss Pepperpot here to join our family. I'll keep you posted."

Beatense saw them stare in desperate want, and Ned didn't even try to hide his anxious worry. "When I see your bankbook then I'll decide, you ass!"

"We're just after someone to sort our recycling," said Shean, taking hope.

The girl told of her Bomb City interlude, and of meeting Renee. Shean of course recalled the child and her fetching paper hat.

In the following lull Beatense saw a nearby table full of magical pretty boys. They sat quietly eating their hamburgers while happily discussing their adventures so far. They were all cut of the highest quality cloth and were thus infused with money. Well mannered, polite kids like this know all about tennis and music lessons, library trips, pets and family trips. Books in the home, symphony concerts, wide green lawns.

Becky brought them the food on a big tray. Her classy black slacks and bow-tied office shirt imparted a trim, all-business slimness to her form. Definitely a skier, her face and neck, her hands and capable arms, that were bared by her sleeves rolled to her elbows, were ginger snap baked. But from her sensibly serious face and primly tailed hair, she looked too practical to get active sun, or even notice her refined and learned looks, so she endured her tan as a Denier. No, she was a Delighter.

Floating her tray with one hand, the tan-embarrassed girl set her stand with the other, with a sure grace that marked her as a pro. She set the plates out, proudly representing the legion unsung staffers who make the world work.

The food was eaten fast, but when they finished Beatense danced with ski crazed impatience as her friends dragged their way back out.

Her friends were greeted by their friends, and she smiled for introductions again and again. But these were wealthy people, mothers and kids with highest DNA.

Then the restrooms. In Men's, Shean and Jesse studied themselves in the mirror. In Women's, Beatense and Tammy left their stalls and went over to the sinks. In the fluorescent lighting both girls glowed rusted black, with golden and coppery sheens.

Beatense admired her face, openly. Then she turned to examine her back, as others watched. Ladies rooms forced women of all varieties together, with the hope that they might be temporary allies. Beatense, Tammy and the other athletes in the room, cruelly abused this silly idea. They were electrically blinding. Me too, once.

Beatense and Tammy came out and thumped down the stairs with the others, out of the lodge. Clumsy in her heavy boots, Beatense galumphed across the crowded yard and retrieved her skis and poles. In crochet only, she stepped her skis on, as people bumped into each other. With her waist working like a demented snake she and Ned began a sword fight with their poles. Tony stuck in his pole to stop them.

Beatense looked at the nearby trail billboard as a new message blinked in.

URGENT A NEG DONORS NEEDED HURRY INTO G/B LODGE

"Hey, Tony, sorry but I got to go back in. That's my type."
"How… How long will this take?" Right away he regretted that.
"It might be a half hour. Ski Spillway and come back up to kill the time."

"Let me come with, Beatense," said Jesse. "Let's all meet here."

They went in. They were led to a meeting room. The donation items, kept on premises, had been hurriedly set up. Two guys already connected very glad to see this newcomer, and they watched closely as she was interviewed.

"Look, I already gave blood just a week ago! But you need A Neg, right?"

"Very. We need it really bad. If you could sign a waiver, miss..."

"Well, I did just eat all twelve inches. Okay, but where is this waiver? Hurry!"

"Th-This here." The attendant gave her the form. Watching her, he said, "You... You do meet the minimum weight, miss, right? Don't answer."

Jesse watched as Beatense's blood pressure was taken. 116/68. Then her finger was poked with the spring pin gadget for the hematocrit test. As the little blood glob sank into the blue fluid, sickening the boy, a helicopter was heard to land outside.

Beatense was warned against strenuous effort after the session, and then she sat in one of the last two donation lounges, facing two guys.

"Hey, dudes. Perfectly fucky way to spend the afternoon, ain't it?"

They laughed aloud and the crook of her arm was rubbed with iodine. Her taut black belly flexed fearfully as the needle was readied. Jesse took a seat, watching in horror. The girl squirmed and Jesse felt his head float as the needle stuck in and as the nurse filled the test tubes. Then her blood ran along the tube into the collection bag. The girl rolled her eyes up at the guys. They were *sooo* glad they came in.

Her scales tipped, and Jesse gulped as the needle was removed. Like the other two Beatense raised her arm in the donor's salute, holding the gauze in place.

"Thank you, miss. You're a hero. Just sit and drink this water."

"You didn't say anything about not skiing, right? It is downhill, heh heh!"

After lots of ice cream Jesse and Beatense were back outside. The girl had a bandage around her arm, as noted by the others as they skied over.

Tony told her how wonderful she was, and she smugly stuck her tongue out at Ned. The blood cooler was run out to the waiting helicopter and it took off.

"Girl, how was it? Does your arm hurt at all?" --/-- "Only when I see Ned."

There were people who paused to take in the busy scene, including the ski racks and the snow banks that were bristling, with countless skis. They turned also to the sweeping view of snow capped mountains far beyond. Anything but the slim waisted lass with all the hair and her hot tan. But then as if to upstage her, the bikini wearing teen age lad beside her scrubbed his browned ripples and chest with snow. He had the face and hair of a lovely girl. But no royal wrapped arm.

Everyone was relieved as the party skated off to the south end of the Gun Barrel lodge, but they did watch the sleek workings of the famed girl's bladed shoulders and long, upward widening back. But the eyes were also on the young bikini girl at her side, who at first glance looked bare. Many girls did that day.

Gunter saw the party coming and he launched a panic dive down Aquarius, that was just back of Gun Barrel. He had to speed, Jesse always bombed this.

Beatense hurriedly poled herself around and along the south side of the lodge, as she watched Tammy's lithe form ahead of her. Shean, Jesse and Ned also got her attention. Meanwhile, it wasn't too easy to get to Aquarius; one had to ski down the slope around the rocks at the side of the lodge and then herringbone (opposite of the showplow) rise back up. Beatense passed everyone in her excitement, and panting from her effort and hemoglobin depletion she emerged around the back of the lodge before the greatest slope in Hammersley's inventory, the fabled Aquarius.

The stirring moment was interspersed with loud calls from the arriving cable cars just above as the naked looking girl was spotted and recognized. She faced these people as they swung by in their cabin pods. The angle of her boots flexed her legs, and this set her hips and gave her back a lanky curve. Her belly was snaking.

Far below the gondola cables the mighty Aquarius lay stretched out, that was as exuberantly steep and wide as it was dazzling in the sun. The distant skiers upon it were mere dots in silent motion. As wide as it was, the slope was actually a rounded ridge with a downward lie, and Aquarius had no edging trees or trees on the slope proper. This removed any frame of reference, giving it the look of being suspended from the heavens. Beyond the slope there was an infinite valley floor with forgotten forests. Beyond these a collage of peaks rose in solitary splendor. One could see remote cabins with chimneys smoking, and tiny vehicles on tiny roads.

Jesse had seen all this many times before. Me too. "Dad, as usual I'll blast this down and slam over to Vack Suck. Okay? Wait for me at the top."

"Don't let the Ski Patrol cut your wire, and don't hit any damn lawyers."

Beatense's heart pounded at the prospect before her, as the shouts of surprise continued from the overhead cars. She was a bigger novelty here than back at the beach. The problem she faced was that she was warned about undue exertion, but skiing was downhill, right? Gravity? Meanwhile Jesse readied himself.

The Ligniter took a deep breath and launched himself over the edge with a sharp jab of his poles. Skating for speed, he dropped into a tuck. Jesse took the slope straight down, flicking from mogul to mogul. Further down he veered over leftward to clear the other skiers and to position himself for his flying turn into the connecting run far down to the right. He blasted by some distant service tractors.

"How does he do that?" Beatense queried. "I can ski, but not like that."

"You think you can ski?" argued Ned, and Beatense shook her fist at him.

They started down. Beatense entered Aquarius at an easy angle, but then she quickly reached top speed. She skidded her edges and popped a turn. She raced a hundred yards more and entered a field of moguls, and precariously rode the mounds up and down. Her gold belly chain danced in bouncing confusion as she worked her skis in a digging wedge to keep from zipping ahead.

She saw smooth snow off to the left. She could go all the way down here, really fast, but then Tammy, who had held back, flew by her as she flexed her strong legs over the bumps. Ned and Shean sped down after her and Beatense watched as the happy kids flowed through their curving turns, alternating right to left. And even Tony had that classic form. Beatense got even by racing all out down the flats, and she caught up to slender Shean of the deep electric baking. The boy was rubbing his thinned arm with snow as he inspected it. The cable cars were too high up to watch.

"How do you guys all ski so good, Shean? That weaving pattern?"

"Parallel. Don't try it here, it's too steep. You got good wide track control."

Beatense felt weak from giving the blood, even though she and Jesse had lots of ice cream while she waited through the mandatory rest. So she eased up her speed over the smoother flank of the mile long Aquarius. She used her ersatz parallel in swinging from turn to turn in a giant slalom. She paused and watched Shean hurtle down, and he expertly bounced the moguls straight-legged.

Beatense kept on. By working her ski edges she braked through her long turns and accelerated out of them. She even threw out puffs of snow with her tails as she made quick little cuts to control her speed. Then for the last thousand feet she went into a hard bomb. She quickly saw the folly of this.

Far ahead Aquarius simply ended. Instead of a long continuing open stretch, a wall of trees and the central support tower at slope end were racing toward her. She would have to ditch. She aimed for an area free of other skiers, but saw that she put herself right in the path of a big snow mound. She tried to turn by it, but she was too close. She hit the hill at an off angle and bucked up airborne in a rolling tumble, then began to fall. She slammed down on the hard snow and pelted and rolled over it to a rough stop. She quickly felt for her chain, and bottom. The others hurried over.

They helped her up. "Beatense! Are you okay?" they variously yelled.

"What do they have that thing right there for?" she in turn yelled.

"It's for jumping," said Shean. "You didn't see it because of the white-out."

Beatense, aching and bruised, stepped her skis back on, and after adjusting her crochet she raised her fist and punched Ned in the arm. He yelled in protest.

"Hey, girl!" said Tony. "Take it easy! We all fall!"

"Tony, I was just pre-empting Ned's plans to rip out my fingernails with a pliers."

"Ned, I better talk to you about that." --/-- "What do you mean, just talking to him? No mention of a punishment?" --/-- "But he didn't do it, yet."

While this dispute took place Shean smiled as he got his map out of his tube.

"Okay, we dive Death Valley down to the Garnet lift, that Jesse is halfway up by now. Death is an Easiest, Beatense, by the way. Like Rowel."

"Good, I need the rest and restoring. Never give blood and then ski."

"I was damn proud of you, girl," said Tony. "I wish I had the type, myself."

Beatense turned to go. Tony watched. Her bared, lean backside writhed with the effort as she dug in her poles, heading over to join the dozens of skiers that were cutting over from Aquarius to the Death Valley portal to the right. Two chairlifts were unloading here, and Beatense watched these skiers as she headed with her friends over to the trail, that was basically a utility route. It was quite narrow, but it headed down across the face of Plymouth through a half mile of lodgepole pines, that filtered the sun. Along the way it crossed two other runs that went on down to the base, for a quick hop onto those twin lifts loading nearby.

Death was gloriously scenic, but anyone with the ability shot down it obliviously. Even the Bomb City graduates let fly, crazily whooping. The Shattuck party entered this trail, joining the chase, and Beatense blasted off after them. Skating for speed, Shean shot ahead down the long trail, looking for an open spot to stop and watch his rapidly learning student. He found a likely place and swirled around into the full brunt of a hurtling impact. He was knocked right out of his bindings.

"You shithead, what did you stop for?" were the words he heard.

It was Beatense! "You were right behind me?" the boy asked stupidly.

On his back the boy lay propped on his elbows, gasping from the collision, and the sight of his breathing belly against the white snow almost caused more mishaps.

"Yeah! I figured you knew what you were doing!"

She was causing her own near collisions. The two lurched to their feet.

"Is everyone okay here?" said Tony, sliding up with the others.

"Well, my tan got badly bruised, thanks to Shean!"

"Don't pin this on me! You have to keep your distance, just like cars!"

"Yeah, Beatense!" said Ned. --/-- "Shut up, or I'll hit you again!"

"But Beatense, you're doing great!" said Tammy. "You caught on so fast!"

The girl reset her crochet. As her party resumed flight she realized she was a respected part of this flying torrent, especially since she was now a speed skier. She was racing past the knock-kneed beginners who were struggling along Death Valley's lethal fairway gradient. Meanwhile the snow was blurring by under the girl's skis, and the shadows of the tall, barren trees were flitting by across her path.

The party burst out from the trees as their trail crossed Flying Pieman. Collisions nearly occurred as the intersecting skiers swerved to avoid each other.

But some skiers purposely veered over to see that bared blackety tan in flight.

One observer was Gunter. A faster skier, he had flown down to the Garnet lift as he tried to stay ahead of Jesse, then he ripped down Pieman to watch the girl fly by.

Good timing, but he was morbidly reminded of what he had lost. Exactly what happened? Suddenly he wasn't even welcome as an old friend. He saw the skinny, rays-clad girl raise her poles, whooping aloud with tangled hair aflutter.

Death swept on to cross Talleyrand, with more close calls, with a drop-off edge ahead. Beatense didn't like this, and she skidded to a lurching stop. Her friends passed her one by one and hit the last six hundred feet of the now full width Death in low tucks. Two fellows who had also stopped patently stared at her. With pole ends lazily dropped on the snow back of her, she stood poised with knees bent, and her back was lazily curved within her actually pain causing tan.

"G-Go for it," one fellow said. "W-We'll m-make sure you m-make it."

"How? By propping me up?" *She answered them!* "Hey, it might work!"

"Wh-What's th-that on your arm there?"

"Oh, my blood was just loaded into that helicopter, if you saw it."

"W-We didn't see it, but you're… You're the Book Girl! A heroine!"

The girl laughed, and she took a deep breath and fearlessly began her descent. The grade was moderate, but her cumulative speed quickly climbed beyond stopping. She rocketed faster and faster. Her golden chain flopped, her eyes wetted and her ears roared. Her skis smacked up, over and down the wave-like bumps, so that she felt like a small plane landing in a rough field. She continued to accelerate wildly, while a raw primeval terror gripped her heart. To fall now and possibly just get injured or possibly just scrape her tan, again, or wait and get killed for sure was the quandary.

She was diving toward the mobbed junction of X To C, Chainsaw, Tuckville, and the Garnet chairlift. Its line was a problem; it was approaching too fast to stop. She had to ditch. She squatted low and tipped over.

The hard impact rolled, spun and tumbled her to a theatrically disgraceful, poorly navigated halt. She heard loud shouts as she lay still, something about calling in the Ski Patrol. Her two friends from atop the hill raced to her side. Shaking, she slowly struggled to her feet, much to everybody's surprise. And of course shock.

"Are you okay?" her would-be coaches yelled, eyes wide with guilty horror.

"Everything was fine until you meddling scumbags said to go for it!"

The scumbags saw a father and his bikini bared teen-age son coming over, and they realized that this girl was called for. They began slinking away over to Tuckville, as the girl was escorted to the Garnet lift-line by her friends.

She cupped her hand and gave a yell. "Hey! The lift is this way, dudes!"

That gesture saved the day for them. Beatense's arm got her waved in as the hero of the day in addition to her fame, and she took a chair with Tony. Ned and Tammy paired up, and the tan, age sixteen Shean singled with an obvious gay. Just to be a jerk he jinkled his stick arm's bracelets and patted his flexing, sunkened belly.

His seizuring partner recognized Shean, from his study of the illicit videos in the secret gay website, Beach Beautiful Boys. I also seizured a gay, butt-cuts me after a hot day of sun flashing deep brown in all directions in that grey enameled stairwell.

Beatense had a thought. "Say, Tony, back in that restaurant I saw Gunter go by out the window there. But it couldn't have been him."

"No, not if he did Spinnaker. How are you feeling after giving that blood?"

"Well, they gave me tacit approval to ski, and that's my priority."

Tony was treated to the spectacle of the girl holding her own stick out for a review. Tightly thinned it was, but its toughly muscled form kept it safely away from being too thin. She slouched forward as far as she could without flipping out of the chair and gazed upon her quivering ripples. They were a fine piece of engineering, tensely laced with steel, and from her belly's appalling slimness it lay starved.

Beatense's slight shape was embellished by her blackety tan and moisture film. Tony didn't dare look at her waif's thighs, as the girl lifted her skis for scrutininizing them. Her belly squirmed from the effort of holding this weight.

Beatense finally hitched back up. "Those son of a bitching skis are heavy."

Chairlifts are richly undeserved by their pampered and spoiled clients. Primeval forests had to be bulldozed down in their helpless innocence to make way for them, and rigging the cable support towers is a logistical nightmare for the low paid, tent housed workers. All this is done so that ungrateful, rich skiers can be carted up for their idle recreation. As they're swept silently upward, suspended as if from hot air balloons venturing too low, they're usually about ten feet above the terrain, but with a steeper climb the free air gap can be fifty feet or more.

The cable was angled sharply upward now, straining, and the moguls that ranged ahead were jaggedly cut and snaggled, like shark teeth. The way they were stacked up behind each other seemed to magnify the Dive's sheer vertical plunge. Beatense feared that they would be coming down this shortly.

"We're running by Vacuum Suction Dive now," said Tony. "It's a real man eating obstacle course here. Jesse should be coming any second now."

"He's coming down this? Tony, these moguls look like they're sharpened!"

"They probably... There! There he is!"

A giant *"Ohhh!"* was exhaled from the chairs as a small figure came flying some distance ahead off a sheer ice face. As the racing boy dropped down through the six foot fall his skis neatly helicoptered him in a 360, so he landed poised downhill like a cat. However, Jesse then hit some ice, and he helplessly fell and rolled and tumbled until at last he fought to a stop. He sat up and retrieved his pole.

The divinity was just a few yards away. The glistening dark cordovan burn of his muscled, pipe cleaner form starkly glowed against the snow.

"Are you okay?" said Tony, to the black tanned whip of boned tensions.

"Yeah. Wait for me up top, can you? Hey, Shean, did you see me crash?"

"Yeah! Awesome!"

Beatense looked away to an unseen audience, shaking her head. She had now seen everything. She looked up at the slope as they continued to grind up beside it, and she was impressed with Jesse's just trying to get down it. Then she beheld a yearling boy come lightly dancing down this death plunge. The afternoon sun dappled his sensation tan with golden glints as the lovely faced youth flexed and twisted in an unrestrained magnum opus of skilled speed. He launched himself off an edge with a roll-over flip. He lightly landed and flew on. Cheers rang out.

Beatense turned to watch him go. "Tony, did you see that kid do that?"

"Yeah. Poor Shean is probably itching to take a run himself now."

Beatense looked back again and saw that boy also turned, watching. With the sun coming from behind her turned head, the ethereal Shean looked near as black bellied as Jesse. His seatmate, still reeling from Jesse, was carefully taking note.

The metal sign redundantly said, **PREPARE TO UNLOAD**. Oh really. Beatense angled her skis for the approach ramp. They hit with a clack and she and Tony zipped down. They skated with the others over by the Gun Barrel lodge to await Jesse.

Shean opened his neck tube and showed Beatense the trail map, again, as her recently met friends skied by and gave a wave. The girl smiled and gave the finger. Then she turned and gave Ned the same gesture. He glowered furiously.

"Okay, Beat, now we take Spillway to the Ruby, that we'll take to Blood. Except we'll take Saddles and Spurs to the Sapphire and re-take Spinnaker."

Beatense adjusted her stretchy red bandage. "Spinnaker, again?"

"Yeah, let's not do Spinnaker," said Tony. --/-- Shean went on, "Okay, Cougar. That will get us to the Amethyst and we can run that up to Majesty."

"Amethytht to Majethty? Thoundth thtupid. Jutht like Ned ith thtupid."

"You're thtupid!" the intricately slender, rather dark brown elf replied.

"Majesty is so pretty, Beatense," said Tammy. "It's like a bowl with trees."

Jesse's bashing down the rest of Vack gave Gunter anxiety. Riding his chair he saw the kid coming like a flash of hot lightning, and he was afraid he would spot him. Luckily he didn't, but then he worried that the kid's flight down the Dive meant his family, and Beatense, were waiting for him up at the lodge. This he didn't count on, so he decided to cut over to X To C once he got to the top. The Shattucks of course would be hitting the upper mountain.

"Thanks for waiting," Jesse said as he finally rejoined the others.

"No time to split up," said Tony. "But look here, after this I don't want you falling when you take that Vacuum headwall. You damn well stay vertical. I pay all that money for your lift ticket and look what shittily happens."

The boy laughed, and Shean's gay friend even photographed the girls.

They made the trek over to Spillway. Beatense, with bared tan clashing against people's sensibilities, didn't wait for the others. Noisily raking out her turns she dove down Spillway, whooshing by the cursed **SLOW AREA** sign that mocked her the day before. She leaped into a stop, throwing snow. Shean and Jesse shot down and stopped by her in swirling, tan flashing circles.

"Nice going, Beatense!" said Shean. "What a difference from yesterday!"

"I can ski lots faster, being able to stop now. Oh, the laggards cometh."

Tony, Tammy and Ned thundered in. Finger aimed, Shean pointed out Blood Cougar to Beatense. This vividly loomed in full sight on the flank of the upper mountain. Skiers far up upon these ramparts worked their way down.

"See, now you have an idea where you are, and were yesterday."

"No need to explain that to me. Ned's the one who's all confused. But golly gee whiz, Wally, that is quite a sight. Gorgeous. It even beats us."

49

INTERLUDE

They raced down the rest of Spill. Beatense going slower, crabbed her skis at an angle, so that their edges scrubbed over the crisp snow with the sound of tearing cardboard. The vibrations of the wedging skis worked her legs in that semi-controlled glide that skiers dream of all summer. She hooked out into Lift Alley and strafed this down to the Ruby chairlift. She tore into the end of the line in a roaring stop. She had no choice but to accept the cattle chute stares.

Beatense and Jesse took their chair and started up. The batching of the singles put Shean and Tammy three chairs back, and Ned and Tony were six back.

"When we get to the top let's ditch everyone and go straight to over Saddles and Spurs, Beatense," said Jesse. "When we unload, head for the shortcut!"

"I thought we were going down Blood Cougar!"

"They run parallel. And no one listens to Shean. Boy, you're black as me!"

The kids shot down the ramp with poles ready, and Jesse led the way down and across Cougar toward a path that cut right into the trees. They entered this at full tilt and the girl suddenly had grave doubts about her chances. Since this pathway had been informally carved out by the skiers, it was dangerously narrow as it snaked its way through the trees, in a steep series of jolting ups and downs.

Beatense chased after Jesse, quite helplessly, as she just missed the tree trunks and boulders crowded close by the trail. Plus she bounced wickedly over the many undulating bumps, flying and hitting and hitting and flying. She could do no more to stop or slow down than to squat down in a futile sliding wedge, but this actually helped because it gave slightly better stability, and she had branches to duck.

Jesse had no trouble with this obstacle course. He was actually working for speed. Suddenly he dropped over the edge ahead, and seconds later Beatense followed him down a steep chute. In terror she shot out of the trees onto the slope.

She stopped and stood panting. Jesse didn't think of her blood situation. "Come on, the others are after us already!"

They sprang off, skating for speed. Saddles and Spurs headed down in a wide boulevard, forming the valley floor between the upper reaches of Molloy and the ridge riding Blood Cougar. Beatense glanced back and saw the others blast out in pursuit. None of them fell on that trail. She worked a long serpentine to go faster. But Jesse bombed into a dive, and continued to accelerate. In full flight, Beatense thought she could stay ahead of the others, but they all caught up and passed her one by one.

"Give it up, lady! You ain't got a chance!" This was Shean, now naked.

"You guys can't just go taking off like that!" argued Tammy, as she and Ned pulled alongside. "We almost didn't see you go down this way!"

The two glided on, and Tony caught up next. Quite a feat, being so old. "Whose idea was this girl?" --/-- "Jesse's. By the way, Shean is naked."

"He's okay, here. This slope is so easy the Patrols don't bother with it."

Beatense decided Tony was right, Saddles was just a nondescript connector route, no one riding up in the gondola would excitedly point it out on the map. Only a few desultory skiers were on it now. Also, it wasn't properly an afternoon slope. Its time instead was morning, when the sun would be positioned at its upper end, lighting the slope like a celestial causeway. This is what makes skiing skiing.

Saddles merged with Rowel to form the bomb run down to the lifts. It was an old homecoming for Beatense, she was last here a lifetime ago. She skidded sideways and crabbed down by sliding her skis, then broke into a hard dive.

She pummeled over the stray bumps at the bottom of the long slope and leaned into a snow throwing slide at the end of the lodge-bound Opal lift line.

Even though Saddles was sparsely traveled, this lift area had a crowd because it was the Molloy gateway. Beatense worked her way through the lift line, getting her usual photos and catatonic stares. Shean drew them too. She rode up with Tony.

At the top of Opal the party gathered. Since Shean's original itinerary was out, the subject of how to get down to Lift Alley came up. They could either make the drop to the lodge from here, as they did heading for lunch, and then take Spillway, or instead they could cut over to the Expert slope, de la luz. Beatense skied over to la luz with Jesse and Tammy, while (despite the crowd) the still bare Shean hung back.

Tony and Ned took the bomb for the men's office at the lodge, after agreeing to then take Spillway down to meet the others. As the three got to the head of de la luz Beatense saw two teen-aged boys who stood in wait.

One was fine and pretty, and despite being airy slight, he was also capably muscled. In this world where thin rules he was one of the Envied. He was obviously a cute natured lad, whose thick tousled yellow hair seemed to exemplify his active personality. Its ends were all brushed out and back like a girl's, and it glowed with a sun halo.

Beatense loved this boy just as much as she was repelled by his friend. He was like me once, an ugly dullard, textbook type who was bucktoothed confused. He was awkwardly underweight and scrawny from undereating as he nervously stood on his beat-up rentals, yet he and his radiant friend probably weighed the same.

And she noticed that while the other boy smiled at the two girls delightedly, Nerd Bird was ignoring her as he stared in too obvious shock at the now also naked, real dark brown Jesse, as that long haired boy glided right to the de la luz drop-off.

The arrival of Shean as nude two almost broke Coonk's neck. He gawked in horror. Beatense waved to Shean and moved to the edge of de la luz, where Jesse waited, and almost pitched over her tips in stopping. This slope fell like a brick dropped down a well, and far below Lift Alley lay in wait. It was actually a continuation of the steep luz. Bikini tied around his neck, Jesse leaped off and bashed the huge moguls down. Nude three Tammy, the traitor, shot off after him fearlessly.

Shean joined Beatense. "Don't panic. Just mentally map out each turn."

Coonk was watching, no time to quibble. The girl adjusted her crochet and then flexed into the slope at a safe angle and cut a quick turn in a flatter area. She moved into the humps and rocked them way up and down, almost breaking her skis. She decided to side-slip every chance she got. She was poised for any contingency in a knees-bent stance, while the shit-sprayed Shean had the same careful technique in patiently working down above her. Each of his exquisite muscles was manipulating through a coordinated rhythm under his baked skin. Coonk was watching.

Beatense halted at the far side and set her ski for the neatest possible turn. She eased forward and rocketed around like a shot. Having given blood so soon after Ivy Street she wasn't sure of her prospects. She bucked and leaped over the moguls as she desperately dug her edges to slow down. She finally got back down to a safer speed and found a flat spot to turn. Incredibly, she was already fifty yards down the slope. She popped a turn and lashed off again, as each foot traveled threatened to throw her down in some spiteful new way. Runaway speeds kept nipping at her, she couldn't relax for a second. Her crochet flopped around her neck.

For most of her turns she could trust in the flatter snow at the slope's edges, but the drawback to this strategy was that once she made it to the edge she *had* to turn even if the snow didn't lie flat. She hated to do it but she resorted to side slipping down as needed, reasoning that this also took real skill. She also scraped downward if her given turn would just smack her into a mogul. One trick she used was to swivel her turns on the tops of the moguls, and then scrape down their fronts, but this wasn't true skiing. Looking up, Beatense saw that Shean never resorted to side sliding, instead always making legitimate carved turns.

He could have taken luz faster, but with blond hair afloat he seemed to like this challenge. Challenge. This was like juggling hand grenades. Sadly these moguls weren't cleanly and predictably shaped, like over on Aquarius. Their spacing was off and they were icy. Beatense edged slowly down with her legs cocked out for better stability, alternating this way and that with each braking situation.

But in spite of her frantic care her tips crossed, and she tumbled and walloped through a chute-way of icy moguls. As she slid one of her skis came off and started down the hill, but Shean pounced on it. The girl came to a stop, and after tabulating her pain she struggled to her feet. Shean brought her ski over.

"Thanks, but I don't know how I can get it on. There's nowhere flat."

"I can hold it. But this is your fourth fall today. No excuse."

Beatense adjusted her crochet again, followed with getting her ski back on. She started off, and as she made more crossings, the decision always was to turn behind the given mogul as it approached, but this would actually cut her uphill slightly, raising the possibility of going backwards. The other choice, to turn in front of the mogul, would take her downhill, not slightly. She quickly learned to finesse the moguls by carving their front sides about halfway up, while taking care to shift her weight to the active ski and dig it into the icy face. Then she had to pivot and head down into the mogul chasm before her, desperately wedging. But progress was in progress.

She was overjoyed when her ordeal at last came to an end.

She and Shean blasted down the last of de la luz into Lift Alley. The skiers who had been watching her slow approach now had to look fast as she shot by.

"Well, I survived that, Shean, so I guess the blood giving didn't hurt."

"You did great!" He pointed to the Ruby lift. "There's Dad and Ned."

Beatense decided she would ride with these two. As she got in the line she looked back up at de la luz, and she was shocked at how steep it looked. Its skiers were tiny dots, some moving fast, others slow, and some dead stopped. Beatense, Ned and Tony took off on their way up Molloy, the back mountain.

"Boy, that de la luz was a killer. My tips crossed and I fell big time, Tony."

"You fall just once on that one, you're a pro." --/-- "She's always falling!"

"Shut up, doorknob nose." --/-- "Beatense, only call him that if it fits."

"But it does fit! Now Tony, I guess I should have talked to you about this before. Ned is so lazy, I'm trying to think of ways for him to be more useful."

"You can be useful by jumping off!" --/-- "What do you have in mind?"

"He needs a list of household chores to do. My childhood is just filled with fond memories of me doing the dishes or washing the clothes..." Ned rolled his eyes up. "Plus I loved doing homework. Ned doesn't have that now, this

being summer, so he needs a few a duties here and there to keep him busier."
Ned heartily wished she would shut up. "And so for starters, he should raise
a puppy."

Ned went rigid.

"Beatense, we went through all this before. Ned already has a horse, for
which I end up forking manure for most of the time. A dog would be too much."

"Dog, schmog! I said a puppy! I'm thinking how this will keep him busy!"

"You think a lot of things. In the first place I'm not so sure I care for dogs. I
was chased by dogs a time or two. That happens when you're a migrant. Plus
they bark and knock things over. Not that we have anything valuable."

"Puppies don't bark, they just squeal and yap a little. Like Ned does."

"But they don't stay little. And they make messes and chew the upholstery."

"So do I. But Tony, you're living in a shack like dogs now, so why not get
one to share in the luxury? Now look, Ned doesn't give you any trouble, hardly.
It's me he has it in for, because I'm so much better than he is, and popular."

Tony shook his head weightily. "Ned, I say you can't have a dog with very
good reasons, but this young lady would think I'm a jerk. Her ideas don't make
sense, so let's look at this from your point of view. If you get a puppy of your
own you'll have to take care of him, you know. That means feeding him every
day." --/-- "I will!"

"And you'll have to clean up his stinky messes until he's trained, by you."
"I will!"

"And if he cries for his mommy you better bring him a bottle of warm milk."
"I will!"

"And if he gets sick you're the one who has to call the vet, and you have
to stay up watching over him all night and give him his medicine." --/-- "I will!"

"And you'll have to teach him to do tricks, and run and play with him."

Ned could certainly face that easily enough. "I will!"

Beatense caught Tony's wink. She smiled widely.

"Okay, it sounds like you're serious about this, son. Now when we get
home ask around and find out who has puppies for sale. Do you hear me?"

Ned reacted by crying out tonelessly, as if he was having a bad dream.
Uhhhh! Uhhhhhh! Uhhhhhh!

"And you better thank Miss Colwell here for this half smart idea of hers."

"I suppose," said Ned, then he melted. "Th-Thanks, B-Beatense."

"Ha ha, Ned. Your puppy will like me best!" --/-- "He will not!"

"I just wish I had someone to play checkers with, by cracky."

Ned thought he better get better acquainted with this unpleasant girl.

"What was all that yelling about?" Shean said, when they all met again."

"I'm getting a dog!"

"What?" Jesse roared. "Really? A dog!? Worthless you?"

"Oh, you luck!" said Shean. "Well, of course he will be a family pet, right?"

"Oh, Ned," said Tammy mournfully. "I wish I could have one."

Beatense looked up at the slope above them, that led up to Molloy's high summit, to the left of Spinnaker's gateway. It seemed that this slope was well cleared, and it looked like a giant, rumpled blanket of vivid white.

"Okay, Beat, time for Blood!" said Shean, another nose-to-toes glistening.

"I gave blood already, Shean." She pointed. "Let's do that slope up there!"

"We will, but we have to take Blood down to get to its lift."

As they started down Beatense realized she could ski by automatic instinct now, especially on Blood Cougar's smoothly groomed ballroom floor. She swung into her flying turns as a true skier now, confident and skilled. She stopped at the cliff rock. She spotted young Ace as he jetted by, and waved Jesse over.

"Hey, who is that kid who just went by?" --/-- "Who? Oh, him down there? Hey, that's Ammo Knight!" --/-- "Ammo? Well, I guess that fits. Try and catch him, can you?" --/-- "That doesn't deserve a response."

Jesse chased after Ammo, and Beatense followed as quickly as she dared. She ran the dogleg further down, that swung off to the right. From this vantage point she could see Lift Alley, and in fact Blood Cougar merged into the run-off bottom of de la luz. The two were waiting just up from this busy junction.

"Boy, major bum if the snow has been this good since we left, Ammo," the nude, panting Jesse was saying. "Anyway, this is my woman, Beatense."

The jaw-dropped boy recognized her. "She... She's the Book Girl! Again!"

Beatense smiled, as she demurely crossed her ski pole over Jesse's in asserting their transcending love. Ammo slid backwards out of shock.

"I cherish you," Beatense said, softly. "You bring me bluebirds of joy."

"And I love you too, Peachie Poo."

"Yeah, right," said Ammo, catching on. "Boy, you had me scared there."

Beatense smiled at this hotshot's realization he had been smoke-screened.

"Anyway, Ace, I mean Ammo, I saw you rip down up on Spinnaker earlier."

This was turf the cool youth understood. "Hey, I can do okay," he said, tipping his head knowledgeably. "Wow, the Book Girl in person! Hey, Tony!"

At that moment they were joined by Tony, who came skidding in.

"Ammo! Nice to see you! I see you met Miss Colwell."

"Yeah. She's got the hots for me!"

"I cherish you," Beatense said, crossing her pole over Ammo's.

Tony rolled his eyes up. "Anyway, Jesse, I say forget Majesty and head over to Bayonet right away. They'll be closing the lifts on us in an hour or so."

"Closing the lifts!" Beatense cried, looking around in panic. "This is how they reward my slope beautification program and my giving blood?"

"I warned you not to," said Jesse. "Hey, Ammo, want to stick around?"

"Maybe," he said, clearly gladdened despite his cool facade. "Ace, hah?"

As she gunned down the rest of Cougar, Beatense recalled her grief on it the day before, and she bemoaned that huge waste of falling so repeatedly. She streaked on to strafe the lower drop into Lift Alley. She was skiing fast;

she passed many skiers toward the Amethyst. This was the longest cable on both mountains, because of its famed trans-passage of Majesty. Beatense got aboard with Jesse and Ammo.

Both boys noted her excited smile.

"Damn, I wish we could do Majesty," said Jesse. "That sucks."

"No shit," said Ammo. "Anyway, uh, h-how do you get so fucking... Tan?"

"Fucking genetic synapses. But where is this Majesty at, anyway?"

"You were looking up at it," said Jesse. "Before we skied Blood Cougar."

"What? *That?* That's what we're not skiing? Damn that blood giving!"

"Bayonet is better. You can ski the actual slope or go right into the trees."

"Tree bashing, hah?" Beatense complacently accepted any dangers.

"Too few for that. But Bayonet is better to take as a beginner, Beatense. Majesty is really tough up there. The moguls are hidden by the powder snow."

"You're a beginner?" said Ammo. "How long have you been skiing, lady?"

"Since yesterday morning, sonnie. I caught on so fast because with me so bitch tan it's a point of pride to beat people down, but you can't do that skiing like some rag doll. So I willed myself to turn into a skiing terror within hours."

"Yeah, on Intermediates, but try an Expert." --/-- "I did, de la luz."

"Ned is actually having fun today," said Jesse. "Not one complaint."

The chairs broke out from the trees and glided over the head of the Cougar and Saddles and Spurs slopes. Ahead lay a vast expanse of arctic white, and Beatense died within. She wanted to ski Majesty so desperately she stared with the horror of a mortal wound. This was truly where the real skiing was done on the mountain.

It was one thing to cruise down nicely groomed packed powder slopes with their tree lined borders, but this was where the skier made his own way, often breaking untouched snow. And still their chair worked ever higher, as the black cables curved upward and disappeared into the immensely inviting white lying above.

All this pounded Beatense's blood, but it was all those bumpy moguls that really gripped her. She hated them, but they did get one's attention.

The unloading ramp came at last, and here there was no doubt that this was the peak. Over atop Spinnaker there was an impression of summit, a feeling, but here, without any obscuring trees nearby, the panorama of mountain vistas roared out for a hundred miles in all directions. This was the top of the world, Serenity Station.

Even the wind got into the act, pulling and buffeting so that the snow flew. Naked Tammy, Jesse and Shean, and nearly bare Beatense shivered with goose bumps as the snowy winds chilled them. Ammo saw that even Ned was joining in the happy clamor, instead of moodily staying away by himself.

"Oh, Tony! Can't we go down this?" Beatense cried plaintively, pointing.

"No, my girl, we cannot. This heads right back down to Cougar."

Shean got out his map. "I wish they still had the old poma lift here, chancy as it was. Then we could do Majesty, Beatense."

"Is this not fiction?" the girl complained. "Why can't we have that pony lift for just now? I don't care if it disappears after we use it."

"Well, why don't we just fly up the mountain then?" Tony thoughtfully added.

"Yeah, we don't need these lifts at all," said Shean. "Bing, up we go!"

"But I like riding the chairlifts!" poor Tammy protested.

"We could de-materialize and re-materialize as needed," said Beatense.

Ammo turned from one to the other, wondering what would be said next by these eccentrics. He felt better when the drift got back down to solid ground.

"Beatense, Bayonet blows this away," said Jesse. "Write that down."

"Okay, but if I don't like it we're coming back here, lifts or no lifts! Ned, shut up!"

"You can ski here if you want!"

Ammo began to get an idea of why there was a change in Ned. A bright, eager faced boy of twelve joined them. "Hi, Ammo!" he said. Just in cuffed butt-cut cut-offs he was perfectly chested and rippled, and saturated with live brown. Ammo said Hi back, wondering how his friend could be so oblivious to all the benefits of that tan.

He was introduced as Gary, I recall him from 1978, and he joined the group.

Getting over to Bayonet meant traversing the barren heights to the western face. Beatense lagged behind as her party reached the transition trail and shot down. She took it more slowly. She came to the top of the long trail, that wound down through a piney woods, and saw glimpses of her friends far below. They flew on and Beatense skidded to a halt and looked around. Alone. She untied her crochet. Naked.

Heart pounding she tied the piece around her neck, under her bandanna.

She shoved off and continued down the narrow pathway. This caused confusion for the fellows that had arrived back of her. *Should we try to catch up?* As expected she skied fast, while they were less confidently sure. The girl's path opened out into what was presumably Bayonet, and she immediately took on that joyful state when skiers no longer fear any phantom hazards lurking within the snow. They simply fly.

Crazed by her bared state, Beatense aggressively worked her skis, and waist whipping she raced down through the winding maze of secretly inter-merged trails of Bayonet. She slashed by little pockets of trees, she scissored through soft pillow-like moguls, and she floated across and down open stretches of uncut snow.

She even noticed the big screen view suspended out in the Beyond.

For scenery, Bayonet was unlike anywhere else on the Molloy back mountain. It was actually like a sparsely wooded Aquarius. With its countless snowy evergreens tucked in at various distances along its chaotic fall, the shimmery backdrop of snowy mountains many miles away presented an infinite sense of space and depth.

Also, with Bayonet so far north remote, its seclusion cast an exhilarating spell of forgotten wilderness, and of wondrous adventure and exploration.

Beatense found that this isolated realm had even greater revelations, discoveries that could distract even self involved sophomores. Off to the right of Bayonet proper lay a rugged No Man's Land of stray, ski-grooved paths, that tenuously clung to the steep, rough side of the mountain.

Anyone venturing out here would feel an even greater weight of distant seclusion, brought on by the pervasive silence. This forsaken world had a timeless, frosty stillness that pervaded the very air. At this moment this was alive with floating snow sparkles, as the altitude chilled water vapor coalesced and froze.

With the others not in sight Beatense guessed that they had come this way, and she headed over and roamed out along a narrow trail. Her heart pounded.

The path's slight incline carried her along slowly but steadily. Yes, Beatense saw her friends, Gary included, gathered in a clearing far below. They waved, then skied into the scattered pines surrounding them. Their laughing banter wafted softly up to their distant witness, who just caught quick glimpses of them as they played an epic game of hide-and-seek. The browned skins of the five kids flashed in the sun.

The girl continued to follow her thread-like ribbon, looking for a spot to turn back. Although her trail had a slight incline, the mountainside itself was steep. This would make turning back difficult. Beatense saw the downward cuts off the trail that others had made long before her arrival, but these tracked into deep powder snow.

The skiers coming before had turned and paralleled down from her path with fast and skilled assurance. And far below Beatense saw no trails like hers heading back toward Bayonet. She was sure she was beyond the Ski Patrol limits.

All she could do was keep venturing out along her grooved path, whose wavy lie carried her gently up and down ever further. She had to find a place to turn back, for the eerie and ominous isolation out here was starting to unnerve her. The snow on both sides of the path was rough, and it would take a lot more ability than she had to make a turn in it. Using her poles she couldn't even rotate herself back around, first because she was being swept along unstoppably much faster now, and second, the mountain's steep lie would grab a deadly accelerating hold of her.

As the girl continued on she kept hoping for a break, just one little flat spot. She finally saw a place to turn, thankfully atop a low rise where she could stop. Her only company was the wide field of snow falling away from her, scattered trees and the glowing, throbbing view out yonder. She stopped and aimed her uphill ski at a sharp angle for her turn. She tweaked ahead with her poles.

Instant roller coaster. She careened wildly down, fighting the thick, uneven snow and her own panicky reactions. But she cut her turn with pure will power.

Panting heavily she finally stopped. She was aimed safely back toward Bayonet and the more populous part of the mountain. All she had to do now was find another path to follow back, one sloping in the right direction. She did see a likely track and crabbed down to it through the deep snow. She started to ski the trail and felt foolish about her panic. *This is a snap!* She came to a broad sweep of lovely, fresh snow, and before she knew it she whipped a turn to head back out. She quickly reached a higher velocity than she counted on, and as she shook and bounced over the deep, gutsy snow, it yanked and twisted at her skis. When she could finally level back out and stop, she leaned on her poles in exhaustion.

As she begged the gods for better terrain she heard a noise and looked up. It was someone she knew! "Gunter! Where ya been? Hi!"

He swooshed down to her, staring.

"H-Hi, B-B-Beatense. N-Nice outfit. Are you... Are you ev-ever d-dark."

She flexed out her breasts and worked her waist at its eye-popping worst.

"This is my way of saying we shudda gotten a motel room last night."

His heart lifted. "Seriously? B-But why a motel?"

"You said yourself your parents had a nasty habit of showing up overnight. But look, I need a favor, could you catch up to the others and let them know I'm on my way? I think they're still in this woods, so if you go out to the main trail and rip it down you should be able to find them. And then ski with us, podner!"

"Okay, Beatense, yeah, I'll meet them at the top of Typhoon."

"Great! And maybe tonight a stylish and poster filled Ye Olde Bunkhouse!"

He laughed and shoved off, and effortlessly skied out of sight.

In envy the girl shook her head and rubbed at her meticulously carved forehead, with a swelling of her tennis ball bicep. She prowled on, looking for a place to turn back. She came to a spread of nice smooth snow. She set her uphill ski and started her cut. Big mistake, deep powder. She rocketed down through fluffy snow almost thigh deep. Ten hellish seconds later her skis caught on some hidden obstacle. She fell like she was tumbling from one snowy bathtub to the next.

She flopped to a welcome stop and lay half buried, until the cold snow threw her into convulsions. Gasping and shivering, she floundered and wallowed as she tried getting to her knees. But she just sank into nothingness. She struggled to unbuckle her safety straps and fought until she was sitting frog-legged with her traitorous skis beside her. She admired her hot baked ripples and the taut slimness of her thighs even now. It occurred to her that sending Gunter on was a mistake.

Beatense drew in her breath and both swam and crawled back up to where she first dropped. With frigid hand she found a pole in the depths and pulled it out. She saw her other pole, its handle just showed where she first fell, ten feet up. She tried getting to her feet to retrieve it, but they just sank and she toppled over. Again she recoiled from the cold. Shaking in frigid spasms, she churned herself up the hill and grabbed her errant pole. On her return trip to her waiting skis she pawed in the snow with her belly curved in a tighter sunk in reaction to its cold caress.

"McKinley was right, a lot of good it does to be beautiful. And rich!"

She lay upon her side and cleaned her boots. She crossed her her poles in an **X** and using them as a prop she battled to get her heavy skis in place so she could somehow get them on by hand. Curled up on her side, she pulled the first ski with all her strength, and she actually heard that blessed click. She pushed up on her poles, then wormed herself up into a low crouch on the single ski.

It sunk down and flexed, but held. Ever so carefully, still shivering, the girl stood. Braced with her poles, she cleaned her free boot again and set it to her other ski. As she toed her boot into place the ski kept sinking into the powder, and the same snow kept her binding from engaging. At last she got it. She was ready to go except for the detail of her nudity. Well, she wasn't the only one.

Beatense was stranded, she couldn't ski anywhere in this slop goulash, but she still had her lift ticket. Shivering, perched as she was, she peered downhill, wondering if there was decent snow around here at all. She did see a thin line of disturbed snow below, a trail, and she began side-tracking down toward it. With each wobbly step she followed a long angled line down the mountain, angling slowly back toward Bayonet. She stopped to pass under a branch, and a tuft of snow fell onto her shoulder. Soft sprinkles sizzled her wet back. She was glisteny wet all over. Still side stepping, the girl trembled on and sidled onto what did turn out to be a trail.

Beatense looked back up at the scene of her ordeal. The saga of her fall was advertised by huge, embarrassing gouges in the snow, that otherwise lay untouched. But fortunately the snow just freshly scrubbed her stinging tan without abrasion. Her ripples flexed with her panting, as she excitedly anticipated scandalously skiing nude right in public as she reconnected with the Bayonet slope. If the Ski Patrol stopped her she could only insist that she wasn't the only one. Heart pounding, Beatense shoved off. Her poking nips eagerly led the way. Her trail sloped back toward Bayonet, but with such a low glide the girl had to keep poling herself ahead, working her triceps, shoulders and waist. After several minutes she came upon a wide, tilted meadow of untouched snow, that flanked the main Bayonet slope further ahead. Reassuringly, other skiers were zipping down here. Beatense cut over toward them at a long angle as she sped over the snowy mounds undulating out before her. Her riding skis were just buried in the soft powder, and their tips spewed up silky comet trails of sparkling diamond dust. Modestly, she did ski the slope's far edge, but the triangular meadow was steadily pinching her over, into continuing her habit as a public nude.

The others were waiting for her at the head of Typhoon. They waited for so long Tony thought of telling the Ski Patrol, despite Gunter's assurances. Then sharp eyed Jesse spotted a distant dot that entered the triangular side meadow.

"There she is, Dad!" he piped. "She found that powder!"

"I knew she would make it!" said Tammy. "Look at how dark she is!"

"She's naked!" said Shean, looking keenly up the slope. "I should talk!"

"I'll kick her ass," said Tony. "Ammo, Gunter, Gary, look the other way."

The bare brave prodical felt like an arctic explorer returning after huge ordeals. Descending the snow field, the girl flew ever closer to Bayonet's bottom. As she got closer some startled skiers spotter her. She slowed up to avoid getting in with them.

50

LAST RUN

In spite of her efforts she regretfully caught the shouting afficionados. With slim thighs tensing to the action of her skis and her gold chain tickling her ripples, her still wet, still waxed tan exorbitantly shined. She never quit being a showhorse.

Swallowing, Ned watched her progress with earnest concern.

Beatense was relieved to see the others waiting ahead. That meant Gunter got the message through! She shot toward them and skidded into a crisp stop. In the late afternoon glare of the snow the free lance cameras caught her black shine.

She placed her arm. "Hi, guys, thanks for waiting. Sorry it took so long."

"What in hell you doing skiing nude?" said Tony. "And where were you?"

She held her other arm protectively. An ever larger assembly gathered.

"Didn't Gunter tell you? Anyway, after he left I fell into this deep powder and lost all sense of conscientious restraint. Like Shean," she added.

She evaluated young Gary. His exertions added a wonderful healthy blush to his brown skin, but as Ammo noted he didn't glance down once for an examination. He himself just got a goldeny tint, but luckily his image carried him in all situations.

"You were lucky to get out of there," Shean said. "That off-trail snow is deadly!"

"Tell me about it. Tony, what am I going to do? I do have clearance for my last run. The Bomb City lift operator got me permission."

They spotted a Ski Patrol come racing down toward them, identifiable even at a distance by his cowboy hat. Shean quickly spelled out their agenda.

"We'll take Typhoon here down to the Emerald lift and ride that up to Gun Barrel! Then we steamroll X To C down to the Garnet! Okay, let's go!"

"Yeah," said Jesse. "They might not let you board the lifts naked, but they can't kick you off the mountain itself. Oh oh, ski your fastest!"

Too late, the Ski patrol caught them as they turned to go.

"Okay, what's the meaning of this? I'm cutting your wire, miss!"

Beatense explained how she saw other nudes, and had clearance. He decided that this was the Book Girl. He laughed and said that yes, she had clearance.

"And I have safe conduct," said Shean. "I always spring ski naked here."

The miscreant boy laughed as Tammy aimed her nudity at the Patroller. She got out Tony's camera from his belt pack and took pictures of her slender friend aglow.

He looked at the little screen. "This is what gets me! All the other colors came in true to life, but am I not more browner than that? Aren't I entitled to just one accurate remembrance of my tan, without having to contrast it in?"

"Well the author had to fix his very shitful Acapulco photo," said Beatense.

"There's always Auto Balance," said Tony tiredly. "Beatense, not you too!"

The shaft of sun posed for the camera. Her out-turned breasts could almost be picked like peaches. Tammy took several pictures. Gunter panted.

"See, the camera works for her," Shean implacably growled of the image.

"We better get going," said Ammo, "before they close the lifts on us!"

Skating for speed Beatense broached Typhoon. This slope angled leftward down toward Lift Alley, away from the Expert Jackstraw.

The upper lifts were closing so everyone was funneling into Typhoon. This was just a trunk route. It had very little charm, all Typhoid did was shuttle everyone back down to Lift Alley below. It was always crowded with beginners.

Beatense still felt excited after her mystical odyssey high atop Bayonet, but the blood donation was catching up with her. She had given too recently and now was working at high exertion at high altitude. At the critical point of turning her edges caught, and too slow in her response in avoiding Ammo she made a high speed fall. She buffeted across the chunky snow, scraping her bared self.

She lay panting as her friends stopped close by her. She struggled back up and continued her grind down Typhoon. She pulled up at its headwall finale, that dove steeply down to join Lift Alley. It had no moguls, that invited flat out bombing, but the girl first addressed the plunge by making a series of turns, dropping a hundred feet.

The others had already blasted the slope except Ned. He was oblivious to her attraction powers. "Get going, idiot!"

At this level Beatense had two hundred yards of the Typhoon headwall left to go, and shooting this straight down would conserve her energy. She accelerated into a dive, hitting downhill racer speeds. She flew by other skiers making their turns. She was far beyond that stage, but still the sensation of paralyzing velocity rattled her.

But the snow was safe packed powder, so the girl zeroed in on Lift Alley like a strafing fighter, following a dead straight line. Seconds later she shot out across the Alley flats. Throwing snow, she careened toward the distant Emerald lift in a leaning hard sweep. Ned made the same turn by rippling his skis sideways.

Beatense got into the line amidst more volleys of stares. As she toured the back and forth line on her wobbly legs, she returned the many looks, and smiled for the cameras. She explained to the lift operator her nudity. He let her in.

"You sure catch on to skiing fast, kid," said Tony, as they rumbled up.

"My legs are sore from twisting them so much to work my edges."

"Finally Ned is joining in the fun. Plus he's actually on fun terms with his brothers, laughing and bantering with them. Oop, fast ride. Here we are already."

When they got to the top they headed toward the lodge. But as they drew near they skied over by the Garnet lift, the one seen unloading from inside the Mainbrace, and here they followed a curious little trail that wound its way through some wind stunted bushes to the head of X To C. It was one's last chance now, with the lifts closing even terrified beginners had to speed up.

Gary said goodbye and went over to Aquarius, with tan causing collisions.

"It's late, we'll have to fly down X," warned Gunter, "to make the Garnet."

But everybody idled down X To C, it's being the prettiest hunk of real estate in Hammersley's inventory. Crowning a broad ridge, this slope formed the north face of Plymouth. X To C presented a wide view of Molloy as it reared majestically up to the right, and also the town, village and ranch valley far off to the left. Long, undulating rows like giant steps lay across the relaxed descent, that slowed up even the fastest skiers as they hit the flats, then sped them back up.

Beatense skied with a crazed fever. She made a long, gliding curve as X To C turned west halfway down the mountain, where it formed the floor of an open, sunny valley that angled down like a half pipe. Here X was jammed with ski vagabonds.

With charms that could keep even ski racers enchanted all their downhill days, X was universally honored and loved. This was the slope that frustrated skiers gaze at longingly in their old trail maps back on the job or in school.

After her Bayonet fiasco Beatense was wildly maddened by the packed powder here, that offered split second control. She lashed into a dead bomb, and when she got going too fast she rode up the widely inclined sides of the slope to slow down.

From these upper vantage points she was poised for really tress-tossing rides, because of the added angle effect. The girl repeatedly slowed to turn into these descents, digging her poles for higher speeds. On and on X To C continued to flow along under her skis, and she soared from one side to the one opposite, first as a jet fighter and then as a skittering little biplane. Craig saw the videos.

Sadly, the Garnet lift at the junction of X To C and Death Valley was closed, meaning Tuckville down and out. A tragic gloom descended over the once hopeful skiers as they drearily watched the empty chairs rattle around the turntable and then march up after those scum who got in under the wire. Slumped in defeat, feeling like she deserved better, bare Beatense leaned on her poles.

"We sure lost our touch," Jesse said. "We should be way up Majesty now."

"My fault," said Beatense, "falling up on Bayonet. Ned, I would pay $100 if you would leave me alone." --/-- "I would pay $100 if you would leave me alone!"

"Well, we're even. So when are you going to live up to your end of the deal?"

"When are you going to live up to your end of the deal!"

"Hold it, you two, no more of this arguing. I don't care whose fault it is, you both you shut up." --/-- "Yeah, Ned." --/-- "Yeah, Beatense!"

As Ammo shook his head at this exchange a pale skinned teen boy in five inch cotton shorts came slamming to a stop, throwing up a rude avalanche of snow. He wore a string of little seashells about his long fine neck, that in turn was enframed by his ostentatiously uncut "how beautiful our son is" blond locks. He had the requisite skeletal muscles, and he looked like a thin girl with his washed complexion. He saw that the lift was closed and took off down Tuckville, skating at full extension.

Beatense and friends took off down Tuck, also skating for speed. Except for its main use of carrying everyone off the mountain at day's end, Tuckville was a morale booster. It was almost two miles long, and the way it meandered down to the snow field fronting the ski village made it seem far longer. Tuck had such an easy descent that the most inept skiers could relax as they toured this trail.

Yesterday Beatense had to brake herself with her poles here, or so she thought, but now she careened down the sleepy Tuck like on a runaway Spook or Windfire. There was a crazed urge to speed, the many dozens of skiers on any given stretch were racing each other, so a crazy mania took hold. Nakedly stared at, Beatense, alongside Gunter, leaned back to lift her tips, and with her waist sinuously flexing she passed almost every skier before her. She took the first winding bend, that then revealed the distant ski village picturesquely ahead.

Then it was hidden, only to reappear as the next curve was swept. Yet again it was hidden by the next sweep, but then at last as the skiers emerged from Tuckville onto the snow field, the still distant village stayed in sight.

Its ranchily rustic buildings made a dream-like scene, meant only for the superior elite in life, and Beatense was certainly in that crowd as she descended toward the town like a landing plane, watching her long, springy thighs.

Decision time came as the long descent continued, whether to ski toward the village and the base lodge, or to veer to the right toward Gold Camp Row.

Ammo broke away from the Shattucks toward the base area.

"Nice seeing you all again!" he called as he arrowed off. "And nice meeting you, Beatense. Great tan, books and videos!"

"Thanks, Ammo, nice meeting you!" the girl called back. "Get some sun!"

One by one Beatense and her friends hooked off the descending snow field into the parking drive of the condominiums. She was bereft that the day had to end, this early, but as she glided along the parked cars and slid to a stop by their building she had a keen glow. The skiers, spotting her and the young Tammy as they drew up, shamelessly halted. Tammy faced them calmly, but within the privacy of her piled haystack Beatense looked away. She actually felt very weak, almost ready to go into shock. A rare switch for her, but it was the blood.

"You did great today, young lady," said Tony, as he stepped off of his skis. "We take people here who never catch on, nor get quite as tan, I might add."

"This was pre-existing," Beatense said, stepping off of her skis. She set them on her shoulder in that skier's way. "But I might have gotten more sun at that."

"Not that any econo camera would catch me getting more sun," muttered Shean, watching Beatense start for the door. "Hey, where ya going?"

She turned. "What?"

"Just put your skis by the van. We'll be leaving in a few minutes."

Her mouth dropped. "Leaving! What do you mean, we're leaving!"

"This was just a two day gig," said Jesse. "You knew that."

"But you can't count yesterday! You yourselves said it was bad skiing!"

"Beatense, there's no choice," said Tony, "the place is rented out tonight."

"Oh, that's a smart move! To whom? Just any creep who comes along?"

"Quick, Shean!" said Jesse. "Grab her skis before she runs off with them!"

"Oh yeah, me wearing these clumsy stupid boots," shouted the girl, as if this was the only consideration. "Ned, I certainly bet that this was all your doing!"

The boy had been neglected for awhile, and he brightened up. "It is not!"

Tony smiled as he set the skis in the rack. This was the first ski trip in five years where Ned was actually delighted. His glaring at his enemy spoke volumes.

That enemy took Gunter aside. "Shit, man, there goes the stylish motel."

"Agh, we never wudda found those corn dogs. Wonderful knowing you."

She felt like she was facing execution as they rode the elevator up. Once in the apartment she changed to her jeans and Tammy's tweed blazer. This was too small for her, and its nipped cut made it look even smaller as it struggled to hide her peach breasts. She also wore Ned's pointy-toed, stove-pipe cowboy boots, with the jeans tucked into the snug fitting shafts. She packed her gear into her backpack, that she slung jauntily over her shoulder as she made her strides out to the elevator, and then on to the van. She handed over her backpack.

"This is such a gyp! Look at all those skiers going by! They get to stay?"

But the girl was gratified to see Jesse also forlornly watch the skiers still coming down. An incredible vehicle pulled in by the van, that was so high slung one had to climb its running boards to get up into it, and despite its yellow paint it had a military look. A slight young woman hopped out of it, with the frail beauty that speaks of a high education bloodline and a dreamily artistic vulnerability.

Petitely refined, she too flaunted a child's jeans size, and looked as if she had emerged from a wasting disease. She had smoky, moody silent-film eyes with a mournfully exotic cast, that was strikingly at odds with her sun freshened, dusky complexion. Her lustrous hair was pencil spiraled, and her urgent cheek points gave her chin exquisite delicacy. It wasn't in her nature, but she had a sensual stature she felt entitled to, as part of her advanced overall character. She wore a white clinic coat that was hanging open, revealing a stethoscope.

"Ramona, hi!" Jesse shouted. "I'm glad we caught you! Just got off, hah?"

"Yes, finally. Hi, Jesse! I wondered if you guys would make it up!"

"Yeah, the snow was perfect! Anything really gross today, ER-wise?"

"Yeah, a big accident. We had to get emergency blood donations."

"Beatense! You were one of the donations!" said Jesse. "I watched!"

Ramona looked at her, even Beatense felt her power. "You saved his life."

"There were four of us, not just me. I also gave just a week ago."

"Well, without you we would have needed blood flown in. But you're…"

"Yeah, Moan, meet Beatense. She joined us for this trip, ending just now."

They exchanged smiles but Ramona seemed puzzled. Beatense knew why. Although she was halfway sensibly dressed, there was no question of her Book Girl identity. As a discerning doctor Ramona was of course above all that.

The others came out and loudly mobbed her, while Beatense, left out, peered anxiously in at the complex controls, gauges and levers of her Pummer. It was a rugged piece of engineering, with grab handles and rounded corner windows, set in black rubber gaskets. A tunnel split the seats, with additional switches and dials.

"But you actually skied after giving blood, er, Beatense?"

"I didn't have any trouble until the end. But this is quite the vehicle, Moanie. How much do these run?" --/-- "Upwards of eighty." --/-- "I just might get one!"

"Just pay for the gas, though. Well, very nice meeting you."

Hoping to buy a Pummer and drive it home, Beatense got in the basic Shattuck van, and watched a squadron of tan, skinny girls just in shorts flying by among the laggard skiers. And more skiers were in sight.

"How can they still be on the way down?" she whined to Tammy, as she and the others clambered in. "It took that long to get down the mountain?'

Tony replied as he set in the last bags, "They waited until the last second."

"How come we didn't? But can't we stay in that tall balcony hotel tonight?"

"Too expensive," said Tony, and he clunked down the lift-gate and got in.

"Don't feel bad, Beatense," said Tammy. "We'll be back next year."

"Yeah, all those months will fly by like nothing," said Shean.

"Months? You said months?"

"Lots of time to let your excitement build up," said Tony. He started the van and backed out. He started down the drive, past skiers carrying their skis *IN*. IN to their lodgings for the night! "Try and let that thought soothe you."

"Oh, yeah, real soothing. And I don't see how that hottie can be a doctor!"

"A resident," said Shean. "But on her way to a smashing career, I bet."

"Aren't we all. But our leaving, is it just because of nowhere to stay?"

"Jad just did the horses these two days," said Jesse. "We have to go back."

"Jads!? That mental case? Give him a call! He can do those fat old oaters one more day! Isn't anyone on my side in this? Ned, speak up!"

"You can stay here if you want!" Actually Ned's family noticed that he spent the whole day laughing and shouting. He was learning that life could be fun.

Beatense glared in reply. "Okay, okay! I miss my beach nudity anyway."

"You would mention that," said Tony, getting tired of this loudmouth.

But he was actually taken by her grand fury at having to leave. This is the most sincere gratitude a guest can show. The sincere guest borrowed a phone and she called her father. After various insults she called Mercaphony per paternal directive, and Mr. Morley said to do *Lazy Lack A Daisy* and *Just Sailing Along.*

Tony stopped the van and everyone was very quiet, Ned too, as she sang. Then taking Chuckwagon he followed this through the busy village. The traffic crept along. Other skiers were sadly leaving too, and with their diesels idling charter buses were kidnapping riders. But sickeningly in-bound buses were pulling in and honking, with noisy skiers-to-be waving from the windows and roof hatches. The bastards.

"I'm just glad I don't have to sit next to Beatense," said Ned, hopefully.

His brothers looked at each other, and Shean tapped Tony on the shoulder. He stopped and the seating change was made. Beatense gave Ned a good jab as she climbed back in next to him. He howled. They continued on their way out of the village, and turned off Chuckwagon onto the road leading out to the highway.

Beatense gazed up at the massive double mountains with their panoramic white entirety. She felt like she was being taken into exile, that a magic chapter of her life had ended, and a new, uncertain one was dawning. But, the last photos had been rushed to platen, and the presses were rolling. Plus, Ned looked (looked) mad.

Ingram Content Group UK Ltd.
Milton Keynes UK
UKHW012332240723
425713UK00013B/249/J